PRECESSION

AGE
OF
DESCENT

A Novel

B. MICHAEL HILL

◨ Gurkbuzzel Press

Alameda, California, USA

Cover and Interior design by B. Michael Hill, via CreateSpace

Edited by K. Kurtiland Brown

Cover photo "Urania's Mirror", from Free-Images.com, acquired by Wikimedia

Interior photo of Tammy by B. Michael Hill, 1978

Author's photo by K. Kurtiland Brown, 2018

◻️◻️ Gurkbuzzel Press, Alameda, California, U.S.A.

Gurkbuzzelpress.com

Publisher's Cataloging-in-Publication Data

Names: Hill, B. Michael, author.
Title: Precession : age of descent , a novel / B. Michael Hill.
Description: Alameda, CA: Gurkbuzzel Press, 2018.
Identifiers: ISBN 978-1-7325334-0-0 | LCCN 2018907777
Subjects: LCSH Life on other planets—Fiction. | Extraterrestrial beings—Fiction. | Human-animal relations—Fiction. | Space warfare—Fiction. | Alternative histories (Fiction). | Science fiction. | BISAC FICTION / Science Fiction / General | FICTION / Science Fiction / Alien Contact
Classification: LCC PS3608.14263 P74 2018 | DDC 813.6—dc23

DEDICATION

For Tammy, the original Alpha Trifid

CONTENTS

ACKNOWLEDGMENTS

I wish to thank the friends, colleagues and family who encouraged me and supported me in the development of this book, specifically A, B, C, D, J, K, L, M, N, R, S, T and W.

The music of various artists contributed to the imagining of this story, including Animal Collective, The Chemical Brothers, Current 93, Etta James, Moby, Mozart, Orchestral Manoeuvers In The Dark, The Postal Service, Prince, and VNV Nation.

Authors, archaeologists, speakers and thinkers who have profoundly influenced my interest in ancient mysteries are numerous. They include, but are not limited to: Robert Bauval, Joseph Campbell, Don Cerow, David Hatcher Childress, Andrew Collins, Walter Cruttenden, Erich von Daniken, Ignatius Donnelly, Enoch, Rand and Rose Flem-Ath, Graham Hancock, Frank Herbert, Homer, Frank Joseph, Christian Knight and Robert Lomas, George Lucas, Craig Marshall, Gavin Menzies, Hugh Newman, Christian and Joy O'Brian, Plato, Gene Roddenberry, Gregory Sams, Giorgio de Santillana and Hertha von Dechend, Robert Schoch, Robert B. Stacy-Judd, Robert Temple, J. R. R. Tolkien, and John Anthony West.

The events in this book take place primarily on the planet Lupus, a world shared by intelligent Canines and Humans. The story posits that Lupus is a sister world to Earth, orbiting a star that is the binary companion to our own sun and solar system. The theory that our sun has a companion reaches far back in time and was recognized by many cultures, including Greek, Mayan, Vedic and Zoroastrian. It is a possible explanation for the Precession of the Equinoxes, the slow relative movement of the stars of the Zodiac over thousands of years. Plato called it The Great Year. We on Earth are on the cusp of the Age of Aquarius. On Lupus, it is the Age of Descent.

For more information on Precession, the Precession of the Equinoxes, and research into the possibility of our sun having a binary companion, please look up the Binary Research Institute, and the Conference on Precession and Ancient Knowledge (CPAK).

i

1 TINDERMATCH

The hanger door wouldn't open. This was not how it was supposed to happen. The target was directly below, seen through the small window of the spy craft. There would not be another chance. The scout and patrol ships were closing in fast. If the payload were not dropped now, there would be no second pass. The pilot wiped the sweat from her brow, her hand shaking. "I've got about ten seconds to decide," she mumbled to herself. She slammed the manual hanger door release again. The control panel was shorted out from the last scout blast she took coming down from orbit at high speed to the city center. The manual release was her only option. "This can't be happening," she screamed, as the hanger doors remained frozen shut. "Damn this!" With no other option available, she did that which she had been sure she would not need to do when she had left Lupus. She keyed the COM panel and auto sent her mission-accomplished message back to her commanders in the rebel stronghold of Shining City. She sent message two, the one indicating she was sacrificing herself in the line of duty. She reached over and armed the payload. Three-second delay. Grabbing the locket from around her neck, she snapped it open and kissed the picture within. "You'll understand, Cornelius. I love you." Then she swiveled her chair over to the helm controls, grabbed the manual steering mechanism, and pushed it hard to descend the ship right into the Lupin embassy. Two-One. The entire city center lit up like a solar flare as the nuclear detonation ripped through the heart of Wror's colonial capital, Bara-Band. The approaching scout craft and patrol ships incinerated like embers above the blast.

2 CORNELIUS

Cornelius dreamed. He was floating in a sky of sound and motion. Up and down he went on the back of a monstrous bird. The sky was dark with storm clouds swirling in a maelstrom. The calls of compatriots sounded close by. He yelled with delight. Then a light brighter than sunlight erupted before him. It carried a blast of heat that burned the thick locks of dred hair from his dark head. He tumbled off the great bird and out of the sky, all the while with a smile on his face and awe in his eyes.

Cornelius awoke with a start. The mid-morning sun streamed through the bedroom windows, the eastward facing wall almost completely a portal to the outside world. Long tan curtains swayed in a warm breeze from two open window panels on either side of the glass wall.

Cornelius climbed out of bed, drawing a navy blue robe around his naked hard black muscled body, tying the sash as he made his way to the window. He ran a hand through his thick black hair, curled, matted and uncontrollable in the morning.

Outside lay the remnants of a wood, dark brown lupin trees standing tall with dark needle-like evergreen leaves, purple on the undersides. All around the big house and down the hills and canyons the wood lay, here and there broken by large elaborate homes of the west Shining City suburb. Across the river five kilometers to the east, scarcely an original lupin tree stood. The sprawling metropolis of the largest city in the Territory of the Shining Star of Lupus covered most of the Okin river valley that opened broadly as the river slowed coming down out of the mountains to the east. Great buildings scaled the sides of twin hills in the distance. But here in western Shining City, a part of the wild world of old growth lupin trees still existed amid the great homes and courts.

A group of children were chasing one another through the stand of lupin trees in the canyon below the house. The game appeared random, or else nothing more complicated than "chase the kid in front of you, and don't get caught by the kid behind you." Cornelius gazed out at the scene for a while, wondering why it at first appeared odd. Then it was obvious. This game was innocent, ancient, primordial.

Cornelius shook his head and realized that before him was a scene of innocent play, bereft of malice and hate. His memory was of a place concurrent with this. But he took comfort in the reality that here was proof; there was hope yet for the Shining Star's covert political cells' plans.

His thoughts drifted back years upon years to the seminal moment of his life, his own childhood in the Lupus Minor city of Bafaria. His family, mother and sister, had just moved to a new flat across the street from the place they had lived since he had been born. Through friends she learned of a larger flat suddenly come available in the building complex across the street. The previous tenants had quickly moved out for some reason. Cornelius never learned why. But the night after his tenth birthday, in their new home just one week, the Security Services came.

It had been a typical operation as far as the military considered it. While the security operatives dressed in full bullet proof body garb assaulted the front door, Cornelius' mother implored her son to hide under the bed with all due haste. Just as Cornelius scurried into the furthest corner beneath his bed, the front door collapsed inward. Gunfire erupted into the front room. The shrieks and screams from his mother and sister were short lived, quickly silenced. Cornelius held his breath. What finally shattered the sick quiet burned itself into Cornelius' psyche for all time. From the main room Cornelius heard one operative shout to another, "Two units liquidated. Let's move to the next assignment. One floor up. Markhab! Let's move!"

Markhab. The name was burned into Cornelius' very being.

Cornelius broke free from the memory. The cause against Markhab and the military government was a banner to which many on Lupus flocked. For many, and particularly for Cornelius, the cause was personal. Cornelius became a mercenary to launch attacks against Markhab. Markhab's regime was institutionally entrenched on most of the Human part Lupus. But even the deepest roots can be extracted from their deep places. Cornelius did not know of all the forces of leverage coming into play against the regime. But he knew his was a part of it.

Cornelius turned his head to look away to the east toward the heart of Shining City. The rebel territory, ever at odds with the rest of Human Lupus, had been his home for two years now, ever since he accepted a job to infiltrate a rebel faction thought to be promulgating open war with the Canine population centers to the north and west. Shining City still lay in the shadow of the mountains, but the sunlight rapidly filled the Okin river valley. Down there across the city in the foothills of the mountains, Naemi must be up already. Ever the early riser, she often practiced marshal arts at dawn. Cornelius wanted to surprise Naemi. She wasn't expecting him back for another three days.

3 MARKHAB

Great clouds rose up out of the sea off the coast of Lupus Major. The wind violently whipped the blue flag of Lupus atop the marble dome of the government building; checkered sable squares on the flag's perimeter boldly outlying the rest in a solid navy field. The building was structured roughly in the same manner as the Parthenon that sits upon a hill on another world. This structure was two hundred and fifty meters in height. Detailed etchings from Lupin history stood out in relief along the border of the building's roof frame, down from which extended huge inner and outer rows of pillars seven feet in diameter. Set within the frame of the inner row of bone white pillars was a massive dark block of lead and steel. It was as if the classical structure were a colossal cage set over an impenetrable interior building. The entire edifice was surrounded by a square of fifty large marble steps, rising up to the heights of the Capitol that overlooked the vastness of the seaport city of Cronapolis.

Established thousands of years before, the city's name, meaning City of Time, was chosen by the early colonists to signify a city that would withstand the march of time and politics. The largest city on the dually inhabited world boasted a population of thirty-five million Humans, and was the base of a huge industrial economy that traded with a myriad of loosely aligned provinces.

Up and down the base of the steps on all sides of the building were crowds of thousands of protesters, signs and banners waving, shouts and cries carrying up to the dark interior building. Media fanned out all around the

5

gatherings. Airships hovered overhead. Security personnel were in force, fully a quarter again as many as the mob. The crush of people represented several factions, pro-government militarists from the Strong Lupus party, accommodation-seeking Lupin Unionists, sympathizers of the rebel Territory of the Shining Star of Lupus, and many other interested and disinterested onlookers that had come out onto the streets. Word had spread quickly of the recent attack of the capital city Bara-Band on Lupus' Human colony of Wror.

Within the dark central interior building of the Capitol, deep down through narrow halls to a random seeming location, the thirteen Commissioners for the People's Politburo of Lupus sat at an elliptical dark lacquer table. Diffused sunlight filtered into the room through fiber optics connecting the ceiling with the sun outside. Men and women, all were dressed in smart tight-fitting military uniforms of black leather and synthetic fabric. Neither medal nor insignia were brandished on the uniforms. Only the sable and navy flag appeared on the upper arms of each. A narrow leather strap crossed the chest from just below the right shoulder down to the left hip, tying on with the leather belt. Silver studs marched down the front, separated by four centimeters between each, from the Nehru-collar to the silver square belt buckle.

The First Commissioner was dressed like all the others around him. But while his fellow Commissioners were busy discussing and exclaiming, the First Commissioner sat quietly, slowly but repeatedly contemplating the cigar in his hand. This was Markhab's habit. It did not matter if the subject at hand was menial or tremendous. He admired the hand-rolled leaves, the exact pattern in the veins, the gentle taper from the center down to the two ends. Gazing at one end, twisting the cigar around, he spied a half-imagined irregularity just as a diamond-cutter would look through his lens. The cigar suddenly stopped twisting. Markhab smiled, and immediately bit the tip off with his front teeth, and in one fluid motion, turned his head to the right and spat the skillfully-severed end behind him where it hit the black back wall. All conversation ceased abruptly. But this show wasn't over yet. No deliberation would commence until the cigar was lit, and Markhab had finally exhaled the longest of all draws of savory smoke, a nearly impossible Human feat, two minutes and four seconds today. Markhab sat back, his chest extended high out in front of him, and stared up at the day lit ceiling, his face one of calm and repose. After the long pause, a gentle yet accelerating stream of white smoke extended up and over the heads of the other Commissioners. Several moments later, following a deep breath by the First, all relaxed and settled into murmurings to conclude their former conversations at once.

Commissioner Menkar, her straight black hair tied tight and back against her olive scalp, immediately spoke the first words to the First. "She was nuked! Not a big bomb. The intent wasn't to lay flat the city. They wanted us to know it was the Lupin Embassy that was the target. Just three blocks in every direction from the epicenter, all the buildings are still standing. The blast was more vertical than it was wide. Our geosynchronous satellite above the city was fried in the directed radiation and EM pulse. One backup is operating, but its coverage is mainly the planetary areas to the south, away from any population centers. Approximately three thousand people dead. Another ten thousand are being treated for anything from acute to mild radiation and heat burns."

Markhab continued to admire his cigar, taking another, shorter draw, while Menkar was speaking. Finally he looked across at her and asked, "Do you believe it was the Canines, Commissioner Menkar?"

Menkar hesitated, then regained her composure. "Unconfirmed, First. We have intelligence that the Canines to the north and west of us, in the region of Canoon, have been conducting advanced nuclear research. "

"Canoon is a hotbed of intent against Human Lupus," said Markhab. The bomb could only have come from Canoon. There are well-known uranium and plutonium mines in the mountains there. I want all river traffic between Canoon and Lupus Minor halted immediately. Board and seize all existing ships on the River of Lupus."

"It shall be done, First Commissioner," said Menkar.

Markhab paused then a moment, looking each Commissioner carefully in the eye. Then he turned back to his cigar. Taking a quick draw and quickly exhaling it in the center of the table, Markhab abruptly turned to his right and addressed his neighbor. "Commissioner Tokez."

The red-haired woman sat up abruptly, giving the First her full attention.

Markhab continued, "The planning for this attack must run deep and broad. There may be many strategists at work here. Run extended algorithms against every communication that passed through the Lupin and Wrorian systems over the past full month. Go back over all Canine intelligence over the same time frame. Get any indications of planning or anything related to me by this time tomorrow. Then I want the last six months analyzed and to me by the day after. We'll start within this timeframe."

Tokez, whose reputation for delivering on impossible cyber-sleuthing was unsurpassed, was unfailing as she replied, "It will be done, First Commissioner."

"Good," said Markhab. Then he turned back to Menkar. "How is this news being received in the rebel Shining Star of Lupus?"

Commissioner Menkar didn't need to clear her throat. "The cities in the Territory are quiet actually. The story is all over the press, but no specific action seems to be taken by the governing councils. My initial assessment is that they do not consider this a concern of theirs. After all, emigration to Wror is restricted to citizens of the three provinces under our control."

"And the Cantons?" asked Markhab.

"Similar situation," said Menkar. Reports from Big City indicate little discussion in the local media."

"Continue your investigations. This could mean they are not involved, or they are involved deeply and are maintaining a cover. I want the mountain passes between Lupus Major and the Territory closed immediately until further notice. Only rail and air ships may transport people and goods between us." Markhab paused and scanned the Commissioners. "All citizens traveling by air ship or rail, traveling to or from our three provinces, are to be cleared before being allowed to continue their routes."

The Commissioners nodded in agreement.

Markhab continued, "I want additional intelligence from the Shining Star and the Cantons included in tomorrow morning's briefing. Offer whatever incentives are appropriate to our operatives there."

"Yes, First Commissioner," agreed Menkar.

"Commissioner Corvus, what of reports from Canius and Canoon?"

The young Commissioner straightened up. At twenty-nine, Commissioner Corvus was the youngest to reach the top echelons of Lupin government. "No news from Canius. Canoon media outlets sporadically covered the attack. There is speculation that it was actually a military-industrial accident. An incident that could potentially be used to foment attacks against Canines."

"Maintain complete surveillance of all communications in the Canine regions," Markhab ordered. "And increase satellite observation."

"It will be done," said Corvus.

At the end of the table to Markhab's left, the eldest Commissioner, General Taurus, spoke up. "First Commissioner." The others around the table turned to look at the celebrated retired general. "Our counterparts on Wror report numerous and mounting requests for emigration back to Lupus. Governor Trian maintains full closure of all air stations, for the time being. I estimate two more days before he is forced to reopen them to planetary use. Only Lupin Defense ships are allowed to and from the planet. This should continue until further notice from this command council." The general never minced words, never beat around the bush. His recommendations were rarely overturned.

"Tread carefully down the path of locking the planet down, General," countered Menkar. "Unrestricted travel of colonists and families between Wror and Lupus was a Governmental Guarantee." Turning to the First Commissioner, she added, "The Guarantee may be responsible for the evident security breach on Wror. But sidestepping the military's century-old Pact With the People has its own inherent risks. We must not allow fuel for civil uprising."

Markhab leaned back in his chair. He was tempted to crack a slight smile. The hawk and the dove, he often thought of Taurus and Menkar. The effectiveness of Taurus' strategies was never in doubt. But it was also true that Menkar was rarely wrong. He finally said, "We will leave the policy of internal travel to Governor Trian for the time being."

Menkar did her job, but she was not relieved. General Taurus was not to be crossed too many times. And Menkar crossed him often.

Markhab listened to more briefings, responded with many edicts and orders. Intelligence was key to Markhab's rule. His colleagues knew that. Only the truth was permitted at conference. Only with the truth, could adequate plans be made to ensure the long-term rule of the military government. The defense faction had held power ever since the last war with the Canines a hundred years before.

The government's hold was strong, through a nationalistic policy that provided for the health of the population, funded advanced scientific research and development, provided for a little-regulated economy that was the powerhouse of the quadrant, and a clean environment. In return, the citizens gave up the luxury of legislative representation. The former constitution was replaced a hundred years before by the adoption via referendum of the military's Pact With the People. The document's inclusive Governmental Guarantees were considered an inviolable bill of rights of the people. To date, Guarantees had only been added to the Pact, never suspended or removed.

When Markhab's cigar was out, the meeting was over. As all the Commissioners began to stand and prepare to leave, the First leaned over across the table to the young Corvus. "Commissioner," said the First, "I want you to call the Drigan ambassador to my residence immediately. The media is not to know. Tell the ambassador it's about 'old legends'. She'll know what I mean."

"Yes, First Commissioner," replied Corvus. "Old legends."

"Quick, Corvus. This is important. Discretion is required."

"Immediately, First." And Corvus quickly left the room, followed by the others.

Menkar paused a moment to gather her things, straighten them out, rearrange a few pages, then straighten them out again. "Old legends," she thought. Then picked up her leather bound sheath of documents, and quickly exited the room.

Markhab remained sitting in his chair, took another cigar from his breast pocket, admired it, slowly turning it over and over.

4 SHINING CITY

The mid-afternoon sun beat down with strength and warmth upon the lush lawn. The expanse of green surrounded a large two-block long rectangular pond. Water lilies broke the surface around the edges and evenly spaced through the center. Large blue fish and black fish swam lazily among the lily beds, occasionally surfacing to swallow up insects stuck in the water's surface tension. At other times, the fish would nearly leap out of the pond, taking great gasps of air and diving back to the meter-depths of the pond.

Tilt-back wooden benches lined the perimeter of the pond. Under the shade of a tall lupin tree, Cornelius sat at one such bench. On a day like today, in the late spring in the Territory of the Shining Star, he was dressed in loose exercise pants and a tank top, his thick frame forcing the shirt to conform, not the other way around.

Next to him sat a man about his same age, mid-forties, in comfortable worn denim, a collared short-sleeved shirt and sandals. He was whistling, trying to catch the attention of a large dark blue peacock-like bird strutting past the pond's edge, eyeing the fish below.

"A low-gain nuke," said the man, Jarbed. "It will look like it's all the Canines have developed at this point. It will take several days to determine where the plutonium came from. The isotopes will give it away. Until then, the whole planet will think the Canines set the thing off. Everyone knows there are plutonium mines in the mountains of Canoon far to the north. When the isotope tests confirm that the material came from the Lupus

12

Minor Materiel Depot, the military government will have to suppress the entire story. But we have the same isotope test readings. We'll make sure Markhab knows this. It will instigate civil unrest from within. The military government will fall. If some Canines get in the way, we can't help that. But the main thing is, change will finally come to sweep aside the dictatorship that has clasped an iron glove over Human Lupus. There will finally be freedom from Lupus Major to Lupus Minor, Aran to the Federated Cantons. It's our destiny, Cornelius. The Shining Star will bring man back out of the timid dark. "

Cornelius was stretching, arching his back to put his head below his knees, grasping the toes of his shoes. His fingers found a sharp tangled bramble seedpod on the sole of his right shoe. He picked it out and tossed it aside. That was from his earlier run to get here through the foothill thickets. Turning his head towards his companion, Cornelius asked, "Did the pilot make it back?"

The young man Jarbed looked sideways at Cornelius, then turned back to the bird at the pond's edge. "No," he said, teeth tightly clenched. Turning back to Cornelius, he said, "Cornelius, it was Naemi."

Cornelius froze, staring into Jarbed's eyes. A quiet moment passed. During this time, the color drained out of Cornelius' face. Finally he mumbled "Gods, Jarbed. Why her? Why HER?!" He started shaking.

"She volunteered, Cornelius. She talked all the others down. Said it was an easy run, and she wanted to make some extra cash smuggling gems out of Bara-Band. She wouldn't take no for an answer."

Cornelius remembered the last time he saw Naemi, two weeks before. She was giddy, saying that she was ready to retire from her terrorist activities. She just wanted to make one more hit and collect the dough to shore things up for the future. After that, it was she and Cornelius all the way. At the time he just relished the change in tempo from Naemi's normally scowling and angry demeanor. She was hot, no doubt about it, and passionate. But she always had a chip. Did she know she was going on a one-way mission?

Cornelius blinked his eyes a few times, to clear them from the moisture welling up. She was a terrorist, but he loved her. The first time he met

Naemi was at a Shining City underground cell number three secret meeting two years ago. He barely remembered the topic at hand. Something about rebel infiltrators in the editorial offices of most of the major media conglomerates in the rest of Lupus. He and Naemi gazed at each other across the steel table in the damp recesses of that secret subway tunnel beneath the city.

When the formalities were over and main business concluded, the group broke up for an hour. Cornelius and Naemi spent that hour, and the following two days and intervening nights, in rapturous embrace. By the end of the second day, Naemi had all the information she needed to know to trust this stranger. And Cornelius knew he had found a reliable intelligence source only three days into his mission.

Cornelius shook his head, stared toward the pool, blinked, then said, "I was to meet up with her tomorrow night. I couldn't get ahold of her earlier today. I didn't know, I," he paused. Taking a deep breath, he turned toward Jarbed and said, "Was there any message for me?"

Jarbed looked Cornelius in the eyes and replied, "It was her personal message, not the standard one. She must have recorded it before leaving. She said she knew what she was doing, had known it was a possibility all along, and was honored to give her life to free Lupus from it's military domination. She ended the communiqué with, 'I know you'll understand, Cornelius. I love you.' I have the original recording in my office. Come around and I'll play it for you."

"Yeah, I just may do that." Then, "Of course I will, Jarbed. After I finish my run. I'll be there in two hours." Cornelius rose, stretched his legs by bending each knee and grasping his foot behind his back. Then he took a deep breath and jogged off to the left into the sun, around the pond and off toward the foothills of the city's eastern edge.

5 OLD LEGENDS

The lift came to a soft landing on the one hundred twenty-third floor of the high rise. The doors opened onto a landing. Opposite the lift's doors was an unobstructed view of the Lupin shore and Capitol Headlands. Located in an exclusive compound east of the capital city proper, this was where many of the government's leaders maintained their residences. The daylight was quickly waning, and the surf far below the window portrayed a blue orange steel palette in the gathering twilight.

Commissioner Corvus stepped off of the lift. He gestured for his haughty guest to disembark onto the platform. The brown leather with fur trim-robed figure slipped past Corvus' outstretched hand and paused in the center of the platform. The guest glanced at Corvus' face, noticing what looked like a black eye covered up by make-up, but said nothing. Turning slightly left, then scanning the room slowly to the center then right, the visitor absorbed the view.

"The First Commissioner will be here presently. You may wait here."

In a quick flowing motion, the woman unfastened her robe at the neck and gently let it fall from her shoulders. Corvus caught the robe and hung it on a coat stand against the wall. Then he moved back into the lift and pressed a button on the interior control panel. The doors softly closed.

Standing straight and stately in a knee-length black satin dress with inlaid pearl, the woman moved forward toward the four steps leading down from

15

the platform. Stopping at the top, she turned to the left to watch the last glimmer of the sun duck down behind the rim of the headlands and the sea. "Marvelous," she intoned under her breath. A sudden noise from the other direction brought her attention quickly back to where she was. A door opened and in walked the First Commissioner, in comfortable yet still official-looking black slacks, shirt and blazer.

"Dania! I am glad you have come," exclaimed Markhab as he approached the Drigan ambassador. She extended both her arms. Markhab took her hands in his, then leaned in to kiss both her cheeks. "You are stunning as ever."

"So you do still know how to be charming to a woman, First Commissioner." Dania released Markhab's grip from her hands, and returned them to her side.

"Please, please come in, Dania, down here where you'll be comfortable. May I get you a drink?" Markhab led her down the steps and off to the left where two leather chairs and a leather sofa entertained an intimate nook. "Brandy?"

"That would be lovely," agreed Dania. "On the rocks, please." She took a seat in the leather chair facing the window, and watched the light drain out of the sky, some clouds still tinged pink in the enfolding darkness. No stars shown out yet. "Terrible business on Wror, First Commissioner. My government is ready to offer any assistance it can. What have you learned?"

Markhab prepared the drinks at the bar against the wall opposite the grand window. Pouring two glasses of brandy over cubed ice, he put the lead crystal stopper back on the decanter and gently set the bottle down on its stand in the caddy next to several other alcoholic beverages resting in lead crystal. He turned back around to Dania and offered her a glass. "This is a delicate affair, Dania. I suspect more than what is obvious."

"My dear First Commissioner, you are being mysterious. State secrets, is it?" The ambassador took a sip from her drink and looked back up at the First Commissioner, staring him in the eyes and not blinking.

"It's probably the Canines," said Markhab, sitting down opposite Dania. "But why all the way to Wror? If they've got nukes, why not send them raining down on us right here."

"Adversaries rarely do what we would have them do, or what we would do ourselves," intoned Dania. "Do you know where the materiel came from?"

"Not yet," said Markhab. "The isotope tests aren't concluded yet. The ground is swarming with my agents, looking for any clues. The entire city center of Bara-Band has been evacuated while we complete our investigation."

"Do you fear a second attack?" asked Dania.

"No. To be honest, this whole situation seems convenient. We received intelligence reports for months about nuclear research in Canoon, but I have the entire planet cordoned off so that no Canines come or leave. They have effectively been under quarantine for two years. So if they can't get in, and they can't get out, how did they get to Wror?"

"They are not without their allies, First Commissioner." Dania took another sip from her glass.

"I just have a funny feeling about this. Nonetheless, at this time the most likely scenario is that it was a Canine attack."

"It is the most logical explanation," agreed Dania.

"Let me ask you about Drigo," said Markhab. "How is the environmental situation?"

"The ice sheets continue to advance. Ever since the equatorial straits became blocked by the advancing ice, the circulation of the seas and gulf streams changed. We have ever more frigid winters and brief cold summers. It's possible the entire world may snowball. Everything is moving faster and faster." Dania turned to face Markhab. The sea levels are falling, humidity is dropping and precipitation is more and more rare. We are caught in a cycle now that is feeding off of itself."

"It's a difficult situation there. But that is not the reason I asked you to come here, Dania," Markhab said, leaning close toward the Drigan ambassador.

Dania narrowed her eyes and almost hissed, "No Markhab. That much is obvious. You are not in the habit of inviting old interests to your eagle's Eyre."

Markhab paused to look into Dania's eyes, took a quick gulp from his glass, and continued. "Nothing escapes your notice, my dear." Taking another gulp, he then continued. "Do you remember years ago, during an intergovernmental conference in Dula City, when that fool Altair nearly ran into us?"

"Of course, Markhab. Altair of Dula. He was drunk, and your quick reflexes saved me from a vodka bath. That was thirteen years ago."

"So it was," said Markhab. "Time does fly."

"What of it?" asked Dania, taking another sip from her glass.

"You and I were having a conversation about colonial history."

"I do remember the conversation," said Dania. "You were talking about the Ordained World."

"Yes, good, good! You remember!" exclaimed Markhab. "The Anointed World, yes. Earth."

"Earth," repeated Dania. "The stuff of children's stories and morality lessons."

"Earth," said Markhab. "Do you also remember what Altair said when he overheard our conversation?"

Dania thought about this for a minute. She was good at remembering things, but remembering the conversations of a drunk was difficult to recall. Then, "Yes. Altair said 'Earth! The shimmering field destroyed them all. And only Humans remained.'"

Markhab's eyes opened wide. "Indeed! I have spent a long time trying to understand those words, Dania. I have conducted my own research about Earth."

Dania sipped her drink again. "And I imagine you learned something. Is that right?"

"Just more stories, legends. I don't know anything for sure. But I learned enough to be intrigued."

"Earth is under permanent quarantine by the Felines. No spacefaring people have been allowed to venture there for thousands of years. The Earth Humans no doubt have forgotten us by now. They probably think they are alone," said Dania with confidence. "And not many people interact with the Felines. So most people no longer remember or believe in Earth."

"You are right, Dania, of course," said Markhab. "But I also believe that Altair's comments spoke of a weapon used against all non-Human intelligences." Markhab sat up straight. "I aim to go there and find this weapon."

"Impossible," exclaimed Dania, putting her drink down on a table to her left. "The Felines permit none to venture there."

"Ah, and why?" asked Markhab. "Why after thousands of years do the Felines care? They have not colonized the planet. They do not mine it for resources, or enslave or even observe the Human population. Why is Earth under permanent quarantine?"

Dania looked Markhab square in the eyes and said, "Because the Humans there killed every single intelligence on the planet that wasn't Human. All the Canines, Felines, Birds of Prey, all of them. The Humans there killed them all."

"Yes. Quite. But how?" asked Markhab.

Dania kept her gaze locked on the First Commissioner's eyes. Something there. "I don't know," she said. "But I suspect you have an idea."

"Old legends, Dania."

"Hm. That's what your young apprentice Corvus mentioned to me when he arrived at my residence to fetch me here," said Dania. "Old legends indeed."

"The shimmering field," said Markhab. "The story barely exists anywhere.

But Altair told me what he knew. A weapon the Humans of Earth developed. To destroy their gods."

"Gods?" probed Dania.

"The sentient non-Humans that inhabited Earth with them, before the quarantine. Before the Felines shut the planet off from all others, making it a legend, a myth, a children's story. The Humans had a weapon that killed all the others. That's why the Felines took the action they did."

"Intriguing," said Dania, retrieving her drink and taking another sip. "And you are going to invade this mythic world, find an ancient weapon, and wield it for yourself? This is something my government would be very interested in. And wary towards any who would possess such a thing."

The First Commissioner took another drink from his glass, finishing the liquor, then setting the glass down on the table. Dania watched him carefully the entire time. The First Commissioner then locked gaze with Dania.

"What do you want with me," asked the ambassador, knowing there was a definite chase to cut to.

The First Commissioner replied, "Lupus does not currently have positive relations with the Felines. I need you to get a team through their defenses and onto the surface of Earth."

"Tell me what else you know, Markhab," intoned Dania, smiling. She reached for her drink again.

6 THE MISSION

Cornelius leaned against Jarbed's desk, listening to the final message sent by Naemi. It was delivered in an even tone, with little emotion evidenced by intonation or word choice. It was a very matter fact statement without detail as to what transpired in the final moments of the suicide mission. The message concluded with the personal note to Cornelius, "I know you'll understand, Cornelius, I love you."

"Do you know what happened? Why she felt she had to sacrifice herself?"

Jarbed shut off the recording from his computer terminal. "No. We haven't been able to secure any intercepted transmissions from the Colonial Defense Force on Wror. Markhab probably has that information by now, but we don't."

"I'll track it down," said Cornelius. "I'd like to know what really happened. Did the CDF know what kind of ship she was in? Was there a visual sighting? Answers to these questions will dictate our next steps."

Jarbed sat back down on the floor where he filled a bare spot, surrounded by a mess of fuses, timers, waterproof shells and explosive chargers. He resumed assembling his bombs, fitting each completed grapefruit-sized sphere with a colorful floating tracker, and carefully setting it aside among a pile of ready devices. After assembling a couple, he got up again.

"Our next steps are already clear, Cornelius." Jarbed reached over to open a desk drawer to his left. "Markhab will have to make some move towards us. Whether that is towards reconciliation, war, or some other means to annex and assume control over the Territory, we don't yet know. But we need alliances regardless of the First Commissioner's intentions." Jarbed removed a black case from the drawer and set it down on the desk surface. Unlatching the side, he opened the case and removed a data syringe. "I'm sending you on a mission, Cornelius." He removed one of several vials from the case and loaded it into the syringe. "Roll up your sleeve."

"What is the mission?" Cornelius asked, pushing back the loose sleeve from his sweatshirt.

"If Markhab comes after us too soon, the entire plan could be jeopardized. We need to get a message to a contact currently in Big City near the great lakes, near the Canius border. You will get there via Lupus City. Renender will aid you. I can't risk sending an electronic communiqué. Markhab monitors all transmissions on the planet, especially any originating from the Territory of the Shining Star. The genetically encrypted message in this fluid will inform our allies of our next steps, and leave a few false leads for Markhab to follow. Our contact in Big City has the decryptor solution." Jarbed injected the data fluid via pressure injection into Cornelius' right forearm. "This will bruise for a few hours, but should dissipate by morning."

Cornelius rubbed his arm and pulled his sleeve back down. "Where do I find this contact?"

Jarbed removed the empty vial from the syringe and put the vial and syringe back carefully into the black case. Locking the latch, he restored the case back into the drawer and closed it.

"This data message will dissipate in your bloodstream within five days," said Jarbed. "There is a roadhouse on the western outskirts of Big City. It is called The Canine Run Roadhouse. The day after tomorrow at four in the afternoon, go into the bar and ask for the bartender Roger. Tell him Jarbed sent you, and that you're looking for Shont. He'll direct you to our contact. If Roger is not there, find out when his shift starts and wait. The contact will be gone by the next morning, so this will be your only window. You will receive your next orders from Shont."

"Got it," said Cornelius, moving towards the door. "I'll leave for Lupus City tonight."

"I'm sending another operative along with you. You'll meet tonight. Good hunting," said Jarbed. He sat back down on the floor to work on his bombs.

"When are you going to set those off?"

"At the Precession night festival in Star City. We set these pretty floats into the Shining Delta, and off they float in the main ocean current just in time to be swept to Aran City with the monsoons. It's all in the timing. And if any of Markhab's warships encounter some, well let's just say there won't be much left to report home about."

"Good luck." Cornelius left.

"Indeed, good luck to you." Jarbed looked at his clock display. About forty seconds passed when he heard the lift doors close down the hall from his office. Glancing back to the door to make sure it was closed, he pressed a touch screen button on his computer and activated a COM line. "Did you hear that?"

A side door slowly opened to his left in the office, and a tall slender woman with long dark brown hair and high cheekbones entered from the adjoining room. She had an almost feline demeanor to her. Her eyes were different colors, blue and brown. "Yes, I heard it," said the woman.

"Go directly to the house. Cornelius will stop there before he heads north to Big City."

Naemi smiled. "In a way, I'm already there."

"He knows there is a decryptor solution there. He'll try and read the message. Make sure he accomplishes his mission in Big City and follows Shont into Canius. Naemi, are you up to the task?"

Naemi looked down at Jarbed and crooned "You never forget the one who broke your heart. I'll have the upper hand, don't you worry about me, Jarbed." She paused, then added, "He'll ask many questions. What do you want me to tell him?"

Jarbed looked up at Naemi. He quickly replied, "The truth. This mission is too important to risk mistrust over layers of cover story. Give him the truth, and he'll follow."

7 NAEMI

Cornelius cut the lights and pulled his ground car around to the back of the estate. The driveway turned away from the house for about half a kilometer, bypassing a stand of lupin trees. The road then turned back around to widen and peter out in a circular parking area. Cornelius had seen lights on in the windows of the house as he approached. They were probably on timers, but he couldn't be certain he was alone on the property

As he parked his vehicle in the gathering twilight and turned the engine off, the lights surrounding the driveway flickered on one by one in a clockwise direction. No motion or movement came from the windows of the house. "Timers and motion detectors," thought Cornelius. He got out of the car and quietly closed the door, leaving it unlocked in case he needed to leave in a hurry.

Cornelius swept his gaze around the perimeter of the driveway. This was a big estate, even by Shining Star standards. Most people in the Territory had large homes. It was a stark contrast to the planned communities and residential block towers that the military government favored in the rest of Human-occupied Lupus. Here in the so-called 'rebel territory', there were no such draconian regulations limiting the citizens' pursuit of self-expression and privacy. Naemi had purchased this estate from one of the original pioneering families of Shining City that had settled the region after the military takeover a hundred years ago.

Cornelius noticed the flowering shrubs that grew around the driveway in front of the lupin trees. The five and six-petaled white blossoms gave off a sweet scent that hung in the still air. Cornelius breathed the fragrance in, enjoying the flood of memories that filled his mind.

He remembered last year near this time when he and Naemi had planted a border of yellow pantha bulbs around all the pedestal lamps. It was long past dark, and the two of them worked together, making their way around the driveway, moving from lamp to lamp on their hands and knees. The planting wasn't finished until ten that night. All the time they worked they were drinking wine, talking, laughing digging hole after hole and dropping in more and more bulbs. The wonderful scent of the shrub flowers filled their nostrils. Cornelius realized he never learned the name of the plant.

He looked down at the base of the lamps. The pantha flowers were largely done flowering. Only a handful still held the twenty centimeter-high stalks with yellow starbursts on top. The rest were fallen over and turning brown. It had been a bountiful winter and early spring for the panthas.

Cornelius turned back towards the house and made his way to the entrance. He stopped at the door and tried to peer through the vertical glass panel and sheet curtain. Nothing looked out of the ordinary. He pulled a small rectangular box out of his pocket and lifted up a panel to reveal a dial and crystal display. Cornelius positioned the device near the touch pad door lock on the right side of the doorframe. He turned the dial clockwise with one hand while holding the device in the other. The box let out a soft whirring sound. The crystal began to display an image of six red interlocking teeth, representing the locks within the door. Suddenly the whirring stopped. The device successfully interfaced with the locking mechanism. Cornelius pressed a button below the dial, then began turning the dial again slowly. At a quarter turn, one of the locking teeth images on the crystal turned green. Cornelius heard a clicking sound within the door jam itself. He pushed the button under the dial again and continued. One by one, all the interlocking teeth displayed in the crystal turned green, and the door lock continued clicking. On the sixth click, the door relaxed and swung out a few millimeters. Cornelius closed the flap on the device and returned it to his pocket. He slipped quickly through the door and pulled it closed behind him.

Naemi was upstairs in the master bedroom. She had been in the house for two hours before seeing Cornelius' ground car pull up into the driveway. She had left the house lights on herself. The outside lights ringing the driveway came on via motion detectors that Cornelius set off when he pulled up in his vehicle.

This was going to be an awkward reunion, even for someone like Naemi who normally prided herself on her detached approach to emotional entanglements.

Naemi moved over to a vanity near the open bedroom door. On the table before the mirror was a framed photograph of Cornelius and Naemi. She picked up the picture and looked at it. Both were in swimsuits near a lagoon, tropical trees around them, soft blue sky over aquamarine water, white sand on the shore. They were laughing in the picture. Cornelius' right arm disappeared in the foreground. He apparently had been holding the camera, taking the candid picture himself. Naemi's expression belied little emotion. Her eyes were cold steel traps. Just as she was setting the picture back down on the table, she heard the front door downstairs click open, then quickly close again. Cornelius was inside.

Cornelius moved quietly through the foyer to stop at the base of the main staircase. He looked around the room, taking in the furniture, curtains, paintings on the walls.

A sudden movement at the top of the stairs brought his eyes quickly into focus on the figure emerging from the shadows on the top landing. His eyes grew wide, and his face flushed. He stared at the woman who slowly made her way down first one step, then paused on the second. Naemi spoke first.

"You look well, Cornelius," she continued, resuming her descent down the stairs.

Cornelius found his voice. He cleared his throat and mustered a strong showing. "You're supposed to be dead! What are you doing here?"

Naemi looked at him, careful to maintain the upper hand. "Waiting for you."

Cornelius did not understand. "But Jarbed...."

"Obviously I am not dead. You are confused."

Cornelius asked again, "How is it that you are here?"

Naemi glided down the rest of the stairs and came to rest within a meter of Cornelius. The two just observed one another for a moment.

"I am part of your mission. I'm to travel with you to Big City. I will help you find Shont"

Cornelius shook his head. He felt so much the pawn in a game whose rules he couldn't yet figure out. Jarbed sent her here? Jarbed knew she was alive? And Jarbed had paired them up for this mission. It smelled of trouble, deceit and danger all at once.

"Come into the living room and sit down." Naemi moved past Cornelius and continued behind him toward the formal living room that opened up on the other side of the stairs. Cornelius followed silently.

The lights were already on in the room. Naemi took her seat on a leather sofa. Cornelius stopped by a wet bar and pulled a cold bottle of alcoholic beverage out of a small cooling unit. "Do you want something?"

"Just water." said Naemi.

Cornelius poured her a glass of water from a tap, then moved over to the sofa and handed her the glass. Naemi took it from him, brushing her fingers against his in the process. She smiled and thanked him. Cornelius tightened his lips and sat down in a chair opposite her.

"Where were you?"

"Preparing for our next mission," replied Naemi. "There are many profound events in motion these days, Cornelius."

"An evasive response. But I am fully aware of events."

"Maybe not to the extent you think you are. Though you are in the thick of it, even if you don't realize it." Naemi leaned forward towards Cornelius. "The message you carry is insurance against Markhab. It's imperative that it reach your contact in Big City."

Naemi held her stoic expression. "Yes I know. But I'm not able to tell you that right now. Please trust me. But you and I will deliver the message."

"Trust you?" chided Cornelius. "That's a lot for you to ask."

"You'll have to for the time being, Cornelius. Now," and Naemi sat up straight, putting her glass down on a coffee table, "Now, let's read that message."

"Do you still have the decryption solution in your office in the basement," said Cornelius.

"Follow me." They got up, Naemi leading Cornelius back through the house to a small doorway off the side of a hallway. "Down here." She opened the door, flicked on a light source, and they descended the steep staircase.

The basement was not a large space. Metal shelving and tables lined all the walls. The shelves were crammed in a disorganized manner with maps, reference books, and strange electronic equipment whose many purposes defied a ready understanding. Two metal chairs were present, sharing floor space with plastic and metal shipping containers.

"What is all this stuff?" asked Cornelius.

"Surveillance devices, med kits, firearms, ammo, poisons. Everything a covert operative would need," replied Naemi, moving directly to the back of the room. She reached a cabinet, bent down to open a sliding door, and rummaged around until she found what she was looking for. "Here is it." She pulled out a black kit not unlike the one Jarbed had used to inject Cornelius with the data message solution.

She cleared a space on a table and set the kit down, unfastening the latch and opening it up to reveal a syringe and two empty vials. A third vial rested snug in its felted depression, containing a pinkish fluid.

Cornelius moved over to a computer monitor on an adjacent table and turned it on.

Naemi put one of the empty vials into the syringe. "Come over here," she said.

Cornelius laid bare his left arm. The right one was still sore from the initial injection. "Don't bleed me to death."

Naemi smiled a cold smile. "Not in this way, in any case." She plunged the needle of the syringe into his arm. Cornelius winced, but by the time he finished in taking his shock breath, the needle was out and the vial was filled with blood. She grabbed a medicated swath of material from the kit and pressed it onto Cornelius' skin at the puncture site. The clotting agent and disinfectant worked immediately. She disengaged the vial from the syringe, and held the vial up to the light. "Still red, Cornelius. You're Human."

"Nice," he replied, pulling down his sleeve over the wound. "I'll take that." He took the vial of his blood from Naemi and snapped it into a side-processing unit beside the computer. "Hand me the pink decryption fluid please?" Naemi removed it from the kit and handed it to him. Cornelius snapped the vial beside the one containing his blood. Then he activated a button, and initiated a program on the computer by typing in some key words. "This should take about a minute."

The computer monitor displayed a rectangular grid with five color buttons below it. The buttons flashed from left to right as a program routine was initiated. The device holding the vials vibrated. The blood and decryption solution slowly drained from each vial, mixing in the device. The computer screen began to show a grainy picture of what looked like stains and shapes. Slowly the menagerie began to coalesce and take on a better-defined shape. A beep sounded from the machine and the vibrating ceased. Cornelius hit a command on the computer's touch screen. The picture came into rapid focus. Words appeared on the display screen.

"Isotope reading 48.2203927414 cross 8. Mineral source, Alairan mines in the foothills of Lupus Minor. Be prepared to release this information if the First Commissioner makes any public announcement that contradicts this data. Project Crott is go. Repeat, Project Crott is go."

"This must be the data from the nuclear device you dropped on Bara-Band," said Cornelius. "You did do that, didn't you? I don't know what

Project Crott refers to though. Do you?"

Naemi didn't say anything in response.

"More secrets?" asked Cornelius.

"Like I said," offered Naemi. "Events are moving quickly. Are you packed for the trip to Lupus City to meet Renender?"

"I'm ready. You?"

"I have a bag in a closet upstairs. Can we take your car back to your house? We should leave it parked there, not here."

"Agreed," said Cornelius. "I already have alternate transportation arranged to get us out of Shining City."

"Then we should leave now." The two of them eyed one another intently for a long moment in silence, assessing the partnership.

"I'm still not fully comfortable with this. And you still need to give me more answers."

"Ask your questions on the way then," said Naemi. "I'll tell you what I'm able to."

They ascended the steps and made their way out of the house.

8 CANOPUS

Far away from the planet Lupus, thousands of rocky worlds slowly orbited a small blue star devoid of greater planets. The star was young, and sat in a region of space occupied by a huge nebula, the Great Aurora Nebula.

The thousands of small rocky worlds floated and orbited within a fifty thousand kilometer wide doughnut-shaped force field that ringed the star from three hundred million kilometers out. Many asteroids had cities rising out of their crater rim walls. One asteroid was larger by far than any other. The huge irregular rock was two thousand kilometers long, eight hundred kilometers wide and six hundred kilometers thick. A huge city and had been constructed over, on, in, and through the large almost spheroid-shaped asteroid some fifteen thousand years before. The result was a diamond shaped gem hung in a shimmering space like an exalted drop of fluid crystal. Her companion asteroid cities ringed the distant star in the shimmering force field of blue and white atmospheric vapor. Over the millennia, countless smaller space rocks had been mined and processed to fill the ringed force field with oxygen, nitrogen, carbon dioxide, water vapor and other trace gasses. The great asteroid city, and many smaller worlds, orbited within the blue and white oxygen rich, humid force field. Secondary protective shields shimmered around the crater cities among the many mini-worlds. On the large asteroid, huge crystal green and red cities rose from the central plateaus on the top and bottom sides of the space rock.

The Feline Eridani often wandered out onto the open plain to play with other Feline children. Today she was supposed to retrieve her brother and return to the city where their mother had summoned them. Galdinier was watching over the herd of dorsein near the crater rim wall. But on her way, Eridani thought it was a great opportunity to take her time and wander through the tall grass looking for grasshoppers. The Ministry of Cycles released them yesterday, part of their ongoing job of regulating seasons and wildlife patterns under the domes of the asteroid city. This year the insects were released two weeks earlier than in years past. Children were fanned out all around the outskirts of the city spires, encroaching on the great central field. The day seemed full of promise, and there was an indescribable something in the air. Something like spring, she thought. And so out onto the great green field Eridani ventured, looking for grasshoppers.

All the settlements of the space city ringed two huge craters of the asteroid, one on the top and the other opposite on the bottom of the asteroid. The open central plain was a verdant expanse of fields, plantings, small woodland and hills. Identical to this scene were the communities six hundred kilometers beneath the asteroid, around the opposite great crater of the underside.

Hugging the great rim wall beneath the dome, many ecosystems progressed down toward the crater floor, tundra, arboreal, rain forest, foothills and grassland. Just above the grassy plain away from the pond crater, a steep ravine cut the rising foothills in two.

Natural cycles were carefully maintained to ensure the population remained healthy and true to the rhythms of a dynamic life on a living world, to continue evolving. There was variation built into the equation as a necessity. But on the whole, entire natural rhythms of circadian, lunar and annual cycles had been reproduced on the space city.

Eridani had walked far from the center of her own compound, which clung to the rim wall behind her. After fifteen minutes of wandering in a zigzag pattern through the grass, Eridani's sight and hearing zeroed in on a quick flutter, high sudden chirp, and pause from the grass directly in front of her. The Feline froze. The cream and light sepia pattern of hair around her face seemed to sink into her cheekbones, lying flat and aerodynamic against her face, head and shoulders. Eridani postured a frozen shape, slowly releasing muscle control little by little to mimic the movement of wind and grass around her. The grasshopper, three meters in front of her, must consider the Feline nothing more than an inanimate object, tossed about by the same wind jostling the grass and grasshopper alike.

The sleek bipedal Feline inched forward in a slightly jerky side-to-side shivering motion. Tendons began to constrict and tense. Then she released. In a blur she performed a precise arching pounce from above directly onto the grasshopper, the Feline child's two hands coming together and down like lightning out of the direction of the insect's blind spot. Eridani counted to twenty, then removed her right hand from the mound she'd made with the two. She felt a twitter of movement under the left hand. In a flash her right hand dove down underneath the left, and her fingers grabbed the body of her pursuit. She pulled the creature out from its hiding place and held it up closely in front of her face. Eridani's eyes dilated and her breathing became quick and fervent. The insect squirmed in her fingers. The more it wriggled, the more excited the Feline became. In a single explosive twitch, the grasshopper tried to escape from its sudden captivity and leap back onto the tall grass. The Feline let out a high gurgling laugh. The hair around her face puffed out. She bent forward to catch the insect in her mouth as she tossed it in. Teeth bit down in a fast crunch, capturing the front half and head of the insect in her mouth with the back half kicking its legs among her whiskers and nose. Two more crunches, and the Feline swallowed the insect. Eridani paused, looked around, and began darting her tongue around her lips. Her hands smoothed the hair back that had been ruffled by the grasshopper's valiant yet fruitless struggle to escape mastication. A purring sound emanated from deep within her throat.

Eridani's attention slowly returned to the environment around her. Off to her right was a small wood. She knew that through the wood and around the rim of a small ancient crater, now a pond, then just up the great rim wall not too far, was her brother and the herd of dorsein grazing in the green foothills.

Eridani came to her senses after experiencing the glimmering rain of tiny leaves lit with sunlight. She sniffed in all directions around her. To her left her nostrils flared. She smelled freshly disturbed leaves and soil. Then, just ahead, was what appeared to be a lithe form appearing first here then there, laughing and running through the thicket. She was difficult to see, but Eridani followed easily. The girl was a calico, and had a scent unlike any other Feline child she knew. Eridani was smitten.

That was when Eridani had seen the other Feline child. She had suddenly run from somewhere ahead out of the high grass and darted into the wood. The child, a girl, slowed, turned to Eridani, and exclaimed in a sweet voice of discovery and delight, "I found some! You won't believe it! Come! Follow me!" The girl then turned and disappeared into the wood. Eridani's nostrils flared wide, her ears craned forward, her eyes fixed to the point between the trees where the girl had just vanished. Leaping forward, Eridani followed in close pursuit.

Eridani lost sight of the other Feline child. She ran through the slender trees. The sway of the branches in the breeze caused a flutter of sound. A mesmerizing feeling of being showered in a fall of sunlight caused Eridani to stop. The leaves shimmered down to the ground from above, catching the day's light in their gentle descent. The dance of shadow and light in the little thicket of wood entranced her.

She zigzagged left, then right, then left, back and forth, yet ever onward. Before long, and in what seemed like an instant, she was out of the wood. The bright "sunlight", enhanced and magnified solar radiation emitted by both the central dome over the great crater, and through the shimmering doughnut force field ringing the asteroids of the distant dim star, the "sunlight", blazed all around Eridani and blinded her for a moment. She stopped and looked ahead, covering her eyes with her hand as her pupils nearly vanished to the vertical slit common among all Felines.

There was the small crater rim. It was rocky in most places along the perimeter encompassing the crater's two hundred and fifty meter diameter. The girl appeared suddenly about twenty meters away, making her way slowly down the steep incline of the crater's inner wall toward the water forming the pond another fifteen meters ahead of her. All along that side of the rim was a field of different textured, shaded, and sized plants. The word "weeds" came to Eridani's mind. The girl stopped abruptly, and slowly crouched down to look at something hidden from where Eridani stood.

The girl turned and looked back at Eridani. She cupped one hand to her mouth to project her voice and ushered Eridani over at the same time with the other hand. "It's here! Over here! Come quick!" The girl seemed excited beyond control.

Eridani considered the scene for a moment. "What could it be?" she asked herself. "More grasshoppers? They're not so exciting to catch again if you've already eaten one." Eridani climbed the small crater wall and began descending to where the girl was crouching and gesturing to her in delight.

Eridani's hair began to bristle as she got closer to the girl. Slowing, she flared her nostrils and sniffed the scene. Ten meters away, she called out "What is your name?"

The girl stood up and replied "Canopus. My name is Canopus. Look what I've found!" and she turned, crouching back toward the ground at her feet once again.

Eridani relaxed a bit. A name was given. She had a name to associate with the new scent. A marker was now fixed in her brain, forever locking the name and scent together through her neural pathways. Eridani approached the small scene beside Canopus' feet.

"I'm Eridani."

The small crater's rim paused in its descent in the vicinity of where Canopus was crouching. A flat step about four meters wide and seven meters long opened above the pond, then sloped down again to the water's edge. In the flat step grew a variety of strange plants. Tall common grasses were thick just down to where the ground leveled off. There the grasses all but disappeared, replaced by tall thistles, creeping dragons that grew up the stems of other plants and flowered among the host plant's own flowers, red brushed flame snapdragons just a few inches tall.

Eridani made her way down among the wild plants toward Canopus. The little step smelled divine. Eridani breathed in the new smells where the multitude of plants and flowers grew. Her eyes glazed over for an instant and she thought she heard her named called. She opened her eyes in a start and saw Canopus directing Eridani's gaze down to a small patch of white flowers growing inconspicuously among a bramble of narrow green creepers, thick with small fan-like leaves.

Eridani's nostrils flared. Her eyes fixed on the flowers, dilated too great for the brilliance of the sunlight around them. Her hair bristled up menacingly high off her face, shoulders and arms. Crouching down to where Canopus was nearly sitting, Eridani got a fresh whiff of the flowers' intoxicating aroma.

"Do you smell it?" asked Canopus. "It's been driving me crazy since I found it first thing this morning. I've been out here since six. The girl's eyes were hyper-dilated. She began to swoon while crouching near the flowers.

Eridani knelt down and craned her neck toward the ground. She breathed in a great breath through her nose. In an instant her eyes grew wide, pupils hugely dilated. Her eyes seemed to roll back into her head. A flush of blood was pumped up to her brain as her heart beat faster and faster. Some sort of pheromone was at work here. She felt a warm flush, then a wave of refreshing cool exhilaration. Her body trembled at the psychotropic visions appearing before her eyes.

"Do you see them? Up in the sky?" asked Canopus. The girl swayed in a stupor, but she was staring intently at something in the sky. "Not in our sky. Not inside the dome, on the other side. Do you see them? Great reptilian birds, meters and meters in wingspan, flying between the asteroids within the force field ring? You can only see them as hallucinations, because your mind has to really believe something lives in the semi-pressurized atmosphere enveloping the asteroid ring.

Eridani looked up. Through a vibrant world of shocking color and moving light, she saw them. Great winged shadows, sweeping their great wings in slow undulations beyond her asteroid. They blocked out the light of the actual distant star in the distance. She felt a shiver and a shadow pass through her heart and body core. Her mind felt dizzy. The sky began to spin. Eridani licked her lips in quick motions with her tongue. A huge feeling of cottonmouth was making her thirsty. She seemed to hear a voice nearby. Turning toward Canopus, words began to distill themselves over the rush of her own heartbeat.

"'There is a sign in the sky. Beware these times! We are not safe from the shimmering field, even here in our ring of asteroids." Canopus seemed to float above the white flowers. A breeze came up, and Canopus dissipated like smoke.

37

Eridani's head spun. She struggled to stand up. Her nostrils were filled with pheromones from the flowers that kept her heart rate high. But as the breeze continued to blow, her head cleared some. Canopus' image ceased dissipating, and settled into her normal lithe Feline form.

Eridani took a deep breathe of fresh air, her head held high into the wind above the flowers. Exhaling the draught of air, she exclaimed "Those are grazimyths." She stood up and moved away from them. "Almost no one ever finds these. This is wonderful!"

"They only flower for a day. I can't believe they're growing here. I've been smelling them all morning, wanting to share them with someone." Canopus broke into a long purring gurgling giggle.

Grazimyths were the only native species on the asteroids. There was nothing here before the Great Construction thousands of years before, when the cities were first carved into the many craters on a thousand rocks orbiting the distant star. After the domes were erected and atmospheres introduced to the small new worlds, an astonishing event occurred. A plant grew out of the old rocky dust and mixed with the introduced varieties. The early Felines called it grazimyth. The flower exuded a molecular pheromone that sent Felines into a hallucinatory high. It didn't last very long, but visions and strange speech were common effects. No other species besides Felines seemed to be affected by the molecule.

Looking down, Eridani saw that the flowers were already turning pink, darkening by the minute.

"They're spent already," exclaimed Canopus. "We are so lucky! Almost no one finds these!"

Eridani focused her gaze on Canopus. She said, "I've never smelled a scent like yours before. Who are you?"

Canopus replied "I'm from Polaris. I'm one of the refugees."

Eridani looked at her strangely. "They say the Polarins are wizards. "Are you magic?"

Canopus giggled and ran away. Eridani followed her with her eyes as the girl circled the pond, and ran off down the far side of the opposite rim. Eridani turned around to face the great rim wall towering above the edge of the plain. She remembered her brother Galdinier, the message from their mother. Taking a deep breath, Eridani exhaled and glanced down. The flowers were now wilted purple veins draped over the long creepers. No scent came from the patch at all. Eridani stood up straight. She turned again to see Canopus disappear behind a boulder. Then Eridani climbed to the rim of the pond crater, over and down the other side, and began marching up a green valley toward the great rim. She knew her brother was in the high ground of this valley. She could also smell the dorsein from here.

9 GALDINIER

Eridani made her way through the ravine where tall trees brought welcome shade and humidity. But that did not stop swarms of small insects from collecting in the air before her. There was a lot to smell here, but she didn't tarry. Only the sunlight passing through the trees above and dancing on the ravine floor distracted her progress. She blinked and shook her head, then focused on the way ahead.

The path along the ravine floor wound great arcs to the left then the right as the ascent became steeper. On the left and crisscrossing to the right and back again was a now dry streambed. When the rainy season was created by the Ministry of Cycles, this path became a creek. For now, it was a direct route to the upper pasturelands.

Finishing up one broad curve from right to left, Eridani came out from under the trees onto a broad hill looking out on a landscape of hillocks about one kilometer wide. Beyond rose the sheer mountains of the crater rim. But immediately before her, a pleasant expanse of undulating green grass spread out on all sides. On the side of a hillock in the distance before her, Eridani spotted a smear of white amidst the green. The irregular pattern slowly moved. It was the heard of dorsein eating their way around the hillock. On the rise of an adjacent hillock just to the left sat a lone figure watching over the dorsein. It was Galdinier.

A warm breeze blew across the top of the hillock. Galdinier sat cross-legged facing toward the rim wall. On the hillock before him grazed the dorsein. Exactly twenty-seven animals slowly ate their way in a roughly forward moving up and over clockwise motion. But they were slow. It was difficult to determine if any logic guided their movement other than choice grasses and an appetite. Galdinier had been here for several hours, and he was watching the herd. Before him on the ground Galdinier had cleared a meter square of dirt, removing all grass and roots. The square was smooth and level. Arranged on the square were twenty-seven small stones. Each stone represented an animal in the herd. Since moving the herd to this location earlier in the morning, he had been sitting before the square. Periodically, as the herd moved, Galdinier move the stones, dragging them across the fine dirt. He had started with the stones in the lower left corner of the square. By looking at each stones' drag line in the dirt, he could see they kept a slow but sure pace with just a few zig-zags to each side, but ever to the left and forward, scaling a gentle hillock and moving around it, heads down and eating the whole time.

The dorsein had been bred on the asteroids for several thousand years. Resembling thick white woolly sheep, the beasts were yet larger. They had necks that could extend out a meter to reach distant grass mounds. The sturdy barrel-shaped bodies had three stomachs to digest the rich grasses that grew on the many domed asteroids within the force field doughnut. Outside the Feline system, the herds had a reputation for being docile.

Galdinier observed the overall geometric shape that the perimeter of the herd formed. It was constantly changing like an amoeba. But each shape represented the same thing, the outline of twenty-seven individuals. Galdinier practiced his geometric mind game by closing his eyes for up to a minute. Then he quickly opened them and stared at the herd. Closing his eyes tight again, Galdinier memorized the fading image on his eyelids. He noticed the outline, and clumping of some dorsein in one location, a few off by themselves. And it was twenty-seven. He opened his eyes again and noticed the direction each beast was pointed. They were more or less random. Maybe a quarter of them were facing up and left, but more were looking in other directions on the whole. Yet they kept their mark. Galdinier saw one dorsein raise its head, let out a sneeze, and walk a couple of meters to some more grass. Identical looking to where he had just been, thought Galdinier. But to the dorsein, one clump was better than another. Galdinier looked down at his map of stone and dirt, and dragged one of his markers a little through the dirt to a new location.

The lines in the sand resembled the twisting climb of plant runners, crisscrossing and interlocking. Galdinier tried to guess what shape the pattern would take in a minute's time. Most of the stones will move a little. Galdinier poked a finger in the dirt in front of each stone, based on the current direction of each dorsein and their ambling progression.

All of a sudden a long and gangly spider speedily scampered out of the grass from the right of the square. It was quickly upon the collection of stones, where the obstacles caused the spider to pause. Galdinier's hair stood straight up, bristling along his spine. His eyes grew wide as his irises expanded to full. He drew in a string of quick short breaths, frozen. There was panic in Galdinier's eyes. The spider must be removed, but not at the expense of disturbing the stones or their tracks. The spider sat in the midst of the stones, moving one leg to touch a stone nearest its many eyes. Galdinier quickly looked up. A desperate thought occurred to him and he quickly swept his gaze among the dorsein, seeking the hint of an enemy, or a giant spider. Stranger things had crept out of the deep holes and crevasses of the asteroids soon after the force field gave them an atmosphere fifteen thousand years before. But on the hillock, no marauding predator snuck in amongst the dorsein. Turning his attention downward again however, Galdinier saw the spider make its way across to the next stone.

Alarm continued to grow on Galdinier's face. His ears flipped back and forth from straight up to forward, then back, then up again. His eyes were wide. Nostrils flared as he took in quick breaths. The spider had an injured leg. As it made its way across the stone and track field of Galdinier's "map", its trailing damaged leg dragged through the fine dirt and altered the stone tracks. Galdinier leaned forward and began to blow air at the spider. Dust blew over the tracks as the spider halted its wavering advance. Galdinier stopped in frustration. He looked left and right, trying to find some means to manipulate and coax the creature off his map. He turned back to face the spider. Pitiful thing. He reached out and plucked the spider up carefully between two fingers. Galdinier raised his hand and dangled the creature before his face. He observed its struggles. Two great eyes locked with the spider's eight. Galdinier brought his nose closer and inhaled. He closed his eyes. He detected a sweet woodsy scent. Then just a little foul. Galdinier opened his eyes just in time to see the spider eject a second spray of venom at him. He jerked his head back and out of the way of the spray. Spiders on the Feline asteroids had little or no toxic venom by genetic manipulation, by design. Galdinier took one more look at the defiant creature, then popped it into his mouth and gave it several good crunchings before swallowing it down. Galdinier inhaled a deep breath and relaxed back into his cross-legged repose.

He looked up at the herd of dorsein. Instantly he saw something not right. The pattern of the geometric perimeter was somehow off. Quickly he realized what had happened. A beast was missing. While he was distracted with the invasive spider's trespassing over his map, a dorsein must have moved around the side of the hillock before him, dropping down the other side out of view. Galdinier looked down at his map and considered whether he should remove a stone, or push it around to circle a mock hillock. The dorsein was still on the hillock, so Galdinier moved a stone in a clockwise circle away from the others.

"Time for a culling of the herd," thought Galdinier. On the majority of large asteroids in the Feline belt, dorsein herds similar to this grazed in the verdant hills and valleys under the domes. Herders like Galdinier kept an eye on them, tracked their movements, identified those that led and observed those that followed. A master-breeding scheme had been in place for much of the past thousand years. The most aggressive of the leaders were separated. A similar separation was performed on the most docile of the followers. The result was three separate herds. The most docile was sold off worlds to peoples beyond the asteroid ring. The middle herd remained as the core of the asteroid herds. The most aggressive dorsein were segregated on a special asteroid as part of a special defensive program.

The downdraft breeze from the rim wall lessened. In its absence, the rich smells and rising warmth from the great central crater valley wafted up to the hillocks and filled Galdinier's nostrils with scent. Among the many plant and earthy smells, Galdinier recognized a familiar and pleasant smell interspersed with the others. It was Eridani. Galdinier turned to his right and looked down toward the ravine that led from the upward climbing hillocks along the crater to the great rim wall. He saw his sister making her way up the side of the hillock on which he sat. Their eyes met as she looked up, and both smiled with the sense of deep understanding and knowing that only close siblings possessed.

"I thought you'd be higher up the rim wall," said Eridani as she approached the crest.

"The grass is rich here," replied Galdinier. "The herd has been content to tarry. It's given me an opportunity to closely observe them."

Eridani paused near Galdinier at the edge of his square map. She glanced down at the tracks left by the stones. Her eyes followed the wiggly tracks to the obvious conclusion. "Lots of leaders, Gald."

"About a third," replied Galdinier. "It's about time for the next culling."

Eridani looked over at the herd on the neighboring hillock. The breeze from the rim wall's heights picked up again. She breathed in the ozone and rocky scents that wafted down. As she did, the lead dorsein on the hillock crest stopped grazing and looked up toward the rim wall to sample the wind. It let out a baying sound, and disappeared down the far side again. Half of the herd picked up their heads and began to follow the lead around and over the hillock. The others shuffled along behind, continuing to graze as they moved.

Eridani looked back at Galdinier, who was busy moving more stones to catch up with the sudden movement of the herd. "What are you doing up here?" he asked.

"Mother sent me," replied Eridani. "She wants us to talk to Father."

"About what?" prodded Galdinier, finishing with his map and looking up at her.

"I'm not sure. I was on my way out to look for grasshoppers when she stopped me and said I must find you and tell you Father wants to talk to us both."

"The herd isn't ready to come down for another couple hours."

"She wants us to meet him as soon as possible," said Eridani. "But that was two hours ago already."

"What have you been doing then?" asked Galdinier. "It doesn't take two hours to get here."

Eridani suddenly beamed. "Oh Gald! The most amazing thing! I found a grazimyth flower!"

The hair on Galdinier's face momentarily stood up and his nostrils flared. His eyes grew wide. "You did?"

"And that's not the half of it," said Eridani fervently. "I saw the flying reptiles above the dome in the asteroid belt. I saw them soar above us!"

"Hm, is that so?" said Galdinier with a quick huff. "Are you sure?"

"Oh don't be that way, Gald," said Eridani. "I sure did. Another Feline showed me. And get this. She was from Polaris"

Galdinier furrowed his forehead above his eyes and squinted at his sister. "What is she doing here?"

"Well, she told me she is a refugee," said Eridani. "But also the smell. She smelled so different. She was so musky, so strong."

"Who is she?"

"She said her name was Canopus.

"Hm. There is not that much room here for more Felines. I wonder why she came?"

"What was she doing?"

"She was in the grassy plain beside the little wood leading to the pond crater. Probably chasing grasshoppers like me. I followed her through the trees. She led me to the grazimyth. We both got lost in the dreaminess." Eridani paused as her eyebrows furrowed. She squinted into space remembering something.

"What is it Eri?" asked Galdinier, noticing the sudden change in his sister's focus.

Eridani saw in her mind's eye the grazimyth flower, smelled the intoxicating scent, looked up at the flying reptiles above the dome. But something else tugged at her mind. A voice. She heard a voice through the trance. She looked back at her brother. "I remembered something. Canopus told me something very strange. I didn't pay attention to it at the time."

"What was it?" asked Galdinier.

Eridani closed her eyes. Her ears bent back and her hair was flat against her face. Images and sounds passed through her mind. The grasshopper. It was so crunchy. The laughing girl. Chasing her into the wood among the shining leaves, the grazimyth. As her mind's eye saw the shadow of the great flying reptiles cross beyond the crater dome, she heard Canopus' voice.

Aloud to Galdinier she repeated, "There is a sign in the sky. Beware these times! We are not safe from the shimmering field, hiding here in our ring of asteroids."

Galdinier stood up and took Eridani's hands. Eridani opened her eyes, looked into his. "What does it mean?" he asked. "What did she mean?"

"A sign in the sky," murmured Eridani. "Suppose she meant the flying reptiles?"

"Nah," said Galdinier quickly. "They fly continuously around the ring, alighting on small unpopulated asteroids from time to time to breed or eat or rest. They're always flying overhead, thousands of them all around the ring. Nothing special about that."

"I suppose not," said Eridani. "Except it was the first time I'd ever seen 'em."

Galdinier thought about that for a moment. "That might mean something then."

Eridani looked over to the dorsein making their way instinctively back down and around the opposite hillock. She turned back to Galdinier and said, "Gald, we have to go see Father. I'll help you bring the dorsein back down to the lower pasture."

Galdinier reached into his right pocket and removed a slender hand held silver plate, rectangular but for the rounded corners. He pointed one face down, above the stones and tracks of his dirt map. A bright flash emanated from the plate. The square map was illuminated for an instant as its picture was taken.

He put the plate back into his pocket and turned again to Eridani. "Ok. I've been sitting here for hours and could use a walk. Where is Father?"

"In the dark city in the crater underside of the asteroid, "replied Eridani.

"Alright then. Let's get these dorsein back down the hillocks. Come on."

10 THE PRECESSION STAR

The two descended into the depths of the asteroid via a rapid turbo lift tube that passed beneath the rim wall city. The lift engaged in a controlled fall for three hundred kilometers. For forty-five minutes they fell. The lift was plexiglass, hard and smooth, an oval teardrop shape. The tube itself was a smooth bore hole down through the asteroid. It was sealed in a clear smooth substance, almost gel like. The lift slid silently and constantly down. The various stratigraphic layers of the asteroid were vividly illuminated in the borehole walls. Layers of dust compacted like sandstone, carbonaceous composites, iridium, hard metals nickel and iron. On they went. Galdinier marveled at the many colors apparent in the rock they were passing through. Ancient relics from the formation of this star system billions of years before. Beautiful. The lift slowed as it finally neared the center of the asteroid, half way on its trip to the underside. The tube ended in a large circular chamber. The teardrop lift emerged into the expanse that was half a kilometer in diameter. The lift was connected at the top and the bottom to snakelike hydraulic attachments. In an artful dance as it cleared the tube's aperture, the attachments snapped in unison and separated from the lift, which then floated in a free fall, drifting in the chamber's anti-gravity well.

Galdinier operated the controls to rotate the lift one hundred eighty degrees. The spherical chamber was precision hewn from the nickel-iron core of the asteroid. An internal carapace of titanium scaffolding curved in a great crisscross around the expanse. Thousands of huge meter-wide lamps were positioned at three-meter intervals from one another on the structure.

They shown out toward the central focus point of the chamber.

Eridani looked out at the dazzling expanse. As she did so, she realized they were not alone. All around them, above and below, dozens of other teardrop lifts were exiting from tubes around the perimeter and entering other tubes on the opposite side. They floated in and out in a constant and seemingly slow motion dance across the expanse. Eridani saw Felines in the other lifts as they passed. Some held single occupants, others from two to four. All were floating through the expanse turning over and over. Galdinier was busy maneuvering the controls. Each lift was fitted with magnetic pulses that automatically repelled any other that got too close. Galdinier diligently steadied the lift's spin, controlling its tumble. He wanted Eridani to enjoy the spectacle.

It really was a surreal interaction of Felines deep within this artificial chamber at the center of the asteroid, mused Galdinier. They passed through the bright center of the chamber, half way to the other side. Nearby another lift slowly turned end over end as it passed within two meters. Two Feline youths with wild spiked hair, dyed to resemble the wild cats of other worlds like leopards and cheetahs and tigers, grinned at Galdinier and Eridani as they passed eye to eye. The lifts' magnetic pulses fired, and the two lifts catapulted away from one another. Galdinier and Eridani looked at each other and began laughing. Their eyes were wide despite the glare of the chamber, and their ears were lowered, pointed away from their heads. The youths in the other lift tumbled away laughing, delight in their eyes.

The lift completed another turn. Its teardrop top turned to face an aperture growing in the approaching chamber wall. Galdinier slowed their ascent to the tube opening. Flexible grapplers automatically reached out, approaching and connecting with the lift, fixing it to the tube.

Despite the moderate size of most of the inhabited asteroids in the force field ring, the gravity of each was higher than the mass implied. Closer to the gravity of larger planetoids, each asteroid had at its core a complex energy source powering the cities as well as providing stronger gravitational forces for the inhabitants. Thousands of years before, the Felines had learned how to harness quantum singularities to create planet-like gravity fields. Resident in the center of each inhabited asteroid was an anti-gravity chamber like the one Galdinier and Eridani passed through now. Deep in the walls of the chamber, machinery held captive in a spinning force field the powerful micro singularity that provided for the life and livelihood of the asteroid's residents.

The lift holding the Feline completed its connection to the other lift tube. They were catapulted up through the rock to the central crater cities on the underside of the asteroid. Up, up, up the lift traveled at great speed, racing to the surface. The trip was another three hundred kilometers. Again the asteroid's colorful stratigraphic history in its lithosphere streamed passed as they gazed out at the sight. On and on it went, from metallic ores to composites, to sandstone. Presently the lift slowed as it emerged to another rim walled city. Up a tall green and red crystal building the lift advanced. On this side of the asteroid, the dark hours held long sway. It was the season of autumn on the underside. A chill came through the lift. Neither Galdinier nor Eridani had left the crater cities of the springtime upper side in many months. Small fires glowed at different points in the distance on the plain. Campers and groups and couples enjoyed the long evenings by firelight. Above them, stars shown through the panels in the domes far overhead. Images of the space outside the nebula were projected on the domes to simulate natural night.

The lift slowed to a stop a third of the way up the rim wall, far above the city spires. A door opened in the lift as if a finger disturbed a sheet of flowing water. The clear walls of the lift undulated and rippled around the opening. Galdinier and Eridani grasped each other's hands and stepped out onto a platform at a cave opening in the rim wall. Before them extended the great crater world of the asteroid's underside. They took a long look at the fires and dark woods of the plain. Here and there small lakes reflected starlight. The light of cities twinkled in the distance on the opposite rim wall. Behind them in the rock opened a wide hall. They turned their backs on the crater world and walked hand in hand down the hall into the rim wall rock.

The cave complex butted up against the edge of the crater dome high in the rim wall. The cave opened up into a large room full of quietly whirring machinery. In the dimly lit interior, lights blinked, dials whirled, screens displayed interconnecting lines of color. The back wall of the cave was translucent, looking out beyond the asteroid to the enveloping atmospheric space of the doughnut force field. The glow from the Great Aurora Nebula flooded the cave in a soft rose-pink glow. In the middle distance between the dome and the force field, distant verdant companion asteroids orbited nearby, some rapidly passing in front, others moving more slowly beyond.

Before the screen of a large console sat an aged Feline. He was alone among the equipment in the room. On the console's screen was displayed a confusing interconnected array of colored lines emerging from the right, intersecting in a trembling circular convergence of lines in the center left of the screen. Some lines passed through the circle, others seemed to pass just near to it, then change course toward or away from the center as if attracted or repelled by the convergence. The Feline followed the moving lines as if they were the unfolding scenes of a play revealing a hidden plot.

Galdren was the Minister of Astronomical and Historical Projections. It was a catchall fancy title for one who observed celestial phenomena, and tracked historical, current and future trends in cosmology. It was an advisory role to the Feline Leadership Council. His observations and projections were considered valued insights in the sphere of wider geo-political interdependencies and policy.

Galdren followed the progression of a blue line that emerged from the central intersection. Its direction was perpendicular to most of the other lines. It originated from the center of the convergence, then spiraled outward counter-clockwise, unraveling around and around until it emerged below all the other lines. As it exited the convergence, Galdren observed a curious change in the behavior of the other lines as they approached the convergence. As the blue line exited the circle, all the other lines began avoiding the central convergence. They seemed to rally around the new line as a new focal point. The original convergence dissipated as the new intersection circle developed.

The echo of footsteps interrupted Galdren's concentration. His ears pricked back behind his head. Turning, he saw his children Galdinier and Eridani appear around a bend in the large central hallway and make their way toward him. Their bodies were illuminated by the rose-pink glow of the dome wall.

"Hello my children!" exclaimed Galdren rising from his chair before the console. He extended his arms to them and said "Thank you for meeting me here."

"It's not often we get to visit you at your work, Father," said Galdinier, accepting a hug from the old Feline.

"What does the future hold for us, Father?" asked Eridani, grinning as she loosed herself from his embrace. She always chided her father, calling him a fortuneteller. Eridani's eyes went wide looking at the projection console.

Galdren laughed. "My new crystal ball portends many events, Eridani. Perhaps you'd like to describe the readouts for me?" He waved his hand across the console screen. The lines continued to flow from the right to the new central convergence at the center, then diverge and exit further to the left.

Eridani approached the console at her father's side. She was fascinated by the ever changing, yet strangely consistent, design the lines presented. Despite her sometimes naiveté, Eridani had a deep understanding of the underlying interconnectedness of disparate events, and the new paradigms that sometimes resulted unforeseen from their convergence.

Eridani watched the play of the lines for a few minutes. Then she turned to Galdren and Galdinier. "Something a long time in coming is happening. Something that has always been, therefore we cannot stop it. We will have to take advantage of a new situation." She turned back to the console. The pattern repeated over and over. A pinwheel pattern spiraled out from the center of the convergence. Lines out of the right diverted by the emerging new event line.

"What lines are these, Father?" asked Galdinier, stepping closer to the console.

Galdren replied, "This is an overall representation of cultural interactions within and beyond our system. Notice how all the emerging lines ripple and twist on their journey from right to left. These are the normal exchanges and evolutions of political thought, artistic expression, behavior and commerce. The central convergence represents a closer examination of the relationships. A different perspective. Those lines on the right show the linear progression. The convergence is like looking at the lines head on. It shows the non-linear view."

"So something is happening, some shared cultural change which will have an effect on all the other events," offered Galdinier.

"It's not just some event," said Eridani. "Look what it's doing." She pointed to the new line below the convergence. It repeated the attraction of lines. "It's creating a new nexus."

"Be careful to not presuppose cause and effect," cautioned Galdren. "I've been studying this for a number of days. It is most likely that the catalyst for the new nexus merely heralds an event, but does not by itself cause it."

Galdinier added, "The news a herald brings may impact many, sometimes more directly, than the actual event represented by the news."

Galdren's ears moved slightly back on his head as his eyes widened. The hair on his face momentarily rose then fell back flat while an exhalation steamed out his flared nostrils. "My children are quite perceptive," he finally ventured.

"Do you know what event this portrays?" asked Eridani.

Galdren's eyes glistened almost imperceptibly in the rose-pink glow of the room. His hair seemed to puff just slightly, and a grin spread across his face. The children glanced at one another and back to their father. They smelled an exciting pheromone.

"I asked you to come here to witness something remarkable," Galdren said hurriedly. He turned to the console and entered some commands on a touchpad to the left of the screen. The rose-pink glow that flooded the room suddenly winked out. The dome wall projected an image of black space filled with stars and galaxies. The children each let out a simultaneous soft gasp in the darkness.

Galdren pointed to a region in the upper right corner of the wall where two stars danced. "These are the twin stars Sothis and Solis. And around each is an inhabited world."

Galdinier replied, "Lupus is the name of the inhabited world around Sothis. Canines live there, with Humans."

"It is said Felines originated there on a world around Solis," said Galdinier.

"Ours is a journey along the stepping stones of an ancient path," said Galdren. And do you know the name of it's sister world around Solis?"

Eridani stared at the two stars her father indicated. She knew something deep about those stars. Something she learned in passing long ago. A footnote in an old record display. She closed her eyes and let her mind open up unhindered in every direction. A three dimensional picture of events flashed through her mind. She saw herself at home years ago studying Feline philosophy. Her brother was at the table next to her taking a practice test on animal husbandry. Eridani yawned in the vision. She was bored. The trigger transcended time. Eridani yawned standing in the cave looking back at the stars. Coming out of the yawn in her vision, her eyes fell upon a line at the bottom of the page she had just read, but apparently overlooked, for she did not remember it. A single simple sentence jumped out at her. She opened her eyes and read it aloud from her vision. "It is Earth, she said."

Galdren smiled in admiration at his daughter. Her abilities at recall were extraordinary. "Yes. And each is the other world's Precession Star."

"Precession Star?" asked Galdinier. "What is that?"

"The Precession Star waxes and wanes over epochs of time, as seen from each world. Sometimes it is quite close, and other times quite far away. It is an ebb and flow, as the two stars revolve around each other in a minuet dance. Each pass is a world age for each. Such a change in the ages is occurring now."

The children stole a glance at one another. The same voice echoed in both of their minds, the words of the girl from Polaris, Canopus. "'There is a sign in the sky. Beware these times! We are not safe from the shimmering field, even here in our ring of asteroids."

11 THE DEAL

A bright sun shone out upon the morning, filling the bay with waves of heat hazes dancing over the ocean waves in the evaporated humidity. The light played games of color and hue reflected off the sea. A few pleasure boats drifted lazily offshore. Several couples pushed carriages or led by hand children along the length of the Ambassadorial pier, stopping to peer over the rails down into the waters below. The pier was extended out into the sea from a protected compound on the coast reserved for off world embassies and residences. Sea birds squawked and fluttered near a woman who tossed breadcrumbs into the air near the pier's end. She was dressed in a three-quarter full tan cotton wrap and dress. Her hair was held back and kept manageable by a red scarf. As she tossed another handful of crumbs into the air directly at the fluttering birds, she observed a lone man in light blue exercise pants, wide-brimmed hat and collared shirt ambling along the pier toward her. The man stopped several meters from her and gazed out over the edge of the pier.

Dania sealed the top of her bag of breadcrumbs and tucked it away in a larger handbag she carried. Moving down the pier toward the lone man, she took a seat on a bench and stared out into the warm sunny distance. Presently the man turned away from the rail and took his seat on the bench next to Dania.

"It's a beautiful morning. Bright and warm," said Dania keeping her gaze directed before her at the sea. "Such warm humid days are a thing of the past on Drigo."

"How is the political situation?" asked Markhab.

"We have risen together to face the global cooling challenge," said Dania. "Our scientists have identified the most probable areas to remain free of ice, including along some of the new shorelines that chase the ever more receding tides. But more and more are opting to relocate to Sabral. Our agricultural plantings there are ever expanding. The entire population of Drigo is employed in the efforts to mitigate and find advantage with the new situation. We fully expect new industries and opportunities for commerce to open up. Of course the transition is difficult, but the alternative continues to stare down at us from the tops of the advancing glaciers across the entire planet. Believe it or not, our dorsein herds are feeling the greatest pain. Their grazing lands have almost disappeared, and they do not seem to be able to adapt to the loss of their grasses."

Markhab turned away from Dania to stare back out at the sea. "We all have our challenges," he said.

"And I have news on your challenge, Markhab," said Dania, lowering her voice. "I have your ship and a pilot to ferry a small team to Earth."

Markhab straightened up his posture and his eyes suddenly grew wide. "So soon?"

"There were difficult strings to pull, Markhab. But it has been arranged. There was a window of opportunity my people were able to exploit," said Dania. "The Felines are, preoccupied. The ship will be ready to depart in a week. Will your team be ready to depart by then?"

"I will summon professor Altair to Cronapolis by military transport."

"The ship is small. There will be room comfortably for five. Is that enough?"

"That will be sufficient," said Markhab.

"Two weeks of supplies will be stocked on the ship. It can be stretched to a month if need be. I trust that will be sufficient time to accomplish your goals?"

"I'm hoping. Will we have an intelligence report available on the Earth civilization? I imagine we can't simply fly a ship down to the planet's surface and expect to be ignored," said Markhab.

"Our pilot will brief the team on intelligence assessments. Data on Earth is sparse, as you can imagine. But we are doing our homework," said Dania. "My government has obtained some smuggled reports of Earth from Feline contacts. But that probably won't include secret weapons hidden, missing, or destroyed thousand of years ago. Does Altair know what he's looking for? Or where? Earth is a big place, as large as Lupus or Drigo."

"Altair fancies himself an expert on the topic of all things Earth. It's a personal hobby of his. He's actually obsessed with it."

Dania took a long quiet look at Markhab. The silence and stare made Markhab feel uncomfortable. He took a deep breath, then ventured, "Dania, why do I sense a caveat to your offer of assistance?"

The Drigan ambassador cleared her throat. "Ever the perceptive one, Markhab." Dania looked about her to make sure no one besides Markhab was in earshot. A seabird fluttered nearby, then moved off beyond the pier. "This adventure of yours could have monumental consequences, First Commissioner. The Felines could quarantine Lupus if they found out what you are planning."

"My government will unite Human Lupus with this tool, Dania. The Felines are not my greatest concern. We must eliminate the threat to Lupin unity posed by the wild Canines. I believe we can counter any threat posed by the insular Felines."

"I want your discovery to be shared with Drigo, Markhab. Together, Lupus and Drigo could use this technology to form a powerful alliance, and change the balance of power in the region."

"You mean Drigo needs an edge to bolster your current vulnerability in the face of your ice age calamity," said Markhab. "No Dania. The plans stay with me. But your offer of alliance intrigues me. Is there something in the short term I can offer you? After all, none of this may pan out."

Dania cleared her throat. "Actually there is, our dorsein herders. Their northern pasturelands have nearly vanished under the ice and permafrost. And Sabral is too warm for the herds to survive. We have ten thousand people, herders and their families, plus the herds themselves in the tens of thousands. There is no place to relocate them. However," Dania brushed back some hair, loosed in the breeze. "I know that a great many of your colonists on Wror are returning to Lupus, or are venturing further to the uber planet of Keldo. They fear battles will meet them on Wror."

"That is an unfortunate truth, and one not widely known. It is a temporary setback," said Markhab.

"What would you say to allowing the Drigan dorsein herders to relocate to Wror? The northern lands would suit them well. And, it could help cement trust and partnership between our peoples during these mutually difficult times."

"Drigans on Wror?" said Markhab. "Our colonists are not of the accepting kind. We carefully screened our emigrants for loyalty. However, we are experiencing a power vacuum and manpower shortfall."

"Of course," said Dania. "Though, there would be meat and wool to sell at market."

"I admit, the local economy could use a boost."

"Do we have a deal then?" pressed Dania.

"I will discuss this at today's Politburo meeting. I'll give you my decision by tomorrow."

"Thank you for considering the request, Markhab." Dania straightened up to compose herself. "Now I must head to my embassy. Thank you for meeting with me."

"It is always a pleasure, Dania." Markhab leaned forward to kiss her on both cheeks. "We'll speak soon."

"I will have more information on your ship in a few days."

"Thank you." Markhab stood back as Dania left the rail and gracefully made her way back to the pier's land connection. He watched her disappear into the street crowd.

12 STRATEGIES

All thirteen Commissioners were present around the conference room's great table. The conversation among the Commissioners was formal and superficial, though many were absorbed in their own briefing materials. Events on Lupus and Wror were unfolding quickly.

Markhab sat resolutely quiet, but not calm. He exuded an air of impatience. There was much to discuss today, and so many things to put into motion. He held his cigar, turned it over in his hand finger to finger, forward then backward. He glanced up and across the table at Commissioner Corvus. The young man was exchanging pleasantries with Menkar. Corvus glanced briefly at Markhab, then was back with Menkar. Finally Markhab put the cigar down on the table and looked around at the other Commissioners. Pausing at Tokez, he began.

"Commissioner Tokez, I want a status on the communiqués from and to all of Lupus around the time of the attack. What have you found?"

Tokez straightened in her chair on Markhab's left and cleared her throat. She brushed her hand over her short shellacked red hair. It had just been cut that morning, and the room felt cold. "First Commissioner, there was absolutely no spike in communications from Lupus under our governance. Transmissions to and from the Cantons and the Territory of the Shining Star actually decreased over the same period until word spread about the attack. As far as communications from Canius and Canoon, very little, and the decryption protocols picked up nothing out of the ordinary. But it is interesting to note," and Tokez looked around at her comrades before continuing, "there was unusual coronal activity on the day leading up to the attack."

"Define 'unusual'," said Markhab.

"There were no observed solar flares or other extra solar activity to account for it."

"Your assessment?" pressed Markhab.

"None, Sir. It appears to be a coincidental phenomenon."

"Has this phenomenon been observed before?" continued Markhab.

"Occasionally, yes. But no correlation to events on the ground as far as I can tell," replied Tokez.

"Then let's save the cosmological weather reports for the science academy briefings."

"Yes Sir."

Markhab continued. "What of communications to and from Wror?"

"All normal chatter, and only between the colony and Lupus Major and Minor," said Tokez.

"Listen to me, people." Markhab turned in his seat and glared at each Commissioner. "We have been attacked. Someone was responsible, and it was probably the Canines. Therefore, regardless of the culprit or culprits, communications must have been exchanged. Think outside the box. Or we'll all find ourselves sucking down radioactive fallout here in Cronapolis before we know it."

Menkar interjected herself into the conversation. "Commissioner Tokez was thorough, First Commissioner. I worked with her on reviewing all communications back to six months prior to the attack. No conversations intercepted were relevant, no date or time stamps were out of the ordinary. We should entertain the possibility that the attack was not coordinated here on Lupus."

"What are you suggesting, Commissioner? What greater enemy do we have than the Canines?" posited Markhab.

"We should simply entertain the possibility. Of course all dialectical evidence points to the Canines, but it's circumstantial at present," said Menkar.

"General Taurus, what are the immigration statistics from Wror?" asked Markhab turning away from Menkar and changing the subject.

The elder Commissioner was ready for his report. "Two thousand have returned since the attack, with another seven thousand in transit. Reports from the auxiliary spaceport of Torth Town indicate fifteen thousand on a number of waiting lists. Including the last figures, that's approximately ten percent of the colonial population." The General rarely needed to refer to his notes. As the oldest Commissioner on the Politburo, he prided himself in knowing all aspects of his areas of responsibility. "First Commissioner, local defenses on Wror cannot adequately rebuke any threat interested in taking advantage of this situation," he added.

"We have one Scorpion battle cruiser in orbit at present. A second will arrive by morning our time," added Corvus. The young security expert was full of confidence. "But the new battlement was meant as a deployment replacement. The Arctus, in orbit now, has been on extended duty already for two local solar cycles." Glancing at Taurus briefly before turning back to Markhab, he added "The attack on Wror was a terrorist action, not interplanetary warfare."

"Keep the new battle cruiser in orbit for a few days nonetheless," said Markhab. "The show of force will be impressive."

"It will be done," said Corvus.

"In relation to our population issue," Markhab began, "I would like immediate high level discussions to take place with the Drigan embassy to invite dorsein herders and their families to settle in the north of Wror."

The other Commissioners looked from side to side at one another, then back at the First Commissioner.

"A strategic move, First Commissioner," said Menkar, breaking the silence. "Assistance to Drigo during its environmental catastrophe, at just the time we need to renew a bold commitment for a Human presence on Wror."

"Precisely," said Markhab, smiling at Menkar, and he thought *Ah, an ally, and leverage against Dania. It will be easier to keep an eye on both her and the Politburo this way.*

"I will brief you on the specifics later," added Markhab. The First Commissioner held his gaze on Corvus, let his eyes glaze over in a moment lost to himself. Suddenly he regained his focus. Turning to Taurus, he said, "I'm told there could be as many as ten thousand seeking entry to Wror. These are traditional fierce mountain families, very insular. But they would fight for their survival if put to it. Taurus, do you see an issue with this?"

It was always a gamble asking the elder Commissioner his opinion. Taurus was a well-respected old guard stalwart and supporter of the harsh military government. A sharp intellect.

The Elder Commissioner replied "That would put us ahead of our prior growth projections, assuming the first settlers began arriving in the next few weeks. The planet's population must be great enough for it to support a viable home guard defense force, answerable to Lupus."

Markhab agreed with the General. Running his eyes among the other Commissioners, he concluded the subject. "Good. This at least solves one problem." Turning to Commissioner Ecko, he asked "Do we have the isotope results from the detonation on Wror?"

The Commissioner sitting at the far end of the table to Markhab's right answered in his usual quiet voice. "First Commissioner, the results only just came in." The dark gaunt Commissioner swallowed, then continued. "The isotopic readings are confirmed as identical to stockpiles from the Lupus Minor Materiel Depot near Bafaria. They are not from ores mined in the plutonium mines of Canoon. Agents in Bafaria are conducting a lockdown and inventory of the warehouses there as we speak."

Markhab looked as if he didn't understand what had just been said. He looked at Commissioner Ecko as if he had made no sense. "The radioactive fuel of the bomb that attacked Bara-Band came from Lupus Minor?" Markhab was visibly uncomfortable. "I want the entire city of Bafaria put under a curfew," he fumed. "There must be Canine sympathizers among the population, and infiltrating the military outpost facilities there." Quickly addressing Commissioner Corvus, he said, "See to it that roadblocks are established in both directions around Bafaria. Close the civilian space and air facilities. Reopen them to limited use tomorrow after strict security measures are put into place."

"Immediately, First Commissioner," replied Corvus. He entered commands into a personal hand held communication device, putting the lockdown into play immediately.

"And order another two military brigades to redeploy to Lupus Minor," added Markhab. Corvus nodded as he continued transmitting his orders.

Markhab gave additional orders, from renewed press censorship, to limitations on civilian freedom of movement, to communications restrictions. The session continued late into the evening. The First Commissioner exercised greater and greater paranoid control as his thoughts kept returning to Lupus Minor as the source of the bomb materiel. It didn't fit into the neat reasoning he had based his assumptions upon. Markhab was overcompensating for his creeping sense of powerlessness against unknown enemy collaborators. In his growing unease, his kept returning his gaze to Commissioner Corvus, who sat with complete attention focused on Markhab throughout the remainder of the session.

13 DOG PLAY

Markhab hummed to himself as he washed his hands and arms in the steel sink that projected out from the black steel and wire mesh wall. It was an old tune from his childhood that came to him during sessions like the one he was finishing up now. The humming was nearly imperceptible over the cacophony of noise. The cold room echoed loud industrial music. It was more a din of clangs, bangs, screeches and bells, with added sounds resembling loud machinery, slamming doors and electronic distortion. The noise was nearly deafening, but Markhab continued to hum his childhood tune, oblivious to the raucous.

The sink ran red with the blood he was washing off. He scrubbed around his fingernails and in between his fingers. The warm soap and water erased the tangible evidence from the torture session. Markhab raised his head and looked at his face in the scratched mirror above the sink. The top right corner of the mirror was cracked where Markhab had smashed the victim's head into it. Strands of thick black hair still protruded from the crack.

Markhab viewed his face on the left and right in the mirror. Some spots of blood, a little gore, were spattered on his right cheek and had begun to drip off as it dried. Markhab lathered warm soapy water on his face and splashed it away. Presently he viewed his now clean face in the mirror and opened his mouth to inspect his clenched white teeth. All clean.

Over the repetitive cacophony of the industrial music, a groaning moan came from the back corner of the room behind Markhab. Looking in the mirror, Markhab watched the body on the cold floor slowly stirring, still in shackles. The naked male form was covered in bruises and blood.

Markhab reached for a small white towel hanging from a hook to the right of the sink and dried his face, hands and arms with it. He replaced the towel. Still humming his lyrical tune, Markhab turned and walked over to face the form on the floor.

This had been an exceptionally good session. Markhab had worked hard to exorcise the demons plaguing him this day.

The form on the floor raised his head to look up at Markhab. A broken plastic-like Canine face peered up through swollen eyelids at the First Commissioner. A faint whimpering sound escaped his lips, still dripping blood and spittle onto the wet blood-splattered concrete floor.

The session had been an excellent example of what could await the Canine scum. Markhab extended his right foot and nudged the left shoulder of the victim. It again whimpered. Markhab smiled. It had been exhilarating on a psychosexual level. He was an excellent sadist.

The First Commissioner moved over to the wall on his right where hanging from hooks and displayed on metal shelves was an array of leather whips, flogs, pipes and shiny cutting equipment resembling crude medical instruments. Markhab passed his eyes over the cutters, paused at a heavy clubbed sledgehammer. He had used that this night. His gazed continued moving toward the right to the whips dangling from their hooks. There hung the cat o' nine tails with its black ball bearings fixed to the ends of the nine loose leather straps. Markhab was good about putting his instruments back after using them. He noticed blood on most of the ball bearing ends.

I need to pay more attention to cleaning up the details of my projects. Despite being a neat freak, Markhab considered himself sloppy. His parents had ever reminded him of the fact so many years ago. He struggled with the secret feeling of inadequacy at times even now. What else had he neglected? He turned to look at the mirror. That needed to be repaired. The floor hosed. The cat o' nine tails carefully cleaned.

No, I'm just getting paranoid, thought Markhab to himself. Attendants will clean the room and set it back to order. But the feeling persisted. He was often afraid that his meticulous plans would come apart from his own neglect. Not betrayal, but his own inadequacy. *Nonsense.* Markhab shook his head and reminded himself, *I've been First Commissioner for thirty-five years. There is always the threat of treachery, but I have carefully mapped out the course of my plans. I will prevail.*

Markhab thought of the expedition about to embark to Earth. Despite the military nature of the project itself, this would be an anthropological achievement in its own right. Earth loomed in near-mythic proportions in the lore of the galaxy. The shared origin world, the place where all species first lived together in harmony. "Sheer folly," said Markhab aloud. "We should not, and we will not, live together. Lupus is a Human world."

The form on the floor groaned again and tried pulling a leg closer to its chest. The leg shivered as it strained, then gave up. Markhab walked over to a metal stand beneath the whips. He opened a metal box on the stand and took out a syringe. He picked up a vial from the box and drew the clear fluid into the syringe. Confident of the dosage, he removed a tube of ointment from the box then closed it.

Markhab turned and walked back to the figure on the floor and knelt down by its side. "Here, time to come back. The adrenaline will invigorate you." He plunged the needle into the form's bare, dirty left shoulder. Markhab put the syringe down on the floor. Reaching forward with both hands, he grasped the face of his victim from underneath the jaw. His fingers groped for a moment before a click was heard on each side.

Markhab slowly pulled up and withdrew the plastic Canine mask from the Human face it covered. A slurpy, sucking sound was heard as the mask came away. Covered in sweat and rapidly gasping for breath now that the mask was gone and the adrenaline was taking affect, the young man's pale face quickly filled with color.

Squeezing some of the ointment out of the tube into his hands, Markhab propped up the figure against his lap and began gently applying the soothing balm. "Easy, easy Corvus." said Markhab softly. "Come back to me." He carefully removed the chains and fasteners.

The young Commissioner, naked and shivering, reached out and held onto Markhab's waist.

The minutes passed as Markhab tenderly coaxed the young man back to full cognizance. "This will sooth your pains," he said. "The regenerator will have you back to normal in a few hours, my boy. A little make up, and you will be good as new." Corvus pushed himself up and looked into Markhab's eyes. "This expedition I am sending you on will be dangerous. Watch Altair. And do not trust this pilot from Drigo. I know nothing about him. You know all that depends on this mission, Corvus. Our utopian society is within reach. Bring back this secret from the ancients, our forebears. We will complete what they were not permitted to finish. But it all depends on you."

The young man cleared his throat, coughing past blood. "I will not fail you, Markhab."

14 SONG OF SOLOMON

It had been two hours since they had returned to Cornelius' house. Cornelius had spent a surprisingly short time packing a small travel pack, a single shirt and undergarment, a pair of socks, razor, two small arms guns with ammo, two knives. Naemi, sitting quietly on a sofa in the main room with her small pack at her side, smiled to herself. It had been she, years before when she and Cornelius had first worked together, who had taught Cornelius the art of packing for an operation. Minimum clothes and personal effects. The tools of the trade took precedence.

The two of them had spoken at length during the drive from Naemi's house. Naemi spoke fast, revealing activities on Polaris that Cornelius knew nothing about. He was surprised to discover that Naemi also frequented Canius, the expansive Canine realm beyond Human Lupus, with no real cities or advanced technologies. It was a seemingly lawless hinterland inhabited by unknown numbers of Canines. The industrial and advanced cities of Canoon, with its rich mineral and fuel resources in the far northern Polar Mountains, in steep, tumbling river and glacier vales, had always been viewed by Markhab's regime as the great danger. Naemi would not elaborate on her visits to the Canine wild, but she admitted to never having visited Canoon.

Finally after packing, Cornelius had excused himself to head down into his basement, "To take care of some personal matters," he had said.

In the meantime, Naemi occupied herself by wandering through the rooms of Cornelius' home. A carnivorous plant sprawled across the top of the piano in the audience room. She remembered a time when Cornelius had been away for three days. Naemi, eager to put into play an experiment to prove something she had recently read, had closed off all the doors and windows to the room. She unleashed a jar of a thousand blood sucking flying insects. One hour later Naemi entered the room and found it devoid of the tiny beasts. But the feeding mouth pods of the "piano plant" were bloated. Naemi loved this plant. It was now more than three times the size since she had given it to Cornelius.

Naemi entered the bedroom. She faced the window wall, touched a button on a pad sitting on a little round table beside her. The lights dimmed to out, and she admired the expansive view. At this hour the darkness of the night accentuated the shade within a shade of the lupin trees spread out around the grounds. But the stars shown bright and furious above. Naemi glanced down and noticed her shadow on the hardwood floors. A shadow cast in starlight. But something grander drew her attention. A tiny star pattern was reflected hundreds of times on the walls, ceiling and floor. Naemi's hand moved to her mouth as a slight gasp seized her breath. She was momentarily spellbound.

Naemi turned to face the window wall again and peered into the corner where the window and the wall perpendicular to it met. The slightest sparkle shone in the starlit corner and caught her eye. Her hand instinctively moved to clasp a pendant beneath the neckline of her silk blouse.

She approached the corner. Affixed to the intersection of walls and at her eye level was a small jewel, a pendant of diamond surrounded by short tentacled arms glowing in a radioactive phosphorescent alloy, shielded behind a clear lead-sodium plaster four microns thick. Naemi knew this, because it was the same as the pendant lying between her own breasts. It was a gift from her on Cornelius' thirty-fifth birthday. It represented the Precession Star, part of an archaic mythical belief story. It had always enchanted her as a young girl on Polaris. Cornelius enjoyed hearing the stories from Naemi's past. He had placed the jewel precisely where Naemi said it would best reflect starlight into the room without being obvious. This was something that drew them close together, dangerously close together. It had better not prove to be a liability.

Naemi came back to herself and realized how long Cornelius had been gone. She had let time slip passed her. She dropped her arm to her side and turned to make her way back through the house to the kitchen where the stairway to the basement was located.

*   *   *

Cornelius had left Naemi after packing his bag, saying he had personal matters to attend to. That was probably true. He had descended into his basement, his meditative retreat, where he could ground himself. His sound proof music and recording studio was where he lost himself, and found himself, in his drum work.

The basement was filled with hi-tech keyboards, an elaborate sound system control console, mixing board and a full band percussion set, acoustical, snare, cymbal and electronic drums. For the past hour Cornelius had immersed himself in an auditory trance of rhythms, distant patterns, voices and beats. The room reverberated. Cornelius sunk into a primal consciousness. And Cornelius beat his drums. At first in an angry chaotic melee, but therein he met a crescendo that opened up some of his hidden demons. Naemi's resurfacing after her "suicide mission" challenged him. And his teacher was pain, deep and severe. But the growth that resulted always proved mind blowing.

Cornelius set in play an electronic melody. He found his groove and his mind slipped down pathways through the subconscious. Cornelius kept time with the drumstick in his right hand counting out a constant rhythm. He stretched his left arm out to adjust the controls on the mixing board. He turned down the volume on the keyboard and string themes, slowed their tempo. He set an electronic harpsichord sound to repeat its melody every six minutes. Then he knocked out an evolving beat, complex and searching, discovering and consuming. His feet worked their base beats into the sound. A steady rhythm with his right, a changing beat with a hint of repetition with his left. Cornelius threw his head back and gazed up at the ceiling, mouth agape, head nodding in a circular motion in response to the music. He saw stars. The studio ceiling was painted navy blue. Glowing stars arranged in constellations shown down on him.

Cornelius played the piece he had been working on for weeks. Naemi had said it led nowhere. But when Cornelius played it, he felt his spirit extend and reach out to new possibilities. His consciousness drifted to feelings that would never go away, anger and passion, love and adventure. He closed his eyes and imagined he was a great sea creature, an octopus, tentacles reaching outward, outward in every direction, discovering, knowing. In his core he held onto the memories and feelings that made him whole. They shined as a starburst from the center of his being. Its colors and hues changed as his tentacles brought him new experiences, new perspectives. The light pulsated to the beat of his music. Naemi entered the studio then and found him in this state.

She had descended the stairs from the kitchen expecting to find Cornelius standing the midst of a mess, open boxes of old mementos surrounding him as he searched for some single treasure. Years before, they had nearly been late for a number of assignments because of Cornelius' little obsessions.

Naemi stopped at the base of the steps and saw the special soundproofing on the door. Anyone else besides her might contemplate what lay beyond the soundproof seal, a machinery shop, weapons testing lab, even torture chamber or secret prison. Naemi knew better. When she released the seal, music flooded out from the studio. Naemi smiled. She slipped in, quietly closed and sealed the door behind her.

An uplifting transcendental music filled the room. But it was not slow. A techno rhythm set to harpsichord. And in the middle of it sat Cornelius, alive, caught up in another world. He commanded the music and led it with his beats. His eyes were closed. Beads of sweat glistened on his brows. His face was flushed.

Naemi positioned herself at the keyboard between Cornelius' right, and the door. Something about the harpsichord music was familiar to her. She strained to remember. Ah, a seven note pattern, here and there in a pair, the second changing from a straight to a sharp, then back to a straight. Later it was repeated. And she thought, though she could not say she actually heard it, the same paring, but to a flat from straight and back again. Naemi remembered that she had once brought over a recording of a modern Polarin musician's latest release. Solomon. This pattern was in one of her compositions. That year the hit had morphed into myriad versions. It reigned in the big techno dance clubs on Polaris, Drigo and Lupus that season. It was the rage on Wror and uber Keldo the next year. She and Cornelius had even danced to it together on a night they spent out at The Casparade in the little coastal City of the Star.

They'd felt high on life that night, and on some impressive performance enhancement drugs she sort of remembered. They were celebrating something. Had it been a successful job? An anniversary? Some holiday? Naemi could not recall. But one thing she knew this moment right now, she was part of him.

Naemi knew how this equipment worked. How and under what circumstances this talent had been added to her repertoire was lost in the whirlwind of her life. She reached forward and slightly adjusted a few settings on the mixing board. With the change of a single command setting on the sound system control panel, she manually took over the electronic music and eased the melody, its cadence and rhythms, to a new place, still based on Solomon's notes.

Cornelius' mind was extended down into an inner universe of possibilities. His hands and feet, his arms and shoulders, were under their own power, yet coming together in a connection as they metered out their respective beats in concert. He was flushed, warm. His face was perspiring. He detected a slight drop in temperature in the room. Evaporation on his forehead, he thought. A vision of Naemi entered his mind, driven by a scent. The scent and the vision started to focus his thoughts, collapse the wave function of untold possibilities of thought. He was returning to "here." Then the music changed.

It changed only a note at first, then the entire tempo changed. The music was off program. It was new, novel, raw. Cornelius followed, took up a new beat, let it spread throughout his percussion. The music kept growing, quickening, changing, then returning to the familiar core rhythm. The idea of soaring up the inside of a giant helix came to him. He thought briefly of the double helix constellation that spanned the northern Lupin sky.

Cornelius opened his eyes and saw Naemi. He almost stumbled, but his inner vision was still intact. Naemi in his vision connected with the Naemi next to him. Had she come out of his vision? Or was it the other way around? She was looking down at her fingers, adrift in her own inner sound. She ignored him as if he were not there.

Naemi's fingers danced upon the keyboard. Her shoulders and body swayed. She had completely taken over the direction of the music. Cornelius found himself stretched in his abilities to keep up. Naemi added a lyrical accompaniment to the melody. The notes struck with her fingers fell into step with those emanating from her voice. Words took shape, consonants interlocked with vowels. Her song was an enchantment of unintelligible words planting pictures of stars and motion in the mind. Cornelius suddenly had it. His drumming accented the direction of the music, led then trailed Naemi's electronic symphony.

Their eyes sought each other out. They were joined in an incredible temporal and spiritual jam session. There was only now. Only here. Cornelius backed off his drumming, switched to an electronic drum set on his left. And if on cue, Naemi launched into a solo.

Cornelius used the mixing board to enhance Naemi's sound. He added echoes, fading, scratches, strobes pauses. Naemi's song was suddenly clear, descriptions of exploding suns, flaming nebulas, wild orbital dances of stars in galactic centers. Then her song changed perspective. They were beneath the starry canopy, rejoicing and singing with the luminous multitude. She kept repeating a refrain.

"We'll seek our souls outside

Beneath the starry night

Watching the stars come out."

Cornelius echoed and faded the last line each time Naemi sang it. He reduced the volume on her music and switched back to his acoustical drums and cymbals. He beat out his own solo finale.

Naemi again followed his lead and supported his set, her fingers dancing to Solomon's tune in a dervish whirlwind around Cornelius' beats.

Cornelius slapped a button on the console with his right drumstick without losing a beat. The lights slightly dimmed and the ceilinged stars pulsated in a rhythmic show above them. Here, then there, now, and now again, they pulsed. Expanding rings of light emanated from the center of each. Cornelius snapped the equalizer back on. Both he and Naemi again were matched in output and clarity.

Naemi ceased singing. Her fingers slowed to join in a long, fading, repeating finale. Cornelius softened his beat. Notes dropped from the melody. Beats dropped from the base. Naemi remained with Solomon's notes. That was all Cornelius supported in his fading drumming. The music trailed until it was imperceptible. Cornelius drummed his last beat. All that was left was a background arrangement of digital rain joined with a passionate palm beat on skin drum.

Cornelius was covered in sweat. Naemi had yet to work up to that. But her eyes were wide and wild. Her nostrils flared in her rapid breathing. She reached out and grabbed Cornelius around the shoulders, pulling them together. In the instance before that, Cornelius caught an at-once familiar, long parted scent. Their mouths joined in a crash of passion, bodies in mutual attraction, embraced in a spin.

As if in response to an internal shockwave, Cornelius pushed Naemi away from him and took a deep breath. His chest heaved. His eyes stung with sweat. He did not see Naemi's arm sweep toward him. Her right palm smashed into his left temple. He head spun right and spit erupted from his wavering lips. She followed by kicking her left foot into his right leg just above the ankle. He was forced off balance. He crashed down onto the floor. A look of surprise on his face rapidly changed into anger, then clarity, passing into blind excitement. Naemi reached down, grabbed one of Cornelius' arms and spun him around on the floor ninety degrees. She fell upon him. He was already poised for the attack.

Naemi tumbled over Cornelius as he used her momentum to put her into spin, allowing him to climb over and onto her. Naemi had only enough room for one tumble before she slammed into the wall. She swiveled her body to turn and face Cornelius. She raised her knee and it slammed into his chest, stopped his advance. She grabbed his shoulders with her hands and thrust him back. As Cornelius attempted to regain his balance, Naemi dove beneath his outstretched arms. Again their mouths crashed together. Their tongues embraced and their heartbeats were in unison. They rolled again together into the wall. The music seemed to grow louder. Their hearts beat furiously. Their bodies writhed. Nails scratched. Teeth met flesh, bit and tore. They were caught in a remembered pattern of violent sex, screams, yells, whelps, shouts and whimpering.

15 LUPUS CITY

The ground car rolled rough over the uneasy surface along the dark road. Since leaving the mountain vale cities of the eastern Shining Star territory three hours before when they crossed the great bridge over the Shining River, the terrain had gotten progressively worse. There was little regular upkeep on the single road that crossed the eastern regions of the Seering Desert. Most traversed the empty regions by air ship. But all flights were monitored by Markhab's satellites. To avoid some detection on the lonely road, Cornelius had secured a special vehicle from Jarbed. The vehicle's surface was coated with an infrared inhibitor, a poly-paint substance only microns thick that absorbed infrared heat signatures. This made the vehicle largely invisible to Markhab's satellites at night. There were no bright external lights. The driver navigated by night vision optics.

Naemi was driving. She had taken over from Cornelius after they'd crossed the river two and a half hours before. Naemi looked over at Cornelius, huddled under a light blanket in the passenger side of the car. "Are you actually asleep?" she asked, somewhat above a whisper.

The huddled figure responded with a broken grunt. Then "If you ask me every half hour whether I'm asleep or not, I won't get much." Cornelius straightened up in the seat. The blanket dropped away, and he attempted to tame his thick hair with his right hand. After a fruitless moment, he gave up.

"We'll be near Lupus City in less than an hour, about the same time the sun will be up. Then I want you to drive for a bit."

"You have no compassion," he feigned to whine.

"There was a time not too long ago when you could handle a little rough housing," Naemi added with a chortle.

"I'm out of practice," Cornelius replied.

"This is just a bit of free advice, Cornelius. Someone in your line of work, our line of work, can't afford to be out of practice."

"It won't happen again," said Cornelius.

"No, it won't," said Naemi. "We both need to be on our guard in these rustic towns and lonely roads until we get to Big City." "That was stupid of us back there. A blow out sex session when we should have been on the road."

Cornelius laughed. "Oh, just because you may not have performed up to par."

Naemi looked over at Cornelius and grinned wide. Cornelius was just able to make out her out in the diode light glow from the driver's console. And to herself Naemi thought, *No, it was a very good thing what we did. He enjoyed it. Hell, so did I. Trust.*

Naemi's thoughts were broken by the loud mechanical sound of a sky runner approaching.

"Cut the engine!" growled Cornelius. "And coast to a stop."

Naemi powered down the vehicle. Her fingers flew across the command console as if it were a keyboard, setting each control to null in a quick fluid motion. Only the air vents she left active.

"The air too," whispered Cornelius. "Off!"

Naemi complied without a word.

The drone of the sky runner's engine grew louder as it rapidly approached the car from behind. Cornelius and Naemi quietly eased to a stop on the side of the road just as the runner passed overhead. Immediately the sound of the ship Doppler-shifted into a lower pitch as it moved away. The diminishing sound was replaced by that of another runner approaching from behind. The whooshing whip-whip-whip of the propeller blades sounded louder and more chaotic than the first.

"Two more," said Naemi.

"From Shining City," said Cornelius. "They must be following the road."

As the two new sky runners passed overhead, they diverge in their paths from the lead ship, moving off to the north. Cornelius and Naemi held their breaths in the fear they'd been spotted somehow. They remained silent until each was certain the runners were not circling back around toward the car.

The air inside the car quickly became stale and the temperature climbed. Naemi reached over and reactivated the air vents. She fell back into her seat, moving her head from side to side, relishing the cool air blowing into the cabin. "They've diverged," she said.

Cornelius felt a sudden chill as the cool air hit the perspiration beading up around his temples and on the back of his neck. He wiped the cooling sweat from his brow and nick with the palms of his hands. He rubbed his arms to force the goose bumps back down. "I'd say one was going to Lupus City, the other to the docks on the Great Lake, and Big City. The strange thing is, there aren't normally such flights at night. The mountains, and weather off the lakes, make it too dangerous."

"Then there's been some move on Markhab's part," deduced Naemi. "The councils and cells of the Territory must be dispatching messages to the western cities."

"Avoiding transmissions that could be picked up by Markhab's satellites," added Cornelius.

Naemi reached her arm toward the control panel and said, "Should we listen to whatever news broadcasts we can find?"

"No! Don't!" barked Cornelius, throwing his hands out to stop her. "We can't risk being detected as a receiver," he explained.

"Then," began Naemi, retracting her arm.

"We'll be in Lupus City soon, like you said," Cornelius reminded her, his voice softer. He grinned as he contemplated their first stop. "Naemi. Do you remember our mission to infiltrate the Titanium Miner's Union in Lupus City and, exposed, Markhab's mole?"

Naemi furrowed her brow and was about to dismiss the comment. She could not see Cornelius' grin, but she heard the change in tone in Cornelius' voice.

"Miner's Union? That was five years ago. What does that have to do with …."

"Six year's ago," Cornelius corrected her. "Who stuck his neck out and pulled strings for us?"

Naemi smiled as she recollected. And Cornelius' plan burst through into her mind. "Renender!" she exclaimed. "Is he still working the transports?

"Right," said Cornelius. And he heard Naemi's smile in the timbre of her voice. "He is our first contact. I last saw him three months ago. Renender can get us reliable news, and will help us get down to the lake and steppes."

Cornelius opened the car door on his side and said, "Let's switch. I'll drive from here.

Starlight filled the cabin through the open door. Naemi followed Cornelius and climbed out of her side of the car into the pre-dawn cold. "Are you all right to drive?" she asked.

The two traversed the car opposite one another counterclockwise.

Hey." he stopped and nodded toward the east. "The sky is getting light. Dawn will be here before long. Let's get going."

Naemi paused to look back behind her into the distant eastern sky, reviewing in the gathering light, the road they had traveled through the night. The driver's door slammed shut and Naemi broke her gaze, followed

Cornelius back into the car.

They pulled back onto the rough road. Cornelius switched off the night vision optics, allowing the view from outside to come into the vehicle.

The further on they drove, the higher the road climbed into the foothills. The only road to Lupus City from Shining City and it's sister communities wound up and around the most eastern spur of the great interior range known as the Canius Mountains. Lupus City lay on the northern flank of the spur.

Cornelius concentrated on commanding the vehicle in the changing twilight, keeping he and Naemi from careening off the road into one of the ever-deeper gorges off the heightening edge.

Neither spoke much as they drove onto into the mountain vales. Naemi looked out the windows and noticed the stars fade and dim and vanish in the gathering light. Before long, dawn's shocking light streamed out of the east from behind the distant Lupin Mountains, in whose still shadows lay Shining City. The last star vanished out of the sky and lofty tops of the Canius Mountains lit up as if by a mighty torch.

As the car wound higher and higher up the ever-steeper climbing road, the light of morning raced down the mountain faces toward Cornelius and Naemi.

Finally, rounding a last bend around the mountain's most eastern buttress, dawn's light crashed through the car's windows. Suddenly before them the great steppes of the Cantons stretched out below them. In the distance was a huge lake with no seen shore.

The road opened up into a great valley where the mountains pulled back from the expansive view. Lupus City spread out in the valley before them.

Lupus City straddled the sides of a great horseshoe shaped valley. For eons, advancing and retreating glaciers had carved this valley, at a time when Lupus had been far wetter and cooler than at present.

When Human settlers advanced outward from their original population centers, some intrepid explorers wandered into the forbidden Canius

Range. There they found the four-kilometer wide, ten-kilometer long valley. It had been completely forested at the time, bifurcated by a swift swollen stream. Its waters cascaded down the one hundred-kilometer sheer drop off the valley's open side.

Lupus City now supported a population of approximately one million Humans. That was small compared to the huge cities to the east. Maps of the Territory of the Shining Star of Lupus most frequently illustrated Lupus City as the northwest boundary of the Territory. Depictions of the vast Federated Cantons also identified Lupus City and its lake port counterpart as the southern boundary. But the citizens of Lupus City held their own view of their place on the great shared world of Lupus. They were their own polity, their own city-state. And they marketed their products to the wider habitation of Lupus, Human and Canine alike.

Spread out from horizon to horizon below the valley's north-facing mouth lay the southern reaches of the Canton Steppes and the southeastern shore of one of the Great Lakes. It was named the Lake of Lupus by the early explorers. Its larger sister body of water to the west was the Dog Lake. Between these two great mountain-fed inland seas, and to their west, was the region of Canius. Many thousands of small communities of Canines dwelt in the northern foothills of the Canius Range, and on the shores of the Great Lakes.

The greatest meeting place of Canine and Human cultures was on the northeast shore of the third and northernmost Federated Lake. There lay the largest Human settlement, Big City.

Cornelius and Naemi were yet far south of Big City and Federated Lake. As the dawn's light swept down into the horseshoe valley, Cornelius slowed the ground car and pulled off to the right side of the road and onto an overlook. Below them was the valley waking up to a new day. No longer did woods of lupin tree and lupin pine fill the flat expanse. Those had been cut down as the first industry to invade the once pristine and insular mini-world took hold. Massive veins of titanium ore were discovered in the steep gulches, canyons and high mountain vales of the upper valley. Farming spread throughout the lower valley as mining scaled the heights.

The political turmoil that was de rigueur of Human Lupus forced the

Human settlers of Lupus City to continually reinvent themselves to maintain their autonomy. The horseshoe valley was the apex of titanium mining west of the mountains of Lupus Minor. But it was also a hub of high-tech, as well as shoddy low-tech, manufacturing. The new industries were spread along the encircling valley, replacing most farming. The city's titanium products were traded for foodstuffs, exotics and luxuries with the wider world of lake and steppe communities far below.

The road down into the valley skirted the edges of the steep mountainsides. It wound first southwest toward the upper valley, then switch backed to the northeast facing the rising sun.

"I haven't been here in years," said Naemi, alert and eagerly taking in the view from every angle through every window. "This is one of the most beautiful places on Lupus. I've always thought so," she added looking over at Cornelius.

Cornelius was concentrating on the curving descent. The road was still rough. "It's a unique place," he said. "The people are genuine, when you get to know them. There are so many business types here though, coming and going everyday. The citizens tend to keep to themselves."

Naemi watched the open plain at the valley's bottom, nodding in agreement at Cornelius' opinion of the valley and its people.

Near the valley's northeast open face, trucks and workers streamed onto the plain from the ringing city. Cargo containers were unloaded and stacked on the steadily transforming staging tarmac. The plain was crisscrossed with paths and circles organically patterned through the closely cropped grass. Away from the main activity on the field Naemi saw a black patrol ship. The sleek insect-like flying machine was conspicuous in its singular presence.

"There's one of the air patrols sitting down there that buzzed us earlier," Naemi pointed out.

"I hope whatever news they brought will have found its way to Renender by the time we see him," said Cornelius.

Turning to Cornelius, Naemi said, "I need some breakfast before we meet

Renender."

Cornelius was silent for a moment as he navigated around the last switchback. Before them now were the first residential neighborhoods and structures on the valley slopes. "That is an excellent idea," he finally said. "I am starving."

The road continued to wind down and to the left. It was much smoother and well maintained now. Tall narrow estates hugged the steep terrain. Each was painted in bright colors unique to their occupant's personalities. Onion-domed roofs topped nearly every home. Each curved surface showed off scenes, patterns and designs in intricate tile mosaic. Presently the narrow road merged onto one of the main traffic loops circling the valley. The road was full of public and personal transports ferrying people to their jobs before the day's airships arrived.

Cornelius and Naemi gathered many stares from the other people on the road. The charcoal grey, low to the ground boxy stealth car was an uncommon sight. Nearly all the vehicles in Lupus city were of a similar elegant aerodynamic form, oblong, graceful, in cool metallic colors.

The car soon circled the valley. Cornelius pulled off onto a side street on the right, descending further. Before long they emerged from the forest of tall slender buildings built on steep inclines and reached the flat plain. Cornelius merged left onto the frontage road. They cruised in the early sunlight along the edge of the plain busy with activity.

Naemi took in the scene. On the drive down into the valley she had especially admired the patterns in the field. Not geometrical, but organic, flowing, incorporating the river and mountain vale surroundings in a harmonious extension onto the plain. Now finally out in the open, the sky arched wide above and before them.

Cornelius pulled the car around to the front of a wide and tapering pastel blue building.

"Is this a restaurant?" asked Naemi, stretching her neck to spot the onion dome on top.

"There's a great café on the eighth floor," Cornelius answered. He stopped the car and set the break. Turning to Naemi he added, "And Renender has his offices here, too."

Naemi's eyebrows went up and she smiled approvingly. "This? It's beautiful! Renender is doing well for himself. I remember that warehouse on the other side." She opened her door and stepped out with Cornelius.

"He bought out his brothers and moved down to the field to be closer to the market. He owns a third of the trade permits down on the landing field." They walked up to the double doors of the building where Cornelius held the door open, entering behind Naemi.

The interior lobby was wide and inviting. A grand staircase directly before them led up to the mezzanine level. A few people were moving about the floor and more could be heard upstairs. The architecture displayed indented lines similar to Art Deco on Earth.

"Come along this way," said Cornelius, leading to the right. "The lift is over here."

Naemi followed, observing details along the way. Surveillance cameras discretely protruded from alcoved recesses high along the walls. There had been no security outside, nor host for that matter, but three suited security guards in attractive navy blue pants and blazers were in the lobby. One was on the left beside the door of a gift shop, not open yet, another on the top landing of the staircase, and the third near the elevators where she and Cornelius were headed. Each maintained communication with the others by communication buds carefully inserted into an ear. They were obvious by their eyes darting one way then the other, lips busy in quiet murmurs.

Voices echoed from somewhere upstairs, largely indistinguishable. But Naemi made out snippets of phrases through the din.

"...And spring peaches at THAT price?" Laughter.

"...Balloon had a HOLE!"

"...Coffee, Miss? MORE COFFEE!"

It was a business breakfast, full of the boisterous banter of trade.

As they passed the edge of the staircase, Naemi read a sign on an easel advertising "Private Reception. Banderlay Stone Fruit Cooperative."

They reached the lift and Cornelius nodded to the guard, smiled and said "A loud party this morning."

"Some businessmen from Banderlay on the Canton Steppes," the guard offered. "They arrived in a flotilla yesterday. Where to?" he added, sizing up both Cornelius and Naemi.

Cornelius replied, "Is Matta still serving up a good cup of coffee in the Café?"

The guard laughed and pressed the lift call button. The doors opened and the guard pressed a command and code onto a panel on the door's side. "She is! Eight floors up for the best cup of coffee in Lupus City."

"Thank you," said Cornelius entering the lift.

"Miss," said the guard bowing slightly as Naemi followed Cornelius. She gave the guard a wide smile in response and a "Good morning."

The doors closed behind them and Naemi said "The best coffee in Lupus City. I can use that."

"Mm," Cornelius muttered and placed his arm around her. "He wasn't kidding. You'll see."

The lift stopped. As the doors opened, the hustle and bustle sounds of a diner met them. The air was thick with the smell of food and strong coffee. Stepping out of the lift, Naemi swept her gaze around the room and inhaled deeply. "Oh this will be great," she said.

A large woman who shook the floor when she walked appeared before them. "How many here, Loves?" She was two meters tall and stocky. She wore a coiled listening earpiece in one ear.

"Two, Matta. Is the coffee strong today?"

The woman bent down and squinted to get a better look at them. The woman's face beamed as she recognized, "Cornelius! Come in you stranger you!" She grabbed him in a bear hug with her enormous arms. Matta glanced at Naemi, then turned back and gave Cornelius a wink and added, "Two it is, eh? You rascal. This way! This way!" She turned, grabbed two menus from a stand, and led Cornelius and Naemi through the half-full restaurant to a bright booth at a window overlooking the landing field. Matta slapped the tabletop, dropped the menus and said "I'll be right back with two cups, Loves. You stay put and enjoy the view." Her voice was hurried but brimming with pleasantries. She quickly turned and disappeared down an aisle, stopping at a table to answer another guest's question.

Naemi grinned at Cornelius, then flipped open her menu. The selection categories included "Hearty Miners," "Broker's Power Stack," "Lake Proud," "Steppes and Gravy." She smiled at the names.

Matta suddenly returned with two big mugs steaming with coffee. Her big arms swung down and the mugs landed with a bang on the table, though not a drop spilled. "What's your pleasure today?" she asked.

"I'll have the Miner's Morning Jumpstart," said Naemi.

"We've got the best in the Valley, Miss!" said Matta nodding. "And for you Love?" she asked, turning to Cornelius and slapping him on the back.

"Night eggs and sausage," he replied. "Easy with the sauce, please."

"You hurt my feelings! That's my specialty!" Matta pretended to sulk. Then changing expressions again, she asked, "What brings you to the Valley?"

"Your famous cooking!" Cornelius flattered.

Matta beamed. "Ain't that the truth, Love!" And she giggled.

"We're here to see Renender. I've brought an old friend. This is Naemi."

"Nice to meet you! And Mr. Renender, he'll be happy to see you," Matta said, and she snatched up the menus from Cornelius and Naemi. "I'll be back with your food in a short while. Stay put, Loves!" She turned and bounded away to the kitchen.

Naemi continued to grin at Cornelius. "She's friendly."

"And strong," added Cornelius, laughing. "She's from uber Keldo originally. Came here two years ago. She says she feels light as a feather here on Lupus."

They both slipped into a few minute's silence, self-absorbed in their coffees' regenerative experience to the senses, rich look, almost remembered aroma, comforting heat, depth of taste. Each sensation combined and revealed themselves in satisfying grunts, hmms and sighs.

Naemi finished her coffee and set the mug down on the tabletop. She relaxed against the back of her seat and said, "That hit the spot. I'm feeling rejuvenated. There was some background flavor I've never tasted before."

"It's the prajaum seed. Matta imports them to add to her coffee. That's why it's the best in Lupus City," explained Cornelius. He slurped the last mouthful from his mug and set it down next to Naemi's.

"Prajaum seed," said Naemi. "I've never heard of it. Is it safe?"

Cornelius laughed. "It uplifts the spirit and adds strength you can feel in your blood. Is that a bad thing?"

Naemi feigned a look of disapproval, but she genuinely did feel energized, ready for the new day. And they had not slept all night. Naemi broke her expression with a burst of laughter and smiles. "I do feel great! Another question," and she leaned in close to Cornelius. "Is it addictive?"

Cornelius joined Naemi in the center of the table and deadpanned, "Just enjoy the coffee, Naemi." Cornelius leaned back, grinning.

"Here you are Loves," belted out Matta, bursting onto the scene. She nearly tossed the plates onto the table before Cornelius and Naemi, and they landed quickly and in just a soft hush. A large glass carafe of more coffee followed. Both plates held mounds of food, glistening in gravies and creams. "Lite, just like you ordered," she winked. "Now those are spring berries on the side," Matta added, pointing to large blue and yellow berries against the edge of gravy a third of the way around the plates. "Eat those up good. They came in just yesterday. DEE-licious!" she laughed and bellowed.

Then Matta leaned in close to Cornelius and Naemi. They leaned in to close the gap, stealing a smile and a grin from one another. "They're from Canius," she said with a nod, a wink and a smile. "Those are good berries, better than any in the Cantons. I'm expecting more today. I'm almost out! Ah, but the airships will be here soon." Matta lifted carafe and refilled the coffee mugs. "Eat up, Loves!" And Matta slapped the table with both hands, laughed and quickly turned.

She disappeared towards the door where a new party stood waiting. She yelled, "Six of you? Come in! Come in! This way! This way!"

"Business is booming," Naemi said. Then they both dug into their meals, scarcely another word exchanged between them until their plates were empty. They were that hungry.

Only the eclectic music from the restaurant's jukebox broke through the slurping, chewing, utensil clanging sounds Cornelius and Naemi made while eating. The music included age old mining songs from the upper valley mining camps, set to base and drum. Popular songs from the Cantons played as well as woodsmen carillons from Aran. Only a few favorites from Shining City, Cronapolis and off world played.

Cornelius finished his second cup of coffee and finally sat back, fully satisfied. "That was a hearty meal," he said. "The kind that sticks to your ribs."

Naemi mopped up the remaining eggs and gravy from her plate with a piece of bread. It disappeared into her mouth. "Mm," was all she could answer until she'd stopped chewing and swallowed. She looked up at Cornelius and said, "Funny, mine looked heavy, but it actually feels quite light. I'm satisfied. Not stuffed."

"Well I'm stuffed," said Cornelius.

The restaurant still bustled with the sounds of dishes clanging from the kitchen, meal orders given and confirmed, buzzing morning conversations about sleeping well or not sleeping well the night before, aches and pains or refreshing new perspectives. A vitality was present in the room. Everyone and everything reacted to the dawn's light streaming through the expansive windows. The verdant valley was tinged with bright pastels and reflected golds in the light of the new day.

As Cornelius and Naemi absorbed the scene, Matta appeared at their side. "How's the appetite, Loves? What else can Matta get you? More coffee?"

"Matta my dear," said Cornelius. "We are stuffed."

"It was delicious," Naemi interjected with a smile.

Cornelius stretched and said, "But we had better get going, or we'll sit here all day admiring the view, and getting in your way."

Matta beamed and shook her head. "It's always a pleasure to see you, Cornelius love. You come back and see old Matta soon. Anytime!"

"Oh that's a promise, for sure," said Cornelius. "What's the damage to my credit?" he asked, reaching into a pocket for his payment card.

"On the house, Love. Both you and the lovely lady," Matta said with a nod towards Naemi. She raised a hand in the air. "Mister Renender insists!"

Cornelius bowed his head and Naemi followed suit. "Many thanks, Matta," he said putting his hand to his heart.

"Well you both look better now, that's for sure," Matta said, and she slapped the table and laughed. "When you came in here, you looked like two people who, well who drove all night through the desert on that nasty old road, just to come see Matta and Mister Renender."

Cornelius and Naemi stole a glance at one another, then cracked a slight smile simultaneously.

Matta went on, "It's my job to make sure everyone gets what they need who comes in here. Matta brings the morning to your day, is what I like to say." She laughed again.

"Such an imagination, Matta," said Cornelius. "Well, I've got to let Renender know we're here, and see if he has time for a visit."

"Oh, he knows you're here, Love. That's Matta's job, too," She smiled at Cornelius and Naemi, and stepped back from the table. Cornelius and

Naemi got up and stood beside Matta.

"Thank you so much, Matta," said Naemi.

Matta grabbed Naemi around the shoulders and gave her a big hug. "A friend of Cornelius is a friend of Matta. May fortune be your friend."

"And you!" she said, releasing Naemi to turn to Cornelius. Matta grabbed his shirt and planted a big wet kiss on his lips, then pushed him back, her hands still on his shoulders. "You rascal! I expect you back here soon! Fortune be your friend."

"Fortune be your friend," returned Cornelius.

"Thank you, Loves," said Matta, releasing Cornelius.

The three of them traversed the diner to pause at the elevators. Matta called the lift. The doors opened and she reached over to enter a command and password.

"Two floors up, Loves. Renender's waiting for you. You both come back soon and see Matta!" She smiled.

"Thank you, Matta. You're the best, as ever," Cornelius said. He followed Naemi into the lift.

The doors closed before them. "Renender is waiting to see us?" Naemi asked. "And what kind of a kiss was that?"

Cornelius laughed with a twinge of hesitation. "Don't be jealous of Matta. She's from Keldo, remember."

"What does that mean?" asked Naemi.

The lift doors opened. Right in front of them stood Renender.

16 CONVOCATION

The large asteroid fell away below Galdren. The aged Feline was alone in the travel pod, heading up, up to the upper curve of the doughnut force field. The pod was a mere capsule eight meters long, three meters wide and three meters high. Micro jets steered the craft through the thin atmosphere within the force field.

The titanium capsule appeared metallic pink, reflecting the shimmering rose light of the force field, and the glowing insides of the Great Aurora Nebula itself.

Not a single star other than the luminous body at the center of the asteroid ring shown through the nebula. Galdren gazed out the forward viewing ports and thought of the singular isolation of the vast Feline asteroid civilization, thousands of inhabited rocks and tens of trillions of Felines. There was some trade with worlds beyond the nebula, and a multitude of spies, informants and allies therein. But for the majority of Felines in the asteroid ring, the small rocks within the nebula were the whole universe. Never mind the Felines of Polaris, that shared Feline-Human world. That seemed so alien.

Galdren fingered the small data pads in his hands, scraped them against each other. He knew that soon the stars would open up to the asteroid ring Felines. He foresaw it in his projections. Galdren was traveling to the Convocation of the Council, the leaders of the asteroid ring Felines, to present his evidence and summarize the future of their civilization, as he interpreted it.

Music filled the cabin of the capsule, classical Feline oeuvres of strings and distant thunder, soft horns and drums, melodies of the small and of the immense. Galdren enjoyed epic music that took a long time to play out. It expanded his mind, allowed him to image the data his projections showed him. Events echoed those of ancient epic mythologies, nearly forgotten stories of the long ago past casting a shadow on the future.

Just as Galdren thought of shadows on the future, the pod was shrouded in a real shadow, then rapidly released to the rose hue of the Feline universe. Flying reptiles of the asteroid ring atmosphere flew between the sun and the pod.

Galdren steered the pod to just one hundred meters from the top of the force field. He then altered course to traverse the ring parallel to the force field. Below him small asteroids, some inhabited and others not, were all covered in a glowing green fuzz that the flying reptiles ate. Galdren saw small ships traveling between the gaps between asteroids. Not a few times larger ships penetrated inward from the outer side of the doughnut force field. Others likewise exited the asteroid ring's shimmering barrier.

The skies to the left of Galdren from the central star lit up. A storm of charged particles bombarded the force field. Sparks lit up the field. The regulators strained to maintain the field against the onslaught of heavy charged particles.

Every one hundred kilometers Galdren passed the copper-sheened field regulators. About five times the size of Galdren's pod, the regulators hung fixed with their oblong shape hugging the force field. Millions of the regulators were stationed along the inner and outer sides of the doughnut ring. Each was powered by a micro singularity. Together they emitted, received and reinforced the field lines. They enabled the existence of the engineering wonder that was the doughnut force field.

Galdren passed five field regulators when looming before him at the top of the force field curve was the Convocation Keep. It was shaped generally like a field generator, but ten times the size. The ship was detailed in organic rococo carvings and structures.

Galdren slowed his pod and approached the underside of the Keep. Gently and without revealing a compartment or seem, a dozen mechanical arms, six to a side, extended down and caught a gentle grapple hold on the pod. They pulled the tiny craft towards a cavity that opened in the center to the Keep's docking bay.

From inside the capsule, Galdren experienced the unsettling sensation of being devoured whole by an immense insect.

An antechamber of the docking bay preceded the vast interior of the Keep. It was itself a large space, a bubble bathed in green light. The hatch sealed beneath the pod and the chamber pressurized with atmosphere. A horn sounded throughout the space and within the pod. Yellow and orange lights were added to the green.

Galdren looked down at his command console and pressed a button that caused the music to cease. He pressed another and a door slid quietly open on the side of the pod. The green, yellow and orange light streamed into the tiny vessel's interior. Galdren gathered his data pads and stepped out of his ship and into the Keep.

The docking bay was an efficient robotic maintenance and storage facility. Many other pods and craft were tucked away in individual maintenance pockets in the walls. As soon as the door to Galdren's pod closed behind him, metal flex arms descended from the ceiling while others rose from the floor. They converged on the pod and began diagnostics, system upgrading, recalibration of maneuvering systems and micro jets.

Galdren walked across the bay floor and ascended a staircase that led up to large metal doors. Convex bubbles protruded from the sides of the doors. About six to a side met Galdren. As he approached the doors, the bubbles suddenly lit up in a yellow and green glow. Vertical electronic pupils simulating the Feline eye dilated within each of the sensors. They all focused on Galdren. A bright light illuminated the old feline from above.

Feathered olfactory-taste sensors flitted out of tiny holes around the eye bubbles, tasting and smelling Galdren, verifying his identity. Galdren reached out and touched a tiny oval on the side of the door. Prints, DNA, pheromones and protein sequences were quickly verified by an elaborate computerized database. Then suddenly the doors slid open and Galdren entered an elevator lift that was a colorful melding of brushed titanium and mother of pearl.

The doors slid closed behind him. Galdren ascended in a beautiful space filled with soft sounds of birdsong, wind and running water. Then the music ceased and the lift slowed to a halt. The doors slid open and a reddish light bathed Galdren.

Before him was the immense and cavernous Convocation Hall. He stepped out from the small chamber. It sealed itself behind him, then descended into the floor, leaving no trace of its passing on the smooth surface. At least twenty stories of space opened up above Galdren, roughly sixty meters.

Galdren was standing in the center of eighty square meters of floor space. He stood bathed in a light tinged orange and yellow. It soon faded and revealed to the old Feline the reddish brown hue of the great chamber. The air was cool and moist. The sound of slight music mixed with that of a soft breeze in tree leaves filled the hall.

One-third of the before Galdren, a sheltered alcove ring glowed red. There were twenty individual spotlights positioned two meters apart in the alcove. Beneath the spotlights sat the Council Members.

"Projectionist Galdren," said a female Feline voice. The sound issued from above, before, beside, behind and below him. There was no point of issuance. But Galdren faced forward and looked up at the row of spotlights in the wall. The female voice continued. "The Convocation Council welcomes you. Please make yourself comfortable." A swivel seat rose from the floor from a spot two meters in front of Galdren. The aged Feline took his place in the chair, still holding the data pads. A glass filled with a sweet smelling liquid rose out of an armrest compartment in the chair and presented itself to Galdren. The Feline slightly swayed his head in the direction of the drink to smell the liquid. His nostrils flared. Fresh juice.

"Refresh yourself with bezen juice," continued the female voice.

Galdren could not tell which Feline had spoken. Each appeared stoic beneath the spotlights in the high alcove above him. He picked up the drink and took a sip. Cool liquid sent fingers of vitality through his circulatory system. The slight muscle tremblings of age relaxed. His heart beat faster. His blood coursed strongly. His mind focused and remained clear.

"I thank you, Eminences." Galdren set his glass down and offered a nod of his head in deference to the Council.

A male Feline, strong and full of command, next filled the chamber with his voice. There was no echo. The walls absorbed sound. "It has been nearly a year since you appeared before this Council. The insight of the Projectionist adds deeper dimensions to our knowledge. Many decisions are influenced by knowing the nature of events unfolding just beyond the bend of our comprehension. Speak to us of what you have seen."

Galdren selected one of his data pads. He flipped on a screen and quickly refreshed his memory with the text of the presentation he had readied. He looked up.

"The turning of long wheels in the passage of time is giving nascence to a new paradigm. Its beginning is already behind us. New powers are rising and old powers are diminishing. The Precession Star returns, following an ancient path. Its light passes through our space, casting its light on the civilizations we know.

"Humans are filling space with trade and the seeking of knowledge. The long quarantine of Earth no longer serves its purpose. Hope and ruin will rise from the Lupin colonies of Wror and uber Keldo. Canines strengthen Humans. Isolation, once our friend, invites distrust, excepting where we engage. "Prosperity and conflict lie before us."

Galdren paused. The small figures below the spotlights in the alcove did not move. Selecting a different data pad, he got up from his chair. He turned to face the empty rear space of the hall behind him. Galdren raised the pad and pushed a button.

The great hall lit up, bathed in a huge holographic projection. It filled all the space of the hall. He turned to face the Council. He was able to make out individual faces illuminated in the blazing light of the projection. Galdren spoke again.

"Before you are the Event Lines of our time. You have seen similar projections in the past. The civilizations of our species. Behold the return of the Precession Star." Galdren turned to face the hologram that was copied from his projection machine. A line emanating from the right traversed the image to the left. An existing active vortex dissipated and found a new focus. It was the same image the Galdren had shown his children.

Galdren continued. "I also repeat a warning. Our small star burns quickly through its life. It becomes unstable."

The projection continued until it played itself out. Galdren raised his data pad and pressed another button. The hologram vanished, plunging the chamber into temporary darkness. Soon Galdren's eyes adjusted to the original reddish light. He turned and saw the spotlights in the alcove above him. He returned to his seat.

The silence was broken by the male Feline who had spoken earlier. "Thank you, Galdren, for what you have shown and told us."

Another voice, female but different from the first, spoke. "We must guard against an unrestrained Humanity."

A male voice added, "The situation on Lupus is untenable. It is confrontational. Dangerous."

The original female voice said, "Felines and Humans have a long history of cooperation when working together. Witness the long peace on Polaris. Such a benign balance."

A new voice, also female, spoke next. "Many Humans flee Wror. Drigans are taking their place. We may offer assistance to help the Drigans emigrate. Transporting two groups of emigrants is as easy as transporting one."

The first male voice said, "Construction of the armored asteroid is nearly complete. We will soon be able to transport vast numbers of peoples."

The other male voice said, "We will extend our presence beyond the nebula. The new world of Wror will be called home by the Felines.

The first female voice said, "It shall be a shared world."

An older male Feline, shakier than the others, added his voice. "We have known about our star's instability for some time. New particle storms, ever more numerous and strong, stream from our sun. They shower our force field as minute high-energy explosions. The instability is increasing, as is the stress on our force field."

A female voice said, "There are many trillions of us in the asteroid ring. We will not be able to maintain the secrecy of such an evacuation."

The first male voice added, "Our sheer numbers will impress others. Our strength will not be questioned."

A female voice said, "The first test will be Wror. The process of selecting suitable families as colonists will begin."

The first male voice said, "The new colonists will debark in the first armored asteroid to come online. We shall ready the craft to pierce our force field and travel to Drigo, where it will pick up the dorsein herders awaiting transport to Wror."

The voice paused. Silence pervaded the chamber. Then the same voice continued. "Galdren. Your son guides the herds of dorsein on the great asteroid."

"Yes," said Galdren. "He has devoted his life to the animals," he added proudly.

The male voice said, "Have your son supervise the transport of dorsein with our own colonists to Wror. He is to make a final culling of the herds. The docile herds shall be presented to the Drigans as a gift, part of Feline assistance is establishing their new homes on a strange and alien world. The other dorsein, those more aggressive, will accompany our own people."

"I will give Galdinier the instructions myself," said Galdren.

The first female voice that had greeted Galdren when he arrived said, "Good then, Galdren. A new beginning awaits the Felines. Ready your son for the departure to Wror."

17 THE CULLING OF THE DORSEIN

The day felt warmer than any in the past several weeks. An increased temperature and generation of additional breezes by the Ministry of Cycles brought a decidedly early summer to the small asteroid. Galdinier sat on a grassy slope, arms behind him propping himself up, head tilted skyward and eyes closed. A deliberate focus of slowly drifting light aimed across the crater dome served as an artificial heat source. The dim star did not produce enough heat on its own to warm the asteroid worlds. The concentrated light radiated enough infrared radiation to be felt. Sun on the face. His legs stretched out on the grass. His feet were bare besides the striped fuzz that grew there. Oh how good the grass felt. He listened to the drowsy whip-whips of grasshoppers and dragonflies whirring on the breeze and grass.

It was midday. Galdinier had been working since before first light. For the past week since his father Galdren had spoken to him about the exciting opportunity to supervise the preparation of the dorsein herds bound for Wror, Galdinier had been busy. Herds were transported from larger asteroids to smaller staging asteroids like this one. Galdinier was culling the herds. The most aggressive were separated from the rest. The meekest were identified and removed before arriving here. The docile herds were already grazing in the small green crater valleys of the armored asteroid. But the herds here were of a different ilk. And Galdinier had faithfully followed the prescribed methods of culling. It was a messy business. But it was also the most effective. Galdinier was resting after culling a herd on another small nearby asteroid. The herd that grazed idyllically down the slope from him numbered his fourth for the day.

Galdinier thought of what it would be like on Wror, a real planet, with a real sky, the passage of real seasons. There would be new animals, dangerous animals. Galdinier had never before been away from the asteroid ring. Few Felines had. The asteroid ring had been inhabited for thousands of years. Where had Felines lived before that? Galdinier slightly furrowed his hairy brows and forehead. His eyes were still closed. Before the asteroid ring? Galdinier was not sure. Just myth and dream stories of wanderings. Endless wanderings. He thought. Maybe. He had not paid much attention to deep history during his early studies. But his father would know. Time was his business. Galdinier knew dorsein. But he did also like stories, and history was like hearing a story if it was told well. Just straight facts like those of his schooling had been dull. Galdinier thought of what he could recall of the Feline mythos. It didn't seem to have any particular order or interconnectedness to the individual stories. Maybe that was the problem, why he never could follow it. He remembered them as disorganized collections of half-recorded yarns.

The breeze picked up and the smell of grass wafted up to meet Galdinier's nose. He breathed deeply, filling his chest and raising his belly in an arch over the grass. He exhaled and opened his eyes.

A quick glance and Galdinier knew there were two hundred and forty five dorsein below him grazing in the small but verdant crater valley floor. He leaned forward and put sandals on his feet. Leather straps tied and secure, he hugged his knees and took another deep breath. The point men would be here soon. Galdinier had to get busy. He rose to his feet and started down the grassy slope toward the herd. This would be another messy business.

The herd grazed in an expanding outward dance that moved clockwise. The collective shuffle of hooves and chomp of grass were the only sounds they made. Here and there one or several heads would rise out of the mass, chewing and looking. Then they would dip back down into the herd, only to be replaced by others in a strange random fashion. Galdinier stopped at the herd's moving edge. The image taken as a whole reminded him of holographic depictions of quantum foam at the sub-Planck scale, remembered from his studies in quantum string and sub-geometry field theory. Now that was a subject that interested Galdinier, spatial geometry.

A dorsein near Galdinier stopped chewing and looked up at the young Feline. The animal stretched its long neck out and smelled the air around Galdinier. It made a lazy grunting gurgling sound, then retracted its neck and resumed grazing in the long grass. Galdinier reached out and stroked the beast's back, gently patting it just beneath the shoulders. He stretched out his other arm and patted the back of another dorsein. The second animal paused, snorted, but did not raise its head. It resumed eating. Galdinier entered the herd, moving through it petting and patting the animals.

The collective herd had no reason to be alarmed at Galdinier's presence in their midst. He was Feline. They coexisted. Without an awkward move, Galdinier slipped a wide chalky marker from a fold in his garb and quickly, gently drew an orange streak down the wool of the animal's back. He moved on to the next beast without altering his pace or bent.

Around and into the herd Galdinier moved. They shuffled clockwise while he made his way to each dorsein in a counter clockwise direction. The close proximity of so many animals clustered so closely together generated a lot of heat. The day was already warm, and Galdinier was perspiring. He frequently wiped his hands against the absorbent material of his pants. Though light, they were thick with multiple layers to absorb moisture. The collected perspiration flowed down internal channels and exited through a back tube in the cuffs overlapping his heels. Small flies hovered above and around the herd. They flew around so much so that he was forced to continually shoo them away with his hands out of annoyance while he also concentrated on patting the backs of each animal. Along with the tiny buzz of the flies, the air was thick with sound of grunts, chews, stomps, shuffles, farts and defecates.

At last Galdinier tested the last dorsein. He stood at the herd's hub. Two hundred and forty dorsein spiraled out from his center. He looked about him and counted sixteen dorsein whose backs bore the orange mark. The last herd Galdinier culled before this had thirty-two. That was large compared to the earliest of the day, two and eight, respectively. But no matter the number, it was still a messy business.

Galdinier turned with the herd and moved through their ranks to finally exit the macro organism that the herd formed. Galdinier kept walking at his calm pace away from the herd in the direction of a small grove of spiny crater oaks. They were across the small plain, slightly up the rim slope. In the shade of the grove on the inward side of the first tree nearest the valley, Galdinier found the rope ladder hanging from a limb in the canopy above. He climbed up into the leafy realm.

Four meters above the ground the rope was affixed to a wooden plank platform. The area was only two meters square. A protective wooden rail bordered the perimeter. It snaked and curved in an organic pattern mimicking the tree's branches. The platform was well hidden from the crater valley behind the leaves and branches. A small table and stool occupied one corner. In another was a box. After raising himself onto the platform, Galdinier walked over to the box and opened it. He took out a pair of binoculars and a small flat but egg shaped remote control signaling device. He set them on the table. Then he unfastened the belt of his pants and dropped them onto the floor. He stepped out of them, then bent down and picked them up. He flung them over the railing near him. The remaining water dripped from the cuff tubes down to the ground. Galdinier was wearing light fabric pants beneath the pair now hanging on the rail.

He went back to the table and picked up the binoculars. He slung its strap over his head and put one arm through the loop. Then he put the signaling device in a pocket.

Galdinier could not see the dorsein from the vantage point of the platform. It was situated too deep near the tree's center. So he crossed the small space and climbed over the rail. He climbed onto a large branch and crawled to its outer terminus. He looked out beyond the spiny oak's leafy edge to the crater valley's bottom and dorsein below. Each leaf on the tree's branches around him sported a yellow-brown upturned spike about a centimeter long.

Galdinier lay stretched out on the limb hidden in the tree's canopy, surrounded by thorns. The stripes in the fur of his face blended well into the spiny foliage. The Ministry of Cycles had ensured Galdinier that the grove of trees was downwind from the crater valley and dorsein herd today.

Galdinier reached into his pants pocket with one hand while steadying himself on a branch with his other. He withdrew the signaling device. On its face on one side were four buttons arranged in a row. The first three were white, and the fourth was red. The red button transmitted an emergency help signal to a support team watching from a nearby facility's upper floor windows. Galdinier pressed the top button and it lit up. It transmitted a ready signal to an anteroom in the facility just within the outside doors.

The facility housed offices and residences for the few animal husbandry men, administrators and support staff that maintained the asteroid and the herds that grazed there. It was located on the crater rim opposite the valley from the grove of trees.

Galdinier looked closer afield at the surface of the tree limb on which he lay. His eyes followed the protruding branches to stems, then leaves and thorns. He was looking for oak ants. They were tiny. They swarmed. They bit. They were non-venomous, but they still hurt. Galdinier hated them. His arms were covered in red swollen bites. Sometimes they hurt and other times itched. Sometimes they felt hot and other times they caused cold goose bumps. During the previous culling, the tree in which he hid had been full of them. Swarms. They were so annoying and distracting. But Galdinier was on a different asteroid now. Maybe there wouldn't be any ants.

He turned his head and focused on a branch to his right. He spied an ant. Galdinier's ears folded back onto the sides of his head. His pupils dilated to fill eyes. His nostrils flared wide in a quick intake of breath. Galdinier's lips were pulled back to bare his teeth and a hiss escaped from his mouth. He followed his hiss with a low growl when he saw two more, then five, then a whole line of ants climbing up and down the branch. For now they were not aware of the Feline.

Galdinier pressed the second button on the signaling device. He drew up the binoculars and looked out across the valley to see the metallic facilities doors slide open. Two quadrupedal dogs darted out the open doors and paused, looking down the crater rim at the herd of dorsein below. They barked. Then two Human men followed the dogs out and onto the crater rim. They each bore a laser rifle slung over a shoulder.

The dogs were bred on a separate asteroid. They had originally been acquired on an expedition to Earth. Access to Earth's resources was reserved to the asteroid ring Felines through their continued quarantine of the planet. Earth was closed off. It was removed and apart. It had been that way for thousands of years. During that time the planet drew many clandestine expeditions by Feline scientists.

The men had been smugglers caught by Feline security. They were contracted into service for a period of time as punishment before being released. So the men believed.

An affinity between dogs and Earth Humans had long been observed by Felines. The same held true with Humans of other worlds that came into contact with the animals. A natural bond formed.

The men who stood on the crater rim had been given specific instructions, shoot only the dorsein with the orange mark. Dorsein were dumb and gentle. That was their reputation throughout the inhabited worlds. Everyone knew that. There were tame herds numbering in the hundreds of thousands on Drigo. This would be an easy job, an easy cull. The men started down the slope toward the herd. The dogs bolted down past the men.

Galdinier held tight to a branch as he shifted his weight on the tree limb to position himself for a better view of the herd. He could make out individual dorsein through the binoculars. They had ceased their grazing. Galdinier could see the beginnings of confusion and alarm spread through the herd. The sound of the barking dogs was the reason. The men and dogs descending into the crater valley were upwind from the herd. The scent of the intruders was carried on the breezes, causing panic. Some of the beasts turned and pushed their way behind their neighbors. Others actually surged forward. Those bearing the orange mark were prominent among them.

Halfway down the slope the men stopped. Galdinier moved his head to bring them into better view. They raised their rifles and the taller of the two men took aim and fired. The shot echoed across the valley. Galdinier quickly brought the herd into view again in time to see an orange-marked dorsein fall. The second man followed the first, and a second shot brought down another animal. The two dogs, circling in opposite directions, began to head off the retreating members of the herd.

The men took aim again and brought down two more orange-marked dorsein. Then two more. The men paused to check their weapons. Distracted, they did not notice the dynamic of the herd change.

The first dog to reach the retreating dorsein came around on the left from Galdinier's vantage point. The dog was running at a trot, then darted straight for a dorsein that broke away from its neighbors just enough to find itself isolated. Suddenly the dorsein spun around. It's neck extended out a meter with lightning speed. Through the lenses of the binoculars Galdinier watched the animal's eyes protrude slightly from their sockets and steel their gaze on the advancing dog. The dorsein's nostrils were swollen, red and flared. Its lips were retracted and cheeks pulled back. White froth filled the animal's mouth and slopped prodigiously onto the ground. Long curved incisors slowly extended down from above, and up from below, the dorsein's front teeth. Galdinier was always amazed when he watched the docile herbivores with mouthfuls of dull, blocky teeth transform into predators. He knew that down there in the valley, the dorsein was emitting a ferocious growl.

Quickly, but not soon enough, the dog realized its misjudgment and tried to pull up only a meter before the dorsein. But its inertia down the crater rim's slope was too great. The dog attempted to turn and its front paws stumbled. The dorsein lunged forward and plunged its teeth into the dog's side, ripping out a chunk of its rib cage. The animal collapsed, and the dorsein fell upon the dog's now dead corpse, casting blow after blow of vicious biting attacks. Its face was red and black from blood and ripped entrails.

Several dorsein near the attack turned at the sound of their comrade's growls and dog's yelps of shock and defeat. As if a trigger had been pulled, the herd became a hunting pack and burst forth in multiple directions.

Galdinier brought the signaling device up close to his eyes. He pressed the third button until it lit up. Then he looked back through the binoculars.

The men had lowered their rifles, aware at first of the dog's howls. They were confused as to what was going on. There issued a sudden but quickly silenced yelp. The second dog fell in a like manner as the first. Then the situation became clear to the men. The nearest of the herd rushed forward up the crater rim slope toward them. The panicking Humans raised their rifles and attempted to fire round after round into the advancing herd. Nothing happened. The men checked the power cells of the rifles. They read empty. The men threw down the useless weapons and started scrambling backwards up the dirt and gravel slope. They stumbled among the rocks. The herd was already three meters away and advancing fast. The men ran as fast as they could toward the facility doors.

Galdinier lowered his binoculars and raised the signaling device to his eyes again. He pressed the second button, which lit up.

The men had nearly reached the facility doors when the great silvery metal doors slammed shut, cutting the desperate Humans off from their only refuge and safety. When the men reached the doors they banged their fists against the surface. Both men fell, swallowed by a growing tide of dorsein swelling around them and engulfing them.

But Galdinier did not see it happen. While preoccupied looking through the binoculars, he had not noticed a line of oak ants advancing down nearby branches onto the larger limb on which Galdinier lay. Just as the men approached the facility doors, several ants traversed up Galdinier's arms and began biting him. They detected residual chemical markers secreted by the swollen sores in the Feline's arms from bites earlier that day. He let the binoculars fall and swatted the tiny crawling jaws off his arms. He frantically held onto the limb with the tormented hand that also clutched the signaling device. The binoculars swayed and banged against the branches beside and below him. The limb swayed a little and Galdinier let out a litany of curses.

He finally subdued the little attackers. He smote the enemy to a decisive defeat by snapping off the branches where the ants had begun to swarm, tossing them to the ground.

Still muttering curses, Galdinier picked up the binoculars and trained them back on the facility doors across the small crater. The herd was disbursing from the attacks, coming together back on the valley floor and resuming their grazing. The only evidence of their ghastly actions was four scatterings of bones and dark wet smears on the ground and on the dorsein's faces. The facility doors bore dark wet streaks, viscous red oozing down to the ground.

"Dammit," cursed Galdinier. "I missed it." He rubbed his arm where the fresh bites burned. Galdinier scanned the herd and confirmed their number, two hundred and thirty nine. Ten orange-marked dorsein remained standing. The sharpshooters had been slow. The surviving marked dorsein would have to be included in a future culling. Luckily, Galdinier was not the only herder charged with this messy business. But it would still be several more days before all the dorsein herds selected to accompany the colonists to Wror were cleared of the most ferocious individuals that could pose a thread to Felines. The gene pool had to remain docile and obedient around Felines. Only Humans and Canines provoked violent responses from these special dorsein herds. They were meant to protect the Felines going to their new homes on Wror.

Galdinier aimed the signaling device toward the opposite crater rim and pressed the first button again, alerting a cleanup team to remove the bones and clean the blood from the doors. Then he pressed the second button and the distant facility doors opened.

Galdinier began wriggling and scooting backwards, making his way back to the platform deep within the tree's canopy. He stepped over the rail and onto the plank floor. With his hands Galdinier brushed his hair, sleeves, shirt and pants, dislodging bark, leaves and stray oak ants. He walked over to the box on the floor and returned the binoculars and signaling device. Then he pulled out a tube of ointment and squeezed out a liberal glob of cream onto his arms. He rubbed it and worked it through his hair into his skin. The cream's cooling effect relieved Galdinier from some of the oak ant bites' discomfort. He returned the tube to the box. Then he pulled down the pants from the rail, folded them and put them into the box and closed the lid. Galdinier walked to the other side of the platform and climbed back down the rope ladder to the ground. He had a shuttle to catch and another asteroid to visit. Another herd to cull.

18 STAR CROSSING

The bonfire blazed hot and inviting in the warm night. Twenty or so Felines sat in small groups, others walked about in couples, talking and telling stories in quiet voices. Off to one side sat a lone Feline strumming a mandolin. Opposite the fire sat another, softly beating a skin drum. Across the valley many other bonfires burned. Extended families and friends gathered around their own fires. Up above projected on the overarching dome was a night sky that held only dim and distant stars. It was dark. A collective hush lay over the valley despite the thousands of Felines encamped in this crater alone. They all waited patiently in the protective valleys of the armored asteroid. Waited to break orbit from the asteroid ring and begin the journey to Wror.

A tall Feline woman stood hunched over a cooking unit stirring a pot of meaty stew. She closed her eyes and inhaled deeply. Her lips elongated into a smile cheek to cheek and her ears pointed forward and down. Another inhalation and she opened her eyes, drew back. "Almost perfect," she murmured. She reached down and pulled a small ceramic vial out of a box of spices. She removed the stopper and sprinkled some brown ground powder into the stew. The woman returned the stopper to its vial and stowed it back in the box. She stirred the pot. Then she raised a spoonful of broth to her lips, smelled it, blew on it, tasted it. She smiled more broadly than before. "Perfect! Dried ground grasshopper is the magic ingredient." She reduced the heat under the pot and covered it with a lid.

Two young Feline girls walked toward the woman from out of the darkness beyond the reach of the bonfire's light. Their giggling and talking and raucous voices broke the woman's concentration.

"Whoa you two wild cats!" the woman said. "Slow down and come eat some delicious stew."

"Alright Mother," said the red-furred Feline girl. She turned to her friend and said, "Come Er. Mother cooks the best camp food."

Eridani smiled and stepped up to the cooking unit to catch a whiff of the stew. "Mm, it smells wonderful!"

In the intervening weeks since Eridani had first met Canopus, the two had become fast friends. The excitement of that first encounter in the central valley of the great asteroid near the small forest, finding the grazimyth and experiencing the hallucinations caused by the flower's scent, was enough to send Eridani on a several-day search for the enigmatic girl Canopus. The girl was finally found shopping with her mother in the crater rim wall city. Now Canopus and her family were on their way to Wror, emigrants joining thousands of others.

After Eridani discovered that her brother was accompanying the herds of dorsein to Wror, she approached Galdren and her mother for permission to join in the exodus. They had approved, thinking it was better to travel with a family rather than alone. Galdren arranged significant compensation and privileges for Canopus' family, who were happy for the assistance in supplies and the extra hands Galdinier and Eridani leant to the family. Galdren would stay in the asteroid ring. His work was with his projection machine and counseling the Feline leadership. His wife was frail and would remain with him.

Canopus' mother used a ladle to fill two bowls with stew. She handed each carefully to the young Feline girls. She found two spoons and added them to the bowls. The girls sat cross-legged on a blanket near the camp stove and ate the stew.

"Canopus," said the woman. "When you're done, take this canteen of water to your brothers and Galdinier down by the bonfire." She picked up a metal canteen and filled it with water from a jug.

"We need more water, too," said Eridani, removing a canteen from around her neck and extending it to her friend's mother. She looked up and asked, "Will we be camping out like this when we get to Wror?"

The woman returned the canteen, now filled. "At first, I imagine yes," she said. "It should be mid-summer in the region we'll be settling, according to the transmigration report. Enough time to establish ourselves."

"Everyday will be unpredictable!" exclaimed Canopus. "Everyday will be an adventure!"

"We'll have this asteroid above us to monitor weather and ensure our safety. Don't worry girls," her mother added. "We'll prosper."

The woman raised a ladle of stew to her mouth, closed her eyes, blew on it and inhaled the rich aroma. She opened her eyes and sipped from the ladle. "Mm. We'll have different foods once we reach Wror. Native foods. Wild game." *This may be the last time I prepare this dish*, she continued to herself. *The little lizard of the asteroid fields, the tiny midnight flower, so delicate, even a few photons damage its blossoms. It opens only in the deepest night on the darkest asteroids. Yes, I shall never make this dish again.*

The two girls finished their stew. Canopus picked up her canteen and said, "We'll be the first Felines in a million years to settle a new world outside the asteroid ring."

Her mother laughed. "Maybe not that long, but a long time, to be sure. Now go and find your brothers and settle down for the evening. I will join you when I'm done cleaning up here. Before long we will begin accelerating through the doughnut force field. We'll be on our way to Wror."

"Yes, Mother," said Canopus.

The girls walked toward the bonfire where a group of young Felines sat, Canopus' brothers among them.

Beside the light and warmth of the bonfire sat Galdinier with his friends Bereth and Beleth, the brothers of Canopus. Walking up to them, Eridani stopped beside her brother and said, "We brought water." She handed Galdinier the canteen.

"Thank you," said Galdinier looking up at his sister and Canopus. Canopus sat down next to her brothers. Galdinier took the canteen and removed the stopper, took a refreshing drink. He handed the canteen back. "Where have you been?"

"Canopus and I walked by some of the other campsites. Everyone is excited about the journey. When do we leave?" Eridani sat down on the blanket next to her brother. "Have you eaten?"

"Yes, with Bereth and Beleth earlier." Galdinier picked up a nearby pebble and tossed it into the fire. He turned to his sister. Both their faces flickered in the light of the fire's fanning flames. "We should be leaving very soon. They're going to turn off the sky projection so we can watch the actual exit out of the doughnut force field and nebula."

"We'll see real stars," said Eridani. She looked up at the dim stars in the black sky projected onto the crater's high dome far above.

The two sat quietly for a while. The mandolin player's music mingled with the snap and crackle of the bonfire, the muted voices around, the sound of drumming. Presently Galdinier reached a hand up to a pocket in his vest and patted a bulge visible in the firelight. A grin crept across his face. "I have a surprise for you." His ears slightly protruded forward and he turned to look at Eridani, excited anticipation in his eyes.

Eridani's eyes widened. Her ears pointed up and forward at her brother. "What is it?!" She scooted closer to him, now eyeing the bulge in his vest pocket.

Galdinier let a moment pass. He knew how to excite his sister and enjoyed seeing the look of suspense in her face.

Eridani licked her lips. Her nostrils flared. She furrowed her brows and gave her brother a piercing look. "Well?"

Galdinier lowered his hand from his pocket to the blanket. Finally he said, "Grazimyth. Father gave me packages of spores, enough to spread across the new land we will be settling."

"Oh, that's excellent!" exclaimed Eridani.

"Not only that," said Galdinier. "I have a vial of grazimyth essence. It's concentrated. Let's sniff it as we move out of the asteroid ring."

Eridani giggled. "This will be a fun trip!" Her ears relaxed and she turned to look at the fire. Her eyes glistened and her mind drifter to inner thoughts.

The evening progressed and Canopus' mother joined the group. The fire gradually burned down. Voices dwindled.

As the evening gave way to early night, something changed in the asteroid. Eridani turned to her brother. Galdinier's ears lay back against his head which was slightly cocked to one side. His eyes squinted, directed toward the ground. "Do you feel that?" he asked looking up at his sister.

"Something feels different," she said.

"The engines. It's starting," said Galdinier. He brought out a small vial from his pocket. He unscrewed its lid and raised the vial to a nostril. He inhaled deeply. Then he did the same with his other nostril. He returned the lid to the vial and handed it to his sister. The young Felines passed the vial among themselves. It eventually was handed back to Galdinier.

The mandolin music and drumming ceased. A faintly audible sound, deep and reverberating, emanated from within the asteroid. A hush lay on the valley of the asteroid crater. A detectable acceleration, a change in direction, could be felt. Then the sky turned a rose hue.

The thousands of Felines in the crater valley raised their heads and gazed up at the dome. Gone were the dim stars in a dark night sky. The Felines beheld the rose atmosphere of the asteroid ring. A smaller asteroid drifted nearby across the field of vision, mossy green in color. Beyond it shimmered the force field. Beyond that blazed the glory of the Great Aurora Nebula.

Expressions and shouts of awe and delight erupted from the young Felines. Sounds of exhilaration were carried on the airs from all corners of the crater valley. Galdinier and Eridani laughed as they saw reptiles fly above the dome of their crater.

From the vantage point of a transport pod hovering at a safe distance from the asteroid, Galdren looked out at the asteroid that shown brightly from light reflected off its surfaces. Rhomboid panels of metallic alloys overlapped around the majority of the asteroid. Domes protruded through the armor sheltering crater valleys within on opposite sides of the floating rock.

The asteroid turned on its axis. Gaps in the rhomboid armor appeared on one side as great metal plates slid aside to reveal the maws of engine exhaust compartments. The inner working of the asteroid's propulsion system activated. Particle streams emanated from the micro-singularity at the heart of the asteroid. The engine rims and surrounding metallic plates began to glow red, then white hot. Steams of visible light flowed through the engine portals. Slowly at first but picking up speed, the asteroid veered from its orbital revolution around the central star and moved perpendicular to its former path.

The rocky body silently and elegantly approached the side of the doughnut force field furthest from the star. As if sensing imminent danger, several flying reptiles escaped from narrow crevasses in the few rocky moss-covered crags and peaks that broached the asteroid's armor. A few moments later the moving body crossed the force field between huge field regulators. Sparks issued from the intersection points and ripples of disturbance spread out in the field from the breach.

As the asteroid plunged into space and away from the asteroid ring, the rocky vessel crackled in a slight contraction. The asteroid's protruding crags instantly turned white as the moss froze in the cold of space away from the doughnut force field's atmosphere. The exterior of the crater domes frosted over as remnants of atmosphere froze and settled, then sublimated in the ambient radiation of the aurora.

The asteroid's rhomboid armor turned a ruddy brass color. A few unfortunate flying reptiles drifted out of crags in the rock, too late to escape to new homes, now dead in the cold airless space outside the asteroid ring.

The armored rock continued to move farther and farther away from its family of sister asteroids.

"Safe journey and success," Galdren said to his children in the departing asteroid. The elder Feline steered his pod around and headed to his home asteroid.

Eridani looked up at the spectacle from the valley floor. "How long will the voyage take?" she asked her brother.

Galdinier lay on his back watching the wisps of auroral gas drift beyond the dome overhead. "A few days to Drigo, then a few more to Wror," he answered.

19 RENENDER

Renender stood fidgeting at the great window of his office. Beside him stood a bronze statue of a boy reaching into a bucket grasping hold of a large bronze fish whose shape feigned a struggle in the boy's hands half out of the bronze bucket. Morning's light streamed bright into the room like silent furies. Morning marked the busiest part of Renender's day. There were the export manifests to review, the import lists to scan. And because of last night's visitor's alarming news, Renender scrutinized all the passenger logs.

Last night. He hadn't slept at all since he'd gotten that call. The noise on the other end was loud. The whip-whip-whip of the scout ship's blades drowned out much of the conversation. But he'd understood the message well enough.

"Please to report the wedding is on. Arriving tonight. Matta's coffee would be appreciated upon arrival." The first part was the coded message he'd been dreading. The part about Matta was more mysterious. Renender had always been prepared to do his part to thwart Markhab's tyranny. Until now Markhab had largely ignored Lupus City. But time and events were coming to a head. This business on Wror changed everything, and the call had come in. Jarbed had come in person.

Renender stepped back away from the window and removed his sunglasses. He turned to his great desk and ruffled through some papers lying on top until he found the manifest. Four names were circled in red, Joren, Gilbraithe, Farroll, and Corvus. Commissioner Corvus.

Renender picked up his glasses and put them back on, turned back to the window. Trucks were already transporting trade goods to the landing field below. Off to the left Jarbed's black patrol ship lifted off the ground. It picked up speed and raced overhead vanishing in the direction of the desert road.

Just after Jarbed had left the building, Renender received the call from Matta that Cornelius and Naemi were in the restaurant below. Renender reran the security camera scans and knew exactly when they'd arrived and to whom they'd spoken.

A chime sounded and a light flashed on the computer screen at his desk. Renender jumped and fumbled with his glasses as he knocked them off his head and caught them in his hands. He turned and patted down his hair, straightened his shirt and vest. They were coming.

Renender placed his sunglasses on his desktop and hustled passed it without slowing. He crossed to the back of the room passed ornate marbled walls. Renender was a tall man, two meters. His bulbous stomach hanging on his slender frame formed a caricature of his own looks. When he moved as quickly as he could manage, his lower legs kicked out in front of him like he was attempting an Earth Cossack dance. Renender reached out his long slender arms and grasped the huge handles of the double doors that adorned his office. His long fingers curled around the handles. He heaved. The four-meter tall doors swung open slowly and silently.

Renender hurried down the marble floored hallway passed glass spun art works of many-hued leafy trees, creeping vines and suspended flocks of tiny birds and winged insects. They clattered in ethereal melodies in the breeze made by Renender as he passed by.

At the end of the hall the way turned left and opened up onto a spacious grand gallery hallway of stone columns between ornately framed oil paintings, forest scenes with mythological nymphs from art masters in Aran province, seascapes near Cronapolis, the inland river marshes near Bafaria in Lupus Minor, the dance of the northern aurora above the great cities of

Canoon in the polar mountains, and more.

Renender hustled his way down the grand hall passed the artworks, looking neither left nor right but focused straight ahead at the lift doors at the far end. He huffed and puffed and wiped the beading and running perspiration from his eyes and temples with a silk handkerchief snatched from a pocket as he mocked a run. He finally skidded to a halt in front of the lift doors. He bent down and grabbed his knees, heaving his chest up and down to catch his breath.

Renender squeezed his eyes shut tight and continued to process how quickly events were moving. Yesterday at this time he was haggling over the price per bushel of sweet berries from Canius with a distributor. Today his shipments down the mountain vales to the lake docks and the Cantons would be monitored by Markhab's men. Manifest lists will have to be turned over. "Permission" to be required for the transport of non-'listed' goods!" Renender mumbled aloud to himself as he thought of Markhab's audacity in the news Jarbed had brought him. The inspectors were already on their way up to the valley in the airships even now, rising up the mountain vales from the lakeside and steppes below.

Renender's breathing slowed after a moment and a smiled crept across his face. "It's a good thing I keep daily 'duplicate' ledgers for just such governmental intrusions," he said to himself. He chuckled.

A bell sounded indicating the lift had arrived at this floor. Renender jumped startled and stood as upright as his tall narrow frame and bulbous gut allowed. His eyes opened wide and expectant. He clasped his hands together in front of him just as the doors opened. There stood Cornelius and Naemi.

"My Dears!" exclaimed Renender. "How marvelous!" He grinned wide and excited. "Stars above, if it isn't Naemi. I can hardly believe it!" Renender reached out his arms and grasped Naemi's outstretched hands as she exited the lift. He kissed her on both cheeks. "It has been years, my Dear. Simply years since I've seen you." Standing back still holding Naemi's hands, he added, "And you are more beautiful than I remember."

Naemi smiled and kissed Renender back on both cheeks. "You look wonderful, Renender. I'm so happy to see you again."

"And always a pleasure, Cornelius. Always a pleasure." Renender took Cornelius' hands and shook them.

"Renender, old friend, thank you for seeing us," Cornelius said.

Renender lost the corners of his smile and he looked passed the two visitors, sweeping a quick gaze at the inside of the lift. "Yes, of course the pleasure is mine," he said, suddenly turning back to Cornelius. "Come in, come in both of you. Let us sit and visit in my offices. Please, follow me." Renender turned still smiling and led Cornelius and Naemi down the hall. A look of concern crept back onto his visage.

Cornelius and Naemi looked at each other then followed behind Renender side by side. Naemi assessed all she saw, Renender so oddly attentive, waiting for them at the lift door, lavishing small talk, the opulence of the surroundings.

"You are doing very well for yourself, Renender," Naemi said.

"Oh, you must be referring to the art!" said Renender. He slowed and turned to answer Naemi. "I have always been a lover of art. I just never had a place to display it properly in that warehouse I used to lease on the other side of the valley." He paused, then added, "Business has been good, too." He turned back and resumed the walk down the hall.

In Renender's grand office Cornelius and Naemi stood at the great window overlooking the landing field. Renender pushed hard against the double doors with both his hands clutching the handles. As they closed, a slight fizzing sound as of air being squeezed out of a tight seal closed in the room.

"I am so glad you are here," said Renender. He did not look up but made straight for the computer at his desk. "May I offer you something to drink?" He pressed a button on the touch screen. An electric status sound squealed from the corners of the room then subsided. Renender relaxed his shoulders and finally looped up at Cornelius and Naemi standing facing him with their backs to the window.

The bright sunlight temporarily blinded Renender and he reached for the sunglasses on his desk. He put them on and sighed. Then he perked up and explained. "Security measures. Don't worry. You must sit down. I have much to tell you and I have not enough time to tell it!" Renender pointed to three chairs that were arranged together near the left corner of the window. He continued to a wet bar against the wall and poured three glasses of water. He brought Cornelius and Naemi their glasses then hurried to join them with his own.

"My dear Naemi. My dear Cornelius. It is good to see you. These are troubling times. And now there isn't enough time. You must listen to me, both of you." Renender took a gulp of water.

"What has happened, Renender?" asked Cornelius.

"We saw scout ships last night on the desert road," said Naemi.

"And they saw you," Renender said turning to Naemi. "It's a good thing they were ours," and Renender smiled. "Markhab is tightening his grip. He's declared martial law in Lupus Minor. And all major transit points are being inspected by the security services. Inspectors are already on their way to Lupus City on this morning's airships. And none other than Commissioner Corvus himself is among them. You both must leave. This afternoon you must be on an airship down to the lake docks."

Cornelius leaned in close to Renender. "Markhab won't relinquish any territory he gets a toe hold on. You can be sure he plans to bring in more 'inspectors.'"

"Lupus City is independent!" said Renender sitting up straight in his chair and thrusting his chin out.

"No one believes that but the people of Lupus City themselves," said Cornelius.

"Cornelius is right, Renender," said Naemi. Markhab wants to surround the Territory of Shining Star. He wants to push deep into the side of Canius. This will be his first move, and maybe his easiest."

Renender shook his head and looked down at his feet. His eyes squinted slightly and he cracked a smile. Devising counter schemes had always been a skill at which he was known to excel. At least he was certain that's what his friends and colleagues said about him in private. Renender was clever. He looked back up at Cornelius and Naemi.

"Markhab's tactics are not good for business. Before any "inspecting" commences by these military-type inspectors, they will have to petition the Lupus City Economic Board and Council. Since the Miner's Union kicked out Markhab's moles, thanks to you two, the Miner's Union now holds considerable influence on the Board. Markhab is not welcome. And business has been good. Look at me." Renender lifted his hands and swept them through the air to take in everything around him. "I have considerable, er, influence with the Board myself these days."

"You won't be able to delay them long. Not with Corvus here," said Cornelius.

Renender quickly closed his eyes and feigned a shiver. He looked back at Cornelius and said, "Just thinking about that monster makes my skin crawl. He's as bad as Markhab, if not worse."

Renender suddenly remembered something important. He turned to Naemi and just looked at her for a moment. "That scout ship that flew passed you last night. That was Jarbed."

"Jarbed!" said Cornelius.

Renender continued without looking at Cornelius. "Naemi, something very big is afoot. Now what it is I don't know." He turned to Cornelius. "But it is bigger than what you and I are talking about here."

Renender turned back to Naemi. "I only have this that I can tell you. Naemi, you are to travel off world. Shont will tell you more. But you must both first get out of Lupus City."

He turned back to Cornelius. "I don't doubt what you say about Markhab's intentions. There are many here in Lupus City beside myself who have no love for Markhab's regime. We are a proud people, we citizens of Lupus City. But I've not become a successful businessman by being naïve to the currents around me. Markhab has supporters here, too."

Renender got up and walked over to his desk. He reached down into the front of his shirt and pulled out a dull grey key that hung around a chain around his neck against his chest. He bent down, pushed the key into a narrow slit in the side of the desk and turned. There was a single distinct "click" sound.

Renender straightened back up and hid the key back in his shirt. He looked at Cornelius and Naemi and said, "Now, I can take care of myself, but you two must safely get away." He walked over to the bronze statue and reached into the bucket. A panel had slid open inside. Renender bent down and reached in.

"Do we just buy tickets out of the city?" asked Cornelius.

"You don't have business licenses or visitor's tickets that the travel agencies issue," said Renender. "You'd easily be pulled out of any line for questioning by some brash military inspector."

"That's how Markhab operates," said Cornelius.

Renender rifled through documents and small parcels in the bucket safe. "Ah ha," he said presently. He stood up and turned back again to Cornelius and Naemi, holding two small green booklets with an embossing of a gold sun on the face, the emblem of the Federated Cantons. "These are identity and travel documents for a husband and wife on a business trip from Big City. Don't bother with the details. Make something up if you need to." Renender handed the booklets to Cornelius and Naemi.

"I run many of the airships between Lupus City and the lake docks these days," he said to Naemi. "Cornelius knows this. I have one pilot in particular in whom I have every trust. You will board her ship this afternoon. Her name is Ferrimay. She will see you safely to the lake docks."

"How do we get to Big City from the docks?" asked Naemi.

"Ferrimay will see you onto a lake hauler captained by an old seaman named Katzer. He is not a pleasant man, but he owes me a number of favors. Tell him 'Renender asks for a couple of tall tales.' This will cash in some of the favors. But you must be on your guards at all times. Markhab will have agents at the docks. And these 'inspectors' represent a new intrusion entirely. You must be discreet."

Naemi opened the booklet Renender had given her. It opened onto a photograph page. Naemi saw herself looking back at herself. The picture was black and white. She was wearing a jumpsuit and a square-brimmed miner's hat. "Where did you get this picture?" she asked looking up at Renender.

"That's the photo from your old Miner's Union ID," Renender said chuckling.

"How did you get a copy of it? I still have mine," asked Naemi.

"My dear," said Renender quite matter of factly. "Whom do you think fabricated the original? Both of yours," he added looking at Cornelius.

Cornelius opened his travel booklet and viewed his picture. "Humph."

Naemi smiled at Renender, feeling a renewed trust in the strange man. She realized that Renender played a more significant role in this entire operation than she had previously realized.

Renender snapped closed the secret compartment in the bronze statue and returned to his chair. "There's something more I must tell you." He paused a moment, then added, "Unless you already know this by breaking all common sense last night when you were trying to sneak across the desert by listening to the radio." He paused again to look at Cornelius and then Naemi. He got no reaction from either, so he continued. "Markhab's state media announced that radio-isotope tests confirmed that the fission material that detonated over Bara-Band on Wror matched minerals from the polar Canoon Mountains. He said a state of heightened security alert was in effect against the "Canine Menace." Renender feigned a punctuation gesture. "You won't hear this on the official news outlets, but the military is occupying Bafaria. Tanks are in the streets, my sources tell me. Military facilities are being expanded west of Bafaria near the great Lupus River. Those are the plains south of Canoon."

Cornelius and Naemi turned and looked at each other at the mention of the radioisotope test results. Cornelius rubbed his arm where the bio-data was injected the day before.

"So Markhab says the Canines nuked Bara-Band," Naemi asked.

"That of course is the assumption he's calling on the populace to believe," Renender answered. "But the situation in Lupus Minor doesn't make sense. It's extreme."

"Is there any active resistance in Bafaria?" Cornelius asked.

"Little to none," said Renender. "That's what doesn't make sense."

Cornelius wanted to tell Renender about the bio-data message in his bloodstream. But it was clear Renender did not know about the true source of the plutonium in the bomb that fell on Wror's capital city. Cornelius decided to remain mum on the fact. The information was destined for an operative named Shont in Big City. Renender was simply going to help him get there. That was his mission.

A wave of exhaustion swept through Cornelius' body. How long had it been since he'd slept? Had it been thirty hours? Forty? It had been a crazy week. Renender and Naemi continued talking as Cornelius' mind wandered, surveying the events of the past few days.

He had spent a week in Cronapolis, melding into his alter ego of Cornelius the purveyor of specialty cutlery. He "worked" out of his state-issued apartment in one of the many residential-commercial high-rise blocks on the north end of the capital. He'd met with his contact M and discussed the general state of affairs within the three military-controlled provinces. They'd mainly talked about the continuing strike by the Orchard Growers Association in Dula City. Support for the strikes was spreading to the other provinces.

Cornelius recalled the long and dangerous return through secret mountain passes back to the Territory of the Shining Star, back to his real home in Shining City. He remembered looking forward to seeing Naemi again, then the discovery that she was dead. Naemi had flown the one-way mission to Bara-Band. Cornelius could scarcely comprehend the rapid-fire events since that revelation, the orders from Jarbed to go to Big City, Naemi being alive, music and sex, the long drive to Lupus City. Cornelius was exhausted. Fatigue was taking over. Renender's voice reentered Cornelius' consciousness.

"I mean, I'm just saying I'm surprised there isn't more anger against the military in Aran. Markhab is stripping the forests of hardwoods."

Naemi countered, "Markhab controls Aran City, without question. The cutters in the forests are glad for the work. Aran's economy is the strongest of the three provinces."

"Excuse me," interrupted Cornelius. "I'm sorry to interrupt. Renender it has been almost two days since I've slept. I need to rest. I need to rest now."

Renender and Naemi looked at Cornelius. Naemi saw the fatigue on Cornelius' face and realized she too needed to rest. She turned and said, "Renender my friend. Cornelius is right. We drove all night to get here."

"As delicious and rejuvenating as Matta's coffee is, I'm afraid it's worn off. We need to sleep."

Renender's eyes widened and he stood up. "Where has my hospitality gone. Of course, you both must be so tired. You can rest here. I have a private room adjacent to this office. You won't need to board the airships for another six hours or so. Please, take rest here." Renender stood up and gestured for Naemi and Cornelius to rise out of their chairs. Renender extended his hand to Naemi and gentlemanly helped her up. "I'm afraid there is only one bed. But it's a large one," he said.

"We'll be fine," said Naemi.

Cornelius looked at her then said, "It will be just fine. I'm sorry to impose."

"Not at all!" exclaimed Renender. He proceeded to the wall behind him and pressed a marble panel. A door opened inward. "Please make yourselves comfortable. I will check in on you in five hours." Renender stood aside, holding the door.

Cornelius and Naemi walked through. "Thank you Renender," said Cornelius.

Renender bowed. "I am at your service Cornelius, Naemi. Let me know if there is anything I can get you." He saw them into the room and sealed the door shut. It was scarcely visible to the eye. He walked back to his desk and deactivated the security field. Then he walked back to the window and looked out at the landing field, bright in the mid-morning light. The airships would be arriving soon. "Let's get this day over with," he mumbled.

Matta was seating a group of grain traders from the steppes when her earpiece burst with static. She grabbed at her ear and snapped at the volume wheel. In the midst of a curse she heard "Get this day over with."

She smiled at her guests, slammed a hand on the table and asked, "Coffees all around? I'll be right back." Matta hustled off to fetch a pot of coffee from the service stand.

20 ARRIVAL OF THE AIRSHIPS

Naemi passed through the door and marveled at the opulence of the room. She stepped into the middle of the chamber and turned around. "Cornelius, this is beautiful. More than that. Astounding."

Cornelius bolted the door from the inside. He turned and faced Naemi taking in the surroundings. "Wow."

The walls all around the main room were opalescent sheets of thinly hewn rock from the vast mines up the mountain valleys behind Lupus City. Slender marble columns tricked the eye by giving the illusion of holding up a domed ceiling painted with beautiful images of flying insects and serpents amid flowering vines. A partially cloudy blue sky was painted behind. Accenting the surroundings were lavishly gold-gilded marble and wood furnishings, tables, chairs, couches, statuary, gold vases and goblets. Sunlight burst in through full wall windows to the right. Built into them was a sliding glass door. A broad patio full of flowering plants in a dozen shades of green invited the eye. Off to the left stood two tall yet narrow doors that hung open. On the left was a bathroom. On the right was a bedroom. Between them was a large recessed niche. Tiny mirrors and prisms arranged in constellations manipulated and recast the sunlight back into the room. One large star cast a purplish light. Cornelius moved closer to the niche and realized the prisms were highly polished precious gems. The room was exploding in liquid light.

"Cornelius, Renender is loaded. Does he really make all this money leasing airship berths?" Naemi asked in a cold analytical tone.

"Yeah, Renender is loaded," Cornelius replied.

Naemi walked to the open bedroom door and looked inside. A massive four-post bed done up in plush deep red velvet and a dozen or more pillows dominated the room. The bedposts were of tall ivory tusks from some great animal, accented in polished black onyx bands and gold gilding. So much gold. The walls were bordered in a red velvet waist high wainscot. Above that extended thin rock sheets embedded with cut rubies and other precious stones. The domed vaulted ceiling was light blue with a red tinge on the lower edges, graduating to a midnight blue at the apex. Stars and constellations were represented by blue and white diamonds fixed to the blue background. A light source behind allowed them to softly shine.

"I think Renender has his fingers in more financial dealings than just airships," said Naemi. She turned back into the main room.

Cornelius stood looking closely at a statue. Two boys writhed in the grip of a serpent. They bore expressions of surprise and ecstasy as the serpent penetrated them. The boys were unadorned white marble while the serpent had bands of precious stones, silver, gold and onyx.

Naemi walked up to Cornelius and smiled at the statue he was admiring. Cornelius turned to Naemi and said, "Oh yes. Renender has all kinds of business dealings."

"All this expensive stuff. Lavish stuff. To the point, Cornelius, can we trust him?" Naemi was completely serious.

Cornelius was surprised. "Oh definitely. I've been in contact with Renender for years, Naemi. I've observed him, inquired about him, cautiously prodded him. For stars sake, Jarbed trusts him. Renender has his, eccentricities." Cornelius looked around the room again. This time it appeared even more lavish than before. It verged on garish.

Before Naemi could respond, the sound of distant music carried into the room from outside. Cornelius and Naemi gave each other a questioning look and simultaneously turned and headed to the glass door and patio garden.

Cornelius approached the door and it slid noiselessly and automatically aside. He and Naemi walked out onto the patio bathed in sunlight. Evergreen shrubs, small coniferous lupin pines and a few wide leafy deciduous plants grew in built-in stone planter boxes on the perimeter. A waterfall splashed behind the trees on the left, cascading down the wall. The floor was polished granite. Two small fountains gurgled nearby in the shapes of amphibians and mythical creatures. They were patinaed in green and red. In front of Cornelius a tiny red and purple iridescent flying reptile with a long beak hovered, its wings flapping faster than could be seen. It turned and hummed away up and over the wall. Then six more flew out of a hanging shrub of red flowers. They followed the first out of sight in a whir of wings.

Cornelius stopped to smell the large red and fragrant blossoms. He inhaled a strong honey-sage and cinnamon scent from the feathery blossoms. "Mm," he murmured, eyes closed. He opened his eyes to look back at Naemi. He swooned and thought he saw a half-dozen Naemis drift in towards their center and merge into one. "Naemi, smell this. I think it's mildly hallucinogenic." His voice slurred.

Naemi came up to him and laughed, "Mildly?" She reached up a hand and wiped the string of slobber that hung out of Cornelius' open mouth.

"Huh?" Cornelius shook his head and wiped his lips with the back of his hand. He slurped and cleared his throat. He looked back at the blossoms and said, "No kidding. That's incredible." He felt clearheaded and steady now. "It doesn't last very long."

"I'll pass on the psychotropic joy ride for now," said Naemi.

"Those flying reptiles must be always high," said Cornelius.

The sound of horns and drums sounded again. It came from the landing field, much louder than before.

Naemi reached the low rock wall first and extended her arm, pointing to a spot in the distance below to the left. Cornelius came up beside her and followed her gaze. Out on the landing field arranged in a formation on one of the gravel pads amidst the grass played a band. Long horns and short trumpets sounded. Long green and yellow banners were steadied by heralds in the warm breeze coming up from the steppes and vales below. A line of drummers accompanied the horns and set the beat. The players wore splendid red uniforms decorated with gold trim, buttons and epaulets. The conductor stood on a small box. The music they played was majestic and patriotic.

"It's Lenguiel's 'Seat of the World.' The official anthem of the City, written by a local composer a generation ago," said Cornelius.

At that moment the distance grew crowded and shadows flashed across the valley. Directly in front of the sun rose one, then three, then nine great airships. The lighter than air oblong balloons in zeppelin shape rose above the valley's drop off. The airships arrived on the morning's thermal updrafts rising from the steppes below.

The band continued to play, and was joined by cheers and applause coming from a gathered crowed of spectators on the edge of the field. Formations of school children in matching uniforms waved tiny flags of Lupus City, light blue and yellow.

The nine airships continued to rise above the valley's cliff edge. Additional airships rose behind and below them. Each was slightly different in form and color from the other, some longer, others wider. All the balloons were painted in brilliant designs, geometric patterns and sponsorship logos. The din from the band and cheerers startled a troupe of valley bunnies. They barked and hopped in all directions away from the ships and their shadows.

"It's stunning," said Naemi. Her eyes were fixed spellbound on the spectacle below them.

In answer to the band's welcoming music, horns sounded from the approaching airships. Each ship sounded its horns with a distinctive note and pitch.

Teams of tether workers in overalls streamed onto the field. Worker triads took positions on the gravel landing pads. Further in the distance across the valley on the other side of the river, like worker teams streamed onto the field. Shouts of orders and replies were added to the growing din. Calls of

"Over here!" and "This way!" and "Watch out, man!" echoed across the field. Then a cacophony of bells rang out from the city around. Ground cars blared their horns. Shouts went up among the populous. The airships were the primary means of transportation between Lupus City and rest of Lupus. It was the economic and social lifeblood of the city for commerce and tourism.

"In Lupus City, the arrival of the airships is greeted like the visit of a king," Cornelius said.

Naemi leaned over the edge and turned her head both left and right to better hear all the bells. She beamed a wide grinning smile. "Ohh," she exhaled.

Shadows and sunlight took turns flashing their faces across the shining and chiming semi-circle city sitting in its mountain vale facing the sun. The airships grew larger and larger. They appeared to approach faster and faster as the passed the lip of the valley's cliff edge. A few moments later they drifted massively passed Cornelius and Naemi. One was only fifty meters away. It was pointed on two ends with red ribbed siding stretching across its latitudes. A giant red "R" was painted on its side. On the rear of the airship a wide rudder operated, and a long gondola hung from the airship's belly. From its sides sprouted long arms supporting propellers. Ringing the gondola, rows of windows revealed passengers observing with amazement their landing in Lupus City.

Beyond the red zeppelin, on the other side of the river, a stub nosed dirigible decorated in yellow and green drifted. More airships floated by.

Cornelius grinned throughout the parade, which is what they were witnessing. "These are the passenger airships, business representatives, tourists, relatives, officials." Turning back to the valley's edge in the direct sunlight, Cornelius pointed. "See? Here come the freight ships."

Ten, twenty, fifty, one hundred. Two hundred and fifty-two airships in all grew from the size of specks around the face of the sun into huge airships. As the first of the large freight balloons rose above the cliff edge, the last of the passenger zeppelins cast down its mooring ropes. A triad team grabbed the ends and tethered them to automatic retractors that pulled the balloons gently and securely onto the gravel landing pads. Passengers exited the gondolas and walked in single files carrying parcels to waiting visitors on the edge of the field. Some waited for public shuttles and others immediately hired private cars to take them into the city.

The band stopped its music and the conductor stepped down from his box. He led the band members off the field. Yet horns continued to sound from the incoming airships. The landing field was alive with sound and people. Teams of tetherers, grapplers, haulers, auditors and supervisors filled the expanse with activity. And the great heaving airships kept rising above the cliff edge, drifting to assigned landing pads, dropping their mooring ropes. The city bells stopped ringing when the band marched off the field. City section by city section, the bells and horns died down.

Cornelius blinked his eyes and caught himself in a long yawn. He turned to Naemi who was now quietly watching the freighter airships begin to disgorge their cargo. Trucks drove off the field to warehouses along the city's perimeter.

Naemi sensed Cornelius watching her. She turned to him and saw him yawn. She realized they both needed rest. "Come on, Cornelius. Let's take a nap."

"You said it," Cornelius replied. "You know, Commissioner Corvus is down there somewhere."

"I know," said Naemi without emotion.

Cornelius added, "But there are just four of them."

"For now," said Naemi. She turned and grabbed Cornelius' arm and led him back across the patio, through the glass door. They crossed the main room and went directly to the bedroom hand in hand. They removed the shoulder satchels they had been carrying, kicked off their shoes and fell onto the oversized bed, lost among the pillows. Both were asleep within minutes.

Cornelius had disjointed and unsettling dreams. He was standing naked in morning sunlight in the open doorway of Naemi's house in Shining City. Classical music played around him. Naemi stood before him in a smart red business dress. Her hair was pulled back. Her red lipstick matched her shoes and handbag. Cornelius could see Naemi's mouth move and she smiled. Her eyes twinkled. Sunlight reflected off her bond eyelashes as she moved. But Cornelius could only hear the classical music.

Naemi leaned in and kissed Cornelius on the cheek. She smiled, waved by wiggling the fingers of one hand at a time, and winked. She turned and walked out the door, the sunlight silhouetting her as her figure blurred.

Then a shiver ran down Cornelius' black. The sun blackened, the sky grew dark and the classical music grew ominous. A cold wind blew through the door and Cornelius was cold. In the distance where Naemi had disappeared, a flash of light burst. Black clouds tinged a glowing red filled the sky.

Cornelius turned away in his dream and he was sitting on the floor, his back to a sofa, watching an entertainment program on his family's media viewer. Animated Canines tossed a hand grenade back and forth. Cornelius was a child back in Bafaria. He wore shorts. On a bare knee was a large scab. Cornelius picked at the edges of the scab, and even though it stung, his attention to it didn't waver. His sister sat on the sofa above laughing at the animation. The smells of good food wafted in from the kitchen.

A loud knock came from the front door. A voice on the other side shouted, "Internal Security. Open up immediately."

On the media viewer, the hand grenade exploded in one of the animated Canine's hands. "Oh no! There goes Gruff!" exclaimed the other Canine. Laughter erupted from the viewer.

Then the walls of the room fell down around Cornelius, the bodies of his dead sister and mother in sight. Cornelius heard an eerie voice echo over and over more and more distantly, "Markhab, let's move!"

Cornelius was crying, his tears pooling around him. They fell larger, collected until they gathered into a great river. Cornelius saw a child's hand place a toy white sailboat into the water. It spun in a circle, drifted, and caught a current. Then a shadow fell upon it. The prow of a great black ship pushed it out of the way. Cornelius saw dozens of black ships sailing down the river. The toy sailboat turned in circles faster and faster until it was overshadowed by the wakes caused by the passing ships. A glittering pink haze scattered light over the scene. Cries and painful moans filled the air.

The waves in the river surged and Cornelius felt the spray of water on his face. He tried to get out of the way but the spray kept landing on him. He heard his name. "Cornelius. Cornelius."

Cornelius opened his eyes and stared up at whom he thought at first was his mother. His heart leapt in his chest, then he saw Naemi standing over him. She was drying her wet hair with a white towel. She flicked water at him with her hair.

"Cornelius," Naemi said. "Wake up."

Cornelius looked up at her, blinking, bringing the world and this reality back into focus. "What time is it?" he asked.

"A little after noon," said Naemi. "You should take a shower. I'm sure Renender will come back soon to take us down to the airfield."

Cornelius scooted himself up in the bed. "Yeah. I could use one."

"The shower's great," said Naemi. "Oh, I made some coffee, too. There's a cup in the bathroom for you."

"Thanks," said Cornelius. He got out of bed and took off his belt, let his pants drop to the floor and took off his shirt.

Naemi got out of his way, noticing him distant and absorbed in some inner thoughts. "Bad dreams?" she asked.

"Yeah," said Cornelius. He didn't offer any more and Naemi didn't ask. Cornelius left the bedroom and went into the bathroom, closing the door behind him.

The coffee was strong. The hot water of the shower pummeled his body. Cornelius ran his fingers through his course hair while the water ran down his face and body. The vivid images from his dreams, and the visceral emotions they evoked, began to dissipate. He soaped his body with Renender's fine scented shower gels. He stood under the falling water rinsing off, eyes closed and mind blank. Calmness returned to him and he moved beyond his prior emotions. Cornelius was in Lupus City. He was with Naemi. He was on a serious and dangerous mission that he did not fully understand, nor did he know where his journey would take him. He turned the water off and stepped out of the shower, took up a towel and dried himself off.

Cornelius came out of the bathroom, dressed and looked for Naemi. With direct sunlight no longer shining into the room, Cornelius noticed recessed lighting behind the rock wall facings. The light backlit the precious stones embedded in the rock.

Naemi was out on the patio looking out onto the field. The garden was in shadow, the sun having passed behind the building while they had slept. The air temperature was starting to hold a chill. A breeze was blowing down from the mountains above the horseshoe valley. But the stones in the patio still radiated warmth.

Naemi was combing the knots out of her now dry hair. She turned at the sound of Cornelius behind her. "How do you feel, dream boy?"

Cornelius chuckled. "Refreshed." He wiggled one of his little fingers in his ear to dislodge some water left from his shower. He drew up to Naemi and looked out at the landing field.

Naemi turned and said, "All the balloons are turned the other way around."

"They're facing the steppes. See all the cargo being loaded on?" Cornelius pointed out teams of haulers passing crates into the freighter gondolas. "The freight ships will depart first. They'll need to unload their cargo down at the docks before the sun sets."

Directly below Cornelius and Naemi on the nearest gravel landing pad, waste trucks drove up to a gondola. Workers connected pump hoses to valves on the side of the gondola. "Lovely," said Naemi. "Our luxury apartment faces a waste transport facility. Funny, the tourist brochure didn't mention that."

Cornelius laughed, and he felt the tension ebb away from his shoulder blades. Then he said, "It's ironic that the whole of Human Lupus has adopted the environmental policies of the military government in Cronapolis."

"The military isn't stupid, Cornelius. They have the long-term goal of governing as much of Lupus for as long as they can. They believe they have a rightful calling." Naemi pulled the comb through her hair one last time then put it away in a pocket.

"That makes what we're doing so difficult. Not everyone is convinced a military government is a bad thing," said Cornelius.

Naemi looked at Cornelius and did not betray a shred of emotion. She said, "Just because you take out the trash doesn't mean your larder is free of maggots."

"Is that a popular proverb on Polaris?" ask Cornelius.

Naemi shrugged and merely replied, "It fit the occasion."

The two of them spent a few minutes in silence watching the activities down on the landing field when Naemi turned her head and looked back into the apartment. "Someone is knocking," she said.

"Renender," said Cornelius. They both turned and crossed the patio back into the main room. Cornelius pulled back the brass locking bolt and the door instantly pulled inward.

Renender stood in the doorway assessing Cornelius and Naemi. "Ah," he said. "Rested and bathed. Renender does appreciate it." He stepped inside, then turned and pushed the door closed behind him. "I do hope you're rested," he said looking at them. "I do not advise you wait for the passenger airships to depart. I'm afraid you need to leave on a freighter ship within the hour. I've learned that Commissioner Corvus is demanding all passenger and freight manifests be turned over to the inspectors, beginning today. Tomorrow's airships will be commandeered by the military, 'For our own protection.'" Renender was clearly distressed. "You will depart on one of the freight ships now. You must be on your way before Corvus begins questioning passengers. I have arranged to get you on the airship 'Valyon.'"

Cornelius looked at the expression on Renender's face and recognized genuine fear in the man's eyes. "What is it, Renender?" he asked.

Renender locked eyes on Cornelius a moment, then broke the gaze and looked down at the floor. "As majority holder of the airship berths, I'm to be 'politely questioned' by a new shipping division of inquiry, headed by Corvus and his closest henchmen."

"I don't understand," said Cornelius.

Naemi looked at Cornelius and said, "They might employ neural mind probes. If Renender is questioned...." Naemi looked kindly on Renender, then turned back to Cornelius and continued. "Invariably then we should be far away from here. The sooner we are away the better."

Renender split his gaze between Cornelius and Naemi and said, "Precisely. You will proceed to Berth twenty-three. Commander Reldere. Go. Now." Renender turned and pulled open the door and lead Cornelius and Naemi out of the private quarters. They crossed the office and back down the hall.

"Markhab's move here is bold," said Naemi. The three of them stood before the lift doors."

"He'll already have agents swarming the docks looking for anyone suspicious," said Cornelius.

Renender shook his head. His eyes betrayed his weariness and stress from all the day's and night's news. "Markhab is giving speeches in Cronapolis. He's 'inviting' representatives from all the Human regions on Lupus to Cronapolis for a conference. He's billing it as a show of Human unity against the Canines."

"It's a ruse," said Cornelius.

"I concur," said Renender.

"Renender. How will we find Captain Katzer's ship?" Naemi was thinking ahead. With Markhab's agents already at the docks, they could not afford to tarry.

"Don't worry," said Renender. "That at least is managed." And he looked visibly relieved and confidant of that fact. Renender extended his long arm and pressed the lift's call button. "Come, I will see you to an escort." He hesitated a moment and looked at Cornelius. Concern crept back into his visage. "My friend Cornelius. I am doing everything I can to get you out of here and off to where you need to be, in Big City. I don't know why, and I don't need to know. But Jarbed was adamant that I do everything I could. You can trust me." Renender reached out and touched Cornelius' arm, turned and reached out to include Naemi. "Both of you."

"Thank you, Renender," said Naemi. She demonstrated gratitude but remained wary of the rapidly moving events.

The lift doors opened. The three of them entered the lift and descended to the lobby.

21 FLIGHT OF THE VALYON

The lift came to a halt and Renender took a deep breath. The doors opened and he stepped out. Before Renender, Cornelius and Naemi, the lobby spread out in a pleasant expanse. Sounds drifted down from the mezzanine where people drank and watched the airships being loaded.

One of Renender's security guards stood in front of the lift. He turned to the three people exiting. "Mr. Renender!" The man stood up straight.

Renender approached the man closely and spoke to him softly, "Please call Mr. Roarsch."

"At once," the guard answered.

Renender, Cornelius and Naemi exited the lift and stood beside the guard, who turned his head and tapped a button on the earpiece he wore. He mumbled, "Mr. Roarsch, please come to Lift Bank Two in the main lobby. Priority One. Renender requests your presence." He tapped the earpiece button again and turned back to Renender. "He is on his way, Mr. Renender."

"Thank you," said Renender. He leaned in close to Cornelius and Naemi and said, "Roarsch can be trusted. He will take you to the airship Valyon. You must board the ship and ask to speak to Reldere. 'business from Renender' tell anyone who asks. Don't worry it will be all right."

Renender hugged Cornelius then hugged Naemi. "I expect to see you both soon." Renender laughed nervously and stood up straight. "Have resolve."

Naemi released herself from Renender's embrace. She spied a man descending the lobby staircase.

The man was stocky and wore a broad goatee that flared back at the bottom corners. His head was bald. He scanned the lobby as he reached the foot of the staircase. Then he crossed the lobby hall directly, at and even pace. "Mr. Renender, Sir," the man said when he reached them.

Renender extended his hand and shook the man's, "Roarsch."

"What can I do for you sir," asked Roarsch.

Renender presented Cornelius and Naemi with a gesture of his hand and said in a louder voice, "These are new kitchen hands for the Valyon. Take them to berth twenty-three immediately. Use the side door."

"Immediately, Mr. Renender," said Roarsch. The man turned to Cornelius and Naemi. They looked back at him blankly. "Come with me."

Cornelius and Naemi filed past Renender, giving him a nod as they followed Roarsch to a side door that led into a service hallway. Roarsch opened the small door and beckoned for Cornelius and Naemi to pass through.

This side of the building was in shadow. The shouts and sounds from the landing field carried loudly in the air. They were in a long parking lot that connected to the front of the building off to the right where Cornelius had parked the ground car several hours before. The adjacent building was only eight meters away. A line of small electric transport carts lined the side of Renender's building on the left.

Cornelius turned to Roarsch and said, "We appreciate your help Mr. Roarsch. We are not familiar with the berth locations on the landing field."

Roarsch gave Cornelius a quiet stare. Renender's security man looked at their clothes. They were not mountain clothes. He noted Cornelius' accent. Roarsch looked at Naemi. This woman might not even be Lupin. She walked almost like a Feline. Roarsch looked back at Cornelius and just said, "Yes." Then, "Come. Get in the cart. I'll take you to the airship."

They approached the nearest cart. It was copper colored and shaped like a big bulbous beetle. Compound eyes formed headlights. Four legs curved back and ended in wheels. The two forelegs extended up and over its back. A canvas top was affixed to the insect arms of the chassis. Cornelius sat in front with Roarsch, and Naemi got into the back seat. The cart was open on the sides.

Roarsch started the vehicle. It was nearly silent. He turned on a touch screen panel and called up a display of departure logs. He scrolled through a list, then paused. He zoomed onto a line and pointed. "The Valyon is departing in thirty minutes. It is in the first launch group near the canyon's edge." He turned to look back at Naemi. "Put those straps on. It is a bumpy ride on the gravel field."

All three fastened themselves in safely straps. Roarsch backed the cart out from its parking space and drove out to the front of the building, left to a driveway, then right to face the field's encircling frontage road. Several trucks rumbled by transporting freight to the airships. Roarsch merged the cart between two trucks and drove left, toward the horseshoe valley's edge.

On the right, out on the field, they passed a huge, ribbed zeppelin, red with yellow stripes. Behind it was a round orange balloon. They drove for a kilometer before turning right down a gravel road and out on the field proper. There were great airships everywhere. All were tied down with ropes and tethers. Teams of workers amid trucks and crates hauled items of different shapes and sizes onto the huge gondolas below every airship. In between the gravel airship platforms grew rich grass, cropped short, which wound its way across the plain. There was no discernable design from the ground level, but these swaths of green formed an amazing organic design seen from above.

Naemi observed the teams of workers diligently moving cargo onto the gondolas. There was no slacking here. Then Naemi noticed that moving along the work teams were people in uniforms. They were conspicuous by the fact that they transported no goods, and carried no tools. They merely stopped others to check for what seemed like identification papers and packing slips.

Roarsch looked back at Naemi through a small mirror extended on an antennae from the cart's carapace. He saw where Naemi was looking. "Transport Inspectors," said Roarsch. "There are normally only about half a dozen roaming around the whole landing field. Today there are about twenty-five. They actually reassigned officers from the city. Tomorrow they will be supplemented by a contingent of military inspectors from Lupus Major. Courtesy of Markhab."

The gravel road took the cart under the bow of a great yellow dirigible. It was shockingly yellow and almost too bright to look at directly with the sunlight reflecting off its sides. Roarsch steered the vehicle to the right around the dirigible. past a team of grapplers stooping to check the tether hooks that tied the ropes to a ground mount. Naemi caught the sight of three Transport Inspectors. They were speaking to a woman wearing a grey and black uniform.

Roarsch looked over to where Cornelius and Naemi's attention was focused. The group of inspectors was only six meters away.

The female inspector in the grey and black uniform looked up and made eye contact with Roarsch. "Shit," he said. He turned and focused his eyes back on the gravel road. He maintained a steady velocity.

Naemi was still looking over her shoulder at the inspector when she heard the woman shout, "Halt." The group turned and started walking toward the cart. Two of the local inspectors raised their hands and shouted, "Excuse me. Halt please."

Roarsch pursed his lips and quickly shot his glance left and right. He was looking for a distraction. He knew it the instant it caught his eye. Approaching quickly on the gravel road just on the right a meter away was a tether grappled onto a ground mount. It was one of the securements holding down the yellow dirigible. "Lean back, Sir," Roarsch shouted at Cornelius. He reached to his waist and pulled out a handgun. Roarsch moved his arm in one fluid motion to exactly where Cornelius' head been, and shot.

The projectile hit the metal clamp that bound the tethered rope and ricocheted away. The clamp bent and shredded like a jagged knife. The strong wind flowing down from the upper valley and mountains heaved the dirigible against its moorings. The damaged clamp cut deep into the tether that stretched taut to head off the wind. The force was suddenly too great. The rope snapped and whipped wildly around. The running inspectors stopped short to stay clear of the menacing rope dancing in the air between themselves and the departing cart. The dirigible twisted in the wind to one side. Shouts and calls from the ground teams lifted up into the air. Naemi saw the female agent pull a communications transmitter from her side and hold it up to her mouth.

"I take it we're not stopping," said Cornelius. He wiped his brow with one hand and stared Roarsch directly in the eye.

"The Valyon is just up ahead," said Roarsch.

Cornelius and Naemi looked up. Looming before them was a massive blue zeppelin. Its sides were ribbed and painted in the center were three huge purple circles. As they drove closer Naemi saw that the ribs were painted with white trim that circled and flowed in the shapes of ocean waves.

Roarsch drove right up to a huge gondola sitting on the gravel landing pad. It was stained a golden yellow. It measured forty meters long and ten meters high. A sign with the number 23 stood at the side of it.

The entire field around the gondolas was shaded in darkness. The massive airships blocked out the light and swayed overhead. Besides the shouts and calls of working teams all over the field, the taut and screech of the tethered moorings filled the air with high pitched squealings and deep grinding moanings.

Roarsch brought the cart to a complete stop while unfastening his safety restraints. "I'll see you to the boarding entrance. Get out now."

Cornelius and Naemi unbuckled their safety strapped and twisted their way out of the cart and onto the ground. Naemi glanced up when she realized that some of the shouts were directed at them. "They're coming," she said.

They ran to the open red doors in the center of the gondola. A metal ramp connected it to the ground. It creaked and rocked. They crossed the distance to the ramp in seconds. Shouts closed in from behind them.

Roarsch led Cornelius and Naemi up the ramp the paused at the opened gondola doors ushering them in. "Hurry inside. Now."

Cornelius and Naemi dashed up the ramp and through the gondola doors. Two startled crewmen standing inside the doors started to raise an objection when neither passenger offered any identification or words.

Roarsch stopped the crewmen and sternly shouted, "These two are okay. This is a Code Blue departure. Orders from Renender himself. I am Roarsch, his chief of security." Roarsch extended his identification badge from his inside jacket pocket and shoved it in the crewmen's face. "Take off this instant!" yelled Roarsch.

The young men's eyes widened. They recognized Roarsch from a recent field-training trip to their employer, Renender's, headquarters. Like many in the valley by this time, they knew that Markhab was sending some kind of occupation force to the city. There were a lot of people trying to get out of Lupus City today.

"Take these two to Reldere," said Roarsch. He jumped from the ramp onto the ground and ran to the cart. One of the crewmen spoke into a transmitter calling in Roarsch's Code Blue departure order.

The other crewman cut loose the ramp behind them and slid shut the gondola doors. A horn sounded from above. It was quickly joined by a horn from the nearest gondola beneath another zeppelin. The whole area erupted in horns, calls and shouts of ground crews. Gates snapped shut and ramps dropped to the ground. Trucks backed away from the circular launch pads all around. Moorings snapped free and a dozen gondolas heaved off the ground. The first launch was aloft.

Inside the gondola of the Valyon, Cornelius and Naemi stood in a wide corridor that opened onto an observation lounge or lobby. A number of people were at the windows on the opposite side. Most wore uniforms of grey jumpsuits. They were the on board transport and maintenance staff for the airship freighter. They all looked up to at speakers set in the ceiling, which emitted a crackling sound from being activated. The voice of one of the ground crewmen spoke.

"Attention. We are cleared for departure. Grab side rails as we lift off," said the crewman. He knew how to take charge of a situation.

Suddenly the whole ship rocked forward. Naemi rushed to a wall with Cornelius quickly behind. They grabbed the safety rail that ringed the corridors and lobby a meter and a half off the floor. Cornelius put his arm around Naemi and whispered to her, "We'll be alright."

"Yeah," Naemi answered. But she was thinking how much trust was being exercised at this moment. She did not know what to predict. Then another thought crowded its way to the front of her mind and she said, "I've never been on a balloon before." Just then the back end of the gondola lifted off the ground. Then the front. She felt her stomach lift out its normal position then settle back down. Naemi held the rail tight while her body swayed one way then the other.

"You're in for a treat," muttered Cornelius.

"Sarcasm, right?" said Naemi.

Cornelius just smiled and held onto the rail as tight as did Naemi.

All of the people in the lobby and corridor held a look of surprise on their faces. Some pulled out watches from their pockets and checked the time, assuming it was later than they thought. Then confusion showed on their faces. The few children aboard giggled.

A door slid open on the left side of the lobby near the windows on the other side of the gondola. A tall woman with ruddy complexion wearing a blue uniform with purple epaulettes burst into the room. She was bearing momentum from running down a flight of stairs. Her voice bellowed into the room. "Who cleared us for takeoff? We're twenty minutes early." She stopped in the center of the room and looked the passengers over. She found the crewmen standing with Cornelius and Naemi and walked over directly.

The crewman on the left spoke up first. "Captain. I made the call to the bridge. These are the passengers who were escorted aboard by Renender's man, Roarsch." He pointed out Cornelius and Naemi.

Cornelius extended his hand. "My name is Cornelius. And this is Naemi." Naemi stood up straight and tall, nodded.

The captain looked at Cornelius and Naemi but did not nod or shake their hands. "So, you're the two," she said. "I'm Captain Reldere. I'll be back down in half an hour. We'll speak then. Stay on this deck." She turned to the crewman who had remained silent. "Apologize to our passengers for the abrupt and early departure. Offer them free beverages for the next thirty minutes. Tell them, we're running ahead of a storm. That at least is true." The Captain turned to the other crewman. "Dardele, come up to the bridge with me."

"Yes Captain," replied the crewman.

"Is a storm really on its way?" asked Cornelius.

Captain Reldere turned back and said, "A spring storm is coming down from the interior mountains. We should have just enough time to unload our freight at the docks before it hits the steppes. You're lucky you're not on one of the passenger zeppelins. They're going to be tossed and drenched by the time they make landfall at the lake docks." The captain crossed the lobby and disappeared back through the door and up the stairs to the upper decks, Dardele with her.

The other crewman turned to Cornelius and Naemi and said, "I'm Watto. You must be important people. Follow me to the concessionary. You can have some refreshments." Watto led them through the center of the lobby passed groups of passengers. He relayed the captain's message on the way. The crowd followed him to the windows and down a corridor on the right to the concessionary.

Thirty minutes later Cornelius and Naemi sat facing one another at a private booth against the wall at a viewing window. The gondola gently swayed. The operation of the airship for the most part was silent. Piped in music provided a background of classical string and wind pieces of various artists and times, one blending into the other. Approximately twenty people sat at tables near the windows around the outside of the concessionary. Two manned concession stands were set up against the two inner walls. Drinks were served at one end, food and snacks at the other.

Cornelius and Naemi drank glasses of a fizzling yellow beverage through straws. The drink was a sweetened root in carbonated water that counteracted motion sickness.

Out the window of the gondola Cornelius and Naemi had witnessed the precipitous drop off of sheer granite cliffs as they had floated beyond the terminus of the horseshoe valley. Ship after ship passed out of the valley and began the long sail down myriad curtained ridges and over long narrow mountain lakes. Swift streams tumbled, pooled, then tumbled further down to join other watery courses.

At the start of the journey the view had been crowded with other airships in close proximity. But as they passed out of the valley they began to spread out, disbursing for the long drift down to the edge of the Canton Steppes and the shore of the great Lupus Lake to the north.

The descending afternoon air currents flowing down from the high Canine Mountains were often turbulent as they interacted with the hot air still radiating up from the steppes. Sophisticated sway compensators built into the gondola's construction dampened most of the dramatic shifts, protecting freight and passengers. Since Lupus City manufactured a great many high precision titanium goods, export officials as well as buyers insisted on strict transport standards for the safe delivery of products.

The Valyon was passing over a purple meadow of shade blooming myrtle growing beside a small lake. Two other dirigibles, one red and the other yellow, floated in the distance. Suddenly at the table Captain Reldere appeared.

"I trust you are enjoying the descent, even on a freight ship," Reldere said. She almost betrayed a smile.

Cornelius and Naemi broke from the view and turned to the captain.

"It's magnificent," said Naemi. She sized the captain up. Renender had sent them here, so this should be a woman she could trust. But trust was not a trait Naemi was quick to adopt with anyone, even under the best of circumstances. Reldere appeared to be a proud able woman with a commanding presence. She appeared fair and understanding, if not graceful in her demeanor.

"We're descending at up to eighty meters per minute in some places, yet the drift remains smooth. It's a credit to the skill of my navigation crew," said Reldere. "Some airships can't stabilize during the entire journey down to the lake."

"How long exactly is the descent?" asked Naemi.

"Four hours normally, depending on the strength of the tailwind," said Reldere. "Of course in inclement weather it could take longer. The airships maintain a formation with lead ships guiding flight teams of gondolas. Each airship has designated emergency touchdown locations all the way down the traverse to the docks. There are plenty of meadows to land on down the mountain courses and foothills."

"The last time I rode an airship was two years ago," said Cornelius. "The trip down was six hours, then eight coming back up."

"You must have been in an old model zeppelin then," said Reldere. "The Valyon is a Mark Eight. The fastest in Renender's fleet."

"Actually it was a balloon. The Ballast, I think," Cornelius replied.

Captain Reldere took a deep breath and abruptly changed the subject. "I invite you up to the bridge. You may enjoy seeing how we operate carrying ten tons of freight with such precision flying and navigation control. Come. Follow me."

Cornelius and Naemi gave each other a questioning glance with raised eyebrows. Captain Reldere was pleasant enough with a no nonsense tact. Both Cornelius and Naemi guessed that the captain wanted to speak to them under more private conditions away from the other passengers and crew in the concessionary.

Captain Reldere led them back to the entrance lobby and through the doors from which she had emerged earlier. A straight staircase took them up twenty steps to the bridge. The three emerged from the back wall. Large oval windows were arrayed around three sides of the large command center. The room encompassed a quarter of the deck. Three members of the crew, a man and two women in uniform, worked at stations near the forward facing window. The view was breathtaking and expansive. The large red dirigible Cornelius and Naemi had been watching from the concessionary floated lower and to the right of the Valyon. A blue and yellow striped airship drifted in front and to the left.

Naemi looked around the large open room. Besides the three of them who had just entered, there appeared to be only the three navigators in front. Hearing a noise behind her, Naemi turned and recognized the crewman Dardele. It had been he who had sounded the take off command directed by Renender's man Roarsch.

"You remember Mr. Dardele," said the captain. "It was his order upon your arrival that launched the first flotilla early. Explain this to me. Dardele knows as much about you as I do, and that's next to nothing, except for your supposed connection to Renender." Reldere extended her arm towards a small table built into one side of the ship, five chairs were set around it. "Dardele, you may join us."

All four sat down, Cornelius and Naemi on one side of the table facing the back wall, Reldere and Dardele facing them on the other side.

The captain began. "This is an unusual day. You are not the first 'special accommodations' Renender sent out to the airship captains under his employ today. Many people are sneaking their way out of Lupus City before Markhab's thugs take over the ships. I imagine there is a small army waiting to greet us at the lake docks already." Reldere noticed Cornelius and Naemi become visibly alarmed.

"Don't worry," interjected Dardele. "The lake docks are socked in with a thickening fog bank. It's typical for this time of year."

"All of our special passengers will help us unload freight when we land at the docks," said Reldere. "We have uniforms for you. After the first delivery to the warehouses, you will all be dispatched to various safe locations, as far as we are able. I will not be responsible for your safely beyond the warehouses." Reldere noted Cornelius and Naemi's silent composure, though their eyes betrayed much. "Most of today's freight ship passengers are merchants, even a few political figures and their families. Now, why are you two so special that the launch order was given as soon as you appeared at the top of my embarkation ramp?"

Cornelius spoke up first. "We are traders from Big City. We're just trying to get out like everyone else."

"We have licenses and travel documents," said Naemi. She reached into her satchel and pulled out the identity documents that Renender had provided. "Show them yours, Cornelius."

Captain Reldere took the documents and looked them over. "Hm. These look brand new. The paper is still clean and stiff. The pictures are old, however. These might fool Markhab's crackerjack team of inspectors at the docks tonight in the fog and bustle, but they don't fool me." Reldere then dropped the documents on the floor and stood up. She stomped her boot on them and twisted. Then she bent down, picked them back up, and bent the pages. She slightly tore a few pages in each. She handed them back to her surprised guests. "A bit more realistic," she added.

Cornelius looked sideways at Naemi, then turned back to Reldere and Dardele. "We must get to Big City in all haste. We are, involved, in this situation with Markhab." Cornelius swallowed, unsure of how much to divulge. He continued, "Renender...."

Captain Reldere cut him off. "I do not need to hear anymore. This thing affects all of us, and tomorrow I will be forced to ferry troops up to Lupus City, compliments of Markhab, 'for my own protection.'"

"Do you know Captain Katzer? He operates a cargo ship on the lake," asked Naemi. "He is to take us to Big City."

"Katzer?" repeated Reldere. She laughed. "Ha-ha. So that's where Renender is sending you. Keep your head down and stay out of his way. That's my advice to you. His ship departs the docks first for the evening cruise to the Channel."

"The Channel?" asked Cornelius.

"It's a narrow shipping passage joining Lupus Lake and Federated Lake," said Dardele. He looked at the captain and continued. "We operate a direct freight transfer to Katzer's ship."

"One of Renender's 'business arrangements,'" said Reldere, nodding.

"I can get them to Katzer's ship as soon as we land," said Dardele.

"See it is done," said Reldere. She stood up away from the table. Dardele followed. "We are about four more hours out from the docks. Dardele will collect you in about three. I trust you will enjoy the rest of the journey."

Dardele led Cornelius and Naemi through the doors in the back wall and down to the lobby. Captain Reldere remained standing and followed them with her eyes out of the bridge until the doors closed. "Renender, do not lose me my airfreight license with any more of these favors," she mumbled under her breath. Then she turned back to the forward windows and gazed out at the passing mountain vales and dirigibles.

22 LAST TRANSPORT

The hardscrabble bedrock was a miserable place. An icy wind flowed down out of the mountains that rose precipitously from the cold sea. The sheer faces of glaciers loomed high and mighty a kilometer away. They poured out of the mountain passes. Even from here the booming crashing sounds of calving ice was carried on the wind. The ice walls marched to the sea several meters each day. The sea itself was nearly frozen over, yet it still heaved and groaned as the waters beneath the cracked ice surface swelled and moved in their dark currents. Snow flurries blew, softly covering the rock shelf. Soon it would blend in completely with the white sky, white mountains and white sea. The temperature was minus twenty degrees centigrade, and it was high summer. This time the year before, a sun drenched-field offered up rich grasses for grazing herds.

The bedrock extended along the shoreline for three kilometers. On both ends, slag piles of ice had been forced out of the way by huge bulldozers. A row of the mechanical behemoths continued to work in the distance. Each was nine meters high and pushed a shovel twelve meters wide. Abandoned at various points in the distance were a dozen bulldozers that had simply succumbed to the punishing environment. Drigo had become a frozen hell.

Galdinier looked out over the cold plain from the top of the ramp of his transport hauler. Three other ships lay on the field behind him, and two others hovered in the air close by, their mighty roaring engines filling the air with the smell of ozone.

About two hundred and fifty Drigan dorsein herders and their families huddled in small groups around a huge metal corral. Inside bayed and shuffled ten thousand restless dorsein. This community had been forced down through the last open mountain pass to the sliver of land beside the sea.

Galdinier was dressed head to toe in a wool and fur parka, his head covered in a blur of fuzzy pelt. With a snow mask betraying only narrow eye slits, it was impossible to tell that Galdinier was a Feline.

The Drigans on the rocky plain before him represented the last group of emigrants to be transported to the armored asteroid in orbit of Drigo. Soon they would escape the advancing crushing ice age. They would all make the final crossing to Wror.

23 ALL THE CARDS

General Taurus finished his coffee and set the empty mug down on the broad table. He wiped his mouth with his cloth napkin and folded it back neatly, setting it carefully beside the empty mug. The general was ever the stickler for detail. Appearances were important to him, both in his personal toilet as well as in the execution of military strategy.

Taurus looked across the table at Markhab. Only the two of them were present. The First Commissioner was unkempt. He had not shaven and his hair had been wet down, not combed. Markhab finished his coffee and set his mug down on the tabletop loudly. He wiped his mouth with the sleeve of his uniform and pulled his signature cigar from a breast pocket. He offered it to the general.

"No thank you," replied Taurus.

"Do you have any vices, Taurus?" asked Markhab.

"Precision and thoroughness," said the general.

Markhab bit off the ends of his cigar and spit them out behind him. The pieces hit the wall and added two marks to the many stains already resident. "Ever the reliable poster child of health and decorum." Markhab lit his cigar and drew in a long drag of the aromatic leaf.

Taurus patiently watched the First Commissioner without saying a word.

Finally Markhab released the smoke in a slow exhalation. It spread out across the table and wrapped itself around the general on its way to finding the corners of the room. The general winced and blinked his eyes, but he did not vocalize any displeasure.

Markhab spoke. "Tell me how our preparations outside Bafaria are progressing."

"Our new base in the canyon lands near the Lupus River is coming together very well," said Taurus. "Some agitants protesting the declaration of martial law have been conscripted for additional manpower. A temporary barracks is completed, and one of two airstrips is nearly ready to receive air fighters from other bases."

"Good," said Markhab. "When will the long airstrip be ready? I want to start bringing in heavy air haulers."

"Within the week," said Taurus.

"Cut a few days off the estimate," said Markhab. "Conscript additional workers from the Polytechnic University of Lupus Minor if you have to. I don't trust that restless student population. They can be a powder keg of unrest." Markhab took another drag from his cigar. The rich farmlands around Dula City in Lupus Major grew excellent tobacco. A thought occurred to Markhab and he blew out the smoke before completely enjoying its effect. "In fact, announce the closure of the university, effective immediately. Put those brats to work constructing warehouses and outbuildings for the new military base facilities. Our defenses must be shored up along the river. I don't want any miserable Canine spies sneaking down from the Polar Mountains."

"The students will make excellent workers," agreed Taurus.

"And put those dirt crawlers from the High Plains Agricultural Institute to work as field hands," said Markhab. "Once we start flying in forward commandos and operations staff from satellite posts in Lupus Major, they'll need a reliable food supply."

"And the rest of the civilians in Bafaria?" asked Taurus.

"Keep them weakened. Reduce their weekly rations by another ten percent," replied Markhab. "Continue conscripting agitants into a useful workforce. Consider sending some to the plutonium mines north of Bafaria."

"We are still unable to get any of our inspectors on the ground in Big City," said Taurus changing the subject. "Stubborn insurgents in the Cantons have occupied the landing fields."

Markhab tapped his cigar over the floor to free the end of ash. "Mongrel Humans," he extorted. "Traitors. They are obviously in league with the Canine rabble of Canius. Desert rats all. Once our new base outside of Bafaria is completed, we can direct regular over flights of the Canton communities and Big City. Rocket their cities with sonic booms. And when we've secured ourselves in Lupus City, we'll control the lake trade economies. It's only a matter of time before the Canton Councils see that they must align themselves with the rest of civilized Lupus." Markhab paused to enjoy another drag from his cigar.

Taurus asked, "What is the situation in Lupus City?"

"Corvus is securing the city as we speak," said Markhab. "With the Cantons and Lupus City under our yoke, we'll finally be able to effectively counter the rebels in the Territory of the Shining Star. When we subdue Shining City, there will be nothing in our way. We'll finally be able to move decisively against the Canines."

The general maintained a pensive look on his face.

"You don't appear convinced that our victory against the rebels and the Canines is finally at hand, General," said Markhab.

Taurus leaned forward to speak. "Even the most careful plans contain holes, First Commissioner. I am concerned that the forces we are redeploying from around Cronapolis to Lupus Minor leaves us vulnerable to a potential uprising by the civilian population."

"Menkar is keeping a tight lid on the media outlets," Markhab said dismissively. "She is setting up Civic Vigilance Committees in the housing blocks and neighborhoods. Vigilance leaders are being trained as rapid response forces to counter any internal threats. They have so far proved successful."

"Don't put too much stock in the civilian population," warned Taurus. "In my experience, civilian loyalties are mutable."

"The situation is well under our control, General," said Markhab. The First Commissioner sometimes grew impatient at Taurus' lack of faith in the command and control structure of Markhab's government. "You worry too much, Taurus. With martial law effectively employed in Lupus Minor, and the population there serving our military needs, we are maintaining firm control over the three provinces."

"The Orchard Growers Union strike in Dula City is still going on," said Taurus. "I would like to send our garrison forces there to finally break the strike and get those workers back into the orchard groves. If we don't guarantee the delivery of the spring harvest of stone fruit to the capital, it could be a catalyst for unrest."

Markhab intentionally blew smoke in the general's direction. "As I said, Taurus, Menkar has the civilian population under her thumb. Stop worrying about security situations outside of your purview. The Orchard Growers Union strike will burn itself out before long. They have no supporters outside of Dula City."

"The Titanium Miners Union in Lupus City supports the strike," said Taurus.

"And they'll be effectively silenced in a few day's time. Corvus is very convincing. Have faith, General. We hold all the cards."

"Faith is not a battlefield strategy," said Taurus. "And Menkar employs unorthodox methods at civilian control. She is guilty in my book of giving away too much control to civilian leaders."

"She keeps pace ahead of events, General. I have every confidence in her abilities." Markhab was becoming impatient with Taurus. "Now tell me about the situation in our colonies, Wror and Keldo. Those are matters that should concern you."

"One of our battleships is nearly full of settlers waiting to return from Wror. We continue to bleed there," said Taurus.

"The dorsein herders from Drigo should be en route to stabilize the Human population on Wror," said Markhab. "Dania informs me that the Drigan transport vessel has already departed. Their numbers will strengthen our presence on the planet."

"I am concerned that we have focused too much attention on Wror and Lupus. I am not comfortable with our level of defensive forces around Keldo," said Taurus. He pressed the issue some more. "I recommend another battleship be deployed there."

Markhab pinched off the end of his cigar. He considered the general's request. In the matter of the colonies, Markhab was acutely aware that he had allowed lax oversight over Wror. Without making any admissions, he did feel that a mistake had been made there which had invited the opportunity for Bara-Band to be bombed in the first place. It was true that Keldo was poorly defended. He had always assumed that the uber planet's massive gravity well was an effective deterrent against off world infiltration. The planet was a difficult place. Outsiders were effectively crippled by its gravity. But doubts crept into Markhab's mind. He would not let Keldo become a target like Wror had.

"First Commissioner?" Taurus said. He observed that Markhab's attention had been drawn away.

Focusing back on the general, Markhab made up his mind. "I agree. Redeploy our second battleship currently in the Wrorian system to Keldo. Keep the other in place until the Drigans arrive. Once their numbers shore up our losses there, give the return settlers clearance to return to Lupus."

"Shouldn't we ensure a battleship remains near Wror at all times?" asked Taurus.

"Governor Trian has Wror well in hand," said Markhab. He had already made up his mind. "Do you have an extra battleship somewhere up your sleeve, General, that I don't know about? We have a ship over Lupus, a ship over Wror, and a ship soon over Keldo. When the battleship with settlers returns from Wror, deploy the ship currently over Lupus back to the colony."

"I don't like the gap," said Taurus. "We should not leave Wror undefended, even for a day."

Markhab was done with the general. "You asked for greater defenses for Keldo. I have provided you with that. Unless you can build me a new battleship in a matter of days, the new deployment will stand."

Taurus knew from experience when Markhab had reached his limit on compromise. The First Commissioner could be impetuous in his impatience. But at least a number of the general's security concerns had been addressed this day. Taurus knew this private meeting was at an end. "I will execute the new security measures we have agreed to right away. Thank you for your time, First Commissioner."

Markhab responded with a grunt and a dismissive wave. He reached into his breast pocket for a fresh cigar and bit off the ends, spitting them out behind him to join the others on the floor. He did not watch General Taurus leave the Commission Chamber. Markhab wished that Corvus would return quickly from Lupus City. *Yes*, he thought to himself. *Another session with Corvus would relax my mood. Especially before Corvus left on his secret assignment to Earth.* Markhab was not ready to share the full breadth of his plans with Taurus. Better to keep that under wraps until the mission was under way. And Professor Altair was due to arrive from Dula in the morning. All the carefully crafted pieces of Markhab's plans were coming together nicely. Yes, victory over the rebels and the Canines was assured. Even Taurus would see that soon. Markhab lit his cigar and allowed himself to savor a moment of premature success.

24 THE AUDIENCE

The sky outside Renender's great office window portended a storm. Dark clouds had moved down out of the high mountains above the city on the heels of the departing airships. The last passenger blimp had departed an hour before. Now not even a sliver of sky was visible beyond the valley's terminus. Heavy clouds blanketed the nearby empty landing field. Only a few teams of maintenance workers were spread out completing grounds repairs.

A small raindrop hit against the window and Renender experienced a shiver. Echoing the turn in the weather was the fact that Renender's most confident employee, Roarsch, had been detained by Corvus' quickly formed advance inspectors. Fortunately all the reports Renender received indicated that Cornelius and Naemi had made it safely aboard the Valyon and were now on their way to the lake docks. They would have Corvus' military brigands to deal with, but Cornelius and Naemi were capable of evading the enemy. And this storm might help.

But Renender knew that time was short for himself. If nothing else would, Roarsch's detention would certainly call attention to Renender. Tomorrow he would not be safe. Corvus would have his military backing. No, Renender had just a small window of opportunity to save himself. He had planned for just such a contingency long ago. After all, this day was not unforeseen.

Renender turned from the window and went to his desk, sat down before his computer. He called up a file menu on the touch screen. He selected a file named DualConfigRen2. He activated the file. After a moment a dialogue window appeared that displayed the command OPEN DB PACKET. Renender turned the computer around and popped the back off. He snapped a lever and gently removed a crystal data disk.

Renender took out the key that he held around his neck and inserted it into the secret keyhole in his desk. He turned the key and the secret compartment in the bronze statue on the floor snapped open. He went to the secret compartment and pulled out a handful of similar crystal discs. Renender selected a disc and walked back to his desk. He inserted the new disc into the back of his computer and secured the backing. Then he picked up the disc that had originally been in the computer, looked at it, turned it over in his hand, then picked up the other data discs. He walked across the room to the far wall where sat a large square metal box. It had a dial on the front and a handle that opened a lid on the top.

Renender opened the box. The inside was fashioned of a ceramic alloy with a hearth at the bottom. Renender dropped the discs into the box and closed the lid. He turned the dial. A caustic crackling sound emanated from the interior. After a moment the discs were fully incinerated. Renender opened the lid and peered inside. A trifling curl of smoke rose from a fine pile of ash on the bottom.

That was that, thought Renender. His business ledgers, personal and professional contacts, all manner of data from his life, were now destroyed. Only the boring commentaries of a manic recluse, peppered with moderately successful business records of a less than high achieving merchant, remained in his computer. That should deflect attention to him in the event Corvus' men somehow took over this building.

Renender looked around the room of his office. He had been quite successful doing business with so many of the factions on Lupus. But his intimate involvement with the political endeavors of the leaders of the Territory of the Shining Star of Lupus, both official and otherwise, wrought the most danger for him. Renender hoped that his extensive business dealings and contacts with enough people would see him through the storm that was coming.

On his desk lay the activation key to the stealth ground car that Cornelius and Naemi had driven here in. Renender smiled. He thought back to his younger years when he worked out of a sparse office adjacent to a dirty airship parts repair shop on the other side of the valley. At night he and his friends would steal, or borrow really, their parents' vehicles. They would race the cars on the field spinning in circles, kicking up the field in dust eddies under bright starry night skies. He and his friends knew how to evade the so-called authorities.

In his life, he had made a point of familiarizing himself with the peoples and businesses of the upper vales and among the deep titanium mines. He was long a benefactor for the Miner's Union. It was a part of the wide net he had cast for himself. Now it was time to call in some favors. Renender focused his eyes back on the stealth car's key. A twinkle sparkled in his eyes. Yes, this would certainly do nicely. But first, Renender had to pass a test. Overcome an evil. He had to find what he could about Roarsch, free him if possible, and face Commissioner Corvus of Lupus Major to do it. He had a growing feeling that was changing into a certainty that it would be a long time before he returned. It was sinking in that the city would be occupied tomorrow.

Renender was struck by the psychological impact the situation had put on his city. He knew from is reconnoitering during the afternoon that Lupus city was wracked by a panicked disbelief. Most businesses were closed. Some people were outraged, taking to the streets in protest. Others frantically provided for their personal security. Oh, some no doubt deluded themselves that tomorrow would be no different than yesterday. But their numbers were shrinking fast. Corvus' arrival, followed by his "advanced arrests," approved by the city's Civic Council based on some obscure protection clause in the city's charter, fed the panic. Renender heard that not a few people attempted to escape to Shining City via the mountain and desert road that Cornelius and Naemi had used. But several early accidents on the crumbled road had done in a few minutes what nature had attempted over years. The road was now impassable.

Renender's gaze hardened. He grabbed the stealth car's activation key, tossed it in the air and caught it, then shoved it deep into a pocket of his pants. He walked determinedly to his great office doors, stooped to pick up a small shoulder sling bag on the way. Renender was packed and ready to go. He would take just the bare necessities. He grabbed the door handles and pulled, heaving the doors open. Each time Renender opened these great doors he always had the same thought, "Why ever did I have such heavy doors installed?" Despite their heft, the doors swung silently open. Renender slipped out into the hall outside.

Down the long hall he began, not hustling this time like when Cornelius and Naemi had arrived. No, this time Renender walked in a calm and deliberate pace. As he walked, his passage disturbed the hanging ornaments on his crystal glass tree. They swayed and clanked against each other. They made a sound of an ethereal breeze through leaves. A bright shimmer caught Renender's eye. He turned toward the glass sculpture and paused. On the far side of the tree hung a crystal broach. It spun slowly in a circle. Light caught in the center jewel's facets and radiated out in a tight beam that struck Renender's eyes and portrayed the colorful spectrum of the rainbow. All this despite the fact that all the lighting in the hallway was recessed. The broach's finely crafted tendrils wove and radiated out from the center jewel. Each slender arm was encrusted in diamond dust. It was Renender's Precession Star amulet. It had been a gift from his mother as she lay on her deathbed. "Take it, dear boy," his mother had said. "It will open impassable doors for you."

How curious that Renender should think of that memory and the jewel right now. He had hung the broach on the crystal tree more than two years ago when he moved his offices into this building. He had not thought of it since. Instinctively, Renender reached out his long arm and gently lifted the broach from the branch where it hung. He brought it up before his eyes and watched how the center jewel played with light. The Precession Star. Renender did not remember very much of the back-story related to this heirloom. Something about an ancient belief in cycles and change. *Curious,* thought Renender. *If nothing else, it might bring me luck.* He hung the broach around his neck and hid it beneath his shirt. He softly patted the hidden jewel and resumed his passage down the hall, turned left at the corridor's end and proceeded to the lift.

Renender stood in the descending lift staring into the middle nothingness between him and the closed doors. He hummed to himself a slight tune that distracted him. He let his mind wander to far away places, exotic places. He remembered odd stories told to him by some of the deep miners who worked far beyond the upper valley, in dark glades and dales beyond the realm of Lupus City. They were half-hatched tales that mentioned cracks in mine walls that led to caves, which in turn opened out to cliff edges above deep crevasses, where narrow well-worn foot paths led up into the mountains to cities shrouded in cloud tops.

Renender publicly scoffed at such delusionary stories. But secretly he found and interviewed firsthand the miners who claimed to have seen such sights. Renender found that each story seemed to hold a piece of a puzzle. It was a mystery, one that took form and grew in his mind. Renender was intrigued. And Renender always believed that a good businessman was a curious businessman.

Suddenly the lift stopped and the doors opened. The din from the restaurant café interrupted Renender's musings. He shook his head and squinted his eyes. They focused on a tall large woman who blocked out half the light entering the lift.

"Mr. Renender. Are you coming in for a bite to eat? I was just on my way out, but I'll stay a bit longer if you need me." Matta was ever so gracious with Renender.

"Oh, Matta," stammered Renender. He calmed his voice and opened his eyes wider, smiled. "No. I'm heading down myself."

"Ah, fine then, Love. I'll just squeeze in next to you all cozy in a keep." Matta blotted out all the light as she entered the lift. Renender was forced to find a refuge in the far corner against the wall. The doors closed and the slow descent to the lobby resumed. Renender scowled, then tried to maintain a forced politeness. This was all very awkward.

Matta turned herself to face Renender. She eyed his shoulder bag and smiled. "Done for the day then, are you Mr. Renender?" she asked.

"Just out, Matta," said Renender. "I'll be back shortly."

Her smile vanished into concern. "Terrible business 'bout that Mr. Roarsch," she said, now serious.

Renender raised his eyebrows. He looked Matta in the eyes. "Yes, but it's only temporary. He'll be released and back at work in no time." He held Matta's gaze until she took a deep breath, slapped the palms of her hands together and looked up at the ceiling, then back at Renender.

"I'm sure you're right, Mr. Renender," she exclaimed. "But these are strange times."

He spoke to her reassuringly. "Commerce continues, Matta. Tomorrow there will be airships, and the day after, and the day after that. Trade continues."

The lift came to a halt and the doors opened. "Ah good. Here we are." Renender was eager for fresh air.

Matta exited the lift first. Renender closed his eyes and practiced even breathing. Matta stood in the open doorway and turned back to face the inside of the lift. "Good evening then, Mr. Renender."

Renender smiled and looked back at her. "Good night, Matta. Good job today. Have a good night. "

Matta beamed in delight. She clasped her hands together in front of her. "Thank you, Love," she said. "See you in the morning?"

"Of course," said Renender. He watched Matta turn and leave by the service door that Cornelius and Naemi had used earlier in the day with Roarsch.

The lift operator turned to Renender and asked "Can I bring your transport around for you, Sir?" The young man's name was Attisand, Renender remembered. He prided himself on knowing each and every one of his employees personally. Attisand was the son of Attis, one of Renender's closest friends from his wild youthful days. The boy's father had been dead ten years now from a mining accident. While Renender had stayed and worked in the horseshoe valley, Attis had moved up into the higher mountains to work in the titanium mines. After Attis' death, his widow and young son moved back to Lupus City. Renender had given the boy a job to keep him from going back into the mines like his father.

Renender looked at the young man and gave a moment's pause before replying. He looked back at the door through which Matta had left. Renender signaled to the man to move closer. "Attis, yes. Bring my car around. But Attis, I have a special request to make of you." Renender searched his pocket and retrieved the activation key to Cornelius' stealth car. He stared at it a second then handed it to the young man. "There is a charcoal grey prototype car a friend recently loaned me. It is parked in the front of the building. I want you to take the car and wait for me up in Sandy Field Park in the upper city. Do you know the place?"

Attisand took the pass key and locked eyes with Renender. "Sandy Field Park. Aye, Mr. Renender. It is above the Councils Building."

Renender stared into Attisand's eyes and did not blink as he continued. "Good. I will take my car and meet you there in two hours. I have a stop to make first at the Councils offices. I do not expect to be long. When we rendezvous, we will switch cars and you will return here in mine. You are to make no mention of this to anyone. Anyone."

"Aye, Mr. Renender," said Attisand, his eyes steeled. Renender need never ask his employees twice.

"Are you going to get Mr. Roarsch released?" asked the young man.

"I'm going to try, Attis. Now call for my car, and for someone to relieve you here. I will see you at Sandy Field Park. Two hours."

"Without delay, Sir," said Attisand. He activated his earpiece and whispered into the device.

Of that I have no doubt, my boy, thought Renender. *Of that I have no doubt.*

The rain was coming down good now. The terraced streets of the horseshoe city flowed in waterfall torrents. The thousands of onion domed building tops caused the rain to bounce and spray in all directions. The streets were bereft of people, yet the city shimmered in fluid movement. Renender's personal little bullet car maneuvered the arcing streets with little heed to the downpour. Such was the expert manufacturing precision of the titanium cars made in Lupus City for its ever-changing climate.

He took a maze of circuitous switchback routes higher and higher into the upper city. He approached the city's midpoint. The area opened up as the buildings fell away for several square blocks. This was the civic plaza. The great edifice that was the joint Economic and Civil Councils Building rose high on Renender's right above the greensward. The building and tower were adorned in rococo style. Atop the tower rose a great onion dome fashioned of titanium. This dwarfed four lesser domes also of titanium that stood on the tower's four corners. All were bordered in gold and black malachite.

On Renender's left, where the Councils Building faced, opened an unobstructed view down to the valley. On a clear day the valley's terminus edge was visible. This was an excellent place to view airship arrivals and departures. At night the many lights of the arcing horseshoe city shown brightly around.

There was no such view this night. The sheets of rain that now fell also blanketed the city in a cold darkness. The storm system swept down the canyons and flanks of the Canius Mountains in a fury. Lightning flashed high above the city in the upper vales where the mines were located. Thunder roared across the sky. It boomed. It screeched. It howled.

Renender parked his bullet car on a side street not far from the Councils Building. He reached into the back and retrieved a rain parka. He put it on before stepping out into the tempest. Then he took a deep breath and touched the pendant hanging around his neck, hidden beneath his shirt. He mumbled what might have been a prayer, but Renender reminded himself that he was not a religious man. He took solace in the importance of his work. He steeled himself against what he was about to encounter and stepped out into the driving rain. Renender crossed the street and onto the greensward. Inside the building, Corvus was waiting.

He reached the other side of the street and up the few steps through an enclosing wall and up onto the greensward. Renender paused a moment to look around. There was no traffic in the district. The rain had driven away the protesters who had gathered on the greensward earlier in the day at Corvus' arrival. Turning and looking up at the Councils Building, Renender saw the presence of many officers from the Civil Guard surrounding it. They no doubt had a hand in dispersing the protesters. The guards were huddled in the many alcoves that studded the outside of the building.

The greensward was muddy where the protesters had marched and stomped. Litter and signs, some broken and some not, lay about. Renender read them quickly as he huddled and marched up to the entrance of the building.

"No to Dictatorship!" read one.

"Lupins Say Go!" read another.

"Throw Corvus off the Terminus!" read a third.

Renender's traverse up the greensward was not unnoticed. Guards policing the building's entrance advanced forward as he approached. One came up close.

"Good greetings," shouted Renender above the din of the storm.

"This is a dark night," said the guard shining a light on the approaching stranger. "Do not be offended that I ask to see your identification."

"Not at all. I am Renender from the valley's Airship Consortium." He retrieved a billfold from a dry pocket and removed his identification, passing it to the guard who turned his light on it. Renender recognized the man. This was a boon. "I know you. You are Lieutenant Robek."

"Mr. Renender," said the guard. "Yes it is me." He handed Renender's identification back to him. "This night is foul and your visit is unexpected. What business do you have in Councils Building tonight?"

"I have business in the Commissioner's office. I am here on the matter of my man Roarsch's detention."

The Lieutenant looked hard at Renender. The man's face was pale, whether from the cold or in reaction to Renender's words, or both, Renender didn't know. "Corvus has him. My men don't have access. Maybe you can help sort out what is happening here. Come, follow me inside."

"Thank you," said Renender. He followed the Lieutenant up to the building's entrance.

"It's ok," said Robek to his guards. "It's Renender." A guard nearest the entrance pulled open the great door on the right. Renender and the Lieutenant withdrew inside.

The interior of the Councils Building was warm. The lobby was large, laid out with beautiful marble floors, walls and ceiling. Marble columns lined the three sides around the entrance. The columns were red and sepia with seams of darker minerals that spread like the vines of a creeper plant. Mineral patterns on the walls reminded the eye of high mountain vales. On all three sides around the entrance twelve wooden doors in ornate frames led off to offices and councils chambers, lounges and meeting rooms.

"Just check in at the Councils desks," said the Lieutenant. He cleared his throat and added "Corvus is in the Civic Council." Robek turned and pushed his way back through the heavy doors, back into the storm.

"Thank you," said Renender. Turning back into lobby he faced the two great desks of hardwood that faced the entrance at an angle of forty-five degrees to each other. They were separated by a space of four meters. An official Registrar sat behind each desk. They were beautiful women, identical twin sisters. On the top of the desk on the left was a sign that read "Economic Council." On the desk on the right a like sign read "Civic Council." Renender approached the Civic Council desk. He removed his wet jacket along the way.

The woman on the left addressed him as he neared the desks. "Good evening Mr. Renender. Do you wish to speak with the Economic Council? The members are in chambers tonight. I can have someone paged for you." She wore a turquoise blue uniform trimmed in gold with wide lapels and matching pillbox hat.

Renender turned to her and smiled broadly. "Good evening, Maurana. Not tonight, thank you." He turned to the Civic Council registrar.

"Good evening Mr. Renender," said the woman in a matching forest green uniform. "How may I help you tonight?"

"Good evening Maurina," said Renender stopping before her desk. "I have business in the Commissioner's office. One of my employees has been held for questioning. I am here to secure his release."

Maurina nodded. "Through the open door just this way," she said extending her arm in the direction of a door on Renender's right. She touched the screen on her desk console and the door swung open quietly inward. "Down the hall to room 118."

"Thank you," said Renender. He walked through the open door and entered an access hall. The door swung closed quietly behind him.

The hall was narrow and unadorned. The floor was a pink and black checkerboard pattern. The ceiling was high. Plain doors lined the walls on alternating sides. No one else was about and Renender's footfall echoed down the length of the hall.

On one side was a door numbered "110 Civil Crimes Investigations." Renender walked on passed further doors "111 Civil Guard Administration," "112 Trade Crimes Investigations." Eventually he came to door "118 Ombudsman to the Office of Military Commission, Lupus Major." Renender faced the door, took a deep breath and squared his shoulders. A bland smile spread across his face and he knocked twice, entered.

"What are the chances that this storm will delay tomorrow's airship arrivals from the lake docks?" The man who asked this question spoke in a deep masculine voice imbued with command. The timbre of his voice said that this man expected answers to his questions. He addressed a short round fat man who stood and squirmed and wiped beads of nervous perspiration from his brow.

The little man was the Ombudsman. He stuttered and stammered a response. "Er, it's a bad storm. Not unusual for spring. It's hard to tell. It's hard to tell."

The other man was Corvus. Almost two meters in height, he was dressed in the tight fitting dark blue and black leather uniform of the Military Commission. It betrayed an agile hard body beneath. At the sound of knocking and the door opening, he stopped talking and looked up, locking eyes directly on Renender.

Renender blinked twice and gulped hard when he saw Corvus. The young Commissioner's strikingly handsome and boyish looks nearly disarmed

Renender. The young man had a pale complexion and eerily cold glow. His eyes were so jet-black. They pierced Renender deep and sowed doubt in his soul. Renender pushed the feeling aside and spoke. "Where might I find Commissioner Corvus from Lupus Major?" he feigned, sweeping his gaze around the large room. Fifteen people stood crowded around the large Ombudsman's desk at the back of the room. Corvus stood behind it, one hand on the high backed chair. All heads and eyes turned in unison at hearing Renender.

Corvus came round to the front of the desk. His attendants shuffled to open a way for him. Renender continued two steps into the room and stopped. Corvus strode up to Renender and stopped a meter before him "Who are you that is asking?"

Renender extended his hand in a friendly greeting. "Ah, Commissioner Corvus is it then? Yes, a pleasure it is to meet you. Yes, a pleasure." Renender bowed just slightly.

Corvus was intrigued by the stranger's bravado. His eyes remained on Renender's as he clasped hands firmly, squeezing tightly as to almost hurt. Renender did not wince. "Thank you, Mister...."

"Renender. From the Airship Consortium."

Corvus raised an eyebrow. "Oh, yes. Renender. I've heard I have you to thank for allowing my protective forces to purchase travel time on your airship fleet at such short notice. I had planned on calling on you. Your arrival is unexpected, yet welcome."

Preemptive, thought Renender.

"Won't you come in," invited Corvus. Renender graciously accepted. "Give us some room," Corvus directed at the crowd around the desk. The attendants, nervous members of the Lupus City Civic Council, hurriedly disbursed but for two women dressed in black uniforms. Inspectors that had arrived with Corvus.

"You will no doubt be relieved to know that Lupus Major guarantees the continued prosperity of Lupus City. Such a splendid place."

Renender could immediately see that Corvus had the city in his hands already by his sheer presence and the fear he evoked. But Renender knew another thing also. Corvus was helpless without his military troop backup. So they both were operating on borrowed time. This storm could be an advantage, a delay. The airships would not fly in such conditions. They had standing orders to ground in safe berths, designated meadows, flats and sheltered canyons.

Corvus offered Renender a chair and the two sat. "May I offer you a glass of water?"

"Er, yes. Thank you," accepted Renender. Corvus was maneuvering quickly for the dominant position. "I have come...." he began, taking a glass offered by an attendant.

"Yes, come. Why have you come?" asked Corvus. "On such a stormy night. Wouldn't you be better off staying home where it is warm and dry?"

"Mm, yes. The storm," hummed Renender. "Always the businessman I guess. I am here on a strictly business matter. You see, earlier today one of my employees was detained for questioning by one of your Inspectors." He glanced at the women standing stoically beside Corvus. "I have come to retrieve him." *That was definitive*, thought Renender. He was maintaining his edge.

"Detained?" asked Corvus. His expressed concern was less than genuine.

"Er, yes," Renender went on. "On the landing field. A misunderstanding I am sure, just as the airships were taking off."

"On the landing field," repeated Corvus. The young Commissioner positioned himself straight in his chair. His demeanor was just detectably less congenial. "I am sure I am not aware of your city's domestic criminal justice trifles. My presence has nothing to do with the efficient running of local services and law enforcement."

Renender knew that one of Corvus' landing field Inspectors had taken Roarsch. This was outright deception. "Yes, indeed," he said. "Nonetheless, my man Roarsch has been detained." *I've reasserted my position*, thought Renender.

Corvus eyed Renender awhile before replying. "I am certain your Councils would recommend any guests remain here for the night, sanctuary against the elements. If you come around in the morning, you can make your case again, assuming the storm has passed by then."

Evaded, thought Renender.

"In fact," appended Corvus, leaning forward across the desk with renewed vigor. "As I said, why don't you come around again in the morning. Shall we say at ten? You won't mind if my colleague Farroll asks you some questions about your business, the airship trade, operations details."

Renender turned to look at the Inspector standing nearest Corvus. She exhibited no emotion. Renender fought against a chill that tried to shake his spine. The room's heat seemed to bleed away from the vicinity of Corvus and the Inspectors. Corvus' eyes sparkled with a cold light. Goose bumps rose on Renender's arms. Corvus continued.

"In fact, if you would be so good as to bring with you some of your records books, you could highlight for us some of the particulars of Lupus City economics, your trade contacts, etcetera. Farroll is very thorough when it comes to accounting."

Renender smiled back at Corvus. "I'm sure that won't be a problem," he said, not wanting to sound too eager or too conciliatory. He exhibited that he had nothing to hide. "Might we make it eleven instead?" asked Renender. "I have shipping manifests and orders to rearrange. Your personnel transports necessitate reshuffling cargo deliveries. It has been quite a busy day and night already."

Corvus' initial enthusiasm at the possibility of swaying Renender to openly work for him waned visibly. "I'm sure you appreciate how busy I am, Renender. I wish as little disruption to the overall economic success of Lupus City's trade with Lupus Major. In fact, I am hoping we can come to broad agreements between the Economic Council, your Airship Consortium and our own trade representatives from Cronapolis. Besides our friendly peacekeepers, I am bringing in a team of economic advisors, comprised of both military and non-essential civilian trade factions."

Renender maintained his friendly outward visage toward Corvus, yet inside he already felt the sure heavy boot of Markhab stomping on the freedoms of Lupus City. Cornelius and Naemi were correct. This was a complete takeover. Everything here validated that. The Lupus City Economic Council would be replaced by Markhab's Military Commission of Economic Materiel. The Civic Council was already effectively dissolved.

"I think it would be best if we kept to the original ten o'clock time tomorrow," Corvus said. "Your punctuality is appreciated in advance." Corvus stood up. The meeting was over. "Thank you for coming here tonight," he added in a more convivial manner. The Commissioner extended his hand slightly to Renender, who had to reach over the desk to grasp it. His hand was cold. Renender felt a cold spike touch his heart and chill him to his bones. His grip weakened. Corvus abruptly released his hand. "Be careful in this storm returning to the valley, Renender. Tomorrow then." Corvus sat back down at the desk. "Farroll will interview you tomorrow."

The cold further darken the room. It clouded his mind. He shuddered. But his inner resolve held. "Of course," he said. "It will be my pleasure."

Corvus betrayed a quizzical look then steeled his eyes on Renender and said "Sleep well tonight."

The words clutched at Renender's heart and turned warm hope into cold dread. He turned seemingly unimpressed and crossed the length of room back and out again to the warmer and more brightly lit corridor. The door to Room 118 closed behind him.

Renender breathed deeply, his eyes closed. He fought for a moment of calm, but it was elusive. The composure he had maintained in front of Corvus quickly melted away. In its place Renender shuddered. Despite the warm hall, he felt cold deep in his bones. It gripped his organs. It filled them with dread. Renender's shoulders slumped and his knees knocked together. His goose bumps spread up his arms, across his shoulders and back, down his legs. His vision blurred from tearing.

He rubbed his eyes dry and stood up straight, taking deep breaths. He had heard of the cold dread the Markhab and his fellow Commissioners evoked in others during face-to-face confrontations. Renender was lucky. It was rare to escape the audience of a Commissioner. He knew it was only because of his preemptive visit. Tomorrow Renender was sure he would not find the situation as accommodating, nor as polite. No, he must be out of the city long before then, before the military arrived on the next day's airship run. Renender turned left and walked back down the hall to the Councils Building's lobby.

The Civic Council Registrar Maurina looked up from her work when Renender reentered the lobby. He walked up to her calmly and said with a smile "Thank you for letting me see the Commissioner on such short notice. He is expecting me back at ten tomorrow morning."

"I'll note the appointment calendar, Mr. Renender," said Maurina.

"Thank you," said Renender. "Until then, good night."

"Good night," said the Registrar. She turned back to her desk console.

"Good night Mr. Renender," said Maurana at the Economic Council desk. "Be careful in this storm."

"Good night," Renender smiled and nodded. His footfall across the quiet hall was the only source of sound. The stillness and warmth were surreal, like the eye of a hurricane. Yet within the rooms and chambers of the Councils Building a curtain of cold was falling on the freedoms of Lupus City, like the rain. He donned his rain parka and left the lobby.

Outside, the temperature had dropped further. Hail fell. Lieutenant Robek watched Renender, nodded at him. He and the other Civil Guards all had their hands to an ear, in communication with one another and others within the building. Renender pulled his rain parka tight, adjusted the hood. He nodded back at the Lieutenant and stepped down to meet the greensward. Ice crumpled under his boots and he sloshed in half frozen puddles of mud. Renender made his way down the slope nearly slipping. He scrambled down the steps and hurried across the side street where his ground car sat.

Renender quickly unlocked the vehicle and scurried in. The ice on his jacket began to melt and water dripped everywhere. He sat still a moment, looked the interior over. The back. Nothing seemed untoward, but Renender was certain the car must have at least been marked or tagged somehow. Corvus or his lesser henchmen would be monitoring his return to his offices and suite down on the valley floor. That is where his car will be at least, after a quick side stop on the way. Renender started the engine, turned up the heat and drove away through the dark icy streets. He drove to Sandy Field Park.

On the top of the Councils building, on the rain-drenched roof, five men were tied by their wrists against five flagpoles. They groaned from their interrogation wounds. Lightning illuminated their wrecked visages. One slumped down to his knees. He had been Roarsch. Now he was broken.

25 DESCENDING THE MOUNTAINS

"I don't know what it is, but there's something about these things that I can't resist." Naemi sank into the seat opposite Cornelius and plopped a jelly doughnut onto a napkin before him. Her grin was partly obscured by a dusting of white. "I think it might be the powdered sugar. They didn't have any plain, which might suit you better."

Cornelius was staring out the window, lost in his thoughts. "What? What's that?"

"Jelly doughnuts."

Before Cornelius could respond, she cut him off. "Dardele is coming," Captain Reldere's man was going from table to table looking for them. She nodded with her head, her eyes still fixed on Dardele.

Cornelius did not turn. He picked up his doughnut and stuffed it into his mouth, dusting his face and shirt with sugar. He tried reaching for a cloth towel with fingers covered in red sticky jelly. Suddenly both he and Naemi lost their balance. Cornelius threw his hands out and onto the table, jerking in his seat. He tried to steady himself. Jelly splattered everywhere. He started laughing and looked up at Naemi. "What was that?"

Naemi was not laughing. She regained her balance. Cornelius cast his gaze quickly around the room. All the passengers had been thrown off balance.

Some had stumbled and some had fallen. Cornelius grabbed a towel and wiped clean his hands and mouth, wiped down his shirt.

"That was the ship."

Dardele arrived at the table, clutching its edge just as the ship heaved again. "I've found you," he said. "There is going to be an announcement soon, but you have to come with me now. The Captain needs to talk to you."

"I thought you said this airship had a superior balancing mechanism," Naemi said. A little sarcasm attempted to mask her foreboding.

"It's the wind," Dardele tried to explain, but another heave left him sprawled on the floor.

Loudspeakers crackled from speakers near the ceiling the Captain's voice bellowed. "This is Captain Reldere. We are experiencing extreme turbulent winds. We are landing in a designated safe berth temporarily. Other ships are doing the same. Secure yourselves for descent."

"Follow me," said Dardele. The three walked through the concessionaire, down the hall to the ship's lobby, and up the stairs to the bridge.

There was both mayhem and cool. Out the forward windows a green zeppelin sideswiped a red balloon. The Valyon's helmsmen averted the danger by sailing over the encounter. Lights flashed and horns blared.

Cornelius and Naemi stood at the top of the landing. Dardele moved quickly over to the right and found Reldere.

The Captain was speaking through a private COM horn. She saw Dardele approach, flicked a gaze at Cornelius and Naemi, then ended the call. She addressed them. "The storm is pushing the air before it down the mountains too fast. We are having difficulty maneuvering in the conflicting gusts. We must reconfigure our ballast before we continue any further." The Captain turned towards her helmsmen and shouted. "Where is the nearest safe berth?"

"Two knots forward. Glade thirteen," answered one.

"That's more of a ravine," scowled Reldere. Prepare for rapid descent." She turned back to Cornelius and Naemi. "You'll not have seen this before." She grinned with a secret pride.

"We're ready," said the other helmsman, pointing. "There!"

The bridge crew and guests looked out the forward windows as the ship just passed over the sharp edge of a mountain ridge. Another lay before them.

"Rudder about!" barked the Captain. "Arms up! Propellers Up!"

Out the side windows Cornelius and Naemi saw a sight. The protruding arms that held the airship's propellers dipped steeply down. Each arm's propellers individually righted itself. The ship stopped in midair. She rotated ninety degrees. Suddenly the arms gave way and pulled up flat then up arced up another forty-five degrees. The propellers righted themselves and also folded forty-five degrees on their own. The downward thrust kicked in and the ship plummeted.

Naemi threw out her arms and grabbed the rail support along the back wall and just missed. She might have hurt herself if Cornelius hadn't hit the floor in a thud first. She fell onto his back and rolled off, catching his elbow in a rib on the way. They both grunted.

The scene out the windows passed quickly. Forested hillside careened bye, interspersed with rock outcroppings on the way.

"Landing mark!" shouted Reldere. The propeller arms suddenly flattened out again, the propellers too. The airship descent slowed to a near halt. Before anyone could speak, the gentlest thump brought the huge ship to a halt.

Cornelius and Naemi found their feet again and stood looking around. Outside was a flat grassy glade only twice the length of the Valyon and just twice as wide. A sliver of a pond full of blooming floating lilies lay against the steep hillside.

"How was that for a landing?" asked Reldere. Then she started to laugh.

Naemi moved toward the Captain. She had had enough of leaving her fate in the hands of others. She wasn't certain what emotion she felt, but she wanted answers. "Is this really about the storm?"

The Captain's smile vanished from her face and her stern demeanor returned. "Saving your asses."

"From the wind?" Naemi was confrontational.

"From your doom," answered Reldere. We've been monitoring communiqués from the lake docks. The military is firmly in control of the landing field and the warehouses. The lake ships are moored several kilometers offshore. Their captains are refusing to approach the docks. Some are returning to the Canius shore, others are turning back to Big City. Captain Katzer is still standing by, but not for long. Communication from Lupus City is down. The storm must have knocked out our relays down the mountains.

Naemi was quiet, absorbing the information.

"What are our options?" asked Cornelius

Reldere stared hard at Cornelius, then briefly at Naemi. "You have only one option, which is why I've stopped here. The storm will only get stronger, but the Valyon can weather it if we resume our course down immediately."

But the approach will be watched," said Naemi.

"For the airships, yes," said Reldere. "But you two won't be on an airship."

"You're marooning us here? Why? To save your skin?" Naemi was blistering.

"Don't be a fool, woman," snapped back Reldere. "You have been provided for. Renender has seen to it."

"What is she talking about?" Naemi asked, turning her accusing eyes on Cornelius.

Cornelius was perplexed for a moment. He understood why Naemi was upset. She was boiling over with drama. She didn't like not being in control of a situation. Cornelius himself didn't know what was going on. Captain

Reldere remained quiet. She was waiting for Naemi's tantrum to play out, for her to calm down. Cornelius saw Naemi's look of consternation. Then something clicked in his mind. He knew something about the airships' emergency procedures from conversations with Renender. There were always contingency plans. He turned to Captain Reldere and said, "Para gliders."

The Captain smiled.

Naemi relaxed a bit, but she still didn't understand. "Gliders?"

Cornelius began to explain. "Renender keeps gliders and supplies at each emergency landing berth, so someone can go for help if something happens to the airship."

"It's also a means of smuggling people away from any inspectors down at the docks," Reldere added.

"Like Markhab's forces now," finished Naemi, nodding with understanding.

"There's a two-person glider not far from here," said Reldere. "Renender was adamant that you not be detained by Markhab's forces. I don't know why, and you must not tell me. But I do know that you won't be safe staying on the Valyon. Storm or no storm, Inspectors will be swarming over the landing field as soon as we touch down."

A feeling of trepidation flowed over Cornelius. He felt it in his stomach. He didn't know how to fly a glider. He looked at Naemi. "I don't…"

"I can fly a glider," Naemi said matter of factly.

Cornelius and Reldere turned to Naemi.

She simply repeated herself. "I can fly a glider."

"You can?" Cornelius did not hide his surprise, nor his relief. "More hidden talents?"

"Something like that," Naemi answered. "I've flown gliders for sport and professionally in the skies above Polaris."

What haven't you done on Polaris, thought Cornelius. *What kind of a life did Naemi have on that world? Was she an agent there, too?*

Reldere sized Naemi up in a new light.

Dardele suddenly appeared at the Captain's side. He nodded to her. She said, "Good. Then you'll leave now. I need to get this ship airborne and down to the docks before the full thrust of this storm arrives. You'll need to do the same. Follow Dardele. He'll see you off and direct you on your way."

"Thank you for this help," said Cornelius.

"No sentiments are required," said Reldere. "I'm glad to see you off my ship for my own sake, as the lady said. But you'll have a chance. Good luck."

Naemi was still evaluating the situation. This could still be worse trap than what awaited them at the landing field. She concluded that she still had to exercise some trust. Cornelius seemed to know what he was talking about. "Let's go then," she said.

Captain Reldere had a few more parting words for them. "Remember this. When you get to the lakeshore, you'll have to find your own way to Katzer's ship. You'll know it by its difference. That's all I can tell you. Now safe journey."

Dardele spoke up and said "This way, now. We can't let the other passengers see you debark. I'll take you down to a side hatch."

Cornelius and Naemi took their leave of the Captain and the Valyon's bridge. They followed Dardele down a different and narrower flight of stairs that circled down a windowless shaft to the gondola's ground level.

Dardele showed as much politeness as he could muster, which was minimal. He hurried. Cornelius and Naemi were nearly pushed out the small side hatch. Dardele remained within the hatchway. "There is a stream behind you against the ridge. Follow it down till you find its sister stream out of the hills on the other side. You must then follow it back upstream to a small bluff. There is the paraglider."

"How far are we talking?" asked Naemi.

"Maybe five kilometers around," answered Dardele.

"Hurry, we've got to beat the storm," said Cornelius.

"Not just the storm," said Dardele, "The night, too. We're about a hundred kilometers from the lake now. Dusk is approaching rapidly and will give way to dark by the time you arrive."

"We'll make it," said Cornelius.

"Be careful," implored Dardele. "Now go." He shut the hatch door and sealed the gondola, leaving Cornelius and Naemi standing in the thick grass outside.

The ship's horns sounded and the great airship pulled itself skyward away from the glad and back into the strong current of air descending out of the mountains. The ship sped away over the ridge and disappeared.

Cornelius and Naemi fell back to the ridgeline across soft ground and high grass. Cornelius splashed into the stream and Naemi stopped at its edge.

The air was muggy and cool, and it was getting colder. Naemi tried to ignore Cornelius' cursing and whining as he splashed his way out of the stream. Naemi stood still on the rounded blue stones that the waters had tumbled and rolled and deposited here. She tilted her head back and stared into the sky above. Dozens of airships sailed across the field of vision. Only the faintest whip-whip sound of the multitude of distant propellers reached the glade. The sound of the wind gusting above was louder.

The glade was protected from the winds, existing in a pocket of calm. A quiet still hung over the area. Naemi came to hear the slight and slender notes of insects chittering and chattering in the grassy expanse. Delicate scents entered her nostrils. Growing blooming greening breeding things. Naemi shook her head and cleared it of tranquil thoughts. No wonder this spot was chosen as a safe berth for the airships.

Cornelius appeared at Naemi's side. "What are you waiting for? Let's get moving." Naemi remained staring at the ships passing overhead. Cornelius retreated back to the stream where he splashed his way to the other side. "It's this way," he shouted back to her.

Naemi panned the glade with her eyes again. Something about the place made her want to tarry longer. A small green damselfly flew up and paused less than a meter away from her face. It observed Naemi, then turned tail and circled twice in the air before darting away towards the pond. The air above it was hazy with the flutter of insects. Smells of honey and jasmine and anise wafted passed Naemi's senses. The humidity seemed thicker. Naemi blinked several times. Each blink felt heavier than the one before. Sharp as a knife her attention was interrupted by Cornelius.

"Naemi! Come on!"

Naemi turned to see Cornelius splash out of the stream's far side beside the ravine's slope. His pants were wet up to the knees. His hands rested on his hips.

"What is your problem?" Cornelius shouted.

Naemi inhaled a deep breath and shook her head. She focused on Cornelius. "I'm coming." She easily found footing on rocks that just broke the stream's surface and crossed to the other side, arriving next to Cornelius completely dry.

"What's wrong with you?" Cornelius asked.

"I just got foggy headed for a moment," said Naemi. "The air is thick in this glade."

"Yeah. Stuffy. Now let's move." Cornelius led the way up the side of the ridge. The going was steep and the ground was soft. Their shoes slid and skidded as they climbed. In places they scaled rocks hands over feet, using their knees and elbows to find two, four and six toeholds on their way. The sound of the wind grew louder and louder. Soon the currents of air roared in their ears. Trees, shrubs and grasses grew at a horizontal slant. The hair on Cornelius and Naemi's heads danced and tousled in the wind. There was a static charge in the air. By the time the two of them reached the ridge top they were fighting against the gale force. They stood five hundred meters above the glade. Rocks outcropped the ridgeline. Twisted shrubs huddled with grasses in the crags between broken stones. Stunted lupin pines struggled for anchorage against the forces of erosion.

Cornelius clambered over the ridge's rocky backbone. He maneuvered around thick brush and thorny bracken. Naemi followed behind, gingerly finding footfall on sturdy stones. She gracefully wove her way through the brush. After some distance along the ridgeline she sidled up to Cornelius. He was bent over plucking thorns out of his shoes and pants. Curses rolled off his tongue.

"Are you still spouting expletives?" Naemi asked half amused, half annoyed.

"These thorns have sharp barbs at their ends. I'm stuck everywhere. Aren't you scratched too?"

Naemi glanced down at her shoes, pants, surveyed her arms. "Nope. Not a scratch. I tend to avoid such things, while you blunder through the bracken."

Cornelius yanked a long twisted thorn out of his shoe where it had penetrated into a sock. "Uhh!" he exclaimed. He dug his fingers under the sock to massage his foot. He looked up at Naemi. Her face bore a smug expression. "I don't blunder," he retorted.

"No?" she asked. It was rhetorical.

Cornelius ignored the comment and surveyed the land around the ridgeline. Down on their left the ridge gave way gently to a bowl occupied by thick groves of bracken and thicket. The steep sides of the mountain spur towered above. On their right the ridge's slope gave way steeply. A gravelly scree of debris blanketed the side like a skirt. At its bottom grew a stand of lupin oaks.

"Let's head down that way," said Cornelius pointing to the trees. Overhead a great red zeppelin soared passed. Mini avalanches of debris cascaded from his unsteady footing. His passage down was labored. Each step he pulled his foot out of ankle deep gravel. He slipped and skidded his way down to the tree line of oaks. Rocks cascaded down after him. He paused to brush the dust off his pants, stomped his feet. He looked up and was startled to see Naemi standing quietly before him. "Whoa. How'd you get down here so fast?" He stooped down to pull off his shoes and shake the dust and pebbles out of them.

"I came down that way." Naemi pointed to a rocky outcropping behind them that skirted the edge of the scree. A clean path was clearly visible. "It was easier."

"Humph" was all Cornelius responded. He hopped about clownishly to keep his balance while shaking out his shoes.

Naemi left him and wandered through the oak grove. Their great limbs bent and creaked against the onslaught of wind. Clumps and sprigs of green-blue tree moss fell around her. They grew in long hanging mats from the high branches overhead. Naemi heard the gurgle of water nearby. She also heard Cornelius behind her stomping over the dried and prickly leaves beneath the trees.

"I think there's a stream through here," Naemi said.

"Good. Let's find it then follow it up to the glider." Cornelius passed her, crunching his way among the great trunks of oak. Naemi followed. Twenty meters on she found Cornelius stooping beside a swift moving stream of milky water, scooping up cupped handfuls into his mouth.

"Is that good to drink? Look at it," Naemi asked.

"Hm? Oh, it's fine." Cornelius consumed a few more draughts. "Cold though."

Naemi bent down and scooped one drink into her mouth with cupped hands. It tasted a little sweet and felt gritty as it sloshed passed her teeth. Her eyes caught sight of a thicket of early berries growing beside the stream up from where they stood.

"Do you have anything to eat in your bag?" asked Cornelius. Naemi was already passing him. At the thicket the berries grew in tight clusters surrounded by twirled spirals thick sharp thorns. Naemi reached into her satchel and withdrew a sharp curved blade ten centimeters long. Its convex side was smooth while its inner concave edge sported tiny graduated florets of sharp teeth. She put blade to stem and cut a berry clump from its thorny cage. She put the knife away and sampled a berry. Its ripe purple juice stained her fingers and lips.

Cornelius came up beside her. Naemi offered him some. "These are sweet."

Cornelius took one and popped it into his mouth. He face contorted in a sourpuss expression and he spat the berry out. "Blaah! That was a bad one."

Naemi ate another. It was as sweet as the first. She bit into a third, just as sweet, and gave the other half to Cornelius. "Try this."

Cornelius sampled it hesitantly. "That one's ok. Hit and miss I guess."

"I guess," said Naemi. She finished off the bunch. All sweet.

"There are supposed to be provisions hidden with the glider," said Cornelius. "Let's move on." He led the way, following the water's edge upstream.

They climbed their way up steeper and steeper grades for nearly an hour. The cold milky water tumbled and splashed and flowed passed. Cornelius loved to be out in nature. It was a calling he'd discovered ever since his mother had taken him and his sister on a vacation to the hills of Lupus Minor. Getting out of the dull grey tower blocks of the gulag city of Bafaria introduced him to a love of the natural world. The terrain he and Naemi passed through here also reminded him of the secret passes the rebel cells from the of Territory of the Shining Star of Lupus maintained to move to and fro the Territory and Lupus Major.

The higher they climbed the closer the ridges and hillsides drew together beside the stream until finally the way ahead was pinched off completely. The stream fell from a waterfall ten meters high above them. Naemi stood looking up at the notch in the hill where the milky water cut through. Cornelius stood beside her looking up then, back down the way they'd come. There seemed to be no way forward.

"How do you suppose we get up there?" he asked.

Naemi watched the falling water and was caught in a half thought, trying to find the other half. Something tugged at her memory. The milky water. She bent down and scooped up a cold handful. Sediment settled in her hand. She took a sip and felt the fine grip against her teeth. "I don't think we do," said Naemi finally. She let the water flow through her fingers back into the stream. "Was the stream water in the glade where we landed as cold as this?"

"No, it was warm actually," said Cornelius.

"It was clear, too," said Naemi.

"Yeah. And your point?"

"My point is, we've followed the wrong stream."

"What?" Cornelius did not show amusement at Naemi's supposition. "We followed the stream on the opposite side of the ridge like we were supposed to."

"Dardele said to find its 'sister stream.' This one is cold and milky. This is not the glade's sister stream."

"Maybe it's the evil twin sister," said Cornelius trying to be funny.

Naemi didn't bite. "We've got to go back down and find the right stream," she said.

"There's got to be a way up," said Cornelius. He was clearly annoyed.

"There is no way up," said Naemi. "This gorge is completely pinched off from the water's course above us. We've got to get back down."

"Why do you keep saying this is the wrong stream? How do you even get off making that case?"

Naemi tried to explain. "Five years ago when we were assigned the detail in the Titanium Miner's Union to ferret out Markhab's mole?"

"Yeah? What about it?" asked Cornelius.

Naemi continued. "That was high up in the mountains. The waters that flowed through those upper vales were milky like this. It's colored with fine sediment released from glacial melt water. The clear waters in the glade where we landed were from some artesian spring. This water," she said bending down and splashing its cold into Cornelius' face, "This water comes all the way down from the high glacial peaks in the interior Canius Range. Simply put, Cornelius, you've led us up the wrong stream."

"Ok, I get it," Cornelius said. Why was Naemi always right? "We've got to double back fast then. Dammit, we've got to find that glider before it gets dark. And I'm hungry."

Naemi pushed past him. "I'll lead this time." Cornelius let her. He was hungry and did not want to argue with her.

Their descent was rapid. Naemi moved with determination at a trot over stone and root and water. Before long they had retraced their steps back to the purple early berry bush.

"Do you want some of this to eat?" asked Naemi pausing beside the thicket. She already hand knife in and snipped off a clump.

"Sure," said Cornelius. "Give me half of that." He shoved the handful of berries into his mouth. Half were sweet and half were sour.

"Were those better than before?" ask Naemi.

"Marginally," Cornelius replied.

Naemi popped the last of her berries into her mouth. All sweet. She bent down to the stream and washed her hands in the milky waters. The gurgling currents carried away the juices in purple red then pink swirls. Naemi watched the colors dissipate in eddies. She followed then down a ways where they slowed in a small pool formed by a barricade of rocks.

Something small and bright red bobbing in the water's edge caught her attention. "What's this?" she asked out loud. She dipped her hand into the cold water and lifted out a strand of red ribbon that held four small red beads of glass or ceramic or stone. She wasn't sure which. Three were solid red while a fourth was orange-striped.

"What did you find?" asked Cornelius at her side.

"I'm not sure," she answered, holding it up for Cornelius to see.

"A funny place for it to be," Cornelius said. "I wonder who might have dropped it here."

Naemi looked back upstream where they had followed the swift flowing water's upper course. "I don't think anyone dropped it here. I think the water carried it down from someplace high up in the mountains."

"Lupus City?" asked Cornelius.

"This water doesn't come from Lupus City," answered Naemi. "Someplace higher up."

"There are no cities higher up, except the mines above the horseshoe valley. There aren't any other people in these mountains," Cornelius stated.

"People," said Naemi. The mountains that rose above them were hide and massive. They could hold many secrets. Naemi gave the ribbon to Cornelius. "Here, you keep this."

"A souvenir? "He shoved it into a pocket. "OK. Now let's find that other stream."

They followed the milky stream down its course and through more stands of lupin oak, lupin pin. Out of the damp clammy darkness of a particularly thick grove of great trees. They stepped into a wide grotto filled with orchid ferns. Their iridescent waxy blooms dangled on the ends of long fronds. Cornelius and Naemi stood in a protected gorge with high rock walls. The stream disappeared around a bend ahead of them. Naemi rubbed her arms to still her goose bumps brought on the chill dampness. "It's cold here," she said.

"It's been getting progressively colder since we got off the Valyon," said Cornelius. "These are pretty though," he said touching one of the waxy blooms. The plant reacted instantly. The bloom's surface chromophores lit up and shimmered in a rhythmic pattern meant to hypnotize its prey. Then Cornelius felt a prick of his finger followed buy a warm numbing sensation. The skin of the blossom undulated and began to curl over itself, recoiling back into the leafy heart of the fern. Cornelius pulled his hand away.

"What's it doing?" asked Naemi.

"I think it's trying to eat me," said Cornelius. "But I'm too big. It stung me though." He raised his finger to see where he'd been pricked. Drops of blood fell from the end of his finger.

"Does it hurt?" Naemi showed some real concern. She couldn't afford for Cornelius to be injured or poisoned. She drew up close to see. "You're bleeding."

"It's numb, but I feel fine. It's a localized reaction. " Cornelius laughed. "It's a carnivorous plant I guess. Dazzle the prey, numb it, then fold it up and drink its blood. I think it injected me with an anti-coagulant. Cool, huh?"

Naemi was genuinely amazed. "Actually, yes," she said. Then Cornelius and Naemi had the same thought at once. They looked down and saw the grotto's floor was littered with the desiccated corpses of moths, birds and small jumping lizards.

"Are you sure you're ok?" Naemi asked.

"Yes." Cornelius flexed his fingers and hands. The numbness affected three fingers and his thumb tingled. He shook his hand. "I think so. It's spreading."

"Let's get away from here while you can still walk," said Naemi. "You don't want to become part of this compost heap."

They followed the stream around the grotto's bend where the walls of the gorge drew close to the water. They had to be careful not to touch any of the waxy blossoms dangling out to touch the unwary passerby. Cornelius tried to keep up with Naemi who almost danced across the mossy edge of the stream. He still managed to get wet.

The gorge opened onto the high end of a boggy field where some last rays of sunlight still shone. The air was thick with a blur of insects, some as large as a hand, other as tiny as a mote. Birdsong carried over the hum of insect wings and insect calls. The field was a shallow hollow, mostly open on the right downward side except for a slight rise that partly dammed the stream's flow and created the bog. On the left other gorges opened onto the field, each spilling a stream to feed the bog.

"You are kidding," said Naemi. "I knew this was a set up. There is no glider. Who would hide a glider so far from the landing field? We are lost."

Cornelius held up his hand to catch the sunlight. The penetrating rays of the Lupin sun warmed his hand. He felt the numbing recede. Sensation returned. He smiled. "Sunlight," he said. "It counteracts the plant's poison. The feeling's coming back."

"Did you hear me?" said Naemi rashly. "There is no glider."

"Of course there's a glider," said Cornelius. "I know Renender. He told me he stows them far away."

"That makes no sense," said Naemi.

"They're for smuggling," said Cornelius. "We're not going to find it under a neon sign with sound speakers beside a snack stand. According to your theory, one of the streams coming out of these gorges should be warm and clear. How many are there?" He counted the gorges around. "Four. Five counting the one we just followed. Let's see."

Cornelius and Naemi kept to the sides of the gorge walls away from the bog, though its edge was difficult to discern, hidden in the bog grass. Gnats and larger insects swarmed around their faces, necks and arms.

"I bet they're bloodsuckers, too," Cornelius said.

They came to the first stream and it was milky. So was the second. But the third was clear.

"It's warm," said Naemi breaking a smile. A little hope returned.

"We'd better check the fourth, just to be sure," said Cornelius. He jumped across the water and scrambled across the gorge face to its other side. He disappeared around the corner while Naemi stayed, swatting gnats away. Presently Cornelius returned. "Yup," he said. "The other one is milky and cold like the others. This one's our girl."

They left the bog and ascended the warm spring's course. Up they climbed for nearly half an hour. The terrain became more and more exposed to the cold wind. Above them the stream tumbled off the side of a barren rocky bluff. Cornelius climbed up its face first and stood on the open ledge. It was ten meters wide and fifty long. The mountain butted straight up one side and towered above them.

"Look!" said Cornelius pointing.

Against the cliff face a dark blue glider sat moored to the rock, its wings folded back against its sides. Cornelius and Naemi ran over to it. The craft looked like a winged tapered tube. The body was more of a cocoon that you climbed into. Hand controls in the open front moved the wings and rudder.

Cornelius and Naemi got to work examining the craft, and looking for food. A small sack stuffed into the foot of the passenger cocoon held packages of dried foodstuffs. "Protein and whole grain bars," said Cornelius. He opened one and sunk his teeth into it. It was chewy. "Oh," he managed, savoring the taste. "Chocolate."

They ate a bar each and quenched their thirst from the stream. It had a sulfur taste but was drinkable.

Satisfied after the food and drink, Cornelius and Naemi walked back to the cliff edge to survey their location. Though open to the elements, the ledge was protected from the brunt of the wind's force by the mountainside. Facing the ledge's open north side, they saw spread below them the last foothills of the Canius Range. Mountain streams converged into rivers that rushed and swelled and met a quick end at the shores of the vast network of Lupus' great inland seas. The Lake of Lupus lay wide and broad below them. A hundred kilometers away lay the Lake Docks. Cornelius could just make out the few bright dots that were the airships making their final descent to the coast. The lake's eastern shore marked the southern fringes of the Federated Cantons. The hidden western shore was Canius.

Cornelius looked up at the darkening sky. Black clouds spread down from the dark mountains. Drops of rain bounced off Cornelius' nose and head. A frigid gust of wind wrapped its icy fingers around the cliff ledge and threatened to knock the two tiny Humans off the edge. They backed away from the drop off and returned to the paraglider.

"The storm is going to kick our butts if we don't leave now. Are you sure you can fly this thing?" asked Cornelius.

Naemi stuck her head into the passenger cocoon and looked at the sparse controls. The wing line ropes connected both above and below to the cocoon around the open control carriage. The rudder lines held the cocoon taut. Naemi stepped back and faced Cornelius.

"Well?" he asked.

"Very little of this is mechanically powered." She snapped open an access compartment just under the nose and reached in to feel around. "There are air pressure pistons and lubricant distributors in here. That's good."

"What does that mean?" Cornelius asked.

"Basically, we've got a rudimentary power steering system. That will make it easier to maneuver, but only just. We still have to supply the power, by old-fashioned elbow grease. And flying in the storm's wind eddies, well," she paused. Finally she said "Yes, I can certainly fly this." Naemi was confident. "You just have to promise me one thing," Naemi said to Cornelius.

"What's that?" he asked.

"No screaming."

"Huh?" Cornelius didn't understand.

Naemi smiled. "I mean it. Bite your tongue if you have to. I don't want to be distracted. Now come on, help me release the moorings and extend the wings.

The two of them worked quickly to untie the craft's fetters.

26 DESTINATION WROR

The Feline Commander held his course steady through the dazzle of star streams. Clouds of proto-quarks swirled in eddies cast in the wake of the ship's passage. The Commander struggled to maintain a straight line, but every so often the ship would zig or zag from the intended course. Each time that happened, the ship skirted the edges of the clouds, causing perturbations. Then the proto-quarks would condense, combine and fuse, releasing energy bursts that further rocked the ship. The commander's striped furred knuckles were white from so tightly gripping the helm wheel. It was such a small device to control the steerage of such a huge ship.

A light flashed on the console near the Commander. A horn sounded. The Commander glared quickly at a monitor display. The gravity well proximity detector was homing in on the ship's destination. The Commander's ears flicked backwards and his whiskers twittered. He slowly eased back on the steerage wheel and switched off the phase modulator. The proto-quark clouds dimmed, the star streams slowed and the great hulk of the armored asteroid emerged from the quantum stream. The once dazzling field gave way to the blackness of normal space as the Commander slipped into an easy geosynchronous orbit above the planet Wror.

The Commander verified his position and activated the asteroid's gyro motion, creating a spin that complemented that of the world below.

The mid belly of Wror loomed over the small domed crater of the armored asteroid. Galdinier stood on a gentle rise covered in soft grass looking straight up. The dome claspers slowly pulled back, retreating into the rhomboid plating, revealing more and more of the wondrous world above him. There was so much planet! The domed asteroid craters that were home to the Asteroid Ring Felines were puny by comparison.

The daylight face of Wror lit the craters in a glow they had not experienced before. A slight breeze blew passed Galdinier. It brushed over the grasses forming ripples. Galdinier heard a baying sound that drew his attention back down to the ground. He looked down the rise at his flock of dorsein. The herd sensed the shifting winds and perceived the strange glow. They shuffled uneasily, anxious from the same anticipation and awe that was sweeping over the thousands of Felines who gazed up, like Galdinier, at the new world above.

The face of Wror was a great green and blue cross in a brown and yellow field. Whereas most of Wror was arid and barren desert, this side of the planet had heaved and belched and torn asunder in epochs long passed. Two great rips, one north-south, the other east-west, formed long rift valleys. High mountains ridged the perimeters of the cross. The deep centers of the rifts were filled by the four long fingers of the Wror Sea. The east-west shores of the sea bordered steep green cliffs of brush and wood. The sea's southern terminus flooded low-lying land covered in thick mangrove and swamp. The sea's northern shores lapped against the edge of a wide fertile valley fed by many rivers flowing down from mountains. In this fertile valley the Humans from Lupus had settled. Huge agricultural farms and communities covered the green land. The farmers of Wror recognized and utilized the natural energy that radiated up through this side of the planet where the crust was thinnest. The energy enlivened and nourished the life that flourished in its green valleys and shallow blue sea. Where the sea touched this northern land, the capital city of Bara-Band had been built at the mouth of the Orod River. The city's central harbor was now a nuked out circle. The far north was not peopled. Not yet. To those cold yet verdant highlands would settle the Human dorsein herders from Drigo.

In the heart of Wror's sea lay a large circular island. Its edges rose steeply from the sea. A huge caldera valley occupied the majority of the island, the mouth of a once mighty volcano. The now dormant caldera was a lush green valley with low hills, streams and lakes. Seen from space, it was an emerald eye in the face of Wror. How like the crater valley homes of the Asteroid Ring Felines. This was the perfect new home to settle. And the planet's radiant life giving energy rose up through the crust strongest here.

Galdinier descended the slight grassy rise and entered the midst of his flock. The Feline herder talked gently to the beasts, touching their heads, cooing softly, offering reassuring sounds. The baying receded to satisfied grunts and snorts. Galdinier's presence always had a calming affect on his dorsein. Most resumed their grazing, no longer concerned by the strange glow from Wror. Galdinier passed through the herd and proceeded to the small crater's rim wall. There he found the access door, entered his code, and passed down an access hall. It was time to meet with the other herders and begin the consolidation of flocks into transports for the descent.

Governor Trian stood with his assembled staff and community leaders on the oratory platform that stood at the center of the city park in Bara-Band's northern district. The park's stage served as the temporary forum for official business, at least until a new structure could be built to replace the governmental buildings that were now dust at the bottom of the nuked crater. Bara-Band will rebuild.

On this day many in the city gathered to watch the spectacle in the sky. The armored asteroid hung above the planet like a glittering jewel, its rhomboid plating catching and reflecting the sun's light.

"My friends," shouted Trian over the din of conversation. "This is the transport from Drigo. Our Drigan brothers have come to replenish our numbers with eager and hardy men and women." The assembled crowd quieted as they drew their attention away from the sky jewel and listened to Trian's words.

"Many have left us to return to Lupus, fearful after the unprovoked attack on our city. But we are rebuilding. We will see Bara-Band's city center return as a new garden." Indeed, architects were making plans to turn the flooded crater into a new harbor. Foundations for retaining walls were being marked around the huge semi-circular crater. Quays and piers and berths would follow. The crater would become a new promenade, a commercial and governmental hub, as it had once been.

"We welcome our Drigan brethren to our promised land we love."

"Look!" Trian's speech was cut off by shouts and hollers. Everyone looked back up into the sky at the glittering ship. A stream of tiny lights issued forth like tiny gnats flying in single file formation. The line of lights drew closer to the planet's surface. As they entered Wror's atmosphere, they glowed bright orange from the friction of their rapid descent. Dozens of contrails streaked across the sky toward the northern horizon. One veered away from the others and approached Bara-Band's spaceport.

"Let us go down and meet our new friends," said Trian.

"What's that?" Some shouted.

"Look!" said others.

"Where are they going?" asked more.

A second line of lights issued from the ship and descended to the southern horizon.

Trian had an uneasy feeling about the second stream of lights. Why were they flying south? The Drigans were only to settle in the north. Trian could not understand what the other ships were doing. And the transport ship itself! It was huge, far larger than he'd expected, visible from the surface like a small moon. But Trian had confirmed with the ship's Commander that this was the transport bringing Drigan refugees and their dorsein.

"Come," yelled Trian over the crowd. "We will ask the Drigans."

Eridani and Canopus had to stand on the tips of their toes to look out the windows of the rapidly descending transport. They were not able to extend their height by much. The harness straps wrapped around their arms, shoulders, torsos and legs pressed their bodies tightly against the foam drop stations. Two hundred Felines were secured in columned rows on this transport alone.

The exterior of the window glowed orange and the view shimmered. The black of space was changing places with Wror's upper atmosphere.

Through the distorted orange glow, the sky grew brighter in hues of blue, indigo, navy, royal, sky, cerulean, periwinkle. The curvature of the horizon gave way to mountains, high and dark green, then green forests and grasslands. Suddenly the four-pointed sea filled the view.

Eridani and Canopus screamed in delight. Their cries were indistinguishable among the shouts and hollers bellowing from the mouths of all the Felines aboard. Canopus' mother, strapped beside, held her eyes squeezed shut. But each time she heard her daughter's voice amid the din, she peeked out through the squint. This time she caught sight of the view out the window. What looked like the green center of a blue cross, the island that would be their new home in moments. She shut tight her eyes again.

The shipped rocked and swayed. It bumped its way down through the atmosphere. The girth and shape of the transport prevented it from tipping and spinning. But the jarring was terrific.

Eridani's teeth chattered and clattered and clanged together. Her rubber mouthpiece was already chewed halfway through.

Topography started to become discernible from what had only a moment before been the flat disc of Wror. Mountains scratched the horizon. The green circle of the green island took form as its cone-shaped mountain was perceived. The scene disappeared, was replaced by white and grey clouds. Beads of water raced up the outside surfaces of the windows and globbed at the top. Then green and blue again. Waves and swells were visible in the sea.

Eridani could make out rocky ridges and the blur of forest on the island's encircling mountain slopes. A thin white line of beach circled the island. Eridani was in the middle of a laugh when her stomach floated up in her chest. "Whoa!" echoed through the hangar of the transport. The descent parachutes deployed. After the initial jolt, the ship began a gentle sway. Its descent passed from a plummet to a fall to a float. The high green of the rim wall mountains blocked out the rest of the view or Wror. Mountain ridges gave way to foothills, to grassland. Slower, then slower, the floating abruptly ended with a soft plush "Plump!" They were down.

The Feline Commander checked his readings as the last convoy of drop transports fell away. A dozen this time. Seen through the planet side view cams, each massive hulk vanished to black dots falling toward the planet. All the Drigan transports were already in situ on the northern high plains. Soon the last Feline transport would be away.

The Commander turned in his seat and pushed away from the console wall. The seat was affixed to the floor on a pedestal that maneuvered around the circular command center in a groove in the floor. He slipped around ninety degrees counter clockwise, then popped back against the console wall at another set of controls. The seat snapped into place. This station operated the ship's internal gyrators. Five knobbed levers faced the Commander, protruding from the bottom of a convex fisheye monitor. The Commander touched one knob and the screen lit up. A dynamic three-dimensional image of polyhedral shapes floated and rotated in the monitor's domed space. There were dozens of blips, each representing an angle, a side, of the great armored asteroid.

The Commander gripped three levers in one hand and slowly twisted them. With his other hand he pulled down on another lever. The images in the screen shifted position in relation to one another. The Commander exercised great patience in making certain no hexagon-crossed paths with a rotating octagon or dodecahedron. An isosceles triangle drifted too near a rapidly spinning cube. The Commander compensated by easing up on the lone knob. The triangle responded by disappearing beneath the cube. Two rhomboids approached one another from opposite sides of rotation. Readjusting his three knobs, the Commander coaxed them closer together in a synchronous dance. He let go of the single knob and reached for the fifth. Pulling down, the rhomboids came together in the center of the geometric sphere, isolated from the rest of forms. They approached quickly and appeared to snap together, merging into one rhomboid.

Seen from outside, the armored asteroid rotated in space above the planet. The many rhomboid surfaces of the asteroid twinkled in the sunlight like facets on a gem. The great hulk shifted from its position in space and moved closer to the planet, just brushing against Wror's outer wisp of atmosphere.

Twenty degrees further around the command center, the Feline Commander matched pitch and fall to a pre-calculated obliquity in the planet's spin. Power drawn from the asteroid's internal micro-singularity pulsed through the lattice network of the asteroid's internal structure, cooling the ship's bulk against the rising temperatures outside. The ship creaked and groaned despite the Commander's best efforts to maintain a stable passage. He couldn't stop the wind to blow or the atmosphere to churn in wakes and eddies from the asteroid's diagonal passage. Through a sliver of atmosphere the Commander navigated his ship. At the asteroid's closest approach to the planet, the rhomboid plating separated slightly in several places. Wisps of gas escaped from the interior of the asteroid. Then suddenly ghostly shape after ghostly shape flew out the gaps in the plating. Ghastly shrieking cries echoed across the skies as flying reptiles found a new home in the airs of Wror.

The Feline commander moved his ship out of the planet's atmosphere. The gaps in the rhomboid plating sealed shut against space's void.

Suddenly red lights and horns flooded the command center. The Commander turned and spun in his seat, dipping into one grooved notch, then another, searching readouts to discover the reason for the alarms. He shook his head to try and stop the piercing ringing in his ears. He slapped a break switch and the sound abruptly ended. The Commander stopped in front of one screen and saw the reason for the alert. His lips pulled back to bare his teeth, and a seething hiss blew passed his incisors. The pupils of his eyes filled to wide dark circles. Coming right at the armored asteroid from the planet's far side was the giant scorpion form of Markhab's battleship.

The Feline Commander was frozen, not knowing how to react. His command dossier stated that the battleship was not supposed to be here. According to his intelligence briefing, it was supposed to have departed two days ago, transporting Human colonists back to Lupus. But it wasn't two days ago. It was now. And it was here.

The Commander's hesitation passed in an instant. This was the first Armored Asteroid, a great Feline ship. The Commander knew what to do. He quickly swung his seat around to another station and locked himself into the notch. The console before him was an oval depression of warm soft putty. Without hesitation he stuck his hands in. The unpleasant tactile sensation was immediate. His nostrils flared. His eyes widened. His ears lay back flat. The Commander bared his teeth and spat out another long hiss.

Centimeters into the putty the Commander felt the neural receptor interface to the ship's main computer hub. Organized electrons carried immense quantities of information per second as they pulsed through the putty. The putty served as both a cooling medium and a contact gateway between brains, Feline and machine. The Feline Commander hated it, but he knew his own physical responses were too slow, and the armored asteroid had to maneuver quickly.

The tingling around his fingertips grew stronger. The temperature of the putty rapidly cooled as the electron bath became responsive to the Feline's presence. The electrons became excited, attracted to the Feline's fingertips. The Commander's eyes glazed and his lids relaxed. The blood pumped through his heart pulsated through his body, passing energy down through the arms, into his hands, out through the ends of each finger. The palms of his hands warmed. Connection made.

The entire crew was robotic. Servers. Handlers, porters, engineers, technicians. The Commander saw out of every eye, every sensor, every capacitor.

A quick beep sounded, followed by an incoming hail from the scorpion ship. The Commander's eyes and ears darted left toward the sound.

"Alien ship. Identify your species."

"Hiss," was all the Commander offered back. He let the message transmit.

The Human ship replied instantly. "Feline ship. Stand down immediately."

At the same time the rhomboid hull plating pulled back in three concentric rings around the asteroid's latitudes. White-hot electrostatic bolts traced complex patterns within the dark crevasses. It took longer than usual to charge full the weapons. A significant amount of power output from the micro-singularity still pulsed coolant through the lattice superstructure. The delay was costly.

The scorpion ship launched volley after volley of EM pulse-on-contact bursts.

Within the armored asteroid, thousands of robots were marching. Many organized themselves into rapid force teams of engineers to shore up systems and ready bulk materiel. Others scrambled to connect far-flung systems with stopgap shortcuts. Robots interlinked arms through corridors, into access hatches, plugging themselves in to vital systems. Like socially organized insect super societies, some robots sacrificed themselves so others could use their bodies as processor data conduits.

As many anterior systems as possible were diverted from normal power flow to fill the weapons systems. Power was drained from tens of thousands of centers around and within the asteroid in a microsecond.

Another white-hot pulse of energy shot out from the latitudinal hull openings at the scorpion ship.

The asteroid shuddered. The shockwave carried enough energy to melt the alloy bonds of the armored rhomboid plating. The shockwave overwhelmed the force fields protecting the crater valley domes. The domes exploded, releasing precious oxygen and life into space. Melt holes pockmarked the already ruddy surface of the rhomboid plating.

Inside the superstructure, melting plating buckled and severed coolant lines and electrical relays. Clouds of superheated gas filled the access ways, a deadly fog contaminated with plastics and incinerants.

Communications was severed among robot teams. Many lay heaped against bulkheads and corridors where steam blasts had thrown them. Others stumbled about in darkened halls and hangar bays, trying to reestablish links to the central hub.

In the command center many monitors were offline, others flickered or snowed with static. Those screens still functioning provided surveillance and readouts of the asteroid and its external environment.

At the interface console sat the Commander. He was frozen, rigid, a smoldering crisp corpse, hands still sunk in the electro bath putty. Ashen whiskers still clung to his face like long fingers of ignored cigarettes. One fell away onto the floor.

The EM buffering systems had been overwhelmed by the pulse attack. There had not been enough power to polarize the asteroid's plating in time, which could have fended off the blasts.

The Commander's head was cocked to one side, dull blank eyes stared at a monitor the imaged one of the transport drop bays. The image showed the last transport still sitting on the drop pad that the Commander had been unable to release. This was the transport that held the stand-alone computer hub intended for the Feline colony. It held medical, technical and historical records to support the nascent settlement, including the communications array. Three robots were visible in the monitor's sight. Two leaned motionless against a wall. The third twitched on the floor.

Another monitor showed the scene outside, and the scorpion ship.

Young Right Commander Balvard screamed in agony. He was pinned to the floor through his left arm. The ceiling strut had broken loose in the attack. Impaled, his arm nearly severed, snapping the bone and ripping himself away from the useless appendage had been the only logical course of action.

"Gods! Cauterize it now! Anything hot. Those exposed wires. See if you can yank them further from the wall. You! Help me get him over to the wall. We'll stop the bleeding by crisping the hole. Now!"

Pain. Such pain. Every moment, every breath, pain. Then the electricity.

A dullness. Slow climb out of darkness. There is a buzzing and tingling everywhere. Not buzzing, voices. Not tingling, pain.

"Aft pincer completely sheared off. Aft carriage punctured through four decks. Penetration only a third of the way through. Our core structure is holding. Aft engines aren't even there anymore."

"Oww!" A deep injection, near where his shoulder used to be. Buzzing fading, whispers. Tingling, a soft tickle. Breathing doesn't hurt anymore.

"Over two hundred crewmen dead or missing."

"The civvies?"

"Over twenty-four hundred."

"Shit."

"You won't believe this. Intermittent, but the quantum stream drive is still up. We can hop scotch our way back to Lupus."

"What's the status of the Feline ship?"

"Quiet. But weapons are still charged. Those open lateral gaps? They're still charged with huge EM potential. One more pulse and we're done for. Whatever is powering that thing, it wasn't damaged by our strike. She's live."

"Transmit to Trian. We're retreating to Lupus. Reinforcements will follow. Get us out of here. Now!"

Dizzying stars. Dancing stars. All a blur. A dull ache, just next to darkness. It feels soft. Soft.

Galdinier stood in grass as tall as his knees. Waves of undulating green shimmered like an emerald sea. The crater valley was a virgin world of streams, lakes, small hills, the odd rocky outcropping. The dorsein herds were already dispersing themselves freely throughout the valley. Galdinier was coaxing several hundred up a pass in the rim wall mountains. He wanted to establish the more aggressive herds along the seaward perimeter of the island.

A breeze picked up and Galdinier inhaled deeply. Ahh. This was paradise. Innumerable different smells filled his nostrils. Strange chirps and clicks and whistles fill his ears.

Galdinier paused in his climb and turned to survey the wide land. Peppered in all directions amid colorful blooms and green were the many drop transports that had brought the Felines, dorsein and supplies to the surface. The transports would serve as temporary shelters until they could be dismantled to build new structures. The Felines would build communities in the encircling mountains, leaving the crater valley green and unspoiled, just as they had lived on their former asteroid homes.

He looked up into the sky and saw the armored asteroid hanging in orbit like a beautiful gem. He felt reassured that all would be safe on this new world with the asteroid above to protect them.

One of the dorsein nearest him sneezed twice. Galdinier looked down and smiled. He made a clucking noise. He resumed his climb, urging the flock ahead. Yes, this was surely a paradise.

27 GURKBUZZEL IS VERY USEFUL

Cornelius lay huddled tightly in the right side of the paraglider's cocoon sack. There was little room to move though the sack was pliable enough. The momentum of the glider's flight created enough force to keep the wing bindings taut. And the gush of wind caused a tremendous roar.

On his left snuggled close beside him in the cocoon sack lay Naemi. Her legs were extended down to the sack's foot where her toes pressed against the rudder pads. Her arms stretched out in front of her, hands grasping the wing struts.

Cornelius turned his head slightly to glance at her face. Her eyes were steeled in concentration, her features locked and rigid. The night vision goggles they'd found among the glider's supplies had been a godsend. The storm had pushed twilight away and smothered them in a vast world of black. Cornelius squinted his temples to adjust his goggle's green depth enhancer. He surveyed the world out the transparent windscreens.

The wide flanks of the Canius Mountains were far behind them. The glider skirted over the tree line of low foothills that cradled small lakes receiving mountain streams that in turn channeled the waters into the burgeoning rivers that fed the great lake. Its shore was a dark line against the horizon about twenty kilometers in front of them.

It was warm in the cocoon sack. So warm that Cornelius wiggled and squirmed trying to stay comfortable. This, despite the biting cold that pushed them down the mountains. Pattering driving rain against the glider was an added force. Soon it was replaced by bullets of hail.

Amidst all this noise Cornelius heard a close-by chattering sound. Even in the green light of his goggles he could see that Naemi was ghostly pale. Her lips were blue and parted. Her teeth chattered in spasms. Cornelius mumbled into the patch transmitter that covered his mouth. "Are you ok?"

Naemi's faint reply eked through his ear buds. "C-co-ld. Cold."

Cold? Cornelius was so hot he was very uncomfortable. He felt like his blood had been getting hotter and hotter since, well, he tried to think. Since that bizarre plant had "bit" him in the mountain ravine prior to their finding the paraglider. And his muscles constantly twitched. He was anxious, and it was getting worse.

Suddenly way off to the left past Naemi he spied through the hail what looked like, well, it looked like another glider! Through the hail and rain and pounding wind, was it possible there were others like him and Naemi fleeing to the lake docks? He couldn't believe it.

"Y-you see them, t-too?" Naemi's voice stuttered in his head.

Other intrepid refugees? It was possible.

A fierce gust of wind pushed hard on the glider. They zigged and zagged wildly. Looking right, Cornelius saw another glider surfing the wind stream. And he could just make out further and lower another. He heard Naemi's voice again.

"C-Cornelius-ius. I'm too cold. Too cold."

Shit, thought Cornelius. But he'd watched Naemi steer this thing. It didn't look hard what she was doing. She was just steering.

"T-take-k ov-over, C-C. Do it."

"How?" Cornelius wanted to help. But how?

"G-grab the strut lines from hands-hands. Do it. Do it now!"

Cornelius first wiped the hot sweat from his brow. He stretched out his hands and put them over Naemi's, which were ice cold. His hot blood caused her to gasp.

"Ohh. So w-warm-m. N-now. I'll l-let go and slide under and around you. W-we ch-change p-laces-es. Wh-when —n I do, p-p-put your feet on the rudder p-pads. Do it."

Naemi pulled back her arms. They were achingly sore, cold and hard to move. Cornelius arched his body over hers and she wiggled to trade places with him.

The glider swung wide as Cornelius tried to assert control over the wing struts. He had to fight against the wind. Naemi made this look so easy. He locked his arms outstretched and grasped each strut ring in his fingers and squeezed, wresting control of the glider from the wind's force.

Naemi was now on his right. "P-pads, Cornelius. P-pads. Rud-d-der. Do it, Cornelius. Do it now!"

Cornelius found the rudder pads and slipped his feet onto them just as Naemi slipped her off. The glider's tail swayed and wagged until Cornelius asserted control. He was flying this thing!

Next to him Naemi struggled into a part-fetal position to try and regain warmth from her body core. She found a nutrition bar in a pouch at her side and munched on it through chattering teeth.

Cornelius' confidence grew with each passing moment. The wings became extensions of his arms via the strut lines. The rudder tail became an extension of his feet via the rudder pads. Cornelius squinted his temples to adjust the view out his green vision goggles and brought the landscape below into greater focus.

About a hundred meters below them the last rolling foothills gave way to flats. Scanning the lake line, Cornelius discerned a flurry of movement through rain and sleet, the lake docks. He squinted again and the vision magnified. Hovering dots swarmed the shoreline. Others lay arranged on a field, bulbous tops bobbing in the storm winds. The airships. Several circled over the lake waters, coming in for landings. A few were still en route on approach. A collection of piers extended from the shore out into the lake, but no ships were moored. Instead, Cornelius saw many dots aligned offshore maybe a kilometer. Squinting again, the scene on the ground came into even closer focus.

Surrounding the landing field three large shapes, Markhab's spider shaped troop transports, formed a triangular perimeter. Too large to land in the horseshoe valley of Lupus City, they were taking over the lake docks.

Cornelius stretched his temples and the view panned out to his normal vision. The lake docs were still some kilometers away, but they were fast closing in. He mumbled into his mouth patch. "Naemi. Are you ok? We're almost there. I need you to be ready to disembark."

The reply was feeble. "I'm doing better. Warming a little. So much heat coming from you. It's helping."

"Yeah, my blood is boiling. I'm ready for it."

Cornelius turned his head in all directions to take in the immediate view. They were now flying in the middle of the ice storm. And he could now count six other gliders making a like-descent. Who were they? Other operatives dropped from airships like he and Naemi? Possible. So long as they staid out of his way.

Cornelius felt completely alive. His consciousness stretched out beyond his body, beyond the rain and sleet and wind. He started hearing voices, snippets of conversation. Where were they coming from?

"Blue glider picking up speed, there...."

"Find his ship, steer...."

"Get between the troop transports and Val...."

"I need another energy bar...."

"More room. I'm swinging wide...."

Cornelius' mind raced as he tried to process what was happening. Was this an effect of that plant's poison? He felt strong as a titan. He wiggled in the glider's cocoon sack. He heard Naemi.

"Cornelius, we're headed right for the landing field. What's next? We have to find Katzer's ship."

Cornelius couldn't hear her well. But her words sunk into his consciousness. He brought the lake ships into quick focus.

"We'll know his ship by its difference. That's what Reldere's man Dardele told us."

"What does it mean?" Naemi wiggled up to peer out the windscreens. "Sixteen, seventeen, eighteen…twenty-six ships I count offshore. They all look the same."

"Can't be. One has to be different somehow." Cornelius flexed his fingers and pulled the wing struts taut in one direction. He eased up on the rudder with his feet. The glider maneuvered into a quick dive and circled left, making a wide arc. They were now flying over the wide mouth of a river a kilometer from the docks.

"Where will we land?" asked Naemi.

Cornelius ignored her. He watched the other gliders, then the ships. Something there. Something was different. "This ship." Cornelius said finally. "I see it."

"Which one? How do you know?"

"All the ships are heading out, but one is moving TO the docks."

"Katzer?" asked Naemi.

Cornelius counted quickly, then said "Ninth from the east. It's coming in. That must be him."

Much closer now. The scene on the ground was wildly chaotic. Hundreds of trooped were fanned out across the storm-wracked field like agitated ants climbing over landed airships to take control. There were skirmishes with crew and passengers everywhere. Several airships were avoiding the field and instead flew out over the lake, making wide circles over the lake ships.

"They're dropping payloads into the water," said Naemi.

Indeed, Cornelius saw them clearly. Drop loads were splashing in the cold dark waters near the ships and bobbing in the waves. The ships discharged dinghies to retrieve them.

"Contraband Markhab is not meant to intercept," said Cornelius.

Bright flashes exploded to the right from the direction of the troop transports.

"They're firing at the airships," Naemi said.

One great zeppelin just coming out of a turn back to the shore exploded from an impact. Flames burst through impact points and the mighty behemoth swooned in mid-air, floundered, then nose-dived while still steering around. It crashed into the cold waters fully ablaze.

Up hillside above the docks descended a blue zeppelin, purple circles adorning its flanks. The nose suddenly burst into flame from an incendiary. Explosions inside the ship caused it to buckle and crumple. It was the Valyon, and it fell from the sky and burned.

The ships were amok, trying to turn and flee. Some crashed together, others crashed below.

Cornelius pulled up on the rudder and wing tips. They were flying low over the beach now, the docks just ahead. He saw where the other gliders were headed. The same pier that the shore-bound lake ship was closing in on. Troops were streaming onto the pier and running down its length.

"You ready?" asked Cornelius. "We're going to take some out on landing. Then we'll have to fight our way through."

"You bet," said Naemi. Her voice was definitely stronger. No more chattering teeth. "Let's do it."

Cornelius was eager for a fight. His muscles quivered. His mind reeled in amazing sharp focus on everything he saw and heard. "Coming in!" he yelled.

The paraglider flew with terrific speed at pier level above the lake waters. Directly in front of them was the mid span of the pier and they smacked into the horde of running troops.

Smack! Pow! Boom! Cornelius slammed into the middle of them on purpose. Twenty-five flew into the air and off the pier. The glider wings snapped, but not before decapitating ten. Cornelius released the strut lines and retracted his arms just in time before the wires knotted and frayed, taking out the eyes of at least two. The cocoon sack rolled and rolled, knocking over more of Markhab's troops. The cocoon smacked into the rail at the pier's edge.

"Oomph!"

"Grr!"

"Arghh!"

Cornelius and Naemi struggled to winnow out of the sack. Mayhem and melee were everywhere. Cornelius was first on his feet. He was hot with adrenaline and a desire to do some real harm. In a flash he retrieved two knives from his satchel. Two men racing toward him choked in their own blood before dropping a meter before the pier's edge. Out the corner of his eye Cornelius saw Naemi dispatch another in hand-to-hand maneuvers. Her grin and the splash of her opponent into the water told Cornelius she still had her game.

Cornelius' eyes flashed wide. His heart pounded and he found his next target. Five more troops ran up the pier's planks. Punching a button on his jagged hand scimitar, the neck snapped out and formed a flared scythe. Cornelius bared his teeth and howled with a mighty cry as he accelerated right into the group. A clavicle snapped, one neck ripped near through, heart blood gushed out of another. The fourth lost an eye when a knifepoint pushed it out the back of a shattered skull. The fifth could not slow before sliding off the pier in the spreading pool of blood mixed with sleet.

Cornelius turned looking for more action and saw Naemi bent over, pulling her knife out of the throat of a man. Cornelius' eyes flashed in alarm when he looked past her. "Naemi! Look out! Hold on!" he yelled. The pier quaked and shuddered.

Naemi slipped in blood and nearly spun off the side of the pier but for Cornelius catching her and pulling her to his side. "Wha-!" she started, shocked and out of breath.

"Katzer's ship. He's rammed the pier. Run!" Cornelius interjected.

They raced to the end of the pier, which was a jumble of matchsticks. Looming high above them was the grey hulk of a lake ship. The matchstick rubble split and cracked as the ship started to pull away. Besides themselves, seven other strangers ran toward the ship. The other glider flyers? Three rope ladders dropped from above. Cornelius sheathed his knives and reached for one, pulling himself up, one arm holding onto Naemi as they both climbed.

Gunshots fired from behind them on the pier ricocheted off the ship's metal hull. Shots fired in return from the deck silenced those below.

A hooded man whose face was hidden concealed appeared at the top of the ladder and pointed a gun at Cornelius' face. "Name your sender or die," the man growled.

Cornelius had no time to think. A shot rang out on his left and a rope climber plunged into the dark waters. Wrong answer? A second climber took his place. Cornelius shouted "Renender!" The hooded man backed away and put down his gun. He offered an arm down to Cornelius. "Her first!" he shouted. He leaned aside of the rope and pulled Naemi up.

She quickly scaled the rungs and grabbed the man's gloved hand and strong arm. Up and over the ship's edge she disappeared. The man reached down again for Cornelius. The man's strength was great and in an instant Cornelius was standing on the deck of the lake ship next to Naemi in the wind and hail.

Gruff voices shouted to each other over the wailing wind. The ship's mechanical grappler arms swung above the deck. One reached down and began knocking apart the splintered wreck of the pier's end, freeing the ship's hull. A second swung wide and further. The sound of cracked wood and bone mixed with shouts of pain betrayed its target. The grappler scraped men clear off the pier.

Not far from Cornelius the other strangers swung onto the deck and huddled together against the outer wall of the ship's main cabin. Hooded crewmen stood guard around them. The man who had helped Cornelius and Naemi shouted to them "Stay down!" He then hurried past, leading some of the crewmen starboard. More crewmen rushed past shouting orders in heavy voices.

Above, the mechanical grappler arms swung again, all six now. At the same time the ship's rudder twisted and the ship immediately pulled away from the pier. More crewmen arrived, this time stopping to bend down on one knee each. They took aim over the edge and fired high-powered rifles at the pier. The gunfire rang out in a constant barrage back and forth, all while the ship tipped and turned away. The bullets and shouting and creaking added their voices to the screaming wind.

Lamps hanging off of metal arms protruding from the cabin swung wildly. The light they gave flickered and wavered. The scene from Cornelius' perspective turned as the ship turned. Soon he and Naemi and the others' faces were lit from the fire burning on the water's surface in front of them. The catastrophic wreckage of an airship ablaze filled their vision. Flotsam was strewn on the water's surface and arms waved in the orange light amid the incendiary rubble.

One of the hooded crewmen on the deck near Cornelius barked orders to others over the din. Then they took off running to port. The ship righted tail toward the pier, bow to open water. Cornelius looked up just in time to see the six winch beams above collect together then swing crossways past each other in pairs. Cornelius squeezed Naemi's shoulder and shouted to her "Look up!"

As each winch crossed paths with its pair, great black sails were released from where they'd been tightly stowed along the beam arms. The winches reached their extreme extensions and the gale filled the sails. Six deafening POPS! Cracked through the air as the wind smacked the sails. The ship lurched forward at tremendous speed. Just then the surface of the black sails erupted in light. A blaze of colors and patterns shimmered across their surfaces erasing the dark. The sails were covered in a skin of chromophores that worked together to pulse and undulate in patterns as complex as any cuttlefish.

Cornelius stood up and looked back to shore. More airships were landing and it was clear the military was seizing control of each ship as it landed. Then one airship actually opened fire on one of the spider transports. The other two spider ships returned fire. The airship exploded in the sky over the landing field. Even on its way down it continued firing at the transport. Just as the flaming airship crashed into a red balloon igniting it, the spider transport blew apart.

"Whoa!" said Cornelius.

"Ditto," was Naemi's reply.

The chromophore sails winked out and the fiery scene on the shore shrunk smaller and smaller in the distance.

The crewman who had helped Cornelius and Naemi onto the deck from the rope ladder barked orders to the others. "Ready the rescue rafts. The Captain's heading to the ship that's on fire. Bossin, take the newcomers down below and out of this storm." He and the other crewmen minus one hustled away.

"Yes Sir," said the one remaining, apparently Bossin. He turned and locked eyes on Cornelius a second, then at the others huddled in pairs or alone. "Come and follow," he barked. "This way, quickly." He hurried to starboard.

The strangers followed. Hesitation was evident, but there was no alternative. Each eyed the other awkwardly. Just ten meters down Bossin unlatched a door and pushed it open, pausing by the side. He turned and ushered to the strangers. "Hurry, Homints! Quickly in. Come and Follow!" His voice was high pitched and squeaky. "Rudders turning. Sails coming down. Quickly in. Come and follow!"

Cornelius was utterly confused. Was this Katzer's ship? Who were these strangers behind him? Homints?

Just then the ship reared into a sharp right turn. Cornelius and the others were thrown against the cabin wall just before Bossin and the open door. Above, the six winches lowered and drew in their sails. The ship slowed. Bossin let out a displeasing "Grrhumph! Hurry Homints!"

Naemi practically slid down the spiral staircase's two flights. Her feet scampered to keep up, slick from the sleet and rain. She had no time to gauge where she would end up before Cornelius tumbled down after her with his characteristic less grace. Then came a third, a fourth, sixth through ninth. Each hopped out of the way as fast as possible to avoid being knocked over from the one behind.

They stood near one end of a very long oval hall. It was not very wide, but spanned most of the length of the ship. The ceiling was three and a half meters high . Recessed lighting bathed the hall in a soft orange glow.

Naemi assumed a defensive stance against the wall opposite the door where the stairwell emerged. A low narrow metal bench protruded from the wall. Low narrow metal benches lined most of the wall space half a meter from the floor all along the hall. Between the benches were spaces that should be doors to other chambers in the belly of the ship, though none were visible. The floor bore a zigzag pattern of chevrons, white on black, or vice versa.

Naemi passed her gaze back and forth across the room. Nothing. Nondescript. It was clean, sterile, bland. What kind of room was this? What purpose did it serve? Just a gathering hall? It was so incomplete. There was a smell though. Naemi carefully looked over the seven strangers as they emerged from the stairwell into the hall. Two strong blond-headed kids less than two meters tall, maybe twins, boy and girl. Maybe still teenagers. There was an older girl with dark hair, red highlights, that hung straight long passed her shoulders. Pale skin and green eyes. There was an older rugged man with very short salt and pepper hair, goatee. There was a husky dark skinned man, tanned from much sun. He had jet-black hair and black eyes. There was a woman with curly auburn hair. She appeared older than Naemi and a little taller. Last was a short tubby man, bald. Naemi inhaled deeply the gathering, mixing scents as all the strangers took up equally nervous and defensive positions in the hall. Confusing scents. But these people weren't what she smelled.

"What now?" Cornelius sidled up next to her, close and in front. Cornelius didn't smell so good himself. Naemi bent her head and caught a whiff of her own armpit. *Yikes. Neither do I,* she thought.

Last down the stairwell was the crewman Bossin, still hooded and protected from the storm. Naemi observed the crewman carefully. He appeared just shorter, slimmer that Cornelius. Naemi flared her nostrils just slightly, twitched her nose. She leaned in toward Cornelius and began to whisper into his ear "Cornelius, this ship. It's…"

Just then Bossin threw back his hood. He was a Canine.

Bossin shook his head to loose ice and water. "You will be safe here. Sit and rest." Bossin's ears were short and pointed. One was bent a little. His eyes were large, round and milk chocolate brown. He had a short puggish nose above a wide mouth. He had short hair striped tan and yellow that repeated in the fuzz about his face and neck. Bossin removed his grey coat, revealing strong muscles beneath a form fitting yellow jumpsuit, tied at the waist by a black leather belt fashioned from the scaled skin of some sea creature. Black waterproof deck boots were on his feet. He had long arms that ended in stubby hands and fingers, thick and well worked.

Cornelius raised himself up in a protective stance in front of Naemi. He tried to take a step back but nearly into Naemi, who quickly stepped out of his way before he stumbled against the bench.

The other strangers reacted with equal surprise. One of the blond twins, the girl, spoke. "We need to see your Captain."

"This is Katzer's ship, isn't it?" asked the rugged salt and pepper man.

"Are we safely away from the lake docks?" asked the bald tubby man.

At that moment the ship leaned into a tilt. Cornelius tried to steady himself but fell onto the floor. Bossin just bent his knees and flexed his body against the direction of the tilt. The ship slowed further.

"We're not stopping, are we?" the tubby man complained. Naemi stared at him. He was too weasely. She didn't like him.

"It's alright. It's all right. Stay and be calm," reassured Bossin. "Stay and be safe. We are rescuing." Bossin turned to watch Cornelius regain his feet, staring at the Canine all the while. "First time seeing a Canine, Homints?" He then looked at Naemi. "Maybe not everyone." Bossin took in the other Humans. "Some yes, some no." He turned back to Cornelius. "I am Bossin. You are cold and wet. Sit and be well. I will take care."

Bossin closed the door to the stairwell. It disappeared with no seam visible. Then Bossin reached up and touched a spot on the wall next to where the door had been. He removed his hand, leaving what looked like a shiny smudge. Suddenly the smudge swirled and swelled large to about twenty centimeters in diameter, a rippled bulbous spiral shell-like structure. It looked roughly textured and glassy green. Bossin reached up and stroked one ridge, let his finger slip along a swirl and followed it around.

The bench behind Cornelius morphed into a gelatinous mass that folded in upon itself and was absorbed into the wall. All the benches did the same. Simultaneously the floor pattern rippled and moved. In the center of the hall a long table with a bench along each long side literally grew up and took form and shape and substance. The walls changed from orange and took on a camouflage visage of greens and black. Tack and netting stretched down from the ceiling, suspending clear glass floats in their embrace. Wide doors stretched open on all sides of the hall revealing chambers and passages to elsewhere in the ship, some going up, some going down, some curving left, some right, some straight.

Cornelius was mentally and physically drained, and confused as hell. "Naemi, what is going on?" he hissed aside to her.

She quickly silenced him with "Shh."

Bossin turned back to face the stunned Humans who gawked and stared and tried to make sense of what just happened. "Gurkbuzzel," he said, though the meaning of the word was lost on those that heard it. "Gurkbuzzel," he repeated. "They're very useful." Bossin's eyes narrowed and his brows furrowed to an expression of frustration. "Please," he finally extolled, this time extending both arms toward the table and benches. "Sit and rest. I will bring you what you need." Bossin moved past Cornelius went through a doorway. "Sit and rest."

As he moved passed, Cornelius caught a whiff of Bossin's scent. It was altogether different from anything he had ever smelled before. Cornelius had never in his life met a Canine, despite being born and raised on Lupus, such was the nature of the separation of species under which he had grown. Bossin smelled musky, of living in close quarters on a ship, and something else, some strangely, well, tangerine, too.

Naemi observed the others. The twins, she decided to call them, exchanged words in whispers. The salt and pepper haired man stared with the same speechless awe as the pale girl. The tubby bald man collapsed onto the bench nearest him, mumbling about being swallowed into the belly of the beast. The dark tanned man appeared the most calm. When Naemi looked on the older auburn haired woman, she was unnerved to find the woman had been looking at Naemi, following her eyes. The woman spoke.

"Well, I suppose we had better find out whom we all are." She looked down at the sniveling bald man, said nothing, then dismissively turned back to Naemi, stepped forward and offered her hand. "Hello. I am Orumnam."

Naemi took the offered hand. "Orum…nam?" she repeated back unsure.

"Yes. I am from Aran City."

At that the young blonds came forward. The boy said "I am Boglei. This is my sister Bogelia. We're from Big City."

The other introductions followed. The salt and pepper haired man was Renchant from Lupus City. The pale girl was Tentz from Lupus Major, as was Klendl, the tubby bald man, though apparently from different cities. The dark tanned man was Ramon from Big City.

The pale girl Tentz said "You know all of us and where we're from. What about you?" She nodded at Naemi.

"Yeah," added the tubby one, Klendl.

Naemi was full of apprehension. This was a confusing, unexpected and potentially dangerous turn of events. Not being on the Canine ship per se. Before Cornelius had the chance to answer, Naemi did it for him. "I am, N. This is C. We're from Shining City." The others did not need to know she

219

was from off world. And Cornelius' story was too complicated. Interestingly, this group represented all the Human inhabited regions of Lupus. And they were apparently all connected in some way to Renender.

"Maintaining a mystery?" the older woman Orumnam said.

"Is Orumnam your real name?" asked Naemi in return. The woman just smiled back and said nothing.

"So all of you flew in gliders, too?" Cornelius asked. Naemi turned to rebuke him with a cold stare. She did not trust these people, regardless of their connections to Renender. Now Naemi harbored more doubts about Renender himself. She withheld the cold stare from Cornelius. She might have asked the same question, though it was obvious some of them at least flew the other gliders to the pier.

"Yes. I've been taking lessons," said blond Boglei, beaming with pride.

"Fighting lessons, too?" the pale girl Tentz asked him.

"We just had to run fast, and remember the password," said his sister.

Interesting thought Naemi. To her knowledge, Renender had said nothing about a password. Had he somehow just told Cornelius? Naemi thought back to the rope ladder. How amazing that they had gotten on. Amazing they were still alive. "Why this ship?" she asked.

"It was the only one to come and rescue us," said tubby Klendl.

Orumnam spoke up. "No doubt we each have our own interesting reasons for being here under such remarkable circumstances. We might let sleeping do…, er, well now," she smiled and fell silent.

"We all have secrets," said salt and pepper Renchant. "No one's too dumb to figure that out."

"Oh don't ask. Just don't ask," whined Klendl.

"You talk too much," said Tentz, slapping him on the shoulder.

"So why are you here, Klendl?" asked Naemi. She was intrigued by the dynamics between the two. She thought to push their limits a bit to find out more.

Klendl whined again and squealed. "I told you not to ask."

Bossin appeared in the doorway. "Stay and be safe. You all are all safe. Take these." His arms were full of blankets, which he passed around. "Put these around you. They will take away the wet and the cold. You will keep the dry and the warm." The Canine boy paused in front of Cornelius and looked directly into his eyes. He cocked his head to the side just a bit, the side with the bent ear. He flared his nostrils and sniffed at Cornelius, smiled shyly.

Cornelius took the blanket awkwardly. Bossin was clearly aroused and did not try to hide it.

Naemi saw the entire exchange, and gave Cornelius that cold stare she'd earlier withheld.

A commotion ensued behind them as several more hooded crewmen emerged from the stairwell door. They bore a Human, dripping wet.

"Bossin! Here!"

Bossin left Cornelius and rushed over to the newcomers. The one who had called set the Human down onto the floor. The crew, four of them, removed their wet hooded coats. They were Canines all.

"Bossin, this one is cold. Give me a blanket, then get some saquash. Warm him from the inside out. Go and hurry."

"Going, hurrying," said Bossin. He delivered a blanket to the speaking Canine and disappeared through another door.

Cornelius drew closer to the Human lying on the floor. He looked up at the Canine and asked, "Can I help?"

The speaking Canine turned his attention to Cornelius. The Canine was roughly Cornelius' height, slightly more muscular. His eyes were piercing, wide bright and sepia in color. His facial hair was a mottled blend of orange, dark brown and black, some grey and white showing through. He wore a tight plaid shirt cut off roughly above his large rounded shoulders.

The fine mottled hair extended passed his powerful biceps, tapering off down his forearms, bare by the wrists. His skin was not quite as dark as Cornelius. "Do you know medicine art, Human?" he asked Cornelius.

"Not exactly," Cornelius replied. "But let's see." Cornelius bent down onto his knees. The Human was facing away from him. Black hair, olive skin. His clothing was a singed and torn uniform. Cornelius turned the man's head and let out a quick gasp. "Dardele!" He called to Naemi. "Naemi, it's Dardele, from the Valyon."

Naemi rushed over, aware that Cornelius had just given away her name. But no time for that now. "Is he dead?"

"If he was dead, we'd have left him in the water," said the Canine coarsely. His voice was deep and gruff.

Cornelius opened Dardele's mouth and cleared his tongue from his air passage. He bent over and pinched Dardele's nose, locked his mouth over the man's and blew. Dardele's chest heaved. Cornelius quickly climbed on top of Dardele and straddled him with his legs about the groin. Cornelius lay both his hands palm down over Dardele's heart and administered cardio pulmonary resuscitation 1-2-3-4-5, pause. 1-2-3-4-5, pause. Cornelius leaned in and locked mouths again. Blew. Dardele's chest rose. Then CPR again. 1-2-3-4-5, pause. Again.

Cornelius looked up at Naemi and said "Can you help?"

Naemi assessed that there was nothing she could do that Cornelius was not already doing. She was about to say as much when Dardele suddenly coughed up a green slurry all over Cornelius' face.

Bossin returned at the same moment carrying a skin flask and a small bottle, maybe smelling salts. Cornelius relaxed his knees to give Dardele some freedom of movement. As Cornelius started to get up, a large hand, missing two fingers, was held out to him.

"That is good medicine art, Human," said the Canine.

Cornelius grasped the hand and pulled himself up. This was the same hand that had helped him and Naemi up and onto the ship. "Thanks."

"I'm Raffir," said the Canine. "I'm the Grit Commander, after the Captain."

"Cornelius." He stepped over Dardele and stood next to Raffir. Side by side the two looked the same age, if Canines aged the same as Humans.

Below them, Bossin tilted Dardele's head up and tipped the flask to pour a red liquid into his mouth. "Shh Homints, quiet and drink. This will give strength."

Naemi smelled the drink. "Saquash. That's a strong drink."

"You know saquash, Human lady?" asked Raffir.

"I've been to the vineyard estates beyond Dog Lake, the far water." Naemi was revealing much by saying that. But she had to find commonality.

"The lady has seen some travels," said Raffir.

The other Humans quietly watched the whole scene, wary of the Canines. Orumnam finally spoke. "So, Naemi. Do you traffic often in Canine lands?"

Naemi turned and looked at the woman, but refused to answer. She turned back to Bossin and Dardele, who coughed and spattered on the floor. He tried raising himself on one arm. "He needs to sit upright," Naemi said.

"Bullgomble," said Raffir. The Canine walked the few steps to the glass spiral and brushed his hand over a part of it. The floor beneath Dardele morphed and took shape as a chaise lounge. Naemi and Bossin scrambled out of the way.

"That's amazing technology," said Cornelius.

"Gurkbuzzel," said Raffir. "They're very useful."

"What is 'gurkbuzzel'?" asked Cornelius.

"Gurkbuzzel. It is a land mollusk," answered Raffir. "Lives along the Canius shores of the lakes. They have chromophores and tactophores. They shape shift and make light."

"Is the whole ship made of them" asked Tentz.

Raffir laughed. "Ha. No. Or they might eat us. We manipulate them for our uses. Sails and this hold. The rest of the ship is wood and titanium."

Bossin closed the skin flask with a stopped and looked up. "We can talk to the other ships using the lights. Gurkbuzzels communicate to each other. We use them to talk."

"Wh-where am I?" Dardele regained lucidity.

"You are aboard the Tarvash," said Raffir addressing Dardele. "We rescued you from the water fire."

"Dardele, what happened?" Naemi pressed him.

Dardele looked up at here, then around him at the Humans and Canines in the room. "Naemi?" He saw Cornelius. "And Cornelius? You made it then."

"You know this man?" asked Raffir?

"We were aboard his airship," said Cornelius. "Earlier in the day."

"You must have an interesting story to tell," said Raffir.

Dardele related his story. "We were circling over the lake, dropping floater payloads into the water near the lake ships. Markhab's spider transports fired at us. They hit the fuel cells and our gas ballast ignited." He looked up at Raffir. "Did you rescue anyone else?"

"Only you," replied Raffir. "The others floated without movement. They are dead."

Dardele bowed his head and shook it slowly back and forth. "Captain Reldere. The Valyon. Gone. Markhab is a beast."

"The beast is strong, and his arm grows longer," said Raffir.

Just then another Canine emerged from the stairwell. "Grit Commander," said a shorter blond Canine, addressing Raffir. "We have retrieved the last of the payloads we could find."

"Then put the sails to the wind," said Raffir. "We will put the lake far between us and the beast's spider men." He turned to the other four Canines who had stood by quietly. "Set full sails out. To north we go. This storm will take us fast. Go and follow." The blond Canine turned and disappeared back up the stairwell topside with his crewmates following close behind. Turning back to the Humans, he said "Sit and rest. You will be safe here. Bossin, give them all saquash to drink."

Bossin handed the flask to Naemi and said "Saquash. Drink and be warm."

Naemi took the flask and tipped it over end, letting the strong red alcohol flow into her mouth. The hot elixir warmed her immediately. She passed it to Cornelius. He took a drink, then handed it back to Naemi who passed it onto the others.

"I hadn't known the lake ships were Canine," said Cornelius, addressing Raffir. "I've ridden the airships down to the docks before, but all the ship crews I ever met were Human."

"The Tarvash is the only all Canine crew to ply the waters between the lake docks and Big City," Raffir answered proudly.

"Then you'll take us to Big City," said the blond boy Boglei.

"The Captain gave the order to rescue any flyers. A handsome price was paid for your heads. We will take you to Big City."

"Not everyone made it aboard," said Orumnam. "The man above me on the rope ladder was shot."

Raffir turned to the woman, who straightened up taller than the Grit Captain. She exuded haughtiness.

"Hesitation is death in a battle like that," he said. "You could just as easily have not made it."

Orumnam took Raffir's response as a partly veiled threat. Her flushed scarlet face amused Naemi.

"You were paid to save us, not shoot at us from above."

"Grr," let out Raffir. "Shoot you still I could. Mind your place, Homints, and you may arrive to Big City still breathing."

"Humph! I won't be threatened," she returned, but she was no match against a ship of Canines. She sunk down onto the bench next to tubby Klendl. She grabbed the flask away from him over his protestations and gulped down a great swig.

"I didn't get any yet. Give me that back," Klendl cried.

Orumnam dropped the flask into his trembling hands. But before he could take a proper drink, the entire ship lurched forward. Saquash spilled all over Klendl's face.

Raffir chuckled, then said "Bossin will give you food and drink and bedding. We sail through the night." At that he turned to leave.

"Will we meet the Captain?" asked Tentz.

Raffir turned and said "You stay out of the Captain's way. He'll have nothing to do with you. You're paid cargo as far as he's concerned. Nothing more." Raffir turned and left, climbing the stairwell topside.

"What now?" asked Tentz. She finished her draught of saquash, the last in the flask, and set it down on the long table.

"Homints have difficulty listening," said Bossin. He moved over to the gurkbuzzel shifting device and flicked one notch on it. Plates, bowls and cups budded off the table's surface in a complete arrangement for eight. "I'll bring nourishment and drink. Sit and be safe." He hurried out of the hall again.

Naemi drew close to Cornelius. He put his arm around her. "Neat device, isn't it?" she said.

"It's bizarre," he replied. "There aren't any buttons or levers or moving parts. The controls appear to be in random locations."

"Maybe it uses electrical signals from the controller," suggested Naemi. "It may sense the intentions of the one using it, then carries them out."

"I've never seen anything like it," Cornelius said.

"Will Dardele be alright?" Naemi asked. The two of them looked at the Valyon's sole survivor. He was fast asleep on the lounge.

"He's fine," said Cornelius. "I could really use some sleep, too."

"We've hardly slept in two days," Naemi agreed.

"And I'm light headed from that drink. What did you call it? Sasquatch?" Cornelius moved over to the long table and took his seat on the bench.

"Saquash," corrected Naemi. "It's a berry wine, spiked with hard cider. Pretty good, isn't it? Rejuvenating."

"I'm relaxed, and hungry, and sleepy. All at the same time."

"Typical man," said Naemi, sitting down on the bench next to Cornelius. But her eyes betrayed fatigue no less overcoming than his.

"How far to Big City?" asked Tentz, to no one in particular.

"Not much more than a day and a half," offered Ramon. "If they sail a straight line. Though passage through the lake channel could slow us down. That's a narrow water way, between this lake and the next."

Bossin appeared again carrying a pot of some liquid. Under his arm was a bundle of leaves from which emanated a pungent fishy odor. He placed the pot in the center of the table and laid out the bundle, revealing a stack of pressed salted fish. "Guaresh and salted poar," he said. "Good for the blood and good for the sleep."

The others took their seats around the long table. Tubby Klendl ladled the soupy brew into a bowl and quickly slopped a spoonful into his mouth. He spat part of it back out into his bowl. "Agh. It's cold."

Bossin chuckled. "Impatient Homints. You must warm it if you want it warm. Use your thermophyte."

"The what?" asked Klendl.

The blond girl Bogelia picked up an odd shaped utensil beside her place and looked at it. It had the appearance of a spatula, but with a wide rippled scoop perforated such that it could not hold, scoop or serve anything. "This?" she asked.

"Thermophyte," repeated Bossin. "Put it to your food and press the button. Not for long. It makes hot fast."

Bogelia applied the thermophyte to her soup as instructed and touch a nub on the handle. Within seconds she had a steaming bowl. "Fascinating."

The others followed suit, and soon all were taking turns slurping and eating their hot meals.

Presently all had eaten, and all were tired. Bossin retreated the long table and benches back into the floor. Hammocks he caused to appear, descending from the ceiling. Each guest in turn took to a bed and rocked and swayed long into the night.

On some occasions Cornelius awoke to movement in the hold. Canine crew quietly entered and took up hammocked repose on the far side apart from the Humans. By the strange bioluminescence of the gurkbuzzel, Cornelius observed them. Raffir and Bossin climbed together into a large hammock and slept with arms wrapped around one another. Individual grunts and quiet groans, creaks and turnings, were the only sounds through the night.

Without, the Tarvash raced northward driven by the storm winds. Her sails flashed and rippled in light that pierced the dark, calling and answering to the flashes from other distant lake ships also driving north.

Standing along on the Tarvash's isolated bridge port above the fierce wolfhound prow with gnashing teeth, the shadowy hulk of Captain Katzer steered his ship. In the cold blinking lights, all that could be seen was the orange yellow of his eyes beneath the furred hood of his coat, the black of his extended nose moist, the glitter of a gold earring hanging from his right ear.

28 MINE CITY

The ground car maneuvered the mountainous heights as if gravity was not a factor. Indeed, neither the wind nor rain nor ice gave the vehicle much pause. Coming out of a sharp switchback overhanging a steep black abyss was deceptively like turning on a dime. The car's sensors judged pitch, velocity, incline, elevation and centripetal torque, to mention a few. Renender had to remind himself this was no bumper car. This car from Jarbed that Cornelius had left could really handle. It had taken the man from Shining City nearly a year to deliver it, the prize winning from a night of gambling. It was too bad that present circumstances limited Renender's ability to enjoy it for long. Ah well, the several hour journey into the mountains above Lupus City proved a fine test of its abilities. Better than spinning doughnuts at midnight on the horseshoe valley's flat landing field.

Two hours had passed since Renender had left Attisand on Sandy Field Park, and the city he knew and loved. Two hours since his encounter with Commissioner Corvus. Two hours along a road strewn with broken vehicles, panicked stragglers walking the lonely lane, beseeching any approaching vehicle for transport to the mines. Renender would not stop for any of them. He was surprised at the number who had taken to the mountains to escape the coming occupation, especially in this storm. But he wasn't surprised that none had gotten far. The titanium mines were a good ways distant. He had seen no sign of refugee, either body or vehicle or refuse, for an hour.

The temperature and humidity in the car was a comfortable twenty-two degrees centigrade. The gyroscopic levitating shocks were so efficient that even at a fifteen-degree grade and ten percent lateral tilt, the ride felt soft and stable, something like a bunch of marshmallows floating on honey. That was a very non-mechanical observation, but that description by Jarbed led Renender to test drive, and immediately covet, the car in the first place.

That was one year ago. Renender had been in Shining City for a business conference. The Free Orchard Growers Union was voting to admit a chapter from Lupus Major. Renender was interested in expanding his own market share in stone fruit, and plug a few titanium opportunities at the same time. It was also coincidentally an opportunity for a clandestine poker game with Jarbed.

An evening of gaming had turned from night to nearly dawn. Bielroth and Tolostok, the other two at the table, had folded two hands before, but stuck around to watch Renender and Jarbed bluff each the other. Jarbed had already won a concession contract for floating anti-mag null buoys, and Renender had scooped him for a cottage in the delta town of Star City. Beautiful place, from the picture. Before the sun climbed over the eastern mountains to illuminate Shining City in its scenic river valley, Renender decided to play bigger. His piece de resistance, an airship for Jarbed's car. Renender's old friend captain Reldere was glad he'd won that hand. Unbeknownst to her, he'd almost lost her Valyon. That was a fine ship, the best in the fleet. But no bluffing on Jarbed's part could beat Renender's hand of a high flush. Still, it'd taken a year for Jarbed to get the car to Renender, by way of Cornelius, this day.

Renender rounded out of the switchback and away from the bald shoulder that overhung the precipitous drop. The road straightened out and bore up a long canyon, sheer of cliff on either side. The road hugged the right rock wall. On the left side was a broken ditch that directed the rain's torrent away from the road, somewhat. But this was a good road. The local Union Mines Road Crew kept it in top working order. That was good for Renender tonight. It would also be good for Corvus tomorrow.

The car's green vision optics displayed an image of the canyon and roadway up ahead, but the picture was distorted by the wind and rain. Outside the car, blasts of water propelled by the wind burst against the chassis in a constant barrage that sounded and felt more like an avalanche of gravel than a deluge of water. Inside on the fuzzy green screen, the bursts resembled something more sinister. Renender imagined nightmare visages of howling, gnashing beasts, ferocious wolves and saber-toothed tigers, huge maws of apes and monstrous birds of prey, all crashing against the screen.

On Renender drove, through ever deeper and steeper canyons, around hairpin curves against sheer rock walls, treacherous switchbacks and blind corners. It was a challenging road in the best of conditions. Traffic was regulated between the mines and Lupus City, up every other day, down every other day. Passing was never advised except at rare designated widenings. Renender hadn't seen one of those for an hour. And Renender couldn't remember which direction this day was designated. Hopefully it wouldn't matter.

The mines. Mine City. It was the last bastion of Human civilization in the Canius Mountains and the source of economic prosperity for Lupus City. A destination in its own right, for the right palate. Mine City was dug into a titanium mountain, shaped and carved and worked into a marvel of a subterranean world. It began at the Portcullis, passed through seven magnificent gates, and culminated in the interior of a turban shaped mountaintop. How much longer until Renender reached the great Portcullis, one of the emblematic features of the mine community? It might be another hour yet.

Renender scrunched down into his seat shifting position, rotated his shoulders, flexed his spine. He wiggled his thighs, contracted his calves, such as he had, arched the crowns of his feet, wiggled his toes. He teased his haunch up just enough to give his butt cheeks some refreshing air, adjusted his balls. He sank back into the seat a little refreshed.

A quick glance at his dashboard and Renender spied a diversion. Not in the dangerous sense driving. Something to help. Music. He hit the button and head banger drums and screeching guitar melodies overlaid with wild youthful baying filled the car. Renender smiled, narrowed his brows and steeled his sights on the road. His knuckles whitened as he gripped the wheel more tightly at ten and one, his head tilted forward on his long neck. He nodded to the rhythmic beats of stomach thrumming bass. He pressed down on the accelerator just enough to feel it.

Renender did eventually pass two widened passing zones in the road for slow traffic, though there was none this night. They were barely designated as such, small one word signs just prior to each widening that advertised briefly to anyone alert enough to catch them on the treacherous turns, "PASS".

Renender had last been to Mine City three months before. It was for a quarterly meeting of the Titanium Miner's Union. Ostensibly in attendance as a notable citizen observer, he took the opportunity to hobnob with the local heavyweights of the union organizers. He maintained relationships with both the old guard and the newer generation of miners. It was always beneficial to remain connected. He was a businessman first and foremost after all.

Balthorelei was the newly invested leader of the Women's Professional Drill Bitters faction. Old Tychlo was still the Gravel Cementer Foreman. Renender also wanted to seek out the Trickle Depth Sounder too, whomever currently held that position. The Depth Sounder probed the furthest recesses of the mines for promising new titanium veins in the deep rock. But the Trickle Depth Sounder was rarely at the Portcullis or Plaza. Two years before Renender had met the then Depth Sounder, a haggard, half crazed and bedraggled fellow named Bordent. Back then he'd already held the lonely position for five years. The man seemed to hold little grasp of reality, at least that's what Renender had thought at the time. But Bordent had had stories to tell, about singing lost cities. How intriguing. Renender also needed to see his friend Jerembor, the Sergeant of Security at the Portcullis.

Hm. Jerembor. Renender would have no difficulty getting through the Portcullis this night. Jerembor was a handsome chap. Off his team, as it were, but the man's brother was a different story. A good five if not ten years older, Jerembor's brother ran a lucrative filming studio whose productions attracted numerous clientele as far away as Shining City and Big City, not to mention Lupus City and the mines themselves. Prurient desires needed an outlet, and Jerembor's brother marketed to that niche. Indeed, Renender had to admit his own leanings had been satiated on numerous occasions as a result of Renchant's films.

Renender did himself a favor by providing an escape for the man. Apparently Renchant had discovered a beautiful set of twins who doted on one another. Orphans no less. Physically sixteen, of course, though with bodies of twelve or fourteen year olds, and with the naïve minds of eight. Exquisite. Renchant had contacted Renender, convinced that Corvus might "sully them," was how he'd put it. The twins would fetch a pretty price together, and Renchant wanted to protect his investment. Only Renchant knew where he'd acquired the children, or "discovered" them, in entertainment parlance. There had undoubtedly been a business deal somewhere along the line. Whatever the exact situation, Renender had secured a means of escape for Renchant and his two investments. And Jerembor knew it. The brother was out of Lupus City by now, safely he had to presume. Nothing was certain.

On the mountain road, just out of a sharp left turn, the canyon walls pinched off to a tight gap just six meters wide. No sooner did Renender start through the gap when a flash of lightning shot through the sky in the narrows above. The thunderclap was immediate and the wave pulse smacked down through the canyon to the floor. The shock bounced the stealth car into the air. It knocked against the right cliff face, then ricocheted into the left wall, finally skidded back onto the road surface. The console dashboard erupted in lights and warning sounds. The sonar proximity detector showed a massive object incoming. Renender slammed to a complete stop centimeters in front of a huge boulder that crashed down the canyon to lodge stuck in a pinched narrow gap. He shut off the music and shut off the alarms and gulped back his heart that had almost leapt out of his throat.

Renender could not tell from the green vision screen if the passage through the gap was still open or not. Certainly the boulder was lodged above the road. He could see the space through to the other side. But was there enough elevation? The car was low to the ground and flat on top. Was it flat enough? Renender turned on forward visible light illumination, grabbed his parka, opened the door and stepped out.

The rain screeched down like scared spitting cats and the storm winds howled through the canyon like mad rabid bats. He was wet and cold to the core immediately. There was less hail than rain now, but that fact didn't make anything better.

Renender reached forward his hands and felt the face of the boulder, slid down and felt the underside. Water cascaded down it everywhere. The surface was irregularly angular, hard. But Renender could see the rock had many fracture lines. Some had slipped, some settled and compacted from the drop. He slipped through the gap to the other side and looked back at the car. Blinking his eyes did little to keep the rain anywhere but obscuring his sight. He reached under the rock again. Yes, there it was. A sharp point hanging down. He could see that the car would make it through but for this point. It would likely dent a groove down the center of the car's roof, if not pierce the chassis outright. Of course, it might stop the car from moving altogether.

He turned and looked ahead up the canyon. How much further to the Portcullis? Kilometers. He'd freeze to death before he'd ever get there walking. Renender turned back and looked on the ground about him. He looked for something with which to knock that point off, anything hard that he could swing. He clutched his arms and shivered.

There! He spied a rounded stone two fists wide holding back a rivulet of water in the broken ditch. Renender bent down and picked it up. It was bigger than two fists. Bigger than his two, anyway, and it was heavy. He swung around, aimed and hit it against the boulder point as hard as he could. He only grazed the side of the point, and his momentum flung the rock through the gap and out of his hands to hit the front bumper of his car. "Dammit!" he cursed.

Was the car scratched? Oh, it didn't matter! Where was that rock? Renender grabbed it and swung upwards at the boulder point again. There was a shatter. Hard flakes of stone broke off. Renender dropped the rock and felt for the boulder point. It was a "W" instead of a "V" now. Was that better? Shit. That was two grooves on the roof of his car instead of one, or worse.

This was frustrating. This was terribly inconvenient. Think! He paced. He looked back through the gap at the car. How much really did he need to knock off to get through?

He bent down slowly. He evened his eyesight exactly level with the boulder points. He looked passed at the roof of his car. Up, down he moved his head. Up, down. He reached out and felt the sharp rock points. They were narrow, and there was a bulge next to them, rough, fracture points, like little fault lines. He didn't need a rock, he needed a crow bar. Renender looked back at the car and smiled. Of course!

He ducked under the boulder and ran to the car door. Inside he popped the trunk and sped around to the back. He peeled back the matting in the trunk and felt for the preformed insert where the – there! – where the crow bar lay. He found the indented finger lift and pulled. Up came the crow bar. How long had it been since Renender had held one of these? Since he last changed his own tire. Stars, that was years ago. Years.

He ran back to the boulder and punched the pointed rock with the flattened end of the crow bar. He punched it again. He ducked under to the other side of the boulder. Smack! He punched it again. Renender felt for the pointed rock again. It wiggled. It was loose. He grabbed the points with his fingers and pulled. "Dammit!" He took up the crow bar again and punched again at the rock. "Out! Get, out! Ugh Ugh. Ugh. Damn!" His last blow missed wide and he hit his head on the boulder's face. "Ouch!" He wiped his bloody brow with his sopping wet sleeve. "I won't die out here!" Renender shouted at the blood and rock and mountain and storm. Round the other side of the boulder he smashed the crow bar into the stubborn rock. He continued to punch, hitting the rocky bulge. "Get out!" he yelled, eyes wide, mouth a mad grin of determination. He punched again at the little rounded bulge. "Agh! Agh! Agh!" Pieces flew off and out and finally it was done.

He dropped the tire iron crow bar and felt the boulder's bottom side. Was it enough? He picked up the bar again. He swung it side to side and back and forth across the boulder's underside. More rock pieces chipped off. He knelt down on one knee and looked through the gap at his car. He saw clear passed the bottom of the boulder and across the top of the car's roof. It was clear! Renender dashed back to the car, tossed the iron into the trunk, slammed it shut and jumped into the driver's seat. "Heat on!" he yelled hitting the controls. And he shivered.

Renender crept the car forward, gently, gently. He didn't hear the broken rocks and gravel crunch under the wheels as he drove over them. The proximity scanner still showed all black but the PP scanner, puncture/penetration, was silent. He kept onward slowly. The car rolled up and down over the rocks in the road. Over, over, up, over. Outside it was scrape, scrape, knock, scrape. Renender made it through. "Smooth like butter," he said aloud, and he sped off.

The heat blasting around and on him in the car felt good but didn't help much with drying. He felt like he was sitting on a sponge in a steam bath. It was certainly not comfortable.

Renender had certainly been comfortable just two nights before. He thought about that last joyful and peaceful night in Lupus City. It had been a date as much as a business deal. An evening of two-step chess in the Economic Association's Clubhouse on the city's chic upper west side flanking the valley's terminus perimeter. Breathtaking views. Oeur d'oeuvres, cocktails, conversation and intimacy in private chambers. Dinner, live music, slow dancing. What a blissful blur that almost was by now. And amid the revelry, Renender had also exchanged two thousand canisters of titanium gas for two thousand bushels of dorsein wool that Ramon had brokered from a Canius-Canton co-op. "The finest grade" the beautiful man had professed. And Renender knew it was.

Ramon had given Renender a coat of distinguished Clements Canton brocade and tweed as a gift. The inner lining and hood was of combed dorsein wool, a skein from the same herd as the profitable wool concession. Why hadn't he brought that coat along with him this night?

Ramon was the heir and first son of the Clements Clan in Clements Canton. Renender remembered that Ramon had breakfasted in the mezzanine of his office building with a delegation of canton orchard growers this same morning when Cornelius and Naemi had arrived. Goodness this was a day! Beautiful Ramon. Strong Ramon. He could fly a glider. He would make it back to Big City.

Renender thought of all the favors he'd had to cash in with Katzer, and they ran deep. Katzer's word was good. And so much, so many lives, relied on it.

On Renender drove into the high vales. He was almost passed the tree line.

Then the road would drop back down again a thousand meters zigging and zagging at a fifteen-degree grade. It was terrifying, but Renender had no time for such paralyzing feelings.

Strangely, he thought of something else he'd thought terrifying. He thought of that scary pale-faced girl with the pale blue eyes and jet-black hair. She looked like a perfect demon, and she was crass, mean. The bitch hated him and called him a faggot to his face. Renender would rather have pissed in her face and set off a grenade in her breeding tube and hurled her off the horseshoe valley's terminus. But she was the mayor's daughter. Tentz was her name. She was a consummate liar. She lied about her age, her interests, her friends, her past, even her parents. She sometimes claimed to be a daughter of the brute Markhab himself. Despite his hatred of the girl, he'd made a deal with her father to get her out of the city. And as a result he now held the sole concessionary rights to each and every one of the airship berths for the Airship Consortium. He doubted that meant much now. But it would prove immensely profitable if he survived to see the military occupation end. The mayor had said his bitch of a daughter could fly a glider, so Renender had given her one.

The road plunged deep into a grove of tessellated Lupin Pine. This species was native to the eastern spur of Canius Range. The trees' boughs bent downward and each leafy branch ended in a six-finger radial. Most of the rain was deflected away from the road by the tree canopy. Here the sub-arboreal road seemed subterranean.

He thought of his cousin Lyshen. He was a tree nut, knew all of them. Lyshen had been Renender's best friend during his adolescence. He'd never made fun of Renender nor ever stopped playing with him. Lyshen even campaigned in Renender's bid for the Student Council Presidency in middle school. He'd won, and immediately started wheeling and dealing. He'd even sold prom king and queenships in eight schools, even fixed several intramural sports matches that year. What a year. Lyshen. He and his wife had a glider. They would make it to Big City.

The road broadened out onto a great exposed shoulder of rock. It angled gently away from a stand of pines on the left. The road was wide here, and the right edge was a cliff that fell three kilometers down. The view was magnificent during the day in good weather. This was neither. Lightning flashed overhead. Thunder crashed out of the sky and blasted against the mountain's open buttresses. The sonic booms shattered bits of the rock faces, the pieces falling and joining the torrent of waters cascading over the road. Renender struggled to keep the vehicle hugging the left while the waters and debris tried to drag the car to the right. "Around and around baby," Renender mumbled to himself. "Hug the left. Hug the left." And the tires kept skidding.

Renender was feeling dryer now. But his butt still felt like he was sitting in a warm puddle. It was damned uncomfortable. He continued on around the bald edge and face of the mountain. It reminded Renender of a bald businessman from Lupus Major, an Orchard Growers Union representative, a valuable, if uncertain, contact. But the man was miserable, on the verge of despicable. He was also desperate to remain free from the grip of his military overseers. The man was wanted for something, that appeared obvious. Whether it was true or not was a different question. Klendl. He was a pig. But he had sold his life into Renender's hands handsomely. The man promised inside economic leverage in the heartland of Lupus Major, access to fields, orchards, vineyards, grasslands. Klendl had already successfully facilitated strike votes in a number of unions around Dula City in Lupus Major's interior. They were attracting Markhab's attention. Renender had provided the man a glider, and paired him with the bitch Tentz.

The road climbed in a dizzying ascent. Lightning revealed the bald mountain face in a dazzling flash of silver. The titanium mountain. And finally before him was the magnificent Portcullis. The colossal seven gates carved from the mountain were the gateway to the mines. The seven walls of arches, columns and plazas were an empiric display of grandeur.

Renender slowed. He did not exactly know what to expect ahead. Much as he had no idea to whom he'd auctioned off the other escape gliders. They'd gone to the highest bidders. One anonymous client had exchanged four hundred military grade pulse explosives. Those were now safely hidden. Renender had taken possession of those personally. Options.

As Renender approached the great Portcullis he thought of those two special friends of his and Jarbed. What a long shot, but arrange everything for them he did. Cornelius and Naemi. They would make it. Thinking on

Cornelius, Renender added out loud, "Just don't do anything stupid." The first gate of the Grand Portcullis reared towering above him.

Legend had it that the approach to the Portcullis and entrance to Mine City was never attempted in the morning to mid-day. The glare of the full sun off the sheer titanium mountainsides would blind any who stared at it. So it was said.

The main rampart was massive. Five huge pointed arches opened in its face, each twenty meters tall and five wide. The pillars in between were square and stood on double square bases. Above the five arches was a row of twenty smaller arches as windows. Electrified torchieres illuminated each window. Indeed, the entire complex was alight in electrified torchlight, flickering yellow, orange and red. The combined effect of seclusion, megalithic construction, storm, and torchlight, leant an air of ancient ceremony to the site. The craftsmanship exhibited great skill, knowledge and also pride. The surface of the rampart about the main arches was finely etched with mostly parallel lines, millimeters apart. Other lines just as fine crossed them, forming geometric patterns. The surface about the row of smaller arches was rough-hewn, complimenting the mountain behind it.

The Grand Portcullis was the first of seven gates leading into Mine City. Each gate was decorated to represent a theme. Renender drove through the center arch slowly. The ground car was dwarfed by the construction, lost in the rain.

The gate was five meters thick. Emerging on the other side, Renender was in a huge open court that spanned thirty meters before him. The ground rock had been excavated into huge blocks and reinserted as cobblestones for a giant driveway. On up ahead loomed the second gate and its great arches. It represented Beauty and Riches. Gems, miner's picks, sparkling rich veins and cave scenes replete with stalactites and stalagmites were carved in relief into the gate and walls opposite and beside. Renender drove the length of the courtyard completely alone in the immensity. More flickering torchlight fought with the storm and gave the place a haunt.

The third gate depicted Mineralogy and Volcanism. Out from its arches and walls seemed to grow protuberances of crystals, geode interiors and the faux openings of lava tubes.

The fourth gate celebrated Exploration. It sported scenes of spelunkers with expressions reflecting the awe of discovery. Stalactites hung down part way from the arch and column tops. Stalagmites rose in clusters around the column bases. Scenes of subterranean lakes and seas filling huge halls of the deeps were carved into the gate and walls.

The fifth gate appreciated and encouraged Science and Technology. Devices from utensils to car chassis to rocket ships were depicted.

The sixth gate was the Gate of Possibility. Only interwoven patterns of harmonic geometric shapes adorned the walls.

The seventh and final gate was the Gate of Remembrance. Great anthropomorphic shapes with indistinct features were carved in high relief. Below them were depicted miners retrieving and mourning the fallen in deep and dangerous places. No individual faces could be discerned. There were scenes of accidents and the dead in repose, friends gathered and bowing around them. Renender drove through the great silent arches of the seventh gate.

The courtyard was unadorned. The spurs of the titanium mountain itself formed the walls. Before him on the opposite side of the huge plaza rose the carved entrance to Mine City. The mountain rock was fashioned into a great spiral onion dome, resembling the spiral shell of a monster mollusk. It echoed the onion-domed tops of the buildings of Lupus City. The top of the structure upheld a spire. The dome itself was one hundred meters above the plaza floor. Steam escaped from unseen vents behind the structure giving the scene an added eeriness. The entire structure from gate to gate to onion dome, as the mountain, was all solid titanium. A great sealed cave formed the entrance to the mines. It was formed as the opening of a shell and was twenty meters tall by five meters wide. The surface of the gate to the cave was carved in the shapes of two great miners, a man and a woman. They barred the way with crossed pick and shovel. The rest of the surface was etched in chevrons.

The entrance was sealed shut. Renender pulled his car up to the gate and stopped. "Closed," he said aloud. "I've never seen it closed." Lightning flashed overhead bounding across the sky, the bolts illuminating the silent sentinels in the gate. Renender reached into the glove compartment and retrieved an infrared key fob. He set the signal frequency, aimed it at the gate and pressed the button. Nothing happened. "Hm." He pressed again, nothing. "How to open it?" Renender mumbled. He searched through the windows of his car for some call box or signaling device. He illuminated the gate with his lights, but the reflection off the titanium surfaces all around him was blinding. "Agh!" The lights went out. But for all that, he could see no way in. Frustrated, and already this far but on the wrong side of the mountain, he climbed out of the car to look at the gate up close.

He stood in the driving rain, bone cold, before the gate ornament of the male miner's knees. He reached out to touch the relief surface. At contact, amber, green and red beams of light swept over the area from hidden scanning sensors, finding Renender and his car. At first Renender froze in the light more out of surprise than any instinct to hide. But only by identifying him would those silent sentries in the gate admit him on a night like this. Renender began waving his arms and shouting "It's me. Renender. Please let me in." Three times the lights swept the area. Then the lights winked out and the great gate opened.

He reclaimed his place in the driver's seat, wet again. But no matter. He pulled forward into the cave tunnel entrance.

Inside, the road was flat in contrast to the crowned road on which he'd traveled the past few hours. The walls bowed out in concave arches on either side, meeting in the round above. Their surfaces were smooth. Electrified amber torchlight gave the tunnel an eerie feel. The road inclined up and twisted around to the left. Up and round, up and round Renender drove. The turn grew tighter the further in he went. The illumination became more intense as the walls seemed to creep closer in on one another. One more tight turn into their pinch and the way fell open into an expanse. On each side the walls retreated and climbed higher. The ceiling vaulted far overhead. He stopped the car.

The expanse formed almost a great semi-circle. In three dimensions he was in a quarter of a sphere. A great wall opposite Renender bifurcated the circle. He was in a great staging hall. On the right, transports sat parked in rows fifteen wide and thirty back. All were laden with full cargos of titanium ingots ready for the foundries and factories of Lupus City. On the left were stationed emergency response vehicles and mountaineering support pods, the kind that grappled onto cliff faces and rappelled into canyons on rescue missions. Near the far back wall was a large area reserved for Guest parking. Renender would be a Guest tonight. He drove on fifty meters and pulled into a parking slot. He set the brake. He grabbed his satchel from the back seat and exited the vehicle, activating the car's security system. He dropped the card key into a pocket in his parka.

In the center of the far wall, rising from the geographic center of the sphere, two colossal statues rose up and straddled the ceiling with outstretched arms, a man on the left and a woman on the right. The stood legs together with their heads bowed between their arms that held up the vault of the sky. Renender looked up to see the stars in their right positions in the night sky of the spring equinox glitter overhead. They were precious stones mined from the mountain and backlit. The hall was filled with a rainbow of light cast from emeralds, rubies, diamonds, sapphires, garnets, opals and more from on high. The great double helix constellation arched across the north and disappeared into the bifurcating wall. The two Atlas centurions formed a central pillar. At their base was a kiosk. Renender approached.

The ornate structure was carved out of the floor from titanium and gilded in gold and onyx. It was only four meters wide, six high, arching in a high spire. Two reception guards in grey and silver uniforms with green trim and epaulettes stood together. A scantily clad woman, tall, long legged, hour glass figured, fair and brunette, stood beside a loin-clothed man, tall, muscular, brown hair with smooth chest and legs but for a treasure trail down around his navel. The two wore sandals that laced to their calves. Gold bands clasped their wrists and biceps. Both appeared in their early to mid twenties. They were the official representatives of the Brothel Guild.

"Good Greetings this night," said the man and woman in unison.

"This is a dire night for visitors," said one of the guards, a short but strong man of blond hair. "What draws you here at such a dangerous time?"

"Good Greetings. I am Renender, of the Airship Consortium. I bear tidings and news, and I seek shelter and counsel." Renender looked at the fine attractive man, the woman, then back to the guard. Saliva welled in his mouth. He swallowed.

The other guard was a tall woman with short-cropped red hair and a freckled face, just slightly shorter than the male guard. She looked on Renender with a scowl. "It is a dire night on a dire day," she said. "We've heard the rumors from Lupus City."

"Commissioner Corvus is there from Cronapolis. His army is at the Lake Docks. They will be in the city tomorrow." Renender shivered, clutching his hands to his elbows. He was still wet.

"I know of you," said the redheaded guard. "You might be someone whose name Corvus knows. It would be ill to allow you to stay here."

The male guard looked at his partner condescendingly. "Renender, forgive my partner. We will not turn an esteemed visitor away on a night like this. Fifty credits for entry. How long do you plan on staying?"

"I would like to leave my departure open, for now," Renender replied.

"One long-term pass then," said the guard. "Three hundred more credits. That's three-hundred and fifty total."

"A bit more expensive than I remember," said Renender. He fished a credit voucher card out of his pocket and handed it to the man. The guard fed it into a machine, confirmed the transfer of credits, then handed the voucher card back to Renender.

"Mine City offers an extensive suite of options to please any Guest," said the attractive scantily clad woman.

"Specialty services to interest any Guest with discerning tastes," added the beautiful man.

"Enjoy your stay in Mine City, Mr. Renender," said the male guard. He reached his arm across the machine console passed his partner and deactivated the holographic bifurcating wall.

Now an open chasm dropped in place of the wall. It was a barrier from left to right. The chasm was five meters wide. On the other side opened up the Great Plaza of Mine City. It formed the second half of the semi-circle chamber in the mountain. On the far side of the Plaza eight tiers of walkways were cut to form a series of promenades. Arches and columns formed the façade. Small waterfalls cascaded down elaborate channels. Ferns and colorful rubber mint plants grew around the water and against colorful tall crystals that seemed to grow out of the ground. And there were the people. People walked together, visited, sat on benches and laughed. They seemed to not notice the five on this side of the chasm. The well-to-do Guests in spa robes or garish designer outfits with their Escorts mixed with merchants, artisans, entertainers, students, security personnel and of course miners looking for places to spend their credits. Some hurried, others walked or strolled.

Occupying the arches and filling deeper recesses were boutiques, information centers, museums and tour operators. Above those were Guest Houses and entertainment centers. There were restaurants and bars, gaming establishments and brothels. Music and song filled the chamber.

The male guard near Renender touched another control on his console and a great titanium bridge, four meters wide and one meter thick, extended rapidly from the opposite edge of the deep chasm. It clanged when it met and attached to this side.

Renender shivered again. "I sometimes forget about that chasm," he chuckled.

"We have our defensive measures," said the female guard.

The male and female Escorts came around, one to each side of Renender, and hooked arms around his.

"Come, Renender, we will get you clean and warm," said the woman stroking his ear.

"Let us pleasure you," said the man. He bent over and kissed Renender on the neck.

Renender took a deep breath and sighed loudly. The three crossed the bridge to Mine City.

From the Plaza view, Renender and his Escorts seemed to suddenly materialize on a pier extending out into a great subterranean lake. The jeweled stars overhead shimmered on the water's dark surface. There was no sign of the carport entrance beyond the chasm.

"My dears," stammered Renender as the trio walked safely onto the solid surface of the Plaza. Beside them was a low sign that stated, *Stay Away From Edge. No Bottom.* "You heard what I said back there. I am not here on a pleasure visit." The bridge clanged into place behind them.

"Nevertheless, we will see you safely to your destination," said the woman.

"We, too, are a part of the Mine's security measures. Do not underestimate our abilities."

Renender looked on the twain again. Both were in the primes of their youth, strong as could be. He looked about him and noticed other Guests, with Escorts. He saw students and tourists, with Escorts. Standing beside stalls and in storefronts, were Escorts. The thought occurred to him that he might not go where he pleased here. "Take me to the Empalasor Hotel. I need a suite, and a bath."

"An excellent choice," said the man, Jeaneau.

At the top level of the tiered Mine City, Renender paused to look out the Empalasor's lobby terrace at the Plaza below. There were the people strolling and enjoying themselves up to the holographic lake's edge, beyond that the deceptive serenity of the cavern with its twinkling jeweled stars shown down on the near still waters. *What would suddenly appear out of that false sea, a day or so hence?* he thought. He turned away from the terrace and checked into a suite.

Renender's suite was large even by the garish standards of many of Mine City's eccentric Guests. There was a receiving room, an inner room for entertainment and reading, and the large bedroom. Tapestries hung from the rock hewn titanium walls. Woolen carpets covered the floors. These softened the sounds and warmed the rooms. The furniture was heavy and wooden. The one element that residents and Guests to Mine City always craved was wood. The subterranean world was quick to impress itself upon Guests. But it was also oppressive in a claustrophobia that was difficult to mask. Even the stoutest craved bits of the world above. Enough natural sunlight was fed down into the depths through fiber optic cables and illuminating sun lamps. Wood, its grain, fragrance and feel, was the luxury.

Renender enjoyed a sweet and sultry hot bath. His Escorts Jeanette and Jeaneau massaged and caressed his physical tensions away. What was left, the mental stress of leaving his home, was muted but not absent. For a time he almost forgot about Markhab, Corvus, Cornelius and Naemi. Almost. The Escorts dressed him in fine orange and brown brocade from the Empalasor's Guest boutique. Renender admired himself in the finery. Such a temporary distraction he thought, considering where he intended to go. He would have to leave it behind. But not just yet.

Thirty minutes later, they were back on the Plaza. Renender wore a suit, smart and chic.

"Take me to see Jerembor," said Renender to Jeanette.

They passed into the Plaza and among the people. Soon he was an indistinguishable personage Escorted through the city like so many others. How many really knew that Corvus was in Lupus City? Much of Mine City was a non-stop parade and party. Here, business deals and fortunes were made, then lost. It was a getaway, a hideaway. It was also knowledge, wealth and discovery, for behind the façade of Mine City were the mines. Wealth there was uncounted. Would Markhab's annexation of Lupus City and the mines mean much difference? Some might not think so, or even care to. This place was rich.

"You Beast!" A woman shouted from a second terrace arch. She leaned out over the edge. She pointed down at them. "Renender! It's you, you bastard!" she wailed.

Renender stared up at her trying to find some recognition.

"My two babies. My twins. I know it was you. Where are they?"

Oh my stars, thought Renender. Those were hers? The ones Renchant has? He remembered her now. She was a gaming mistress, Tolstoi. She was from the Rogert Quick Picks gaming room. But what...."

"Under my very nose, you son of a bitch! While I waited on you!"

The crowd slowed and attention turned on the woman and Renender's party. A group of rowdy university students stopped and shouted "Hey what's up?"

She had been the table master, three months ago when he'd last been here, Renender remembered. That's when Renchant and he made the deal to guarantee safe passage for three. Those investments of Renchant's, those kids, they were hers. Renchant set me up for sure. "What did I do to…."

"Mr. Renender," said the woman at his side, sternly with grace. "You have a reputation."

"I can take care of this," leaned in the male Escort. He scanned the second terrace around the screaming woman. He was looking for, there! Another Escort, just to her right. A scantily clad woman as sexy as his partner accompanied an elderly woman, a Guest, bedecked with diamonds in a loose beige dress of sequins hanging off her frame. They were headed toward the screaming woman, outside Rogert Quick Picks. He gave a discreet whistle like bird song, a secret signal.

The Escort near the screaming woman heard, turned, saw and reacted. She slipped away from her paying Joan and swiftly, gracefully, appeared at the screaming woman's side. She whispered something in the woman's ear, kissed her cheek, smiled, gently touched the woman's chin. At the same time with the other hand she withdrew from a secret pouch a tiny gilded tube and sprayed a fine mist in the woman's face.

The woman stopped screaming. She relaxed into a stupor of euphoria and slumped down, guided by the Escort who said soft words to her, and deposited her onto a bench. The woman slept.

Another Escort arrived and assisted. The female Escort slipped back in the arm of her Joan. "Forgive me, Madam, but the woman was just carrying on…." She winked down at the man on Renender's arm.

"Nice," whispered Renender. He glanced at both his Escorts and nodded approvingly.

"Let's get out of here," said his female companion. They exited the Plaza and disappeared up a stairway through a rococo garnished arch. A tiny sign beside the entry read in a flowery script *Bazaar del Fundo, Especiale*s.

Such cryptic phonetics, thought Renender.

The carved steps led up to the second terrace. But this section was closed off to the main second tier promenade. A bazaar opened up, revealing advertisements for high-end tastes, special pleasure services and copulation rooms, associated with boutiques to browse and look busy in.

They passed several Escorts, some with their Johns and Joans. Just passed a sign advertising Specialty Dentistry and through an arched doorway Renender was led into a dark smoking club. Stacks of books in cases and art on walls looked down on leather chairs, couches, tables with games, ashtrays. Above all drifted smoke, agitated by hushed conversations. As outside, many of the well dressed were attended by the scantily clad. About the room, glasses clanged on tabletops, ices jumbled, pipes and cigars started, followed by coughs, and whispered conversation. The sign above the door read *Men's Lantry Smoking Club, Women Admitted.*"

Renender turned his head to the woman on his arm, smiled and asked "The Sergeant is here tonight?"

"He's off duty," the woman replied, smiling back.

The rooms were sided in dark hewn rock surfacing. Torchieres gave just enough light that kept the chairs, couches, tables and bar private.

The Escorts took Renender passed a table of four, a man and woman with their female and male Escorts. They played the card game Jarmble High Stakes. Passing one couch revealed a conversation snippet. "When he comes home, if he's carrying her pheromone, the robot will isolate him in the foyer. He won't survive being carved into a gourmet rack of tenders, one thousand pieces. That's about how much he's worth." Renender chuckled to himself. People always scheme.

They passed a table where a handsome blond haired man in his forties sat. He sported a goatee and a sapphire earing in his right ear. Next to him sat an older hefty man puffing on a cigar and talking.

"I hear the Orchard Grower's Union strike is spreading to more regions in

Lupus Major. Several chapters in the Cantons are funneling them credits."
The man took a deep draw from his cigar, held it, eyes half closed. He held
it. He exhaled. Then he coughed. "You know what that makes the Union?
The Opposition. The Enemy." He took another draw from his cigar and
noticed Renender.

Renender's party stopped at the table in between. The man on his arm
spoke. "My gentlemen, please forgive this interruption." He turned to the
blond man. "Your audience, please."

Jerembor turned and peered up and them. He recognized Renender and sat
up straight. He leaned in toward his smoking comrade and said softly "If
you would excuse me, Pillar." Then the blond man stood up and offered his
hand to Renender without calling him by name. "Come, let us talk."
Jerembor led them to a private booth under darker lighting against the wall.

"Jeanette, Jeaneau," Jerembor quietly said. "A moment please." The Escorts
released Renender and sank back into the shadows of the room.

A waiter appeared and silently poured Renender and Jerembor two cups of
tea then retreated. Jerembor leaned in and said, "Renender, you are here. I
know I won't like it. Tell me the situation in Lupus City."

Renender looked around the room. No one was near, but the place was
busy. It was deceptively private in the dark. He picked up his cup of tea,
blew on it, smelled it, closed his eyes. Oh, it was meerchamomile. Ahh.
Warm and soft and comforting tea. Renender sipped. He savored. He
opened his eyes and looked at the man across from him.

"Jerembor. You will be cut off tomorrow. And besieged the next day.
Corvus sits in Lupus City. The Councils have already cowed to him. The
occupation has begun." Renender sipped his tea. Then he added "There
was a commotion in the Plaza when I arrived. The rough side of a delicate
business deal. A complete surprise."

"It doesn't matter," Jerembor cut him off. He whistled to a waiter and said
"A Smokey. Triple." Jerembor turned back to Renender and asked "What
else?"

Renender replied, "I brokered the spread of the Orchard Grower's Union strike."

Jerembor stared at Renender without saying another word. Jerembor could play it cool, too. He picked up his cup of tea, held it under his nose and eyes with head bent down to catch the steam in his face. He smelled the extent to which the brew had steeped. The steam caused his eyelids to flutter. The water was still too hot to sip without burning his lips or tongue. He blew gently over the surface of the tea. The waves set off by the contact with his breath met the cup's circumference and rebounded back to meet at the center of the cup. It repeated. Jerembor now took a sip. Damn, it was still too hot and he burnt his lips and tongue. He set the cup carefully back down onto the table. Only then did he look back up at Renender.

Jerembor straightened up in his seat, squared and flexed his shoulders, arched his back. Then he calmly returned his attention to the private space over the tabletop between them. His eyes darted over Renender, noticing the attire. It was plain, for Renender. "You bought those clothes here. Did you not pack your own? A step below your usual de rigueur. Are you trying to stand out, or blend in?"

"I don't intend on staying, Jerembor, if that's what you're worried about. I realize my presence is a likely liability right now."

"You could be a bargaining chip, too," Jerembor said. He took another sip of his tea. He couldn't taste it now. "We have plenty of accommodations for a Guest like you. Some more discreet than others."

Renender considered Jerembor's statement. Was that his position? He knew there was no escape from Corvus, even here in Mine City. Renender's hopes rested on the slimmest of possibilities. "Is that your offer to me?"

The blond man scratched his goatee, leaned back in his chair and stretched out both arms over his head, then clasped his hands behind his head. He smiled. "Not mine, friend, but that may be the Adjunct Mayor's offer to you. By now, I'm sure she knows you're here. You won't be allowed to leave."

Renender threw back the rest of his tea and swallowed. It was lukewarm. He set the cup down on the table with a slight clang. Too loud, he thought. Then, "I wasn't planning on leaving by the front door."

Jerembor furrowed his brow in confusion and said, "I don't understand."

"You don't have to," Renender said. "Just do your job. I won't interfere, or be a nuisance." He leaned in, signaled Jerembor to do the same. "In fact, you may wish to impound my ground car. Keep it safe, out of the way, away from the Adjunct." Renender retrieved the auto's key card from his parka and slipped it across the table to Jerembor. "Here. Pretty black one in Guest Parking. Ask your lovely goon squad to point it out, wherever they are," Renender said looking around the darkened space mockingly. They were beautiful, wherever they were.

"You're kidding," said Jerembor, taking the card and slipping it into his shirt pocket. "Should I ask you any questions?"

"About the car?" said Renender. "It's mine. You can ask about that."

"Not the car," said Jerembor. But he got the point. "Since you're cooperating, and NOT considered a flight risk…where would you go? You may book any lodging you wish."

"Thank you," said Renender. "First, I want to look someone up. Have you seen Tychlo?"

"That old coot?" Jerembor laughed. "You two go way back. Yeah, he's around. Hangs out at the Geode Club. He's probably there now."

"Thanks, Jerembor. You stay safe. Corvus will want to keep the mines open, and this little underground cash cow paradise in business, too. Though he might be planning some management shuffle. Mind your options."

"As you, my friend." They shook hands. As Renender got up, he added "Your brother made it out."

Jerembor paused a moment, then visibly relaxed. "Thank you," he whispered. The he whistled, and Renender's Escorts emerged from their shadowy repose. "Renender may enjoy any of the fruits we have to offer."

"Yes Sergeant," said Jeanette. And the three left, leaving Jerembor to finish his tea. He sat back down. Finally the cup had reached a temperature he could enjoy. But he still couldn't taste anything.

On the way down the carved steps back to the Plaza, Jeanette asked "Where do you wish to go now?"

"You will not be retiring soon, Mr. Renender?" asked Jeaneau. "The hour is late."

"That it is," replied Renender. But he yet had much to do. "I will go out for a drink first. There is a friend I hope to meet. You may escort me to the Geode Club."

"That is not one of our finer establishments," said Jeanette. "Are you sure you wouldn't prefer the Empalasor's VIP Lounge?"

This one spends too much time trying to steer me where she wants, thought Renender. *No doubt the Adjunct Mayor had faith she'll keep me under a tight reign with this one.* "Perhaps after," he said with a smile. *Better to feign compromise with her.* The three descended to the fifth level where the Geode Club operated.

The club was dark and full of cigar smoke, more than the filters could adequately scrub. The tables were round and metal, and wobbled unevenly on the floor. The chairs too were metal, with cushions that only hinted at comfort. Only the bar itself sported wood, a structure of cabinets and compartments backed with a mirror reflecting assorted spirits.

The bartender was a middle aged haggard man, pale faced, with long grey hair slicked back behind his shoulders. Renender and his Escorts sidled up to the bar.

"Well, Renender. What a treat. How are things holding up with you?" the bartender asked.

"Mack, it's been awhile," Renender replied.

"That it has," said Mack. "I hear there's trouble come to the valley. I hope you didn't bring any with you." He turned his back to reach up and retrieve a cut glass bottle of rose colored liquid. He turned back and drew a glass from below, presenting it to Renender. "Cursple?"

"Please. Thank you, Mack."

The bartender poured the drink and slid it to Renender. He looked at the two Escorts and asked "You?"

"Just water, please," said Jeaneau. Jeanette just shook her head.

"Anything special I can do for you tonight?" Mack asked Renender. He handed a glass of water to Jeaneau without looking at him.

Renender sipped his drink. Cursple was distilled from rose nectar with blossom hints. A couple of drinks usually went down fine, but a third was often enough to knock him on his butt. *Just one for tonight*, Renender thought to himself. "I'm trying to stay as far away from trouble as I can get," he said aloud.

"This is a good place to get away from trouble behind you," said Mack wiping clean a glass with a bar towel. "But most people find new trouble here. I'm just saying."

"Mm," acknowledged Renender, taking another sip. He leaned in toward the bartender and said, "Actually Mack, I'm looking for an old friend, Tychlo. Is he here tonight?"

Mack gave a nod in the direction of the back of the club. "Side table on the right, near the stage."

"Thank you," said Renender. He pulled out his credit voucher card from a pocket, inserted it into a reader in the shape of a geode sitting on the counter. It displayed a price glyph. Renender authorized the purchase, then added thirty-five percent for a tip. He returned the card to its hiding place. Tilting his head to Jeaneau he said "Some privacy please. Wait here." He left the bar and the Escorts and Mack to cross the room.

Jeanette moved to protest and reached for Renender's arm. Jeaneau countered it in mid-reach with his own and shook his head.

"I'm not letting him out of my sight," whispered Jeanette, angry she'd been reproached.

"Then don't," said Jeaneau back. "But give the Guest his privacy."

"Renender is not here as a Guest," snapped back Jeanette. "He has a reputation for sinister dealing, scheming and political maneuvering."

"Then he's in good company," came back Jeaneau. "He fits right in."

"Hey, you two be clear about something," Mack butted in. He filled Jeaneau's water and gave one to Jeanette. He tapped the top of the geode reader with the palm of his hand and said "Registry says he's a Guest, so he has Guest's rights. No customers of mine are going to be harassed tonight. Tomorrow may be a whole different story, but we'll be civil and normal tonight."

"Humph," Jeanette let out. But Mack was right. Tomorrow would be a whole different story. She grabbed her water and turned to lean her back against the bar facing the stage and Renender.

The Geode Club had about fifteen tables organized loosely around a small stage in the back. Amber, white and blue lighting illuminated a woman in a red dress. She crooned into her microphone a sultry song to the slow cadence of the three-man band behind her. They wore black suits with red lines and buttons, square black hats atop.

There were maybe twenty people in the club maximum. Most were miners with no Escorts. Near the front at a dark table against the right wall Renender found an old man, unshaven, balding with slicked back white strands of hair and a patch over his right eye sitting by himself. A bottle of brown Brunel spirits was on his table, half full, next to a glass of water and a shot glass. The man leaned back in his chair facing the singing woman, his head slowly bobbing in synch with the music.

"Tychlo, you sot," said Renender. He pulled a chair over from the next empty table. It's feet scraped against the floor. He sat down.

The old man turned in surprise and squinted his one eye at Renender. "Who?" he asked.

Renender leaned in. "Old friend. When are you going to come down the mountain and ride in one of my airships?"

Old Tychlo relaxed with a laugh. He grasped Renender hand, which held his drink, and caused it to spill. "Re-nen-der," he said slowly. "I haven't left the mountain in thirty-five years. You're not getting me off solid ground."

"Nor out of it," Renender added.

"What brings you up here? You here to negotiate higher union dues? They're too high already." Tychlo gave Renender a chuckle.

"Enjoying the local amenities," Renender said. He sipped his drink. "And looking up old friends."

"Oh? Do I owe you money?" Tychlo asked.

"Nooo," said Renender. "But maybe a favor or two."

"Ah. Those troubles down in the city," said Tychlo. "I've heard. Markhab is making his move. Finally sending his cronies in for the spoils. I always knew it was coming. You can't hold back military types from wanting to rule the world." He picked up his bottle and poured himself a shot of Brunel, three quarters up. "Wet your whistle on this," he said presenting the glass to Renender.

Renender shook his head. "I'm not mixing my drinks tonight. But thank you."

"What are ya drinkin?" asked Tychlo.

"Cursple," said Renender.

"Not bad," said Tychlo. "She's a cunning mistress, Cursple. Lulls you into complacency before she deprives you of your memory."

"I'm only having the one," said Renender.

"That's how she gets you," said Tychlo. "Now Brunel, you know what you're getting into with the first swallow." Tychlo tossed back the spirit, chased it with his water. He gasped, shook his head. "Yeah."

"How's your health?" asked Renender.

"Never better," answered Tychlo.

"Keeping busy?"

"As much as ever."

"Doing what?" Renender chuckled. "You're retired."

"I'm still a miner by rights," said Tychlo. "Just 'cuz I lost an eye doesn't mean I don't fill a valuable position."

"When was the last time you were on a dig?"

"Oh, been maybe four years, since I lost my eye."

"As I said." Renender took another sip from his glass.

"I'm a consultant these days," said Tychlo. "But admittedly, I'm not consulted much."

Both men laughed. They paused in their conversation to watch the singer, the band, listen to the music.

Finally Tychlo spoke up. "I know Renender is a busy man, an important man, with a lot on his mind. Military toughs moving in on your territory. That's got to bite. Tell me about these favors I owe you."

"They're inquiries mainly, Tychlo," said Renender drawing his attention back to the table. "First, what is the situation with the Brothel League's Escorts? I was here just a few months ago. They were fine then. But now? Now they act more like escort thugs. Where I want to go, what I want to do. I feel countered and questioned at every move."

Tychlo shook his head, gave a glance across the room at Jeanette and Jeaneau at the bar near Mack, then looked back at Renender. "Nasty turn of events there, I'll agree with you. Not long back now the Adjunct made an arrangement with the League for added security. More zones are out of bounds now for the average Guest, and being escorted is now a requisite condition rather than a privileged amenity. Miners are still exempt, for now. But merchants and entertainers are encouraged to have Escort attaches assigned to them. It's only a matter of time before freedom of movement is curtailed for everyone. I've said all along, it's only a matter of time before the police state comes here. And now with this business in Lupus City, it'll accelerate.

Renender sipped from his Cursple. "Hm. Earlier when I arrived I witnessed an impressive coordination of organization and efficiency in incident control."

"Eh, what's that?" asked Tychlo confused.

"Sorry. They definitely seem to be in control," Renender clarified.

"In the Plaza for sure," said Tychlo. "But I've seen them poking around in the inner tunnels lately, places an Escort has no business being."

"Those two at the bar are with me," said Renender. "I can't lose them, but I need to."

"That won't be easy," said Tychlo. "They go through extensive drills regularly. They are definitely in control here."

Renender finished his Cursple. He watched the singer and band again. They were wrapping up a set. "Do you know what Balthorelei is up to these days? I'm going to need her help."

"Ha-ha. That's an easy one. She's been singing this whole time."

"What?" Renender looked back again at the stage. The band was separating for a break. Tychlo whistled to the woman in the red dress and motioned for her to join them. She retrieved a bottle of water from the floor beside the band equipment and approached.

"Well, well, well. Renender from the Valley. What has cracked open your hell to bring you all the way up here?" she said taking a seat.

Renender got up and gave her a kiss on her cheek. "Balthorelei, where did you learn to sing so well?"

"Just 'cuz I blast holes in rocks all day doesn't mean I don't also fancy some of the finer things. Not unlike you, you old devil."

"You have a marvelous voice," complimented Renender.

"And she looks great in a tight dress, too. Even out of one eye," Tychlo added, inviting a punch in the shoulder from Balthorelei.

"What's with the two Beauty Goons at the bar?" she asked.

"I'm afraid they're here with me," admitted Renender.

"He's looking for a way to shake 'em," said Tychlo.

"Good luck with that," said Balthorelei. "They've turned into a home grown goon squad. Where would you go, even if you could lose them? Only a rodent or a snake could slither out of this place. It's a trap, especially now."

"What will you do when the occupation begins?" asked Renender.

"Adapt," said Balthorelei. "What else? There's no way out."

Tychlo nodded in agreement. "You might very well have come to the wrong place at the wrong time."

"On the contrary," said Renender. "I'm betting on the chance I've come to the right place at the right time. All I need is a little help, a little information, and some luck ditching the Beauty Goon Squad." He jerked his head in the direction of the bar.

"A plan," exclaimed Balthorelei. "I like it already. What do you have in mind?"

"Who is the Trickle Depth Sounder these days?" asked Renender.

"Bordent," said Tychlo. "I know, still on the job. He's nearly as old and wily as me," he laughed then started coughing.

"Is he here? In the city I mean? Or still crawling through tunnels in the mines?"

"He's around I think," said Tychlo. "I saw him not two days ago. But if he's here, he won't be for long. Not with the military coming in. He'll slip back out through some crack and disappear for a good long while, till things blow over, or till he runs out of supplies and comes back for a restock."

"This isn't going to just blow over," said Renender.

Balthorelei listened quietly to the exchange, looking back and forth between the two men, then over at the bar and back again. She caught on to what Renender was proposing. "You aren't serious," she blurted out, interrupting. "You'll never survive in those cracks. And Bordent won't tolerate company. What's the use of even trying? You'd perish for sure."

Renender just grinned, then said, "I don't mean to get stuck in a crack. I mean to slip out through a crack and out the other side."

"Ho-ho," began Tychlo, but he caught himself in another cough. He took a drink of water to recover.

"There's nothing for you out there in the wilderness, even if you did find a crack to slip out of," said Balthorelei. "You'd be giving everything up for a sure and miserable death, by freezing, starving, accident. You'd never find your way back. Pointless."

"I don't bank on anything unless there's a chance for a payout," said Renender.

Tychlo stared at Renender awhile without saying anything. The table was quiet. He scratched under his eye patch, then squinted his good eye at Renender. "You haven't lost it, have you my friend? Really, you believe those wild stories?"

"What stories?" asked Balthorelei.

"There's a chance," said Renender. "I've done my homework. I just need to lose the Escorts, and connect with Bordent."

"You mean those outlandish rumors of singing cities in the clouds? Fantasies of men lucky enough to find their way back, but without their minds."

"Maybe," said Renender. "But I intend to find out."

One of the band members called out "Balthorelei. We're ready to go back on."

"I'm coming," she called back. Turning back to the conversation at the table she said, "Boys, I've got to go. Renender, you're as crazy as Tychlo here, and old Bordent. But I can get you easily passed the Escorts. Tell me when it needs to happen."

"As soon as possible," said Renender.

"If Bordent is here, he'll be at the Commissary. I can check for you," said Tychlo.

"I get off in an hour," said Balthorelei.

"I have a feeling those two won't let me stay here much longer," said Renender. "I'll be at the Empalasor's VIP Lounge."

"I'll meet you there in an hour then," said Balthorelei getting up. "And we'll get you to the Commissary." She leaned over and gave Renender a kiss, then left back for the stage.

"If Bordent's there, we'll get you away from the Plaza and into the mines," nodded Tychlo. "You've always done right by me, old friend. You can count on us."

29 A DAY ON THE WATER

Softly the ship swayed, no longer driven by the wild winds of the cold storm. Gently, rocked Cornelius in his hammock of gurkbuzzel flesh. His conscious mind was at rest as his subconscious mind dreamt.

The little boy Cornelius stood in front of his mother's full length mirror, bare-chested, flexing the young muscles a little boy is proud of, admiring his form, imagining days when he would be a man. Young Cornelius posed with his head turned to his left profile. He sucked in his stomach, pushed out his chest, tucked in his chin, and squared his shoulders.

The sound of the front door opening and the rustling of bags were heard. Cornelius' sister ran barefoot down the short hall to their mother's room. She stopped in the open doorway. "What are you doing? I'm going to tell Mom."

"Shut up, grub. I'm the man of the house. I'm going to grow up big and strong. Look at these muscles." Cornelius raised both arms up and flexed again, this time making his face into a grimace. "Grr. I'm going to fight monsters and bad men."

The sure and comforting clip-clip of their mother's shoes on the wood floors approached down the hall. She stopped in the doorway and watched her children. "What is going on in here?" she asked with a wide grin.

"Cornelius is being ridiculous," said his sister.

"Look how strong I am, Mom. I'm going to grow up big and strong. I'll protect you from monsters and bad men. I'll fight the wild Canines."

"You're stupid," said his sister.

"Shut up, grub," said Cornelius back, with his usual dismissive line. He stuck his tongue out at her.

"You're already the man of the house," said his mother. "I couldn't ask for any greater protection."

"See?" said Cornelius, aimed at his sister. "I'm going to be a hero, just you wait and see."

"I will have to," agreed his sister. "Because you're just a skinny boy now."

"I am not!" Cornelius protested.

"You're strong, Cornelius." But the voice was different. The light shifted and the walls disappeared. In their place the sunlight was intense from overhead. It sparkled bright on the sea in front of Cornelius. He stood on wet sand looking out at the ebbing horizon. "Do you work out regularly, or have you always been so muscular?"

Cornelius turned to see Naemi standing beside him on his right. He beamed a smile at her that was partly a blush. The two of them wore loose fitting white cotton pants that stopped just above the ankles. Red drawstrings hung in wide tied loops to keep the pants up. Neither wore a top. Cornelius' broad chest and muscles, strong neck, shoulders and arms darkened easily in the bright light of the Lupin sun, his already dark brown tone glossing to ebony. Naemi's also muscular frame sported plump upturned breasts. They were white and shone dazzling in the sunlight. Her areolas perked to attention, both from the heat of the sun and from the heat she felt near Cornelius.

A wave lapped at their feet and both jumped back in surprise and giggles. A shade crossed the sun and Naemi looked up, pointing. "Cornelius," she said. "Look."

Cornelius raised a hand and looked up just in time to catch some great winged shape fly overhead.

But the sun was gone now. And Naemi was gone. Bright stars in a black sky shown overhead in the place of the sun and blue day. The double helix constellation rose in the east. The horizon was partly obscured. A circle of standing stones stoically surrounded him. A masculine voice, strangely accented, spoke to his left.

"Through the fourth gate the sun will rise this morning. It will set in the fourth gate on the other side. From this gate the leaders of the multitude of stars will emerge. There are six in the east and six in the west. All of them follow east after the other. Their names are Cordin, Baramethis, Tordal...."

The man who spoke was silhouetted against the field of stars. In the east the orange glow of dawn harkened and the man's face was revealed, dark blond hair with brown stripes. His strong nose betrayed his Canine species.

As the light grew brighter, Cornelius grew sleepier. He felt himself sinking, eyes closing. Slowly down into a quiet darkness fell his mind even as the bright sun rose, its light streaming through the fourth gate.

Cornelius' gurkbuzzel hammock stretched itself from the ceiling and lowered Cornelius onto the floor. Like the gentle comfort of a mother's arms, it deposited him silently onto the floor of the hold of the Canine ship Tarvash. Cornelius stirred, stretched, and yawned. He opened his eyes and saw he was lying on the floor. He was awake.

The girl Tentz, with her jet-black hair and pale skin, sat across the room on a bench observing Cornelius. "You sleep a lot," she said.

Cornelius drew his fingers through his thick hair. He was hot. The room felt hot. The gurkbuzzel hold had resumed its innocuous and sterile pastel form. Metal benches lined the walls. Tentz sat on one, eating something that looked like a biscuit. Two doors were presently open in the hold. One let to the lavatory, the other topside.

"What time is it?" Cornelius asked.

"Afternoon," responded Tentz.

"Where is everyone else?"

"On top. The storm's over and the sun's out." She took another bite of her biscuit, dusted the crumbs off her dark blue blouse. She stared at the floor a moment, then turned her attention back to Cornelius. "Did you know the floor eats crumbs? Look." She broke off a piece of her biscuit and dropped it onto the checkered surface of the floor. Cornelius leaned forward and watched as the floor turned slightly fluid beneath the crumbs, absorbing them. Like flies pulled into amber. "Neat, huh?"

Cornelius stood up. "How does it tell the difference between a crumb, and me?" he asked.

"Maybe people don't taste good," the pale girl replied.

"That assumes we've been tasted," said Cornelius. He moved toward the lavatory door, calling back, "Excuse me while I relieve myself." Out of his peripheral vision, Cornelius caught Tentz watching him intently with almost a school crush fascination as he disappeared through the narrow door.

It was two steps down to the latrine. Cornelius let out a steady sigh as his full bladder emptied into the urinal trough. He let go a couple of farts. He ignored the face in the mirror in front of him. He thought about the strange dreams he had, haunting dreams. Cornelius shook his head to scatter the remnant memories. His stream of piss reduced to a trickle. Cornelius focused his eyes better and looked around. He suddenly noticed that the facility was no ordinary latrine. Like much of the rest of this strange ship, it was a gurkbuzzel structure. He knew he was in one of the strangest situations he'd ever found himself; on this slug skin Canine boat with strange people, Canine and Human. Big City was his destination. He needed to find out if he was in any trouble here. Who were these people? Were the Canines actual allies, or otherwise? Renender sent them all here. Now what? Cornelius had wiles of his own to draw upon. The girl Tentz was slightly rebellious but clearly impressionable. Cornelius thought to turn this situation to an advantage.

He gave himself three shakes to the right for good luck, and watched the drops absorb into the fleshy urinal. "Strange place," he murmured. He fastened the drawstring ties to his under shorts. The red drawstrings from his dream flashed through his mind and were gone.

Cornelius removed his well-hidden switchblade knife from a tiny pocket in the seam of his pants. Facing himself in the mirror, he felt his face, sideburns, chin and neck. A couple days worth of stubble. He stopped the basin and filled it with water. He looked around for something for lather, soap. Nothing. The walls glistened a little. Cornelius pressed his fingers onto the spongy surface of the gurkbuzzel wall. A white something oozed out. Cornelius smelled it. Shaving gel. "Gurkbuzzel is very useful," Cornelius said. With a steady hand and concentrated gaze, he sliced through the stubble and cleaned himself up, leaving his growing sideburns and a goatee and mustache.

Back in the hold, Tentz had finished her biscuit and was focused on feeding the floor crumb by crumb. Cornelius stood in the doorway and casually buttoned his loose trousers, watching the girl the whole time. When he was done, he leaned his shoulder against the doorframe seductively. "Why aren't you topside with the others?" he asked.

Tentz looked up. She pretended not to smile, but Cornelius saw it through her embarrassed efforts to remain aloof. *This girl definitely has a crush on me*, he thought. That got him aroused, and he shifted his weight to his other leg, leaned his other shoulder against the opposite door jam.

"I don't like the sun," she answered.

"You're very fair," said Cornelius. He smiled. The left corner of his mouth went up and that creased his dimple. Tentz stared hard at him for a second, then looked away quickly, embarrassed. *Gotcha*, Cornelius thought. "So where can I get one of those biscuits?" he asked. "I'm hungry."

Tentz got up and walked over to the door where the spiral staircase led topside. She scratched the wall and the gurkbuzzel control device spiraled out in its strange fashion.

Cornelius stood upright in the doorway to the latrine, his arms dropped to his sides. "How are you doing that?" he asked.

Tentz traced an arc on an inner ridge of the shell like surface of the device with a finger. Above Cornelius, a drop formed out of the doorframe. It congealed into a biscuit and dropped. Cornelius caught it in his hand.

"What?" he exclaimed. He held the biscuit up to his nose and smelled it. "It's warm," he said. Then, "Butter," surprised.

"We've been eating slug skin," said Tentz. But she did not make the gross face Cornelius expected. "It's not bad," she added.

Cornelius took a bite. It was delicious. "Cornbread and butter," he said. Crumbs fell to the floor and the floor ate them. He grinned, and his smile was rife with pleasant surprise. "With honey."

"After everyone else left, and you didn't get up, I started playing with it. Anyone can use it. The gurkbuzzel just reacts. Cool, huh?"

Now we connect, thought Cornelius. "Completely," he replied. Tentz betrayed a smile, but smothered it immediately, which made Cornelius chuckle inside.

"It's just another gadget," she said dismissively and shrugged her shoulders.

Cornelius turned his thoughts to other things. "Well, I'm going to look for my friend Naemi."

Tentz grew visibly annoyed at the mention of Naemi. She resumed her unimpressed, aloof demeanor.

Lust dashed, thought Cornelius. *Temporarily. I'll access those emotions again later.* "I'm going up. You're cute. I'll see you later." He strode past the suddenly incapacitated girl and ascended the spiral stairs.

Cornelius heard the sounds first, shouting, hollering, laughing, yelling, banging, and drumming. And when he emerged topside, he saw that the scene on the deck was like a carnival. So different from the ominous and treacherous events of the night before.

Canines climbed the foremast, the mainmast and the mizenmast. They hung off the rigging, hung off the jibs, mending sails and rigging. The previous night's winds had loosed lines and snapped ties, tearing gurkbuzzel from shrouds and sprits. Some Canines mopped the main deck while others polished fittings and bells, brass leads, heads and cover caps. Water ran in rivulets passed Cornelius' feet, disappearing down scuppers.

And there were Canines in the water. Some maneuvered in tiny dinghies to check the outer hull. Many were just swimming. There was a huge splash and Cornelius saw the next in line of a row of young Canines dive off a plank extended through the gunwale. Cornelius saw they were near shore. Near a Canius shore, about half a kilometer away.

A crewman bumped Cornelius while leading a troupe of Canine youths starboard toward the diving plank. There were seven, all naked, boys and girls, just adolescents. Half were dripping wet and all were giggling, and their downy fur was of an astounding variety of color. There was a golden girl with tightly braided hair on her head strung with small white shells. There was a boy all red and brown with one white leg. He was tall and thin and sported a mohawk on his head. Two small girls were spotted white and black; three silver boys came next, shiny and rotund.

Following up the rear came Bossin. He paused near Cornelius and said "Homints finally wakes when the sun is straight up."

"Hey Bossin," began Cornelius. "Where...."

"Forward, forward up the steps. Food and friends. Go and follow," said Bossin. He hurried past not waiting for Cornelius.

Past the amidships cabin, the deck was bi-level. Four steps led up to the forecastle deck, above the fore cabin. The upper deck hosted a crowd of Canines feasting and socializing, crew joined apparently with Canines from the shore. The visiting delegation was dressed in robes, colorful and striped. Men and women wore elaborate headdresses, some feather plumed, others with interwoven laurels. And there were more children, some clothed, but most naked, wet and laughing, taking turns jumping and diving off a second higher ship plank. The Human twins Boglei and Bogelia were among them, naked like their Canine counterparts, even more so, being Human.

Cornelius paused beside the starboard gunwale on the lower foredeck near the lower diving plank, taking in the scene. Good cheer permeated the atmosphere of everyone around him, and he laughed. He looked up. The bright Lupin sun shone through a cerulean blue cloudless sky. Shore gulls squawked and dove amongst one another through the airs about the ship. A pleasant breeze blew.

Across the deck on the portside, Cornelius spotted chubby Klendl standing with a pair of visiting Canines in light blue robes and light blue turbans. They stood near a pile of stone fruits of different varieties arranged on the deck. Over the many sounds of the many people, Cornelius could hear Klendl's conspicuous whiny voice asking, "These are how much a bushel?"

More laughter broke out among the crowd on the forecastle deck. Cornelius climbed three steps, hugging the gunwale, and looked about him at the greater view revealed to him.

The Tarvash was anchored midway in a small sheltered bay. Across the water, amid the tall cattail grasses, cypress and pines, stood huts and tents and boat launches. Smoke rose from cooking fires at various intervals along the shore. The moving forms of Canines could be made out on the beach. But closer, on the waters of the bay, there were Canines on surfboards, Canines on wind sails and Canines on kite sails. In fact the Tarvash was surrounded by small craft of all kinds moving and bobbing.

There was movement overhead and shadows raced across the deck of the ship. Cornelius looked up to see the portside winches maneuvering boxes and bundles onto the deck near Klendl. Cornelius approached his fellow Human and observed the loading and unloading of trade goods. Rafts of fruits, nuts, meats, dry stuffs and assorted items were hauled up to deck, the bundles guided by the Canine crew. Other goods were offloaded to waiting empty rafts below.

Before Cornelius reached Klendl, Raffir appeared at his side, proud, bare-chested, barefoot and wearing short pants. He was eating a skewer of roasted meats and vegetables. He thrust one at Cornelius and said at the same time "Cor-NEElus, done sleeping? Eat!" Cornelius took the offered skewer as Raffir led him away from the working Canines portside and back to the starboard. "Too busy back there. Enjoy the view below on starboard. Look."

Eating the tasty meats and vegetables, Cornelius looked over the gunwale where children continued to dive and splash and play. He noticed several rafts that the children clung to, and was surprised to see Naemi sitting on the edge of one next to Canine women doing the same, their feet in the water, flowers in their hair, bare breasted. They were calling up to the men on the ship, waving chains of flowers, offering greetings and charms and wiles. Cornelius laughed and waved down to her, calling. "Naemi! What are you doing down there?"

Naemi caught sight of Cornelius and returned his wave. She grinned, and turned to the young Canine woman beside her and said something in her ear, pointing up at Cornelius. The women burst into laughter. Both then waved garlands at him, coaxing Cornelius down into the water.

"Careful there, Cor-NEElus," said Raffir. "Sirens. They try to ensnare a sailor's soul, drag him back onto land to make husbands out of them. Men who fall under their spell are no longer men of the sea, and they don't return." His straight face erupted into a laugh, with his jowls pulled back and his tongue lolling out. He drooled a little and his eyes got wet and cloudy from his laughter. "Your friend Naemi there," Raffir added nodding in her direction. "She's one of them. You watch out now." Raffir poked Cornelius in the ribs and laughed some more.

Cornelius was caught up in the good cheer and jibing. This was the same stern Raffir from the night before? Powerful, dominating, and now he was chummy. Raffir's laughter was contagious. "Raffir," attempted Cornelius through his own laughter. "Where are we? What's going on?"

"This is Somet," answered Raffir. He grinned at Cornelius, grinned down at Naemi, grinned at the day. "We trade here, and all up and down the Canius shore. Not just the Lake Docks. Not just Big City. This is one place of many places."

"It looks nice," said Cornelius. "Have you ever been there? To the shore?"

"Nooo. I never been there," exclaimed Raffir, and he was completely serious. He made the point clearer. "Never closer than this. See this earring?" He tugged on the gold earring dangling off his shaggy right ear. "This says I never touched land. Not ever, in my life."

"Never touched land?" repeated Cornelius as a question. He was confused. "Never stood on a shore? Never walked up a hill?"

"No," said Raffir leaving no doubt. "Most of the boys on this vessel, they've touched shore, came from there even, made a change in their life for some reason and are here now," Raffir stomped a foot on the deck.

"Were you born on the Tarvash?" Cornelius asked.

"Found," said Raffir. "After a storm. Floating in a box. So maybe I was born on the water, and maybe I wasn't. But if you ask me, I never touched land."

Cornelius just looked at Raffir. Never touched land? But the ship trades with communities up and down the Canius shore he thought. Interesting. Cornelius noticed Raffir was busy looking for something in a fold of his breeches, short as they were. "What are you doing?"

"Ah, found it." Raffir held up what looked like a skinny dark leathery sheath. "Here, have a taste. Open up."

"What is it?" asked Cornelius. Raffir didn't wait to answer.

Raffir tipped the sheath over Cornelius' open mouth. A slithery slippery something slid down his throat. Cornelius swallowed it before he could tell what it was.

"Sap eel," said Raffir. "It gives a happy feel."

Cornelius felt warm inside, and happy. He was already happy. Now he was feeling euphoric.

"Don't worry," said Raffir. "We're shored here for a few good hours more." Raffir pulled out another sheath and downed a slimy eel himself.

Cornelius' mouth was full of sweetness and everything seemed extra bright. He felt warm. But he was also cool. It was hard to describe. Then the blue Lupin sky seemed to open up even bluer than before. And the hot Lupin sun blazed even hotter from above. Cornelius felt wonderful. He looked at Raffir. The Canine was saying something. His mouth was moving. But Cornelius couldn't hear anything. Raffir's eyes slid up into the back of his head. He started drooling. At least Cornelius thought that's what he saw.

He turned to look out at the lake water. The children were diving into the air, into the water, in slow motion, graceful and swanlike. Beyond them, he saw sunlight reflecting off the wind sails and kite sails of the Canines zigging and zagging on the lake's surface. Some maneuvered themselves in wide circles around the Tarvash. Cornelius watched intensely at their prowess, the muscular strength and skill they employed. Then he heard music.

An accordion sound accompanied by drums and flutes. Cornelius looked past Raffir toward Klendl and the fruit pile. Renchant and Ramon were there too. Nearby were some young Canines in red and orange robes. They had joined with some crewmen to bang on the drums, sound out chords on an accordion and blowpipe. Music and laughter filled the deck. Cornelius turned back to Raffir, who was still speaking. This time Cornelius could hear him.

"Now Captain Katzer," he went on, and he straightened his back and raised himself tall out of respect. "That's three generations in that man, maybe four as some say, that never touched the shore, nor soft nor solid land. Life on these lakes, Human, it's beautiful."

Cornelius caught the music again. He liked the tune, though he certainly didn't know it. There were words, but they were repetitive and nonsensical, in fact quite funny. Cornelius grinned widely at the musicians, at Raffir, at the activity off the side of the ship.

Passed Naemi and her siren calls, passed the splashing of Canine and Human children, Cornelius focused on the wind surfers and kite sailors. The wind picked up and was refreshing on his face. He suddenly turned back to Raffir and exclaimed, "I want to do that."

"Raffir laughed. "Wind skimming. I've never done it. Too much skirting towards shore. And most start from there. Bossin has tried it though, a few times."

"And?" asked Cornelius.

Raffir laughed again. "Isn't it obvious? A Canine with the wind in his face? He loves it."

Cornelius chuckled. He didn't brave a comment on the species stereotype, but he was glad Raffir had bridged the divide. "How do I start?"

Raffir grew serious. "I will show you!" Smiling again, he added "You will skim circles around your siren Naemi."

"She'll think I'm a show off," said Cornelius.

"Come. I will take you to Bossin." Raffir slapped Cornelius on the shoulder. "Let's check on business things, and find the pup. Come and follow."

Along the starboard amidships they passed Dardele who was leaning on the gunwale, lost in a gaze toward shore. "Dardele!" exclaimed Cornelius.

The only survivor of the airship Valyon turned his absent gaze toward Cornelius and Raffir without saying a word. Images from the disaster of the night before flashed through Cornelius' mind. But they were difficult to hold onto. The happy high from the sap eel kept them disconsolate. "Come my friend. Join me in some water sports?"

Dardele half smiled but shook his head no. He turned back to the shore, to the sky above.

"There is food on the forecastle deck," Raffir said to Dardele. And stone fruit too, near the musicians, near the fat Human."

Dardele nodded in response.

Raffir leaned in to Cornelius' ear and quietly said, "He has much to grieve over. Come, we will find Bossin. Come and follow."

Raffir led Cornelius to stern. There a group of Canine shipmates worked together to guide a crate of goods hooked onto a winch off the lazarette deck up and over the port gunwale and down to a raft of waiting Canines below. Through the slats of the crate Cornelius could clearly see canisters of titanium gas, each bearing the mark of a big red "R." Renender Enterprises.

Rounding the back of the amidships cabin another group of crewmen were receiving a net of tightly woven round reed baskets. Raffir stepped up to the winch operator and said, "Easy. Easy." Then shouting up the forward length of the amidships deck he called "Bossin. Bossin. Here. Gurkbuzzel arrive." The net hovered just above the deck surface. One of the crew guided it carefully down. Raffir came over and reached up to the winch hook, releasing the ties. As the net was released, thirty round baskets rolled and spread out in a tumble. Raffir laughed, his big hands affixed to his hips. Bossin rushed down from somewhere forward, attempting to corral the baskets back into some semblance of a pile.

"Bossin, get these up to the sail spouts immediately. And the hold, too. Set and flip sails," Raffir ordered.

"On it, Raffir," replied Bossin. And he added in a singsong voice "Sticky, gooey gurkbuzzel fright. The sails will be bright against the sky tonight."

"What does he mean, Raffir?" asked Cornelius, his hands on his hips like Raffir. A basket of squirming somethings rolled toward him and came to rest at his feet.

Raffir swiveled his torso toward Cornelius and replied. "The sails were damaged in the storm last night. The gurkbuzzel must be replenished." Nodding toward the basket at Cornelius' feet, he added "Go on, open it up. Look inside."

Cornelius reached down and pried the lid off the basket. Inside was a squirming mass of flashing glowing dark green and spotted gurkbuzzel slugs, slithering over and in and out and among each other. Hundreds and hundreds of them. Sticky and gooey. "Wow, that is cool." He was fascinated. Cornelius sniffed at the wriggling mass in the basket. It had the scent of tangerine.

"Not too bad a smell," said Raffir smiling.

Then overhead all six winches of the Tarvash rotated, stretched out and released their sails, horizontal to the deck, forming a kind of umbrella ceiling. Sunlight filtered through the gurkbuzzel sails, casting a spotted green hue onto the deck and people and goods. Yellow sunlight shone through tears in the sails.

Bossin organized teams of deck hands to take the baskets, each an armload, to the six winches around the ship. At the nearest winch to Cornelius, Bossin unscrewed a small hatch in a pipe. A gasp of air sounded from a pneumatic tube. He then reached into the basket and lifted out squirming slimy handfuls of slugs and dropped them into the tube. The slugs made loud slurping sounds as they were sucked up into the tube. When the basket was empty, Bossin picked up another and began the process again. Slug mucous dripped between his fingers onto the deck.

"Now look up, Cor-NEElus," directed Raffir.

Overhead, the slugs were ejected onto the flat surface of the sail like a mass of squirming shrapnel. They spread out, joining with their kind making up the sail, filling the tears and strengthening the whole. The sail above Cornelius rippled in excited waves. "That is amazing."

"We help the gurkbuzzel, the gurkbuzzel helps us," said Raffir.

"That must be a lot of work collecting the slugs," said Cornelius. "Expensive maintenance."

"We trade what the people of Somet here want," said Raffir. "You mean money though. Just like a Human. Money is only good in Big City. Nobody else uses it. We trade like any honorable lake ship crew." Raffir winked, flashing his big eyebrows at Cornelius. "And Bossin was right. The sails will be bright tonight. Come," he said, grabbing Cornelius by the arm. "Time for water skimming." He turned his head and yelled back to Bossin. "Bossin. When you are done here, show Cornelius what you know about water skimming."

Bossin pointed his face and nose into the air and howled, letting out an "Aroooo! Hooooo!"

Raffir led Cornelius forward, passed the musicians, Klendl and his ongoing inquiries over stone fruit prices and trade arrangements. *He reminds me of Renender*, thought Cornelius. Renchant and Ramon were opposite, on the starboard side, watching the children continue to leap off the ship, some doing somersaults midair. The Human girl Bogelia dove next, followed by a Canine girl. Boglei was next. He was facing the Canine boy behind him, apparently, sharing a joke. Both broke into giggles and laughter. They leapt into the air together, both splashing cannonball into the water with great impact. Calls and hollers rang up from below.

They're getting along so naturally together, Cornelius thought of the Human twins and their new Canine playmates. *Nothing like the mean kids I see in Cronapolis.*

Cornelius followed Raffir up to the forecastle deck where the visiting shore Canines were gathered. Raffir left Cornelius to speak to a stout Canine woman in an elaborate orange and blue headdress puffing on a fat cigar. "I have a passenger who wants to try water skimming." He nodded back at Cornelius. "Human. Would it be possible for one of your boys to help?" The woman bent her head around to look at Cornelius, thick clouds of puffy smoke wafting out of her mouth and nose.

While Raffir continued his negotiation, Cornelius drifted over to the starboard gunwale and peered over, looking for Naemi in the water below. She was not difficult to spot, but her raft had drifted further away from the ship, too far to call out to.

Raffir nudged Cornelius in the arm with his elbow and said, "I've got you a board and a kite sail and a rope." He sported a broad grin that stretched the length of his face from jowl to jowl.

The smoking woman let out a call or howl out over the ship.

"Look," said Raffir pointing.

Cornelius looked out at the many water skimmers tacking back and forth out in the bay. Presently a red kite sail broke ranks and approached the ship. As the skimmer drew closer Cornelius saw he was a tall well-toned Canine youth wearing a red speedo. The board he was on was also a deep red. As he neared the ship, he released his hold on the grip rope that connected to one of the kite sail's ends. The rope flew out and snapped in the air. The kite sail straightened out and lost its pull, the wind no longer pushing against it. The kite sail drifted downward and the rider quickly lassoed the grip rope, loop over loop around his shoulder and elbow as he neared the ship, all the while maintaining his balance on the board. He maneuvered into a turn by shifting his weight in a lean. This caused a skid wave, which slowed his approach to such a controlled degree that his board merely tapped the side of the Tarvash. The rider lassoed the last bit of rope and the sail touched down into the water beside him. He grabbed hold of the side of the ship and called up.

"Taklaso?"

The smoking woman, her face surrounded by cloudy puffs, called back. "Sobe Tomo. Lend us your board. Benso Homints beg Tarvash."

"I vouch," Raffir called out after.

The board rider looked up at Cornelius and smiled wide, his now evident long brown hair falling over his face. He knocked it back behind his shoulders with a shake of his head and waved at Cornelius, calling up "Beme Homints."

Cornelius was excited. He waved back but didn't know what to say. He turned back to Raffir and said "Now what?"

Bossin appeared at their side with his own intricately carved board under one arm and trappings around the other. His board was a rich brown mahogany color with iridescent gold flakes glittering through the resin polish. The front was curved up slightly like a ship's prow. Showing through the resin were stamped symbols that looked like a "W" with an arrow on the right arm.

"Down into the water, Homints," said Bossin. "Come and follow." Bossin began stripping down to a brown and yellow speedo.

Cornelius asked sheepishly "Is it cold?" He followed Bossin's lead and began disrobing to his own shorts, taking off his shirt, pants, and shoes. Cornelius had always thought of himself as strapping and strong. But now he looked a little soft next to Bossin's toned and tight muscles from life on the Tarvash.

"Maybe cold," replied Bossin with a smile. "It's wet." Bossin slid his board over the gunwale where the boy Tomo, standing balanced on his own board, reached up to guide it down. Without a flinch, Bossin dove over the side and pierced the water in a perfect perpendicular with nary a splash. He surfaced and scrambled onto his own board, balancing into a stand. He waved up at Cornelius. "Jump Homints. Come and follow."

Cornelius bound the drawstrings of his shorts tight, grinned at Raffir, and dove sideways into the water near to where Bossin had. His splash showered Tomo and Bossin, who erupted in hollers. Cornelius emerged grinning. He snapped his head back to shake the excess water out of his thick hair. He swam freestyle over to Bossin's board. Bossin stood with one foot each on his board, one on Tomo's. He tried helping Cornelius up, but the Human lost his balanced and careened backwards into the water. A gathering audience on the amidships deck added their laughter to that of the boys in the water.

Tomo and Bossin instructed Cornelius on the proper form to balance on the board. After several more unsteady attempts Cornelius was finally able to stand on his own, his toes and heels finding anchorage in the straps and dimples fashioned on the board's surface. The fit was not exact, Cornelius' feet being larger and of somewhat different shape than those of his Canine instructors.

Tomo fastened the harness straps of his kite sail around Cornelius' broad chest, over his shoulders and around his waist. The towline was connected to the back of his board. While Tomo was doing this, Bossin posed and feigned maneuvers on his board, all the while maintaining his balance. Before long Cornelius was able to imitate Bossin, impressing the now large crowd of onlookers from the ship.

Tomo left Bossin and Cornelius and swam out to a raft from which to watch. He reached the one Naemi was on.

Next Bossin and Cornelius lay flat on their boards and paddled away from the ship. They practiced standing and balancing again, this time where the breezes were stronger. Finally satisfied that Cornelius was ready to give the wind a go, Bossin tugged on his kite sail lines in such a way as to release the kite to the wind. The sail grew full, lifted off the water's surface, and the ropes grew taut. Bossin took off, immediately maneuvering into tight practice circles around Cornelius, explaining resistance and counter-resistance techniques. Then Bossin pulled Cornelius' sail ahead of his board and gave the signal for Cornelius to yank up on the lines. The sail caught wind. Cornelius braced for the forward tug, held his positions, his toes and heels doing their work for him. Cornelius was off.

Bossin artfully kept pace beside Cornelius, shouting tips and techniques.

Naemi sat on her raft beside the young Canine woman and now Tomo. Her legs dangled in the cool water, her hair pulled to the back away from her face, which, with her breasts, tanned in the sunlight. She watched as Cornelius joined the circling group of a dozen or so Canine skimmers. She was impressed by his quick grasp of technique. Then again, he was quick with the glider too.

For Cornelius, the experience was exhilarating. The wind was in his face and the sound it made roared. It was joined by the snapping and creaking of the ropes, the popping and shearing of the sail, in response to his pulls, tugs and strains. He might have fallen more frequently if Bossin hadn't proved so adept at instruction, anticipating Cornelius' weaknesses, providing timely advice before Cornelius even needed it. Bossin was close enough for encouragement yet far enough away to give Cornelius breadth and maneuvering room to increase his confidence through ever more taxing moves.

Cornelius matched Bossin's zigs with his own zags. Then the wind picked up and changed direction. The kite sail pulled up abruptly, and Cornelius with it. His stomach did a somersault as he rolled into one too. His feet maintained their grip on the board and he slammed back into the water, still careening forward with the sail. "Wahoooo!" he yelled.

Right next to Cornelius, Bossin somersaulted out of the air and landed with a splash. They laughed together and they heard even from their distance a chorus of cheers from the ship.

The other water skimmers drew near, running circles around Bossin and Cornelius. Then the whole party circumnavigated the ship. Rounding the stern, Cornelius caught a brief look at a beautiful naked Human woman standing on the private captain's deck, hand to forehead shading from the sun. That wasn't anyone he'd seen in the gurkbuzzel hold. Who was she? Long dark hair moved in a breeze. She had curves in all the places that got Cornelius' fires going, long neck, supple breasts, enticing shadow zone, legs not too long. Beautiful. Cornelius smiled and waved and yelled "Hello!" And she waved back. Then she was gone, hidden by the rest of the ship.

They skimmed close to shore next, and Cornelius was near enough to clearly watch a group of young Canines kicking a ball in the sand in a heated team game. He passed children building sand castles. He passed women in colorful wide brimmed hats strolling along the water line.

Cornelius and Bossin followed the others back out into the bay side by side. They looked like mirrored twin images, one Human one Canine. They skimmed out beyond where the Tarvash was anchored, to the reef line of fresh water coral that helped shelter the bay. Each skimmer approached a rocky outcropping of jumbled boulders at the end of a natural jetty, a spit of land fingering out from the rest of the shore. Suddenly each skimmer yanked hard on one towline and their kite sails dipped. Each ricocheted off the same imagined point in the water.

The wind shifted and Cornelius' kite sail moved. He skimmed right over a massif of glowing red freshwater coral just centimeters below the water's surface. He turned his head and looked down to admire it. Bossin was just beginning to tack hard in his own getaway from the rocks when he suddenly found Cornelius rushing at him directly in his path. Bossin tried to compensate but there was nowhere to turn.

Cornelius looked up in complete surprise that matched the shock on Bossin's face. There was only one course and Cornelius tensed himself for the collision into both Bossin and the rocky jetty.

Waves, Human, spray, boards and Canine flew up. The kite sails of both skimmers miraculously snapped out from their safely leads and slowed, drifted down and settled on the water. Cornelius was underwater in the second of three tumbles before his hand touched the hard surface of rock. He deflected himself away, completed his third tumble and broke the surface into the sunlight, gasping for air, spitting and shaking his head, looking left and right wide-eyed for Bossin.

Bossin was a few meters away and struggling to stay above water. Cornelius swam over and swung his arms around the Canine's waist. Cornelius kicked and gyrated to move his body upward with Bossin firmly attached. A few motions and Cornelius brought Bossin up onto a rock shelf just below the surface, the rest of the rock forming a wall at their back. Cornelius hauled the spitting and coughing Bossin up onto the portage and to safety. Cornelius perched himself beside the Canine. Both sat with their rumps just a couple centimeters under the surface of the splashing water. Cornelius used both his hands to strain the water out of his hair, his fingers like combs. He shook his head and wiped his face and let out a great sigh. "You ok Bossin? I'm really sorry. The wind came up and I couldn't slow. I didn't know what to do. I'm sorry. You ok?"

Bossin breathed deeply to regain his breath. He opened his eyes and squinted into the sun, wiping his furry brow clear of water. Then he laughed. "Homints. Wind. Water. Too much."

Cornelius laughed with him, then looked about for their boards and sails. They were floating nearby, jostled by the waves. "I'll be right back," said Cornelius, and he swam out to retrieve them.

Within minutes Cornelius returned, paddling on Tomo's board while pulling Bossin's by its towline. Once back on the rock shelf, he began reeling the ropes in, pulling hard to drag the sails through the water. Grabbing one sail, he felt it. It felt like nothing, wet. "What are these sails made out of, Bossin?" he asked turning to the Canine.

Bossin was preoccupied and didn't respond right away. His head was tilted and his fingers fidgeted at his right ear. He ceased laughing and his smile was gone. Finally he held his gold earring in his hand and just stared at it. After a moment he looked up at Cornelius and replied "Skimming sail is strong and light. Silk from the milk spider."

Cornelius was impressed that anyone would have such patience as to weave fabric from spider silk. He was about to say as much when he noticed that Bossin was growing increasingly somber. The Canine clenched his fist around his gold earring and was about to launch it into the lake. Cornelius squatted down beside Bossin, gripped the clenched fist in his own and stopped him. "What are you doing?" Cornelius asked quickly.

"No good now," said Bossin despondently. He slammed his back against the rock wall behind him and splashed the water with his free hand. "Gurrbot-desh. Land. It's the end. Bossin is no longer in brotherhood of the Tarvash. My beru, my spirit, no longer floats. It falls to the ground like a stone."

Cornelius understood the symbolism. His conversation with Raffir had done that.

"No good for Bossin. No good for Raffir," said Bossin.

"You have touched rocks before, haven't you Bossin?" Cornelius asked. "We're still in the water. These rocks are in the water." But his reasoning wasn't convincing even himself. "Come, let's go back, Bossin." Cornelius had to make an effort to smile. "Come and follow," he added, shaking Bossin's shoulder.

Part of the sky then seemed to get dark, like a curtain just two shades off from what it was before. The curtain like change came from the north and raced across the sky. As it passed by Cornelius and Bossin, they each heard a crackle in their ears. Bossin covered his with his hands. Cornelius watched the curtain move into the bay onto shore and proceed south. The freshwater coral nearby erupted in color and shone through the water, brilliant red and fuchsia. Trees along the shore seemed to glow greener and fuller. Then it was all over.

"Wow. What was that?" asked Cornelius.

"We better be going," said Bossin. "A quake is coming. Get the ropes and sails attached and back up." He smiled at Cornelius. "Come and follow."

On the way back in to the boat, skimming the surface with his newfound skill, Cornelius watched as the rafts and boats of the shore Canines headed in away from the Tarvash. Bossin drew up to the ship first, approaching with nearly the same skill as Cornelius had seen Tomo demonstrate, albeit with much less enthusiasm. When Cornelius came up along side, he tried to skid into a like stop. He managed to do a fair job, staying balanced and grabbing the ship's side. His board still hit the ship with a thump. A tiny splash at his side and suddenly Tomo darted up to the surface to reclaim his board. A few words exchanged, and Tomo skimmed off back to shore. Cornelius ascended the rope ladder after Bossin.

The welcoming party was less welcoming than Cornelius expected. Naemi was the first to greet him.

"You're a show off," she said. She shoved Cornelius' clothes at him. Her hair was gathered to one side and bound into a braid with a string of water hyacinths. "Did you have an accident out there?"

"The wind picked up and I lost control just a bit," Cornelius replied. He began to get dressed.

"Mm hm," Naemi responded.

"What have you been up to all morning?" Cornelius asked.

"Morning?" Naemi ran her fingers through her still wet hair at the end of her braid. She flicked the moisture at Cornelius. "I tried to rouse you, but you wouldn't wake up. Near first light Raffir, Bossin and the others got up, so I did, too. Bossin prepared a light meal on deck while you and the others, Humans, slept. We sailed into Somet Bay and Raffir prepared for a trading stop. Those people who were up there," she said, nodding at the forecastle deck, "with the elaborate costumes? They're the Village Elders."

"You seemed to be getting along with the locals quite well," said Cornelius. "Have you been here before?"

"Not around here," said Naemi. "This region is called the Heklado, the Place Between the Lakes. This part of Canius is new to me."

"Hmm," Cornelius responded. "What was all that stuff you were doing on the raft with the Canine beauties?"

Naemi laughed. "Sirening. It's a custom for the single Canine women to coax sailors off their boats. It's a sport."

"I don't think the sailors feel the same way about it," said Cornelius. "Bossin—." But Raffir suddenly appeared, none too happy.

"Cor-NEElus," he bellowed. He came quickly up and pushed Cornelius against the gunwale, almost knocking him over. Raffir growled, his jowls pulled way back baring his teeth. He seethed. "You took Bossin to land." He reached out and pushed Cornelius again, this time with the tips of his fingers.

Cornelius tried to move defensively away as possible, but he had nowhere to go but overboard.

Raffir continued his rant and rage. "He is Hekbet. Land dog." And Raffir spat the words out at Cornelius and spat onto the deck at Cornelius' feet.

"What's going on?" demanded Naemi. She shoved Cornelius aside and stood face to face with Raffir, matching his anger with her own. She meant to protect Cornelius, but what new mischief had he gotten himself into?

Raffir stood tall staring at Naemi, chest barreling out. He puffed his cheeks and let the air blubber out from his lips in a noisy flutter. Then his lips pulled back just enough to bare teeth. A low growl issued forth.

"It was an accident," pleaded Cornelius. Naemi threw up her arm to keep him silent.

"Bossin is apart now. No longer Shes. Hekbet."

"I don't understand," said Naemi.

"I'll explain it to you," said Cornelius.

"Keep quiet," said Naemi. She accompanied it with a quick hard glance. Cornelius complied.

Raffir gave a huff. A horn sounded from above and his demeanor changed. He turned back to the two Humans. "We are heading out," he said. "Stay out of the way." Raffir quickly left them alone.

Naemi faced Cornelius and said, "You've got some explaining to do. Now."

"Yeah, yeah, I said I would," Cornelius blurted out. He was angry at Raffir, though understood the reason. He also knew he was not in a position to pick a fight with Raffir, or any other Canine while he was on this ship. "Our boards hit." Then he remembered something else and he grew exited. "Did you see the flash? The curtain? The crackle?"

Naemi looked at him strangely. "The what?"

"You didn't see it? Hear it?"

"No."

"Why do you think all the Canine visitors left for shore?" Cornelius asked.

Naemi didn't understand where this nonsense talk was leading. "Because it was time for them to leave," she said annoyed.

"Maybe that, too," offered Cornelius. Cornelius finished putting on his clothes, and the two moved away from the gunwale to the middle of the foredeck. "So what have you been doing today?"

"What have I been doing?" Naemi asked exasperated. "I've been gathering information. I was up before dawn following Bossin, getting on his paranoid sarcastic good side. I found out that the gurkbuzzel room makes a lot more things than just furniture and utensils. Did you know that Bossin was born on the Tarvash? Though he wouldn't say whom his parents are.

"I followed Raffir up here at the break of day. He commanded the ship into the bay and made trade preparations. I watched the delegation of Elders and traders come out from the village. Captain Katzer met them with a banquet. I was able to get chummy with Raffir. He told me there are dozens of these settlements up and down the lake's western shore. We're lucky we've only stopped here today. We're headed to the channel through the rift valley next, then on to the next lake and Big City. Normally, the Tarvash trades up and down the Canius shore. We could have been stuck on this ship for a couple of weeks before reaching Big City."

"I suppose we have Renender to thank for that," said Cornelius.

"So the question is not *what have I been doing*, you lazy oaf. The question is what did you do to undo all the rapport and confidence I worked all day to build with the crew? What happened with Raffir and Bossin?"

Cornelius decided to egg Naemi on a little more. "And what were our fellow Humans up to?"

Naemi opened her mouth to answer, then pursed her lips and tilted her head, squinting her eyes at Cornelius. "Are you making fun of me?"

Cornelius gave her a blank face and said "Why?"

"Why?" Naemi pressed.

"Because you do know." Cornelius said. "You're very good at gathering information." He stopped in their walk and gloated.

"That's right, I do know," said Naemi. "And don't grandstand. I'll push you over the side."

"Alright, alright," said Cornelius raising his hands.

A couple of crewmen came up to them and stopped to check the winch riggings. One turned to Cornelius and Naemi and said "Sails going up. We're headed out." A horn sounded again from above. Overhead, the six winch arms of the Tarvash did their dance in the air and unfurled the gurkbuzzel sails. They flashed in patterned lights. Though the breeze was light, the six sails filled with air and the ship slowly pulled out of the bay.

"Is there any food left?" Cornelius asked Naemi. "I'm hungry."

"There's Klendl's pile of stone fruit," Naemi replied.

"Come on," said Cornelius. He led Naemi away from the crewmen working. On the port side they found Klendl standing with Ramon deep in conversation, but no stone fruit. "Hey, uh, Klendl. Any food around?"

Startled, Klendl abruptly stopped his conversation and turned to stare at Cornelius before responding. "Hm. Cornelius is it? Our hosts have removed the provisions below decks. There was plenty to eat earlier."

"I was busy doing other things," said Cornelius.

Ramon spoke up. "Bossin would probably fix you up with something to eat if you asked."

"Yeah, maybe," said Cornelius. "He's probably busy helping Raffir though. But thanks. Maybe I'll run into, uh, yeah. Maybe I'll see him. See you guys later."

Naemi gave the men a friendly smile and casually slipped her arm around Cornelius' waist, leading him toward the portside midship.

Cornelius looked at the arm hooked around his waist and said to Naemi, "What's with the corset hug?"

"I wanted to convey the symbology of ownership," said Naemi. "There's a strange dynamic on this ship."

"There are a lot of strange things about this ship," Cornelius said. "And along those lines, I think Tentz is hot for me. So if you don't mind, I'd like to do my part to gather information, by appearing single, available." Cornelius removed Naemi's arm from his side with a finger and a smile.

"Homints." The voice came from behind them, moving closer quickly. It was Bossin. Now face-to-face, he was not smiling. He spoke with little emotion. "You should go down below deck before Raffir comes. He's on rounds. He's looking for you. Stay away from Raffir."

"Listen, Bossin," began Cornelius. "I'm sorry. Let's sit down together and talk about this."

"You did not know. You are just Homints," replied Bossin. "I was too close to the rocks. And you are not a very good water skimmer."

Cornelius started to protest, but Naemi put her hand on his arm to stop more words from coming out. "Where is Raffir now?" she asked. She still had little idea what Cornelius and Bossin were talking about, but Bossin was talking, and that was more important than Cornelius driveling on.

"Raffir is working near the lazarette." Bossin turned to go. He hesitated, turned and opened his mouth to say something more, but no words came out. Bossin left.

"Let's get off the deck," said Naemi. "Then you can explain to me what is going on."

"And you can tell my why you're so paranoid," added Cornelius.

They doubled back around to the to the foredeck. Klendl and Ramon were gone. They went around to the starboard side of the ship and to the cabin door leading below decks, to the gurkbuzzel hold. Just as Cornelius was opening the door to let Naemi pass through another horn sounded from high above. A dozen voices then followed, bellowing into the wind. Up on the roof of the cabin a dozen Canines stood facing forward, arms extended out at their sides, legs apart, and chests out, heads up. They shouted in unison.

"Ho-Ho Tarvash Go. Into the winds that blow. To the rift channel and to

Big City we go."

The Tarvash rounded Somet Bay's headlands and sailed into the open waters. The wind here was strong. The gurkbuzzel sails flashed rapid bright circle patterns. Cornelius looked over the gunwale and spied the rocky spit where he and Bossin had been. Then it disappeared from sight behind the headlands.

"Come on," said Naemi. "Come and follow."

Cornelius gave her a disapproving look, then they ducked into the cabin.

At the bottom of the spiral staircase, Klendl blocked the entrance to the gurkbuzzel hold. The man was in the middle of some impassioned speech. Trying to scoot passed, Cornelius bumped into Klendl's shoulder, stopping him in mid sentence.

"Excuse me," Cornelius offered.

Naemi slipped in behind Cornelius and barely brushed the air near Klendl. She followed Cornelius to the back of the room to take a seat at a table.

The gurkbuzzel hold had been transformed into a tavern, with round oak tables arranged between a bar at the stern at one end of the room and a stage toward the bow. The Humans sat at several tables, and many more were empty. High on the walls all around were large displays of teeth, jaws and tusks from lake fauna, with tanned skins and bleached bones in between.

"What is this all about?" Naemi muttered sideways to Cornelius.

Klendl, annoyed at being interrupted, continued his diatribe. "So why are we all down here again? Are we prisoners now, to be taken up into the sun for a few hours only to be pushed back down into the belly of this beast for the duration?"

"Maybe it's too windy out on the open water?" That was Boglei, the little blond boy twin.

"An actual passenger ship from the Lake Docks to Big City would allow free roam," said Ramon.

From where Naemi was sitting, she could see nearly all the other Humans. No Canines were in the hold. Renchant, Boglei and Bogelia sat at a table nearest to Naemi and Cornelius. Ramon sat at a table by himself, as did the pale girl Tentz, near the exit. Klendl moved to stand near a table by the stage, where Dardele sat, quiet and lost in his own thoughts, ignoring the others.

Then Orumnam emerged from the stairwell into the hold. "Pardon, Klendl," she said. She sat down next to Tentz.

"That's the first time I've seen Orumnam all day," whispered Naemi to Cornelius. "She was gone before I even woke up."

Next Bossin descended from the stairs. Klendl turned and scooted out of the way towards Dardele's table. Klendl stood for a moment hesitating about something, then sat down without a word.

"Aren't you going to ask him?" said Bogelia.

"Ask Bossin about what things?" said Bossin. He turned to the table where the girl sat. Klendl remained silent and fidgeted in his seat.

"Why are we in here again?" Bogelia asked.

"Here?" said Bossin. "Is it unsafe? Is it unkind? Here you have everything you need until Big City."

Orumnam spoke. "Bossin, do you mean that we are to remain in this, room, for the remaining duration of our journey?"

Bossin avoided making eye contact with the wild haired woman from Aran, but he answered. "For now, Raffir says. So for now, stay. Stay and follow."

"That doesn't make any sense," said Boglei.

"But why?" asked Ramon. Tell us that. Give us a reason other than 'Raffir says.'"

"I think it's something Cornelius did," said Klendl, finding his voice.

Bossin became visibly upset at the mention of Cornelius' name. He huffed and snorted through his nose. He avoided looking in the direction of Cornelius' table. And he did not respond to Klendl.

"Maybe it's because of the quake," said Orumnam.

"What quake?" asked Klendl, alarmed all over again.

"Didn't you hear Raffir up on deck talking about it just before the Canines from shore left?" continued Orumnam. "I heard him talking about signs of an impending quake. Isn't that right, Bossin?"

Cornelius turned to Naemi and said, "See? I told you."

"Shh," said Naemi. "She wasn't there."

"If you were, then why didn't you know about the quake?" added Cornelius.

"Yes, yes," answered Bossin, still not looking at Orumnam. "That is coming. The coral said so. And the wind said so."

"And the trees," whispered Cornelius.

"That's preposterous," said Klendl. "There was no quake. And you can't predict one."

"It's all true. You'll see. Homints can't hear the telling of things when you don't listen and see." Bossin was tired of all the questions. "Raffir says Homints stay here, so Homints stay here. No trouble for Bossin. Bossin is already trouble. Homints stay. Stay and follow."

"But there's nothing to do here," whined Klendl.

"I will bring music and spirits for listening and dancing and drinking. No more complaints. Stay and follow." Bossin turned and activated the gurkbuzzel device with an intimate swirl of his finger in a groove of the spiral. A dozen meter wide portals opened in walls all around the hold. Out the portholes was the outside seen from topside. There was a gunwale, and sea and sky.

Klendl was so surprised he fell out of his chair.

"Wow," said Boglei and Bogelia together.

Bossin crossed to the opposite side of the hold to the bar. He busied himself by sorting through bottles, looking for something.

Naemi longed for a private talk with Cornelius, to find out what he'd really done to upset Bossin and Raffir. That was undoubtedly the reason why they were all now confined to the hold. She was confounded that the very people with whom she was locked up, she distrusted the most.

A dozen crewmen suddenly surged down the spiral staircase into the hold. They were loud and they were boisterous.

"Dobe Bossin. Dobe!" called out one of the Canine crew, a man older than Renchant, or at least as weathered.

Several of the others took up the greeting and chanted "Dobe Bossin! Dobe drink!" They sidled up to the bar, greeting the Humans on the way. But each avoided the table where Cornelius and Naemi sat. Indeed, it seemed like the floor stretched itself between their table and all the other tables, ostracizing them further.

"Great," said Naemi to Cornelius. "I was the Human these Canines trusted most. Now I'm a pariah by association. And it's all because of you."

Bossin served up drinks, the bartender for the crew shift.

One Canine at the bar threw back a shot of sap eel in rum. He slammed his empty glass on the bar and called out to one behind him. "Dallay Shome. Music!"

"Tien!" shouted another. "Music."

The Canine named Shome downed his own shot glass and deposited it onto the bar. Then he strutted to the gurkbuzzel device and gave it a good whirl with his hand.

The wall behind the stage rippled and a display case of musical instruments formed out of it. There were drums, flutes, banjos, guitars, a xylophone, tambourines and assorted clickers and scrapers. The stage floor rippled and a small piano grew out of it.

Shouts went up among the Canines and five stepped forward to claim instruments. Two began tuning banjos. Another slung a set of drums around his waist. One sat at the piano and started picking out notes. The fifth picked up a scraperboard and pick.

A Canine at the bar shouted "Play Dobbin Storm."

"No, play Tycho Day," said another.

The Canine at the gurkbuzzel device countered them both and called back "Nay, neither. Bard's Big Fish!"

The two acquiesced to cheers of agreement among the rest of the crew.

Ten more Canines stepped into the hold from spiral staircase. "Dobe Bossin. Drinks!" they shouted.

The room stretched wider and more tables grew out of the floor. The musicians on the stage shouted in unison "Hey Ho!" And the music and singing began.

The words were difficult to individually make out, but the story itself was not hard to follow. A lone fisherman with a tall tale of a catch too big to be true. The tempo was lively with a toe-tapping beat.

Bossin began serving up food along with the drinks.

Amidst the rowdy song and revelry, Naemi found the privacy she had been seeking. "Now at least we can talk without being easily overheard," she said. She looked Cornelius in the eye and said "Well?"

Cornelius was nodding his head to the music, grinning and slapping a hand to his thigh. Naemi's stare brought him back. "Oh that," he said. "Really, it's less than you might think." Cornelius leaned closer to Naemi and continued. "I was skimming on the water, out by the rocky spit that forms one side of the bay. Bossin was in front of me. But the wind changed and I didn't compensate in time. Our boards slammed together."

"You mean you hit him," clarified Naemi.

"Well, technically we were both moving." Naemi's look told Cornelius she'd already made up her mind on how to interpret the story. "Ok, my board hit his." It was easier to tell Naemi the story from the perspective she was more apt to believe.

"Then what happened?" she asked.

"We rested a bit on the rocks. Bossin got a little upset at the idea of not being on the water anymore."

"A little upset?" pressed Naemi.

"I don't think he gets off the boat much," Cornelius added.

"Is that why he's so good at water skimming?" Naemi was being sarcastic now.

"That's when we saw the coral light up," said Cornelius, growing more animated. "You should have seen it, Naemi. It was amazing. The water lit up red and orange and violet. Everything around, the moss on the rocks, the ferns, even the trees on the shore, lit up and glowed like they were caught in an electrified field. The sky crackled."

"That's when the Canines from Somet departed the ship?"

"Yeah. Then we came back in, too." Cornelius left out the part about seeing the beautiful Human woman.

"And Bossin?" asked Naemi.

"He's fine," said Cornelius. "He'll be fine."

"Apparently Raffir doesn't think so," said Naemi.

The other Humans were eating and drinking, singing and socializing with the Canines. But Cornelius and Naemi were neither observed nor attended to.

"It sort of seems like we're not welcome," said Cornelius.

"Personas non gratas," said Naemi.

"What does that mean?" asked Cornelius.

"It's a saying on Polaris," answered Naemi. "Means the same thing."

"Well, I'm still hungry," said Cornelius. "And I don't think Bossin is going to serve our table. Why don't you go to the bar and see if he'll at least serve you. Bring something back for me."

While Naemi was at the bar speaking with Bossin, Cornelius tried to make eye contact with Tentz. But the girl, not seeming so pale anymore, was focusing all her attention on eating and watching the others. Everyone but Cornelius.

Naemi returned with a plate of meat and cooked tubers.

"What this?" asked Cornelius.

"Red claw rat and hollow crunch root," said Naemi. "And yes, they're real. Bossin said they bartered for it at Somet."

Cornelius cut a piece of the steaming root and savored its butter taste. "Man, this is good. What's the significance of it being called 'hollow'?"

"Don't ask," said Naemi. She cut a piece of the meat and ate it.

"I just did," said Cornelius, taking another bit of the root.

"Fine," said Naemi. "It's hollow because it's inhabited by a juicy yellow grub." She watched in amusement as Cornelius slowed his chewing, then forced a swallow. "Good, isn't it?" It was rhetorical.

"Yeah." Cornelius switched to the meat.

They ate and enjoyed the food, the fresh bounty from Canius. It all smelled delicious, tasted delectable, felt wholesome.

The view out the portholes reflected a late afternoon, the gurkbuzzel approximating the day outside. To starboard, shadows cast by the ship's sails rippled their elongated shapes on the water.

Cornelius licked his fingers, his mouth still full of meat. "So what's the rest of your story?" he asked Naemi. He held back a burp, unsuccessfully, and licked his fingers again. He'd given up using his utensils.

Naemi was finished eating. She'd only eaten the meat. Her utensils were clean and neatly laying side by side in parallel on her plate. "My story?" she asked.

"Yes." Cornelius wiped his fingers on a cloth indiscriminately. "You said you knew what all these people were up to today. And you were going to tell me about it." He nodded out at the crowd.

"Oh. Most of them," Naemi said. She was about to say more when Tentz suddenly appeared at their table. She looked sallow, her eyes bloodshot.

"You've been looking at me. Well stop it." Tentz then spun on her heels and returned to her table, faced the stage and ignored Cornelius and Naemi again.

"What the…," began Cornelius.

"I thought you said she had a thing for you," Naemi said accusingly. "You do have a way with people."

"There's something weird about her," said Cornelius.

"I knew that the moment I saw her," said Naemi.

"She seems out of place," Cornelius went on.

"You know who's out of place," Naemi returned. She looked and nodded directly at the pudgy man sitting on the far side of the hold with lost Dardele. He was devouring his food with both hands. "That one. Klendl."

"Everyone looks out of place here," Cornelius said.

"He's fat." Naemi wasn't listening to Cornelius. "He's piggy. Soft. It's obvious. How could he fly a glider, run the length of the Lake Dock through gunfire and invasion, climb a rope ladder onto a strange ship, in that storm, with the rest of us?"

The current song from the band ended in a crack of cymbals, tambourine shakes and laughter. The Canine called Shone called across the room to the bar. "Bossin. Come here and sing us a song."

Shouts and claps and whistles rose up in agreement. Canine and Human yelled "Song!"

"Song!"

Bossin dismissed them with a wave and "No. No Bossin singing. Bossin is sad this day."

"Then sing us a sad song," someone called out.

"A sad song!" many more repeated.

Bossin stopped what he was doing. His gaze was down at the floor. Then he looked up. "A sad song," he yelled to Shone. Bossin shook his hands dry and crossed the room of agreeable people to the stage.

Cornelius and Naemi both looked at each other, then back to Bossin.

One of the two musicians with a guitar struck a chord, then waited while the room fell silent. He strummed a slow dirge, a forlorn prologue. The second guitar player handed his instrument to Bossin and surrendered his seat. The other musicians left the stage to join the audience.

Bossin slung the guitar strap over his shoulder. He held the instrument gently. He ran his pick down one string, from nut to bridge.

Bossin joined his music with his fellow guitarist's, bringing the somber tempo down lower than it already was. He sang.

> "That. That.
>
> Up, down, sideways.
>
> That. That.
>
> Swimming forward, backward, sideways.
>
> That. That.
>
> Rocks that never rock.
>
> Time is still. Only water breathes. Not me.

That. That."

There were words of praise from some tables. All the Canines were quiet. Bossin continued.

"No siren called me to land. But the ground took me.

That."

Naemi turned to Cornelius and said, "So you think he's fine?"

"I said he'll be fine," Cornelius returned.

"He's not fine," said Naemi.

Then the floor heaved. The room swayed. The tables and chairs and bar and instruments melted. The walls and ceiling and floor undulated like the inside of a bladder that someone just sat on. Spots ran across the gurkbuzzel surface. Humans and Canines tumbled into one another. Stomachs rose in chests. The lights dimmed.

"What's happening?" yelled Naemi. She wasn't the only one asking.

"Hands to deck!" shouted Shone.

Bossin was at the door, securing it open with the gurkbuzzel device. The rest of the Canines ran out and up the staircase, holding tight to the rails as the ship continued to sway. When the last Canine was out, Bossin faced the others and said "Homints will stay." Then he too went topside.

Cornelius climbed out from under Boglei and Bogelia, with help from Renchant. He looked around for Naemi. She was standing apart, holding her own. Cornelius came up to her as the gurkbuzzel hold reset and morphed back into its sterile pastel form.

"I'm fine," said Naemi, before Cornelius could ask. "You?"

"Yeah." Cornelius looked around. The others reached for the metal benches and sat, checking themselves for injuries. The emergency snapped Dardele out of his gloom. He moved from one to the other making sure everyone was all right. Back to Naemi Cornelius asked, "Are you going to stay?"

Naemi hesitated, considering the question. Before she could answer Cornelius was already moving toward the door.

"I'm going to see what's going on." He disappeared up the stairwell.

"Everyone else stay here," announced Naemi to the others, assuming charge.

"Not because you said so," countered Orumnam coldly.

Up topside the sky was dark. It was much later than the view out the gurkbuzzel portholes had portended. Cornelius clutched both sides of the doorframe and struggled to not fall backwards or forwards as the ship rocked. He bent his knees to compensate but ended up on them.

A voice from a crewman on the cabin roof bellowed down. "Pivot sails! Hold Position!" It was Raffir. He was not aware of Cornelius below.

Cornelius backed down the stairwell a little. He was barely in a position to see what was going on. There was little light, little perspective. The ship continued to rock, and from where Cornelius could see over the gunwale, lights in the distance twinkled and vanished and twinkled again. Cornelius took a chance and stuck his neck out the cabin door and peered up and out.

He could make out what he thought were the lights of other lake ships. Their lights twinkled here, there, over there. Some were closer than others. It looked like the nearer ships dipped below some great darkness, then reemerged. Further out, the next line of ships did the same, then the next. Way out in the distance was a flood of white lights. It was the Channel Locks, the end of this lake and the gateway to the next, and to Big City. Cornelius watched the furthest line of lake ships' lights dip and blink. Then the bright lights of the Channel Locks went out. And they stayed out.

A wave, thought Cornelius. *A quake tsunami.* He crept out of the cabin door and ran towards the bow of the ship. No Canines were in sight. Hopefully they were busy working the winches and the sails, securing ropes and gear. Cornelius strained to see more but little made sense. Then the sails of the Tarvash burst forth their light, illuminating everything, including Cornelius.

He turned and ran as fast as he could down the amidships towards the stern. He ducked down beside a lifeboat and peered over its upended keel. Bright flashes signaled back and forth from the Tarvash and nearby lake ships. Blinding flashes erupted from the Tarvash's sails in rhythms. The ships were communicating with one another. One more blinding conflagration coincided with the heave of another wave and Cornelius fell over and rolled. The small of his back slammed against a protruding eye-ring at the base of a gunwale followed by his head hitting something. Utter darkness ensued.

Cornelius fought hard against the pain. He hurt all over, particularly the whole that was his head, skull, brain, and mind. All the rest of him hurt, too. His legs, His back. Just the act of considering the information his neurons were transmitting made his mind swirl. Thoughts were a jumble, or simply weren't there. 'One. Twelve. Yellow pancakes. Blue sky through dark leaves. Rain.' Rain reminded him of water, reminded him of the ship, reminded him of....

Cornelius opened his eyes. Bright pointed lights overhead. They spun, but maybe that was just his mind reeling. They slowed. They stopped. Most of them. They were the stars. That's right. Though some of them still moved across the sky. They moved in different directions, in different orbits. So tiny. Markhab's satellites. Always watching. What did they see in the dark?

Then the sky blazed with light so bright Cornelius let out a cry. It was the gurkbuzzel sails. Cornelius scooted up onto his haunches and reached back with one hand to feel for the gunwale and the eye ring. A figure stepped in front of the light, silhouetted. Cornelius put his other hand up to the light to try and shield his eyes. A strong hand was thrust down at Cornelius. He grabbed the hand and was helped up to his feet.

The Canine before Cornelius was tall, almost two and a half meters, taller even than Raffir. His face was long, his hair also long, golden brown. It was parted straight down the middle of his head, cropped close around the ears, which were ten centimeters tall, erect and directed forward. From the right ear dangled a gold earring. His eyes were large with piercing gold irises around his black pupils. His nose was longer than Raffir's or Bossin's, or any of the other Canine crew.

His wore a full-length coat, black with great triple lapels and big black shiny buttons. A silver sash extended from his left shoulder and crossed his chest, connecting with a silver belt.

"When my Grunt Captain gives an order to remain below decks, I expect that order to be followed." It was Captain Katzer. "You are the one called Cornelius?" Katzer spoke unhurried with measured words.

"I am," answered Cornelius. "Thank you, Captain."

Katzer observed Cornelius for a few moments, sizing up the Human, determining Cornelius' character.

Cornelius was not sure what to do or what to say. He remained quiet, frozen under Katzer's gaze.

"My wife tells me you spoke to her today."

"Your, wife?" Cornelius was confused. Then he remembered the beautiful naked Human woman he had seen and called out to while he was water skimming. Naemi said the Captain's wife was Human. "Uh...."

In the same measured voice Katzer said, "Why would my wife even have an opportunity to speak about you?"

"I only..." Cornelius stammered, and he knew that was the wrong thing to say, to admit.

"My wife should not have cause to speak of any of you," Katzer continued. "I will not permit you to remain on the Tarvash."

"I..." started Cornelius. Then "What? I'm really sorry. It was an accident. I...."

"It has also come to my attention that Raffir is looking for a reason to kill you. You have taken honor from Bossin. I am not inclined to temper Raffir's intentions."

Cornelius could not believe what he was hearing. What was he to do? Fight Raffir in a duel? The outcome of that was quite uncertain.

"On the other hand," Katzer added, "I have made a personal pledge to Renender to see to your wellbeing. I owe Renender many things, but he did not vouch for your behavior. And magnanimity was not one of the things I promised him."

"But we're in the middle of the lake," complained Cornelius. He had no more composure.

"On the contrary," said Katzer, "We have arrived at the Rift Channel Locks. But there is great damage because of the tsunami. Many ships are damaged and the locks do not work. No ships can make the passage until repairs have been made."

"But I have to get to Big City by...." Cornelius was frantic.

"I understand your destination and your need," added Katzer. "I will give you fifteen minutes to be off the Tarvash. Raffir should be around by then, and you will not want to meet him. You will take one of my lifeboats. I owe Renender that much."

"A life boat?" Cornelius looked at the upturned lifeboats stacked nearby, below which he'd crouched before blacking out.

"There is an overflow channel that runs parallel to the locks on their west side. It flows freely through the rift to the next lake."

Cornelius took a deep breath. One door closes and another opens, the ever-apparent long reach of Renender's influence. "Thank you," was all he uttered.

"Fifteen minutes," said Katzer. And the Canine turned and walked away in the bright lights of the gurkbuzzel sails portside towards bow.

Cornelius thought fast. There wasn't much to think about. Find Naemi, and get off the ship, fast. Cornelius ran up the deck of the ship starboard. He heard shouting ahead of him, and slammed right into Naemi who appeared out of nowhere, running, out of breath. In unison, each exclaimed, "We've got to get off this ship!"

Cornelius grabbed Naemi by the shoulders. She grabbed onto his.

"Now!" hissed Naemi.

"I know," said Cornelius. "Captain Katzer...." he began.

"Tentz is dead," said Naemi quickly.

"What?" exclaimed Cornelius. "How?"

"I killed her," said Naemi hurriedly. "We need to go. Now."

Cornelius was quick. "I have a boat."

30 THE GREAT ESCAPE

All was silent but for the pat-pat, pat-pat of sensible shoes hurrying down the floor's course concrete surface. A lone bulb of light hung from overhead illuminating this stretch. The hall was like a tunnel, long, straight, stark white. One bulb hung every hundred meters. Big numbers were painted in green on the sidewalls and floor under the bulb marking its spot in the line. "120." That was not even halfway yet. Renender stopped a moment to catch his breath. He bent over and grabbed his knees with his sweating palms. *Breathe. Breathe. Catch your breath,*" he muttered to himself. Renender glanced up at the wall on his left at the security camera. The status light was red.

"Fifteen minutes," old one-eyed Tychlo had said. "We can keep them down for fifteen minutes. But you've got to reach the end of the line by then or you risk being caught on the security tapes, if anyone bothers to check them. And they might."

Keep going, Renender told himself. And he hurried off down the lonely hall toward light "121."

It was an excellent plan from the start, and was executed better than he could possibly have imagined.

The Empalasor Hotel's VIP Lounge was electric with energy tonight. The pending occupation was on everybody's mind and tongue, and both patrons and purveyors were doing their utmost to forget it this night.

Socialites, businessmen, and those who prey on both, filled the eighth level bar overlooking the Plaza and holographic lake cavern. Music, chatter, laughter and shouts filled the room. The walls' sound absorbers could barely do their job muffling and diverting the echoes from the titanium walls.

Renender stood at the bar with Jeanette close at hand. Jeaneau was some distance away. Not two paces further sat the Adjunct Mayor herself, leaning over the bar snorting a white line of kokol blow. One of her many advisors said something in her ear and she leaned back bursting into laughter, nearly tipping from her seat. Her entire entourage joined in the laughter, even if they hadn't heard the joke, and the laughter spread out around the room like ripples in a pond.

A woman in a green sequined dress, some-when in her fifties, staggered up to Renender, her drink and ice trying desperately to stay in her glass as she waved it about. It looked like a tempest in a teapot. "Excluse me you handshome Slir," she slurred. "Is this seat taken?"

Renender recognized her as the woman who's Escort incapacitated the screaming woman in the Plaza when he'd first arrived. She was certainly as close to being a mess as inebriation made possible. Renender wasn't sure how amusing this would be, but he decided to ad lib a little while he waited for Balthorelei. He took a sip from his drink of Cursple, glanced passed Jeanette toward the entrance and the elevators, then turned back smiling and replied, "Why as a matter of fact, I was just looking for you, Alice."

The woman blinked, suddenly trying to determine if she knew Renender somehow, embarrassed that she also might have forgotten that her name was Alice. It somehow didn't sound right, but she'd had quite a few drinks. Maybe it was, and she'd just forgotten. She smiled back and said, "Oh you must be one of my clients. I'm a veterinarian, you see. I meet so many people all the time."

"Of course," said Renender. He winked at the woman and grinned widely, letting his dimples do their work.

"How is your...." and the woman who may or may not be named Alice trailed off, trying to remember Renender's animal's name.

Renender grasped at the first thing he could think of. "My cave marmelot, Jaspar," he said proudly. "You corrected an astigmatism in her left eye."

"Marmelot. Marmelot," Alice said, not exactly remembering if she had actually seen one of those in her practice. "That's the one with the tentacle thingies on its face?" She wiggled her fingers in front of her nose at Renender.

"Uh, no. That's a star-nosed mole."

"That's it," said the Alice. "How is he?"

"The marmelot," Renender corrected her. "She's fine."

"Oh good. Such a beautiful creature, with soft golden fur," Alice beamed at remembering the pet she had not seen and that Renender did not have.

"Course, reddish fur," corrected Renender.

"Simply beautiful," said Alice. "Simply beautiful," she added with exuberance. And she hoisted her glass and toasted Renender. "To the mole!"

Renender raised his glass smiling and said "The marmelot." And both drank.

"Honestly!" said Jeanette not so under her breath. She had observed the entire exchange at Renender's side.

More laughter erupted from the Adjunct Mayor, and Renender turned just in time to see a delivery boy step into the room carrying a large bouquet of flowers. They caught the Adjunct's eye and she let out an "Oooh!" People turned and added their own.

The boy scanned the room looking for someone. A server stepped up to inquire for the boy, then pointed Renender out in the crowd.

Renender gulped.

The boy nodded and started into the room through the throng, holding the flowers high and uttering "Excuse me's," and "Pardons." Nearing the Adjunct, the titular mayor turned to him grinning and extended her arm to impede the boy's advance.

"Who's the lucky Guest?" she asked loudly so as to draw attention and grandstand.

"A Mister Renender," the boy replied.

"Renender?" said the Adjunct, laughing. She turned in Renender's direction and shouted over the crowd's din, "Renender is our distinguished Guest in the City tonight. An admirer?"

Cheers and clapping broke out. Some because the Adjunct Mayor said his name, only a few because they knew him, and no small amount because an Escort slipped on a fallen ice cube, did a back flip, rolled, and landed a perfect ten.

"Oh, that's my Escort," groaned Alice. "She's a show off."

The Adjunct turned back to the delivery boy and asked, "Who sent them?" Then she had a brilliant idea. "Never mind. It doesn't matter. Here now, just throw away the card and say they're from the City, thanking Renender for choosing to stay with us tonight." In a softer voice closer to the boy she added, "I'll tip you double what you were offered. She motioned to one of her advisors who promptly thumbed some credit vouchers off of a roll out of his pocket and handed them to the boy.

The boy shoved the credits into his pocket and turned tail out of the lounge with a quick "Thanks."

Renender's face was frozen in a hardened smile as he watched the Adjunct handle the flowers.

She took the bouquet out of the delivery boy's hand, got up, and moved toward Renender. "On behalf of Mine City," she said presenting the flowers to Renender, "May your stay with us be delightful, and full of pleasure at every turn." It was the City's current marketing slogan.

Renender took the bouquet from the Adjunct, bowing slightly and thanking her with some modesty. He quickly eyed the base of the tubular vase. There neatly hidden was a small glass vial attached to the stem of one of the flowers, the blooming rubber mint, sticking up above the others. Safe, and at present, unbroken. Renender imperceptibly sighed and raised his glass in toast to the Adjunct. The room followed, another excuse for another drink. The Adjunct Mayor reciprocated, sipped her drink, and returned her attention to her clique, bending down to another line of kokol blow.

Renender turned to his Escort and said with a hint of sarcasm, "Jeanette, be a dear and take these back to my room." He thrust the bouquet at her.

Jeanette huffed and looked around. "Where is Jeaneau? Oh, fine. I'll be RIGHT back," she said, and she forced herself through the crowd toward the entrance.

Renender turned back to the woman in green at his side, leaned in close to her and said, "Alice, I bet those were really from you." He raised his glass to her.

The inebriated woman blinked in partial confusion, then blushed, smiled and giggled with an "Ohh." She wondered if she had sent them, and then decided that yes, she did remember. She blinked again and raised her glass to Renender and took a drink. "To the City's Guest!" It no longer occurred to her that her name was not Alice.

Jeaneau finally appeared at Renender's side.

"There you are," said Renender. He leaned over and planted a wet kiss on the Escort's cheek.

The woman who wasn't, but now maybe was Alice, gave Jeaneau a queer look, which she then also gave to Renender. Momentarily put off, she looked passed Renender and moved off into the crowd again, stopping a stranger and asking rather loudly, "Carron is it? How is your marmelot? Or is it a mole?"

The startled stranger gave Alice a glassy stare and replied, "What?"

Renender smiled at the exchange but was interrupted by Jeaneau who asked, "Where's Jeanette?"

"She's running an errand for me," said Renender off handedly. He reached down and pinched one of Jeaneau's nipples, which caused the Escort to gasp and smile.

He brushed Renender's hand away and asked, "Are you hungry? They're serving wings against the wall over there." He nodded in the direction Alice had gone.

"That sounds good," answered Renender. The businessman and his Escort mingled and managed their way through the crowd toward the far wall. Indeed, just as Jeaneau described, laid out in exquisite detail on a table were platters of roasted wings and crisp hors d'oeuvres. Alice was there gorging herself. With one hand she held a plate of wings and celery sticks with nut butter. Out of her masticating mouth she told a story of a bat with four wings to an unsuspecting man younger than Renender. In the other hand Alice's glass danced in the air.

Renender caught the young man's eye and smiled. The young man smiled back. Then his attention refocused on Alice who was making a point about the importance of well-groomed feathers. "You don't say?" replied the young man.

Jeaneau offered Renender a plate of wings. He ate some and said, "Oh my, these are good," discarding some bones onto the plate.

Jeaneau smiled and nodded and helped himself to more. "Do you see anyone here you recognize?" he asked.

Renender turned back around to face the room. Scanning the self-absorbed crowd, he was surprised he recognized more than a few faces. "Yes. There is Bienda, a microelectronics exporter from Lupus City. With her is her husband, whose name is Blent, something. He's a software writer, for a racy pornographic enterprise." Renender shifted position in his pants as he remembered the man's work well. "Behind them nearer to the musicians are the Gort brothers. Strange to see them here. They're artists, sculptists. Amorphous figures in cinnabar. I've seen their work in a Lupus City gallery not long ago."

"Any good?" asked Jeaneau.

Renender considered a moment then said, "I'd like to see them try something else." He was being polite. Looking back toward the entrance he said, "There's the Adjunct, of course." And behind the Adjunct, wearing an amazing one-piece burgundy wrap showing off her curvy lines stepped Balthorelei into the room. Her hair was made up tall and sparkled with diamond dust. A broach of gypsum roses added a stunning touch. Around her hair, wrapping her head was a matching burgundy lace mobius brimmed hat that completed her look. Renender beamed in delight. She was right on time.

Balthorelei ordered a drink at the bar. She cast a smile in the direction of the Adjunct who sat nearby, spellbound by the beautiful woman in burgundy. Balthorelei didn't say a word other than to mouth a "Thank you" to the bartender. Then she made her way to the other side of the room and stood near the musicians. The singer recognized her and he craftily ended his song, the musicians following suit. A guitarist reached down and helped Balthorelei up onto the stage and the singer proceeded to introduce her.

Oh, this will be good, thought Renender.

"Ladies and Gentlemen," began the tall slight man in an equally burgundy pinstriped suit. "We are lucky tonight!"

The noise of the crowd lessened a bit. The man continued.

"Singing her way through the most exclusive venues, may I introduce to you a Diva in her own right, Mine City's own gem, Night Breath."

The man's clapping against the microphone in his hand sounded throughout the room and prompted the crowd to give up a joyous welcome. Renender noticed the Adjunct come up from another line of kokol blow, brush the white off her nose, and join in the clapping cheering welcome.

Night Breath, thought Renender. *How wonderful.*

"Isn't that the woman you knew from the Geode Club?" asked Jeaneau.

"She sings the circuit apparently," said Renender casually. Then he added, "I had no idea she'd be here." Renender eyed Jeaneau. It would not be wise to underestimate the levels of an Escort's curiosity, or resourcefulness in satisfying it. "Another crisp with nut butter, please." The Escort did his bidding.

"Thank you, Tom Nikkel," Night Breath's voice projected throughout the lounge as she took the mike from the pinstriped man. "And hello to all of you! I'd like to sing you a favorite song of mine, and I bet it's a favorite of yours. It's an old song from more northerly parts. If you've not heard it before, you're gonna like it."

Night Breath turned slightly to the drummer behind her and gave him his queue. Turning back she caught sight of Renender. Night Breath winked, gave him a nod, then beamed to the crowd and began.

Renender smiled outwardly, but not as great as inwardly. His pulse quickened as he listened to Night Breath's song. It was a ballad, and Renender knew the verses well. Many in the crowd would. It was a popular nursery rhyme. The crowd sang along.

"There were two maids named Fen and Men,

The bluest and palest millers 'neath the northern Lights, who deigned to take the Grotte Mill up one night.

"Fen grasped the handle left while Men grasped the lever right.

Together they fought 'gainst the Grotte Mill's stubborn weight.

"Grunting and groaning they heard the Grotte give,

Then round the mountaintop they sang.

Round and round from top to bottom

Till the turning Grotte did stick and was stuck in spot.

"Fen, she hollered.

Men, she did shout.

Together they heaved and hoed.

Sweat burst forth from the brow of Fen,

And blood boiled red in the face of Men.

"Harder they heaved till the Grotte by torque was freed,

And finally the mill turned and gave some more.

The corn was crushed, the barley ground, the wheat to powder was ground, ground down.

The Grotte turned down near its lowest grind,

And one last great turn did Fen then try.

Beneath was ground only gristle and gore, and Men with her might leaning to her task turned the mill once more, but naught but salt came out. The salt piled high and the Grotte was stuck at stop at the very bottom of its wheel.

And Fen then laughed, and Men laughed too, and they both took a spell to rest.

Then Fen took the place of Men, and Men took the place of Fen, and they began to twist the Grotte Mill up again."

The crowd roared. The song was always a favorite in beer halls, and tonight's high-heeled clientele showed just as much exuberance and abandon. Night Breath's next cancion threatened to bring the house down. Big Bessie's Rumble, a Lupin City favorite about a down and out girl who takes on a group of thugs just out of military cadet finishing school. It put every last Guest of the Empalasor's VIP Lounge into a frenzied shout and dance.

Renender was a good dancer, and his Escort Jeaneau was hard pressed to keep up. Even the woman who wasn't Alice slurred the right words and danced with her glass held high.

Renender spun round, loosed himself from Jeaneau and slipped his arm around the waist of the woman not named Alice and whispered into her ear. "My dear Alice, you are positively at your best tonight. I've never seen you move so."

Alice in the green dress accepted flattery as her cause célèbre and broke into a childish giggle just as Jeaneau twirled back into Renender's grasp.

Night Breath reached her crescendo and the room bellowed with her.

"Their heads rolled round while Bessie's head held high – Boom! Chuggalugga Boom, Bessie, Chuggalugga Boom!"

Applause and laughter erupted all around with one final

"Boom! Chuggalugga Boom, Bessie, Chuggalugga Boom!"

A cackle of laughter at Renender's ear caused him to turn. The Adjunct Mayor and her dance partner were next to Renender and Jeaneau and Alice smack dab in the center of the floor. "It's a party to remember!" Renender called out to the Adjunct.

Beaming through her narcotic-driven haze, the Adjunct agreed, adding, "A night to remember. Let's make it last. We may not be having many more such festive nights."

Renender smiled and brushed the comment aside. "There's always a niche for business, and profit and merry-making, under any regime, Adjunct."

"Too true. Too true, Renender." Then she said, "May I buy you another drink?"

"I would be delighted. Thank you. But please, Alice here needs another as well."

The woman in the green dress was hanging on Renender's arm again, this time more for balance. She took note at hearing her name, or not her name.

"Alice dear," said Renender. "May I present the Adjunct Mayor. Adjunct, Alice."

Alice beamed, and the Adjunct bowed, sure she was being introduced to a maven of Lupus City's business community.

"Why, you're right after all," said Alice. "A marmelot for sure."

Renender laughed at the joke and his laughter, lost on everyone, spread wide.

Night Breath began her final number, and Renender smiled at its recognition.

"Aaat Laaast...."

They moved back towards the bar with Alice in tow. Jeaneau spoke into Renender's ear, serious amid the pomp. "Where did you say Jeanette went?"

Renender replied absently, "On an errand. I said that. Some flowers or something. Yes, she went back to the room."

"She should be back by now," said Jeaneau.

"Well, possibly," said Renender.

"Let's go back to your suite," said Jeaneau.

"You can go, my boy. You're my Escort, not the other way around. I'm staying here with Alice and the Adjunct Mayor. This party is just getting started."

Jeaneau looked torn. He was assigned to Renender. But so was Jeanette. Where was she?

"Go on. I'll be right here when you both get back," said Renender. "We'll have a grand old time."

"Alright," said Jeaneau. "I'll be RIGHT back."

"Yes my boy," said Renender. That's exactly what Jeanette had said. Renender watched Jeaneau exit the room. He then glanced at the stage and saw that Night Breath was watching, too.

She crooned the finishing words to her song, "For you are mine. At last."

"Brava!" yelled Renender. And the crowd followed. *Beautiful song. Beautiful voice*, thought Renender.

"Thank you. Thank you very much," said Night Breath into the microphone.

Tom Nikkel took back the mike and said, "Night Breath, Ladies and Gentlemen," to more applause.

Balthorelei left the stage and left the lounge.

* * *

"244." The end of the line. Renender was exhausted. He panted, gulping breaths. His knees were shaking. He bent over and grabbed his kneecaps. He looked up. The cameras were still off. There were three of them here at the end, one at ceiling level on each side wall, and one above the green double doors with large letters reading "SEPTUM." Renender stood erect, glanced at his wrist. No watch. He faced the doors, stepped over the huge painted "244" and pushed against the doors' release hatch. The doors parted, "SEP" and "TUM" on either side. Renender strode through. The doors clicked shut behind him just as the red lights of the surveillance cameras turned to green.

The Septum was an anteroom to the deep tunnels beyond. There were no cameras here. A bare bulb hung from above as the only illumination. The ceiling was broken, vaulted here, low and jagged there. In the oval chamber five meters wide opened five rough hewn holes each as tall as Renender. Each led in a different direction, down, left, straight, up, right. In between the holes, separating one from another were narrow bands of vestigial rock, septums.

Renender put his hand into the top of his shirt and reached in. He pulled out the key that the Trickle Depth Miner, Bordent, had given him in the Hypogeum. The bulky, flat, upside-down pear-shaped key was jagged all along its perimeter, as if some rodent had taken more than a hundred tiny bites out of it. The key was made of titanium, of course. One tiny notch near the bottom was edged in brass.

"Start here," Bordent had said. "Follow each notch clockwise with a fingernail. Don't lose your place! Each notch corresponds to the wall on your left. Always keep left! Even if you don't want to. Otherwise you'll be lost. Follow the left wall. Follow the notches to their end. Don't be driven mad. You'll be tempted to. It will seem the easier way." Then, "Start in the

Septum. The first hole on the left."

Renender took a deep breath. He let it out slowly. "Ok. Let's do this," he whispered as he adjusted his backpack. He started in. He started down.

* * *

Renender tarried at the VIP Lounge not more than ten minutes after Balthorelei, Night Breath, finished her set and followed Jeaneau out. Her reappearance at the elevator banks, quick wink and finger signal told him it was time. Renender took his leave of the Adjunct Mayor and offered to walk the woman not actually named Alice, out. She agreed with little trouble, and didn't bother to remember about her own Escort. They departed, Renender doing most of the walking.

"What's this?" asked Balthorelei at the open elevator.

"A favor, and perhaps an alibi, a diversion," said Renender. "What is your room, dear Alice?" he asked.

"Oh, well. Let's see. It's on the ninth floor. Tenth I think actually," Alice answered with some difficulty. "You are the singer," she added. "You sing so pretty. So nice."

"There are only eight floors." Balthorelei was impatient.

"We'll get you a nice cup of coffee, at the second floor lounge," said Renender, holding Alice steady.

"Oh that would be so lovely," she accepted.

The lift settled at "2" and the doors opened.

"We'll get you a good strong cup of coffee, dear," Renender said to Alice. "It's been a lovely evening. Thank you for your intimate acquaintance." Renender kissed the woman on both cheeks.

Alice giggled and blushed and attempted to straighten her dress and hair, in case she had indeed just been intimate with a man and just didn't remember.

Renender and Balthorelei, one on each side, helped Alice out of the lift, around the corner and onto a seat at the café bar.

Balthorelei wanted to finish this business as quickly as possible. "A double espresso for the, green lady here," she called out to the barista even as the girl started to mouth her own greeting.

"Coming right up," said the girl, pleasantly. *Won't get any tip out of her*, she thought of Balthorelei.

"This needs to be fast," said Balthorelei to Renender.

"It will be," he said. Then to Alice, whose head was drooping over the bar counter, eyes half closed and drool commencing an escape from her flappy lips, he cooed, "And just who are you really, Alice dear? Hm?" Renender reached into the hem of the woman's dress where her pocketbook was cached away in an inner pouch. He opened it and pulled out the woman's ID. "Well, Daljones is it. From Lupus City. I like Alice better."

Balthorelei pulled on the card and took a quick look. "A veterinarian?" She gave Renender a most quizzical look and asked, "What is she doing with you?"

"We danced," Renender said. He pulled one of several credit ID vouchers from his own pocket, and switched it with Alice's. He hid the card and pocketbook back in the dress pouch. "She is under the impression that I, or rather my pet marmelot, is a patient of hers."

Balthorelei looked blankly at Renender for a moment, not having to ask the next question.

"I may have mentioned it," Renender said with a sly grin on one side of his cheek.

"Really," said Balthorelei. "We have business."

"Yes, yes. Just a bit of fun," said Renender.

The barista returned with a steaming cup and set it on the table in front of Alice.

Renender keyed in his own credit voucher for the drink. Then he added twenty thousand more credits. "Alice here has had a bit to drink," he said to the girl. "Don't let her fall off her seat. This should cover about anything else she might want. Give her the special treatment."

The barista saw the huge tab he'd left. "Are you sure you want to leave that as a tab? An amount that size is reportable. Now if you left it as, say, a tip, then we don't have to report it, and I never saw you."

Renender liked this girl. She would go far. If only he had the time to watch her abilities develop, she could be a valuable person to know. But Renender knew what he was doing. "I'll leave it as a tab. But I like your style." He keyed in ten thousand and logged it as a tip. "I'll check in on you again."

The barista was sufficiently impressed. Not bad for a slow night. But then again she had the uncanny ability to detect the slightest con among Guests, and the skill to use the mask of an efficient and pleasant server girl to maximize her turning tricks. That's what she thought the barista's trade really was. And it turned her on to manipulate people so easily.

"Are you kidding?" said Balthorelei.

"It's all part of the plan, Balth. All part of the plan." Renender winked back at the barista, who used a towel to wipe Alice's dribble off her counter. He and Balthorelei quickly headed out and back to the lift. They were on their way up to his suite in seconds.

At the door to his room Renender asked, "Was it difficult?"

Balthorelei shrugged. "The bitch tried to scratch me just before passing out. Your boy toy tried to hit me. But hey, most of the guys around here do." She smiled. "Nothing I couldn't handle."

Tychlo came around out of the bedroom as Renender and Balthorelei entered. "Ah, you're finally here," he said smiling. The patch over his eye moved up and down as he spoke. "I've got everything here tied up pretty well."

"Where are they?" asked Renender.

"In there," said Tychlo nodding toward in the direction of the bedroom. "Come and have a look."

The bed was yet unused. A vase and flowers were on the floor, water spilt. Petals yellow and blue lay about, curled up at their edges. A lingering scent both sweet and musky hung in the air. In the center of the room in two straight-backed wooden chairs, cushioned for comfort, sat Jeanette and Jeaneau side by side. Their ankles were bound to the legs of the chairs, their waists tied around the backs, their hands wrapped in cords behind them. Tape covered their mouths. Their eyes were blindfolded and their heads were slumped over. Both were naked.

"Are they out?" asked Renender.

"Out cold," replied Tychlo.

"Why are they naked?" asked Renender. He looked at Jeaneau's penis, erect with some precum glistening at its head. Jeanette was visibly moist in her corresponding anatomy.

"They are Escorts," replied Tychlo. "They weren't wearing much anyway." He saw Renender's attention. "It's the fainting gas. It brings on an erection. Makes women moist. It's a versatile drug."

"I can see that," said Renender. "How long will they be out?"

"No telling," said Balthorelei. "Another hour would be nice, but it's not a guarantee. We need to hurry. Bordent's waiting for us in the Hypogeum."

"Ok. Wait for me in the other room," said Renender. "I'll be right there."

Balthorelei and Tychlo left him alone with the comatose and immobilized Escorts. Renender eyed them closely, noting the slow rise and fall of their chests as they breathed. Up close in front of Jeanette, a lock of her hair hung down, tickling her nose.

Turning around, Renender approached the spilt vase and flowers. On the end of one of the flower's stems was still affixed the jagged remnants of the small glass vial that had held the fainting gas. Balthorelei had been right. Jeanette, in her arrogant manner, would deliberately handle the bouquet roughly and inadvertently crush the vial. Innocently, or not, she would steal a whiff that would debilitate her just enough for Renender's co-conspirators to overwhelm her. Jeanette was more than a match for any one of them. It had taken two, plus the gas, to subdue her.

Renender bent down and picked up the stem. He caught just enough of a whiff of residual gas that he suddenly felt light headed. He dropped the stem and his mind whirled. His breathing quickened and he gasped to bring in enough oxygen to dissipate the fainting gas in his lungs. His face flushed. He felt euphoric. His penis hardened in his pants, aching for release. Renender grabbed himself and was taken to a whole new level of ecstasy by his own touch. He was hyper sensitive. He shook his head wildly. "Wow," he said aloud.

Turning back to his captives, he crouched down in front of Jeanette. He brushed his fingers against her moist dripping vagina. Her trimmed pubic hair glistened as if sprinkled with dew. Renender's eyes detected movement from her face and he jerked his fingers away from her. He eyed her closely. Nothing more. Perhaps it was just a tic, a muscle spasm in her face. Renender smelled his fingers. Delicious. He shook his fingers in the air and wiped them on his pants. His penis responded with renewed throbbing.

Renender turned his attention to Jeaneau. The man was absolutely still but for a six-centimeter string of precum dangling from his penis. Renender reached down and grasped the Escort's tool. He didn't move or react in any way. Renender cupped Jeaneau's smoothly shaven balls, squeezed them a little, and then pulled on the meaty shaft. A thick stream of fluid ran out the opening of his penis. Renender scooped it up, brought it up to his nose and smelled it. "Mm," he moaned. Then he licked the wetness off his fingers.

"Renender, come on!" came Balthorelei's impatient voice from the other room.

Renender sighed. He reached out and squeezed one of Jeaneau's nipples. The boy flinched, causing Renender to jump back. "Coming!" he called out to the others. He quickly left the two Escorts to join his companions.

Balthorelei had changed out of her burgundy dress and into drab grey miners overalls. She handed a pair to Renender along with a hooded cloak.

"Put these on," she said. "And then let's get out of here."

Renender changed quickly. He grabbed his small satchel and they vacated the suite.

* * *

There were few people about the Plaza at this hour. There was a flower seller with his cart, the same boy who had delivered the bouquet to Renender in the Empalasor's VIP Lounge. Two miners were sitting on the steps of a shuttered business sharing puffs off a roach. At the edge of the holographic lake, their legs dangling over the drop off, two students sat crouched over. One comforted the other who was puking into the abyss.

"We need to stop by the flower seller first," whispered Tychlo.

The boy was busy clipping the ends off stems over his pots of water. He looked up and recognized Tychlo. "Hey there Pops. Back for some more blue rubber mint and roses? Only thirteen credits for a return customer."

"No, no. Not right now," answered Tychlo. "Do you still have that bill of sale from the flowers I bought, like I asked?"

"Sure Pops," said the boy. "I kept it blank just like you asked."

"Good. Here," said Tychlo. He pulled a card from his pocket and handed it to the boy. "Run this through as the identity of the purchaser. Okay?"

The boy took the card, looked at the name and whistled. It was the Adjunct Mayor's card, the one she'd slipped into the bouquet in the VIP Lounge.

Tychlo turned to Renender. "Here's where you come in again."

"Got it," said Renender. He pulled out a credit voucher ID and ran a tab. Twenty thousand credits. "Send all these flowers here to a woman named Alice. Uh, wait." He pulled Alice's ID card out of his pocket. "Daljones. Find out where she's staying and deliver all of them yourself."

The flower seller was having a great night. "Now you're talking. You've got it Pops."

"Something else. Mess up the bed. Knock a few things over. And, uh, masturbate onto the sheets. I'll make it worth your while." He keyed in ten thousand more as a tip.

"Kinky stuff, man. But I'm into it. It's cool. It's cool. You guys sure are cookin' up some kinda prank. With the Adjunct involved. Hot tamale. Let's do it."

Renender wished he could be there, watching the boy, or even better, watch it on a closed circuit channel. "Do it now, then take the rest of the night off. Enjoy yourself."

"Hurry," said Balthorelei. He's waiting." Her voice was almost a growl.

"One moment," said Renender. He headed over to the edge of the lake. He took all his identity cards and credit vouchers out of his pockets. The trappings of his life, who he was. He kissed them and tossed them over the edge. "Goodbye," he called after. He rejoined Balthorelei and Tychlo. The three of them departed the Plaza leaving behind the flower seller, the vomitus youths, the smoking miners, and Renender's past.

* * *

Balthorelei and Tychlo led Renender through a maze of corridors deeper and deeper into Mine City. Renender tried to keep his face hidden under the hood of his cloak, but he had little confidence in the disguise. To his eye, they were a suspicious trio, slinking about in a hurried manner, obvious to avoid anyone they encountered. They kept going for what seemed like an hour through tunneled streets that got narrower and narrower as they progressed deeper.

Finally they came to a checkpoint beyond which only miners were allowed. The guard was a stout woman, red hair. She looked up from reading a glossy magazine as the three approached.

Balthorelei greeted her. "Bendeth."

"Balth...." began the guard.

"Shh," cautioned Balthorelei. "Bendeth, this is the one."

The guard nodded. She bent down and picked up a backpack and moved around from the back of her station. "Take this," she said to Renender without any pleasantries. "Now quickly, into the Hypogeum. The next shift change will be soon. You'll be able to blend in." She sized Renender up for a moment. "Just barely." She stepped aside to let the three of them pass.

"Thanks Bendeth. I owe you." Balthorelei gave the guard a kiss on the lips as she passed.

"I'll see you later tonight," said the guard. "Sing me a good song at the Club."

"You've got it," said Balthorelei.

Passed the guard station, the corridor teed off left and right.

"Left," whispered Tychlo. And the others followed him.

The hall was twenty meters long in this direction. Rooms opened off the hall on each side, doorless dormitories, locker rooms and equipment storage chambers. At the end of the hall, the great red granite frame of the miner's inner sanctum rose above them. Behind the solid stone edifice was the Hypogeum. Its dimensions were huge and it bulged out from the wall in stone as if massively inflated from the inside. The Hypogeum was a place of quiet, of chanting, of prayers, of smoke, of whispers. Before entering the dangers of the deep mines, and upon safely returning, many miners tarried in the Hypogeum to whisper prayers, some of safe return, others in thanks, and others in mourning. Sconces of bright red flames burned on each side of the stone door. Balthorelei picked up three small sticks of incense from a dispenser and lit them in the flames. She handed one to Tychlo, one to Renender, and kept one for herself.

Renender's first impression on entering the Hypogeum was a feeling of somber and personal insignificance. He had the sense of being humbled, dwarfed amid the chamber's dimensions. The Hypogeum was fashioned into a sphere with a corbelled ceiling and an uneven floor of steps and levels and benches. The ceiling was on average fifteen meters above the floor. The diameter was thirty meters. Great rectangular mustabas inset the walls within extruding cornices. Twenty-four mustabas lined the walls around the perimeter. Most were false doors, though some did lead out and away. Visibility was hampered by the low light and the thick incense. The walls were multicolored with only veins of titanium, which sparkled and reflected the candlelight from votive offerings glowing dimly in some of the mustabas. Low frequency chanting was more felt than heard, and among the repetitive droning were the fragments of many whispered voices.

A menagerie of blending scents hyper-activated Renender's olfactory senses from different incenses, floral and woody and sweet. There were also smells of body oils, fresh and pungent and rank, burnt oils, juniper and cedar and candlewood, vapors, steam and wax and burnt wood smoke.

The air in the Hypogeum had a taste. It was part smoky wood taste and part like flesh.

Renender's body shook from the physical vibrations pulsing through the room.

"I can't see him," whispered Renender to either Tychlo or Balthorelei, whomever was nearest. He couldn't tell.

"Just wait," replied a voice in the feminine beside him. "Let our eyes adjust."

Presently Renender's eyes did adjust, and what he saw amazed him even more. The warm smoke ladened air was alive with vibration. Ripples as on a pond's surface marked the passing sound waves from the whispers and chants of nearly three dozen people, miners in prayer. The rhythmic chanting formed visible sine waves that caught the smoke and channeled it throughout the chamber. One such wave emerged from a mustaba opposite Renender and reached out in slow motion. He watched as it came closer and closer and finally engulfed him. The visceral feeling deep in Renender's gut from the sounds brought on emotions of melancholy.

His mind flickered with unsought remembrances of regrets. A moan escaped him as he relived an unbidden memory of his conversation not long ago with Naemi. Cornelius was asleep in the bedroom adjacent to his offices in Lupus City before they departed on the airship. His own words rang in his ears. "Once aboard Katzer's ship, you may encounter a particularly nasty little girl. Her name is Tentz," he had said. "Find a way to kill her. You would be doing me a great personal favor. Don't let Cornelius know I've asked you to do this."

"Any special reason you want me to do this? Why you want her dead?" Naemi had asked.

"Yes," Renender had replied. But he had said nothing more.

Now in the Hypogeum, Renender's body shook from the memory. Maybe the brat never made it to the Tarvash. At the least, Orumnam might intervene and try to stop Naemi. Renender shook his head to shake away the thought. Other regrets took their place and filled his mind, each demanding recognition. The experience was unbearable.

The chanting increased. More voices joined the resonating cacophony. Renender's head throbbed, his breathing erratic. One voice made its singular presence distinct from the others. It was the faintest whisper, but Renender heard it clearly. "You have half the answers," it said. "But you do not yet know the full question. You led that boy to the wolves." The voice pulsed on the sine wave from the opposite side of the chamber.

The visible smoky wave dissipated when another intercepted it at a right angle. The Hypogeum filled with a new chant "Om, yom-om-m-mom-om." On it went.

Then just audible to Renender's dizzying mind he heard "Here. This way." It was Balthorelei. She tugged on his sleeve and pulled him to the left through the smoky haze, down one step, up two, down three. He slowly felt his way through the stone obstacle course. Balthorelei paused though Renender could not tell why. Then, "Here you are," she said.

Emerging from a suspended waving river of smoke was the wrinkled shrunken hardened face of the Trickle Depth Sounder, centimeters from Renender's nose. The mouth spoke, crackled and worn. "Rr, ar-Renender."

"Bordent?" Renender asked.

"I suppose so," said the slight miner. "I'm still Bordent today." He coughed.

"Let's sit over here," offered Tychlo. He found a bench beside a mustaba moderately lit from seven votive candles.

"Put your incense in the offering basin," croaked Bordent in a course whisper and he coughed again. "I can't breath in here." He didn't say anything until the sticks stood upright in the ashes of the offering basin. He watched the smoke rise up in curls. "Those are prayers, and you are going to need those, every one of them." All his words were directed solely at Renender. "And this," he added. The man struggled to pull an awkward, jagged, bulbous shape on a chain out from under his shabby shirt. He pulled it over his head and held it before Renender. "This is the key, Renender. It will lead you to the place you want to go. To Them."

"It's real, then," Renender said.

"Real?" countered Bordent. "As real as any vision of madness can be. You may doubt what is real, what is unreal. If you think you can tell the difference, you may lose your mind soon enough. Keep your mind open. Do not despair from what you see, from what you hear, from what you *think* you see, what you *think* you hear. You will doubt. You only have half the answers."

Renender was listening carefully, but he perked up at that. "Wait. What's that?"

"No more answers. They are unimportant now, until you know the whole question to ask." Bordent groped for Renender's hand, grabbed it and thrust the key into his palm. He wrapped Renender's fingers around the key. He found the thumb and pushed Renender's nail into a groove. "This is the key. This is the beginning. Only the beginning." It was a shiny brass groove in an otherwise darkly burnished titanium surface. "Follow it left and clockwise with your left hand, always feel for the surface on your left. Always keep left. If you become lost, you may be lost forever. Maybe you can find your way back to the beginning. Maybe you can try again. Maybe not."

"Where is the beginning," asked Renender. "Is it this place?"

"No," croaked Bordent. "The Septum. First passage on the left. That is the beginning. But there are many eyes between here and there."

"He means the security cameras," said Tychlo. "I can get you through them. You'll have to hurry."

"There are always eyes watching," said Bordent. "In the dark. Even when you think you are alone."

The chanting in the room changed. The incense laden smoke waves became more chaotic. Whispers turned to voices. Movement was everywhere.

"The shift change," said Balthorelei.

"It's time," said Tychlo. He grasped Renender's sleeve and led him to an adjacent mustaba. This one was not a false door. It led out and away.

As Renender pulled away from Bordent, the wrinkled old Trickle Depth Sounder let out a final warning. "Remember. Stay left. This is the beginning. The beginning." As Renender slipped out of the Hypogeum he could still hear "The beginning."

* * *

The way forward was easy enough. A hundred meters down the passage, first on the left in the Septum. Renender felt the rocky wall on his left and kept moving further in. There was only a distant light from behind that was the Septum. Ahead the passage continued to descend into the dark. The space between the walls gradually narrowed.

Suddenly the wall fell away on his left, and then quickly surfaced again. A small gap. It led away from the main passage. *Stay left*, echoed in Renender's brain. He faced the gap. He took a deep breath. Out of his backpack he pulled an illumination ring. He yanked on it, activating the bioluminescent solution in the tube. It let off a warm green glow. Renender put it around his neck and it sat on his collar. He reached into the sack again and pulled out a headband with a forward bulb on a pivot ball. Renender squeezed the bulb a few times and it glowed green as well. He put it on. Next he brought out a rubber protective skullcap. He put it on his head. Pulling on the brim, it stretched to any sized. He chose three centimeters, and angled it down, longer in the back. Renender reached into the backpack again and retrieved a high-energy nutrition bar. It tasted like chicken jerky and chocolate. It was interesting.

Renender flung his backpack over his shoulders. He brought the key out from beneath his shirt. He placed his thumbnail over the brass notch. He then moved it up a notch clockwise. The beginning. Renender brought a ten-centimeter long knife out of his pack and strapped it to his belt. He used it to scratch a scar into the edge of the notch. He was determined not to lose his way.

A deep low rhythmic sound reverberated around him. The tunnel trembled. A temblor. The temperature grew cold, a heavy chill. Renender looked back the way he'd come. In the distance out the passage opening, he could see the green door that led from the Septum back to the long passage of security cameras. Eyes. The light began to flicker. He turned and looked into the dark gap. One last deep breath and he slipped through.

* * *

Daljone's Escort, Juliard, landed on her feet in a perfect dismount, after slipping on an ice cube at the Empalasor Hotel's VIP Lounge. She had done this before in practice at the Escort Guild Academy. But this was actually an accident. Nice to know the lesson was well learned.

Sergeant Jerembor had asked Juliard to keep a watch at a distance on Renender. She easily got Daljones liquored up while waiting for Renender to show up at the Lounge. Then she juiced Daljones up some more while watching Renender do little more than sip a single drink while scoping out the room with his two Escorts in tow, Jeanette and Jeaneau.

Juliard had finally sent Daljones over to flirt with Renender. The rest was amusing as much as it was interesting. Renender immediately pretended to actually know her. He kept calling Daljones by the ridiculous name Alice. The Escort Guild's stooge, the Adjunct Mayor, was flipped out as usual on kokol blow. The Guild supplied good stuff. Surprising though how she had flowers delivered to Renender. That was unexpected. The Adjunct was too independent. But that would soon change.

Ten minutes after the walk on performer, Night Breath, left the Lounge, Renender and Daljones suddenly left together. They entered an elevator with Night Breath, who must have tarried in the Lounge, though Juliard was pretty sure she'd remembered the singer actually leave after her set.

Inquiring after them with the Adjunct Mayor, Renender was apparently being a gentleman and taking Daljones to her room. Juliard had had enough of the VIP Lounge, but wanted to give Daljones and Renender a little space for a period of time. So she decided to check in with Jerembor.

* * *

Sergeant Jerembor leaned back in his chair and rubbed his eyes. It was early, six a.m. He was in his office at the Mine City Security Precinct looking over the dossiers of the night's catch, pick pockets, rabble rousers, gambling cheats and drunks. For them it was late, six a.m. There was a knock at his door. He yawned, shook his head to wake up. "Come in." The door opened and he saw it was an Escort. "Juliard. What brings you here at this hour?"

"I just need a place to hang out for a bit," Juliard said. "My Guest is occupied."

Jerembor offered the Escort a seat. She was dressed in her standard uniform of rope sandals, a gold G-string and matching support bra, gold armbands and a gold braided headband. "Daljones?" he asked. "Really? With whom?"

"Renender," said the Escort.

That got Jerembor's attention. "Excuse me?"

"Yeah. I got Jonesie drunk and sent her over to engage Renender in some conversation. They seemed to hit it off. In fact they might actually know each other." Juliard reached behind her to work her bra clasp. "Do you mind?" She removed her bra and loosed her breasts. "Need to breathe."

"I don't mind," said Jerembor. He'd seen and been with more pairs of breasts than a man could count. But he never got tired of seeing them. He returned to the subject. "What is Renender doing with Daljones?"

"Taking her to bed I imagine," Juliard fidgeted in her seat. "Do you have a cigarette?"

"I thought you weren't supposed to smoke when with a Guest?"

"Are you a Guest?" Juliard said in jest.

Jerembor ignored the comment. "Renender is gay."

"Yeah? A lot of straight men are. Don't box yourself into corners," Juliard said with first hand knowledge. "I bet you…"

Jerembor wasn't exactly going to deny anything. "And a lot of gay men are straight? I'm not buying that. His reputation is well established."

"Then why did you stick Jeanette with him? I thought he swung with 'em both." Juliard didn't buy anyone who was too sure of their sexuality. It meant they had deep dark dirty little secrets that a good Escort could always find.

"To keep an eye on Jeaneau. The boy can please, and I had to assign someone to Renender who could keep her wits about her." Jerembor prodded Juliard for more information. "Renender and Daljones are where exactly?"

"In her suite I presume," said Juliard.

"You presume?" Jerembor thought he'd made a good selection when he assigned this Escort to such a simple task.

"That's what he told the Adjunct Mayor," said Juliard.

"He didn't tell you?" asked Jerembor.

"I asked her," said Juliard. She grew annoyed. "Listen, I'm doing my job."

"Is that why you're here and not with Daljones?" asked Jerembor.

"I just thought I'd give them a little time together," she said. "It's what an Escort is supposed to do when her Guest meets another Guest. Unless they ask me to join them."

"Renender would not ask you to join him," said Jerembor. "Unless he was scheming something."

"Well since he didn't ask, I guess he's not scheming. He's probably going down on Jonesie right now." Juliard was serious too. She knew how men worked. Even the *gay* ones.

"It's more likely he's going through her financial records and client lists about now," said Jerembor. "The man cannot pass up an opportunity for business." There was another knock at the door. "Who is it?"

The door opened a crack and another officer stuck his head in. "Just me. Racko. Here are the reportable charges from the last few hours." He handed Jerembor a paper report.

"Isn't Karver here? Given them to him," said the Sergeant.

"Yeah, ok," said the officer. "You wanted to be informed if a Mister Renender made a large purchase though."

Jerembor and Juliard became interested.

"What'd he buy?" asked Jerembor.

"He set up a tab at a café in the Empalasor," said Racko.

Jerembor grabbed the paper and scanned it, looking for Renender's name. "Where..."

"Here," said Racko pointed to a line on the page. "About an hour ago."

Jerembor turned to Juliard. "I guess they're done now. How long ago did you leave them?"

"A little over an hour," said the Escort. She became anxious and looked at the Sergeant. "A quickie?" she said.

"I don't think so," said Jerembor. "You'd better check on your Guest." To Racko he asked, "Any charges since then?"

"This is the standard report. You want to look real time?" asked Racko.

"Yeah." Jerembor turned to his computer and called up a real time display of high-end charges in Mine City. Renender's name came up again. "There's another," he said pointing. "Fifteen minutes ago, in the Plaza. Flowers."

"Flowers?" asked Juliard. "Over twenty thousand credits worth?"

"Exactly twenty thousand credits," said Jerembor. "What's he doing?"

Juliard got up. "I'm going to check on Jonesie."

"Yeah," said Jerembor. "I'm coming with you. Racko, keep monitoring Renender's account and all high-end transactions. Call me if anything else shows up." He grabbed his earphone from off his desk and inserted it.

"Will do, Boss."

* * *

Within minutes Jerembor and Juliard were walking the halls of the Empalasor. Juliard led, making no allowances for Jerembor to keep up. She suddenly stopped when she noticed the door to Daljone's suite was ajar. She waved her hand behind her to motion Jerembor to slow, and she silently mimicked a "Shh."

Jerembor came up beside and passed Juliard, taking the lead. He felt for the can of servo at his waist. That spray could incapacitate any thug, or businessman. It wasn't as elegant as the Escort's fainting gas. This left a discoloration around the burning eyes for a few days. He pulled out the servo and got to the door. He peeked in, servo ready.

The room was one of the smaller suites at the Empalasor. Jerembor supposed a veterinarian didn't bring in much, or this one didn't splurge on accommodations when visiting Mine City. The only wood furnishing in the main room was a coffee table. Everything else was titanium, fabric and plastic. Couch, chairs, tables were all manufactured. Jerembor saw that the room was overflowing with flowers. Vases of them were over stacked on the coffee table, sidewall tables, bar counter, on the floor. All kinds of flowers and arrangements. He then noticed the coffee table was askew in relation to the couch, and a coffee mug was lying on the floor. Foul play? Juliard was breathing down his neck to get a look. The room was empty of people. They both entered. "This explains the purchase at the flower seller," he whispered. Juliard checked the vases of flowers. No card on any of them. A sound from the bedroom froze them in their paths. Juliard started in first, with Jerembor right at her side.

Moans and loud hard grunts preceded what they saw next. A fully naked boy was kneeling on the bed, head tossed back and eyes closed, wanking on his huge meat of fifteen centimeters. Even Jerembor did a double take. It never felt good to be so outgunned. He was glad he had his clothes on. Juliard eyed the boy's size with the view of determining how easily she might handle such a penis on a Guest. But that was a fleeting thought. This was not her Guest. The boy let out a shout and an "Oh No! Yeah!" and ejaculated in four rivulets of spunk all over the sheets. He broke out laughing and opened his eyes, amazed at his accomplishment. Then he saw the others. "Holy shit!" He pulled a sheet up, but it was cold and wet. He let it drop. "What the hell. Who are you?" He asked.

"Who are YOU?" Jerembor sent back. "Where's Daljones?"

"I don't know what you're talking about," the boy said.

"He's the flower seller," said Juliard. "He delivered some flowers to Renender up in the Lounge earlier."

The boy was climbing off the bed and reaching for his pants when Daljones stepped into the room, disheveled and still fairly drunk, but just sober enough to feel the headache she'd suffer through the next few days. "Wh-who are all of you? Oh Julie!" Daljones stopped short when she saw the boy, the mess on the bed, and the obvious reactions on everyone's faces. She blushed and became horribly embarrassed at the scene that must have taken place. The flowers, the boy. Did she have sex with him? She wasn't remembering so much about the night. But it was so obvious. "Get out. You're invading my privacy." She directed it mainly at Jerembor and Juliard. The boy dropped his pants, turned on by the situation and attention. Daljones wasn't too drunk to appreciate his size.

"Where's Renender?" asked Jerembor. "You were with him."

"Who?" said Daljones. The name was vaguely familiar. She couldn't be sure.

"Are you alright?" asked Juliard coming up to her.

Daljones belched. It's then that she noticed her green dress was covered in grease. "Oh, it's from the fried chicken," she said. "A lovely girl fed me in the café. Gave me everything."

"Renender's doing," said Jerembor. To the boy he asked, "Where's

Renender now? You were with him not half an hour ago."

The flower seller could tell from Jerembor's tone that these were not casual questions. He lost his hard on. His began to put his clothes back on. "I don't know who you are, man. But I'm not answering any of your questions."

"I think you should all leave," said Daljones. She'd had had quite enough of an evening, and was feeling not so well all of a sudden. "Out."

"I'm out of here," said the boy. But Jerembor stopped him.

"Not so fast wonder boy," he said putting the palm of his hand on the boy's chest. "Why are you here?"

"No more kinky shit," said the boy.

"No kink," said Jerembor. "Answers."

"Like I said, who the hell are you?" said the boy defiantly, hands on his hips.

Jerembor fished out his ID and flashed it at the boy. "Sergeant of Security."

"Oh. I was just delivering the flowers. That's all. This was just, just for fun," he said looking back at the bed.

"They're beautiful!" exclaimed Daljones. "You stay, hon. Everyone else goes."

"Finish putting your clothes on," said Jerembor. "You're coming down to the precinct with me. Pronto." He looked at Daljones, said to Juliard, "You too." He pulled a pair of handcuffs out of a pocket and said to the boy, "Anyone who doesn't can wear this nice bracelet."

"I already have a bracelet," said Daljones. "Nicer than that."

"Come on Jonesie," said Juliard. "Turn around sweets. We're moving out."

To Juliard, Jerembor asked, "Where is Renender's suite? We should check there, too."

"I don't know," replied the Escort. "But I can find out." She activated the intercom beside the bed and called down to the lobby. "Yes, this is Daljones' room. Yes. Oh fine, thanks. Can you tell me in what suite the gentleman Renender is staying? He, left something here and I'd like to return it. Oh that's kind, but I'd like to deliver it myself. 8012," Juliard repeated, looking at Jerembor. "Thank you, dear. That's all." The Escort disconnected the call. "Did you get that?"

"Yes. Come on, you're all with me."

* * *

The door to Renender's suite was still open. Sounds of bumping and thumping and clanging and voices came through the open door.

"Ouch! You stupid fool. Now the leg is on the rope. I can't move now." It was a woman's voice.

"Use your fingers to untie the knot. That's why I scooted closer." A man's voice.

"I can't get it."

"You have it. Just pull."

A grunt.

"There."

"Got it."

Jerembor entered the suite with Juliard, Daljones and the flower seller close behind. In the open doorway to the bedroom, two Escorts, naked and tied up, lay among fallen chairs covered in ropes.

The flower seller broke out into laughter. "Pops, this place is one kink fest to be sure."

Jeanette looked up at the audience and exclaimed, "Jerembor! Well don't just stand there. Untie us."

Both Jerembor and Juliard moved forward and began loosing the two

333

Escorts from their bonds.

"What happened here?" asked Jerembor. "How did Renender overpower both of you?"

"He had help," said Jeanette, rubbing her wrists after they slipped through the rope.

"That singer," added Jeaneau. "And a one-eyed man." He got to his feet.

"Tychlo," said Jerembor.

"And Night Breath," said Jeaneau.

"A bitch and a half," said Jeanette. She spat onto the floor in disgust. Then she noticed the flower seller ogling her nakedness. "What are you looking at?"

The boy was no stranger to trouble. He looked away.

"And they had gas," Jeanette added.

There was a crackle in Jerembor's earphone. "Sergeant Jerembor," he said. There was a pause as he listened. "Racko, talk to me." Another pause, then, "Yeah. Ok. I'll be right there." He disconnected, turned to the others and said, "We've got him. Come on, altogether now. We're stopping at the Club Especiales, in the Bazaar del Mundo." And to the newly freed Escorts, he said, "Put something on."

* * *

The bouncer at Especiales saw Jerembor and his entourage approach. The two-plus meter tall muscular he-man with no neck turned to the cashier at the glass windowed entrance. "Here come the cops," he said in an unexpectedly high voice. "With friends."

The cashier pushed a small blue button under her counter.

"Speemout," said Jerembor to the bouncer.

"Sergeant," Speemout the bouncer replied. "You don't normally avail yourself of our services." He eyed the three Escorts, Daljones and the flower seller. "What's the occasion?"

"Just looking for someone," replied Jerembor. "This won't take long."

"They all coming in, too?" asked Speemout.

Jerembor looked his companions over, and then replied, "Yeah. Any problem?"

"Not with me," said Speemout. He stepped aside to let them through.

"Uh, six of us," Jerembor said to the cashier.

"Is Mine City Security paying for all of you?" the cashier asked.

"Yes," said Jerembor. "On our tab."

The cashier's machine went "Ka-Ching!" six times. With little emotion the cashier said, "Enjoy." She handed out six small towels to the party. "No stains on the furnishings," she added. "Wipe them down when you're through."

"Thanks," said the flower seller.

"Rooms or lockers?" asked the cashier.

"Neither," said Jerembor. "We won't be long."

"I'll take a locker," said the flower seller. Then, "No, a room, since the Sarge here is paying."

The cashier tossed a key at the boy who caught it with a quick swoop of his hand.

"Come on," said Jerembor.

The main room was dimly lit. Techno music pulsated around the vast space and laser lights danced across the ceiling. A DJ's voice made provocative statements to the beat of the songs. Go-go girls and go-go boys engaged in mock sex acts atop tall pillars with wide perches. Above them two trapeze artists, a naked woman with fans and a naked man with feathers, maneuvered along wires invisible to the people below. And there were scores of people. Some were in towels, others in briefs, but most wore masks of bizarre and macabre faces, large noses, elephantine ears, horns and tails. Women and men wore strap on dildoes and fornicated on the floors, on tables, on chairs. The ceiling erupted in a brilliant flash of golden laser light and a voice boomed across the hall. "Showers!" The trapezists were joined by six others who proceeded to urinate onto the floor. Several umbrellas were quickly raised by some prepared Guests, while others writhed and reveled in the golden showers.

Jerembor darted to a wall followed by the Escorts. Poor Daljones was drenched and began shrieking. The flower seller had shed his clothes and found a mask on the floor. He put it on and danced a wild rumpus amid the golden showers hollering in delight.

Racko met Jerembor against the wall. "Sergeant."

"Racko," said Jerembor. "Where is he?"

"This way, hurry."

Down a corridor of open rooms where the only illumination came from small red diodes in the floor Jerembor and the Escorts followed Racko. Daljones and the flower seller were no longer with them. Moans, groans, laughter and screams variously sounded out from the different rooms. Jerembor and Racko ignored them all. They stopped beside the only closed door off the corridor.

"Here," said Racko. "I traced his last card usage here."

Jerembor tried the knob. It turned, and left a cold slime of lube all over his hand. He wiped it on his breaches. He went in.

The room was well lit. A naked quartet played classical music on strings and wind pipes in the center. A naked young girl tended a bar on one side. A small blue light flashed on the bar. Along the opposite wall at a small table, five naked girls and boys gorged themselves on candy, cotton candy, lollipops, gummy dorsein and gummy worms. A door near them was ajar. A squeal was heard through it followed immediately by three small hairless animals, one darting left, one right, and the other under the candy table. The kids screamed in surprise.

"Through there," said Jerembor. He made the distance short with quick steps.

Through the open doorway Jerembor and Racko could see the naked back of a man bent down over something, another animal that squealed and squirmed on a rotating dais. Standing on ladders on each side and in front were a half dozen naked children clapping and laughed as the grown man ploughed into the squealing beast. There was blood on the floor and blood on the walls. Six more children, drugged and dazed, sat in the bloody pools playing with naked bloody dolls.

"Renender!" shouted Jerembor. "Enough. You're coming with me."

There was no answer. The ladder children laughed and clapped some more.

Racko moved forward and placed his foot on the dais, spun it around.

"Renend...," began Jerembor. But the word fell flat. It was not Renender. "Who," he began.

"Mack!" said Jeaneau and Jeanette in unison.

"Who?" asked Jerembor.

The bartender from the Geode Club climaxed just as he spun around to face the security and Escorts. His laughter echoed in Jerembor's ears as he realized his hollow victory. Renender was not here. They had been duped.

"I don't understand," exclaimed Racko in disbelief. "How does he have Renender's number?"

"Renender doesn't pay for drinks," said Jerembor.

Jeanette thought back to when she and Jeaneau escorted Renender to the club, before he separated to sit with the woman and the one-eyed man. Then she remembered. "Renender keyed in his credit number at the club for a drink."

The lights in the room began to flicker. Turning around, Jerembor saw the lights in the outer room did, too. This wasn't normal. He ran out into the hall. The red diodes flickered there as well. The musicians stopped playing and looked around. So did all the children. The walls trembled. The techno music in the club stuttered and stopped. Then a siren blared out.

"Let's get out of here," Jerembor said to Juliard right beside him. "To the Plaza."

* * *

Hundreds of people filled the Plaza. Most shivered in the cold air. There were miners and businessmen, Guests and Escorts, security personnel and students. They all looked out to the cavern lake from whence a roaring sound got louder and louder. Jerembor could see his breath condense in the air in front of him.

"What's going on?" asked someone behind him.

"Did a quake shut off the heat?" asked someone else.

"Is it a cave-in?" asked another.

The roaring subsided, but was quickly followed by clicking sounds. It sounded like drumsticks hitting metal drum rims. The sound came from multiple directions.

"No. It isn't," said Jerembor. He reached into his shirt and pulled from around his neck a pendant of a radiant star. The Precession Star. He closed his eyes and kissed it.

The holographic projection of the bejeweled cavern lake flickered. It crackled. It was gone. The chasm opened before the crowd in the Plaza. Beyond that was the entrance, loading and parking facility for Mine City. Military Spider Transports crowded the facility. There were eight of them. Others emerged from the spiral tunnel. Two still climbed over the loaded titanium ingot cars.

One man stood hands on hips facing the crowd from the chasm's edge. He wore a black leather uniform. His face was boyish. He smiled in an expression of eager delight. And he was extremely pale. His face shined with an inner cold light. Very cold. So cold that all of Mine City shivered. Corvus was here.

31 ISLAND OF THE PLACALOTS

The small brown striped mammal sniffed the breeze. Its pudgy three-nostril nose wiggled and twitched. A quizzical look beset the animal's face. Something different was out there. What was it? Was it dangerous? Was it safe? The animal's small circular ears rotated independently three hundred degrees around, listening to something different, a new sound, a chirping sound. The chirping lilted. It was a song.

The small animal cocked its head to one side, trying to figure out the nature of the chirping song. The new scent on the air smelled sweet. Smelling this new smell felt very nice. With the chirping music, everything felt wonderful. And there was a new sound. A whirring.

The little mammal relaxed a little, slumped to one side. It's nostrils still twitched and sniffed, but its eyes were glazed over. The animal did not become alarmed when the black bag swooped down out of the sky and covered the world in darkness. The chirping song grew closer.

Galdinier had his prize. This was his seventh catch of the afternoon. He had learned that the afternoon was the best time to hunt for the little mammals the Felines on Wror called placalots. In the heat of the day, the little grazers were fat and fed and lazy in the warm humid sun in the caldera valley. They seemed to have no natural predators, at least before the arrival of the Felines. Already the valley was no longer a-wiggle with placalots. They were becoming scarcer to find.

Galdinier picked up the squirming bag. He cooed a clucking sound. The placalot became docile. The Felines had been surprised to discover such a simple vocalization had such a profound calming effect on the little creatures. And the Felines' natural pheromones were also easily manipulated such that the placalots' flight instincts were suppressed. And the placalots were delicious.

Off to Galdinier's right many meters sat another placalot, wiggling its nose, head cocked to one side listening to another chirping song. A couple of meters in front of the animal, the tall grass rustled. Galdinier could see the Feline crouched down, partially concealed, slowly making her way forward. It was Canopus. Many meters beyond her was her brother Bereth. Away on Galdinier's left was her other brother Beleth. A dozen Felines were spread out across this part of the valley. Taking in the whole scene, Galdinier watched the other Felines pop up one after another with wriggling bags, then duck down again.

* * *

Canopus squatted uncomfortably on a clump of grass that hid a stone. The stone poked at her in the most uncomfortable place possible, squarely into her right buttocks. If she squirmed too much or moved too suddenly, she'd startle the placalot she was trying to snare. But oh it hurt! Canopus leaned to the left, reached behind her and fiddled with her fingers until she found the offending rock. It wouldn't move. She let out an exasperated sigh and scooted up. And the grass was too thick. It was too tall. It caught her whiskers and poked her eyes. She shook her head. But Canopus had lost her focus on the placalot. She'd stopped clucking, and her pheromones were off. Her placalot hopped away.

Canopus maneuvered to sit cross-legged, back straight. She looked around for the nearest next placalot. Then she caught a whiff of something else. Right in front of her she was surprised to find growing a small clump of grazimyth. Its tight curl of flowers shone with a light of their own. Galdinier had scattered grazimyth seeds all about the caldera on the day of their arrival on Wror. The young planet that pulsed with life nourished each and every seed. The hallucinogenic plant spread quickly throughout the valley. The Felines had already found it growing in the foothills and mountains, too. The placalots avoided it.

The grazimyth's unique scent molecules had a potent effect on Feline chemistry. Canopus' mind reeled. The herb had evolved into a stronger drug on Wror. Canopus held her head. Her vision pulsed in different colors, red, pink, blue. Her skin tingled. It felt like it rippled, as if her skin were the surface of a wind blown sea. The waves passed out of her body and rippled out among the grasses, placalots, Felines, outward toward the hills. Everything was fuzzy for a moment, then suddenly Canopus' vision sharpened into remarkable clarity. And the valley was full.

Canopus saw placalots everywhere. There were thousands and thousands. Some were striped brown, the ones she was hunting. But for every brown placalot there was also a spotted red, mottled blue, and a pink and white variety. The brown ones glowed with an inner warmth. The others had auras that danced and waved like flames, taking to life before Canopus' eyes like a breath blown over embers. The multitude of placalots sat nibbling on green grass and blue grass and purple grass. These were grasses Canopus had not seen before.

There were insects on the air. Big hand-sized twirley-whoopers with two sets of wings all moving independently. Canopus had seen finger-sized versions before. These were much larger. The insects landed on hummocks of blue grasses and purple grasses, and devoured huge swaths of foliage with their clicking mandibles. Canopus could hear the chomping. She saw that the insects flew to the green grasses to release their droppings, which helped to feed the grasses. The green grasses in turn fed the brown placalots. There was an intricate web of symbiosis revealed to the Feline. And spreading throughout the caldera valley, she saw bunches of white grazimyth, pulsing with light.

Canopus looked up higher. The sky was filling with mists and clouds, purples and blues and reds. High up in the sky was the shining day star of the armored asteroid, quiet and ever present. And everywhere were flying reptiles. Immense lines of the winged beasts stretched across the airs like highways from one horizon to the other. Some lines traversed south to north, others east to west. Some flew circles overhead. They were as clear to Canopus as the many colored placalots and the different grasses around her. The reptiles circling overhead were closest. Canopus easily saw their azure and crimson scales. They even had feathers. She'd never before seen them so defined, and she'd never seen so many either, not among the Asteroid Ring, not above the skies of her home world of Polaris.

Over the caldera valley, the reptiles circled in great concentric orbits around the Feline colony. Canopus could see that some flew in circles up while others flew in circles down. A quintet of reptiles flew closer to the ground than any of the others. They swept over the grassy landscape from south to north. One broke ranks from the rest and careened straight down out of the sky.

The placalots took notice. The red and blue and pink animals started up a high-pitched shrieking alarm. Then they stampeded off in different directions. The red placalots ran west. Their blue cousins ran en masse east. The pinks congregated into a frantic huddle rotating in a clockwise circle. Then came the otherworldly screech. Canopus threw her hands over her ears; the sound was so blood curdling.

Clouds spilled over the mountains and flowed into the caldera valley. The air thundered and the sky drew dark and cold around Canopus as the winged beast blotted out the sun. The beast saw the Feline and dove right at her. Canopus saw it in great detail.

The beast had an elongated head fringed with black and white feathers. Its beak was long and hooked like a bird of prey. And within the beak the beast sported rows of razor sharp teeth. A red forked tongue darted out. The flying beast shrieked again. This time the thunder shook the ground. The reptile's black eyes pierced Canopus' mind. She instinctively directed her head just enough to point her pineal gland, her third eye, at the beast. Canopus' forehead felt numb. She felt paralyzed. She felt her mind exposed. Intruded. An angry hungering presence crowded out her thoughts. It was the reptile. It spoke directly into her mind.

"Feline. Who…are you? I will have you and know."

Canopus felt absolute terror. Yet she was frozen in place.

The pink placalots quit their circle dance and darted north. The flying reptile shrieked again and its hot breath blew across the grasses. The creature diverted its attention from Canopus and aimed its flight at the fleeing placalots. In that instant Canopus was able to feel panic. She ran, away from the placalots and their monster pursuer, and dove into a clump of two-meter tall blue and red flax grass.

The flying reptile passed just overhead. It reached out with its five-taloned fore and aft claws. The hooked feet snatched a pink placalot on the run. The reptile then flapped its massive iridescent wings. Arching its back into the air with the squealing placalot firmly in its grasp, it rose high up into the sky. The reptile shrieked again and Canopus cowered in the grass. The thunder this time brought on rain. The beast's tail waved back and forth, its bony diamond shaped end cracking the air in its wake.

* * *

Mists of water soaked clouds spilled over the distant ridges of the caldera valley's encircling mountains. It joined a bank of heavy clouds already hugging the mountain passes and interior foothills. Shades of winged reptiles, all but invisible but for their shadows, crossed in front of the sun. Galdinier looked up and saw three shapes dim the bright sun ahead of the fingers of clouds. They reached up and tickled the face of the sun. Then the azure sky of Wror fell away, replaced by the dark mass of the monsoon. The Felines were learning to quickly adapt to the fast changing weather on a real planet. Rain began to fall.

Bereth called from his spot in the grass. "Galdinier! This is going to drench us!" Galdinier's bag squirmed. He put his face close to the opening and clucked to the animal inside. The bag stilled.

"Run!" yelled Galdinier.

Shouts of "Rain!" rose from the other Felines popping up out of the tall grass, each with a squirming bag.

"To the settlement!"

The Felines raced one another back to the shelter of prefab buildings, drop containers, tents and tarps. These were arranged in a circle. The enclosure they made was no longer a neat grassy field; it was now a great muddy expanse. A makeshift sidewalk of crisscrossing metal sheeting on the mud under flapping tarps kept most Felines out of the mud.

The settlement was temporary until proper villages were completed in the encircling foothills of the caldera rim. Distant "Boom! Boom! Booms!" echoed across the valley. Feline engineers and munitions experts blasted rock and ridge day and night to set foundations for new cities. It would be weeks before habitable lodgings were constructed, but already stoneworkers were marking marble and granite outcroppings for cutters, shapers and movers. The new cities would be glittering wonders in bright stone. In the meantime, the muddy camp sufficed as home.

Galdinier ducked under a tarp spread over the space between two drop containers. He leapt up the three small steps holding his squirming bag before him. Canopus' mother was there to meet him and the others returning wet and out of breath, laden with placalots.

"How many did you catch today?" she asked.

Galdinier came to a stop beside her and shook his head, shaking water out of his hair.

Bereth, Beleth and Canopus appeared out of the sheets of rain and huddled under the tarp flaps with Galdinier.

"Mother, take these please," said Canopus. "I'm soaked."

"Child, you look more frightened than wet." She took the squirming bags from her children. Cluck-cluck coos calmed the animals within.

"I'm ok Mother," said Canopus.

"Galdinier, did you find any new herbs?"

Galdinier wiped his hands over his face and whiskers. He took off his high water boots and started unbuttoning his overalls. He stopped to pull some green sprigs with roots out of a pocket. "Yes. Two new ones," he answered. He handed the herbs to Canopus' mother. "Maybe these will help."

"Something in this paradise must be useful," she said. "Besides placalots.

Galdinier asked sheepishly, "How is she?"

"Still with fever," said the older Feline. "A bad one. It's just our luck that the only drop container that did not drop was the one with medicines."

"It's still up there," said Galdinier. "If we could only get to the asteroid."

"No use dreaming," she said. "Come on now. All of you get out of that wetness and come in. You'll find her in bed. I'll be there." She turned and disappeared down a metal clanking walk amid the shadows and tarps.

Galdinier let his overalls drop to the floor. He stood naked with Bereth and Beleth, while Canopus undressed further in. Most of the fuzz on Galdinier's body was patterned like his face and head. But in his long chest was shaved the letters alpha and omega. Many of the young Feline males, including Bereth and Beleth, had shaved logos and messages onto their bodies after arriving on Wror. For them it marked a beginning of their new lives on the nascent world. Galdinier and the others donned dry clothing, made of native fibers and placalot skins and furs.

"How about this storm?" said Galdinier.

"It just appeared out of nowhere," said Canopus.

"The coastal dorsein must be soaked," said Galdinier. "I'll have to check on them when this monsoon passes."

Lightning flashed overhead followed by a Boom! Crash! The sound reverberated through the metal and tarp village. Shouts and hollers, cries and moans followed from the Felines within. Then Boom! Boom! Boom! The munitions teams in the encircling mountains continued their work regardless of the weather.

"I'm going in," said Canopus.

Galdinier and the others ran after her.

The interior of the settlement was like a Kasbah of narrow alleys that met and crossed. It was humid within. Rainwater dripped and ran down from holes in the tarps, forming rivulets and pools everywhere. Galdinier passed groups of Feline children. Children made up the majority of Feline colonists. There were thousands of them. He knew most by name in this section, which constituted a neighborhood. Besides being responsible for the colony's dorsein herds, Galdinier was also a section leader.

"G, when will you take me to the mountains?" asked one Feline boy.

"How about when it stops raining, Beed?" replied Galdinier.

"I want to go to the sea!" asked another.

"We can go together, Teed," said Galdinier.

"G, can you make my sister well again?" asked a third.

That last one stung. So many Felines were sick with fever. Many had already perished. "I'll try," said Galdinier. He hurried along the narrow passages. Deep in the warren he and his companions at last came to the drop container that was their destination.

"Galdinier," said Canopus. "Out in the valley, just before the storm came on. I saw something, something frightening."

"Yeah? What was it?"

Canopus stopped at an open door. She looked in, then back to Galdinier. "It can wait."

"Come in, come." It was Canopus' mother. Canopus entered. Galdinier followed. Bereth and Beleth remained standing in the doorway.

The room inside was piled high with supplies. Boxes and containers and equipment vied for space among beds. Bright light from rigged sconces on the walls did little to lift the gloom that hung heavy in the air. There were no windows. A hole in the roof let in water that dripped into a pail. This was Galdinier's home, and Eridani's along with Canopus' family's.

Canopus stood beside her mother, who was bent over a bed. There lay Eridani bundled up and shivering from chills and fever.

"How, how is she?" asked Galdinier. He spoke softly with a broken voice.

"She's asleep," said the woman. "In and out, but quiet now."

Eridani coughed and sputtered awake. Only a moan escaped her lips and she was quiet again.

The woman wiped the girl's forehead and cleaned her mouth of spittle. "She's been like this."

"What of those herbs I brought?" asked Galdinier.

"I'm making a tea with them now," said the woman. "It may help."

Boom! Boom! Boom! The shelter rumbled and shuddered from the distant munitions.

"We'll be able to move to the new cities before long. Weeks, maybe less," said Galdinier.

"If we make it that long," said Canopus. "Thousands are sick, like Eridani. So many have died."

"Shh," said her mother. "Don't speak of such things in here."

"Some of the other section leaders are speaking of going to the Humans. Maybe they have medicines that can help," said Galdinier.

"There's been more than talking," said the woman. "A group set off this morning for the coast. They're tired of waiting."

"What?" exclaimed Galdinier. "But Humans can't come here. The dorsein. We can't have Humans here."

"We'll see," said the woman. "But there's nothing you can do to stop them. Someone has to try."

The quick glow from lightning burst through the door. Thunder rattled the settlement. Eridani let out a moan.

"Galdinier, please fetch us some clean water," said the woman. He went out, passing Bereth and Beleth still at the door.

Just a few moments after Galdinier had left, the room shook. A loud din as of breaking glass and metals scraping together sounded. A flash of light erupted in the center of the room. In the glare stood the tall shape of a man. It stepped out of the light. It was Feline. It was Galdinier, but somehow different. He wore a navy blue uniform. His faced was aged with many cares and his right ear was notched in two places, as from a bite or an accident.

"What is this?" whispered the woman to Canopus. Canopus stared without saying anything.

The stranger looked about the room and found Eridani. He quickly went to her and kneeled beside the bed. In his hand he held a steaming cup of liquid that smelled sweet. He lifted her head and gave Eridani a drink.

She drank, opened her eyes and murmured, "Galdinier. Thank you brother," and put her head back down and went back to sleep.

The stranger set the cup down on the floor and stood up. He looked into the eyes of everyone present, Canopus, her mother, Bereth and Beleth at the doorway. Then Galdinier returned.

He moved passed Bereth and Beleth and entered the room holding the container of clean water he had fetched. He stared at the strange Galdinier, dumbstruck.

The stranger in the center of the room stared back. He took a step forward toward the Galdinier at the door. He spoke, and his words rumbled like thunder. "I'm up there," and he looked up and pointed. Then an arc of bright light enveloped him. He was gone. The shattering, crashing sound ceased.

"What just happened?" said Canopus. She was afraid and her ears lay flat against her head.

"It was…." started Bereth.

"…Me!" said Galdinier. He hurried over to her sister, but she was fast asleep again.

Canopus' mother came up to him. "Child, don't tell anyone about this."

"He said he was from 'up there'," said Beleth. "Did he mean the armored asteroid?"

"Maybe the Humans have a ship," said Canopus. "Someone can go up there."

Canopus' mother sneezed, then she shivered.

"Mother, are you alright?" ask Canopus.

"I'm fine, dear."

"No Mother," said Canopus. "None of us here is fine."

Galdinier looked up at the ceiling and thought of the armored asteroid ever resting in the sky above the Feline colony, silent and motionless.

32 THE CANINE ALPHA

Trifid, the Alpha of all Canines, sat on a wide knoll a few meters above the sprawling Canius Plains facing east. Small plains lupines, spry purple flowers only a few centimeters tall, radiated out as a carpet from where Trifid sat cross-legged. They had an iridescent sheen. Some dimmed in regular intervals, corresponding to hardly noticeable ground vibrations. The Three Ugly Women were directing Alpha's Fifty-Guard Regiment in raising a fallen megalith on the Henge Plain, over a hundred kilometers distant. The lupines reacted to the acoustic rhythms of the Guard's deep percussion drums. Trifid could hear the creaky voices of the women carried on the wind.

"Rr. More to the right," said One.

"Tilt the stone back-Grr," said the Second.

"Rrah-No!" said the Third. "Lean it forward. Forward!"

"Rr. It needs to be swiveled more, Sister," the First One said. "The rising sun must shine through this notch three days before Precession."

"Precession is more than a month away, maybe more-Grr," said the Second.

"Rrah-Look! This day's shadow would be shorter if it was that far away. Look at it now," said the Third.

"We're late-Grr," said the Second. "It's already here. They're already here."

"Rr. Not yet. But it's your fault the stone fell down. You should have called the Alpha sooner for his help," said the First.

"Rrah-It's up now," said the Third.

"Rr. Time to get the Stilt Walkers to prepare their stories. We need their orations," said the First.

Alpha Trifid smirked over listening to the Three Ugly Women argue. Yes, the henge stone was fallen. Time might have gotten away from those three old timekeepers, but they would make adjustments to their calculations. For ages, they had kept the Canines in pace with the movement of the stars and Precession. They would continue to do so with their customary sarcastic alacrity.

Trifid looked down at the tiny lupine flowers around him. The dimming rhythm of the lupines stopped. The henge stone must be in place.

Trifid untied a small leather pouch hanging off his belt. He shook a few pale yellow sun dried seeds, pointed on one side, onto the palm of his hand. They were latties. He popped them into his mouth and crunched them, swallowed. He refastened the small pouch tight. Trifid's golden eyes dilated just a bit and his brow ridges relaxed.

The latties caused Trifid's Canine muzzle to glisten from extra mucous discharge. The snot dripped onto the ground. The green leaves of the lupines turned up on their tiny stems. Trifid could see narrow pink lines iridesced on the purple petals, revealed in the ultraviolet spectrum now opened to his eyes. Insects used these sight lines as guides to the nectar chambers within each open bud.

The Alpha looked up at the northern sky. He could see the ghostly carapaces of invisible Canine ships from Puppis mark out their trails across the blue Lupin sky. They were traveling from the Polar Cities of Canoon to larger ships in space over the planet, invisible ships that Markhab's satellites and the Humans never saw. Puppis, the small hidden Canine world, was in regular contact with the polar Canines of Lupus.

The long hairy ears of the Alpha sported centimeter-wide holes on their outer sides. Each was filled with a stone plug, a petrified bone encrusted with blue agate crystals. His ears' downy fuzz rose on goose bumps caused by an almost imperceptible high and distant screech. Turning to look at the southern sky, Trifid saw a shimmering flock of flying reptiles. They were several hundred kilometers distant, outpacing a quake-curtain. The curtains emanated from shifts in the planet's tectonically active lake region. Quakes had rocked the lakes for three days now. Trifid could hear the tinny horns of Canine lake ships.

A breeze picked up and he smelled a faint pungent hint of tangerine on the air. It was mixed with the sweat pheromones of a Human. Images of a dark man with thick black matted hair flickered in Trifid's mind. He associated the smell with the image, then both were gone. Trifid knew that this Human was on his way to meet the Alpha. It was arranged, though the Human probably did not know this.

Trifid shifted to face northwest. He could hear far away horns, scrapers, and noisemakers carried by the Canine Stilt Walkers on their migration across the plains of Canius to the celebration place for the coming Precession Festival. Trifid easily made out the clip-clip-clomp-clip of the hundreds of stilt legs marching. They were still three days distant, but a line of dust kicked up by their passage was just visible on the horizon.

Beyond Canius, the ever-shifting sands of the Seering Desert grated against rock and dune.

A sound of falling rocks entered Trifid's awareness. Southward in the Canius Mountains, someone was crawling through caves, disturbing stones near the Canine monasteries. It was another Human. He was on a personal quest. His fate was already laid out before him and behind him. The man was yet to guess at all the questions for which he sought answers. Trifid felt somehow that both these Humans' fates were entwined with his own.

Far away to the east, Trifid heard the crack and crash of hardwood trees in the dense forests of Aran. Humans were felling the forest giants. Mixed with the crashing sounds were the laments taken up by the Forest Canines. Their anger seethed. Trifid sensed it as readily as the suffering cries of Humans in the gulag cities of Lupus Minor.

South beyond the mountains, the waves of the great ocean lapped the sandy shores of the coastal Human cities, Aran, Cronapolis, Star City.

So many Humans. So many Canines. Such tenuous bonds tied them together.

Suddenly Trifid heard a loud clamoring crash nearby. It sounded like breaking glass and sheets of different metals scraping together. It was altogether unpleasant to hear. The carpet of lupine flowers around Trifid dropped their petals. Tingle vines curled up out of the ground and pushed the lupines aside. The vines rose in response to the racket. Trifid's eyes grew wide. He saw something he has never seen before.

A Feline appeared out of thin air only five meters away. He was a young man, strong and able in age and physique, wearing a blue jumpsuit. He walked with a deliberate gait. Somehow the Feline did not seem to be aware of his surroundings. He walked as though he saw things Trifid could not see. The clashing sound of glass and metal followed him for several paces. For a moment the Feline slowed. His head turned toward Trifid, then his ears darted back as if listening to something. The Feline seemed to notice Trifid, made eye contact. Trifid saw that one of the Feline's ears, the right one, was notched in two places irregularly, as if he'd been on the losing side of a biting fight. Resuming his direction, the Feline turned back. He dropped something from his hand that fell onto the ground. Then he vanished as suddenly as he appeared. The sounds of breaking glass and scraping metals ceased.

"Hello and good-bye," said Trifid aloud. Alpha shook his head. Things seemed as they did before the apparition, except for the mass of tingle vines. Trifid got up and made his way over to the place where the Feline disappeared. There were footprints in the vines. Trifid's bare feet itched from the vines' toxins.

Littering the ground where the Feline disappeared were seeds. Trifid bent down to pick some up. Holding them in his hand, he allowed his breath to warm and moisten them. A whispered word, and the seeds wiggled and spun in his palm. They sprouted and grew and budded and flowered in moments. A fragrance rose up to Trifid's nostrils. The small white blossoms' scent tickled the inside of his nose.

Trifid squatted down and poked holes into the ground with a finger and gently inserted the roots of each new plant into a hole. He passed his hand over the plants and utters whispered words. The plants' roots took hold and the small herbs began to spread, replacing the tingle vines.

Alpha Trifid rose up tall arching his back. Facing the sky, he put his hands on his hips. The ephemeral shadows of high and distant flying reptiles passed over him and across the landscapes of Lupus. Trifid filled his lungs with a deep breath of fresh grassy air, held it a moment, then let out a long slow howl. "Aroooo!" It was loud, and grew louder and louder the longer he yelled. Trifid sustained the howl for an hour.

The sound of it circled Lupus. It connected with distant mountains, gravelly lakeshores, sandy riverbanks and ocean beaches. It passed through forest mists and races above great cities. The yell circumnavigated the sphere of Lupus. Completing the circuit, the sound met Trifid's ears from the other direction. Trifid allowed the call to die down in diminishing, receding echoes.

His ears were flat and his eyes were wide. He ran in clockwise circles, ever wider. With a shout he broke out of the turn and ran with the wind behind him. He ran to the west, to the Three Ugly Women and his Fifty-Guard Regiment. He must tell them what he's seen, a Feline on Lupus, come and gone!

33 THE CHANNEL RIFT

Cornelius dreamed. He climbed a tall ladder up, up into a whiteness, a void without interruption. As he climbed higher into the featureless white, a rushing sounded all around him. It grew louder with each step. It was the sound of wind, though Cornelius felt none. When the sound was a roar pounding upon his eardrums, he stopped. This was the place. Cornelius determined that the sound circled about him clockwise. Presently a new sound added itself to the roar, a sound of glass breaking. The whiteness shifted into a million faceted mirrors all spinning wildly around him. The sound of metals clashing against each other joined the sound of breaking glass.

In each facet of mirror was a reflection of Cornelius. Some faced him while others were side views. In yet others he saw his back. Each reflection showed Cornelius doing something different, each in a different place, each in a different time. Some facets moved around more slowly than the others. These he could follow, a ragged Cornelius running through forested lands with a monstrous wolf beast at his side, Cornelius pouring tea for Naemi in Mine City, Cornelius engaged in a knife fight at the Lake Docks, Cornelius with Naemi aboard a scout ship in the skies of Wror.

The faceted mirrors turned to white tiles and covered Cornelius in a whiteout again. He resumed climbing the ladder.

The sound of wind died down. The din of breaking glass and metals ceased.

As Cornelius continued to climb, the ladder disappeared. Cornelius clung onto scaly legs while his own feet dangled. He struggled until his feet found anchorage on great talons. Cornelius then climbed onto the back of a great winged beast. He settled between great wings arching up, then down. They were in flight.

From the beast's head Cornelius heard its voice. "In a stream of stars, I am lost."

Cornelius responded. "I will guide you out of this fog."

The fog dissipated, revealing a world far below. There was a great long river originating in glaciated mountains, running through passes and plains, through a mighty forest and down to the sea.

Cornelius soared up and down on the winged bird's flight. He heard a tap-tap-tap sound. A moment later it became a bump-bump sound. A distant voice joined it.

"Cornelius. Cornelius." It was Naemi.

Cornelius awoke. He rubbed his eyes. He still heard the bump-bump, and a roaring sound.

Naemi spoke again. "Cornelius. How long are you going to sleep? Time to wake up."

The up and down from his dream continued. Where did dreams end and waking begin?

Cornelius cleared his throat. "Ok." He looked at Naemi. She appeared different. She sat perfectly straight on a bench on the lifeboat. But her eyes! They flashed different colors in quick synchronized rhythms. What was she trying to do, just sitting there staring at him, flashing different colored eyes? They were intensely focused on Cornelius. And she hummed a strange private tune, barely audible. In addition to her uncanny eyes, Naemi wore an elaborate girdle ill concealed under her cloak, holding an impressive array of knives and swords that Cornelius had not seen before. Cornelius clambered up to a sitting position opposite her. "What is up with your eyes, Naemi?". He stretched his arms and flexed his biceps, turning his head to stretch his neck.

Her eyes slowed their rhythmic dance, then settled to one green and one brown. "You're a ham," she said. Then both her eyes turned blue.

"You're eyes?" asked Cornelius again.

Naemi was silent for a moment, looking at Cornelius. One flashed blue, then the other. Then she said, "Would you believe me if I told you I lost my contacts on the Tarvash last night?"

Cornelius stared at Naemi. One of her eyes went soft brown. "No, I wouldn't," Cornelius said. "You don't wear contacts. I've known you for years. You're eyes have never looked like that, and you've never mentioned contacts to me."

"I'm from Polaris," Naemi reminded him. "My eyes are, different, from yours."

"Bullshit," said Cornelius. "We're both Human. Humans don't have eyes like that."

"Not on Lupus," said Naemi. Her mind wandered, back to her life before joining Cornelius aboard the Tarvash last night, before G pulled her from that life on Polaris. She thought of the debacle of her life, the offer of redemption from the Magistry. Then followed the implant procedure, and the hunts that followed, hunting Ferals.

Shouting sounded from lake ships anchored offshore in the lake mists beyond where Cornelius and Naemi bobbed up and down in their boat. Small craft were emerging from the mists carrying crews for repairs of the broken lake docks.

"Beme, Bossin. Bolo toar. Beme."

"That sounds like Raffir," said Cornelius.

"We don't need to be found," said Naemi.

"Agreed," said Cornelius. He looked around. "We'll get back to your eyes later. Where are we exactly?"

"See for yourself," said Naemi.

Bump-bump. The little boat rocked up and down on small waves. The boat was tied by a toe-line to a tall titanium wall. The boat kept rocking and knocking against the wall. Bump-bump.

They were in the small lifeboat from the Tarvash. It was about four meters long, painted white on the inside, white with blue horizontal stripes on the outside. The inside paint was full of scratches. Two metal benches occupied the little boat.

"The famous locks?" asked Cornelius.

Naemi nodded. "And broken in the tsunami. Repairs have been going on all night and morning, while you slept."

"The quake," said Cornelius. Memories of the night and day before came back to him. "Where are we, exactly?"

"At the sluice gate," said Naemi. "You told me last night that Captain Katzer told you to come to this place. Remember?"

Cornelius stretched again, let out a groan. He remembered. The Canine captain of the Tarvash had sent them here in this lifeboat. From here they were to journey through the Channel Rift Valley. It was that or face Raffir's wrath back on the Tarvash.

Cornelius asked, "How long have you been up?"

"About half an hour," she said. "You sleep a lot."

"So people keep telling me," said Cornelius. He swiveled to look around.

Bump-bump. The little boat banged against the sluice gate.

Cornelius felt his stomach grumble. "Is there anything to eat?"

Both of Naemi's eyes flashed blue. She reached behind her and drew out a small waterproof pouch from below her seat. "Just this." She handed Cornelius the bag.

He took the bag, opened the locking seal. He reached inside and pulled out

358

a small brown brick wrapped in muslin. There were seven bricks in the bag.

"It's all there is," said Naemi.

"Seven is a strange number," said Cornelius. "Did you eat one already?"

"WE ate one. Last night." Both of Naemi's eyes flashed green. "Remember?"

"Ok," said Cornelius.

"You need to be more alert," said Naemi. "You're too foggy-headed when you wake up."

Cornelius was nonplussed by Naemi's jibes. "I've been having some crazy dreams, Naemi."

"About what?" The tone of her voice feigned interest.

"Us. My mom sometimes. Lots of strange things I don't really understand."

Naemi was curt with her reply. "Don't let dreams affect your waking self. We have things to do."

"Come on," said Cornelius. "Ok. What do you dream about?"

"I don't dream."

"Everyone dreams," said Cornelius. But Naemi wouldn't be drawn any further into the debate.

Cornelius unwrapped the brick, broke off a piece and handed it to Naemi. She took it and started eating. Cornelius bit off the end of his. It was chewy. The taste was not exactly pleasant. It tasted of pressed fishmeal, lake weed, and some substance that made Cornelius think of dung.

"It's nutritious," said Naemi.

"It'll do," said Cornelius, finishing his swallow. He wrapped the rest of the brick in its muslin and sealed it back in the bag with the others.

He stood up in the boat and began untying the knot in his drawstrings.

"You're going to have to forgive me," he said. "I need to piss."

"Yes," was all she said. She turned around in her seat to face the other direction.

Cornelius sighed the liberating sigh of release. His stream was steady, splashing onto the grey green waters of the lake. The boat rocked as waves sloshed against the lifeboat's hull. The boat bumped against the sluice gate. Bump-bump. Bump-bump.

A slight breeze blowing out of the fog was chill. Cornelius shivered and rubbed his arms. His stream fell to a dribble. He shook himself three times for good luck, then hid himself back in his pants and fastened the drawstring. He turned back to Naemi and found her observing scratches on the interior of the boat. She hummed to herself as she flicked the scratches with a fingernail. "Idle musings?" Cornelius asked.

She flicked a scratch, then sat back in delight. "There!"

A sculpted green shell swirled out of the boat where the scratch had been. Both Cornelius and Naemi exclaimed at the same time, "Gurkbuzzel!"

"Of course, it's a gurkbuzzel boat," said Cornelius. "No wonder there are so few supplies on board. Not even a life ring."

Naemi touched the shell. A red and white life ring emerged out of the boat's hull near Cornelius.

"Look at that," said Cornelius. He sat back down on his hard bench. Then he reached forward and gave the shell a swirl with one of his fingers. The two benches grew red plush covers. "No need to be uncomfortable," he said grinning.

More voices called shoreward from boats emerging from the foggy lake mist. They were closer now. Cornelius looked behind Naemi at the titanium sluice gate and wall. "Have you looked over the gate yet?" he asked. "That's our next move, right?"

"I have seen where we need to go," said Naemi.

"Ok. Let me look then." Cornelius stood and steadied, just, on the bobbing boat. He grabbed onto the top of the wall and hooked his arms over it to look beyond.

The sluice gate butted up against a nearly sheer cliff of grey and red rock on the right. Built into the rock face were the gates, bays and passageways of the lock system. Jumbled debris and detritus clogged the locks. A kilometer off to the left, the waters of the southern lake roared over cataracts in a massive falls structure, forming a lake. Here the Channel Rift River began.

The sluice gate opened onto a narrow and nearly vertical "S" shaped sluice or channel. With dismay, Cornelius realized that opening the gate would plunge the lifeboat down the sluice for about a kilometer, ending in a splash in a lake.

Beyond the lake, in the headwaters of the river, Cornelius saw eight lake ships queued for the locks that now were damaged. Small boats ushered forth from the ships, with Humans and Canine repair crews ready to join those arriving from the southern lake ships.

Surveying the lands alongside the river, Cornelius saw a dry rocky terrain to the east, a verdant canopy of mangroves to the west.

Naemi's voice carried from behind Cornelius. "Well?"

"Uh, there's a slight drop," said Cornelius. He sat back down in the boat next to Naemi. The boat bumped against the sluice gate.

"Slight?" Naemi had never trusted Cornelius' choice of adjectives to describe a situation.

"A kilometer," said Cornelius, turning to look at Naemi. She maintained a cold stare. "There's a channel."

"Hm," was Naemi's only response.

More shouts sounded from the small boats approaching from the lake. "Bossin bolo toro. Beme...."

"They're getting closer," said Naemi.

"Bala beme, Bossin!" Raffir's voice was even closer now.

Naemi was very agitated. She grabbed Cornelius' bicep tightly. "I know what we have to do," she said. "I've been here before." Her eyes turned green. Before Cornelius could respond to her statement, Naemi was in action. She bent down and stroked the gurkbuzzel device. "Buckle in!" she ordered. The lifeboat seats morphed into side-by-side bucket seats with cross straps. Naemi secured herself in an instant, though the tussling and pulling of straps loosed her breasts from her blouse.

Cornelius was caught up in her previous words. "You've been HERE before?" Not hesitating to follow Naemi's lead, he snapped his straps across his chest and yanked them tight.

"Secure your bag," said Naemi. Then she reached for the gurkbuzzel device with her foot and tapped it with her big toe. A long white pole two meters long emerged from the boat's hull. She grabbed it and thrust it up to the top of the sluice gate. In one quick motion Naemi knocked the latch up and over the lock. The gate burst open swinging wide. The boat tipped in the rush of water and was sucked through. In the midst of the rush of water, the pole slammed back and was reabsorbed just as the boat plummeted.

"Naemi! Holy shit!" shouted Cornelius.

Naemi had just a moment to tap the gurkbuzzel device again with her toe. Three masts sprung out of the boat and released a three-point glider sail. But the boat crashed against the sluice channel's rock wall, throwing Cornelius and Naemi out of their seats, suspended in air by their straps. Arms and breasts were flung toward legs. Steerage ropes dangled in front of them. Naemi grabbed these as she was knocked back into her seat. The rope ends formed into straps and gloves and enveloped Naemi's hands. She pulled hard. The sail flapped loudly above them as the boat again struck the channel's rock embankment. Cornelius and Naemi were thrown forward again in a rush of water that drenched everything and everyone. As they crashed back into their seats, the craft was airborne.

The glider boat tipped and rocked, throwing out most of the collected water. Skillfully working the ropes, Naemi leveled the boat out and they flew. With a slight tip forward, the glider drifted down and away from the sluice and toward the roaring falls. The sail flapped hard in the wind and erupted in bright flashing patterns of green and blue luminescence.

Having just caught his breath and swallowed his stomach, Cornelius yelled out, "You've been HERE before? And you've done THIS before?" He was caught up on the subject.

Naemi was busy operating the ropes. Sorry she'd mentioned it, she turned to Cornelius and said coarsely, "Yes. I said I'd been to Canius. This was the way." Her eyes were orange.

"What is it with your eyes?" asked Cornelius again.

"Not now, Cornelius," said Naemi.

The glider boat neared the roaring falls. The deafening wall of water cast spray all about them. The water and downdraft of wind pushed the boat down toward the center of the cascade lake below. As Naemi leveled out their descent, a great electrical flash filled the view before them. Where the eight queued ships Cornelius had seen earlier were anchored, twenty were now queued.

"What the hell!" exclaimed Cornelius. But another electrical flash erupted, and the twenty ships became two hundred, lined up in the distance as far as the eye could see. "Get us out of here, Naemi," he yelled.

Naemi did not need to be so told. There were lake ships and skinners, small boats and rafts. She was reminded of this place in another time. Five hundred ships including military carriers, with combat craft buzzing the skies. Those weren't here, not yet, and Naemi didn't want to find out if they'd appear again this time. This time, she might make it where she'd failed before. Naemi leaned forward scanning the skies for other aerial craft. Seeing nothing, she looked down at the channel's left bank. There a narrower channel, edged close on both sides in mangroves, ran parallel to the main river.

"What are you looking for?" asked Cornelius.

"Safe portage," said Naemi. She guided the glider boat down towards the narrow channel. They passed over the lake, and over the first of the ships in the main river. Horns sounded from the ships and shouts rose into the air from smaller craft.

"They see us," said Cornelius.

"They won't follow us into the narrow channel," said Naemi. That's where we're headed."

"How do you know that?" asked Cornelius.

How indeed. Naemi had vivid memories of an earlier attempt at getting to Big City this way, with Cornelius. That time, only one of numerous attempts, Naemi had tried to commandeer a lake ship. It had not turned out so well. But she had learned a lot about the ships, for example, that the military maintains an agent, oft in secret, aboard each ship. Naemi now had another chance to get through. She hoped it was her last. But she owed Cornelius some answer at least. "Raffir told me, while you were surfing. By treaty, they cannot enter Canius."

"I was kite boarding," said Cornelius. For now, her explanation was satisfactory.

The glider boat continued to descend away from the main river. Soon it dipped below the edge of the mangroves and the lake ships disappeared from view. The glider's wings barely fluttered in the still air despite the boat's forward motion. They glided two meters above the narrow river channel's surface, then one. Naemi brought the boat gently down in the center of the channel's current with barely a change in velocity. Only a "whoosh" sounded when the hull made contact with the water.

"Nice landing, huh?" Naemi complimented herself. Cornelius started to unclasp his safely straps. Naemi was already out of hers.

The air on the river was humid and still. The sun was not yet high enough to shine onto the water. Even so, the air was warm, and despite the calm, the air was filled with sound and activity. Frogs croaked, seemingly in the thousands. Bree-whistles, little reptiles only three centimeters long and two wide, piped to each other as they darted from one side of the river to the other in aerial dives. Bright red beetles, their wings polka dotted with white, buzzed about the mangrove roots at the water's edge. Yellow and white striped moths fluttered near the surface of the water's midstream.

Naemi bent down and rubbed the gurkbuzzel device. The little boat responded immediately. The sails folded up and disappeared into the mast, then the masts sank back down into the floor of the boat. The bucket seats returned to padded benches. At a second touch, a new mast rose up producing a proper sailboat sail. A rudder emerged at the boat's aft.

"Slick," said Cornelius.

"We're on our way to Big City now," said Naemi with a smile.

"Cornelius looked up. "Nice sail, but there's no wind to speak of."

"Why don't you blow?" suggested Naemi.

Cornelius smiled. "You mean like this?" He stood in the boat, hands on hips, and filled his lungs with the humid air. Barrel-chested with full puffy cheeks, he leaned forward and let out his wind in a slow stream aimed high at the sail. At that moment the sun broke out over the canopy of mangroves flooding the channel with bright hot light. The yellow striped moths began flying in spiral columns up and over the river toward the mangrove trees on the banks. Great fish jumped out of the water, gulping air and moths. And along with all this commotion, a strong wind blew up out of the south. The gurkbuzzel sail snapped taut and full. Cornelius and Naemi tumbled back onto their benches as the little craft sped north down the river.

A surprised Cornelius laughed and looked at Naemi. "Did I do that?"

Naemi gave him a steady look, but did not seem surprised. "Proud Cornelius called the wind to blow."

Naemi's typical non-plussed attitude, thought Cornelius. He leaned over and gave the gurkbuzzel device a spin.

"What are you doing?" asked Naemi.

"No reason not to travel in style." At that, the little boat morphed into a twenty-five meter long yacht with two great sails and two tall masts. A great steering wheel stood at the prow, where a straight titanium spear jutted out five meters. And Cornelius and Naemi found themselves sitting aft in luxurious chaise lounge chairs.

"Frivolous!" said Naemi.

Cornelius got up grinning. "If we're going to do this, let's do it right." He stood and headed to the wheel. "Come on." He took the wheel, playing captain. But the wind blew steady in the right direction, and he had little actual steering to do.

Naemi came up beside him and said, "Ok, let's get your questions out in the open and out of the way."

Cornelius turned his head to face her and said, "You know my questions. You do the talking."

Naemi's eyes turned green. She took a deep breath and began. "It's like this, Cornelius. You are to get to Big City, as planned."

"This is the plan I already know."

Naemi continued. "You are to provide the information encrypted in your bloodstream to Shont."

"Again," said Cornelius.

"And Shont will arrange for you to disappear into Canius."

"Canius?" said Cornelius.

"Yes," said Naemi.

"Why?" Cornelius began, but Naemi interrupted him.

"You saw the lake ships in the river change, become more numerous?"

"What WAS that?" asked Cornelius.

"From this point out, things may change around us. ARE changing around us," said Naemi.

"Why? What's causing it?"

"They are local manifestations of changes to the past, or present or future, depending on your perspective. Anyway, that's the simplest way I can explain it."

"So your eyes," started Cornelius. "Are they a result of some change in your past?"

"No," Naemi replied. "Actually a change in my future. But not because of that," and she waved her hand toward the main river channel to the east. "My eyes won't change for a year or so."

"I don't understand," said Cornelius. "You're talking in circles."

Naemi sighed. This was a lot for Cornelius. She was patient. "Last night while you were on the deck of the Tarvash, I was with the others in the hold."

"Here we go," said Cornelius.

Naemi continued. "While you were on deck, there was a change."

"Like that?" Cornelius imitated Naemi, waving his hand eastward.

"Yes." This is where the story would get even more confusing for Cornelius, she thought. "I, came through. Me, the Naemi standing beside you. I came through to help, myself."

Cornelius just stared at Naemi for a long while saying nothing. Naemi waited. Then Cornelius said, "You 'came through.' What does that mean, exactly?"

"I came through, came back, in time," said Naemi.

"Why did you kill Tentz?" asked Cornelius.

Naemi allowed herself a secret smile. "Oh, a number of reasons. But one, she was not Human. She was gurkbuzzel."

"What?"

"I didn't know it at the time actually," said Naemi. "And I don't know how long she was not Human. All I know is that when she died, her body sunk into the floor and was absorbed.

Cornelius tried hard to suspend his disbelief of Naemi's fantastical tale. But he had a thought about this part of her story. "Yesterday morning when I awoke, Tentz was in the hold with me. She stayed there when I came up on deck. You were in the lake with the Canine women."

"I remember," said Naemi. And she did, more or less.

"As far as I know, she was still down there when Raffir and Bossin dumped the new gurkbuzzel slugs into the hold."

Naemi followed Cornelius' logic. She smiled at the thought of the girl alone in the hole, smothered in slugs. Renender would have appreciated such an end for her. "She must have been absorbed, eaten, and regurgitated, in a manner of speaking."

Cornelius was disgusted at the thought, and his face showed it. He looked away east just as another electrical flash erupted, though the mangroves concealed most of the flash. "What do you suppose just changed over there this time?"

"Maybe more lake ships," said Naemi. "Maybe Markhab's military has ships there now. He has already launched his attacked against the rest of Human Lupus. Lupus City, Shining City, Big City. He may have all of them soon, or already."

"You said that Raffir killed me once before," said Cornelius. "And earlier you said you've been here before. How many...."

Naemi cut him off. "More times than I care to quote you, Cornelius. You need to get to Big City. Both of us do. So far, it's proven difficult."

Cornelius looked to the north where lay Big City in the far distance, too far to see with a Human's eyes. He considered the tale Naemi had told. He was not so quick to believe Naemi's stories, so many of them proved false. But this one was not even believable, and therein lay the difference. Naemi had a habit of making plausible claims to mask her secrets. This story was ridiculous. Did that make it true? He looked back at Naemi. She was strangely quiet, patient. She was definitely not herself, yet she was. Cornelius chuckled at the paradox.

"What's so funny?" she asked.

"That was quite a story," he said. "Even for you. Let me assume, for the sake of argument, that what you're saying is in fact true. Why tell me at all?"

"You mean besides the fact that you insisted?" replied Naemi.

"Yes, besides that," said Cornelius. "Why not tell me earlier? Why didn't Jarbed tell me? Does he know?"

"Jarbed knows as much as he needs to," she said. "And yesterday's Naemi would not have told you. But I can see from here on out that you need to know. Perhaps it will help."

"So Jarbed is not the leader of some futuristic forces?" asked Cornelius.

"Don't be silly, Cornelius. This is not a comic book." One of Naemi's eyes turned brown.

Cornelius had more questions. "Does Markhab have this technology, too? Is he changing time? Is this some temporal war against Lupus Major?"

"Markhab does not have this technology, as far as I know," said Naemi. "Only G has it."

Only G has it, thought Cornelius. He tried thinking of the people he knew, anyone whose name began with G. "Who is G?"

Naemi's eyes went grey. She hesitated answering just a moment, which let Cornelius know she'd let some information slip that was not intended for his ears. "You don't know G. Never mind about him." Her eyes softened to green. "Anymore details would distract you. And it's not relevant to our current mission."

"You know," said Cornelius. "So why not me? Do I get snatched out of time like you?"

"No Cornelius. And that's not the point. You are to do this on your own, so to speak. Unsullied."

"Unsullied?" asked Cornelius.

"Sorry. It's G's term. Never mind. This needs to happen all in your own timeline, continuous."

"Unsullied," repeated Cornelius.

"Yes."

"What's in Canius?" Cornelius asked.

Naemi paused, then said, "Alpha."

"What's that?"

"Not what. Whom. The Canine Alpha."

"A leader of the Canines? I thought there wasn't any."

"The Canine Alpha is the spiritual leader of all Canines on Lupus," said Naemi. "You are to cooperate with him to defeat Markhab. That's your mission. That's all I can tell you."

"What does 'cooperate' mean, Naemi?"

"We need the Alpha to defeat Markhab. He will help, but only if you go to him."

"Is he expecting me?" asked Cornelius.

"I don't know," said Naemi.

Cornelius then chuckled. "Your claim about losing contacts is more believable."

Naemi just glared at him with grey eyes.

"I've heard enough for now," said Cornelius. His mind was too full of crazy information. "I'd like to be alone for awhile. Why don't you go relax back there." He waved to the chaise lounge chairs in the aft of the yacht.

Naemi didn't complain. "Yes, we've talked enough." She turned and left Cornelius manning the wheel.

Naemi tapped the gurkbuzzel device and it offered up a big white floppy hat and wide black sunglasses. She put them on and took her seat on a chaise lounge chair. Despite the wind that Cornelius seemed to have called forth that propelled the yacht forward, the sun felt warm. Naemi gazed awhile at the wake left by the yacht. The river teemed with fish. Naemi watched as the fish took turns jumping the wake and waves. Facing aft, the mangrove banks kept receding as more mangroves came into view. She saw flashes of light among the boughs and roots of the trees. Gurkbuzzel slugs? Naemi then chuckled to herself at the irony of her position. Her view was of where they'd been, not where they were going. Time and again she'd made this trip back in time to aid Cornelius. Always the past was repeating itself, and Naemi was always repeating herself. How tiresome it was always coming back. Was this really the best way? She'd have to speak to G about it next time she was aboard his time ship. She had no doubt he'd pull her back in time again, and again.

The yacht sailed northward for over an hour with Naemi dozing in her chair.

She awoke to the sound of her stomach complaining about being empty. She stretched her arms, wiggled her feet and got up. Resting her hands on the yacht's starboard safety rail, she watched the large fish alternate between surfacing and submerging. One particularly large fish more than two meters long seemed to keep its eyes focused on Naemi. She entertained the thought that the fish might make a tasty meal. She just had to catch it.

Naemi nonchalantly backed away from the rail and from the eyesight of the fish. She reached the gurkbuzzel device and gave it a good spin with her hand. In place of the pair of chaise lounge chairs, a massive fishing pole on a pivoting turret with chair rose three meters out of the deck. Naemi climbed up the metal ladder of the turret and swung her legs over the fishing pole, straddling it. She smiled. She liked this position. She leaned forward and grabbed the two buttoned handles jutting out on either side of the pole. She looked down at the water for the fish. It was still there looking up at Naemi on her mount.

Naemi locked her gaze with that of the fish. Her eyes were wide and she began humming. Then her eyes began flickering in rhythmic procession, one blue the other grey, then grey and green, then green and brown, brown and yellow, yellow and yellow, green and green, blue and blue. All the while

Naemi hummed.

The fish responded by making kissing motions and sounds with its huge mouth at the river's surface. Its fins and tail maintained their motion to keep pace with the yacht. Then its eyes grew cloudy. Naemi swiveled the fishing pole and aimed it at the fish. She pressed a button on the left handle. The fishing line shot out from the end of the pole and splashed into the water near the fish. The hook sank but a green and yellow floater bobbed. The fish sank beneath the surface and disappeared. A moment later the floater disappeared and the line pulled taut. The turret and Naemi pivoted sharply to the left. Naemi fell back into the chair. Her eyes stopped their flashing and turned a dark green.

Naemi retained control of the pole by grasping both handles. The huge reel in between spun and spun and rattled as the line went out of it. Naemi pushed a button on the right handle and the line stopped with a snap and a jerk and a shudder. She pressed another button and the line began to retract. Naemi never stopped humming. The pole bent down to the water as its catch was dragged and pulled. The floater surfaced and rose into the air. A moment later the huge fish emerged splashing and writhing.

Two and a half meters of massive struggling fish fought against the line. Its huge mouth gasped for oxygen. As its tail exited the river following the floater into the air, the fish brought Naemi's pole further down toward the water. Naemi heaved her shoulders and torso, applying torque pressure against the pole handles. The fish writhed in the air as it just cleared the yacht's rail. It swung over the deck and hovered in mid air, thrashing about.

Naemi leapt off the turret and pulled a long curved blade from its scabbard around her waist while still in mid air. She landed with a thump on the deck firmly on both feet. In a strong and fluid motion grasping the blade with both hands, she swiped at the moving fish, cutting right through its midsection and ribs. The fish slammed down onto the deck, its guts flying out. Loosed from the fish's belly, inertia carried the bloody mass of guts and gore through the air. Naemi ducked to miss the mess. It soared over the yacht's rail and splashed into the river. Other fish immediately surfaced and began to feast.

Naemi stood over her catch dead at her feet, its bulging eyes glazed and opaque. Naemi reached down and released the hook caught between the fish' gaping mouth and gill slits. The freed hook retracted to the end of the pole.

Naemi cleaned her blade by wiping its bloody edge on the fish's scales, then returned it to its scabbard around her waist. She calmly walked over to the rail and looked overboard at the aquatic feast of guts. The tumultuous water was smeared red. Naemi spied a lone drop of gore clinging to the rail. She wiped it up with a finger and held the crimson stain in the sunlight where it glistened. Her eyes flashed yellow, and she cleaned her finger with one deliberate and savored lick. Turning back to admire her handiwork lying motionless on the deck, she called aloud, "Lunch!" Her eyes settled to blue.

With a turn of the gurkbuzzel device, Naemi transformed the fishing pole and turret into a butcher-block table, sink and grill beside the fish. Bending down, she slipped her right hand into the fish's mouth feeling for the gill slits from the inside. Her fingers poked through the gills. With her left hand, Naemi reached inside the open belly and heaved up, but the many kilos of fish were too heavy for her to lift. She pulled out her hands, goopy with gut juice, and stood up to reassess the situation. A better strategy occurred to her. She returned to the gurkbuzzel device. A quarter turn and the butcher table sunk back into the deck. Another turn and the table reemerged, this time from beneath the fish. Now the fish lay on top of the table, complete with cooking utensils and seasoning.

Withdrawing her knife again, Naemi began scaling the fish. With each scrape-scrape-scrape, the scales flew into the air and over the rail of the yacht. Minutes later the fish was ready for slicing. Grasping her blade with both hands, Naemi chopped. The head came off, the tail was severed. Naemi threw these overboard, instigating another feeding frenzy in the river. Naemi chopped the rest of the fish into nice thick cuts of steak. She arranged the steaks on the grill and lit the fire. Seasoned and turned, aromatic smoke wafted above and beyond the yacht.

Naemi placed some of the cooked steaks onto a gurkbuzzel platter and packaged the rest for eating later. She added utensils and a sprig of floating river garnish to complete the presentation. Then she carried the platter up to the bow of the ship where Cornelius was still by the wheel.

Cornelius was sparring with the wind before the steering wheel. The wind tussled his hair and the sun danced off his black and bronze skin. He held himself in attack poise, one leg before the other, one arm before him aimed at an imaginary opponent, the other held behind with a long blade in hand. He reacted with a forward thrust of his knife hand followed by a body spin, ending with an air kick. He repeated this by exchanging the knife to his other hand and leaning on his other leg. With each thrust and stomp and kick he let out a loud grunt, or "ah-HA!", or "take THAT!"

Throughout his sparring exercises Cornelius contemplated one of two possibilities, one, the bombshell of time travel, multiple Naemis, and a mission with more than planetary consequence, and two, were they all half-truths or lies?

Cornelius found the prospect of her story being true as the more appealing. Time travel! What Human had not wished such a thing possible? Indeed, as a boy he had fantasized about it, to go back and save his mother and sister from a horrible and senseless murder. Someone Naemi mysteriously referred to only as "G" had a time ship. The possibilities flooded Cornelius' mind.

Naemi came up beside him. "The wind is a most worthy opponent. Are you winning?"

Cornelius turned and smiled at the platter of cooked fish presented by Naemi. "Food! Where did you get that? It's not gurkbuzzel food, is it?" He sheathed his blade.

"Not a chance," said Naemi. "I caught it while you were up here playing swash buckler."

"Playing what?" Cornelius asked.

"It's just an expression," said Naemi. "Is the boat steering itself?" she said, noticing that Cornelius was not really manning the wheel.

"My wind seems to be driving us exactly in the right direction. No need to touch the wheel. But I have been watching it," he said.

"Your wind," repeated Naemi. "Yes, I suppose you called it."

"Wouldn't that be nice," said Cornelius. But despite his confidence in the wind and the yacht's direction, he took a moment to grasp the wheel. As he held the wheel's spokes, his fingers sunk gently into the wood as if it were becoming soft. "Strange," he said. "The wheel is soft."

"Maybe it's you," said Naemi. "Come on, let's eat."

The two sat cross-legged on the yacht's deck and enjoyed the feast. The meat was fatty and sweet. It was delicious. Cornelius eschewed the use of his knife and fork, if he even noticed they were available. Naemi fumbled with her utensils around the fish bones, then abandoned them and joined Cornelius main-au-bouche, complete with slurps and grunts of satisfaction. Naemi licked her fingers as Cornelius called forth deep belches. Naemi joined in with a demure burp of her own.

"Too bad there isn't more," said Cornelius, still masticating.

Naemi's eyes turned a pale blue then went green. "Oh, but there's lots more. The fish was huge. We've got food for the rest of the day."

They basked in the sunlight, the breeze and the sounds of the river. Then Naemi cried out, "The yacht!"

The gurkbuzzel yacht burst into an array of competing chromophore patterns. The deck undulated, then the yacht itself collapsed, morphing back into the small lifeboat sans mast and sail. Cornelius and Naemi tumbled together onto two small benches, Naemi's package of more fish steaks falling beside them. The wind ceased.

"What's happening?" Naemi exclaimed.

"The gurkbuzzel boat must need replenishing, just like on the Tarvash," answered Cornelius. "It needs to eat."

"Eat what?" asked Naemi.

"Slugs," said Cornelius. "Gurkbuzzel slugs. But where do we get more?"

Naemi had the answer. "The western shore. I saw their flashings earlier, among the mangroves. We'll have to collect them ourselves."

"Great," said Cornelius with some disgust, remembering the baskets of writhing slimy slugs that Raffir and Bossin had unloaded the day before.

The strong wind that had driven the yacht forward ceased to blow when the yacht collapsed. The little lifeboat idled listlessly in the center of the river channel, barely moving in the slow waters.

"We need paddles," said Naemi. "And baskets." She began searching the scratches on the inside of the boat again, flicking several before finding the one that caused the gurkbuzzel device to erupt in a swirl.

"Do you think it'll respond?" asked Cornelius.

"Let's give it a go." She gently touched the device, not sure of the outcome.

As if responding to its own need, the boat reciprocated. Two paddles and two baskets emerged beside them. They breathed a sigh of relief.

"Let's get to it," said Naemi. They seized the oars and began paddling to the Canius shore.

The paddling was the easy part, once Cornelius and Naemi ceased working against one another and got in synch. Within minutes they were at the edge of the mangroves. But where actually was the shore? The rigid interlocking and stilt like mangrove roots stood in the water. They marched back some indeterminate distance. No terra firma was visible. The overgrowth obscured much.

"What now?" asked Cornelius. "Where are your slugs?"

"Hiding from the sun?" offered Naemi. Indeed, it was late morning if not noon. The sun was hot overhead, and the air even more still and humid than before. Large black flies buzzing near the roots greeted their arrival. They soon enjoyed swarming around Cornelius to his annoyance. They left Naemi alone. "Come on," said Naemi. "Let's tie the boat up and move in."

Cornelius leaned forward and grabbed the boat's toe line. He reached for a sturdy root and secured the boat with a tight knot.

"Follow my lead," said Naemi. She grabbed a basket, slung it over her shoulder and somehow secured it there. Then she stood, the boat not rocking much, and stepped onto a root, grabbed an overhead branch, and climbed into the tangled foliage.

Cornelius demonstrated less grace. With his own basket secured to his shoulder, his first footfall slipped off a root and he fell out of the boat, splashing into the water with one foot still in the boat. The foot in the river sank into mud. "I'm stuck!" he exclaimed.

Naemi was already several meters ahead when she was forced to turn back and aide Cornelius. "Really, Cornelius. Have you any balance?"

"Don't start!" he said exasperated.

Naemi pointed out which root and which branch Cornelius should grab. Just as he was hauling himself up, the branch snapped and he tumbled back into the river again. Naemi said nothing, just waited patiently. Before long Cornelius joined her in the mangroves, quite wet. But wherever he seemed to be, the black flies followed. He tried swatting at them to little avail, except to teeter himself and almost topple back into the water again.

"Ignore them," said Naemi, who had no flies around her. A few minutes later she called back to Cornelius. "I've found the ground."

Cornelius emerged from the tangle of mangroves to find Naemi standing on a mossy bank in the sunlight. Behind her grew willow trees, and crawling and flashing among the branches and leaves were hundreds of gurkbuzzel slugs.

"Are you ready?" asked Naemi.

"You've found a gold mine," said Cornelius.

They set their baskets down on the mossy ground, opened their tops, and began collecting slugs, dropping them into the wicker receptacles. Cornelius scooped up fistfuls of slugs at a time. Before long his hands and arms were dripping with slime. He shook the goo off after dropping each fist full into the basket.

"This is messy business," he said.

"Is it?" said Naemi absently. She was having no problem with slime. She glanced over at Cornelius and saw him struggling. "Pick them up like this." She picked each slug up by the midsection and dropped them one-by-one into her basket. "They tend not to excrete this way."

"Nice technique," said Cornelius. He tried her method, but ended up with just as much slime as before. He returned to grabbing fistfuls.

They worked their way around the willow trees until both their baskets were full. They secured the lids and stopped to rest. They could see that beyond the willow trees the landscape quickly opened up into a rocky landscape. Trees gave way to shrubs and grass, thick blue hummocks. Low hills rose in the distance. Amid the rock outcroppings, sulfurous steam rose.

"This is a different place entirely," said Cornelius.

"The channel rift," said Naemi.

Scattered here and there were circular pebbly areas without grass or large stones. Within them arrays of straight thorny sticks in sunburst patterns radiated out from the center of each. There were dozens about. The sticks were about two meters long, making the circular areas four meters in diameter.

"What do you think those are?" asked Cornelius.

"Piles of sticks," said Naemi. "We should leave them alone."

Cornelius was already at the nearest clearing and bending down to pick up a stick before Naemi had finished speaking. Just as he touched one, the whole arrangement snapped up and together into one upright structure, prickly and tight, with Cornelius' hand caught inside. "Oww!" he cried out.

Naemi came running over. Cornelius' hand was bleeding, caught and impaled on the sticks' spikes. "Are you ok?" she asked.

"No, I'm not!" said Cornelius. He grimaced in pain. From an orifice at the sticks' center on the ground a red fleshy tongue rose up to lick and catch the drops of blood dripping from Cornelius' hand. "Help me get free of this thing. It's alive!"

Naemi immediately unsheathed her long blade. She hacked at the trunk of sticks, but none shattered. "They're as hard as iron," she exclaimed. With each knock the spikes pinched Cornelius' hand even more.

"My hand's going numb," Cornelius said. The red tongue, over a meter long now, lapped and slurped the blood that now more freely dripped.

"It's an anti-coagulant," said Naemi. "You could bleed out." She hacked and hit at the sticks harder than ever.

Just at this dire moment, the most amazing thing Cornelius ever beheld thus far in his life occurred. A horrible din broke the air like a hundred glass windows shattering. Undertones of scraping metals vied with the glass to be loudest. Then a bright arc of light erupted right in front of him. Out of it stepped a Feline.

Naemi gasped. "G!"

The Feline was Cornelius' height though more slender of build. He was garbed in a navy blue uniform, buckled at the waist. His right ear was double-notched, perhaps from some accident. His eyes were wide, green with huge vertical pupils set in his black striped and short auburn hair. He held in one hand a tubular instrument. The Feline gazed intently at Cornelius and Naemi struggling in their predicament. With his full attention momentarily just on Naemi, his voice bellowed like ten thousand drums echoing off a rock face, "GET BACK!" Cornelius' eardrums hurt from the pain of the loudness, but he could not cover his ears. Naemi, dazed by the audio blast, jumped back away from Cornelius.

The Feline jumped into action. Tightly gripping the instrument in his hand, he spun with force and released a metal whip. At its end were three autonomous spikes. Cornelius turned his face away as well as he could. With a mighty CRACK! The pronged metal whip exploded into the stick creature. Shards and shrapnel burst in all directions. A high-pitched scream came from the center orifice and the red tongue fell limp to the ground amid the stick carnage.

Naemi looked up. Cornelius was freed. She ran to him where he was getting up holding his injured hand, having been thrown from the force of the crack whip. His hand was swollen and turning black at the puncture site. A reddish black fluid oozed from the wound. They turned back to find the

Feline observing them intently, seeing Cornelius' injured hand and Naemi's near helplessness beside him.

Looking directly at Cornelius, the Feline tossed the tool to him. Cornelius caught it with his good hand. To Naemi, the Feline stared into and through her, blasting her mind with knowing and judgment. He uttered another cacophonous demand. "HEAL HIM!"

Naemi covered her ears while Cornelius cried out, "Owwww!"

A moment later the Feline vanished. The arc of light went out and the crashing sound of glass and metal ceased. All was quiet as it had been before.

"What just happened? Who was that?" asked Cornelius.

Naemi took a moment to regain her composure. She rubbed her temples. "I'll get to him later." She trained her now grey eyes onto his hand and said, "Cornelius, let me see your hand again."

He extended his swollen hand for her to see.

"It's turning purple," she said with shaking voice. "There's poison in it."

"I don't feel anything," added Cornelius.

"I have to get the poison out." She took a small blade from a sheath at her waist.

"What's that for?" asked Cornelius, jerking back his hand.

Naemi did not answer him in words. In one almost choreographed flurry of motion she tensed her face, pursed her lips, steeled her eyes that went purple, yanked back Cornelius' hand and held it in a vice grip. With her bladed hand she swung up, and with a delicateness she was not known for, punctured Cornelius swollen hand and sliced a centimeter long incision. Naemi swung her blade hand away and squeezed Cornelius' hand. Stringy pulp and ooze and digestive enzymes, pus and blood erupted out. It ran over both their hands. Naemi put her mouth to Cornelius' wound and sucked. She spat. She sucked and spat repeatedly until only normal red blood came out. The bloated skin of Cornelius' hand deflated to normal size. All this happened in seconds, and Naemi released Cornelius' hand.

Cornelius had barely enough time throughout the procedure to wear a mask of surprise. As his freed hand fell away from Naemi's grasp he exclaimed, "Holy shit Naemi!"

"Your flesh was starting to rot, Cornelius," she said, spitting the taste of bitter out of her mouth. "That stick plant's tongue was lapping up your juices as your hand decomposed in digestive enzymes. You have an uncanny ability at finding all the carnivorous plants on Lupus. I just saved you. I just saved you, again."

"You're effective, I'll give you that," said Cornelius.

Naemi then pulled a tiny needle that was concealed in her clothes. She ran her fingers through her hair and pulled out a strand. She strung the hair through the eye of the needle and asked, "Is your hand still numb?"

Cornelius flexed his hand slowly. "Kind of," he said. "Though less. The feeling's coming back. Do you mean to sew me up with that?"

"Yes." Naemi extended the thread to Cornelius. "You need to urinate on this, to sterilize it."

"You're kidding," said Cornelius.

"I could do it, but you might think that's gross," said Naemi.

Cornelius laughed. "It's still gross, but I'll do it." He snatched the needle and hair from Naemi and turned around, stepping a few paces back. He undid the drawstring of his pants and let loose his stream.

"Clean out the hand and wound, too," said Naemi.

"Uh huh," Cornelius replied. The cleaning done, Cornelius shook his hand to dry it off. All put back together, he returned to Naemi, handing her the dripping needle and thread.

"Relax," she said. She took Cornelius' shaking hand and carefully sewed the incision closed. She tied off the end and cut the excess hair with her knife, then sheathed it again, along with the needle. "There you go, Cornelius," she said finally, smiling and flashing blue eyes.

Cornelius looked over the needlepoint work. "Thank you, Naemi. I really mean it."

"You can't say I'm not useful," she said.

Cornelius chuckled. "And everything you said earlier, it's true."

"Yes," said Naemi. "Now come on. We've got a task to finish. The gurkbuzzel slugs. Let's get them back to the boat."

With the baskets of flashing squirming oozing contents hooked to their backs, the two maneuvered their way back through the mangroves. Cornelius asked again, "Naemi, who was that?"

"I call him G. He is a time traveller I met. That's all I am prepared to say."

Cornelius looked at the strange whip device given to him by G. He turned it in his hand. Then he put it away.

Naemi led the way back. She lumbered along the mangrove roots with knees and elbows extended like a lumbering reptile. Despite Cornelius' injured hand, his return was a bit more dexterous. He walked primate style on the roots, with hands grabbing branches above. As Naemi neared the boat, she lost her footing on the same root that had given way under Cornelius on the way out. She tumbled into the river completely submerged, her basket of slugs bobbing on the surface where she'd just been. She splashed out of the water and climbed into the boat spitting water and grumbling curses. Cornelius held his tongue from voicing comments about balance and grace, though a half dozen thoughts came to mind. Naemi was not quite herself, not even this new Naemi. She was quiet and pensive. Now back in the boat, they were ready to replenish its gurkbuzzel shape changing abilities.

"How do we do this?" asked Naemi.

Cornelius stood on one of the benches. "Let's stand on these and just dump the slugs onto the floor of the boat."

"And then?"

"Well, I imagine they'll just be absorbed," said Cornelius, working to keep his balance.

They unfastened the lids of their baskets and shook the slime and slugs out. The slugs slithered about, crawling over themselves, onto the sides of the boat and the benches. Some found themselves on Cornelius and Naemi's feet, starting up their ankles.

"Nothing's happening," said Naemi, shaking one foot, then the other, teetering the boat. She lost her balance and fell onto the slug mass. "Yuck!" she screamed.

Cornelius could hardly contain himself. He broke out in uncontrolled laughter.

"Not funny!" Naemi exclaimed. But she began laughing, too.

Cornelius straddled both benches and stood over Naemi as she scrambled up, knocking red and pink flashing slugs away. Cornelius bent down and flicked the gurkbuzzel device. The grateful boat shimmered. The slugs joined and were absorbed into the boat. With rippling patterns of green, the boat groaned and grew and morphed back into the yacht. The toe rope to the mangrove root snapped and the boat tipped to one side as it grew. Cornelius found himself standing beside the navigation wheel at the bow. Naemi lay at his feet, full of slime.

She got up in silence, trying to brush the slime away with little results. Then she turned to Cornelius and mumbled, "I seem to be a bit off my game today."

"A bit," said Cornelius.

The boat leaned and banked to one side.

"We might be stuck," said Naemi. They walked to the back of the yacht. Naemi looked over the aft side nearest the mangroves, then up at the quiet and flaccid sails. "We need wind."

Cornelius came to her side. "Wind, eh? Shall I give it a go again?"

"Blow, Cornelius," she said.

He filled his lungs with a huge breath and released it in a steady stream into the sails. Suddenly a strong wind raced at them from behind. The sails filled and popped. The yacht creaked and pulled away from the shore. The wind blew fiercely, and carried on its gusting voice was a long low canid howl.

"Cornelius! We're going to smash into the other shore!" shouted Naemi.

Cornelius grabbed the wheel. He leaned all his weight to aft trying to compensate for the wind. "I need your help," he yelled back to Naemi.

She joined him and together they turned the yacht just in time. The keel scraped the river bottom and the starboard side knocked against mangrove roots. The titanium prow ripped off branches before finding the channel's center.

"Did you hear that voice on the wind?" asked Cornelius. He stood at ease before the wheel.

"Yes," said Naemi. "It sounded Canine."

"What does it mean?" asked Cornelius.

"I don't know."

They raced northwards on the river for more than an hour. Cornelius and Naemi took turns keeping the course straight in the wind. When Cornelius was not at the wheel, he inspected and practiced with the metal whip the mysterious G had given him. It was a remarkable device. Its reactions seemed to be guided by the intentions of the handler. Before long Cornelius snatched falling leaves and blossoms out of the air with its three pronged fingers. When Cornelius had the wheel, Naemi sat by herself, feet dangling overboard, dwelling on her own thoughts. The channel's banks opened up as the mangroves gave way to grassy and rocky terrain, desolate after the lush forested river. As they progressed, the banks drew towards one another. The water flowing through the narrow channel moved swiftly and turbulently. The yacht rose and fell and rocked in the choppy water. Spray doused Cornelius and Naemi, and Naemi was the first to notice a difference.

"Cornelius, the water is hot."

"Look at the shore," said Cornelius at the wheel, pointing to one shore. Steam rose out of cracks among the rocks. Rivulets of steaming water flowed from the steam beds into the river. The air smelled of sulfur.

"This is a geologically active region," said Naemi.

A curtain of shade in the cloudless sky raced passed them out of the south. A rumbling sound followed, then the rocks on the banks exploded.

"A quake!" yelled Cornelius.

Naemi, looking behind, saw a huge wave roaring towards them. "Hang on!"

The wave hit. The yacht was carried up onto its crest and sped onward at a tremendous clip. Cornelius struggled at the wheel to keep the center of the river. But as the channel narrowed the water rose and the wave ignored the river's bounds. The yacht could crash on unseen rocks. He turned and shouted, "Naemi! Go back and collapse the yacht. Do it now or we'll crash."

Naemi quickly scooted to the back of the ship while clutching the portside rail. When she was close enough, she dove at the gurkbuzzel device and gave it a good slap. The yacht promptly collapsed back into a small lifeboat, no sails unfurled. Cornelius tumbled beside Naemi. He grasped the rudder and tried to guide the little boat. Without the sails to propel them forward by the might of the wind, the boat slipped behind the wave. The boat skidded over the submerged right bank and bumped over innumerable rocks.

"To port, Cornelius! Port!" shouted Naemi.

Cornelius tried to comply, but the water carried them to more danger. Straight ahead was a whirlpool. The floodwaters were being sucked into a crevasse. Cornelius could do little to change their predicament other than to shout, "Hold on!"

The boat smacked into a submerged rock and was flung into the swirling vortex. Naemi lost her grip and careened half over the starboard side of the boat nearest the vortex. Cornelius reached for her with one hand while holding fast to the boat's rim with his other. He grabbed Naemi by her wrist, but the grip was tenuous. Out of the corner of his eye he saw a vertical boulder emerge out of the sinking water. In a split second he let go the boat and released his metal whip at the boulder. Then he jabbed its handle into the boat, knocking against the gurkbuzzel device, which partially absorbed the whip handle. The whip swung round the boulder and locked onto itself. The boat jerked out of the water. Cornelius hung on as tight as he could to Naemi, fighting against falling out of the boat himself.

Naemi struggled, a writhing body of arms and legs. She managed to scramble aboard more or less in one piece. Cornelius clicked the whip's control button and the boat was reeled over rocks and swirling water to the boulder. The whirlpool's floodwaters receded down the crevasse leaving the boat clutching the boulder. All was quiet for a moment but for the panting of Cornelius and Naemi. Then, just as they'd caught their breaths, a deep rumbling sound emanated from the crevasse. Suddenly a jet of steaming water erupted out reaching more than ten meters into the sky before raining down hot water onto the boat below. They were on the edge of an active geyser. Only Cornelius' quick thinking flick of the gurkbuzzel device produced a great purple umbrella that protected them from being scalded.

After a few seconds the geyser spent itself, and Cornelius retracted the umbrella. He and Naemi scrambled out of the boat. They were perched on a cleft above the crevasse on a rocky rise. Cornelius released his mechanical whip from the boat. With a click of its switch the whip loosed itself from the boulder and retracted into his hand. The boat settled among the crags.

"A handy device," said Cornelius of the whip.

"G must have known we'd need it," said Naemi.

The air was thick with the smell of sulfur. The wind yet blew, but far more mildly than before.

"There's no telling when that geyser will erupt again," said Cornelius. "We should get this boat out of here and down to the river."

Cornelius surveyed their position from where they stood. About twenty meters away was the cliff edge leading down to the channel. He marched to its edge among the loose debris left by the receded waters. A broken path led down the cliff face and terminated on a gravel beach. He returned to

Naemi. "There's a way down. We'll have to carry the boat." He tried to lift one side. The boat was heavy, but it budged a little. Naemi just stood by watching. "Are you going to help?" asked Cornelius.

Naemi smiled with green eyes. "There's a better way," she said. She bent over the boat and spun the gurkbuzzel device. The boat shrank down to a toy size ten centimeters in length. She picked up the boat in one hand and said, "Let's go."

Cornelius laughed. "That didn't even occur to me."

They headed down the cliff to the gravely beach and were at the water's edge in minutes.

The afternoon passed into evening with nothing more that could be called an adventure befalling Cornelius and Naemi. They remained in the lifeboat, feeling it safer than the yacht in case another close brush with disaster occurred, and so as not to deplete the energy of the gurkbuzzel slugs. Naemi was largely introspective. Cornelius continued practicing throws and catches with his mechanical whip.

As they continued their journey, the sun slid low in the western sky. The banks of the river channel grew lush again, this time with willows and aspen and ash. To their delight, they found preserved on the floor of the boat the remains of Naemi's fish catch, still wrapped and fresh.

After eating and watching the sunset over Canius, Cornelius broached a subject with Naemi that had been on his mind. "The past few days have been quite an adventure for us. I am glad we've had each others' company."

Naemi did not respond.

Cornelius went on. "You said there are, expectations for my part in this affair."

Naemi took awhile making up her mind how to respond. Her eyes turned a soft brown. "Cornelius, you are the key here. You may not see it from your current perspective, but you will continue to discover abilities you did not know you possessed. You will kindle hope in others, as others will kindle hope in you."

"Do you mean like the wind? You knew I could do it, cause it to blow, didn't you?" Cornelius asked with a little awe.

"I knew it," said Naemi. "I'd seen you do it before, though of course you don't remember."

"I hope these abilities will be sufficient for the work ahead."

"Haven't you learned yet, Cornelius, that you can be more than the sum of all you expect yourself to be? I am only a peripheral player in this opus." Naemi shivered in the cool of evening.

"You are an important player to me," said Cornelius. He reached for the gurkbuzzel device and called forth two warm fur parkas, and turned the benches into a bed. They donned the warm robes and snuggled together watching the stars come out into the sky. The double helix constellation filled the sky before them. Along the river's banks a glittering display of lights danced from thousands of hovering and darting fireflies. They joined their myriad flashes with the slow moving arcs of starlight. Cornelius bent close to Naemi and planted a gentle kiss on her cheek. She did not protest. They made love among the celestial and terrestrial lights. Sleep quickly took them after, and the little boat continued along its northward journey in the channel's current.

A misty morning greeted them many hours later.

34 THE CAPTIVE

A bright cold frost had descended upon the Human capital of Cronapolis. The multi-block Forum around the military complex was nearly bereft of visitors. Only a few guards marked out checkpoints at various locations around the huge edifice. The streets were hardened with ice, and ice and frost clung to sills and windows. It was unseasonably cold despite spring in the equatorial capital. Under the haze of the frosted sky, a lone figure, tall, stood feet apart and hands on hips before the steps to the square marble building. Commissioner Menkar looked at the heights with a childish grin of delight on her face. She was pale yet glowing, with ice shimmering on her eyelashes and frost exhaling from her mouth. Ice frosted her black uniform.

It was not usual for one, nor any, of the Commissioners to be out in the open, even beside the Headquarters, where they might mix with the common population. But the cold was keeping the people in their homes and places of work.

It was exhilarating to be alone in the Forum. Sound was muffled under the blanket of chill. The tops of the white columns that lined the black marble block of the Military Headquarters were lost in the low crystalline fog. The building itself glowed eerily opaque, reflecting nothing.

Menkar shouted at the building, "Now for a little artistic improvement!" She raised her hands out and over her head. She grinned from ear to ear, her eyes opened wide, her pupils turned from black to burning white. Her whole face radiated a white energy. Rays burst out from her face and struck the building. The radiation's warmth melted the snow and ice, creating running, dripping stalactites and stalagmites around the entire structure. Then Menkar changed the hue on her face to a pale cold blue. Another burst of radiation blasted the building with frost. The Headquarters now looked to be inside a massive ice bramble reflecting ghostly colors and sounds.

"I like it!" Menkar said aloud. She marched up the great steps to the black edifice. Her boots glowed and melted the ice underfoot with each footfall of her ascent. By the time she reached the black entrance doors and flung them open, a thunderous waterfall rushed down the steps behind her to the Forum below.

Two guards stood at attention just inside Headquarters. Across the expanse of the dark interior lobby two officers sat behind a massive dark marble desk. They played a game of cards to pass the time. The surface of the desk and the men behind it were lit from narrow beams of light shining down from niches overhead. Around the lobby, more recessed lighting from a trench cut in the stone floor's perimeter dimly shone up to the dark ceiling.

The doors burst open. The officers stopped their game, dropped their cards and stared at Commissioner Menkar standing imposingly at the entrance. Water cascaded around her and ran in a torrent down the great steps. She entered and a great cold entered with her. Ice crystals reached across the hall's expanse and dusted the officers' uniforms, hair and faces. The doors shut tight behind her.

The guards at the door had quickly brandished their rifle firearms, but relaxed when they recognized the visitor.

"It's just me," Menkar said sternly. Then she marched up to the great desk.

"Commissioner," said one of the officers. He shook his head, knocking ice onto the desk.

"Boys," she said, and nodded.

"What were you doing in the Forum?" asked the other officer.

"Surveillance," said Menkar. "I'm going to the satellite room. Call the elevator."

"At once," said the first officer.

A moment later Menkar was descending into the building's lower floors. The lobby reclaimed its warmth after she left.

The officers took up their card game again. "That was weird," said one.

"Something's happening," said the other. "The Commissioners are all acting strangely lately."

"And what's with this weather?" asked the other. "It's mid spring. Why is it so cold?"

"Don't know," said the first. "Your deal." And he cut the deck of cards.

In the satellite imaging room, Menkar bent over the readouts from the past day. The room was more a large command center. It was twenty meters wide by thirty meters long. The walls were twelve meters tall to the ceiling. Two separate mezzanine levels bisected the room on either end. Menkar was the only person present. The temperature in the room was comfortable. Green dials and screens with radar sweeps lined the consoles. The walls displayed monitors revealing contours of the planet from aerial vantage points. Right now Menkar was focused on the great lakes region. There were intriguing movements of lake ships about the locks between the southern and northern lakes. Comparing images over several days, she determined that a quake or some other disaster had visited the locks.

"Now that's odd," she said aloud. Several images showed a queue of ships. Different images showed differing numbers yet no additional flotilla was extant to provide the additions seen in later pictures. It was a puzzle. One image could be revealing, or just a bad image, a disturbance caught by a satellite's eye, a flash of light over the area of the ships, but seemingly without a source. Menkar viewed the same area from another satellite's vantage point. The angle was less precise but the resolution was higher. The light was everywhere. Blurred within the light appeared to be dozens of ghost ships, partially translucent.

She stood back from the images and considered what she was seeing. A glare in the captured images? Ghost images superimposed on themselves creating an abnormal optical effect? Menkar switched to images from a different satellite, this one over Big City. Similar distortions were visible in several images. There were the Hornet fliers overflying the city, crashing sonic booms against the buildings. Spider transports advanced from the across the Cantons, aiming for the city. But in several satellite images, hazy bright light bursts showed even more ordnance, surface and air support, emerging from some nether place.

Menkar turned to a different console, called up military orders for the Canton assault. Something was oddly out of synch.

19:45 The night before - 26 Spider transports fuel up from their base in Lupus Minor.

21:08 - 37 Spider transports take off from Lupus Minor.

08:16 This morning - 56 Spider transports approach the outskirts of Big City.

A similar situation was occurring with the fliers.

20:11 Last night – 18 Hornet fliers take off from Lupus Minor.

00:18 This morning - 28 Hornet fliers pass the halfway point across the Cantons.

02:20 This morning: 36 Hornet fliers approach Big City.

Menkar scratched her head. Where did the ever-increasing number of fliers and transports come from? All the records appeared to be in order. But there was nothing to explain the additional forces. She called up readiness orders. At each time interval, all appropriate approvals confirmed the numbers. But in each report, the numbers increased. Ships don't just materialize out of thin air just because they're wanted. Menkar called up a new satellite image. Timestamp 09:19. The Spider transports surrounding Big City numbered seventy-eight. And forty-four Hornet fliers were over the city. *Did we even have forty-four Hornet fliers stationed in Lupus Minor?* She checked further. Yesterday's records showed a total of eighteen. But reports confirmed a total of twenty-eight that night. And now fifty-six today. This was very odd. Menkar would have to speak to General Taurus about the figures. *Was the military hiding assets from itself? That would be just like Taurus*, she decided.

There was one task Menkar had to complete before anyone intruded on her work. She stood before a holographic globe of Lupus hovering in an open space in the center of the room. Hundreds of holographic satellites in varying orbits, geostationary, polar, equatorial, circular and elliptical, soared around the planet like gnats, or electrons around a nucleus. Menkar extended her hand and, with a finger, intersected the path of one satellite. Its pole-to-pole orbit crossed both Lupus Major and the northern polar Canine region of Canoon. On a wall console behind the holographic globe, specifications of altitude, velocity, orbit schedule and other details of the satellite's function and motion displayed. Menkar turned the chronometer dial that marked time and progress on the hologram. She adjusted the date forward approximately one week out to Precession Day, the date celebrated by Canines, and some Humans, marking the Precession Star's aphelion, or furthest approach, to Lupus' star.

The holographic image of satellites around Lupus quickly advanced. Menkar then traced with her finger the chosen satellite's path from Canoon to Lupus Major. The chronometer's readout reflected the times that the satellite flew between the two regions, 21:08 – 03:23.

Menkar pressed a black button on the console to lock in the time parameters. Then she manually typed into an open display field, "lock open/feed flow positive-duration." She pressed the black button again. The readout changed to "Accepted."

Menkar smiled. This little surprise would wake up her stodgy co-Commissioners. A little insurrection is good for keeping them on their toes. Anyone with an unscrambled receiver will be able to tap into the Precession Festival Concert broadcast from Canoon. That will not reach many people within the military run provinces, but the broadcast would be received for the duration of the satellite's over flight, unless someone turned it off. Her little prank may not last long, but she would make her point.

Menkar turned back to review more satellite images. Her frosty breath iced the monitor screen. A chill fog filled the room. Creaking, buckling sounds in the walls, ceiling and floor followed fingers of ice that crept up and along seems and cracks. The temperature fell by as much as twenty degrees as wave after wave of sheer cold swept through the room. Footfalls echoed outside the door. She spun around and faced the entrance just as the double doors were pushed open from the other side. Frost and ice crystals shattered into the room and scattered on the floor. Markhab stood in the frame.

"First Commissioner," Menkar addressed him in a somewhat relaxed manner, though her eyes were like cold steel. "I am reviewing the satellite images of our sorties over the Cantons and Big City."

"How is our little game playing out?" asked Markhab.

"Extremely well," answered Menkar. "Surprisingly well, in fact."

"General Taurus' acumen in planning and execution should not be considered surprising," said Markhab.

"It is true," said Menkar. "Our cloak drapes quickly over the remaining Human lands."

"Only the true enemy will remain to be defeated," said Markhab. He looked around the complex at its humming beeping flashing whirring equipment. Then he turned back to Menkar. "The Forum is full of jumbled broken blocks of ice and drifts of snow. You've been enjoying your newly acquired abilities?"

"The gifts bear chilly fruit," said Menkar. "Practice will make perfect."

"Don't block the satellites' view of our city with your fog drifts. Nothing should crawl or creep that we don't know about." He stared a long moment into Menkar's cold bright eyes, then turned to leave. "I am visiting the lower chambers. I'll see you at the briefing."

The waves of cold lessened after Markhab departed. Creaking and resettling of walls and the building's superstructure followed the temperature differential. Ice cracked and melted, dripped and ran, sloshed and pooled onto the floor.

Menkar stood still and listened to Markhab's departure. Eventually she heard the lift open, and then close to take the First Commissioner below to the bowels of the military complex. *To play with his toys*, Menkar mused. She raised her hands and arms, lifted her face to the open door and hallway. A blue ghoulish light leapt from her face and illuminated the space before her. She exhaled a cold vapor from her lips that flowed and bent and shattered and solidified in the air before her. When she was done, a frosty curtain of sparkling diamond-like ice sealed the room from the hallway. Menkar liked her privacy.

* * *

Markhab liked his privacy, too. The smooth black walls of the building's lowest levels frosted over at Markhab's stomping passage. The normally stifling hot and humid environment was now a cold and clammy fog. The internment cells lining the hallways served as Markhab's personal pleasure redoubt. Internees provided a regular supply of disposable participants for Markhab's games. Fluctuations in temperature and humidity, sometimes lasting days, other times switching between hot and cold, humid and dry within hours or minutes, kept the prisoners off balance, compromised their immune systems, and made them pliable to suggestive influences.

Waves of cold spread out from Markhab and his boots echoed loudly on the metal floor. He had recently learned this trick of channeling a frozen dread from deep within. He channeled waves of cold outward into his immediate environment. He had in turn taught the trick to his Commissioners. The effect this ability had on the general population was impressive. Warmth and comfort were transformed into cold and insecurity. Doubt and self-doubt filled a person's mind and battered his will. Across Cronapolis, truancy in factories and schools was nearly eradicated. Curfews were more regularly observed. North in Bafaria of Lupus Minor, the pathetic population was completely subdued. There they were nearly complete building the military's new super complex, defensive battlements and offensive forward structures. And Corvus had easily subdued Lupus City and Mine City with waves of cold and dread. The noose was tightening all around Lupus.

On either side of the hall down which Markhab stomped were small fortified doors or hatches to internment cells. Each hatch was half a meter wide, one meter high, and separated from neighboring cell doors by only three meters. Small round concave viewing lenses in the center of each door gave fish bowl views of each cell's interior.

Markhab stopped at one lens to peer in at a captive. The lens iced up as his face neared the glass. He scratched at the ice with his fingernails. Inside was a naked Canine female, one of the first snatched from the ground in the wide net cast across the Cantons. Many had been captured and brought to Cronapolis for interrogation. Real Canines. Markhab grinned at the huddled woman cowering in the cell. The Commissioner's lips quivered and a little drool spilt from his mouth to the floor. It froze in the fall and shattered on the floor. His eyes were radiant as his mind flowed with prurient intentions. The Canine rocked back and forth with arms around knees. Feet squatted in a foul puddle of water, waste and blood. Her nose was broken and an eye was missing. It'd been roughly gouged out. Scab and infection covered it.

The Canine sensed Markhab at the door. She slightly lifted her head in his direction, ears pointing toward the door. In a move of astonishing speed she threw herself at the hatch snarling and biting. Blood spattered over the lens from a ravaged mouth of broken, twisted teeth and gaps where others had been forcefully pried out.

Markhab jumped back. What resilience the Canines had. Markhab put his face to the lens again and focused his inner dread, projecting it outward. The Canine fell back, knocked hard by waves of cold. The bloody puddle froze. Fingers of ice crawled up the walls. For an instant snow condensed and fell in the cell. What a surreal sight! Markhab grinned with pleasure. He ceased projecting, and a stifling heat returned to the cell. The Canine collapsed in shivers and sweat, defeated.

Markhab turned away from the scene in the cell and resumed his march down the internment hall. At the end of the corridor was a special cell with a very special prisoner, one of Markhab's most closely held secrets.

The door to the cell was full size. No window pierced its surface. Massive bolts and rivets and heavy metal cross bars reinforced it. A great locking wheel to the left produced a seal. Above the wheel, a small keypad granted access. Whatever or whomever was held inside was dangerously special.

The First Commissioner stood before the door. His lips quivered and his eyes were wide and furtive, darting left and right in nervous anticipation. Moisture beaded on his temples and upper lip. Then a wave of frigid cold blasted through the door and wall. "Blasted" but without destruction. Markhab's perspiration froze on his face. He frowned. He bent his forehead towards the door and closed his eyes. A wave of cold issued from his forehead, hit the door and passed within. Another blast came at him from the other side. Markhab was pushed backwards a step. He frowned even more.

Regaining his composure, Markhab entered a code onto the locking keypad. There was a click. He then turned the wheel. A hiss of air was released from the seal. He pulled the door open. Eerie black lighting flooded out into the corridor. Markhab stepped inside and sealed the hatch closed behind him.

This room was larger than any cell, but it too was a cell. Humming buzzing quivering equipment convulsed and sighed around the walls. Hoses and wires ran across the floor and connected the various machines. The room was circular, twelve meters in diameter. Two technicians silently manned the equipment. They wore insulating robes that protected them from the violent cold waves. The robes reflected iridescent light in some angles and appeared plain and drab from others. Both looked up when Markhab entered, then immediately resumed their work.

The machines in this room maintained a confinement field opposite the door, a spherical force field of shimmering light six meters in diameter. Inside something indiscernible moved. The mainly formless something floated in a stream of mixed reality. General Taurus' footmen had caught the shape with an anti-proton containment beam near the military's new forward operations in Lupus Minor. Anomalous energy readings in a canyon above the great river drew the curiosity of some scientists. Markhab had the "anomaly" captured and transported to Cronapolis.

It turned out to be a most amazing find, a captive Bird of Prey.

The ancient beasts were the stuff of legends. Birds of Prey were supposed to have vanished in the early days of Lupus, shortly after the Feline Quarantine of Earth and its Precession Star. Only vague wispy remnants of the ancient Birds remained in the form of flying reptiles, but most people could not even see those. They lived in a nether world, neither fully here nor fully not. Markhab had found a way to communicate with this captured being, to his profit.

Ripples in a mist within the containment field swirled and turned over like blurry pixels of a flock of birds turning in the wind. At certain moments a form took shape, almost Humanlike with great wings. For a moment the image held, then scattered like tufts of dandelion seeds caught on the wind. Another wave of cold blasted through the containment field. Frost momentarily formed on the robes of the technicians, melted then ran off as drips and rivulets onto the wet floor.

Markhab shivered. Then he straightened his back and addressed the creature within. "That won't free you."

Vocalizations came through the field. It sounded like cold calculating laughter. "Are you enjoying the tricks I taught you?" said a voice.

Markhab smiled. He wanted to encourage the creature to share more of its knowledge. "They have proven useful in population management, crowd control."

The creature chuckled. "Children at play. Have you come for more games?"

"Information," said Markhab.

The creature sounded like it was grumbling. "My knowledge is old."

"How did you enter this stream of ephemeral existence?"

"That is an ancient tale. It started on Earth. Do you know that world?" asked the creature.

"It exists," said Markhab. "Beyond a Feline blockade."

"The Mammals started it. We adapted to survive. We seek to return."

"How is that to be accomplished?" asked Markhab.

The form of the creature pulsed and scattered and reformed. It made a loud hissing sound. "What would have doomed us saved us. It can release us."

The creature's unspoken words meant much to Markhab. He knew of the ancient weapon of the shimmering field that doomed Humans on Earth to a millennial blockade.

"Where you captured me, that is a good place. Lots of resonite."

Markhab's ears perked up and his eyebrows rose. Another clue. Resonite? He would share this information with Professor Altair.

"Interesting," said Markhab. He feigned boredom and shrugged his shoulders.

"Tell me, Markhab Human," began the creature. "How many others of my kind have you, found?"

"Only you," said Markhab, too quickly he decided. The truth came out too fast. He could have played the creature with half-truths, but it was too late.

The creature's form twisted and tumbled behind the force field. It laughed and the laughter grew louder. The creature was clearly amused by this information. "Of all my kind you might have found, you found ME." Laughter echoed in the room and waves of cold flooded out. The creature's form momentarily collected into a visible golden winged form tall and proud. Then the gold melted away into black and was lost in a haze of dissociated pixels.

Markhab remained silent.

"You are lucky to have found me," said the creature.

"Or are you lucky we found you?" Markhab turned the statement back onto the creature.

"I don't require your existence," hissed the creature. "But you might require mine. Some assistance, eh?" The hiss continued.

Markhab didn't follow what the creature meant, but he grew slightly uncomfortable. Doubtless the creature would notice.

A whine of electrical feedback produced by the equipment sounded in the room. The technicians hustled trying to find its source and mute it. The feedback grew louder and baser. It actually sounded like the howl of a Canine. Markhab looked over his shoulder at the door. Was his Canine plaything in the other cell making that noise?

The creature laughed some more. Its pixelated form rose tall and took Humanoid shape again with full outstretched wings. Colors collected into gold sequins.

Then it screamed. The screech was mind shattering, absolutely painful. It wrenched the mind's neurons and sinews from the base brain. The equipment shuddered. The building groaned. The technicians covered their ears and cowered on the floor. Markhab stood still and amazed. He was motionless and his mind emptied. Then a voice intruding on his consciousness spoke. "I can teach you this trick, too."

Markhab smiled pleased. The screech faded as a memory. The force field held.

35 THROUGH THE CAVES

"Plink.

"Plink-plink plunk.
"Plink-plunk.

"Plink."

That's 367 times now.

"Plink.

"Plink-plink plunk.
"Plink-plunk.

"Plink."

368.

"Plink-PLINK.

"Plink-plink plunk.
"Plink-plunk.

"Plink."

An extra "PLINK". The pattern changed. Number one.

Renender shifted his huddled position in a semi-dry cavity beside a stalagmite curtain. He'd been counting drops of water, drips and drops, for over an hour. Was that all? The drops fell into a pool or pond, lake or sea. He couldn't see the other side. The drops made it sound, feel vast. He started counting the new pattern.

"Plink-PLINK.

"Plink-plink plunk.
"Plink-plunk.

"Plink."

That's two.

"Plink.

"Plink-plink plunk.
"Plink-plunk.

"Plink."

That's back to the first pattern! That's one.

Renender had enough. His neck and shoulders were sore from being cold and hunched. It was going on an hour since he'd taken this break. Some break it was, obsessively counting water drops. Were his eyes even open? The world appeared brighter when his eyes were closed, maybe from some electrical impulses originating in his brain. When his eyes were opened, the darkness was complete, incredibly so. He knew his eyes were opened, because he'd stuck his fingers right in his eyes checking to be sure.

He'd been in the caves for days it seemed. Minutes and hours and days had so little meaning here. His food rations were only stocked for a few days, so at least weeks had not passed, unless his eating was that sparse.

"Enough of this infernal darkness!" he said aloud. There wasn't really an echo, just a muffled stirring each time he spoke coming from many directions around. Renender pulled on his bio light necklace. A wobbly green glow spilled out from the activated microbes within. Shadows fled, and Renender looked out across the body of water in this cavern. The drips and drops continued somewhere out there beyond his sight. His own movements drowned out the sounds. He looked at the chronometer on his wrist. He'd been two and a half days in these caves. It was time for a snack.

The nutritional crunch bars he'd brought didn't crunch anymore. They'd absorbed moisture during the passage through these caves. Renender feared they'd mold and make him sick. That hadn't happened, yet. In the meantime, until they started to smell funny, he ate them.

Now thirsty, Renender bent down by the side of the water and scooped up a cupped handful. It tasted delicious. Deep within the pool strange movements caused small eddies and distortions. Renender had noticed this earlier. With his headlamp, he'd identified translucent fish and fat water slugs. The slugs sometimes flashed lights red or green or blue, some sort of communication, Renender thought.

He gathered up his few belongings and strapped on his pack. Around his neck beside the precession star amulet his mother had given him, dangled the pear-shaped key guiding his passage through the caves. He grabbed it, looked at it and sighed. His scratches along the notched perimeter were almost all the way around. He was close, but close to what? He ran his fingers around the key. It was such a simple representation of a map through this mineral labyrinth. Was trial and error involved in its making? How many times did the original user get lost? These were questions he'd like to have asked the Trickle Depth Sounder miner who'd given it to him, old Borden. Renender noticed something odd. The key easily recorded the scratches marking his progress along the notches. Otherwise, the key was smooth. Hadn't it been used before? Shouldn't it have been used before? The thought struck him, what if this was a hoax? He could surely perish. And Corvus was in Mine City now far behind him.

Renender scratched his head, scratched his scraggly beard now taking over his face. He turned in a clockwise circle, then stopped and reversed counterclockwise. He sighed. He was tired. He sat down again in the hollow by the water and closed his eyes. He started counting drops again.

"Plink.

"Plink-plink plunk.

"Plink-plunk.

"Plink."

That's one.

* * *

He dreamed, or teetered on the edge of dream. What was the girl from the coffee shop in Mine City doing talking to Matta at her café in Lupus City? Looking for a job, maybe. Then Alice sat down. But Alice wasn't her name. What was it? There was food served at the table, but it was all wrapped too tightly in cellophane. He tried to pull it apart to get to the food, but he couldn't pull apart the wrapping. He tried and tried and struggled with his food.

Then he was searching for something, searching. He felt he was being followed. Shadows were after him. He mustn't be caught. Nothing must be found. He was in his office. He frantically tore up any papers from his desk and files he could find. He broke apart data disks. Everything must be destroyed.

Renender sensed someone was behind him. He turned. It was a lovely boy, an Escort. "I'm Jeaneau," he said. He wore almost nothing. The boy slowly undressed Renender. They kissed, they danced. There was music. It was an old song, something about a great mill wheel in the heavens that turned ever so slowly, ever so unremittingly. Then Jeaneau laughed and yelled "Boom Chuggalugga Boom Bessie! Chuggalugga Boom!" Renender laughed too.

Then the lights went out and the music stopped. It grew cold, very cold. Renender tried to find Jeaneau, but the boy was gone. A different voice permeated his awareness. It was a biting, unforgiving voice, full of terrifying cruelty and wicked delight like a child filled with evil intent.

"Where did it come from?" the voice insisted.

Renender didn't understand. But an idea formed in the center of his being where guilt hid and distress dwelt. He knew what he had to say. The cold was intense. He felt his own hands and feet, nose, eyelids and lips freeze. Then they burned from the cold and fell off in grotesque flakes of rotted black skin. Confess and the cold might stop. Confess and it would be over. He thought it, then he said it. When he said it aloud, he heard himself scream, "I did it! I arranged for the nuclear material to be brought downriver, through the forest. From Aran City, Orumnam delivered it to Shining City. Because of me, the rebels attacked Wror. I did it!" But the sound of his voice was pathetic. It wavered. It was a confession made only because no one could hear it.

His guilt and distress only grew. "Traitor!" screamed a vision of the wild woman from Aran in his head. The cold grew worse. Orumnam's face changed and it was Corvus. Renender's heart froze. He fell backwards and he hit his head on a wall. He shivered. It was still dark, but he was awake. He heard a familiar sound.

"Plink.

"Plink-plink plunk.
"Plink-plunk.

"Plink."

Awake. How long had he been out? Renender pulled on his necklace. Its green glow lit the surroundings of his hollow again. He was naked, shivering in the hollow with his clothes tossed haphazardly nearby. All around him were the wrappers and remains of his nutrition bars, the only food he had. In the fits of his dream he'd torn through all the wrappers and thrown them to the ground. Now to his disgust he saw in the dim green glow slimy slugs crawling all over the food and wrappers on the ground.

Renender scrambled up. He groped for his clothes and flung them on. Already they were more dirty rags than garments. He managed to salvage half the nutrition bars. The goopy trails left by the slugs disgusted him enough to abandon the other half. The slugs could keep them.

It was well past time to move on. Checking his chronometer, he saw he'd been out for six hours. Being in the caves was maddening. He wanted to feel wind and smell air, stand in sunlight. He needed to get out.

With the pack slung over his back, he started down the path around the pool. He fumbled while getting the key out and trying to find the place for his thumbnail on its perimeter. Then he tumbled over a low stalagmite. His pack fell into the water. Cursing and grumbling, Renender gathered up what he could of the food now scattered along the shoreline. Without another look left or right, he marched forward down the path. He did not notice the narrow cleft in the rock wall on his left.

* * *

The air initially seemed cool and fresh as he proceeded further. Past the lake, Renender ducked into two large tunnels that opened on his left. That meant only three more notches remained before the key ran out. Was he that close? He kept a good pace, even quickening and furthering his progress out of anticipation of this trek being at an end. The way forward veered down. Renender trotted on. Twice he slipped on the increasingly damp rock surfaces. The walls around him, the stalactites and stalagmites, were slimy with water and strange growth. Despite relatively large tunnels and spacious galleries, the air grew increasingly close, dank and hot. Unpleasant smells assaulted Renender's nostrils, yet he pressed on. Another left passage, then another. Was the end just before him? Could it be?

For a long while, maybe an hour, Renender continued. His eyes started to sting and some fog in the air that he could just make out in his headlamp hovered in the high recesses of the rock ceiling. The smell was rotten. It was hydrogen sulfide. He slipped again and tried to slow his fall by grabbing onto a slimy pillar. His hand sunk into spongy ooze that burned his skin. It was acidic. Renender caught his balance by banging his shoulders into the column. That got the spongy ooze into his hair, onto his neck and over his clothes. His eyes burned. He coughed. But he was close! Slipping and nearly running through the hazy green gloom he found another opening on his left. Was this it? He ducked inside.

A long drop with rough almost step-like terraces led down to a forbidding body of water, or some liquid. It smelled very foul and a vapor rose from it. Long tentacles of drippy ooze hung from the ceiling. Illuminated in Renender's headlight, the tentacles sparkled from the shiny sulfuric beads hanging from their ends. A drip here, a drop there, punctuated the otherwise muffled hush of the cavern.

Renender's throat burned. He wiped his tearing eyes, but the acid hanging from his sleeves stung them more. Through the tears and pain he looked at the key in his hand. His thumbnail was on the brass notch, so this must be the end. But it was not the end he hoped for. This was a tomb. Renender frantically looked around for another gap, another corridor, some place that led further, or away. There was nothing. He reached into his bag and retrieved a nutrition bar. He broke off a piece and threw it into the lake. It sizzled in a flurry of bubbles. The acidic water dissolved the organic matter away. This was NOT the place he needed to be. Somewhere along the way he must have missed a turn. He had to go back before he became a casualty never to be known or seen again. He turned round and hurried higher, back up the way he'd trotted down. Renender stumbled and tripped, coughing and wheezing all the way.

More than an hour passed and the air grew sweeter. There even seemed to be a breeze. Renender's breathing became less labored, though his skin still tingled and his throat was sore. His eyes were fairly flushed clean from all his tears, but the skin around them felt puffy and tender.

At last Renender stopped to rest. He let himself slide down against a curtain of minerals and slump in a heap at its base. He spent some time just breathing. When the loud sound of his breath softened from rasps to sighs, he heard a familiar sound.

"Plink.

"Plink-plink plunk.
"Plink-plunk.

"Plink."

He was back to where he'd camped earlier that day, or night if it was night. Renender crawled to the edge of the lake. He began splashing water onto his face. He decided to submerge himself altogether. He waddled in on his haunches. It was not very deep and the bottom was hard, but not sharp or jagged. He rolled in the cold clean water, feeling the burning sensations fade, replaced by refreshing coolness. He gulped mouthfuls and belched happily. Finally he crawled back out and sat in the hollow where he'd slept hours earlier.

The dilemma now was what to do next? Which way to go? He brought out the key and stared at it. Amazingly, the thumbnail notches he'd recently scratched onto its surface had faded. They were gone. The remaining scratches represented his journey from the beginning up to his present whereabouts. Renender chewed the less slimy half of a nutrition bar. After a swallow he leaned back against the rock. With his damp skin and clothes he noticed something he'd not been aware of before, wind.

Renender perked up. Somewhere nearby was the source of the fresh air he'd noticed the last time he'd been here. He stood up and slowly turned around, gauging where the fresh air might be coming from. It seemed before him, down towards the way he'd just come. But he was skeptical. There was nothing down that way but bad air, hot and foul. Nonetheless, there was a breeze of sorts, and it smelled sweet.

He stepped slowly around the vicinity of the downward path. He held his hands out in front moving them this way and that to find the source of the moving air. It did not take him long to find the cool out-gasp that issued from a cleft in the rock wall. *Now how did I miss that?* he thought.

The cleft was only a meter long, beginning a meter above the path. It was a third of a meter wide, stretching at a diagonal from top left to bottom right. *Only just big enough to squeeze through.* Renender gathered his few things, then he gripped the sides of the cleft and heaved himself up and in. There were four notches left on the key.

The cleft was a crack in the titanium seam of the mountain. While neither very tall nor wide, it followed a fairly straight route for about fourteen meters. Renender was glad to not be very much wider than he already was, though a little thinner would certainly have helped. The light from his bio headlamp and necklace shown with a rich silvery green glow reflected from the rich mineral veins. The look was not unlike starlight through fine green leaves in spring. Though it was spring, this was no sylvan forest. But the sight was beautiful.

As Renender scooted through the rock cleft, its terminus brightened with each progressive scoot. At last with a final push from his feet that loosed rocks, metal crystals and debris, he emerged hands and head first, dropping like a worm onto a smooth metallic surface. He fell with a grunt onto a two-meter wide path that arced left and right in a circle. The wall in front was as the outside of a sphere. Standing up and surveying this new place, he saw he was in a narrow carven space between two great titanium spheres, one within the other. The metal was intruded by a dark green mineral that suffused the rock. His every footfall and noise was amplified greatly in this passage. He was struck by the feeling that he was inside a great bell. This was surely a man made space, whether by Human or Canine hands, or some other being he could not know.

Renender placed his thumbnail on the fourth to last notch in his key and marched down the left path around the sphere. His heart raced with long held back anticipation. Someone built this place. It was no ruse. For days Renender had pushed from his mind what he might find at the end of his journey. Now his hopes burst forth from his heart and mind and he almost ran the circular way.

About a third of the way around the sphere, a carved cross was cut into the wall on his left. A bright green glow shown through it. Renender ducked to look through the cross. He saw a great domed chamber a hundred meters high, a hundred meters across. Its otherworldly beauty dumbfounded him.

The walls of the chamber were covered with bioluminescent bacteria that hung in clumps to the green and titanium façade. Flashing slugs crawled over them. Small streams of water flowed down the walls and converged in a green glowing pond in the center of the space. Out of a rocky outcropping in the midst of the pond rose a mass of green pylon like crystals growing in diagonals in all directions toward the ceiling. The translucent crystals towered more than eighteen meters into the air.

Renender climbed through the cross opening that represented the third to last notch on his key. He skidded and slid down the slick mushy walls to the damp surface of the cavern floor. In his green headlamp, the crystals refracted and reflected light in all directions. He noticed that the surrounding walls also sprouted large irregular silver-grey crystals of titanium. Renender walked up to a large green crystal nearest him. He thrummed it with a flick of his fingernail. A single chime quickly moved others to chime, and soon the whole cavern reverberated with a sweet harmony of tones.

Renender was so struck with its beauty that his hand by its own volition laid its palm upon his heart. Only slowly did the sound fade away. *Amazing*, he thought. *Resonite crystals. The mountain must be infused with the mineral.*

Suddenly concerned that he might overlook another opening, Renender looked back and up whence he'd come through the cross opening. To his dismay he saw that he'd climbed through but one of over two dozen cross cut openings that circled this chamber. He began to panic. He'd come through one of those cuts, but which one? He pumped his headlamp to more fully activate the luminescent bacteria within it. Then he saw the scar he'd made in the mushy growth on his way down. That was where he'd come through, and the cross cut beside it must be the next passage. He needed to get back up there.

He tried scaling the wall but found himself quickly sliding back down. He stepped far back and gave himself a running start. That was less effective than the first try. He looked around for loose rocks that he could stack at least part way up. There were few to be found. Even they slid back down as Renender put his weight upon them. *Get a hold of yourself, 'Ender,* he thought. *There is a way back up, even if it takes awhile.* He closed his eyes and breathed slowly and deeply. After a few minutes the sense of panic dissipated. He opened his eyes and looked up, this time with renewed sight. In the scar he'd make through the mushy growth on his way down, he saw uneven horizontal seams of resonite within the titanium. *Just maybe.* Together they formed a narrow ladder with each mineral rung centimeters from the next. He stepped up and sank his rough torn fingernails into the mushy growth, finding narrow cracks and catchments in the wall. Into the largest seams he carefully placed his feet. Slowly, slowly up he hauled himself. He did not slip and he did not falter, such was his concentration and determination. *Don't rush this, 'Ender.* He did not.

Though sweat ran from his temples, the pits of his arms and the soft behind his knees, he persevered. Slowly and methodically he scaled twenty-five meters up the wall. He was now above the giant green crystals, but he dared not glance any direction other than where his fingers next must be. At length his eyes were parallel to the cross cut. Carefully finger-by-finger he reached up and grasped the opening where he'd come through, one hand then the other, wrists, elbows and full arms, he held on. Then with much less effort than he'd anticipated, he swung his body to the side and reached through the next crosscut. He heaved up and hauled through and disappeared through the hole. His key had two notches left.

He was in a new shaft, tiny and extremely narrow. Incredibly steep steps only a few centimeters long but forty tall led up and away from the green crystal chamber on one side and the titanium sphere on the other. Renender followed this passage up. He was terrified of slipping. He was careful not to.

He climbed the narrow stairs for over eighty meters, though he was not measuring his progress. He was far over the top of the crystal cavern. Then the steps ceased being steps. Renender crawled forward on hands and knees about three meters. Then he slumped down cross-legged on the level stone. He was in a passage that ran straight ahead, one meter wide and five tall. He could stand here, though he didn't yet. He was thirsty. He was hungry. He was exhausted. He brought out Borden's key and saw quite clearly there were two notches left. But besides the fact that he was clearly *somewhere*, and that *someone* had been responsible for carving this strange structure through which Renender crawled and climbed, what if he'd taken the wrong way again? He could have died last time. He had no idea what kind of a place he was in. He brought forth from his pack broken pieces of nutrition bars and some water. *Take nourishment now, at least.*

After resting for half an hour, it was time to move on. The sooner he discovered this was the wrong way, the sooner he'd backtrack, however long he needed. Renender stood up and marched on. The air in this tunnel was cool and fresh. It even flowed from somewhere up ahead. That was encouraging. For two hundred meters he walked in a straight line. No indent or alcove opened from the smooth surface walls either on the left or on the right. As Renender went on he saw in his headlamp that huge stone double doors punctuated the end of this tunnel. They were all grey and sported no markings that he could discern. And they were ajar.

Renender poked his head inside. In the light of his lamp he saw a hall with six or seven passages radiating in different directions from the door. Just before darting into the hall, he was startled to find a half-meter wide by two meter tall opening on his left. On his LEFT! He might have missed it, and been lost in some greater maze.

He squeezed into the new passage. It represented the second to last notch in his key. The air was still and close. Nothing moved. Two meters in Renender faced a solid wall before him. Then he noticed something peculiar. On his left and on his right were markings, each different. On his right at eye level was cut and embossed in titanium, a square. Each side was a line that did not touch the others. To his left was cut and also embossed in titanium, an eight pointed star. It looked like his precession star amulet. Renender touched the center of the carved cut with a finger. It lit up. He took out his star amulet and held it dearly in his hand. Then he put the amulet to the star on the wall. There was a CLICK! The whole wall moved!

With very little effort and very little friction, the door in the wall swung outward. LIGHT! Light burst forth into the close antechamber where he stood. Renender shut his eyes tight but the searing brightness still attacked his brain. Nonetheless, he moved in. The last notch. It was some minutes before he could make anything out. His eyes adjusted to the natural light after so many days crawling in a green gloom. He was in an open cave. Dust and leaves lay scattered about the floor. The final opening was ten meters ahead. Through that opening Renender could see white and blue. Clouds and sky! But this cave, this space, was surprising. On each side was a row of statues that looked carved out of titanium and resonite. They were figures of men and of women, Human, with men on the left and women on the right. Ten statues stood there in all. Some held books, some brandished arms, some looked and pointed at the visible sky. Around the neck of each was carved a star amulet, just like the one he wore.

Renender slowly walked the meters passed the Human statues. He was filled with a reverence he did not understand. How ancient was this place? No tale of Humans on Lupus included lore about this place, yet here he was.

A breeze picked up and Renender smelled a sweet fragrance that reminded him of the flowering hallucinogenic shrubs on his terrace garden in Lupus City. Ah the delight! Then two tiny fluttering flying reptiles rushed the cave in swoops and calls, one after the other. Renender laughed and laughed. He had not laughed for days. He held before him the key of Borden. His thumbnail cut a line in the last notch. Next was the brass notch of the beginning. Renender stepped forth onto the cave's threshold into the light of the sun. As he held the key he watched in amazement as all his scratches near the notches faded. When it ceased the key was smooth again, ready for a new passage through the caves. Then Renender looked out onto the world before him. It was terrific.

He stood on the edge of a nearly sheer cliff face. Across from him beyond a deep wooded valley was another sheer cliff face, and it was carved. A huge Canine, mad and snarling on all fours was carved clinging to the cliff top. To the right was another cliff top; this one carved in the likeness of a wild saber-toothed Feline crouched in a pounce. To the left was yet another, this as a winged Bird of Prey, part dragon in appearance, menacing the others. Then Renender looked straight up from where he stood. A vampiric ape-man with protruding teeth and pointed ears silently screamed across the valley at the other stone beasts. What was this place?

Foggy mists curled around the deep valley below him, but even through their reaches Renender saw buildings. They were red with up curled corners. He saw that a path lay before the cave entrance. With his eyes, he followed its winding course down into the valley. The sound of swift moving streams rushed up to meet his ears. Looking up and much further afield Renender could see other four-pointed cliff faces, more and more across these Canius Mountains. On each were carved figures like those around this valley, so many stretching on and on.

It was too much for Renender just now. Around the cave entrance grew huge shrubs of the hallucinogenic flowers. There was a stone bench. Renender sat down upon it and he swooned. The last thing he thought he heard was bells and hurrying feet on the path.

36 BIG CITY

Naemi sat at the back of the boat with one hand on the rudder. The sail was up and the boat cut a quiet path through the water, fog and morning grey. The water sliced away by their passage sounded a gentle "whoosh" on each side. It lulled.

Cornelius was still asleep, sprawled out at Naemi's feet. He twitched at times and he ground his teeth. An arm flailed, slapping Naemi's thigh. She looked down at him. Her eyes were blue-grey. One flipped purple. She shifted position in her seat and kept steering the boat through the quiet nothingness.

They'd travelled the rest of the length of the river through the night. They were now sailing in the river's mouth where it emptied into the northern great lake. Naemi tried to stay parallel to the eastern shore. She couldn't see it, but she figured it wasn't too far away. When the sun came up and the fog burned away she would adjust course as needed. It wouldn't be long now. Maybe Cornelius would wake by then.

* * *

Cornelius dreamed.

He was falling. He must have crashed out of the window of a building a kilometer high. The sound of breaking glass was all around him. Glittering shards tumbling in the air with him fell toward the ground.

Thud! Cornelius landed on the ground with knees bent, on his toes, and leaning forward suspended on his fingertips. He looked up. A flat expanse stretched around him to the horizon on a predawn morning. East the sky was rapidly turning orange and all the stars had fled. Trails of dust hovered in the air all around him. The sounds of engines cruising and idling churned the air. Motorcycles circled round and round. At that moment all the engines were cut. The sun burst into the sky just as the figure of a tall man was silhouetted. Cornelius could not see who it was, a dark sun god. There was a buzzing. It grew louder and louder and...

"Ow!" yelled Cornelius jumping up and nearly out of the boat fully awakened from his dream. "What is it? I've been hit by a dart! Down! Down! Cover!" Cornelius dove to the bottom of the boat.

"Bees," said Naemi. She was calmly sitting up straight in the boat.

The sun had risen on a morning just freed of its cool foggy mists. The air already felt warm. The boat drifted quietly near the shore, a beautiful shore. Shrubs of berries grew above the watermark. Orchards of flowering fruit trees marched row upon row for kilometers beyond the lakeshore. The trees were huge with wide girths and laden with blossoms, flowers of all shapes, pastel pinks and reds and whites. The air was thick with the smell of sweet nectar. Pollens swam in the breeze and caught the sunlight in shimmers. The sky and air droned with the buzz of bees. They flew thick and fast.

Bees swarmed over the boat, which seemed to lie just at the insects' furthest extent from the orchards. Cornelius squirmed on his back at the bottom of the boat swatting the air. Naemi sat still, unaffected.

"Why are we so close to them?" exclaimed Cornelius.

"Because they're attracted to us." Naemi looked sown at him. She flashed both her eyes yellow. Then one turned brown, the other grey. "They're attracted to you." Flash-flash, her eyes turned green.

"I've never been called a flower before," he said. He slowed his swatting at the air. There weren't any bees within reach.

"No one's calling you a flower," said Naemi.

Cornelius laughed and sat up. He took in the beautiful world. To the right and south the orchards marched into the flat distance. Where they became hazy, fields of edible grasses grew to the horizon. They were well beyond the mouth of the Channel Rift River. Naemi had taken them through while Cornelius had slept. To the left and north the orchards continued, with different varieties of fruit blossoms in the many rows of trees. Maybe five kilometers distant were the many and varied lofty spires of Big City.

It was situated on a buttress jutting out into the lake. Seen from the south as Cornelius and Naemi did, the city rose from the rounded buttress and soared skyward. If it were situated in the sea, it would resemble a huge anemone. Towers reached heights of five hundred meters. A massive harbor was constructed in the lake by two arcing bulwarks of stone. From above it was shaped like the horns of a beast drawing near to one another at their tapering termini. But Cornelius and Naemi could only see the southern jetty. Myriad windows in the skyscrapers caught the dawn's light and reflected it in all directions. As the land around warmed, waves of heat caused the city to shimmer like a mirage in the distance. Lake ships crowded about the harbor.

"It's beautiful," said Cornelius. "I thought Cronapolis, even Shining City, were great cities. This is even grander."

The bees had retreated from pestering Cornelius in the boat. They joined their billion brethren among the trees. Cornelius looked past the first few rows of trees and spotted in the distance a great mound oak, wider than two rows and higher than any other trees in the blossoming orchard. He had an idea.

"What do we have for breakfast?" he asked Naemi.

"Cold fish," she said.

"Yeah. How 'bout something sweeter?"

"Like?"

"Let's put to shore and I'll show you."

Naemi encouraged the gurkbuzzel sail forth from the hull, but there was precious little breeze. Cornelius sent a puff of breath at the sail. In a few moments they'd crossed the remaining stretch of water and skidded onto the gravelly sand. The two Humans jumped out and Cornelius pulled the boat up the bank and out of the water. The air was alive with buzzing bodies.

"What's this about?" asked Naemi.

"Honey," said Cornelius with a sly childish grin. "I used to sneak honey from the orchards near Bafaria when I was young. I'm pretty sure I can still do it."

"Where is this honey?" Naemi looked all around but didn't know what she was looking for.

"It's a good bet there's some in that mound oak just over there." Cornelius pointed to the great tree a few rows in. "But first we need a torch."

"For what?"

"To smoke them out." He bent down and spun the gurkbuzzel device. The boat offered up a firebrand, flame alight. "Follow me!" Cornelius bounded across the beach and up the bank, passed the berry shrubs until he was several rows of trees inside the orchard. Naemi trotted along behind him. The bees were busy just above their heads among the blossoms. "Smell that fragrance, Naemi," he said. They stood and inhaled the orchard's sweet breath. Apple and citrus and stone fruit, peach, apricot, and pear, the many varieties scented the morning air. "This is a blissful place." The warm blue sky peaked through the laden branches that vaulted over the two, their tips touching and intermingling mid rows.

"Let's see your oak tree," said Naemi.

"Snap a few green branches with leaves and blossoms," said Cornelius. "I need fuel for smoke."

Naemi jumped and snatched branches from one tree then another. From afar she looked to be dancing to music that only she could hear. "Is this enough?" she finally asked, arms full of fragrant bows. Bees hovered around her bouquet.

"This way," said Cornelius, and they walked further into the orchard.

The mound oak, or great mound oak, was among the oldest, tallest and most massive species of tree on Lupus. They had tremendously long life spans. The specimen that towered above Cornelius and Naemi, and all the many trees around, was upwards of three thousand years old, though six was not outside of the realm of possibility. There was not another nearby for kilometers. What fortuitous events and environments enabled this giant to germinate and thrive in this place was anyone's guess. But the trees were revered and were never cut down.

Cornelius and Naemi stood beside the great girth of the oak's trunk. It would take six people to link hands and circle the base.

"This is the biggest oak I've ever seen," said Cornelius.

"It's an old soul," said Naemi. Turning to look at Cornelius, she asked, "So where's your honey?"

Cornelius scanned the tree and observed the bees flying to and fro. At last he spied a cleft in the trunk fifty meters up. "There," he said pointing. "That's where our honey is."

"How do you plan on getting it?"

"Climb?" Cornelius offered.

Naemi considered the predicament. "You mean me."

"If you wouldn't mind."

This was a task for which Naemi was not unprepared. "Ok, but you owe me."

"Many times over," said Cornelius with a broad smile.

Naemi dropped her bundle of branches onto the ground. She proceeded to search through her belt of blades until she located a round disk of intersected grooves. She unlatched the disk and maneuvered with the fingers of both hands a series of pushes and pulls on the disk's sides. The disk responded with a series of clicks and snaps. Two segments separated. Naemi popped the center of each and they expanded to form toe clasps with four sharp curved talons. She hooked these onto the toes of her sandals. Next she popped the remaining two pieces and they formed claw like gloves. She attached the gloves to her fingers and thumbs. Then she clicked her heels just right so that a single reverse facing talon emerged from the back of each sandal. With not a word to Cornelius, she snatched the firebrand from his hand and held it between her teeth. She scampered up the trunk of the great tree like a well-seasoned cat intent on prey.

"That a babe," yelled Cornelius after her.

Naemi ascended the trunk with ease. Climbing trees in this manner had been part of her training by the Magistry back on Polaris. She had apprehended many Ferals like this.

She climbed up and up. The razor sharp talons easily pierced the ribbed bark. The only sticking point, so to speak, came from her spur blades exiting the back of her sandals. They provided necessary support against falling or sliding down, but she found she had to jerk her legs up by bending her knees and yanking more than she liked.

She paused a moment to call down to Cornelius, the firebrand still between her teeth. She could scarcely speak clearly. "So w'at does ho'ey 'ook 'ike 'ot i' a jar?"

"Wax," yelled Cornelius back. "It's encased in wax."

Wax, thought Naemi. She didn't see any wax, nor any waxiness.

"Follow the bees."

Yes, of course, she thought. On she went up. Now the great trunk split into two thick branches, trunks in their own right. Just a bit up on one there was a crack in the wood. Bees lackadaisically flew in and out and around it. "Found it," she yelled down.

"Ok," said Cornelius. "I'm going to toss you up some branches. I'll use the whip."

"Then what?"

"Light them, douse the hive with smoke."

"And then?"

"Just reach in and cut out some honey. Some wax. Piece of cake."

"Cake?"

"Never mind. It should be a cinch."

Naemi chose not to respond. Presently a silver cord whistled in the air and came into view. A wad of branches came right to her and she grabbed them with a metal claw. She leaned her head in and lit the branches from the firebrand between her teeth. She waved the smoking branches at the hive entrance. The bees did seem to calm. She laid the branches at the entrance to the hole and retrieved a knife from her belt. Easily enough she reached in and felt a waxy resistance. Slice, grab, out. She had a ten-centimeter tall block of honeycomb. Honey oozed from ruptured cells.

"I'm dropping it, and the brand," yelled Naemi. She let them go.

"Hey!" Cornelius shouted. But from the tree somewhere above Naemi the sound of breaking glass erupted.

"Nut-Nut honey-butt. Will Naemi share some honey-nut?"

Another voice giggled nearby. "Ha-ha! Naemi. What are you doing up here?"

As much as a Human Polarin could, Naemi's ears almost flattened. Goosebumps rose on the back of her neck. "Hiss".

"I see you."

"I see you."

There were two small pre-pubescent boys in camouflage overalls sitting on a horizontal branch five meters above Naemi. One was Human, the other Canine. Their bare feet dangled in the air.

"The question is, why are YOU here," said Naemi looking up at them."

"Time to play," said one.

"Play, ha-ha," said the other.

"You'll get in the way and make a mess of things," said Naemi.

"Maybe," the Nut-Nuts said in unison, giggling.

"Go back. Go back now," said Naemi trying to sound commanding.

"No," said one.

"There are lots of us this time," said the other.

A commotion sounded from Cornelius on the ground. "Naemi. Get down here fast. I need you."

"Better go see."

"Better find out," the Nut-Nuts giggled.

Naemi pulled her heel blades out of the tree and scuttled down fast. She landed on her clawed feet with a clang, crouched with clawed hands poised for anything. "What?"

Cornelius stood three meters from her, hands on his hips. Beside him were two small boys, one Human and one Canine, fighting over the honeycomb. They were identical to the two high in the tree.

"They appeared out of nowhere with a sound like breaking glass. Just like G."

"G. Ha-ha," giggled one.

"This is good," said the other, sticky fingers in his sticky mouth.

"Who are they?" asked Cornelius.

"Cornelius doesn't remember us," said one.

"Can't remember what hasn't happened yet," said the other.

Naemi relaxed and her eyes flipped to blue. "Trouble, nothing but," said Naemi. "They're the Nut-Nuts. Only there are more of them up in the tree."

"What are Nut-Nuts?"

"They're combative, disrespectful, troublesome kids, from G's ship. They got out."

"We left," said the sticky one.

"You know why," said the other.

"We told you we'd come back."

"We're here to help."

"You'll get us killed," protested Naemi.

"Not all of us," said one. The other giggled.

"You said it yourself," observed Cornelius. "Combative and disrespectful."

Naemi removed her claws and blades and returned them to her belt. Then she marched over to the sticky boy and grabbed the honeycomb, what was left of it, out of his hands and mouth. "This is mine," she said. She broke off a piece for Cornelius.

"Hey!" said the sticky Nut-Nut.

"Mm, wonderful!" intoned Cornelius. "Just like the honey from Bafaria."

"It's ok," said Naemi. "Too much wax though." She spat out many pieces and picked at her teeth with a fingernail. "You're just remembering the taste from then, not tasting this." She spat out more wax.

The sticky Nut-Nut wiped his mouth with his hands, then wiped his hands on his overalls. Suddenly two Nut-Nuts dropped out of the tree onto the ground in a tumble, both laughing. All four Nut-Nuts then clasped hands and danced in a circle singing a rhyme.

"Round and round the circle we go. Light in the middle and more to go.

Dibble dabble dally-doe. Nut-Nuts, Nut-Nuts, Go Go Go!"

The thyme was followed by more laughter. A bubble of light burst forth in the midst of their circle. The sound of glass breaking filled the air. Another pair of Nut-Nuts appeared, same as the others. They joined hands in the circle and continued the song.

"Dibble dabble dally-doe. Nut-Nuts Go Go Go!"

And more appeared. Six, eight, twelve, sixteen, eighteen, twenty. Then amidst their song and dance a banquet appeared, roasted bird with barbeque sauce, fresh bread, more honey, butter, orange juice and pie.

"Oh wow, I am starving," said Cornelius. The honey had only stoked his hunger. "Come on Naemi. Don't pass up a good thing." They started eating.

While they ate, the Nut-Nuts played and sang.

"Herry derry dally-doe, Nut-Nuts come and Nut-Nuts go. Come to help. Come to show. Nut-Nuts, Nut-Nuts, Go Go Go!"

They jumped rope, played tag and kicked a ball.

"They're strange," said Cornelius, his mouth full of bird and bread. "But helpful so far."

"So far," said Naemi. Her eyes turned blue-green.

Then with no warning all the Nut-Nuts took off running through the trees toward the lakeshore.

Cornelius looked wonderingly at Naemi, then they too ran after the others. About the trees as they ran, the buzz of the bees grew louder and louder until it sounded like jets overhead. Then they heard the sonic boom, and another, another. It sounded like the sky cracking open above them. Now clear of the orchard and in the bright sunlight, they witnessed the commencement of the attack on Big City.

Hornet Fliers careened across the sky at supersonic speeds. Their velocities shattered against the sound barrier booming and rumbling. Bees and birds and many other forms of wildlife turned the formerly placid landscape into harried blurs of motion. And the flying ships kept coming. Aerial columns of transports in bloated spider forms like gorged ticks swept into view. Four lines broke away from the main force heading south. In a matter of seconds they were over the orchards. Cornelius and Naemi dropped to the ground and covered their ears. The lines of ships passed overhead and on, screaming by, quickly vanishing into the southern horizon.

"I'll bet you those are headed for Shining City," said Naemi. They rose to their feet and looked south, helpless to act. Explosions sounded to the north. They turned and saw smoke rising from Big City where bombs rained down. Horns blared from the city and from the many lake ships around the port. The ships turned with full raised sails heading away to deeper and maybe safer waters, until the Hornet Fliers had them in their sights. Bombs dropped onto the lake waters and many found their marks. The lake ships rocked from the bombs and seething waves, and burst into exploding flames.

"Cornelius!" yelled Naemi. Her eyes were crimson red. "You can help them. Wind!"

Cornelius opened his eyes wide at the realization of what she meant. He COULD help them. He inhaled mightily, puffing his chest out, then he let loose a gale. The lake became a tempest with a driving wind to the northwest. The lake ships that had avoided the first bombardment snapped their sails in the wind and sped away. The Hornet Flyers were tousled in the turbulent airs and broke off their attack. They circled back around toward the city. Before their eyes Big City literally disappeared. A bubble of light enveloped the city. A second later it was as if the city and the harbor had never been. Only trees and a wild landscape remained, with waves dashing against distant rocks and crags.

"What just happened?" asked Cornelius.

Naemi's attention was elsewhere. "Cornelius!" She pointed at the sky where a Hornet Flyer was coming in on a wide arc from the lake to where the city had been. It was almost right overhead.

Without even thinking about it, Cornelius spread his arms and spun in a tight circle around, around, around. The air about him blurred in a turbulence that rose higher and higher. Just as the attack craft came overhead, he released his hold on the tornado. The flyer buckled in the air and ripped apart in a magnificent explosion, sending burning debris onto the beach, the orchards and the lake. Off toward where Big City had been, the many flyers few in confused circles, searching for their target.

"Where are the Nut-Nuts?" asked Cornelius.

"Unreliable as always," answered Naemi.

"Can we use the gurkbuzzel boat?" He and Naemi ran to where they'd grounded the little boat, but it was gone. In its place was a puddle of slime and trails leading up the bank to the prickly berry bushes. Flashing and flickering slugs were crowding in a heap in the shade of the shrubbery. "Now what?"

"We run for the city, or where it should be," said Naemi. "We still have to find Shont. Run." They raced north along the shore, but soon crossed back into the orchard for safety and cover, and to escape the residual waves from Cornelius' storm that sloshed onto the beach.

Half way to Big City the orchard gave way to fields of early sunflowers two meters tall. Cornelius and Naemi moved more slowly now that they were out in the relative open. The circling Hornet Fliers could spot them. But a new surprise approached. Coming at them at full run were hundreds of people in twos, threes and more. Behind them came still more, Humans and some Canines, fleeing the city, wherever it was.

"You're going the wrong way," someone shouted at them. "There's nothing that way but disaster."

But Cornelius and Naemi pressed on. Two Hornets banked in the sky and flew over the running masses. Then there were explosions. Bodies and body parts flew into the air amid shrieks and cries. But then a ripple of light burst among the sunflowers. Two columns of Nut-Nuts appeared a hundred meters long. They brandished a dizzying array of weapons, shoulder to air missile launchers, automatic crack rifle guns. They began firing up at the bombers.

"This way! This way!" some shouted at Cornelius and Naemi. They ran through the columns of Nut-Nuts. One flyer was hit and fell crashing, exploding into the field of sunflowers and people.

Near where the line of Nut-Nuts ended, people emerged out seemingly nowhere. There was just the landscape of rocks and grasses, trees and streams, and suddenly people running and screaming.

"You'd better do it," said a Nut-Nut. "There's another bomber coming." It barreled down out of the sky at a steep angle. Six Nut-Nuts working as a team took it out with volley after volley of missiles.

Cornelius and Naemi clasped hands, looked trustingly into each other's eyes, and stepped through. What they entered was a gluey membrane that so successfully deflected light and sound that everything within was hidden from everything without, and vice versa. The membrane was a maze of colors. It was like walking through a rainbow, if you could first catch one. Colors clung to Cornelius and Naemi, clumped then let go. Many other forms crowded and blurred the already hazy view, residents of Big City escaping in the opposite direction. What seemed like a sizeable distance to traverse was actually less than a millimeter thick, and they were through.

Before them was Big City, grand metropolis of the Cantons. Hornet Fliers that had passed just as easily through the membrane rained missile upon missile at the city. Inside the invisibility shield, light was distorted. The sky was off purple. People were running everywhere.

After a moment of silence that seemed to take an age to understand what he was seeing, Cornelius said with too much brevity, "I feel like we're in one of those globes that snow when you shake them."

"That's a bad joke," said Naemi. "Our lives are in danger here. We have to get to the other side of the city."

A Hornet bombarded a steel and glass skyscraper not many blocks ahead. As if watching in slow motion, its flagged turrets bent and angled in a collapse. The superstructure weakened and gave way, the entire edifice crumbling under its massive weight. Clouds of smoke, ash and dust billowed through the streets. Hundreds more bodies, arms and legs akimbo, tumbled from the once great heights. It was not difficult to imagine hearing the helpless cries of innocents tumbling to their deaths far below. The scene of destruction was repeated on skyscraper after skyscraper around the city.

"This way," cried Naemi. She led Cornelius through the throngs of people along the embarcadero concourse beside the harbor. Not a few people, Humans and Canines together, were jumping off the concourse into the water after the few small bobbing boats that were already too full. There were no large boats anywhere near and the lake ships were gone. Cornelius paused to watch someone struggling in the water below him. He jumped in.

The woman struggled to stay afloat while holding onto a baby, its head barely above the water. Cornelius surfaced right beside her, but he was distracted by her wild kicking and flailing. "Easy, easy," he said. He slipped an arm around her waist and drew her to a quay nearby. They sat on a stone step at the water's side, waves sloshing. The woman wailed over the dead infant in her arms. Cornelius could only hold her. And others kept jumping in.

A bomb fell into the harbor and exploded in fire and spray. Cornelius was thrown clear of the wall and foundered in the churning waters, surfacing near another quay, bruised but unbroken. Not far from him the woman he'd just saved broke the surface, bobbing in the water face down.

"Cornelius!" Naemi' voice carried down to him. "Are you ok?"

Cornelius nodded. "Yes." He picked himself up and climbed broken steps to the concourse above, his knives clanging from his waist belt.

Everywhere was melee and mayhem. Those deadly Hornet Fliers that found their way through the shield to the city easily found their way out again. Their communications did not carry across the shield's barrier, but before long the entire force was in the attack. Just beyond the harbor Cornelius and Naemi could see two more Fliers emerge into the sky out of nothingness.

"A city-wide invisibility field is nice, but it's not stopping the attack," said Cornelius. "Where are the city's other defenses?" There was gunfire and rockets rising from various places around the metropolis, but the flying gunships made quick grist and rubble of any perceived or source of any real resistance. "Ok, there's some."

"It won't be enough," said Naemi.

But the shield did have resilience. Bombs dropped onto it did not penetrate, and the Hornets did not know where the generators lay.

"If we move along this concourse north, we'll be able to slip west to our rendezvous point with Shont," said Naemi. But when she turned to face Cornelius she saw that he was already moving east, deeper into the city center. "Cornelius!" she shouted. "We've got to get THROUGH this, not further IN it!"

Midway along the curve of the concourse opened up the main public forum of the city center. It was the grand Zocalo, a kilometer square grassy and flowering park space. The center feature was Big City's Great Ziggurat, its religious and civic center. It was one hundred meters tall, four sided to the cardinal directions, with central stairways on each side climbing three hundred and sixty steps each, passing the four main platforms, leading to the top.

Moving towards the base of the ziggurat in jerky slow motion like a stop action film were hundreds of female citizens, dragging, leading and carrying babies. They were called to the ziggurat by a priest or leader who stood on the stairs at the first platform level. As Cornelius and Naemi approached, they could make out what the man was saying, his exhortations booming out of a megaphone at the gathering crowd below him.

"Hither Citizens! Hither! Our doom is upon us. Gather at the gods' temple in this the End Times. Climb the sacred steps and enter Paradise."

"What is he talking about?" asked Cornelius.

Naemi pieced together the motions and intentions of what was happening. Women in high angled heels they wore as shoes crept across the Zocalo at the fastest pace they could manage, which was quite slow. Their arms jutted and flailed as they maintained shaky balance. Their ankles wobbled and shuddered in their high-heeled shoes. Many stopped at a building on the Zocalo's perimeter where a group of proctor teachers from a school or nursery were handing out babies to queues of the women.

"Baby Pickers," said Naemi with disgust. "And goat walkers."

"What do you mean?" asked Cornelius.

They stood at the terminus of an avenue that ran from the concourse to the Zocalo. They watched as woman after woman in their strange almost paralyzing shoes, mainly Human but some Canine, marched up the ziggurat's steps at the call of the supposed holy man.

Now on the second platform, he called to his flock, "Endure this oblation. Prepare yourselves for blissful release."

Naemi leaned closer to Cornelius. "That is one of the religious nut cases one so easily encounters in Big City, in the Cantons. The people here seem prone to gullibility." She pointed at the women. "Look at those shoes! They're meant to inflict constant pain and discomfort throughout the day. They spend money like mad on ever more tortuous devices to inflict on themselves. And do you know why they do it? Their preacher here calls it 'fashion' and right worship for their gods. It's the trickery of an economy of nonsense, a dangerous thing that gets out of control."

Cornelius thought on this a moment. "Religion is just routine for those who cannot lead in their own lives. True faith of the heart does not require a religion."

Naemi looked at him and said, "It's ritual they crave."

The preacher was on the third platform now, calling down to the mass of women and infants trudging like zombies up the ziggurat's steep steps. Amid his message, bombs and gunfire, smoke and Armageddon, continued around them. "The hour of our deliverance is here. Forth to be saved."

"His flock is called the Goat Walkers, because they can't walk like people.

"Goat?" asked Cornelius.

"I think it's some animal, like a dorsein. Imagine a dorsein trying to walk on its hind legs."

"And they do that on purpose?"

Naemi nodded.

"And Baby Pickers?"

"They pick babies from the nurseries and daycare centers to go with them, to be saved with them. Who knows whose children they have."

The preacher was now on the top platform of the ziggurat. He held his arms high and wide and called to the gathering throng around him. "Be cleansed from your sins. Cast your souls into Paradise." He snatched a child from the arms of a woman near him and flung the baby over the opposite edge. Cries were lifted up from the others. The woman then cast herself off the edge of the platform after the baby. This was repeated over and over. Bodies of the dead and dying piled up on the ziggurat's face. Blood ran down the steps. And still the women came and still the women climbed.

"This is beyond insane," said Cornelius. He looked around. "There are no Nut-Nuts here. Maybe they can't pass through the field."

"I don't know that that should make a difference," said Naemi. "But there are plenty enough of them outside the city."

"Then this is our fight."

"This is NOT our fight!" said Naemi.

"But we're here."

"But…." She stopped short. Cornelius was already in a spin. A tornado gathered around him. He aimed it at the Hornet coming in for an attack on the ziggurat. It exploded, raining shrapnel onto the pyramid and across the Zocalo. Plenty of people were part of the collateral damage. There were a dozen other flyers in the air above the City. Cornelius proceeded to take them out as well.

Naemi did not stand by idly. "Cornelius, lend me your whip." She grabbed it out of the air as he tossed it to her. She took aim at a low flying Hornet and released the whip. Its claw end caught on a part of the flyer and Naemi was hauled into the air. She leapt onto the windshield. In a sudden motion that defied explanation she kept her balance and grabbed two of her longest and strongest blades from her belt and thrust them with all her might through the Plexiglas straight into the pilot's skull. The ship plunged toward the Zocalo. Naemi jumped just before it careened in fire against the ziggurat. More casualties. Then Naemi chose another target, loosed the whip, and jumped again.

Before long there was one Hornet remaining above the City. Cornelius took one more aim and sent a tornado directly into its path. The craft smashed into a nearby skyscraper. Debris flew in all directions.

"Whoa-ho! I got him!" yelled Cornelius in the midst of a victory dance. But it was short-lived. Where was Naemi? Then he saw her. He ran to the base of the ziggurat. She lay in the grass pierced through the chest by errant shrapnel from Cornelius' last target. Blood gurgled from her chest and from her mouth and nose. "Naemi!" he cried and laid his forehead onto hers. "I'm so sorry," he sobbed. "I should have listened to you." Naemi could only blink, one pale blue eye and one soft brown, growing more opaque.

Beside them both a flash of light erupted, accompanied by the now familiar sound of breaking glass and scraping metals. A new Naemi emerged from the light, younger with normal eyes, though wide and wild. She rushed to the dying Naemi's side.

"Oh sister self, this is a sad end. But all is not in vain. You did well. I'll take over from here." And the light went out of the downed Naemi's eyes.

The new Naemi stood up. She looked around at the state of the city that now had quieted a bit. "A pity," she said. "I would have liked to see Big City before this." This Naemi apparently had never been here before. Then she straightened and turned to Cornelius. "You are Cornelius. I'm sorry, but we can't stand on ceremony for my former, well later, self." She took the dead Naemi's knives as her own and hooked the belt around her waist. "I take it this is yours," she said, handing Cornelius back the whip given to him by G. "It's time we met up with our contact."

"Not yet!" snapped Cornelius. He was pulling himself together. "There's one more thing." He selected a throwing knife from his own belt, took aim and cast it with all his strength at the preacher on top of the ziggurat. Even from this distance the blade found its mark in the man's throat. The preacher tumbled down the side of the pyramid among the bodies of his flock. The women still on their way up paused as if a spell had just been broken. "Now we can go."

Naemi nodded. "This way then."

They dashed back to the harbor concourse and followed it around north and west through residential neighborhoods. The damage here was less than in the city center. With the attack suspended for now, people were out and exploring.

"We can't be sure there won't be more attacks," said Naemi. "More spider transports may be moving across the Cantons to Big City as we speak."

Skyward from the direction they were headed, another Hornet emerged from the shield, but it was badly damaged from a surface to air attack. It came in low billowing black smoke. The flyer dove and crashed into a block of homes. More casualties.

"It looks as if the Nut-Nuts are still busy outside the City," said Cornelius.

"The Nut-Nuts?" asked Naemi. "They're here?"

"You've missed a lot."

Mainly Canines populated the northwest side of Big City. Many were not going to wait for another attack to happen or not. Families and other groups were fleeing, their destination roughly to the west, to the nearby Canius Plains.

After following the throngs, Cornelius and Naemi came to the edge of the city. Here people vanished into the invisible barrier. Cornelius clutched Naemi's hand and they stepped through. Fluid rainbows of color swirled around them, and then they were out.

Fields of red ripe strawberries stretched before them full of people making their way west, not a few picking strawberries as they went. A normal blue sky was above them now, dotted with a few remaining Hornets. But here and there teams of Nut-Nuts kept up their attacks.

Cornelius and Naemi walked along the tracks of a rail line that came out of the city's shield. Turning back at a rumbling noise, they saw a train appear on the tracks rattling toward them. They waited as the train neared, slowed and stopped. The doors opened automatically and they stepped on. The cars were full of huddled Canines, adults and children and a few Humans, sobbing and crying and grieving.

They stood holding onto an overhead handrail. The train resumed its course northwest to the furthest outskirts of Big City, away from the devastation.

37 AFTERNOON IN CRONAPOLIS

The military capital was resplendent with banners and streamers, flags and pennants. Crowds filled the Forum and bands played victorious marching music. Ice cream was freely given out to children. Fountains and water spouts arched high into the sky. A cold layer of air hovered above the crowds, turning the sky into a rainbow of kaleidoscopic colors as water spray froze and fell back down as radiant prisms, melting just above the heads of the people, turning to a delightful mist that dusted eyebrows and eyelashes. "Union! Union!" shouted the crowds. "Peace! Love! Victory!"

Deep within the military edifice another celebration took place.

Menkar sat directly opposite Corvus at the afternoon Commissioner's Briefing. Power emanated from her. Frosty tendrils danced around her shoulders and head. The black walls of the room behind her held onto a sparkling layer of ice. Her eyes shown with a cold glow. Only two-thirds of the Commissioners were present, the others maintaining forward command positions in Lupus City and Bafaria.

Menkar's mood alternated between being furious at having been kept out of the loop on the attack against Shining City and the rebel territory on the one hand, and admiration that the action seems to have been a near complete success. But she still had her own questions. She was determined to get answers today. She glared across the table at Corvus. *The little beast looks just so smug,* she thought to herself. *I wonder what he has been up to in Mine*

City. Practice throwing escorts or miners into the bottomless chasm?

Corvus, radiating his own cold glow, sat next to the First Commissioner, who was just finishing his ritual cigar puffs. General Taurus sat two seats away from Menkar.

Markhab shifted in his seat and began. "My friends, this is a Day of Days. Our hammer has fallen against the errant Human lands. I will let Taurus run down the list of glories this day."

Taurus cleared his throat. "Before dawn, our Hornet Flyers set off from our forward bases in Lupus Minor. They crossed the Cantons to Big City, joined by additional Hornets at auxiliary bases along the way. At Big City they separated into two attack forces, the second continuing south to Shining City and its sister cities along the Shining River. At this time I can report that our forces have swept aside the rebel resistance. Shining City, what's left of it, belongs to us. Our Flotilla Fleet is en route to the Star City delta for mop up operations."

"Can you say the same for Big City?" asked Menkar. The tendrils of cold about her head jumped and danced.

"Our intelligence is still coming in," said Taurus.

"My intelligence indicates uncertainty," said Menkar.

"Explain," said Markhab.

Menkar was happy to have her pulpit. "Satellite reconnaissance indicates that a battle was engaged, but the outcome is less than conclusive. In fact our satellites are not showing any city at all in situ, Big or otherwise."

"How is that?" ask Markhab.

"I was hoping Taurus could enlighten us," said Menkar, turning to look at the general. The frosty air about her mouth reached halfway to him. All other faces turned in suit.

But Taurus was fully confident and did not turn on Menkar's attempt to position him in a corner. The general merely removed the "walls" that made the corner. "Commissioner Menkar is quite right. Satellite imagery and

435

limited reconnaissance hint at the complete elimination of Big City. Why this should be I cannot speculate. But we have Spider Transports on the ground moving across the Cantons. They will soon be on the scene."

"Cowed, ruined or eliminated, we will have defeated the Cantons," said Markhab proudly. He leaned back in his seat and puffed on his cigar.

Taurus continued. "My fellow Commissioners should know that our Flotilla moving on Star City is pushing against the seasonal monsoons. It will be a few days before we can engage the rebel remnants there. In the meantime, our Spider Transports that are even now scaling the mountain border will herd the rebels south.

"A Day of Days indeed, my friends," said Markhab. He glanced quickly at Corvus, then addressed the others. "But things must keep moving in the direction of our momentum. I want immediate preparations to commence for moving ALL of our operations, command and control, to our new base in Lupus Minor. The unification of Human Lupus will have put the Canines off balance. There is no time to waste. In a few days, I want to stare down the maw of Canoon with the cry of victory on our lips. Meanwhile, I have other plans in motion to ensure our final victory. I'll give no further details at this time." He panned the room, staring into the eyes of the other Commissioners.

Menkar spoke up before Markhab's gaze fell upon her. "First Commissioner. Lupus Major must remain secure during these operations."

"Of course," said Markhab. "And is Lupus Major secure?"

His response hit Menkar like an accusation. "It IS," she answered defiantly. "Completely." Her face blushed, which caused a rising column of steam to envelop her. The ice on the wall behind her melted and ran down in streams, collecting in puddles on the floor.

"Then our plans are infallible," said Markhab, and he added, "I will personally oversee the transfer of prisoners held in these Headquarters to Bafaria. They may represent assets of special opportunity." He said no more of the matter. "I think we are done here. We will convene at our evening briefing.

38 THE ROADHOUSE

There was less whimpering than one might expect from a train laden with Canine refugees. Most conversation consisted of speculation on Markhab's next moves and the future of the metropolis of Big City. The city was injured but not broken, invisible but not gone. Many spoke of what awaited them as they headed west. Where in Canius might they go? There were no cities, no ready-made havens for the influx of Canines who would be streaming in the hundreds, thousands, onto the open plains. The population in Canius was nomadic, with temporary settlements occupied mainly by groups of extended families, trading with related clans, loosely associated with autonomous tribes. But the refugees were not in Canius, not yet.

Cornelius and Naemi were pressed together in the crowded train car. Though the windows were open, arms reached through for a hold from the throng hanging on the outside of the train. Legs dangled from those riding on top. Through the appendages, Cornelius could make out hundreds of Canines running alongside the clattering train in the strawberry fields outside. Within, the heat and smell of bodies permeated the car with musky smells. Most inside were quiet, including Cornelius and Naemi.

Music wafted through the train from somewhere in the back of the car. Naemi pressed up tight next to Cornelius. Yes, the train was crowded, but it wasn't that crowded. This Naemi was young, but how young? Cornelius' skin tingled in contact with her, his breathing shortened. He looked down at her. She was several centimeters shorter than her other incarnations. Her eyes were half-closed, her breasts full and round, her nipples raised and hard. She squirmed against Cornelius' body. Was he the only one on this train who sensed the erotic tension? The meat in his groin stiffened and Cornelius squirmed. A barely audible gurgle and growl escaped Naemi's pouty open lips. He pressed against her, dry humping her through his pants. The knives hidden in his vest clanged against the knives hidden in hers. This was insane. But oh, how good it felt.

Cornelius held his balance steady by gripping the overhead rail with one hand. With his other hand he clutched Naemi's neck and back of her head, massaging her scalp and fondling her wisps of hair. Her breathing was hurried with uneven staccato breaths. Her body shook. She grabbed Cornelius' back and dug in with her fingernails. He bled. Her knives clanged against his, almost melodiously, producing a range of tones based on the length of each knife against each knife.

Cornelius pushed hard. His eyes were closed and his head was thick with heat and noise. He thought of the many times he and Naemi had made love, the different Naemis with whom he had made love. He heard a jumble of sounds ranging from murmurs to shouts to booms. Cornelius imagined he had an audience at a performance art premier. There were clapping and hoots and hollers. Cornelius moved his free hand down Naemi's back and pulled her closer to him, nearly impaling her but for the fabric of their clothes. He struggled to overcome the resistance. Naemi loosed her wrappings, reached down and freed Cornelius from his bindings. Her pants fell about her ankles and his did the same. He rushed in. She bit her lip and barely muffled a scream. Then she did scream. Cornelius lifted her and wrapped a leg around her waist. He thrust. He thrust again. He swelled. He ploughed. He howled and shuddered in his release. Naemi shook and erupted with her own flood of moisture. They were both drenched. Cornelius shook his thick mane of hair, casting beads of sweat in all directions. His thick beard glistened. His eyelashes reflected light in prisms of moisture. Salty drops hung from his nose. He opened his eyes and laughed.

He expected applause from the crowd of voyeurs, but there were none, only the backs of many Canines. Cornelius was confused. He looked at Naemi, held her gently. She swayed and smiled, murmured softly to herself, almost a purr. Cornelius looked further down. Naemi's legs dripped blood in her vaginal wetness. His penis hung limp and also dripped blood. Cornelius was shocked. He'd made love to Naemi many times. But this time, she was....

She opened her eyes, saw Cornelius' expression. "Yes," she whispered. "A virgin."

Cornelius kissed her forehead. Then the train erupted in voices.

"Spider transports!"

"Look! Something else is attacking!"

Cornelius tried to move away from Naemi to look out the windows while pulling up his pants and tucking himself inside. Between arms and legs and bodies he could just make out two transports crawling across the strawberry fields, moving like great bloated ticks over the landscape.

"Something's going on," Cornelius said.

"Outside," said Naemi, moving to conceal her body.

Cornelius looked up. Just above them was an emergency hatch with a wheeled lock. He reached up and grasped the wheel with both hand and heaved. It barely moved. "It's stuck."

"Try turning it the other direction," said Naemi.

Cornelius did, and the wheel moved. It spun and the seal opened. Cornelius pushed up and out, displacing four Canines who had been standing on its outer surface.

"Hey!"

"Hey!"

"Hey!"

"Whoa!"

"Sorry!" yelled Cornelius from below. With his fingers he grabbed the exit's rim and jumped. He strained his arms and drew his knees up. Naemi pushed on his rump from below. Then his feet caught the rim and he heaved himself up and out.

Canines were sitting, squatting and standing on the roof of the train, seven cars in all. They gave way for Cornelius. Behind him Naemi leapt up in one jump and landed on her feet on the roof beside Cornelius, standing graceful.

They were at the edge of the strawberry fields. Grassland spread out to the horizon stretching away into the green of the Cantons. Crawling toward them across the grasslands were great metallic behemoths carried on long spider-like legs. These were the Spider transports carrying the occupation forces of Markhab's military. Cornelius counted dozens in his line of site, and there were many more. But they did not come unchallenged.

A rumble and tumble and roar echoed out of the north. Distant sounds of ground impacts rolled and were rolling closer. A shudder ran through the ground, though the riders in and on the train felt no additional temblors over the racket and rattle of the little train's passage. But they heard the rumble vibrate in the air.

"Something's coming this way," said Naemi.

"More than one something," said Cornelius.

"A lot more."

Along the horizon, little clouds of dust peaked here and there. As the minutes passed they could see glints of sunlight reflect from many points along the northern horizon.

Far up in the polar regions of Canoon, the Canines had long prepared a defense against a land attack by Humans. Tens of thousands of great opalescent spheres ten meters in diameter had been stacked and pressed against ingenious nets at the mouths of many deep canyons. The spheres were fashioned from a substance as strong as titanium, yet as supple as rubber. And they were careening across the Cantons.

After Markhab sent his Spider transports across the Cantons from Lupus

Minor to sweep up resistance and take over Big City, the Canines made their defensive move. The nets were retracted. The sound of their release was like an ice dam breaking that had held back a glacial melt water sea. The mountains shook and the Polar Cities of Canoon shook. Innumerable avalanches swept through the snowfields down the mountain faces, changing the landscape. Wonton destruction was neither the aim nor the method of the spheres. They bounced over lakes and streams, swerved around towns and herds and fields. They followed natural ways through the Cantons toward their intended targets, the Spider transports.

Multiple spheres converged onto individual transports, and the results were breathtaking. The crash of sphere against sphere against transport shattered all into jagged wreckage. The spheres then melted in all their pieces, then grew hotter and melted further into brimstone that incinerated the transport debris. When it was all over, only steaming, evaporating ponds remained. Once dry, only a dimple and a stain remained. Nothing and no one were left of either sphere or transport. And they came and they came.

Cornelius and Naemi stood half-crouched on the roof of the train with the Canines, maintaining their balance while watching the great spheres approach, ricochet and roll across the fields. Three huge spheres rolled in from due north. Two curved off to the right where the closest Spider transport to the train clambered closer. The third sphere hopped the tracks ahead of the train's front engine and then rolled passed left of where Cornelius and Naemi were standing. Shouts of fear and wonder rose from the Canines. Then the sphere made a right turn and jumped over the cars, over the heads of the train's riders. Its surface was a smear of opalescence capturing and reflecting light and color. Cornelius saw his and Naemi's distorted reflections as the sphere passed overhead. Then it thundered to the ground on the train's right side and rolled to meet its two companion spheres converging onto the transport. Boom! Crash! Crack! Sizzle! Fwoosh! The train shuddered from the explosion, knocking some Canines from their perches. Cornelius and Naemi fell to their haunches to keep their balance. Around them other spheres met their marks and more transports exploded.

As the attacks and counter attacks ensued over the next few minutes, the train slowed and came to a stop just before the tracks gave out. The doors opened on the train cars. Canines disembarked, and Cornelius and Naemi slid down from the roof with the others.

"I think we're here," said Naemi.

"Where's here?"

"Our destination," said Naemi. Indeed, the train had stopped before a hard-packed dirt field where rose an odd building bearing a great sign that simply read "Roadhouse."

The train had taken a course that left the lakeshore far to the west. Only grassy fields were visible in all directions away from the Roadhouse, crawling with transports and rolling with spheres. Cornelius and Naemi walked slowly toward the building among the crowd of anxious, desperate and weary Canines from the train, and others catching up on foot. Dust devils whirled and danced around the structure, but they were not caused by wind. Heard among the booms and crashes from the battles between spheres and Spiders was the rumble of motorcycles, hundreds and hundreds were on the move. Many others were parked around the Roadhouse. And odd motorcycles they were. Each had innumerable strangely shaped metal parts affixed to their chassis. Each bike looked different, like creatures that glued bric-a-brac onto themselves for protection. The bric-a-brac looked like discarded parts and pieces of machinery of many designs, with no hint to their former or future purposes. As Cornelius and Naemi approached, they saw from where the parts and pieces came. They were from the Roadhouse itself. It's walls and roof were covered in an amalgamation of the metal parts. And Canines were swarming over its surface, seemingly oblivious to the battles and crowds descending on them, removing each piece. Other Canines were busy affixing the parts to the motorbikes.

"What's going on here?" asked Cornelius.

Naemi was quiet for a while taking in the activity. This was not the Naemi who had traveled into Canius in her past. This Naemi, a newbie, green behind the ears as some would say, was trying to understand what she was seeing.

As they reached the edge of the grass and entered upon the hard packed ground, Cornelius felt a strange sensation move through his body. His mood lifted, he stood taller and straighter. The air even seemed to smell sweeter and fresher than he remembered it could. He stooped down and removed his shoes.

"Why did you do that?" asked Naemi.

"I want to feel the grass and ground beneath my bare feet, between my toes," said Cornelius.

"Hm," replied Naemi. But she followed suit.

"Nice, isn't it?"

"I guess so. Come on, let's keep going."

As they neared the Roadhouse, they saw that Canines had set up tables on the left. On them, food, water and blankets were provided to as many of the now homeless as could be cared for. The needy and hungry formed themselves into queues, some of the longest waiting for first aid. Many other refugees simply stood and blinked at the strange and welcome sight, while others wandered with a curious aimlessness, watching the dismantling of the Roadhouse, or the battles in the distance.

"I'm starving," said Cornelius. "We haven't eaten since this morning with the Nut-Nuts."

Naemi looked at him. "You didn't eat with *me*, not really."

It took a moment for the fact to sink in for Cornelius. "Yes, that's right. Well, still you must be hungry, too. Watch." Cornelius pulled out his mechanical whip, aimed at the nearest food table, and sent the clawed end flying. It grabbed two items and sailed back through the air when Cornelius pressed the retraction button. "Catch," he said. He caught one, and Naemi caught one.

She looked at the food she'd caught. It was steaming. "Nice." Naemi was impressed. "You have interesting abilities, Cornelius. What is this?"

Cornelius took a bite. "Some sort of bun with cooked meat inside. It's good."

They ate as they walked, stuffing the food into their mouths. Still holding their shoes, they marched up to the swinging mid-riff doors of the Roadhouse and went inside.

The interior was dark after the brightness of the noonday outside. Windows faced east, west and south. Tables and chairs were arrayed on the right, booths on the left, with a large open space in the middle that served as a dance floor on wild and festive nights. A long bar with stools took up most of the far wall opposite the entrance. Closed doors stood on either side of the bar. The walls sported pennants and pictures of Canine sporting teams, something like lacrosse as well as something like rugby. Older Canines sat at the bar nursing drinks.

"This is the place?" asked Cornelius.

"It must be," said Naemi. They headed to the bar just as two Canine men entered behind them in animated conversation.

"Don't bother packing the stuff in here. Besides the liquor, everything else can stay."

The one speaking was not as tall as Cornelius, and was stockier and full of muscles with a healthy gut. His face was hard to describe, rather misshapen and not at all pleasant to look at. Actually, he was downright ugly. He shuffled rather than walked, one leg being shorter than the other. His companion was much more recognizable as a Canine, with an extended snout and a mane of brown hair.

"Go help Gerats with the work on the roof. Everything's got to be ready to go as soon as possible." His friend nodded and left. Then loudly to the Canines at the bar, "Alright mates, it's last call. This bar is closing." He walked passed Cornelius and Naemi and took up station behind the bar, pouring shots and filling pints for the die-hards on the stools.

Cornelius plunked himself onto a stool with Naemi beside him.

"What'll it be?" asked the barkeep. "Make it quick. I've got a lot of packing to do."

"A cold beer," said Cornelius.

Naemi gave him a quick disapproving look.

"What? It's been a hell of a day."

The barkeep slammed a huge frothy stein in front of Cornelius. "And for you little lady?"

"I'll have the same."

"You will!" exclaimed the barkeep, wide eyed and grinning. "The drink for the pretty lady is on the house."

"His too," said Naemi.

"Now listen, I make the rules here, Dearie," the barkeep began.

"We're friends of Shont," said Naemi. "After you serve my beer, let her know Naemi is here, from Shining City. She's expecting me. I have her, Asset." She aimed a sidelong glance at Cornelius. His face was deep in his stein. He coughed and sprayed froth all over himself and the barkeep.

"Hey hey now. Watch your manners. Friends of Shont, eh? We'll see. We'll see." He wiped the foam off his shirt.

Cornelius bent close to Naemi and whispered, "Asset? I'm the 'Asset'?"

"You'll understand," said Naemi.

The barkeep set a frothy stein in front of Naemi. "Now you two stay right here while I go and check your story out with the Misses. Naemi, you said? I'll be right back." He shuffled to the closed door to the left of the bar, knocked once, and disappeared inside, closing the door behind him.

"You could have been nicer," said Cornelius. "Demanding free drinks." He shook his head and took another gulp from his stein.

"We don't have any money," said Naemi. "And Shont needs to see you. And one other thing, I don't think he's a Canine."

"Hm?" Cornelius downed his stein of beer, leaving frothy suds and brew dripping down his bearded chin. "At least the beer's good." He belched and wiped his face, chin and shirt. "How much of this mission do you actually

445

know about? I mean, you're a new Naemi. Did you speak with Jarbed?"

"No." Naemi finished her beer. "G gave me instructions. I know all I need to know."

The door into which the barkeep had gone burst open. A tall old Canine woman, grey of hair, stood in the doorway barking orders to someone behind her. "Get everything packed up now. We haven't much time." To the few patrons at the bar she shouted, "Bar's closed. Everyone out." The old die-hards grumbled, finished their drinks in final swallows, and climbed down off their stools and headed for the swinging doors. Cornelius and Naemi too started up, but the old woman said, "Not you two. Come in here."

Cornelius and Naemi shared a glance, Cornelius gulped, and they obeyed. The barkeep shuffled passed them and started collecting liquor bottles for packing, the bottles clanging as the door closed behind the two Humans.

The room was small, crowded with boxes. Besides overflow storage, this room was also an office, with a large desk set against the far wall. A lone window beside the desk brought light into the room. Alongside the old woman was a large stout Canine with a very long snout. His hair was iridescent purple and green.

"So you're here, finally," said the woman. "I was losing hope. We won't be staying here much longer. No more time to wait, or to waste."

"You must be Shont," said Cornelius, stepping close to the woman and offering his hand. "I'm Cornelius, and this is..."

"Naemi. Yes, I figured that. Yes, I am Shont. You said your name was, Corneze?"

"Cornelius."

"Shont, we came as quickly as we could," said Naemi.

"We had a few adventures getting here," said Cornelius, smiling and putting his hand down.

"Adventures? Your adventure is just beginning," said Shont. "Well Naemi, let's see what you've brought us." She nodded to the iridescent Canine, who moved to set up a piece of equipment, a tangled array of metal boxes, tubes and lasers connected with wires in the corner. "Pelax here is one of the Longfaces, from Canoon. He has a nice appearance, don't you think? He's readying our bio-reader to see what information this Corneze carries in his blood."

Pelax turned on the reader, which hummed and lit up with blinking lights. While he was busy doing this, Shont sized Cornelius up. She grabbed his shoulders and gave them a good shake, felt his chest, arms, then grabbed his private parts.

"Hey!" exclaimed Cornelius. "Ouch. Well, you did buy me a drink first."

"Hush," said Shont. "I'm checking the goods on our acquisition."

"I can vouch that he's certainly man enough in that department," said Naemi.

Shont laughed. "I can tell that he is. Well built and strong, I'll give him that."

Cornelius stood still while Shont felt his legs and thighs.

"Let me see your teeth," said Shont, shoving her fingers into his mouth and looking at his gums, teeth. "Hm. Healthy enough." She turned to look at Naemi. "You're younger and shorter than Jarbed indicated." To Pelax she said, "This one won't fit the uniform we've got. You'll have to find another."

Pelax nodded. "It's ready," he said finally. He slid a chair around beside the apparatus.

"Sit down," Shont said to Cornelius. "Let's see if you've brought us anything we can use."

Cornelius removed his belt full of clanging knives and handed it to Naemi. He sat in the chair and put his arms on the rests. Pelax prepared a long needle to extract blood. It was attached to the machine by a long clear rubber tube. Cornelius stared at the needle and exhibited a degree of apprehension.

"Don't worry, the needle is sterilized," said Pelax.

"I wasn't thinking of that," said Cornelius, still looking at the size of the needle.

"Is the knife-man afraid of a little prick?" asked Shont.

"This may sting a little," said Pelax. He jabbed the needle into Cornelius' arm. Cornelius jerked with a start. He watched as the red line of his blood flowed up through the needle, down the tube, into the apparatus. It started to beep.

Shont moved over to peer into a readout screen on the machine. Pelax adjusted some knobs. "There it is." Pelax removed the needle from Cornelius' arm and placed a small bandage over the tiny wound. Cornelius rubbed his arm.

"That wasn't so bad," said Naemi.

"Yes, easy for you to say." He and Naemi bent close to the screen to try and see what Shont and Pelax were seeing.

The machine imaged, isolated and magnified the message-carrying molecules attached to Cornelius' double helix DNA. Pelax turned some more knobs to inject a green catalyst to decode the data Jarbed had injected into him five days prior in Shining City. It seemed so long ago. There were more beeps emanating from the machine.

"It's coming through now," said Shont.

The screen showed a single strand of coiling DNA. Attached to one base pair, a three-atom molecule was stained green. The enzyme attached to the molecule and detached it from the helix and floated free. Pelax fine-tuned the amplification and zoomed in. Another enzyme grabbed onto the molecule. Suddenly thousands of data points streamed out of the molecule like viruses loosed from an infected cell. Pelax then sent pulses of laser light into the sample to read the data freed by the enzyme. The screen rapidly filled with strings of numbers, with the machine providing a translation that could be read.

"What is it?" asked Naemi. "What does it say?"

Shont read aloud the translation. "It's the radio isotope of the material used in the nuclear device detonated on Wror. It matches exactly that of the radioactive materials from Bafaria, Lupus Minor to you Humans. It proves the material did not come from Canoon.

"I thought we knew that already," said Naemi.

"It was strongly suspected, but not known until now," said Shont.

"Is that all?" asked Cornelius.

"At the moment," said Shont. "Pelax, zoom in on Corneze's DNA again. Look at the place where the data molecule was attached. What's that there in the cavity or dimple where it was lodged? What do you see?"

Pelax fiddled with the knobs some more, increasing the magnification. He rotated the DNA on the screen until the dimple showed clearly. A brown mark was embossed onto the DNA itself. "It looks like a glyph."

"A glyph?" asked Cornelius and Naemi in unison.

"It's a memory engram, not part of the data molecule itself. The engram was hidden under it," explained Pelax.

"What does it mean?" asked Naemi.

"We'll find out in just a moment," said Shont. "Pelax, activate the glyph reader."

Four large lenses protruded from the top of the apparatus, casting four beams of red light into the room. They swiveled in rotation until they focused a projected image behind Cornelius' left shoulder.

"I'll get the light," said Shont. She closed the blinds on the window. Then she, Pelax and Naemi came round to stare at the image near Cornelius.

"What is it?" asked Cornelius, craning his neck to try and see.

"It's very small. Pelax, try and make the image larger." A few turns of another knob and the image filled the room. It was an architectural plan of a large facility. Shont walked around the room, in and out of the rooms and corridors of the projection. "I don't know what we're looking at," she said in frustration.

"I can give us some perspective," said Pelax.

The image scaled down and settled in a topographical map of hills, canyons and a river, a large metropolis showing itself on the perimeter. Additional facilities revealed themselves around a large circular field.

"It looks like a space port," said Pelax.

Cornelius got up from his chair and studied the projection. "The topography is familiar. I think, I think this is outside of Bafaria. There's a huge canyon outside the city that the great river flows through."

In the image a flashing vertical line extended out of the projection into space. The projection realigned itself to a perspective above Lupus.

"What does that indicate?" asked Cornelius pointing to the line.

"That's what I want to find out," said Shont. "Pelax, can you see how far that line extends? I want to know what it's pointing to."

"One moment."

The image of Lupus fell away into the distance, but still the straight line went on, this time with breaks in the line at regular intervals. Within the breaks, images of great space ships blinked.

"Scorpion battleships," said Shont. "But look how many there are. I thought Markhab had only two such ships. This indicates a much larger fleet." Pelax continued to adjust his controls. The image left Lupus altogether and continued out into deep space. "Follow that line, Pelax." And he did. Rapidly moving into view was another planet, much larger, surrounded by many more Scorpion ships. Then the image changed entirely. A projected fleet of Scorpions raced from the planet to surround numerous planetary targets.

"If I'm reading this correctly, it's a battle plan against those other worlds," said Shont.

"Look at those symbols by the targets," said Naemi. "That's Lupus, that one Wror, Polaris, Sabral, and...Earth!"

"Markhab means to attack the worlds outright! By conquering and uniting the Human worlds, shared or not, he means to break the Feline blockade of Earth. The rest of us won't have a chance, neither Canine, nor Feline." She looked at Naemi when she mentioned Feline. "That big planet must be Keldo. That's his secret, his grand scheme. We've got to get this information to the Alpha as soon as possible. Naemi, your next mission is more important than ever. Naemi and Corneze, you've done well."

A rumble in the distance grew louder, drew closer. Just then there was a creaking, tearing sound. The roof suddenly gave way and peeled off in a racket of metal and voices. Four Canines peered down into the room.

"We need to go," said one. "Now!" The rumble outside was much closer now. The four Canines leapt off the roof.

Shont yelled to Pelax, "Did all this write to the disc?"

"Yes."

"Then grab that disc and let's get out of here." Pelax ejected a crystal disc from the apparatus and tossed it to Shont. She burst through the door to the main bar with the others quickly following. The barkeep was pushing a dolly crowded high with boxes of liquor across the floor to the entrance.

"Roger darling, put that down and get out of here with the others. We're leaving now!"

"But it's for the festival in...."

Then the walls came down, yanked to pieces by the Canine demolition team. Workers quickly extricated the mechanical parts and pieces, and hurriedly carried them off and attached them to nearby motorcycles.

"Get all the refugees onto available bikes and move out," shouted Shont.

Cornelius exited the roadhouse last. He ran passed Shont as she slowed to help the barkeep Roger. *Roger*, thought Cornelius. *Strange name for a Canine. Maybe....* His thought was cut off, for he saw what all the sudden hubbub was about. Only meters away, a Spider transport that managed to survive annihilation by the spheres approached the Roadhouse. Refugees screamed and scattered. Canines directed as many as possible onto bikes and pull carts. The air crackled with the sound of engine starts. Dust filled the sky as the host moved out, west to Canius.

"Pelax!" yelled Shont. "Take Naemi, now. Roger, take Cornelius. I'll...." But Shont spoke no more. A great shadow covered her from the sun. The right leg of the Spider transport's eight-legged frame crashed through what remained of the Roadhouse and hit the ground, piercing Shont through the chest. Her body was crushed and she died instantly.

Roger broke away from his run with Cornelius and returned to Shont. "Oh my love, oh my love, no more, no more...." His voice trailed off, but he noticed in her hand the crystal disc. He grabbed it, touched his fingers to his lips and to Shont's, and took off running as the Roadhouse collapsed onto and around Shont's body. "Come, my boy," he said catching up to Cornelius. "We must go."

"Wait," said Cornelius. "Where's Naemi?" A dozen meters ahead stood Naemi with Pelax in a large open space. Cornelius ran towards them. He watched as Pelax took an elaborate ring off his hand and gave it to Naemi. She put it on. Pelax was explaining something to her. She touched one aspect of the ring and suddenly she and Pelax were in shadow. Directly beside them appeared a space vessel. A hatch opened, and Pelax and Naemi started up its ramp.

"Wait!" cried out Cornelius. Naemi hesitated on the ramp. Cornelius ran to her, embraced and locked lips. The kiss was so long that both Pelax and Roger had to pry them apart.

"No time now," said Roger. "Away!"

Pelax pulled Naemi into the vessel. The ramp retracted and the vessel slipped back into invisibility. The ground and air buzzed and a breeze whipped up as the ship took off.

"But where...." began Cornelius. But he saw his danger. Spheres were rolling in. He ran as fast as he could with Roger to the waiting motorbike.

The transport rested on the wreckage of the Roadhouse. Knee joints in its mechanical legs bent, causing the entire Spider carapace to squat. Hatches opened along the transport's perimeter. Occupation troops were just beginning to flood out, but not fast enough. A giant sphere leapt into the air over Cornelius' head and joined two more rolling in from the south and the east. Crash! Sizzle! Fwoosh! The sounds erupted from the glowing melting steaming collision, then all grew eerily quiet. Nothing but a stain in the ground remained where the Roadhouse, the Spider, and the body of Shont had lain.

Cornelius raced into the west on the wheels of the Canine host.

39 THE VALLEY THAT MY VILLAGE CALLS HOME

A jumble of strangeness filled Renender's dreams. He sat in the center of a circle of accusations in a large cavern. On one side was a group of marmelots all named Alice. On the other was a group of star-nosed moles not named Alice. The Alices demanded to know why he had gone away, while the not-Alices demanded to know why he wanted to return. There were so many questions, and Renender had no answers for either camp. Each new question was louder than the last. Renender couldn't remember why he had left, and he equally couldn't remember why he wanted to return. From whence and to where? He just didn't know. Above him flitted colorful butterflies glowing in the darkness. He wanted away from this circle of interrogation, but he could not move from the place where he was. He wanted to escape from the questioners and all their questioning. Couldn't he just find a place that would give him peace? He wanted to get away from all the probing, all the pestering, all the cacophonous haranguing. The voices melded together and Renender covered his ears from the din. One voice rose louder over the rest, and the rest died down to murmurs, to whispers. They sounded like the wind in trees, like the babble of brooks. And that one voice was distinct. Renender had the feeling that someone was shaking him, drawing his consciousness out of the cave of marmelots and moles.

"Sir, are you all right?"

Renender moaned.

"Sir, do you need help?"

Renender stirred.

"Sir, may I help you?"

Renender opened his eyes.

"Sir, can you get up?"

Renender was now fully awake. He sat up on the stone bench where he'd been sleeping, blinking his eyes in the daylight. A breeze picked up and stirred the boughs of pines. The sound of water was nearby. A Canine face peered close to his own. "Huh? What?"

"Sir, are you all right?"

The Canine stood up. "Ah, you are awake."

The Canine was tall, two meters tall. He was lithe yet strong, with broad shoulders. His face was black and tan striped, with bright green inquisitive eyes peering down a black snout five centimeters long. He was dressed in colorful fabrics of red and brown. Red ribbons hung off his shoulders as epaulettes, and from a belt woven of flax. Over the Canine's shoulder was slung a woven net in which he carried three large pink-speckled eggs. On his back hung a crossbow. The Canine had a long single braid of black and tan hair that was tied at the end with beads of black glass.

Renender rubbed his eyes. Was this part of his dream? "Where am I?"

The Canine smiled. "You are here." It was an easy answer.

"But where is here?"

"The mountain path," said the Canine. "Not many Humans come here. Are you visiting the monastery?"

Renender stood up. "Monastery? I, I don't know."

"Did you come through the caves?"

Renender looked behind him at the cave opening, below the huge stone statue of a monstrous Human beast. That was real. Renender remembered his dark journey through the subterranean world.

"Easy now," said the Canine. "It is clear some darkness is behind you. You may come with me. I will take you to a place where you will find light and peace."

"Who are you?" Renender was fully awake now.

"I am Aleph," said the Canine. "And who are you?"

"I am Renender, from Lupus City."

"Hm. I don't know that place. But perhaps you can tell me along the way. Come, can you walk?"

"Yes," said Renender. He slung the satchel that lay on the bench over his shoulder and took a few steps along the path, then paused. He looked down into the valley at the distant red-tiled roofs of a Canine settlement. Dappled sunlight danced with the sound of tinkling water. Fragrances filled the air, drifting on the breezes. An almost inaudible hum or ringing seemed to echo through the mountains, as from a deep bass bell, or was it his imagination? It was there and yet it wasn't. It was felt more than heard. Renender sighed. What a peaceful place.

"Come," said Aleph. "We will walk." The two proceeded down the path.

"What is this place?" asked Renender after some moments walking in silence.

"This is the valley that my village calls home," said Aleph.

"Does it have a name?"

Aleph crinkled his brows as he contemplated the question, trying to think of an answer. "No, I don't think so. At least I've never thought about it before. I don't remember anyone calling it by a particular name. I suppose its name is 'The Valley That My Village Calls Home.'" He smiled. "Yes, that sounds right."

"Do you think it's strange it doesn't have another name?" asked Renender.

Aleph looked a little puzzled. "Not really. There are other valleys that my village does not call home. That's the distinction. Isn't that the purpose of a name? To give a distinction?"

Renender was silent for a minute. "It's logical," he finally said.

The two continued down the mountain path in near silence for about fifteen minutes. But the valley was not silent. Reptiles, insects, wind and water filled the air. As he walked, Renender was surprised to realize his knees did not bother him at all. In fact he felt strangely rejuvenated the further down they went. Each new footfall was steadier than the last, and his senses seemed to be sharper than he'd remembered them being, for many years in fact. Cares lifted from his mind until he almost couldn't remember why, or if, he'd ever been in a hurry about anything.

"Look! Here's one of my favorite streams," said Aleph. The Canine darted off the side of the path and down a slight ravine. Here a small waterfall tumbled down the mountainside and formed a pool with a pebbly beach before the water tumbled down again from the other side. Aleph carefully set down his net of eggs, his crossbow, then shed his clothes. He laughed as he splashed naked in the cold clear water. He submerged himself in the pool, then darted straight up and out several times, laughing each time he shot up. Tiny rivulets of beaded water ran down his black and tan lithe and hairy body.

Renender followed, apprehensive at first, until he realized with some surprise that he'd shed his own clothes and skipped into the water after Aleph. "Oh! It's cold!" Renender exclaimed.

"It is?" said Aleph, and he laughed. "Yes! It is! Ha-ha!" And the two began splashing each other with the cold crystal clear water.

After a few minutes of horsing around, they started turning over rocks and exploring the bugs and larvae they exposed. Then, ankles and toes and fingers sufficiently cold, they plopped down on a mossy rocky bank in the sun to dry.

"The sun feels so warm and nice," said Renender. He looked about and noticed the lichen covered bark of trees, hanging mosses and broad leaves shimmering in the breeze, shimmering almost to the ringing he felt, but he couldn't hold onto the thought for long.

"How long were you in the caves?" asked Aleph. "I've peeked in a few times. It's full of leaves and dust and spider webs, and strange statues. It's much nicer out here in the sunlight and fresh air."

Renender had to think about it a moment. "Caves? Oh, yes. Well, I don't really remember just now. I think, I think I was there for awhile, searching, crawling, escaping."

"What were you escaping from?"

"Uh, hm." A shadow passed over Renender's mind as he tried to remember. Only pieces of images came to him. "I remember a cold glowing face, a young man in black leather, very scary." A shiver ran down his spine as he saw the image in his mind. "But there was also music, dancing, a smoky chamber. It's, it's hard to remember now exactly."

"The music and dancing sound fun," said Aleph. "All that in the caves?"

Renender thought hard. "Yes, somewhere in the caves." He looked up at the mountain from where he'd come. "Yes, there was fun. I remember having fun." Renender smiled.

"What were you looking for? You said you were looking for something."

"I was, yes. Looking for, looking for, hm. It's a little foggy now. But I think, I think I was looking for, help. Yes, I was looking for help."

"Help with what?"

"I'm, not sure exactly. It seemed important. I'm sure it was important."

Two singing flying reptiles flew into view. They perched on a tree branch overhanging the pool and started to serenade. Renender and Aleph watched and listened for a while until they flitted away.

"Come on," said Aleph. "Let's go. I'm dry now. Are you?"

"Yes. Ok, let's go." The two got up and retrieved their clothes and belongings. Renender struggled with his pants. They seemed too long, and too loose. He rolled up the cuffs and tightened the belt he had. His shirt was extra billowy. Aleph was doing the same.

Another fifteen minutes passed with Renender and Aleph not speaking much. Before long the path leveled off.

"Let's run," said Aleph. He took off at a gallop, while carefully hugging the net of eggs to his stomach. Renender followed. They ran for about fifty meters until the path ended at a rocky outcrop. They ran to the finish laughing and laughing.

From the outcrop, they looked down onto the inhabited valley floor. Streams fell down cascades and watered gardens and trees. Little houses with red-tiled roofs and upturned corners lay clustered around a big stone building with a tall bell tower. Little columns of smoke curled up from cooking fires. Fragrant smells of good food wafted up to their nostrils.

"What's that?" asked Renender pointing to the big building. He laughed at the sound of his own voice, for it sounded higher than normal, as if he'd inhaled helium from a balloon.

"That's the monastery," said Aleph, in a voice equally high and funny sounding. "That's where I live. Come on, let's go down."

Stone steps led down from the rocky outcropping. They trotted down, sometimes skipping one and two steps at a time. Renender's pants fell down to his ankles more than once and his arms got caught in his oversized billowy shirt. His star necklace dangled low against his skinny smooth chest. By the time they reached the bottom, they were two young boys, Human and Canine.

The stone steps terminated at a well-manicured lawn about twenty meters wide and fifty long. At its edges grew lighting fig trees, not quite yet in radiant bloom, and the skeletons of flame maples, their spindly red arms arching over the grass. A small brook that tumbled down the mountain wove its way around the lawn and formed its outer border. Irises, daffodils and herbs grew along its tiny banks. A small red arching bridge led over the stream to the cluster of red-roofed cottages and the big monastery building on its small hill.

"This is a very nice place," said Renender. He set down his shoes and let his feet enjoy the soft grass. It was cool and soft. A little warm breeze blew through the valley. From all around, in hidden and secret places, the tinkling sound of bells was all around, barely heard, a sound on the wind.

"This is home," said Aleph. He too set down his shoes, net of eggs and the bulky crossbow. "I'll introduce you to the others."

Renender didn't have time to ask who the others were before the sounds of laughter and play came from doors opening in the cottages nearest the bridge. Canine children burst out, chasing one another in a game of tag. Some saw Aleph and Renender standing on the lawn. Hollers of "Hoy! It's Aleph!" rang out, and the group of children ran over the bridge and across the lawn toward them.

"Hallow!" yelled Aleph at their approach. Boys and girls in candy-colored outfits with red ribbons surrounded Renender and Aleph. There were about twenty, half girls and half boys. All were smaller, seemingly younger, than Aleph. But one could not tell by looks alone. How old was the boy Aleph? And how old the boy Renender?

"Who are you?" said a boy to Renender.

"You look funny," said a girl.

"He's a Human," said Aleph.

"No way!" said a girl.

"You have no hair," said another.

"Not much anyway," said a boy.

"Look at his nose!" said another. "It's hardly there."

"There are no such things as Humans," said a girl, the smallest of all.

"I'm real," said Renender. He ran passed the littlest girl, touched her shoulder and leapt aside laughing. "You're it! Ha-ha. I can play tag, too."

The clustered group broke up in laughter and chase as "It!" passed from one to another. They ran about in and out of doors, around the cottages and trees and shrubs. The game went on for a long while. In the midst of the play, Aleph broke off and returned to the grassy area to collect his and Renender's things, including the net of eggs and crossbow, and took them up to the monastery. Meanwhile the other children continued to play as the shadows lengthened in the valley and evening came early, the sun disappearing behind the mountaintops.

Renender ran behind a big fig tree, out of breath with a big smile on his face. He was having fun, so much fun, even though his pants kept falling down. Then a loud chime rang out from the bell tower of the monastery. Its sound echoed throughout the valley. The children stopped their game and they congregated before the steps to the big building.

"What's that for?" asked Renender.

A boy replied, "Time to eat. And time to sing!" Then the boy broke out in a melodious song, a falsetto carried from his voice to the air as effortless as breathing. The others took up his melody, and soon the whole troop was singing on their way up the stairs. Renender could not understand a word they sang, but he was lifted by the song and the moment, and almost floated up the stairs.

The monastery stood on a slight rocky hill rising above the grassy valley. The top of the hill was leveled and the building's foundations were great pink stone blocks cut with precision at some time in the distant past. A wide staircase of twelve wide steps, rising from the ground to the first floor, reached great double doors. Granaries, pantries and kitchens were on the first level.

The children entered the main entrance through the huge doors. Inside, the light was dim, but lit with torches. A hallway led to the store rooms, and another staircase led further up to the main hall. Up these the children ran singing, until they emerged into the great room. High vertical windows let in the fading light of the setting sun. The expanse was largely empty. Huge woven carpets covered the wooden floor. At the far end blazed a mighty fire in a huge stone hearth. To its right was a spiral staircase leading up to the bell tower. To the left of the hearth was another spiral staircase leading down to the lower floor and onto further subterranean rooms. A long low table sat off center in the hall. There were no chairs, but about thirty soft cushions were on the floor around the rectangular table. On these the children would sit and eat, or sit and read. Indeed, along the opposite walls were huge bookcases filled with old scrolls and books. On the table was laid out a modest feast, and Aleph stood beside it waiting for the noisy hungry children to assemble. There were bread rolls and soups, salad and sweet drinks, as well as bubbly water. Plates and bowls and cups were arranged before each cushion.

One child took Renender aside and gave him clothes that fit his small childish frame. "That's a pretty star," said the boy, referring to Renender's amulet.

"Thank you," said Renender. "I, I think someone gave it to me."

The children sat at favored places. Renender hung back, not knowing where he should sit, but Aleph motioned for him to sit at his side near the head of the table nearest the great fire. The chatter and laughter of young voices died down. Then Aleph said, "This evening was my turn to prepare our meal. For the main dish, I've made a special omelet from the eggs of the ice dragon. It was a great trek to the snow and ice fields high above our valley. With stealth and cunning I stole into the cave of the ice dragon while she was out. I gathered these eggs for our feast. On the way back down the mountain, I met a new friend, Renender." Aleph grinned at Renender and gave him a wink. "Renender, too, was on a quest, and journeyed through caves and darkness. I found him near the Cave of Humans. Now he joins our merry group. We thank the mountains, we thank the gardens, we thank the skies, the sun and the stars, for our happiness and our nourishment and our health. With thanks, let us eat."

"Eat!" shouted all the children. And the feast began.

Renender was famished. He couldn't remember the last time he had eaten anything. Looking down at his plate and bowl, there were no utensils. But he quickly realized none of the other children had any either. So he ladled soup into his bowl, scooped up a heap of omelet onto his plate, alongside a pile of salad, and dug in with his fingers. He picked up his bowl and slurped his soup like everyone else. The meal was scrumptious. The bread was warm, and there was honey dripping in glowing sweetness. The salad was full of spiky ticklish leaves and fragrant tasting herbs and flowers tossed with a sauce like sweet vinegar. The soup was thick with greens and mushrooms. The omelet tasted magical. Never had he eaten such a dish. His mind was filled with visions of cold blue skies and cold bright stars over fields of ice and snow. Renender almost thought he heard the cry of the dragon in his musings.

Amidst the chitter and the chatter of the children, Renender asked Aleph, "Where did all this food come from? Did you really make it?"

Aleph laughed. "We all know how to cook here. The valley and meadow has all kinds of things to eat. We'll show you tomorrow, and then you can learn to cook too."

Renender grinned, leafy greens sticking to his teeth. He was glad. He loved to eat, and would love to know how to make such good food.

After the last sticky finger had been licked, and the last satisfying burp burped, the children heaved their happy selves up off the cushions and began gathering their dishes and leftover food for cleaning and storing. Renender offered to help, but he really didn't know where anything went. Aleph was close to the fire and beckoned for Renender to join him. Aleph stoked the fire with a poker and watched the sparks crackle and fly up.

Renender looked up at the high tall windows. Any light coming in from outside was fading fast. As he stood there, the light changed from blue to indigo to black. Now only the reflection of light from the great hearth inside glowed in the windows. He turned to Aleph and asked, "Does anyone else live here? Any big people?"

Aleph stood by the warm fire and fiddled with a toothpick in his teeth. "Big people? What do you mean?"

"Big people. Like grownups."

"No, there are just us. I don't know what grownups are. Is that a Human word?"

"I guess so," said Renender. "Human kids don't live by themselves."

"Why not?" asked Aleph. "There are thirty of us here in our valley. You know all of us now. We take care of everything. There is nothing for 'big people' to do. They might just get in the way, if they're so big."

"I guess I meant older," said Renender. "How old are you, Aleph?"

"Oh, I'm very old I guess." He laughed. "We've lived here a long time." Pointing to the bookcases, he said, "Do you see those scrolls and books? We wrote those. I can still remember getting ink on my fingers. We haven't made any new scrolls in awhile. They're very old now. Sometimes Uriel makes marks in some of them. She watches the stars in the sky to see when it's the next time to ring the big bell."

"Ring the bell?" asked Renender. "What does that mean?"

"The big bell in the bell tower," said Aleph looking up at the ceiling. "Every once in awhile we have to ring it. Uriel knows when."

While Renender and Aleph were talking, the other children returned in ones, twos, threes and fours to the great hall and the wide hearth. More wood was brought in and the fire roared and blazed magnificently. Two boys rolled in a barrel of cider, and cups were distributed so everyone could enjoy the strong apple freshness. Others brought out rolls of bedding and pillows. They all made themselves comfortable in a semi circle around the hearth.

"Stories!" cried out a girl.

"Stories!" shouted the rest.

Aleph spoke. "Renender, we like to tell stories most nights before we fall off to sleep. Will you be the first and tell us a story? Something from your village perhaps, or a favorite story you know?"

"I. I don't know," stammered Renender. "I don't think I know any."

"Everyone knows stories," said a girl.

"Tell us a fun one."

"It doesn't have to be long."

"Make it exciting!"

"Ha-ha. Don't pressure Renender too much," said Aleph. "It's ok, Renender. Go ahead."

Renender thought and thought as hard as he could, as fast as he could. In truth, he didn't remember much before the morning when he met Aleph up by the mountain cave. But by and by a short tale did enter his thoughts, coming almost unbidden.

"Ok. Here's one." And Renender began.

> "Two children sat opposite with a pail of water between.
>
> The one held a paper sailboat,
>
> The other a hard-shelled snail.
>
> The boat set out gently on the water in the pale,
>
> The snail manned the boat, guiding the course of the sail.
>
> A tempest arose and the sailing snail stood steadfast and brave,
>
> Foot firmly planted on the paper deck, never mind the fierceness of the gale.
>
> The boat took on water, the paper deck collapsed.
>
> The snail climbed the rigging to reach the top of the mast.
>
> When all was nearly lost, the waters of the pail convulsed.
>
> The snail flowed forth on the headwaters of the tide
>
> Till grounded on rock he found himself safe,
>
> But never again did he see his boat, all torn asunder as papier-mâché."

"That's what I had," said Renender, a bit embarrassed.

"I liked it," said a boy. "It rhymed."

"Just sort of," said a girl.

"Thank you, Renender," said Aleph. Then he told a story. It was a tale of primeval forces, battles in the heights, of lightning and rock, thunder and rain, of ice dragons and sky dragons, tales of renown that few or none other than Aleph knew or remembered. The tale was written in an old book.

The fire in the hearth roared, the flames licked higher. The shadows of the children cast onto the walls flickered and danced in ghoulish and macabre forms.

When Aleph was done with his tale, it was Uriel who lifted up her voice and told of the movement of stars and of planets that circled and chased one another, met up and conjoined, then parted and sped away. The tale then wove around the happenings of two giants, Gr-Fen and his mate RR-Men, who turned a great wheel of stars in the sky. Renender felt almost that he'd heard such a tale once or more before in a land and a time he no longer remembered.

The fire finally died down to slow flickers and glowing coals. Some children had dozed off and more were succumbing to the slumber of night. Renender tried to stay awake, listening of Gr-Fen and RR-Men reach the bottom, then turn the wheel up again. And then Renender too succumbed to sleep.

He wrestled with fitful dreams during the course of the night. On some occasions the sound of one of the Canine children muttering in her sleep brought him out of his own reveries, or the stirring of another squirming about trying to find a comfortable position. Now it was a late hour, or perhaps an early one. A howling wind was sweeping down the mountain flanks, pummeling the valley with hard gusts. Bells tinkled in the wind. The monastery groaned and creaked from the onslaught. Only embers lit the hearth, but the wind found its way even there, and embers glowed ever brighter. Then a sound carried on the wind cried out in the night.

What was that? Renender sat up with a start. Shapes were moving about in the great hall. Faint shadows crossed the floor. The sound again. Other children sat up. Suddenly the fire blazed forth. Aleph stood beside it, tossing wood onto the embers where they burst into crackling flame.

"Shh," Aleph cautioned to the others.

The cry sounded again outside. It was the screech of some beast.

"Ice dragon," one child said.

The others whispered it also. "Ice dragon."

Aleph seemed to transform in flicker of the fire, once a boy, now a man, a great warrior. Aleph ran from the fire, leaping over bedding and heads, across the hall to disappear down the great stairs. The place was alive with motion.

"Stay here by the fire," said Uriel nearby to Renender. Children that had run down the staircase returned grown, carrying tall spears. Most of the Canines remained children, and Renender remained a child. He was frightened. The sound of the wind battering the walls from outside was louder. Then BOOM. BOOM. Something was on the roof. The great bell in the bell tower chimed. There were shouts from the lower hall.

A warrior came up the great stairs. "It is on the roof. Stay here."

Renender huddled with the other children near the downward spiral staircase, blankets and pillows heaped around them. The wind wailed outside, with innumerable bells straining to be heard. Renender thought he heard bells somewhere below him. Then the wild cry of the ice dragon sounded again. Clomp, clomp, clomp sounded the beast on the tiles of the roof. Renender peered up at the tall narrow windows. Something was there. Then he saw it, the bright glowing red-orange of the beast's eye in one window, its other eye at the next. Renender felt it stare right through him, and his heart was struck cold. It saw him.

The sky behind the dragon lit up. The beast turned its gaze away from the windows and away from Renender. It leapt from the high roof of the monastery and landed upon the green.

There was shouting outside. Aleph's voice carried on the wind. "The lighting figs!" As by magic the valley erupted in light of its own. Each fruiting fig was lit from a source within. Then the red maples loosed flames of red as buds and blossoms and leaves sent fireless flames to mingle with the yellow of the lighting figs. Through the windows inside where Renender was, the entire valley looked aflame. The ice dragon screeched again, and battle was met with the warrior Canines before the monastery's great doors. The shouts from outside grew louder and more urgent. The beast screamed. It climbed the great stairs outside and threw itself against the doors. The building shuddered. The children inside howled in fear. The Canine warriors fought against the dragon outside.

A mortal fear struck Renender's heart each time the beast screeched, and he remembered the terror of its eyes. The dragon threw its girth against the great doors again. Renender heard the timbers creak and snap and break. Light flooded up from the lighting figs and flame maples. A powerful steam and stench rose from the shattered doors and the beast cried again. It started to slither up and in, but was met by more warriors just inside the first hall.

Renender was terrified. He was not safe. He bounded away from the others and raced down the spiral staircase to the levels below. Where would he be safe? Where could he hide? Down and down and down he went, several levels below ground level. He darted down a dank hall lit dimly only by torches. He slowed. He could hear through the stone foundations and walls the destruction caused by the beast, the fierce fighting of the Canines.

Then Renender perceived a soft tinkling sound from the far end of this hall. Bells, strange tinkling bells. They called to Renender, urging him closer. He crept along the hall until he came to a closed door at its end. A light shown from under the door. Renender pushed. It gave way. He tumbled into a narrow room lit by torches.

Torches lined both walls, and the walls drew nearer to one another the further in. Renender moved further in. At the far end was a dais, and on its platform was a strange thing. A white suit as of silk was suspended on a perpendicular stick frame. It was a body suit. As Renender looked at it, the suit took on a dizzying array of colors, pulsating to the sound of tinkling bells, reacting to the struggles outside and the plight of terror in the hearts of the Canines.

Renender ascended the few steps and stood before the suit, completely mesmerized by its magic. He reached up with a hand and touched the glowing fabric with just one finger. A flame shot out and filled Renender with electricity. Brilliant light exploded into the room, through the monastery, into the face of the dragon. The big bell tolled. The ice dragon released a blood-curdling cry of hate and defeat. The walls of the monastery shuddered. The beast was overwhelmed and withdrew. And when the blinding light had faded, Renender stood alone wearing the suit. They were one.

40 THE HENGE PLAIN

The afternoon and evening since the Roadhouse seemed unending. The dust had been choking and, to Cornelius, near unbearable. Riding behind Roger on the Human's motorbike over hill and dale had rendered Cornelius' butt one big bruise. Hill and dale indeed. It might have sounded pleasant, but this was an entirely off road trip, for there were no roads in Canius. Maybe it had been fun for the ones riding at the head of the refugee columns. For everyone else following behind, including Cornelius, it was all choking dust.

That was yesterday. During the night a rainstorm swept through the plains. Cornelius and Roger had huddled together next to the bike with a tarp thrown over all for protection. It'd been late, and the storm gave no opportunity for tents. But there had been no respite from the rain and neither had slept much. It was now near the end of the next day, and the rains still fell, sometimes driving, sometimes drizzling. Everything was mud, and they'd had to stop many times to free tires and bikes from the sticky mud. Cornelius wished for the choking dust now, but the rain wasn't letting up anytime soon.

The wind was getting stronger, the rain harder, and the temperature colder. Cornelius shivered behind Roger. Despite the reptilian leather jacket a Canine had leant to him, Cornelius was still cold. His front was a little warmer, protected from the blast by Roger's back, but not by much. Carrying on a conversation was well nigh fruitless over the din of wind, rain and the many motorcycles. The troop was heading up a gentle incline to a broad hilltop, a place without protection from the wind, but at least the rain flowed away. Cornelius dwelt in his own thoughts, there was little else to do. The landscape was fast dimming as the sun, hidden all day above the storm clouds, proceeded to set, casting the gloomy world into a near complete darkness. The terrain leveled off and Roger cut the engine. They stopped. Kickstands went down as all the bikes parked.

"We'll camp here for the night," said Roger. Cornelius nodded and they climbed off the bike. "The sun had better come up tomorrow or we'll have a problem with fuel." Solar collectors powered the bikes, but they'd been useless the past day with all the cloud cover.

Tents were quickly going up so cooking fires could be lit. There were many mouths to feed. Cornelius helped as best he could. Everyone had to pitch in. Tonight the cooking fires would be a challenge, again.

Cornelius and Roger worked quickly setting their tent and securing it in the mud beneath the wet grass. Then they assisted in the common work to make certain everyone was fed and any first aid rendered. Cornelius helped set up the kitchen tents. Despite several attempts, he could not get a fire lit. Eventually three motorcycles were brought in so their batteries could be used as impromptu cookers. The bikes would not be able to travel far come morning without the sun to power them.

That night in the cooking tent some older Canine women brought in a group of children while Cornelius was trying to light fires for the cooking pots. They were orphans, or at least children who had been separated from their families. Last to come in with the group was a small Human child, alone and lonely, despondent and removed from the rest. Their Canine handlers intended to feed these children first before the tent was swamped with all the others looking for a steaming cup and hearty bowl. But the longer it took to light the fires, the more people started to arrive, and to wait. The little Human wandered over to Cornelius.

"Are we going to eat soon?" asked the boy.

"Huh? What? Oh, hello there," said Cornelius noticing the little boy. "It won't be too long now. We'll be getting these going here soon. It's very wet."

"I'm hungry," said the boy.

Cornelius tousled the boy's head. "And you're cold. Wait right here." Cornelius retrieved a cup of hot broth water from a pot. "Here, this will warm you up until the food is ready."

The boy eagerly took the cup from Cornelius, holding it and its steaming contents in his little hands. "Thank you, Sir."

"Now what's your name?"

"Nuttin," said the boy.

"Nuttin? That's an unusual name.

"I named myself that," said the boy. "Because I have nothing. Nuttin at all."

"You'll be ok," said Cornelius." This journey is hard on all of us. But we'll all be ok."

A Canine woman came over. "Corneze, can you help us with the stew? Everyone is starting to arrive."

Cornelius nodded. He turned back to the little boy and said, "Nuttin, I've got to help the others now. But I'll look in on you later."

Cornelius was busy with the kitchen duties for over an hour. When he was done and finally took time to eat for himself, he looked for the boy but couldn't find him. Cornelius eventually made his way back to his own tent. Roger was already there.

Cornelius changed into some dry clothing, though it was only a poncho that came down to his calves.

"How much further do we have to go to get to where we're headed?" Cornelius asked Roger.

"That's a hard question to answer," said Roger. "The Alpha isn't in any set place."

"Is there a rendezvous point?"

"Not that I know of."

"Then we're just hoping to run into him in all this expanse?"

"It's not that haphazard, My Boy. The Alpha will find us. He'll know we're out here."

In the few days since the attack and flight from the Roadhouse, Roger had taken to calling Cornelius 'My Boy.' Cornelius hadn't been called 'Boy' in many, many years, except by Renender on the occasion where a situation was critical or dangerous. Did they think he couldn't handle himself? Roger took a personal responsibility for Cornelius since the death of his wife Shont.

"Roger, can I ask how you and Shont came together? I mean, it's not that common for Canines and Humans to marry, is it?"

Roger became sullen for a moment. He often was melancholy, and Cornelius had been reticent about broaching any subject involving Shont.

"I'm sorry if the subject is too sensitive for you. I…."

"No, no it's ok. It was several years back. I had managed some establishments in Big City, but I wanted a change. You see in my youth I'd been rather reckless, and had gotten into some bar fights. I wasn't always on the winning wide. As you can see, my face isn't so attractive. I'm not one to shy away from a fight if I think I'm in the right. But like I said, I don't always come out on top. Well, after awhile it was obvious to me that Humans tend to shy away from a face that's not too pretty. Business suffered. Some of my Canine associates suggested I work more exclusively with a Canine clientele. They put out feelers and got me an interview for a position at the Roadhouse. Shont took an immediate liking to me, and well one thing just led to another. Shont was a widow, and I guess she just saw through my physical appearance. I mean, who else would be interested in such an ugly man besides a Canine? They're just a more accepting lot."

"I see," said Cornelius. "Thank you, Roger."

"No worries My Boy. I think I'll take a little walk if you don't mind."

"Ok. I'll be here when you get back, if you want to talk some more. Don't get lost out there."

"Mm," answered Roger with a grunt. He donned a rain parka and floppy hat and left the tent, walking out into the wet night.

Cornelius putzed around the tent. It was a three-meter cube with the top pointed to facilitate the off-flow of rain. Not that much room, especially for two, but Cornelius had stayed in much smaller, and it was better than the tarp from the night before. What made it so claustrophobic was the weather outside. Cornelius had very few belongings of his own, just his knives and his satchel. He rummaged through his little bag. There was the titanium whip from the enigmatic G. He had a razor and a small mirror, neither of which he'd used for days, not since he and Naemi, the older Naemi with the blinking eyes, had traveled down the Channel Rift. That seemed so long ago now. He looked at himself in the mirror. What a grizzled face looked back at him. Maybe tomorrow he'd attempt a shave.

A soft keepsake cloth bag was also there. Cornelius took it out. He untied the little drawstring and withdrew his treasure, the Precession Star amulet that Naemi, the original Naemi he'd known for years, had given to him. It was warm to the touch and had an inner glow. It was a curious object really, made of a precious metal, probably titanium, but maybe silver, and a precious gem, possibly diamond. He knew that the current Naemi had a matching amulet. He fingered the contours of its shape. Where was Naemi now? What adventure, what assignment was she on? Would he see her again? Also in the little bag was the red ribbon he'd found in the stream in the Canius Mountains on their way to the find the glider in order to get to the Lake Docks. What an adventure this week had been, and it wasn't over. He put the objects back into his satchel and bedded down for the night. Sleep came quickly.

Cornelius woke in the dark early hours. The absence of the sound of rain woke him up. There was still plenty of noise. Roger was in the tent snoring. Others snored in nearby tents. The wind still rapped against the tent flaps. Cornelius pulled on some trousers under his poncho and slipped out into the night.

The rain had indeed stopped, for now, but heavy black clouds still filled the sky and threatened still more rain. Wind still howled and lightning bolts pierced the gloom, reaching down from the blackness to pierce the wet ground. Thunder rasped the air.

Cornelius squatted on the balls of his feet in the wet trampled grass before the entrance to the tent. Little lights twinkled here and there, signaling some of the refugees were still awake. Most was blackness all around except when the lightning blazed across the sky. Then light reflected from the hundreds of motorbikes like gleaming gems on the ground.

Against the black horizon, shadows moved in the shadows. Amid the wind and thunder, Cornelius could hear what sounded like the bellowing of huge beasts. When the lightning struck, he could see what looked like a herd of gargantuans, strange monsters out of the wastes of Canius and the world of disturbed dreams.

Some drops of rain began falling again. Cornelius was so annoyed. He looked up at the black sky. It was so close he felt he could touch the heavy clouds if only he stood and reached up. He stared into the black horizon. Just in the foreground of the shadows within shadows he thought he could see a solitary standing figure. With each lightning flash the figure appeared closer, or more vivid. The eyes stood out, eyes that glowed blue-white in the dark, eyes that reflected the lightning. The rain fell harder. The howls of shadowy beasts were more frantic. Cornelius was mesmerized. What was out there? The driving rain obscured whatever it was he thought he saw.

He'd had enough of the rain. It suddenly occurred to him that maybe he could do something about it. He stood up. He inhaled. He blew a steady breath into the night. The winds changed direction. The black clouds rolled back, dragging the storm away far to the northwest. Why hadn't he done this long before? Stars filled the opening sky. Starlight twinkled on his wet eyebrows and eyelashes, on the many pools of water, on the wet tents and bikes. And in the distance Cornelius saw the bright eyes of the mysterious figure in the far distance. He even thought he caught the glint of starlight reflected in a smile. Then both eyes and smile disappeared, as if the figure had turned around, or simply vanished altogether. Without the cloud cover the air grew noticeably colder. Cornelius turned and lifted the tent flap and returned to bed.

Drums woke Cornelius up. Drums before dawn. He roused himself from a thick sleep. The drums were close, but as far as Cornelius knew, there were no drums among the possessions of the refugees. Drums. What did it mean? He looked around. Roger was gone. Then he heard shouts, calls and yells. Was there trouble? A great clamor was raised in the camp. Pots were banged and pans were clanged and anything in the camp that could be added to the clamor was added to the clamor. And there were the drums.

Cornelius threw off his poncho, an arm getting stuck on its way out, then it was free. He pulled on his trousers. One leg got stuck and he fell over onto the bedding, cursing. He got back up and got into the trousers. Where was his shirt? Never mind. He flung open the tent flap and ran outside.

People were everywhere, looking and pointing, facing northwest. The light was blue-grey. Dawn had not yet overtaken the world, but it was coming fast. The east was orange. Cornelius pushed his way through the crowd to behold the source of the drumming.

Marching up the north side of the hill was a procession of Canines, more than fifty strong in military style formation. The Canines were tall and strong. Some held aloft banners of green and brown, their pennants fluttering in the light breeze. Others carried spears, and others carried the drums, beating them in unison. Boom. Boom. The Canines all wore huge headdresses of long iridescent feathers. The feathers bounced and swayed over their heads in rhythm to the drumbeats. Boom. Boom. Besides the headdresses, the Canines wore only loincloths. Their feet were bare and they wore no baubles, bangles, anklets, bracelets or necklaces. Some did sport piercings of smoothed and shaped bone in various places on their bodies.

They stopped at the edge of the hilltop. Cornelius pushed through to the head of the crowd, then he stumbled and fell upon one knee, his fingers catching his fall. The drums abruptly ceased. Cornelius looked up and saw a great Canine larger than the others, with a more elaborate headdress, break from the formation and come forward. Cornelius raised himself off the ground and stood. And as he stood, the nascent sun blazed forth from the horizon bathing the Canine procession in golden light. Cornelius' own shadow cast a single shade onto the great Canine, such that in the Canine's eyes, Cornelius was a dark silhouette. But in Cornelius' shadow, the Canine radiated a light like a star's corona that can only be seen in an eclipse.

One voice out of the procession called to all present, "Make way for the Alpha. Alpha Trifid is come."

Some of the refugee Canines behind Cornelius gathered themselves together as a delegation and moved passed Cornelius, approaching the Alpha. Most of the Humans held back. The great Canine raised a hand and the delegation halted. Then the Alpha spoke. His voice was a bit higher pitch than Cornelius expected, but the timbre of his voice fell upon all ears that heard him as melodious and full of gaiety.

"Weary and hungry travelers. You will rest here this day. Ease your tired muscles, relax your cares, and fill your bellies." Then he extended both arms toward the refugees, palms raised. "Here is beauty and bounty."

To the amazement of the refugees and Cornelius, the ground about them sprang to life. Flowers sprouted up, lupines and clovers, irises and bluebells, red flame flowers, daisies and lilies. Spring peas curled and unfolded, spreading along the grasses in tendrils, ripening fresh for the eating. Cauliflowers, carrots, tubers and sweet herbs also appeared. All good things ready and ripe for picking and eating. The Alpha commanded a power over nature that was as close to magic as Cornelius had ever seen. Then the Canines in the Alpha's party separated. Six of the mighty host came from the back carrying an immense burden, the carcass of a great feathered, tusked beast.

"This juvenile hunta died in the night's storm," said the Alpha. "Prepare knives and fires. You will feast today."

Murmurings in the crowd of refugees turned into cheers of praise. The Canines with their burden of meat entered camp, and the refugees met them, with others beginning to scour the hilltop to harvest herb and vegetable.

"Where among you is Shont?" asked the Alpha. Many then fell silent, and Cornelius felt a pit growing in his stomach. The Human Roger stepped forward and passed Cornelius.

Bowing low, Roger approached the Alpha. In a low voice he said, "Lord,

Shont is not among us. Your mother fell by the evil of Markhab in the battle at the Roadhouse."

The Alpha was silent for a moment and he bowed his head. Then he stepped forward and said, "Roger, walk with me please." The two then parted company from the crowd to speak in private. The rest of the Alpha's troupe broke up and mingled with the refugees, assisting them in their needs and preparations.

Cornelius found himself standing alone, knowing not what to do. He was shocked to learn that Shont was the Alpha's mother.

The Canine woman who tended the orphan children came up beside him and said "Corneze, you can help in the kitchen tent."

Cornelius finally had an opportunity to demonstrate some of his knifing skills not in combat. Outside of the main kitchen tent, Cornelius helped the Canines, refugees and Canians, to butcher the great beast. It was strung up on poles made of the spears of the Canians. Cornelius had never seen a beast like this, had not even heard of a hunta. The cut its throat and drained the blood into vats. It would be made into blood sausages. They skinned the beast and gutted it. The hide would later be tanned. They removed the intestines and cleaned them for the preparation of the sausages that would then be smoked. The butchers carved out shanks, the brisket, flanks and ribs, all the way down to cuts of loin, rounds, tips and hocks. Strips of flesh were hung on poles to dry in the sun as jerky. After a few hours the beast was fully rendered into meal-sized pieces. The remaining bones of the skeleton were reduced to pieces fit for boiling. Nothing was wasted.

Cornelius was splattered with blood and gore. Somehow he'd gotten more than the other butchers. And the flies seemed to be attracted to him best. Just lucky he guessed. He gathered his knives and headed down the western side of the hill where he was told a rocky path led down to a stream. On the way, he passed the motorcycles on the edge of the camp. As he watched, mechanical arms unfolded from the bikes' chassis, releasing solar panels that faced the sun, to charge the many batteries that had been drained to dangerously low levels over the past few days of darkness.

His entourage of flies followed him the whole way down the hill. Swatting at them proved futile. He found the stream, whose source was a spring bubbling out of a crevasse in a rock outcrop that looked like the remnant of a crumbling old wall. A short distance from the spring was a deep pool shaded by willow trees overhanging the water. Water hyacinths swayed and bobbed on its shores. Cornelius stripped and waded into the pool. It was a comfortable tepid temperature. After a few minutes of splashing and dunking, he was cleansed of the blood and gore. Wading back out, he took up his clothes, shaking off the flies, and began washing them, agitating the water to loosen the mess. While he stood in the water, tiny fish nibbled at his toes and the hairs on his legs. The water was stained red; the stream soon carried the effluence away. He wrung out the excess water from his pants and shirt and laid them out on rocks to dry in the sun. The flies were gone. After he cleaned his knives, he lay down naked on the soft grass, his dark body enjoying the warmth of the afternoon sun. Cornelius gazed at the few white fluffy clouds slowly drifting by, seeing in them shapes of feathers and feathered canyons until, with drooping eyelids, he napped.

"There he is, over there," a voice called out. Cornelius awoke with a start, and for a moment did not remember where he was or why he was naked. He jumped up, found his pants on the rock and jumped into them. Two people drew near from around the side of the hill. One was Human. It was Roger. The other was one of the big Canian Canines, still wearing only his loincloth, but no feathered headdress. He was immensely muscular. His fur was dark brown, almost black. They came up to Cornelius as he was putting on his shirt.

The Canine spoke, his voice gruff. "Corneze, is that your name? I am Rokket, Captain of the Alpha's Fifty Guard. Come with us."

Cornelius extended his hand, but Rokket offered no handshake. "What's up? What's going on?"

"Everything's fine, Cornelius," said Roger. "Please come with us. It's about the information you carry. The information you brought to Shont."

"Oh that. Yes. Yes, ok." He was about to gather his knives, but Rokket got to them first. He picked them up, studied them.

"These are good blades," said the Canine. "Are you a warrior? These are not a cook's knives." He handed them to Cornelius.

"I am. Quite a good one, too."

"Hm. We may see one day. Come. You will see what we must do with your information. This Human has told me what you brought."

Cornelius attached his knives to his waistband and followed Rokket and Roger.

They walked around the base of the hill until they reached its eastern side. Here there were more rocky outcrops that resembled an ancient crumbling wall. Just beyond a tumble of stones an actual stone entrance into the hill appeared, cave-like, clearly once constructed by people long ago. They entered, pushing aside vines and roots, and ducking beneath spider webs. Torches recently lit flickered in alcoves as they moved deeper into the hill.

"Someone carved this place into the hill?" asked Cornelius.

"No," answered Rokket. "This is a pyramid, very old. Over time it became a hill."

"A pyramid? But it's immense. I thought there were no cities in Canius."

"Long ago there were many cities here. Many pyramids, before Humans spread into what you call the Cantons. There were great wars long ago. Now there are no cities in Canius."

They ascended a steep gallery. The passage was wide and they walked three abreast. The ceiling was high and sloped with the floor. At the top was a wall with a short narrow entrance to another room. They ducked inside. They were in a small antechamber with another short narrow entrance. They ducked inside and found themselves in a large room lit by many torches. The walls were smooth, constructed of huge blocks of red granite and quartz. A stone platform also of red quartzite granite stood in one corner. Something that might have been a device rested on the platform. In the wall on the right was a metal ring.

"What is this place?" asked Cornelius.

"It is a communications room," said Rokket.

"Communications? Surely nothing this old still works."

"Some things are built to withstand time," spoke the Canine.

Voices sounded strange in the chamber. They didn't really echo, but they weren't exactly muted either. It was as if the sound, or energy of the sound, was being transmuted, or transferred to someplace else.

Rokket spoke. "Roger, hand me the disk that contains the information you told the Alpha about." Roger complied. Rokket looked at the crystalline polyhedron disk. "Interesting thing. If I didn't know this contained information, I might think it a toy." He moved to the apparatus on the platform.

The apparatus seemed simple enough. There were two granite crystalline slabs twenty centimeters tall sat upright facing one another with a gap of thirty centimeters. There was a groove parallel to the slabs in the center of the base on which they stood. A depression slightly raised like a little cup fed the groove. Rokket positioned the disk on the groove so that it too was parallel to the slabs. He then placed a piece of wood on either side to keep the disk upright. Rokket turned to his side where the metal ring hung on the wall. He pulled it. A sound of flowing liquid within the walls could be heard, but none emerged into the chamber. The air in the chamber felt charged. Their skin tingled. Then he turned to Cornelius.

"Corneze, you carry this information in the blood that flows in your veins. Use one of your knives to cut the palm of your hand. Let the blood flow into the cup so that it may touch the disk."

"My blood? The information should have dissipated by now. It was only to last five days."

"We will see."

Cornelius shrugged, then retrieved a knife from his waistband. He grimaced, made the cut and grimaced again. He held his palm over the cup letting the blood drip into the depression. It flowed into the groove and spread out to touch the disk and both crystalline slabs. Rokket, Roger and Cornelius stepped back. Lights danced across the room and a projection just as Cornelius had seen at the Roadhouse with Shont appeared all around them. Lights ran up the walls of the chamber. Rokket looked intently at the images.

"What's happening?" asked Cornelius.

"The power of this pyramid is synchronous with the natural energy emanating from the heart of Lupus, the core. It is transmitting the message. It is sympathetic with the planet's magnetic field. The data is being picked up and transmitted through the planet's magnetic field so that it may be received."

"Received by whom?" asked Cornelius.

Rokket turned to Cornelius. "The Polar Cities."

"Canoon?"

Rokket nodded.

Cornelius was concerned. "What if Markhab detects it?"

"The Humans do not have this technology," said Rokket. "It is ancient."

The crystalline disk shimmered and glowed and vibrated. This continued for a few minutes while the three stood in silence. Suddenly the disk shattered. Cornelius and Roger gasped.

"It is done," said Rokket. He pulled the metal ring on the wall again. It was warm. The humming in the chamber died away and the static electric feeling in the air subsided.

"Neither of you are to speak of this to anyone, especially no other Humans. It is the will of the Alpha that none know this."

Cornelius and Roger nodded. Cornelius asked, "Why are you explaining all this to us?"

Rokket replied, "The Alpha wants you to know. Now we go. We return to the others for the communal feast."

In silence they left the chamber the way they had come. To himself, Cornelius wondered what the militant Canines in the Polar Cities would do with the information. He felt a sense of dread in the pit of his stomach.

The feasting on the hilltop campsite had already begun while they were in the pyramid far beneath the camp. Indeed, some had already eaten so much that they waddled about groaning, belching. Some had already retired altogether even though the sun was still up. Roger was very hungry and headed straight to the main kitchen tent for food. Cornelius went to his tent first to lay down his knives. He retrieved his star amulet from its little bag and put it around his neck. He took the red ribbon and attached it to his waistband. Then he too joined the others.

There was much laughter and camaraderie among the refugees. The Canians ate too, but they sat removed in a group away from the others. There were salads of fresh herbs and lettuces, roasted hunta and stewed hunta, and refreshing spring water for all to drink. Cornelius looked for the boy, Nuttin, in the hopes of eating with him, but the boy had made a friend of a young Canine boy. The two were running about playing, along with many of the other children. So Cornelius filled a plate with as much food as it would hold and took a seat near a bonfire by himself and ate. When he was done, he got seconds. Then he sat quietly watching the goings on and listening to various conversations. Many wondered what the party would do on the morrow, whether they would remain at the encampment, or travel again, to where none really knew. As the sun was setting, one sought him out. It was the Alpha.

"Corneze, I want to thank you for making such an arduous journey to bring me the information so important for so many." The Alpha's eyes were bright and sparkled in the light of the setting sun and bonfire.

Cornelius stood up. He found himself suddenly nervous, apprehensive. Voices hushed around him. "Sire, I merely did my duty, completed my assignment as instructed."

"A well done effort," said the Alpha smiling. "Sit with me a moment."

As the sky darkened, Cornelius saw that the Alpha emanated a glow, just as he'd seen upon the Canians' arrival at dawn, an internal light that shimmered, sometimes faded, and sometimes burned brightly.

"Tell me, where are you from?"

"My home is in Shining City, in the Territory of the Shining Star. Do you know of it?"

"I know of it," said the Alpha.

Cornelius shifted position, and his necklace slipped out from his shirt at his neck. It caught the light from the fire.

The Alpha's eyes widened. "Shining Star indeed. I see you bear an ancient amulet."

"It was a gift from a friend, one who made the journey with me, at least as far as Big City. The Roadhouse, actually."

"She is a good friend then. She did not come with your party?"

"No. She had other plans I guess. Another mission. I don't know for what, or to where."

"I see. No doubt you will see her again. And I see you bear a ribbon from the mountain Canines. Do you often travel our paths?"

Cornelius looked down at the ribbon on his waistband. "I found it while journeying through the mountains below Lupus City. A curious thing."

"The monastery Canines do not idly let fall their talismans."

"I did not see any monasteries."

"Yes."

"Sire," began Cornelius.

"Alpha. You may call me that. I am not your Sire. Not yet anyway," and he smiled.

"Alpha, then," continued Cornelius. "Let me express my sadness at the loss of Shont. I did not know her long, or well."

"Thank you."

"If I may ask, I am surprised to know that a Canine from Big City was the mother of the Alpha of all Canines."

Alpha smiled. "You are surprised that the Alpha of all Canines is not the heir of a kingly family? We have no such hereditary royalty. The Alpha is chosen, or perhaps discovered, identified, is a better way of putting it. I suppose you could say I was born to be Alpha Trifid. Though in the beginning I was only Trifid."

Cornelius nodded. "I understand. Or at least I think I do."

"I believe you do." Alpha turned his gaze northwest to where the sun had set. He turned back to Cornelius, an eager smile on his face. "Corneze, do you enjoy running?"

"Running? Well yes. I mean, I run to stay fit and sharp."

"But do you enjoy it?"

"Yes, I enjoy it."

"Good!" Alpha suddenly stood up. "Will you run with me? Come, let us run together, you and I, as the stars come out. They will light our way."

Cornelius hesitated. Dare he turn down any request made by the great Alpha of all Canines? He didn't think he could, or should.

"There are plenty others here to help with the cleanup, if that is your hesitation."

"No, not at all. Well, permit me to at least tell Roger, in case he looks for me."

"Roger can take care of himself. And he does not need to know all of your doings and whereabouts, now does he?"

"No, you are right," said Cornelius. "Alright." He stood.

"Good! Then come. Let us run!"

Alpha was already halfway down the hill before Cornelius started, but his heart was already pounding in his chest. Cornelius leapt over a sleeping refugee and bounded after Alpha. They ran and ran. Cornelius was amazed at the distance the Canine covered with seemingly little effort. Cornelius even had the distinct impression that Alpha was pacing himself so that Cornelius could keep up, that Alpha could run much faster if he wanted. Cornelius wondered how long he could hold out, but realized he was not tiring at all.

Several kilometers away from the hill they encountered a wide stream with mud banks on either side. Alpha leapt over its entire width, landing softly in the grass on the far side with nary a muddy toe. Cornelius wasn't sure if he'd make it only half way and splash into the center of the stream, or just make portage in the thick mud. When he leapt, the uplifting momentum was exhilarating, and his footfall landed in the same patch of grass as Alpha's. The Canine's laughter carried back to Cornelius, and Cornelius ran faster.

For hours they ran and never once stopped. The wide canopy of heaven with its billions of stars lit the world for them in a twilight that blazed. Ahead of Cornelius, the figure of Alpha Trifid reflected all those lights and he softly glowed. The fields of grassy slopes across which they ran twinkled from the myriad night flowers that opened their petals and drank in the rich starlight. Cornelius ran faster and came near to Alpha. Cornelius was astounded to see that never a blade of grass nor stem nor petal of flower was crushed underfoot of Alpha. Indeed, at each of the Canine's footfall, blades, stems, twigs and stones curled away so that Alpha only treaded on the soft rich ground. Cornelius looked down and saw that the same thing was happening for him. He laughed and Alpha laughed. Then Alpha pressed forward with a speed like none other, a blur in the night, and Cornelius matched his speed.

He didn't think the night could be so beautiful. Every outcrop of rock, lazy river, even tusked hunta stood out as if painted in silver in a rolling landscape of green-black. Even the green-black of the grasses that filled the lands of Canius had their own many hues under the starry sky.

They came to a stretch of land filled with white flowers spread like a carpet, and spreading still. Cornelius and Alpha were silhouettes flying across the soft surface. On they went until the topography rose higher to a plain sloping above the lands about. Presently it leveled off and Cornelius could see in the distance a collection of menhirs, sentinels of stone on a secret sacred plain. As they approached, the great stones grew higher and more massive, filling the area with silver light, collecting and reflecting the starry expanse above. Finally Alpha slowed his pace until he merely walked, and Cornelius walked beside him. Neither's breath was labored despite their hours of running.

"What is this place?" asked Cornelius, the first time he had spoken.

"This is called the Henge Plain," answered Alpha.

They came to the place of monolithic stones, hewn and transported here by ancient hands in a faraway time. They walked quietly among the stones until Alpha chose one great stone in front of which he sat. Cornelius sat beside him, their backs against its smooth surface. They sat within the circle facing east. As they sat in silence, a bright star broached the horizon. Solis, the brightest star in the skies of Lupus, rose and it cast its light on the stones. The henge blazed in silvery light. Cornelius' star amulet hung about his neck resting on his chest. It caught the light of the star and refracted the light, filling the interior of the henge in a night rainbow of color. For the first time, Cornelius noticed that one huge stone on their right was set slightly off from the others so that, from their vantage point, the star's light did not shine upon it. But the light reflected from Cornelius' amulet did, and the stone was bathed in the rainbow. It seemed that images took form and danced on the stone's face.

"Show me, Corneze, what you have shown the others. What message did you carry to Shont?"

On the surface of that stone appeared the projection that Cornelius had now seen twice before. The plans of Markhab's new base in Bafaria showed in rich detail. The lay of that land, the streets and buildings were crystal clear. Alpha meticulously studied every detail. There was the spaceport field, and the straight lines of light that pointed away from Lupus, illuminating the armada of ships around faraway Keldo, and the plans of Markhab's to bring all Human worlds under his sway. These were all laid bare for Alpha to see. Strangely, none of it appeared disturb the great Canine.

The image focused on the environs of Bafaria. One block of the city came into sharp focus and centered on a building, a tenement of many apartments. One window came into clear view and through it, Cornelius and Alpha saw a little boy, a Human, playing placidly by himself. The doors to the apartment burst open and the boy hid under the bed. An older woman and a little girl ran in fright as two men burst in, showering bullets through the rooms until the woman and daughter fell.

Then a voice. "Markhab, Let's go. On to the next one."

Tears streamed down Cornelius' face beside Alpha as he relived the memory of his mother and sister's deaths.

The projected image fell back, showing the new military complex recently built. One structure, low and massive with no windows, took center stage.

Alpha stared at it with huge eyes wide open and white, searching. He sniffed the air, his nostrils flared, trying to detect something he thought he could detect from all this distance away. Something shimmered in the image. A low growl escaped the Alpha's throat, ominous and threatening. The growl echoed off the stones, angry. In the shimmering projection, huge wings, silver and black, fluttered and beat. The image of a creature filled with hate and evil intent became sharp, its cold bright eyes stared back at them and a cold laughter filled the henge. Alpha howled into the night, a challenge, directed squarely at the winged image so clear on the stone. In answer, the winged creature answered the challenge and let out a shriek and distorted the image. It curdled Cornelius' blood and shook the stones. Alpha howled into the night louder, overpowering the shriek until both died away. The projection ended and presently silence filled the space of the henge. Only the starlight was left.

The two sat in silence with their thoughts side by side with the menhir at their backs. At length Alpha spoke. "You have enabled me to see much, Corneze. The path before us is now clear."

"What was that? What, WAS that?"

"Fate, Corneze, my fate. And maybe doom."

Cornelius' mind reeled from all he had seen and heard. "How was all this possible?"

"The light of the Precession Star reveals many things to those who seek its mysteries, seek answers to questions. In this place, on Precession Night, much is revealed."

Cornelius thought on those words. He remembered snippets of legends told to him by his mother so long ago, which echoed stories in the tales of history still told by the people in the Territory of the Shining Star. The Shining Star!

Alpha saw the realization in Cornelius' eyes. "The cycles of time are long, Corneze. And on THIS night, a cycle comes full circle, ending one age and heralding another. Some time ago I caused that stone over there to fall. My Fifty Guard raised it again and set it back in its place, but slightly offset, so that others would not know truly when the Precession Star would fill this space and reveal its secrets. Only I knew. Now my questions have been answered. Others will come here on the night they believe Precession to be, to revel and rejoice in the starry night of a new age's dawning."

"When will they come?"

"Tomorrow, Corneze. We shall enjoy the great Festival of Precession at this place tomorrow evening. Only you and I have experienced the mystery of Precession on this, its true anniversary."

"Why do you so freely answer all my questions, Alpha?"

The Canine looked curiously at Cornelius. "Corneze, has it not occurred to you that none has the will to deceive you? You command honesty in all whom you encounter." He smiled. "Much like me. Stand up. I want to show you something."

They stood and Alpha pointed to the surface of the stone against which both had been sitting. There in relief were carved two figures side by side looking east, just as Cornelius and Alpha had looked east, one the figure of a Canine, the other the figure of a Human.

"What does it mean?"

"Lupus is and always has been a shared world. Its history and its fate is that of two peoples, yours and mine, Human and Canine."

The two looked at the figures carved into the rock. They faded as the Precession Star crossed higher into the sky until they were no longer visible.

Cornelius and Alpha kept their silence. Presently drowsiness overcame them both, for they had exerted much this night. They lay down together in the circle of stones and sleep took them and they were not cold.

41 FORBIDDEN PLANET

The lift carrying Commissioners Markhab and Corvus up to the Diplomatic Spaceport atop the three hundred story Diplomatic Residence in Cronapolis just passed the half waypoint on its ascent. The glass-walled pod that snaked around and around the circular tower normally afforded its passengers a three hundred sixty degree panoramic view of the coastal metropolis, but an icy fog had pervaded the equatorial city, keeping citizens shivering in a gloom.

"General Taurus' campaign against the Cantons has been a complete failure. Not only does Big City appear to have been barely affected, all of our Spider Transports were destroyed by those Canine balls," said Markhab.

"You have to admit, it's an ingenious defense. Why didn't we detect them with our satellites?" asked Corvus.

"We did!" said Markhab. "They just looked like ice and snow fields."

"We shouldn't assume that anything we think we see is what we think we're looking at. Another case in point, the floating mines that sunk our ships as they approached Star City." Corvus readjusted the large bag slung over his shoulder.

"You need to remind me of that? Taurus' ineptitude has single handedly wiped out our offensive advantage."

"We still have Shining City and Lupus City." Corvus straightened the diagonal military belt on his black uniform. "The source of the rebellion has been crushed. Don't forget that."

The lift reached the two thirds mark on its spiral ascent. The fog finally gave way to a warm blue sky. "Ah, that's nice."

"Don't make any mention of these facts to the Drigan pilot," said Markhab. "Dania tells me he is one of her best, with an abrasive personality. Apparently he has no regard for the pedigree of his passengers."

"I can deal with the pilot," said Corvus, admiring the lofty view. The ocean was calm and inviting at this height.

"He's also probably a spy for Dania. Keep the details of the mission, what we're looking for, and how we might use it, strictly top secret. This is an "archaeological survey." If any secrets do get out, or the pilot suspects, you know what to do."

"Of course, First Commissioner."

"Transmit your information back to Lupus as soon as you receive it. Don't wait to return home. And one other thing. Make a stop on Wror on your way back. We've had no word for too long from our Scorpion ship in that system."

Corvus nodded.

The lift arrived at the spaceport platform. The door opened. Markhab and Corvus stepped out into the hot midday sun and equatorial humidity. Before them two rows of guards in full diplomatic regalia complete with sounding trumpets led them from the lift to the landing pad.

"Whose idea was this?" asked an annoyed Markhab.

"Mine," said Corvus with a smile. "We must keep face with our allies, even if we think they're spying on us."

Several lifts led up to the circular hub of the spaceport. A circular walkway many meters wide ringed the hub. Three walkways projected out to meet three large circular platforms in a cloverleaf pattern. Two platforms held ships. One was empty. At the end of the trumpeting row of guards, the Drigan delegation stood awaiting Markhab on the empty platform. Among them was a confused looking man with too many bags and boxes and equipment. Arriving at the delegation, Markhab motioned to the guards to cease their trumpeting.

Four Drigan diplomatic guards in full regalia of purple uniforms, medals and gold crested caps stood two to a side of a tall woman in a full-length fur coat.

"Dania my dear," said Markhab. They kissed on both cheeks. "May I introduce Commissioner Corvus. And this is Professor Altair. This is Ambassador Dania of Drigo."

Corvus beamed his boyish smile and gently shook Dania's hand.

Altair did the same, but with an awkward stumble. He attempted a bow and a curtsy at the same time, neither elegant. "A pleasure indeed," mumbled out of his mouth.

"You have come through with flying colors, Dania. But where is the ship?"

Dania smiled. She pressed a gem on a ring she wore, and a ship materialized behind her.

"Ah!" Markhab looked at the large white bulk of a modified delta wing design. No windows or doors or seals were visible. No markings were apparent. It rested on a tripod of legs.

"Yes, here it is. You will find everything in order for your perilous journey." Dania turned specifically to Markhab.

A ramp opened in the ship's underside. Down stepped a tall svelte blond in a form fitting purple Drigan uniform. She gracefully descended the ramp and stood beside Dania.

"Gentlemen, may I introduce your pilot. This is First Captain of the Drigan Reconnaissance Fleet, Naemi."

Markhab, Corvus and even Professor Altair were visibly bowled over by the sex, and sex appeal, of the pilot. Dania smiled, knowing that this was just right. Naemi held a steely gaze that attempted to unnerve the Commissioners. There was no second chance for a first impression, and she had been well briefed by Dania, and by G.

Dania broke the tense moment. "Naemi, this is First Commissioner Markhab, and Commissioner Corvus."

"Commissioners," said Naemi with a curt nod to each as she shook their hands.

"And Professor Altair," said Markhab.

The Professor stammered and flushed as he shook Naemi's hand. "A plea-pleasure Captain. I tru-trust you will keep us safe on both sides of our adventure."

"I will keep the 'adventure' to a minimum, you can be assured," said Naemi.

Markhab singled out two Lupin guards nearest the delegation. "These are Sergeants Blem and Blum. They will also accompany you on this expedition."

Naemi nodded to each, who nodded back.

"Now that introductions are out of the way, tell us about this very special craft."

That was Naemi's queue. "This is the latest model spy ship, equipped with technology designed to be invisible to the most sophisticated detection systems, including total environmental dampeners. As you saw, it can be completely invisible." She touched a gem on a ring on her finger. Suddenly the ship blurred and became completely invisible.

"Remarkable," said Professor Altair, feeling in the air for the ship. He hit his head on a wing.

Naemi touched the ring again and the ship rematerialized. "No known detectors have ever penetrated our dampeners. This mission will be successful."

While Altair was being impressed by the invisibility cloak, Corvus had his eye on Naemi's ring. *Now that's an interesting little trinket,* he thought. Then he joined the conversation. "I see there are no markings at all on this ship."

"Stealth and secrecy are the primary functions of this vessel," said Naemi. "And speed. This ship has outpaced and out maneuvered even your own Hornet Fliers and Scorpion Ships," she added with a glance at Markhab.

"We may have to do something about that," said the First Commissioner, attempting to make light of the comment.

"What about weapons?" asked Corvus.

"Minimal," answered Naemi. "Evasion and flight from danger are our primary defenses."

"That will hopefully be adequate," said Corvus.

"Though we do not know the extent of Earth Humans' technologies," said Professor Altair.

"That is the great unknown," said Naemi. "But we will get answers to even that question on this mission."

"Fine, fine," Markhab said finally. "Let us not belabor the start of this mission anymore."

"As you wish, Commissioner," said Naemi. "With no further ado's then, let us board." To Dania, she added, "With your leave, Ambassador."

Dania nodded.

Naemi led the way up the ramp, her tight-fitting uniform leaving little to the imaginations of her all male passengers who followed, but imagine they did. With Professor Altair the last to file in, huffing and complaining as he shouldered, carried and dragged his equipment all by himself, the ramp was raised.

Dania and Markhab retreated from the platform to the hub, their remaining guards following.

"And so the expedition begins," said Dania.

"I am indebted to you for your assistance," said Markhab. "Will you descend with me for a lunch in my private quarters?"

"That would be splendid, Markhab, except that I am recalled back to Sabral for the usual consultations with my government. I regret that I am unable to stay even for the afternoon. My ship is ready even as we speak."

Markhab was surprised to hear this news, but he did not question the Ambassador. "When might I expect your return?"

Dania showed her lovely smile and replied, "At my earliest opportunity, I assure you. But I remain available to assist you further in any way I can. You have only to ask." She and Markhab embraced and kissed one another on both cheeks. Then Dania led her party to the ship waiting on the other platform.

"That's it then," mumbled Markhab to himself. He entered the lift with his guards and descended into the cold and foggy city below.

* * *

Naemi retracted the ramp just as Altair dropped his many carry-ons onto the floor of the ship.

"No helping the scientist, eh? I thought I was the indispensible member of this expedition."

"When you've found what you're looking for," said Corvus.

"How much do those things weigh?" asked Naemi.

"Not nearly enough," said Altair. "Your weight restrictions were punitive. I had to leave a lot of important equipment behind."

"What you have will have to suffice," said Naemi. She sealed the ramp hatch and pressurized the ship.

The five of them were in a rather large bay. Four bunks, two above and two below, were against the sidewalls. A single table was at the back with three chairs around it.

"Here is where you will eat, sleep and socialize. This bay is equipped for your needs." Naemi walked to the table and activated a wall console and monitor. "This unit will provide you with a library, music and games for entertainment. Food and water is dispensed here." She pointed to a small counter with a cupboard and sink. "A lavatory is behind this panel." She touched a button on the wall, which opened a narrow door to a toilet and sink. "Food and water will be rationed on this trip. So be mindful of your consumption."

"There are only four beds here," said Altair. "Where are you sleeping?"

"I sleep in the bridge section, behind this door." Naemi moved toward the front of the ship, activating the door panel. Inside was the command center with two seats. A cot was set up on the right side, a small table on the left. "No one is allowed up here without my permission."

"As you wish," said Corvus. He selected a bottom bunk and set his bag down on the bed. The others selected their own berths.

"Are there any windows?" asked Altair.

"Here," said Naemi. She touched a button below a wall panel near the lavatory. It slid open to reveal the bright blue sky of Lupus. "There is another on the opposite wall. Now, if you'll excuse me, I'll prepare the ship for takeoff." She left them without waiting for an answer. Sitting down in the pilot seat, she closed the door behind her.

"Let's settle in," said Corvus.

* * *

Naemi activated the locking mechanism as soon as the door to the cockpit closed. There was a small mirror on this side. She swiveled around in her chair and looked at herself and said, "Well done, Naemi. You have the beast in your maw." She then turned back and started running down her checklist. Life support systems, check. Fuel and power cell at maximum, check. Navigation arrays, check. Communications, check. Engines and thrusters, check. Secondary and tertiary systems, check.

Beep. Beep.

Someone was requesting entrance. "Damn," she whispered. Swiveling around again, she released the lock and the door slid open. It was Corvus. "What do you want?"

"I would like to be here at our take off, if you don't mind."

Naemi did mind, but she held her thoughts to herself. She felt she had to be, somewhat, accommodating. There was no sense in dooming the mission before it had even begun. "Fine."

Corvus took his seat beside her. "I'm glad we're getting off to a good start, you and I."

"You may be here, but don't touch anything."

Corvus nodded.

Naemi completed her checklist while Corvus watched her intently. He had a cold glow about him that Naemi found unnerving. But he also had an eagerness about him, like a wary adolescent. That could be dangerous, she decided. She activated the communication link with the military authorities. "This is Captain Naemi from Expedition One. Request permission to depart."

"You have permission," said a voice from the speakers.

Naemi cut the link and turned to Corvus. "All ready, Commissioner?"

Corvus nodded and grinned. "By all means."

Naemi activated the thrusters. The ship was aloft. They plied upwards through the atmosphere, the sky getting darker as it lost its hue. Soon stars were all about and the planet dropped away, the blue, brown, green and white world shrinking into the distance.

"Setting coordinates to Solis. Activating stealth mode. Initiating a quantum tear. Entering the proto-quark cloud in three-two-one."

The ship momentarily vibrated, then the view out the cockpit shimmered and the ship sped through the mist of the subatomic soup.

* * *

In the main cabin, Professor Altair sat at the table pouring over old records, notes and not a few books that covered every centimeter of the table's surface. The door to the command cabin slid open and Corvus joined the Professor. The two guards sat on a lower bunk playing cards.

"I see you're already at work," said Corvus, taking a seat opposite the Professor.

"What? Oh, yes, of course. There's no time to waste." He circled an obscure phrase in one book, quickly cross-referenced a passage in a different text, found a comparison in a third, then wrote furiously in the margins of his notebook. "Resonating minerals, yes yes. Specially carved structure, yes. But what's the catalyst? What's the catalyst?"

Feeling bored and ignored, Corvus got up and moved to the bunk where the card game was in progress. "Blem, deal me a hand."

* * *

Naemi sat in her command chair pushed back against the locked door, her feet up on the console. The cabin was filled with pink light from the ever-swirling vortexes outside the ship. The navigation and propulsion systems knew how to find the right path to their destination, even if one could not discern fore from aft by looking out with eyes.

Dramatic string and horn music was piped into the cockpit, and Naemi played a game introduced to her by G. Before her were four disks a centimeter wide and half a centimeter deep floating in an electromagnetic field. She flexed one finger held aloft, gently manipulating the field. One disk rotated in a clockwise tumble, another counter-clockwise. Another swung vertically over the others, and Naemi was manipulating the fourth to move in an opposite direction without getting too close to the others. She increased all four's tumble speed. She brought them all close together, then started to move them apart when a buzzer sounded from her console. At the same time, the door buzzed. She abruptly moved her feet and sat straight up in her chair. Two disks knocked into one another and careened off in opposite directions, slamming against the walls. "Damn." The other two dropped to the floor. She scrambled to pick them up while at the same time releasing the door. Corvus stood in the doorway.

"Am I disturbing you?"

"It's ok," said Naemi. "I was just about to call you." She tossed the four disks onto her bed cot and cut the buzzer. "Our first obstacle is the Feline blockade." A few touches of the controls and the ship eased into a normal star field of space.

Corvus took the seat beside Naemi. "I don't see any ships."

Before them was mainly empty space except for a small planetoid in the distance.

"There," said Naemi pointing out the planetoid. "That's an Oort cloud object, at the edge of the Solis system. There are thousands of such objects fully encircling the system, much like around Lupus' sun. Long ago the Felines mined them around Solis." The ship slowed to a moderate gliding speed in space relative to the planetoid. "There's a proto-quark cloud field detector in the mines."

"I thought you said nothing could detect this ship?" Naemi ignored the question. "What now?"

"We coast through, carefully." She kept her eyes on the sensors.

"Can we be sure they're still active?"

"That's a testable hypothesis." Naemi launched a probe and let it drift away from them before activating its engines. As soon as the probe moved by its own propulsion system, an alarm sounded in the cabin. "Detection!"

A pulse of light erupted from the planetoid, emitting a powerful laser beam at the probe. It exploded in a pulverizing burst of light and debris.

"I see it's still operational," said Corvus. "Fascinating."

Naemi adjusted several controls and the lights dimmed. Suddenly there was a knocking at the cabin door. "What now?" she said, letting the door slide open.

It was Professor Altair. "Captain. Is there a curfew on this ship? I need lights to continue my work. And," he added turning to look behind him, "Blem and Blum wish to continue their game."

"We need to reduce as much EM radiation as possible. We can't risk being detected by any mines."

"Mines? What mines?" said Altair, craning his head into the cockpit and staring out the view screen.

"We've entered the Feline blockade," said Naemi.

"Come now, Professor," said Corvus. "Your scribbling can wait. I'm not ready to be reduced to space dust just yet."

Naemi gave Corvus a reluctant appreciative smile. "Go back, Professor, and relax." She closed the door on him.

"Captain. How long must we coast?"

"Until we've reached the other side of the mines' field perimeter."

"Are we talking minutes? Hours?"

"At coasting speed? It could be days."

"There must be an alternative," said Corvus, exasperated.

Naemi thought a moment. "There is another way, but it's riskier. If we're detected, then we're toast, and our mission will already have failed."

"What is it?"

"Feline command codes. But there's no guarantee the codes haven't changed since we obtained them."

"Is that why you didn't use them? Is there a way to test it? With another probe, perhaps?"

"We have limited probes."

"How many?"

"One more."

"Try it. I'll take full responsibility."

"That's a comfort, if we're dead," said Naemi with her usual sarcasm. She paused. "But we can try."

She set the controls to release another probe. It detached from the ship and drifted slowly away. When it was several kilometers from the ship, she activated a coded pulse from the probe.

Through the view screen, dozens of previously unseen mines floating in space blinked on. Their red lights glared menacingly. Naemi and Corvus held their breaths, but no attack came. The mines swiveled in space tracking the probe. Moments went by.

"Well?" said Corvus.

"Now let's see," said Naemi. She activated the probe's propulsion. It lit up and moved forward. The mines continued to rotate, but no lasers fired. Minutes passed and the probe retreated further until it disappeared into the inky blackness. "Ok, Commissioner. Now it's our turn." Naemi transmitted the same code. Many of the mines swiveled to face the ship. Naemi held her breath and heard only the fierce beating of her heart in her chest. She slowly activated the ship's propulsion systems. The ship crept forward. The mines' red eyes followed them, but no lasers.

Naemi and Corvus sat in silence for half an hour. Finally Naemi said, "I think we're clear." She increased the ship's velocity. Still nothing from the mines. "We're out of their tracking range now."

"It seems it was a risk worth taking," said Corvus.

"It would seem."

Corvus turned to Naemi. In a biting accusatory tone he said, "Explain to me why you lied about this ship's ability to slip through the Feline blockade undetected."

"We slipped through," said Naemi, answering the cold interrogation with an equally cold answer.

"What else did you lie about?"

"I wasn't lying," said Naemi, lying. "Feline defenses are always being upgraded. I was not going to unnecessarily endanger us by *assuming* we could just sail right through. Caution is to be exercised."

Corvus said no more, but kept a distrusting eye on everything Naemi did.

The ship streamed at high velocity toward the inner planets, first passing the realms of the gas giants, then innumerable asteroids. A small red planet took form in the view screen and grew larger and larger. The invisible craft swung wide around its south polar region. From this approach the most megalithic of Mars' natural features were out of view. There were no towering peaks of the sentinels of the Tharsis bulge; no great hemispheric rip across the belly of the world, only the beautiful serene spiral of the southern ice cap. One side was blurred by a fog of sublimating carbon dioxide ice; the other side was obscured by a localized dust storm. Admiring the beautiful swirl pattern of the ice, the thought occurred to Naemi that it resembled the Precession Star broach that hung around her neck, hidden beneath her uniform. Mars looked quiet, at peace with itself and the planetary neighborhood.

A buzzer sounded from the console, startling Naemi.

"What is it?"

Naemi checked her readings. "E-M proximity warning."

"Feline ships?"

"Checking." Naemi enhanced her scans of the planet, but was confused by the results.

"Well?"

"No," said Naemi after some moments. "It's not Feline. I'm guessing it's Human."

"Where?" Corvus' face flushed with eagerness, a child's curiosity.

"Multiple signatures on the surface, and several satellites in orbit. They appear to be all automated. Low power output. I'm guessing most are solar powered. One of the satellites has a small neutron signature, nuclear powered."

The door buzzer sounded. Naemi opened it and Professor Altair stepped in. "I saw a red planet out the window. Where are we?"

"An outer planet from Earth," said Naemi. "We've detected electronic devices on its surface."

"Are there any life signs?"

"No, I'm sure of that. The structures are quite small, smaller than this ship."

"Sounds like reconnaissance scouts," said the Professor. "Earth Humans must be reaching out to touch the stars, to find their lost brethren."

"You're too much of a romantic, Professor," said Corvus.

"If the Earth Humans were really venturing forth into space on their own, the Felines wouldn't stand for it for long," said Altair. "They'll see it as a threat and punish them again, send them back to another stone age for their arrogance."

"A nihilist too?" Corvus quipped.

"Me?" The Professor laughed. "I like to think of myself as an eternal optimist. But be assured, the Felines have no intention of letting Humans from Earth unite with us. They mean to isolate the Earth for all time."

"We'll see," said Corvus. "That's an awfully long time, and they might get sloppy. All schemes eventually meet their end."

Naemi was surprised to hear this come from the little tyrant. She bit back a grin. If Markhab were eventually taken down, then this little tyrant would fall, too.

The arc of Mars passed out of view and the ship travelled on. Within minutes traveling at subluminal relativistic speed, the blue orb of the Earth appeared.

"It's beautiful," said the Professor. Oceans and landmasses, swirling atmospheric storms and ice structures of the world filled the view screen.

"I'm detecting hundreds of orbital satellites," said Naemi. "Geosynchronous and otherwise. They're Human. No Feline signatures detected from any of them. I'm swinging us around to the dark side of the planet."

As they passed the meridian from day to night, they all gasped. Terrestrial lights of Human population centers outlined and filled the continents.

"This is amazing," exclaimed Altair. "How many Humans are down there? They seem to have consumed the planet in cities."

Naemi checked some readings. "Billions. Maybe tens of billions."

"A Human population poised to burst into space and join their brethren," said Corvus, glancing at the Professor. Naemi was less upbeat at the prospect.

Corvus turned to Naemi. "Do we have a dossier on the Human civilizations of Earth?"

"Yes." Naemi accessed an information file. "I have a summary. More than two hundred separate political units with overlapping alliances. Hundreds of different languages, several politically aligned religious movements. Numerous active conflict zones."

"In other words, a fractured population."

"There are global organizations, including a United Nations."

"Military capabilities?"

"Conventional and nuclear, including supersonic aircraft. Communication is near real-time via satellite. Extensive surveillance capabilities."

"Open up the frequencies on the receiver," said Altair. "Let's see what we can pick up in the way of radio chatter."

"Will that identify us as a receiver?" asked Corvus.

"Unknown," said Naemi. "But we are invisible. Let's try it." She activated the communication system's radio wave calibrator.

Corvus reached out and grabbed Naemi's hand. "Be sure it's receive only," he said sternly.

Naemi stared into his cold eyes, but did not protest her outrage. "Of course," she replied with gay mockery.

The air in the cabin erupted in static and voices. The din was a cacophony of different languages and music. Naemi reduced the volume and scanned the frequencies for anything cogent.

"Do you want to listen for anything in particular?" Corvus asked Altair.

The Professor stood with his eyes closed, face smiling. He appeared like one who just discerned for the first time the subtle pattern in the melody of a favorite song. "Ah, can you hear its sweetness? Its determination? The sound of our lost Human brothers and sisters, declaring to the cosmos their existence, their resilience."

"Really, Professor. Is there anything we should be listening for? I don't want to be wasting time listening to gossip," said Corvus.

"Do you have anything we can key onto? Any cities? Words? Anything?" asked Naemi.

The Professor checked his notebook. "There are so many."

"Give me something."

"I have no way of knowing if any of the ancient places still exist."

"Professor."

"Ok. Ok. Try Jericho."

"Thank you." Naemi keyed in the name to the communication sensors. After a moment she said, "I've got something." She piped a live communiqué over the speakers.

"That's absolutely right, Iskander. And for anyone just

tuning in, I'm Lev Levi...."

"And I'm Iskander Hussein...."

"We're here at the commencement of the new archaeological dig at Jericho."

"As part of a week-long series of events marking the tenth anniversary of unification and the creation of the Nation of Abraham, we're here to bring you a first hand look at the opening of the Jericho Temple."

"Uncovered just last year during construction of a new housing block, the Temple is estimated as being ten thousand years old, far preceding the earlier known occupation at the site going back eight to nine thousand years."

"Financed entirely by the Gaza Bank, this is the largest joint excavation by the Ministry of Antiquities."

"The Directors of the Jericho Dig are descending the ladders and scaffolding to the lowest level of the site. They'll inspect the entrance to the Temple before the work crew gets started unsealing the Temple Door."

"But before that happens, Lev, Rabbi Schumann and Imam Muhammad will lead the officials, crew and bystanders in joint prayers, honoring the ancestors and blessing the site."

Corvus turned to Professor Altair. "What does this all mean?"

"I don't know. Some sort of official science event. It may not mean anything at all.

The female voice continued.

"Long before Stonehenge, long before the Great Pyramids of Egypt were constructed, this temple was already extant in situ for millennia."

The Professor interrupted. "Did you hear that? Pyramids. That's where we need to go. Where did she say they were?"

"Some place called Egypt," said Naemi.

"Where is that?" asked Altair.

"I'm checking," said Naemi. "We have the Feline surveys of the planet to help us. Got it." A geo-political map of the region appeared on the screen. "There," said Naemi pointing to a location on a large South to North flowing river system snaking through a desert region. "That's Egypt. And there, that's where the Pyramids of Egypt are located."

"Set a course for that place, Captain," said Corvus. "We have our first exploration site."

Naemi brought the ship down in wide circles. If anyone had bothered to look up into the fading twilight of the Egyptian evening, they might have noticed the spiraling contrails lit by the sinking sun. But that is all they would have seen. The ship was still invisible. Soon the Saharan winds dissipated the clouds, but not before the ship had landed.

Professor Altair was ready with his equipment before the exit ramp, carrying his notebooks, scientific devices and a bag containing additional, no doubt important, supplies.

"What are you doing?" asked Naemi, entering the room from the cockpit.

"I'm ready to start my scientific investigation," replied the Professor.

"One little bag," said Naemi. "That is all. We mustn't draw attention to ourselves."

"Then we'll need other clothes," said Corvus. "Your purple uniform, and our black, will also draw attention."

"Correct," said Naemi. She opened a wall compartment and brought out sets of clothing. "Contemporary Earth Human garbs. Put them on." She handed Corvus and the Professor their bundles.

"What about us? Asked Blem.

"One of you at least should stay with the ship."

Corvus nodded, half undressed already. "She's right. Captain, give some clothes to Blem. Blum, you'll stay here." Blum nodded.

Naemi disappeared into the cockpit to change. In just a couple of moments she was back, dressed in a loose fitting pant and blouse outfit of black linen. She wore laced sandals on her feet. The men also had linen clothes, though of white. They had no additional shoes with which to accessorize, and they looked a bit strange in their black leather boots.

"It'll do," said Naemi. She opened the exit hatch and lowered the ramp, which was invisible outside the ship. "We stay together. And don't forget to activate your translators." She handed them each a small clip. "Affix these to your right ear."

They carefully marched down the invisible ramp and set foot upon the sands of Earth into the dry and dusty Egyptian evening. The ramp closed quietly behind them.

They stood in a bare sandy area next to one of three small pyramids. Towering above the small pyramid behind it was the Great Pyramid. To one side rose the mighty hulk of the Sphinx.

"Amazing," said the Professor. "This could be one of the four great Colossi of the Four Directions." He stopped to scribble into a notebook. "On a savannah beside a great river, each of the four species erected a colossus to represent Humans, Canines, Felines and Birds of Prey. It was part of the Tribute Jubilee, the great festival long ago where the genocide against the species took place. After the Jubilee, only Humans were left on Earth."

"Some party," said Naemi.

"This looks like it might have been either the Canine, or Feline Colossus."

"But look at the head," said Corvus. "It's Human."

"And far smaller in scale than the rest of the body," said the Professor. "Later Humans may have refashioned its visage to Human form."

The sandy area in which they stood was cordoned off to prevent the many tourists milling about the area from getting too near the small pyramid that was undergoing some form of renovation. Scaffolding and ropes were erected all around it.

"Hey!" shouted a voice. It came from a uniformed officer standing nearby. "Keep away. See the sign, Misters? Keep away."

Only now seeing the cordon, and the illegible sign, Corvus led the others over the cordon and toward the officer.

"My apologies," said Corvus.

"How do we enter the great pyramid?"

"There, there," said the officer pointing to a queue of people around the edge of the small pyramid. "That way to the Great Tomb of Khufu. Get in line with the others. Keep away from here."

"Again, my apologies," said Corvus. He nodded to the others and they headed toward the queue. As they left, another guard came up to the first.

"What's going on here?"

"Nothing. Tourists."

"They're probably Americans." The two enjoyed a laugh.

Coming up to Naemi, the Professor asked, "What's an 'American'?"

"I don't know," she replied. "It's probably a derogatory term. Ignore it."

The queue straddled several merchant tents selling trinkets and blankets. Others sold food. Smoke fragrant with the smell of roasted goat filled the air. They took their places at the end of the queue and slowly shuffled ahead along with tourists of every size, shape, color and dress.

"Pyramids are ancient, sacred sympathetic structures," began the Professor, eager to share his knowledge. "They are designed to tap into and amplify the natural energy frequencies of the planet. The energies they are capable of accessing, and manipulating, can be staggering."

"What are they used for?" ask Corvus.

"Lots of things. Anything from lighting up a city to communicating with other pyramids."

"Communicating?" asked Corvus, suddenly interested. "Did you say there are pyramids like this on Lupus?"

"In Canius, yes," said the Professor. "But they were destroyed long ago. As I'm sure you know from your satellite images, there is nothing at all left of the ancient cities in Canius."

Nothing we see is as it seems, thought Corvus, remembering his conversation with Markhab over the energy balls of Canoon that had so easily swept aside their invasion forces in the Cantons.

"Salaam! Salaam!" greeted a date seller to Naemi. "Pretty lady, these are the most succulent dates to be found anywhere in Egypt. Enjoyed by the Pharaohs who built these marvelous structures. Here, try." He held out a plump date for Naemi to taste.

"Go ahead," said Corvus smiling. "Indulge."

Naemi took the date from the seller. She held it, eyeing it suspiciously.

"Eat. Please nice lady. It is a gift." Naemi took a bite.

"Well?" asked Corvus.

"It's sticky, but very sweet." She smiled to the seller. "Thank you."

"You like?"

"Yes, I like."

The seller beamed his approval. "Best in Egypt. You honor me, pretty lady."

The line moved on, and so did Naemi and her party.

A nearby disturbance attracted their attention. A flightless bird ran between Naemi and the tourist in front of her. It was fast followed by a cat, which in turn was chased by a dog. *Canine, Feline, AND Bird of Prey?* Naemi looked long side at Corvus, who smiled and shrugged his shoulders. *Species, in miniature.*

A deafening sound from above took all by surprise. Jets from the Egyptian Defense Forces streamed overhead crackling the air with supersonic bursts as they broke the sound barrier. Multicolored lights turned on, their beams illuminating the faces of the Pyramids, large and small. Military marching music blared from loudspeakers.

"What's going on?" asked Naemi, turning quickly to Corvus and the Professor. But none of them could know this was not unusual. No one broke from the queue and fled to safety. If anything, the scene was stranger. The tourists, sellers and guards just smiled up into the sky and clapped at the jets and pyramid, laughter and delight passing through the crowd. Naemi was confused.

Ahead of Naemi in line was a large woman with two teenage children in tow. The kids were preoccupied with small electric devices. They paused only briefly to look up with everyone else, then they returned their attention to their toys. The woman bit off juicy pieces of goat from a kabob, sauce smeared across her lips and cheek. She was dressed in a light blouse, and pants that only reached to the tops of her calves. The woman noticed Naemi's perplexed expression, and started up a conversation.

"Is this your first time to the Pyramids?"

Naemi nodded, still confused.

"It's my third," said the woman. Then glancing up, she looked back at Naemi and said, "Oh that. Don't let it alarm you. Just part of the celebrations for the anniversary of the unification of Israel and Palestine. Momentous times in which we live, eh?" She bit off the last of the kabob and dropped the stick onto the ground. "I promised my little monsters here I'd take them on a big trip once my divorce was final. I'm a free woman now!" She wiped her mouth with the back of a hand, smearing more sauce onto her cheeks. "Amazing place, Egypt. It's so old! Where are y'all from?"

"We've come a long way to see the pyramid," said Naemi. She didn't want to further this conversation more than was needed.

"You sound like you're from Europe," said the lady. "But that's not that far, really. Oh! Maybe you're from Australia, or New Zealand?"

Naemi remained silent.

"My husband, my ex-husband I mean, has family in New Zealand. That's a long ways away from anywhere. Well, maybe not from Australia."

Naemi smiled and nodded, then turned back to Corvus and the others.

"You're very likeable," said Corvus, now at ease.

Naemi just grunted.

The line moved closer to the entrance, heading part way up the face of the great pyramid.

"Truly a massive undertaking," said Professor Altair.

"They say it only took twenty years," said the woman. "All this five thousand years ago, too."

"Oh, it's only that old?" said the Professor. He seemed disheartened. "I wonder why it took so long to build."

That comment elicited a quizzical look on the woman's face. She was about to say something when a guard interrupted with an announcement.

"Alright. The next ten of you can go. Come on."

Naemi's party entered behind the woman and her kids.

In a minute they were in the Grand Gallery of the pyramid heading up the incline.

"Just look at this architecture," said the Professor. "Exceptional precision. Just what one would expect."

The party diverged from the gallery and moved horizontally into the Queen's chamber. The room was quite small, and barren except for a corbelled cornice in one wall. Two small openings near the floor revealed the room's star shafts.

The Professor was already examining the cornice.

"What do you think it is?" asked Corvus.

"I'm not sure. I've never been inside a pyramid before. But from old drawings of the former pyramids of Canius, I'd say it might be a communications center. Minus the equipment."

"Do you notice how the air feels strange?" asked Naemi. She felt dizzy. Sound was muffled in the chamber, not really producing any echoes at all.

"It's charged somehow," said the Professor absently.

After another couple of minutes, the party exited the Queen's chamber and resumed their ascent in the Grand Gallery. At the top, the party ducked into an antechamber, then ducked again in a larger chamber.

"There it is," said the lady ahead. "The King's chamber, and the tomb of the king."

The professor was all over the place, inspecting the open and broken sarcophagus, the smooth walls, and two more star shafts. Then he joined Naemi, Corvus and Blem in the center of the room.

"Well?" asked Corvus.

"This certainly isn't a tomb," said the Professor, with a sidelong glance at the large woman. "A power station of sorts, yes. But if that lady is correct, it's too young. Just too young."

"Then we're wasting our time here."

"Just a few minutes more, please," said Altair. He moved passed Naemi, who was staring up into the ceiling shaft at the exposed corbelled roof. Arriving at the sarcophagus, Altair observed the precision workmanship, the crystalline granite. He took from his pocket a small titanium wand. It was a pen on one side, and a ping resonator on the other. He struck the sarcophagus and listened, admiring the pure tone emitted from the granite structure.

Naemi's mind reeled as she felt increasingly dizzy. Her eyesight blurred for a moment. She felt almost inebriated. Her vision registered double, triple images of the room and everyone in it. There was Corvus, impatiently standing in the center of the room with Blem. But strangely, she saw their right sides, and their left sides, and their backs. The Professor, too, seemed to display three angles. So did the large lady and her nonplussed kids. Then Naemi gasped. From two angles, she saw herself. She blinked her eyes. Rubbed her eyes. She tried to make sense of what she was seeing. As the pure tone resonated through the room from the Professor's ping, Naemi felt disembodied. But she quickly realized what she was seeing.

There were three Naemi's in the room, each with a different vantage of the scene. And Naemi could see all three versions of herself, though apparently no one else could. A moment later, she had another revelation. These Naemis were not the same. One was slightly older, the other older still. The oldest had strange blinking eyes. *Like the eyes of members of the Magistry on Polaris*, she thought to herself.

Naemi, and Naemi, and Naemi each saw through the eyes of the others. Naemi rubbed her temples, and the others did as well. Triple vision was difficult to process. The mind was not necessarily built for such perspectives. Naemi looked at Corvus. From this angle, the pale handsome blue-eyed devil faced the Professor who was busy over the sarcophagus. From Naemi's second angle, Corvus was in profile, his boyish pug nose and broad forehead recessed from the broad shoulders and bulging chest. From the third angle, Naemi looked from behind, right at the Commissioner's bubble butt. *Pretty packages often conceal horrific gifts.*

Two Naemis suddenly turned their startled faces to the large woman who had just said something remarkable.

To her uninterested kids, she said, "The star shafts point to special stars in the sky. One points to Sirius, the Dog Star, and the other to the pole star, which right now is Polaris. Is either of you listening to me?"

All three Naemis walked up to the woman, though only the youngest Naemi seemed to be visible to her. "Excuse me. Did you say Sirius, the Dog Star? And Polaris?"

"Yes!" said the woman with delight. "Someone at least is interested in the

Egyptians." She gently bopped one of her kids on the head.

"Time's up, folks," said the guard who had accompanied them. "The tour is over. Let some more people enjoy the mysteries."

The party made their way back down the Grand Gallery and outside where the long queue of tourists still waited to go in. Naemi said nothing of her apparent split existence. The two apparitions of herself walked quietly beside her, one on either side, alert, looking this way and that.

"Now what?" asked Naemi.

"We go back to the ship," said Corvus. He looked around and noticed that the Professor had wandered off to the near stall of a bookseller.

Coming up to him, Corvus said, "Professor, time to go." But the Professor was flipping intently through the pages of a book on antiquities.

"Look at these pictures," he said to Corvus. "Look at the symbology. Images of Felines, Canines, and Birds of Prey. Remarkable."

Naemi started to glance in his direction when something else caught her eye, or a Naemi's eye. Weaving in and out of stands of tourist trinkets was a robed man. His flowing clothes barely concealed his bulky chest, but it wasn't muscles that had drawn Naemi's attention. Blinking lights and wired rods were just visible through his open robe. The man nervously pulled the fabric closer across his chest.

Naemi prided herself on what she called her sixth sense. But with three Naemis afoot, she effectively called upon an *eighteenth* sense. Naemi sniffed the air around her. The smells on the night air were alien and unusual, but one smell was familiar, even on this strange planet, explosives. One Naemi broke off to the right, another to the left, circling around toward the mysterious man. Youngest Naemi stayed put, on high alert. She heard the Professor still speaking to Corvus.

"Such remarkable ruins. Why, there's even...." The Professor stopped speaking, apparently in shock at the picture on one of the book's pages. "This! This is the gate!" He turned to the seller. "Sir. Where is this? Where can we see this?" He held the book open so the seller to see the picture.

The seller squinted at the page. "Oh. Tiwanaku, in South America. Very far away."

"How far?"

"On the other side of the world. Are you going to buy that?"

Naemi with the blinking eyes had circled around the mysterious man, and they were now heading right towards one another. The other Naemi was quickly coming up behind. Naemi beside Corvus and the Professor tensed, sensing that something was about to happen. Naemi with the blinking eyes stopped directly in front of the man. Suddenly he seemed to see her, and tried to move around the woman who somehow materialized right before him, but his way was suddenly blocked by an identical woman. Twins? He turned again, but the first woman still blocked his way.

"Hey," he began to say, but the woman started to hum, and her eyes flashed colors in his face. He slowed, just long enough for the second Naemi to yank the robe off his shoulders. Panicking, the man reached for a cord and....

Naemi hissed in Corvus' ear. "That man has a bomb!"

But she whispered too loudly. The word BOMB spread through the crowd like lightning. Panic broke out.

Corvus turned just in time to see the man pull a ripcord. In a moment, a brilliant flash of light erupted from the man. But Corvus was as fast as lightning. His steely eyes grew suddenly pale blue, and a frightening light as eruptive as the bomb burst forth from his eyes. Waves of freezing light rippled through the air, pushing and pushing through as fast or faster than the bomb and its destructive debris flying outward. Whatever the icy waves encountered, immediate freezing ensued. Shrapnel froze and hung in the air, slowed down by the waves, falling to the ground in slow motion. Stalls and food and people froze on the spot. The fire from the blast was caught in the waves and burned dimly like cold prisms in an ice prison.

Naemi stared amazed at the sight. Blem grabbed Naemi's arm, and the Professor's, and pulled them down to the ground. People were rushing away, but others were fast approaching, security officers.

"Sir, let's get away, now!"

Corvus' eyes returned to their steely blue. He looked about him quickly, caught sight of the incoming security officers, and ducked down with Naemi and the Professor. "You three run. I can take care of this." He pushed Blem out of the way and stood up to face the guards. Blem, Naemi and the Professor darted away to the right.

As she ran, Naemi ran up beside Naemi and joined body to body, disappearing into her being. On her other side, the other Naemi approached, and she too merged body to body. Naemi felt momentarily dizzy, but shook it off and kept running. Then she heard the shriek.

The chaos of people yelling and sirens blaring was nothing like the thunderclap that split the air and shattered its roaring shriek in the ear of every bystander. It was a paralyzing sound that touched upon the very foundations of fear residing deep in the animal brain of all Humans, and it came out of Corvus' mouth. Terror gripped each soul. Images of giant hunting Birds of Prey from the deep past of Humanity's shared journey flashed in the minds of everyone who heard the shriek. Like a great eagle striking paralyzing fear in its prey, the mob, and security officers, froze in place. Corvus ran as fast as he could.

It would only be a few moments before the most resilient Humans shook off the effects of Corvus' screech in the night. Corvus already heard shouts behind him and the fast thump of boots on sand. Naemi, the Professor and Blem were just rounding the small pyramid ahead. The ship was close. As Corvus rounded the corner, his pace suddenly slowed. Naemi, Altair and Blem had run headlong into three guards. Blem lunged at two guards at once, mowing them over. He had almost regained his footing when the butt of a rifle slammed into his shoulder from the third guard. He winced in pain. Naemi and the Professor kept running, but Blem was lost.

Corvus had little time to think. His reflexes reacted to the situation immediately. He spun around and stood his ground, taunting his pursuers, who were only a dozen meters away brandishing firearms pointed directly at his head. Laser guidance lights danced on his face and chest. His eyes turned pale blue, he extended his arms, and a brilliant wall of light burst from his hands. A wall of ice materialized and pushed forward toward the guards. Grating, grinding sounds from bulldozed sand quickly were met with cries as sand and ice engulfed the guards.

Corvus dashed the last hundred meters toward the sandy field where the invisible ship was located. He could see Naemi and the Professor disappear up the ramp. There were more and louder shouts behind Corvus, then gunshots rang out into the night. He leaped over the stunned body of Blem, and came crashing down legs extended feet first into the chest of the guard who had clobbered Blem. The guard grunted and loosed the breath in his lungs as Corvus somersaulted onto the ground and kept running as fast as he could.

When he reached the ship, he spun around to see several more guards jumping onto Blem to immobilize him. Corvus did one better. With an angry flash of his eyes, cold fire streamed from his face. There was the sound of a sharp crack, and Blem and five guards froze in place, entombed in ice. Then Corvus spread his arms wide and stuck them over his head. The ice tomb rose into the air. Corvus turned and directed it to the river, throwing with his arms the ice tomb and its contents, which smashed into the river. He yelled in rage, his face glowed a pale preternatural blue, and the Nile froze in its course all the way down to the muddy bottom. Waves, knife sharp, stood motionless on its surface.

Corvus ran up the ramp. He dove inside and the ramp closed and the hatch hissed sealed just as the force of the Nile's waters upriver crashed against the ice, ripping and crushing against itself, heaving fragmented bergs onto the shore. Nearby, in a whirl of flying and stinging sand, the ship ascended into the night.

42 PRECESSION PART 1: MAGOG

Renender stood on the narrow slippery shelf of rock at the foot of the waterfall, exhilarated by the force of the torrent. Two days had passed since his coming to the Canine children's secret village. In those two days he had explored the potential of the newfound powers imparted by his mysterious magic suit. Tag-you're-it was an easy game to win when one could disappear and reappear at will. But it wasn't all play. He put his super-Human strength to work repairing the damage done to the monastery by the ice dragon attack. Now he was about to show off again in front of Aleph who waited patiently at the top of the waterfall.

"Anytime now would be fine," yelled Aleph, his voice barely heard over the great roar of water crashing around Renender. But Renender easily heard him just the same.

Renender ducked his head out of the curtain of water to gaze at the river's tumbling course to the lower valleys below. He ducked his head back in again to the little space behind the wall of water. He took a gulp of air, readying himself for his next feat. Attached to his waist were two reed baskets, open at the top. He cautiously turned himself around to face the rock wall. He lifted his arms, and leapt.

Like a professional athlete in a competition, he swam straight up through the rushing downpour. Plop! Plop! Plop! went his baskets the whole way up. When he leapt free of the rushing water to land right in front of the startled Aleph, his baskets were laden with fish that had swum down the waterfall from the pool at the top.

"I have dinner!" said Renender proudly.

"We could have just caught them up here," said Aleph.

"But where's the fun in that?" said Renender, and they both laughed.

"Hey! You're perfectly dry!" exclaimed Aleph.

"I swam between the water drops," said Renender. The abilities of the magic suit seemed to have no bounds.

Aleph took one of the baskets, the fish still flopping inside. Aleph and Renender made their way up the path beside the pool to the village. It had been decreed Renender's turn to prepare the communal meal this day. On the way back, they collected wild mushrooms and herbs. By the time they reached the village in the later afternoon, all their provisions for the feast were in hand, and basket.

"There you are," said Uriel to Renender, standing atop the steps of the monastery. "I found the book I was talking about, the one that tells the story of the suit."

Renender had been excited to hear about the alleged book. The night before, she had been unable to find it.

"Great! Let me just put these in the kitchen."

"Don't just leave the fish in the kitchen," said Aleph. "You have to do ALL the preparing."

"Ok," said Renender. "After dinner?" he said to Uriel.

"That's fine," she replied.

* * *

In the kitchen, Renender and Aleph emptied their baskets of fish onto the long wooden table in the middle of the room. The mushrooms and herbs went into large bowls. Then Renender just stood there.

"What's wrong?" asked Aleph.

"Nothing," said Renender. "It's just that I don't know how to, uh, I don't know how to...."

"Gut the fish?"

"Yeah."

"I can show you." Aleph went to the knife block and selected a slender blade. He laid out a fish and began to show Renender his technique. "First, the blade is very sharp, so be careful." He positioned the blade just passed the gills. "Slice forcefully down here." He tossed the head into a large bowl on the table. "Now for the insides." He held the fish in his hand and cut through the midsection. "All you have to do is reach in and pull out the guts." He demonstrated, scooping out the innards in a quick motion and dropping them into a slop bucket on the floor. He chopped off the tail. "And you're done."

Renender watched Aleph's skill with great fascination.

"It's easy actually. Here, now you try." Aleph handed the knife to Renender. He turned to fetch another knife from the block. When he turned back, he stopped short, mouth agape. Twenty-seven fish lay in a neat row, beheaded, betailed and gutted. The bowl of fish heads was full, and the slop bucket was full of tails and guts. Renender set the knife down on the table and looked at Aleph.

"Like that?"

"They're all done!" Aleph poked several fish, seeing that each was prepared just as he'd demonstrated.

"Did I do it right?"

Aleph laughed, setting his knife down. "Yeah. Just right."

Renender smiled. "I'm a quick learner." He started gathering pans and ingredients.

"You can't cook them with the scales on," said Aleph. "Here, they come off like this." With his knife, Aleph held a fish over the slop bucket and scraped against the scales' growth. Scales dropped into the bucket. "Think you've got the hang of it?"

Renender took his blade. In a flurry of motion, he scaled the other twenty-six fish in a matter of seconds.

"Wow," said Aleph. "You are fast."

Renender grinned wide, pleased with himself.

"I'll take out the slop bucket and bury this stuff in the garden. Have fun with the rest of it."

"I'll see you at dinner," Renender called after him.

Two hours later the children were all gathered around the table in the big hall. They chatted loudly amongst themselves in anticipation of Renender's first prepared meal. They all fell quiet when he emerged from the back spiral staircase carrying a large steaming bowl. He set it on the table, then ran back down the stairs, returning a moment later with a platter laden with breaded fried fish. Delectable aromas filled the hall and everyone's stomach grumbled. Renender took his place at the head of the table with Aleph and Uriel on either side.

"My friends," began Renender. "It is my great honor to present you with a fine feast of my own making. I swam the great waterfall to catch the fish before you tonight. Mushrooms and herbs I picked along the fragrant path. They were gently simmered to make this fish head soup. We thank the ground and the water, the sky and the sun, for the feast we partake together this day. We give thanks."

"We give thanks!" all the children said in unison.

"Let us eat!"

And they did eat. The fish fillets disappeared in minutes, followed by slurp-slurp-slurping of the soup. No one said a word until the meal was finished. Bread rolls soaked up the bottom of each soup bowl. Finally satiated, the Canine children and Renender sat back on their cushions burping, smiling and happy, bellies full and taste buds impressed.

"Thank you, Renender!" each said. Renender was pleased with his culinary skills.

* * *

After the grand meal, while some of the children attended to the cleaning of dishes and others went out to play, Renender, Aleph and Uriel were alone in the great hall. Evening bled the light of day from the room and Aleph started toward the great hearth to stoke the fire.

"Aleph, my friend," said Renender. "Let me." He stared into the hearth, feeling the heat of the coals in his soul and awakening the desire for more. Renender reached an arm toward the low flames. Tongues of fire burst from his outstretched fingertips. Then they flew forth into the hearth, waking the fire. The flames burned high, lapping up into the flue. Two logs levitated from the woodpile and dropped dead center among the flames. The wood crackled and spat. The hall basked in brilliant heat and light.

"You know such tricks," said Aleph.

"That's just it, Aleph," said Renender. "I don't know how I know. There's a power in me I don't understand."

"Then maybe I can help you," said Uriel. She was at the great bookcase. From a shelf just above her head she retrieved a big dusty book, bound in soft brown leather. She laid the book on the table. "Come here, both of you."

They came to the table and sat on cushions on either side of Uriel. She caressed the front of the book. "This tells the history of the suit, and of the Shadow Warriors who once wore them."

"Shadow Warriors?" asked Renender.

Uriel opened the book. The pages were leather. Drawn in colorful detail were images of warrior Canines glowing in powerful suits just like Renender's. Strange letters of a script unknown to him lay at the bottom of each page.

Uriel turned the pages slowly, taking in the images and reading the text. "The earliest days on Lupus were peaceful. But the Birds of Prey tried to control the other species. When they could not, they sought us only as carrion for their tables. Some Humans proved easier to sway, and some turned against the Canines, though not all were so beguiled. Most Humans made pact with the Canines, and they put their strengths together to fight the Birds of Prey. They devised uniforms of power, and so the Shadow Warriors were born.

"The Shadow Warriors gathered before the forested plains of Bafaria to drive the Birds of Prey from those mountain eyries that were their homes. From the low plains to the high heights battles ensued. Thunder and lightning filled the lands with burning fires and death. Gog was defeated and thrust into the void. The rest of the Birdmen sought refuge in the Mountains of Canius. The bells of the mountains tolled. The Watchers fell, and the heights were filled with sky dragons and ice dragons. The Shadow Warriors met them in battle until all but a few were subdued. The rest fled to hide in the fields of ice. Magog escaped and set fires on the mountains. Most Shadow Warriors fell, but one stood with breath still in his lungs. The last battle was fought in a deep valley, where Magog beat down the last Warrior of Shadows. Then it was that Casimir of the Red Falcons rallied. The Canines of the valley woke the Anthroforms, and both Magog and Casimir with their hosts disappeared into the void."

Uriel turned to the final page where was depicted the suit in its catacomb compartment where Renender found it. In the picture, a small boy faced the glowing suit on its dais. Uriel read the final caption. "The suit always remembers." She closed the book.

The three were silent for some moments. Finally Renender asked a question. "Did you know the suit was here? Before it found me, I mean?"

Aleph answered very matter of factly. "Of course. I put it there myself, when the last Shadow Warrior died."

Uriel nodded.

"But according to this book, that was a long, long time ago."

"It was a long time ago. But I remember it like it was yesterday."

"What do the last words mean?" asked Renender. "'The suit always remembers.'"

"It means the suit remembers everyone who has worn it," said Uriel. "It remembers the times it fought."

Renender closed his eyes. He tried to remember what the suit might remember of its past, but try as he might, he could only think of the taste of fish in his mouth and the fun he had swimming up the great waterfall. Then he heard shouts below him. He opened his eyes.

"Whoa! What are you doing? What are you doing?"

Renender found himself floating in the air near the rafters. "How did I get up here?" he asked aloud.

"What were you just thinking of?" asked Uriel.

Renender floated down to the floor and settled cross-legged on a cushion. "I was thinking about this morning, swimming up the waterfall."

Both Aleph and Uriel said in unison, "The suit remembers."

"The suit remembers," repeated Renender. And they all fell quiet.

The light had by now fully receded from the windows, and the rest of the children returned to the great hall. They began pulling out their blankets, settling into a cozy circle before the great hearth, which still burnt fiercely.

"Who'll tell a story?" asked one.

"Choose among yourselves," said Aleph. "Uriel and I have something we want to show Renender. We'll be back later."

The trio exited the monastery and selected the path up the flanks of the mountain whose peak formed the bestial Canine Anthroform. They ascended to the top, transforming into adults on the way. Below the Anthroform, a semi circle of stone benches faced outward, and on these they sat. The stars above were close and bright. The night air was not too chill, and no wind blew. The three could discern the outlines of the Anthroforms on the mountaintops around. Their rock faces reflected the ample starlight, but their frightening grimaces were shrouded in the night.

Behind them opened the cave into the heart of the Canine Anthroform. In it were the dark shapes of statues, like those Renender had passed on his way through the cave beneath the Human Anthroform.

"Aleph," said Renender. "With my now older eyes I understand much more of what you and Uriel have been telling and showing me. I think I understand your places here."

Aleph said, "The years are gentle on us down in the valley, but I know the outside world is full of trials for the peoples out there. When I first found you, you said you were looking for help, but you did not remember exactly why. Do you remember now?"

Renender did not have to think long. The occupation of Lupus City, and the calculating terror of Corvus and Markhab, was quick in his memory. "Yes. A great evil has entered my city, and from that I fled."

"After tonight, Renender," said Aleph, "soon you will be able to return to your city. I think now you know that the help you sought has found you. You came to us, and the suit found you. It will aid you in your task."

"But," said Uriel, "you must help us tomorrow."

"What happens tomorrow?"

"The bells will ring again in these mountains," said Aleph. "And we will need your help to fight against what follows."

"And what is that?"

"The void will open," said Uriel.

"And the Birds of Prey will return," finished Aleph.

"But why will they return?"

"Because it is Precession Night," said Uriel.

"It is time for us to finish what started long ago," said Aleph. "We must be prepared to fight, if it comes to that. The suit must fulfill its destiny. Then you will be free to fight your own fight, and perhaps to meet your own fate."

"But look now," said Uriel. She pointed northeast to a cleft in the mountaintops. There, a bright blue star was just beginning to shine through. "It is the Precession Star. The time has finally come."

"I heard stories of Precession as a child, stories my mother told me," said Renender. "It was she who gave me this amulet." He touched the gem star hanging around his neck. As he touched it, the light of the Precession Star refracted and reflected in the facets of the gemstone. The reflected light grew in luminous tendrils that stretched across the valley to illuminate the other mountain top statues. Soon all four Anthroforms appeared animated as the red, green, yellow and blue light danced on their surfaces. The air felt electrified and full of movement, though it was not certain whether they actually moved, or the effect was an illusion of light. Then Renender underwent a change.

The refracting colors of light streamed over the suit and pulsated until it was a dazzling rainbow of living light. He stood, and at once Renender grew. His body stretched until his head was level with the heads of the Anthroforms. He looked into their eyes. Something sparkled back. Renender looked passed them. He had a distant awareness of the movement of ice dragons, cries of Humans in Mine City, even below, the voices of the Canine children telling bedtime stories. Then Renender shrunk back down to normal size, and he was again sitting on the stone bench beside Aleph and Uriel.

"What are the Anthroforms?" he asked.

"They are guardians," said Aleph. "Carved out of the titanium mountains long ago, very long ago. So long ago even I have difficulty remembering."

"Why are they in the form of beasts?"

"They were not always that way," was all Aleph would add.

The Precession Star moved out of range of the cleft in the mountain peaks. Renender's amulet ceased its refraction. The suit stopped pulsating.

"I will help you," said Renender. "Then I will take my leave."

Aleph and Uriel nodded. The three got up and silently made their way back down the mountain path. Again as children, they found their beds beside the warmth of the great hearth and they took their sleep with the others.

Dawn did not take long in coming. The children were up quick and tidied their bedding away with haste. Much had to be done this day. Breakfast was sparse but satisfying, bread rolls with butter and honey, fish paste on tender greens, and refreshing water.

When the dishes were done and put away, Aleph gathered all together to assign work details. The great bell atop the monastery had to be cleared of vines, swept of dust and emptied of spiders. The ropes had to be checked and reinforced, and this was not the only bell in the valley. Hundreds of smaller bells hung throughout, atop cottages and walls, and hanging from rocky outcrops along all the mountain paths. These, too, had to be inspected and cleaned. The valley chimed with the sound of tinkles high and low, near and far.

While this was going on, Aleph led others to a stock room in the catacombs where a great number of arms were cached. There were spears and axes, bows and arrows. These they sharpened and readied for use. They brought them outside and laid them against the outer walls of the monastery, against huts, and in many strategic places round about.

Shortly after noon Aleph announced lunch, and all the children gathered on the grass beside the stream to picnic in the sun. They feasted on capered salad, dark bread and spring berries. After a short but ample rest, the work resumed.

Renender worked on clearing the bells at the top of the mountain paths. Grown tall and adult, and full of memories, he started near the Canine Anthroform. There was not much to do. The path was apparently well traveled and the Canines kept the path and bells well cleaned. He moved onto the next Anthroform, the dragon-like Bird of Prey, by leaping into the air and soaring over the valley, landing on his feet next to the cave. There were statues in this cave, Bird of Prey chieftains brandishing spears. After the bells were inspected and cleaned, Renender sat on a large stone. He could hear the voices of Canines along the paths, talking and singing. He heard Aleph and the others laying out the arms. Like the night before, he could also hear the movement of the ice dragon, or were there more than one? They were trudging across ice fields, leaping over crevasses and scaling rock walls. Everywhere was motion and preparation.

Another leap, and the bells around the saber-cat like Feline Anthroform were at hand. Curious, thought Renender. In this cave there were no statues of warriors, only what looked like the remains of levers and gears jutting out of the rock walls. The bells around here were the most overgrown.

Last was the peak topped with the vampire-like Human Anthroform. Here was the cave where Renender had first appeared several days before. *Soon I will make my way back through this labyrinth,* he thought to himself. Anticipation began to fill his being. Anticipation for whatever Aleph was going to set in motion this day, and anticipation for returning to the Human cities beyond these mountains. He would have much to do. The bells were quickly found and cleaned. Then Renender descended back down into the valley, again a boy in a magic suit.

The afternoon was getting on and Renender was hungry, though it was not yet the traditional time for dinner. Today would be different. As Renender trotted down the mountain path and reached the grassy area beside the stream where they had lunched, he saw another picnic feast had been laid out. Uriel had prepared this meal. The children all sat in a circle around the food. Renender took his place beside Aleph and Uriel again.

"I had the pleasure of preparing this meal. Rice bread made from grain harvested by hand. We have a salad of water hyacinth sprouts and ground cover nuts. Filleted fish, caught in the traditional manner with line and pole," Uriel said, smiling in Renender's direction. "Sweet seed-bread from last season's squash. Refreshing water from ice melt. We thank the ground, the air; we thank the sunlight and waters of ice and stream. We give thanks for this meal. Let it nourish us body and soul this day, this night. We give thanks."

"We give thanks!" said the children in unison. They heartily consumed the food.

The sun was fast moving over the mountains, and shadows lengthened in the valley. The remains of dinner were quickly dealt with. Then all gathered at the foot of the monastery steps. Aleph prepared to speak.

"My friends. It has been a long, long, long time since we last rang the bells with vigor in this valley. It is time to do so again. We must all be prepared for what will follow. You know where our weapons are stowed. We will remember how to use them. Are there any questions?"

The group was silent, though all harbored many questions.

"Alright. It is time. I will ascend the bell tower and start the bell. It must ring continuously. Each will have a turn. Renender, you shall help, too. Be the last. Ok, let's do it."

Aleph headed up the steps and into the monastery with several Canines following.

"You can stay here with me, Renender, until it is your turn," said Uriel.

Renender nodded.

After a few minutes, the clamor began.

Aleph rang the bell atop the monastery. The pure circular tones rang out across the valley and up into the heights. ZING-ZING-ZING-ZING. Its resonance was picked up by each of the hundreds of little bells. The sound kept riding up the mountain faces. Feedback perpetually fed back into the system, increasing the pitch and decibels.

What happened next, Renender would find difficult to recall, even years later, for it seemed his whole experience moved in slow motion, as seen from a great distance. When the bell started, his consciousness was pushed aside from within by a Canine personality taking center stage in his psyche. *The suit remembers,* he thought. The suit glowed and shimmered. It radiated a kaleidoscope of colors outward from Renender's Precession Star amulet. He remained aware of many things, but they felt far away. The Canine children marched up and down the monastery steps, each taking a turn at the bell.

Aleph came up to him and said, "Renender, it is your turn."

Renender scaled the steps. The Canine girl ringing the bell ran in a tight circle around the bell's base, pulling a rope that dragged a titanium ball around the titanium-resonite bell, its movement made smooth by greased ball bearings. She was growing tired, and released her hold on the rope. Renender's hands curled around it. Now he circled the bell, his strength pulling the ball faster than any of the other children had been able to do. Faster and faster he went, and the resonating sound took visible form. Wave upon wave of sound shimmered in the air around and above the valley. Everything and everywhere echoed of bells.

Renender's mind filled with memories not his own. Fires and battles in mountain heights where Canines and Birds of Prey were pitched in life and death struggles. These came from the suit, remembering long ago deeds of renown like to those illustrated in Uriel's book. Still Renender ran in a circle around the bell.

High above the valley, the waves of sound pushed higher into the sky. A percussion wave forced the air into a column up, up into the atmosphere, punching upwards until the airs of Lupus bulged away from the planet in this place.

The first of Markhab's satellites to intersect the percussion column veered out of its assigned path. The turbulence knocked it hard, creating an out of control tumble. The satellite's trajectory was unstable and it plunged through the atmosphere, burning up and lighting the sky with streaks of fire. Other satellites, compensating for the gap in surveillance, automatically adjusted direction and course. They too, one by one, were knocked off course and plunged through the atmosphere in flames. Renender kept ringing the bell. Satellite after satellite fell. *And the Watchers fell.*

The column of sound and air rose even higher. Then the sky itself shimmered and blazed. Everyone looking up saw ghostly columns of flying reptiles stream from all directions of the sky to the percussion column. The sound of the resonating bells tore a hole from this world to one long hidden. And the winged hosts broke through.

Birds of Prey streamed out of the blinding portal, descending straight towards the valley. Cries that curdled the blood screeched down.

Below the bell tower, the Canine children were transformed. Each grew to manhood or womanhood, great warriors clad in mail. They ran for their spears and axes and bows. The Birds of Prey plummeting to treetop and ground barely had time to realize their escape from their long and tortured sleep before they were set upon by the Canine warriors. Metal and arrow met talon, beak and wing. Battles pitched all across the valley.

The Birds of Prey were almost three meters tall with wingspans of five meters. Their wings were iridescent Black and Silver. Their faces were covered with striped down, with lipped beaks and tube nostrils for mouth and nose. They had arms with hands like those of Canines, Humans and Felines, but their feet were clawed talons. Each had a feathered tail. They flapped and flapped and stirred the air into mighty winds. Many dove at the Canines, snatching spears out of the hands of the warriors, who had to scramble and dodge as they sought new arms. Arrows flew up and found many targets. Then with a shrieking roar, the mightiest and most feared of all Birds of Prey exited the sky portal and dove straight into the valley.

Magog, tyrant of history, joined his legions and led their muster. But quickly behind him, a new host of Birdmen appeared out of the portal. It was Casimir, friend to men, with his host of Red Falcons. They joined the battle and fought on the side of the Canines. Red and amber wings crashed against the Black and Silver. But Magog's host was far larger, and now it was joined by another terrible foe.

Ice dragons slithered and bounded down the mountain paths. A dozen of them, with green and red scales, horns and teeth, entered the valley. The biggest was thirty meters long, the smallest twenty. Their rock-splitting shrieks momentarily paralyzed the Canines. But the cries of the ice dragons were met by a new sound.

From the cave entrance below the Feline Anthroform, a great light shown forth, erupting with the sounds of glass breaking and metal sheets grinding against each other. A Feline with a double notch in one ear stood and watched the battle. Behind him, a dozen mechanical robots emerged from the light. They set to work pulling and straining to move the ancient levers in the cave. A deep CLICK sounded, and roaring resonating sounds burst forth.

In caves beneath each Anthroform, massive titanium and resonite bells, a hundred meters in diameter, rang in the deep. The mountains rumbled. The Anthroforms moved and changed. Their once-hideous forms morphed into mighty warriors in true forms of Canine, Human, Feline and Bird of Prey Red Falcons. Then from the other three caves, the armed statues came to life and issued forth. Statues of Canines, Humans and Birds of Prey joined the Canine warriors and Red Falcons. They ran down the mountain paths and attacked the dragons.

Renender saw all that was happening. Still he rang the great bell, faster and fast he went. The suit blazed in blinding hues. Renender released the rope and leapt down from the high tower. As he did, he grew in girth and height until he met the Birds of Prey face-to-face in the air. He swatted at them like they were flies.

On the mountains, the statued warriors routed the dragons. The beasts snarled and growled and loosed rocks onto their attackers, but they were pushed back up the mountains where they attempted to regroup beneath the Anthroforms. The animated colossi reached down and snatched up the dragons. The beasts shrieked in fury as they tried to dodge these new foes. The colossi threw the dragons down, breaking their bodies against the rocks. As dragon scale struck stone, lightning flashed into the sky. Thunder clapped across the vastness. The mountains shook.

The Birds of Prey under Magog's command regrouped and barreled down again into the valley, but Casimir's forces took up the space they vacated, pushing the Black and Silver host back down faster than they willed, blocking any retreat. Some Falcons sped up, and passing the dark host, they bent their wings and careened just over the ground, picking up golden spears from against the monastery wall and other caches, and quickly ascended again just centimeters from the ground. They clashed into Magog's host head on.

The chaos of shrieks and screams filled the valley, and the great bell still tolled, spinning round and round from the momentum left by Renender.

Magog's host tumbled through the Red Falcons' spears to the valley's floor where Aleph's Canines waited for them. Just above Aleph's head, Magog countered his descent by wildly beating his wings. His host followed suit, and the gale scattered dust, leaves and debris among the Canines such that they had to shield their eyes. Magog stood, wings beating, suspended in the air. The King of the Birdmen laughed. The Canines were enraged, and they shook their spears in the air.

Uriel hid behind a bush. She raised her bow and took aim at the great Birdman. She let her arrow fly. Magog looked in her direction and laughed again. His eyes were bright and cold and fierce. He extended an arm out toward Uriel and caught the arrow in mid-flight. He then threw it back down. Uriel ran. The arrow clanged against the stones behind which she had been crouching. It burst into splinters. Magog then signaled for his host to move against the Canines, who ran for cover, scattering in all directions.

Renender stepped forward all alone to take their place. He stood still, smiling, a lone figure. Magog made right for him. Fire was in Renender's eyes and his suit blazed. He reached out with his hands and grappled with Magog, grabbing onto his wings. Magog struggled, slashed at Renender with his taloned feet. But Renender held firm. Magog shrieked, and his cry shattered the glass windows of the monastery. Renender just smiled and did not let go. He saw passed Magog, saw red wings fast approaching, the figure of Casimir flying down, spear in hand directly at Magog.

"Welcome back Magog, King of Birds." The sound came from Renender, but it was not his voice. "Today you meet your end."

Magog thrashed in Renender's arms. He spat and squawked. He raised his head and stared directly into Renender's eyes. "YOU die this day," shouted Magog.

"Not yet," said Renender. He straightened his arms and braced himself.

Casimir's spear plunged into the back of Magog, whose surprised eyes widened in shock. His mouth agape, a feral piercing cry issued from his beaked lips. The point of the spear stuck through Magog's chest cavity, the Birdman's heart dangling from the end of the spear.

Renender dropped the Bird of Prey. Magog's body crashed against the rocks beside the stream at Aleph's feet. Aleph raised his axe, swung it round over his head three times, and brought it crashing down, severing Magog's head at the neck. The head rolled loosely in the stream's turbulent waters, bounced between rocks, then was carried down and away towards the fish pool. There, hungry fish attacked the head, ripping skin and flesh, eyes and feathers.

Casimir's host sped down, routing the now leaderless Black and Silver host. They scattered in confusion. Many were slaughtered outright, their bodies falling to the ground like autumn leaves in a wind. Those that managed to escape fled any way they could, away to distant places. Casimir and his Red Falcons gave chase until none were left in the valley.

The ZING-ZING of the great bell slowed, its momentum finally spent. The smaller bells around the valley stopped ringing, with only residual tinkling heard here and there. Renender shrunk to normal Human adult size. The shimmering air calmed and cleared. The Anthroforms returned to their stoic poses on the mountaintops, no longer in beastly guises. The lone Feline and his robots vanished in a burst of bright light. The statued warriors returned to their respective caves. No dragon remained alive in the valley. The quiet was itself deafening.

The Canine warriors assembled themselves on the monastery's steps. Not all had survived. In all, thirteen Canines had lost their lives.

Presently the Bird of Prey called Casimir returned. His followers held back, hovering in the air. Casimir landed on the grass before Aleph.

"Well met in battle, friend Casimir," said Aleph. "I waited long years for this day."

"It was but a moment for me since we chased Magog's forces into the void," said Casimir. "How is the world?"

"Changed," said Aleph.

"Other Birds of Prey will find their way back," said Casimir.

"All of them," replied Aleph.

"The Red Falcons will help." With that, Casimir beat his great wings and launched himself into the sky, leading his host away over the mountains.

Renender stepped up to Aleph's side. His consciousness returned as that of the suit retreated to the background of his psyche.

"You have aided us well, Renender," said Aleph.

Renender stayed silent. He looked about him at the carnage and the fallen, Canine and Birds of Prey. Then he looked at Aleph and simply said, "I will help with the cleanup."

"Appreciated," said Aleph. By the light of many lit torches, the work began. First the bodies of the slain Canines were taken to the side of the monastery and laid out in a row on the ground. Blankets were drawn over them. Then the heavy work began moving the huge carcasses of the Birds of Prey. Aleph directed that they be piled together in a heap on a gravelly surface on the opposite end of the valley. They piled leaves, branches and wood atop the heap, then the whole thing was set ablaze. The bonfire blazed into the night, its smoke filling the valley with a horrible stench. Feathers floated everywhere.

Aleph directed a mass grave to be dug in the valley below the Canine Anthroform. There the Canine dead were interred.

When all was done, Aleph came to Renender. "Now is the time to return to your own people and help them in their time of need. Come, we will walk the path to the cave together."

On the upward path Renender said, "I came here on the slim hope that I could find help for my people. I did not know what I might find, if I found anything at all."

"You found more than you bargained for," said Aleph.

"That is for sure."

"We needed your help as much as you needed ours."

"It seems my coming was part of a bigger story."

"There is always a bigger story to be told. It's all a matter of perspective."

They reached the entrance to the cave beneath the Human Anthroform. Inside, the statued warriors who had so recently fought against the ice dragons stood in their two rows, still and stoic, as if none had ever moved.

"I have a question," asked Renender.

"What is it?"

"The Feline that appeared. Who was he?"

"I don't know the answer. But wherever he came from, he too, is part of a larger story."

"I have another."

"Yes?"

"Are you the Alpha of all Canines?"

Aleph smiled. "Once I was. That title long ago passed to others. But I am still here."

Renender nodded, not sure of the meaning of the answer, but satisfied nonetheless.

"Go with speed, Renender. Help your people. And if our paths should cross again, we will meet as friends."

"Yes."

"I have some advice for you."

"I'll take it gladly."

"Aleph smiled again. "Remember, keep to the right."

Renender laughed. He'd left the titanium key that Bordent the Trickle Depth Sounder had given him in his small bag in the monastery, but Renender did not need it anymore. "Keep to the right," he repeated.

"Farewell then, Renender. For now." They embraced and Aleph left him. As the Canine walked down the path to the valley that his village called home, he shrunk to the form of a child. He turned a corner and was gone.

Renender stepped into the cave. His mind's eye formed a picture of the maze of twists and turns through the caverns. With lightning speed, he passed through. He passed the cavernous chamber of green slugs, the chamber with the pool where he had slept, and all the caves beyond. In minutes he stood in the Septum facing the green door. On the other side was the long hall leading back to the Hypogeum. Renender pushed the door open and went in.

43 PRECESSION PART 2: TIAMAT

Cornelius dreamed. He was running from a pillar of light under a star-filled sky. Wings were all about him, huge wings, black razor sharp wings. He ran, hiding his face and battling the wings. For a moment he was clear. Then a gruff voice spoke from nearby, full of malice.

"Corneze."

"You!" Cornelius answered. A black fist struck out and made contact with his head. Stars reeled.

Cornelius awoke. He sat up. He was sitting in the circle of henges. The sun was high. It was midday. He half expected to hear a rebuke from Naemi as her first words of the day. *You sleep too much.* But Naemi was not here. He smiled, amused that he would think of her words.

Alpha Trifid was nowhere about. Last night they had sat here together, lain here together.

Small white flowers grew all around the hill of the henges. He hadn't remembered noticing them last night, but his attention had been on so much else. Surveying the Henge Plain, Cornelius saw that the plain was circular with a ridge of hills all along the perimeter. The hill on which the henges stood rose up from the center of the circular plain. The whole plain was an ancient impact crater of immense size. A curious fact.

He heard a commotion somewhere in the distance, shouting, yelling, war drums, and lots of other noise. He stood up. Looking through the henges, he saw down on the plain below beside a grove of mound oaks, a huge gathering. People were everywhere. Many tents were arranged in rows. There were many fires, and smoke rose high into a sky without wind. Nearby were hundreds of motorbikes. To the left of the tents were numerous large crowds of people fighting. The camp was under attack! Cornelius ran down the hill with all his speed. He had no time to notice that in each of his footfalls upon the ground, blue lupines sprouted, grew and blossomed amid the white flowers.

Cornelius quickly traversed the couple of kilometers and reached the encampment. The sounds down here were completely different. The smoke from the many fires carried the smells of cooking. The yells around the fighting were cheers mixed with much laughter. The jostling groups of Canines and Humans were wrestling contests. The drums came from bands of musicians. Cornelius stopped. It was a party.

While Cornelius had slept the morning away, the refugees had traveled the distance from the old pyramid hill to the Henge Plain and set up a new camp. *Naemi was right,* Cornelius thought. *I sleep too much.*

He was famished. After his all night run with Alpha, and sleeping so late, his stomach grumbled as loud as the beats pounded out by the drummers.

A Canine woman walking by on her way to one of the kitchen tents heard his stomach and said, "Corneze, Sir. That's a mighty groan. Come with me and I'll fix you a heaping plate of food."

"Ah, that's just the thing. Lead the way."

The tent was big and very wide without sides. It was filled with steaming pots, bowls of fruit, bunches of vegetables and hanging smoked carcasses. Men, women and children were coming and going in a bustle. The many hands snatched up morsels of whatever they passed. The woman heaped slices of dark meat onto a plate, with raw carrots and roasted nuts. She tossed a tomato and a sprig of green on top and presented it to Cornelius with a smile.

"There's plenty more," she said.

"I will be back," replied Cornelius. "Thank you so much." He grabbed a cup and asked, "Water?"

"Out that way by the rocks. You'll see a flag. There's a spring."

"Much obliged." Cornelius headed off in the general direction, popping the tomato into his mouth. He came across Roger at the spring.

"There you are, My Boy," Roger said. "I was wondering when you'd turn up. I've got all your things packed neatly in my tent. Just let me know when you want them, and I'll walk you there."

"Thanks Roger," said Cornelius. "How are you doing?"

"I've eaten more in the past couple days than I have in a week." Roger laughed, rubbing his belly. "Quite a party."

"Sure is." Cornelius filled his cup three times from the spring, satiating his thirst. He set about devouring his meal. Burping profusely, he chuckled and said, "I'm getting more. Do you need anything?"

"Not at the moment," said Roger. He winked and nodded in a direction off to the left. There they spied a half naked young Canine woman bathing behind a towel near the spring.

Cornelius smiled and nodded. Then he left Roger to his spying, and headed back to the kitchen tent. He was just about done piling another serving of meats onto his plate when two children bounded in, knocking over a pot of hot water and spilling a pile of apples.

"Whoa!" cried Cornelius holding up his plate lest it fall over. "Nuttin, is that you?"

"Yep!" said the Human boy.

"Get out of here, you two," said a cook, reaching to retrieve the overturned pot.

"Who's your friend?" asked Cornelius.

"I'm Burnut," said the Canine boy.

"Burnut and Nuttin," said Cornelius. "You're as mischievous as Nut-Nuts. That's what I'll call you. The Nut-Nuts."

"I like it!" said Nuttin.

"Nut-Nut! Nut-Nut!" they both yelled, running out of the tent laughing.

Cornelius helped to restack the apples into a neat pile, then hovered around the kitchen until he was stuffed. He put down his plate and headed towards the sound of drumming, grabbing an apple to eat on the way.

An area designated for lavatories was set at the edge of the camp. A few groups of motorcycles were arranged around several dug holes, providing an element of privacy. Cornelius found a vacant hole and proceeded to relieve himself. The piss splattered and showered the nearest bike. Only then did he see the piss-stained sign that crudely read *Don't Piss On the Bikes*. "Oops," said Cornelius. When he was done, he shook himself three times for luck, and went to check out the drummers.

There was a group of Canines and Humans playing flutes, string mandolins, and one with a violin. Nearby, four different groups sat with drums, bongos, bass beaters and stick pans. The combined sounds competed for attention in a chaotic rumble. Cornelius walked up to one group and asked if he could join in. A Canine lad gave up his drum and Cornelius sat on the grass with others, first observing their styles and skills. One boy had a beat that Cornelius liked. He started drumming, using his palms and knuckles on the side rim and center. He put out a beat he'd been working on back in Shining City. It was lively and up-tempo. Soon the others picked up the beat and offered their own complementary sounds. Their heads were nodding in rhythm and everyone was smiling. Before long, the other three groups broke up and came over. They plopped down and joined in. Those with string instruments and flutes added to the music. People came wandering over to watch and to listen. Some energetic youths did acrobatics nearby, and not a few danced, while more stood and clapped. All through the melody, the grasses and flowers growing about pulsed in rhythmic harmony with the musicians.

Cornelius took up a solo. He belted out a beat that got everyone really moving. He was in his element. Another group showed up with tambourines. The party was going. Among the crowd, he observed three old bent wrinkled hags, ugly women, shuffling through the throng away in the direction of the hill of henges. Then some distance away horns sounded. They were answered by horns blowing somewhere in the camp. The drummers stopped as people ran to see who was coming. Cornelius stood up with the others.

"Stilt Walkers!" some cried.

"Desert Stilt Walkers!"

Arriving from the south was a strange assemblage of persons. Maybe a hundred Canines decked out in long feathered plumes that bounced from the odd movement of the walkers on two-meter high stilts. Pads were affixed to the feet, and bells hung on the long stilt legs all the way up to the Canines' feet. The Walkers maneuvering on the stilts wore hats shaped like umbrellas. They carried bulging backpacks.

Alpha Trifid suddenly appeared from among the crowd. "Ahoy wanderers," he cried out to the Stilt Walkers. "Welcome to the Festival. Rest! Eat! Enjoy!"

The Stilt Walkers formed themselves in a circle. Then each leaned to his neighbor on his left, kicking down his right stilt. Then jumping forward, each released his left stilt. The air was filled with the sound of their jingling bells. Soon the entire party stood on the ground, while their stilts lay in a perfect circle of counter-clockwise sticks in the shape of a sunburst.

The lead Walker moved forward and embraced Alpha. "We have traveled five days from the Lakes. We are headed to Canoon."

"In time to join the festival," said Alpha.

"Feliz Precession," said the Walker.

"Feliz Precession," Alpha answered.

The Walkers unslung their backpacks and laid them beside their stilts. Some rifled through their bags for personal possessions. Cornelius, watching intently, caught a glimpse of shiny metal canisters in the bags, each with a bright red R on the side. *Renender Enterprises,* thought Cornelius. The lake ship Canines on the Tarvash had transported similar canisters. *Titanium gas?* wondered Cornelius. *What is that for?* Alpha led the troupe into the camp.

The arrival of the Stilt Walkers caused considerable excitement. Even down from their stilts and out from under their umbrella hats, they stood out as an odd group. They wore brown leather harnesses around their toned and lithe torsos. Each bore billowy silk pantaloons tied at the knees with high-strapped leather sandals. The hair atop their heads was matted masses of dark brown dred locks. The rest of the hair on their bodies was a fine downy light brown.

Cornelius resumed his drumming with the other percussionists. The rest of the musicians took up their instruments. The party resumed. Some of the Walkers started leaping and rolling. They climbed on one another's shoulders three and four high before leaping off in all directions. Others engaged in a wrestling dance form of capoeira. Others drew glowing orbs from pockets in their pantaloons, tossing them high into the air, juggling seven or more at once. Amazed children gathered close. At the forefront were Cornelius' new Nut-Nuts, tumbling and dancing and laughing in imitation of the Walkers.

The afternoon wore on and Cornelius tired of his drumming. He relinquished his drum to a young Canine and headed over to the crowds encircling the Canines engaged in bouts of wrestling. The yells and cheers were loudest here. Several of Alpha's great warriors tested one another's strength and agility.

The first wrestling duo was both refugees, a Human and a Canine. Neither seemed to be very skilled. They went through the motions, circling, dodging, ducking and circling again. Their comrades cheered them on and they got a little braver. The Human lunged, grabbing a Canine leg and toppling his opponent. They rolled in the grass until the Canine finally found an advantage, quite by accident. He stumbled and fell on the Human, pinning him down. A Canine referee called the play, and the Canine jumped up, fists raised high as his fans cheered his victory.

"Who'll bout with Chumps?" the referee asked the bystanders.

Cornelius stepped forward. "I will." He jumped into the center of the circle, moving left then right. Cornelius and his opponent faced each other, locked arms and went at it as soon as the referee whistled through his teeth.

The crowd cheered. Many had encountered Cornelius over the past several days, and directed their enthusiasm to him. The bout was over quickly with a win for Cornelius. Now he danced about, fists in the air, yelling "Yeah! Yeah!"

"Who's next?" shouted the referee.

A Canian warrior stepped forward, grinning and full of rippling muscles. The warrior was a hair taller than Cornelius, and much more massive. At the whistle the bout began.

The two struggled, locked together, twisting one another in a tight circle. Cornelius tried several times to knock the Canian's legs, but the Canine's legs and thighs were like tree trunks of furred muscle. Cornelius broke off contact. The Canian head butted Cornelius' chest. Cornelius tumbled and rolled beneath his opponent, grabbing an ankle, lifting the foot off the ground. The Canian tumbled. Cornelius held onto the ankle and fell, pinning him. The referee called the match in Cornelius' favor. The crowd roared with cheers.

He jumped and danced, grinning and laughing. His grin faded when he recognized his next opponent. It was none other than Rokket, Captain of Alpha's Fifty Guard. Although Rokket was not that much taller, Cornelius felt dwarfed by the Canian. The referee brought them together. They locked arms at the shoulders, the whistle sounded, and the bout began.

They circled each other, sparring a bit, sizing one another up. Cornelius felt tense. This wouldn't do. He needed to remain limber. Rokket lunged and butted Cornelius' chest hard. Cornelius stumbled back. The Canians in the crowd roared. This was the only crowd now. The other wrestlers had joined the audience. Cornelius went for Rokket's feet. They refused to budge. Rokket flipped Cornelius over and nearly had him if Cornelius hadn't rolled between Rokket's legs and jumped back up. They sparred again.

Rokket spoke in a low growl for only Cornelius' ears. "Human Corneze thinks he has the Alpha's confidence now. We will see."

What is he talking about? Thought Cornelius. *Is this personal?*

Rokket lunged again and Cornelius quick-stepped to the side, but Rokket grabbed Cornelius' midsection and tossed him into the air as easily as if he'd lifted a child. Cornelius thudded onto the ground with the wind nearly knocked out of him. He rolled just in time to avoid Rokket landing on him with full force. Instead, he caught Cornelius' leg. Cornelius rolled over three times to avert getting his ankle broken. This bout was not just for fun. Rokket wanted blood.

Cornelius managed to free himself. He jumped to his feet and lunged at Rokket, knocking him backwards. The refugees roared and applauded. Rokket was clearly furious. Cornelius searched for an advantage. In the corner of his eye he spied a small sharp stone lying in the grass near Rokket's foot. Cornelius backed up just enough so that Rokket stepped onto the pointed stone. The Canine howled and wavered. Cornelius slammed into the Canian's shoulder. Rokket went down. Cornelius landed on him with his full weight. Rokket snarled in Cornelius' face, the Canine's breath hot and menacing. Rokket's arms and legs were pinned by Cornelius' hands and feet lying spread-eagled on the warrior.

Then Cornelius felt some force enter Rokket from the ground itself. The grass glowed an ethereal green. Both were flung up from the ground from an almost magical force. Cornelius was flung ten meters into the air and fell back down onto the ground in a thud. Rokket pounced on him. Cornelius struggled, then with his own surprising roar, evoked the same magic, throwing Rokket onto the ground. Rokket growled. The bystanders roared.

"You think you have the power?" said Rokket. Then he lunged at Cornelius.

The two rolled and somersaulted on the ground. Cornelius jumped up and over the Canian. Cornelius lunged again, this time exhaling a powerful breath. Rokket tumbled backwards and fell onto his back hard. He lay dazed. Cornelius pounced on him, but Rokket had feigned defeat. Cornelius found himself beneath the Canine. He squirmed. He arched his back. He could barely move. He turned his head this way then that. He caught sight of Alpha watching from the circle of bystanders. Cornelius drew his legs up and pounded Rokket with his knees. Rokket tipped over. Cornelius leapt up off the ground high into the air. With a flick of his wrist a whirlpool of air and dust flew into Rokket's face. The Canian blinked and sneezed.

Cornelius experienced his final move in slow motion. Rokket made to charge directly at Cornelius' mid section. Cornelius swerved and Rokket hit the ground. Cornelius was on him, definitively this time. He was face to face with the Canine. Cornelius growled in mockery, his hot breath taunting the Canian who growled and squirmed, to no avail. The referee called the match for Cornelius.

The crowd was wild. Cornelius experienced a moment of confusion. Rokket got up and ambled away. Cornelius was apprehensive, as if this was another feint, not the end of the game. But it quickly passed.

An eerie sound wove its way among the cheers and congratulations. Slowly, everyone became aware of the sound. It was singing. All eyes turned to look in the distance. There, up on the hill beside the henges were three figures, beautiful even at this distance, lovely female Canines in flowing white robes. There was a twinkling in the air above them. They were flying kites. The diamond shaped kites were of some reflective material that caught the westering rays of the sun. The singing grew louder. The Canines and Humans in the camp moved en masse toward the henges.

Cornelius, still huffing and puffing, took one step forward with the crowd, then stopped. Something seemed strange. The sun was just dipping below the horizon, but didn't set any further. The Humans and Canines drifting toward the henges slowed their march, and then stopped. Cornelius turned in a circle, and was startled to find Alpha standing beside him.

"Alpha. What's going on?"

"You and I shall compete in a match. You bested Rokket in a fine challenge, the best of my Fifty Guard. Now I shall challenge you."

"I have no desire to meet you in a challenge. It is not necessary."

"To the Canines, especially my Guard, it IS necessary." Alpha nodded in the direction of the crowd, frozen in their movement. All faced the henges, all but the Canian Guard. They faced Cornelius and Alpha, watching with frozen gazes.

"I challenge you, Corneze. Let us begin."

Reluctant to carry out his challenge, yet equally reluctant to disobey the Alpha, Cornelius capitulated. They locked arms at the shoulders. A whistle sounded from Alpha's lips. The match commenced.

Cornelius and Alpha began by each trying to dislodge a leg of the other. They knocked knees and ankles. They pushed against one another. Finally they broke their arm locks and circled. Cornelius lunged at Alpha, who was knocked back a few steps. Alpha lunged at Cornelius, knocking him off his feet. Cornelius flew backwards from the blow nearly a kilometer. What was going on? The eerie singing from the three women continued. Words came to his ears. *So you think you can be the next Alpha?* Cornelius didn't understand. He rushed at Alpha, covering the distance in two seconds. He slammed into Alpha, throwing him back. Even from this distance, Cornelius heard Alpha growl.

They raced towards one another and both leapt into the air and collided, arms and legs and heads akimbo in a furious tumble. They landed on the ground in a heap. Then each leapt into the air again, straight as bullets. In his ascent, Cornelius spun, creating a hurricane funnel. Alpha did the same. The funnels collided and both Cornelius and Alpha were thrown out as the funnels dissipated. When Cornelius hit the ground he gouged out a huge pit. Alpha landed on his feet on the rim. He raised his arms into the sky. The moisture in the air condensed, filling the pit with torrential rainwater. Cornelius rose to the surface on the back of a mountain that rose from the pit and soared skyward. The new mountain knocked Alpha off his ledge. Lightning crackled around the mountain peak, the accompanying thunder booming across the plain. Alpha howled and the mountain's roots collapsed, tons of rock crumbling into sand.

Cornelius struggled to stay atop the collapsing sand. He raised a new mountain, and stood on its peak. Alpha rose on a mountain equally high. As they faced each other across a dark abyss, the sky wheeled. A boom echoed in the far south. Looking in the direction of the far distant Canius Mountains, a beam of light pierced the atmosphere. Lights across the sky streamed toward the light. They were Markhab's satellites. One by one they encountered the atmospheric disturbance and plunged through the air in fiery descents. Cornelius was in the midst of calling up a new tornado.

Alpha wrenched away the top of his mountain many times his own size and held it aloft above his head ready to throw it at Cornelius. They both saw that twin blazing orbs of satellite debris were headed right towards them. Cornelius and Alpha's eyes met, they nodded in recognition of the danger, and directed their fighting now at the incoming debris. Alpha heaved his boulder at one of the satellites, and it exploded in the sky in a shower of fireworks. Cornelius launched his tornado at the other with similar results.

Alpha turned to Cornelius. "It would seem, Corneze, that we are…."

"Equals."

"Equals."

As they each turned toward the henge, the time spell was broken, and the crowd gathered at the hilltop. Cornelius and Alpha ran down their respective mountains, which collapsed as sand behind them. They met in the circle of henges beside the three kite flying Canines.

The satellites continued to fall in the distance, raining down on Lupus like fireworks.

"Fireworks for our celebration of Precession," called out Alpha. Then to Cornelius he said, "I know what is in your mind. The movement of Canines on the surface of Lupus will no longer be seen by Markhab. He has lost his eyes on the world. For us, for tonight, they are fireworks."

The Canians, Stilt Walkers and refugees were in celebration. There was more music and drums and dancing. Bonfires lit the base of the hill, their lights reflected in the twinkling of the airy kites. As the night and revelry wore on, distant booms and thunder were heard. Lightning etched the southern horizon. At one point a frightful shriek was carried on the air.

Cornelius saw that the Canians were restless and uneasy, though the others kept partying. He asked of Alpha, "What is happening away to the south?"

"You are observant," said Alpha. "Be wary now. A new danger comes fast towards us."

"What danger?"

"On the wing, attracted by the flashing light of our kites and fires. Stand with me now, our backs to the henge."

There was a sound of flight on the air, of frantically beating wings coming closer.

"To arms!" yelled the Alpha. "Everyone!"

Spears grew out of the ground around the hill beside every man, woman and child, like they were new saplings. Each grabbed their spear and thrust it skyward. The three women released the strings of their kites, and shrieking, metamorphosed into three bent and wrinkled hags. The kites, instead of floating off into the sky, turned to walking sticks and fell before the women, who picked them up and swung them at the sky. Then the Black and Silver wings attacked.

There was riot and confusion all about the hill. The refugees stabbed at the darkness above. They did not know what foe or foes befell them. Streaks of silver flashed here and there in the air. Bright eyes came and went, filling terror in the hearts of those who saw them, however briefly. Claws reached down out of the blackness to maim and tear, and then withdrew. And always there was the flapping, flapping of wings. Yet no other cry was heard than the cries of the refugees. The air grew very cold, a ghastly chill drawn down by the wings.

"What is this thing?" asked Cornelius standing beside Alpha.

"They are many things, many foes," answered Alpha tensely. "They are the Birds of Prey."

"Gods and stars," exclaimed Cornelius, and he looked up, making out individual shapes now that he had an idea what to look for.

The Fifty Guard was interspersed among the rest. They leapt high into the air, stabbing and knocking the Birdmen. Those killed or mortally wounded fell among the refugees, causing more panic, their first glimpses of Birds of Prey other than from books, stories told to frighten children.

"We must call a greater power to help us this night," said Alpha. He started to glow. In fact the entire hill, the entire plain, pulsed with light. Streaks of it flooded down from the rim of the plain and merged on the hill, the henges glowing like the Alpha glowed. And Cornelius glowed, too. Tongues of fire leapt from Cornelius and Alpha's eyes.

"We call the great mother of these beasts to drive away her evil brood. Cornelius, look up into the sky with me, now!"

As they both bent their heads, beams of light shot out from their eyes straight into the dark sky. The beams merged far above in a crash of thunder. A portal opened in the sky. Out of the portal emerged the gargantuan form of a dragon sparkling in golden scales. Huge wings beat the air and the monster writhed and turned in the sky above the henge. Beams of golden light shot out from the flaming orbs that were the creature's eyes. The pulsing light on the henge plain went out. Cornelius and Alpha stood as two dark figures among the henges.

"What new beast is this? Foe or friend?" cried Cornelius.

"Neither, and both," replied Alpha. "Tiamat is danger." Then calling out into the night, he yelled, "Mother Tiamat. Reign in your brood!"

A great hot wind surrounded Tiamat. She let out a piercing cry, and fire erupted from her throat. Then were heard the sudden and maddened screeches of a thousand Black and Silver Birds of Prey. The shrieks froze the blood of all who heard them. They carried snow and ice on their shrieks. Hail fell, hard and smoldering among the refugees.

Long spears grew out of the ground beside Cornelius and Alpha. They each took up arms and leapt into the air, shouting challenges at the winged horde. Mortally wounded Birds of Prey fell among the people.

Cornelius plunged his spear into the heart of a Birdman, and both fell to ground. Cornelius yanked his spear from the felled creature. As he prepared to launch himself into the air again, a gruff voice from behind called out.

"Corneze!"

Cornelius spun around, "You!" It was Rokket.

"We have unfinished business, you and I," growled Rokket.

"This is no time for vendettas," cried Cornelius.

"Do you deprive me of my honor?"

"You deprive yourself of honor. Fight WITH me, not against me."

"You think you can be Alpha. We will see." Rokket lunged at Cornelius and struck a blow with his furry black fist squarely into Cornelius' jaw.

Cornelius was flung into a group of panicked refugees. Spears shattered about him. Rokket was beside him in an instant with a spear raised high in his hand. There were too many innocents nearby for Cornelius to summon a wind. Instead, he growled and called forth that ground force that had served both Cornelius and Rokket in their previous bout. They both bounced up into the air. Cornelius grappled with Rokket and loosed the Canian's spear from his grip. Cornelius fell to the ground with Rokket falling next. Cornelius aimed the spear directly at the Canian and braced himself for the force of impact. But before it could find its mark, black talons grabbed Rokket in midair, carrying the howling Canine up into the night. A few moments later pieces of the warrior torn asunder by the Birdmen landed among the refugees, who scrambled away, splattered in gore and pummeled by body parts.

"Corneze! To me!" It was a call carried on the air from Alpha among the henges. Cornelius fought his way to the hilltop to stand beside Alpha.

"We must drive her back, Corneze, before the whole plain goes up in flame. Again, eyes to heaven!"

The plain pulsed with light again and the two raised their fiery faces to the sky. The beams of light struck the dragon Tiamat. From her blood curdling screeches she belched fire, setting her brood of Black and Silver Birdmen aflame. The sky was full of burning bodies and feathers falling to ground. A portal opened in the sky above Tiamat. The great dragon fought against the powerful beams issuing from the Alphas on the hilltop.

"More, Corneze!" cried Alpha. Alpha raised his arms, and the hilltop groaned. The henges swayed and wobbled, becoming separated and teetering over.

Cornelius knew what he had to do. His face still pointing skyward, he spun his body around. A terrific wind raced around the hill. By the force of the tornado, and Alpha's power, the henge stones rose into the sky. Faster and faster they sped upward until one after another they struck Tiamat. Again and again the stones were taken up into the airs after striking the dragon. Again and again they pummeled the golden-scaled body of the beast. At last, Tiamat could find no other safe repose than was offered by the sky portal. She screamed a last great scream into the night air of Lupus.

"Away, holy mother. Away to your wide secret halls. Away!' cried Alpha.

Tiamat's great barbed tail flung down and crashed into the hill. Where her tail struck, bodies of unfortunate refugees flew in all directions and the hill was shattered. A flash of light and grating sound of metals accompanied the crash. Cornelius and Alpha were thrown off the hill. Their beams of light were extinguished. The dragon disappeared into the sky portal. It closed, and darkness covered the plain. Only the embers of bonfires and cooked corpses twinkled here and there. The rush of flapping wings retreated far to the northeast, a small remnant of the Birdmen who had survived, barely.

The rest of that tragic night was a long and mournful wait for the dawn. Caring for the wounded meant first finding them. A few Birds of Prey suffered living through the night before the sun rose. Those that could speak were interrogated as to whence they'd come, where those who had escaped had planned to rendezvous, and what was the nature of their plans. Any still alive at dawn were finally given a merciful beheading, ending their suffering torment. As the sky brightened in the east, the destruction wrought was fully revealed. The henge stones were a jumbled pile of broken monuments. The hill was rent, and hundreds were known to have perished. Of the Alpha's Fifty Guard, there were now forty-nine. Two children, the very ones called by Cornelius, the Nut-Nuts, were missing, assumed smashed by the falling henges or crushed by the vengeful tail of the golden dragon, which was where they had last been seen by any witnesses. Bodies were gathered, piled and burned.

Alpha held a small council of his Guard and representatives of the refugees and the Silt Walkers.

"Roger, you will ready the refugees for a journey south to safe lands of the

Canines in the wood along the shores of the Western Lake. Take only those motorcycles that can be spared after the metal works have been stripped and transferred to other bikes. Silt Walkers, you will proceed to Canoon with all haste, as you had planned. The main host of bike riders is to travel to the great river below Canoon where my Guard will gather for an assault against Markhab's forces in Bafaria, and any other foes that may be there."

Later, surrounded by his Forty-Nine Guard, Alpha offered the position of Captain of the Guard to Cornelius. "My Guard will be fifty strong again. Though you be an Alpha in your own right, by tradition you may accede to Rokket's position, having bested him fairly in a wrestling bout." Cornelius accepted, at once being Alpha's equal, and also his immediate representative among the Guard. None protested.

"After we have eaten and rested and been assured of the readiness of the refugees to depart, we shall race by foot to Canoon and there await the meeting of the host on motorbikes. Our movement may now go unseen by Markhab. There our battle plans shall be made and put into motion."

Thus the sorrowful first day of the new age began.

44 PRECESSION PART 3: KISS OF THE BAT

A crouched figure slinked in the shadows cast by a streetlight through the metal gate in the concrete wall. It was night in Cronapolis. No stars showed through the thick fog blanketing the capital. Water collected on the barbed wire fence atop the wall, dripping to form rivulets down the course surface, down the sign that read "Power Station Gate 14" and warned "Trespassers Will Be Shot On Sight." Wet trees and bushes grew close together along the wall.

The night was quiet. Only the silvery drops of moisture falling onto the gravel ground made any noise. The crouched figure on the inside of the gate shifted position, and a twig snapped. There was a quick intake of breath. Then the figure quickly leapt over the wall, somersaulting over the barbed wire. His long black cloak snagged on a barb, a piece of fabric remained dangling. The figure dropped to the ground and disappeared into the dark foliage. He looked back and up at the torn fabric. Nothing to do about it. He opened the cover of his wristwatch, an amber light suddenly revealed. Then it was shut off. "Sine cosine, cosine sine," murmured the figure. He quickly, softly moved through the foliage, darted out across the wet dimly lit street in soft and quiet moccasins, and disappeared in the trees on the other side.

Here was a low building one story high that stood back from the trees and followed the road nearly a kilometer. A window faced the direction from which he'd just come. He peered in at the lower right corner. Two guards sat at a table in the interior room playing cards. He was lucky they were engaged with their game and did not spy his dash across the road. He looked up at the tree above him with its sturdy bough overhanging the roof. With stealth he jumped, grabbing a branch and hauling himself up. In a moment he was crouching on the roof. There was movement below. The window opened. He heard voices.

"What is it? Is someone out there?"

"I don't see anything."

"Probably one of those boosles. You know how they scurry about at night, looking for anything to eat. Come on, it's my hand, and I'm winning."

"In your dreams."

The window closed and the guards retreated back to their game. The figure on the roof quickly scampered over shingles to the building's far side. Here was a narrow interior alley, across from which was another low building. He leapt, easily clearing the alley. He ran across this roof until, at its far end, he came to a metal ladder built into the building's side. Down this he scaled. At the bottom was another dark alley. He crept against the wall some distance before finding a large dumpster. He pushed against it, opening a space by the wall. Revealed on the ground was a grating. He moved it aside and slithered down, navigating his descent beneath street level by an internal ladder. His head below the opening, he reached up and pulled the dumpster back into its place against the wall. The grating he put back and climbed down, down to a network of sewer catacombs.

The weather and climate in Cronapolis this past month of spring was a perpetual hoary frost that chilled to the bone on the best of days. But the strange weather pattern over the city did not penetrate to these tunnels. Here it was overly warm, humid in the extreme, and full of noxious gasses. Effluence floated by in the streams of waste, with boosles munching on scrap and croaches jumping and clicking.

He pulled an air filtration mask from a pocket in his cloak and strapped it over his face. He breathed and allowed his shoulders to finally relax. He calmly walked down the main line, which was illuminated with a modicum of light from glow strips hanging from the ceiling a meter above his head. They supposedly had an average usage life of up to two hundred years. No one had ever been down here to inspect them or replace them since the sewer had been laid. But there were plenty of vagabonds much like himself who ventured here for much the same reasons as he, to move invisibly beneath the city and hide out when they needed to, and to stay warm. It was from one such hider that he had learned his greatest secret.

He walked the distance of ten city blocks, maneuvering around flotsam, pools and slime, and avoiding curious bristly boosles and the ever-present croaches. Now a small passage intersected from the left. He followed it a ways, then stopped at an outcropped block of concrete pillar. He put his hands and shoulder against the wall behind it and pushed. The wall gave way. He slipped and closed the wall behind him.

It was pitch black inside, but he knew this was a tubular tunnel angling down with a slippery floor. There were regular overhead beams that he grasped to stay upright and guide himself down. He descended. Fifty meters later his reached the bottom. He groped along the wall on his right until he found a dangling string. He pulled. A standing lamp connected to a large battery lit up a great stone corridor. It was eight meters wide and four tall. There were folding chairs, a heap of blankets that served as a bed when needed, and piles of reading material. A neat row of canned foods was stacked against a wall. He had a number of hiding places, but this was his favorite, his most secret. Craven was home.

He took off his cloak, tossing it onto a chair. He took off his shirt, revealing his skinny body in the light. From a box he pulled out a nice buttoned down shirt, purple with threaded sequins in a design about the collar and down along the row of buttons. He tossed his old shirt into the box. Lifting his wrist to his face, he opened the watch head. The two intersecting squiggly waves of light pulsed on the watch face. "Sine cosine, cosine sine," he said softly. He chuckled, smiled, closed the watch head, and proceeded to button his shirt.

Tonight was a special night. He was going to meet his girlfriend, the mysterious Moona, and enjoy a hedonistic night at a clandestine, and very illegal, party. It was Precession Night, and although any observance was strictly banned, there were plenty who found ways to celebrate. Maybe Moona's friend, Cornelius, would be there too.

Craven put his coat on, a hat, and turned off the lamp. He activated a setting on his watch, causing variously angled beams of light to feed his sight. The passage gently curved to the right. The walls and ceiling were dug through the bedrock and topped with enormous flat lintels twenty meters long each that spanned the passage. All the lines were precise, the curves perfect. Craven had learned by exploring that this was one of six immense tunnel systems that spiraled through Cronapolis' underside. They originated at dead ends beneath the outskirts of the city at sixty-degree intervals in a perfect circle. They all converged at one point, around a six-sided column directly beneath the Acropolis' Forum. But Craven wasn't going that far tonight. He was going to the rave, and he and Moona were going to share something special, intimate. They were going to share the joining of consciousness by the Kiss of the Bat.

Living on the streets, and under them, for years introduces one to many unusual things. Such were the bats of Cronapolis. These mammals were somewhat domesticated, many being kept as pets by certain underworld elements. They were excellent message carriers. And a veritable Cult of the Bat had grown up in recent years, right beneath the noses of the military Commissioners and their bureaucratic spies and lackeys. The method of carrying messages was both brilliant and surprising. If one holds a thought in one's mind, and allows oneself to be bitten by the bat, the images and content of said thought is encoded in the animal's saliva. The next person to be bit, or 'kissed', by the bat, hopefully the message's intended recipient, received the message directly into the bloodstream. The original thought and image associated with the message manifests in the recipient's mind, message received. The trick was not to get pulled in the dark morass of the bat's own thoughts. There was a danger there, a labyrinth of madness. It was akin to a bad trip, or an overdose, but in fact far more frightening for the host. Craven had seen not a few friends succumb to the allure of the bat mind.

After walking a distance of about a kilometer along the curved megalithic passageway, Craven stopped. In the wall on his right was a round shaft like the one he used to enter the tunnel where he kept his bedding and supplies. He scrambled up the ascending incline for fifty meters. A good push against the wall forced an opening into the city sewers again. The light from his watch caused a hoard of croaches to scurry in all directions, but not before some met their demise under Craven's footfall. The dank of the sewers was a marked contrast to the neat and dry tunnels below. He donned his air mask again.

He made his way deliberately and without haste around the dark puddles and refuse. Fifty meters on he found his exit point, a metal ladder leading up to street level. He turned off his wrist light. At the top was a grate that he shoved aside, climbed through, and replaced.

He stood in the middle of an alleyway with several parked ground vehicles. No one was in sight. He calmly walked to where the alley intersected with a larger street. This was a mixed business and residential district. Because of the late hour, cold temperature and military curfew, the streets were quiet. He walked along a couple of blocks, keeping to the shadows cast by the few streetlights. He turned a corner and stopped at the entrance to another alley. Before him was his destination, a side entrance to a warehouse. He stood concealed in a shadow and waited.

A couple came into view, walking up the alley from the other direction. Craven watched as they secretly looked around to make sure they were not being followed. They stopped before the warehouse door, knocked, exchanged a few words with someone on the inside, then entered. The door quickly closed behind them. This was where Moona would also enter. He would wait.

Ah Moona. She intrigued him from the first moment he saw her, throwing stones at a storefront window so she and some companions could loot it. Craven had watched from a safe distance, amazed at the girl's bravado. And the only thing she'd stolen that day was two gloves, one blue and one green. Was she color blind? Ah Moona and her disheveled beauty and her ignorant wit. She seemed to know so much, but hardly anything about living on the streets. But the streets were where she claimed to live.

That was three months ago. Their paths had crossed infrequently, but frequent enough that he'd introduced her to some friends of his, and she introduced him to her strange friend named Cornelius. "He sells knives," she'd said. "The kitchen kind. Mainly in the agricultural city of Dula." He liked Cornelius, and he didn't believe the cover story at all. She must know it had too many holes in it. "No, we're not sleeping together," she'd answered once to his question. That night she and Craven had slept together. Oh it was bliss. Now they were an item, though he still didn't know where to find her or how to get in contact with her. They would meet only by prearrangement, the times and places always named by her. Tonight they would meet at the underground club, because he had asked her. And it was Precession Night.

Craven shifted his weight from one leg to the other. Someone approached from the alley. It was a woman, black hair in ponytails, a scarf, and a faded blue dress under a loosely fitting coat, and there were the blue and green gloves. It was Moona. She stopped, looked around, almost looking right at him. He held his breath. She approached the entrance of the building. Craven watched as she knocked, gave the password, and entered. The door closed quickly behind. Craven cleared his throat, straightened his shoulders, and stepped out of the shadows to follow her.

* * *

Commissioner Menkar rode the lift up to her residence in the seaside military sector of the city. The ride was anything but smooth. The lift ascended too fast. At times it jumped in its magnetic casing, other times slowing and dragging. It rocked and slammed against the sides of its conveyance. Menkar sat hunched and crouched in the corner on the floor. Then she catapulted to the ceiling and fell back down again. Her body slammed into one side of the pod then another. Any other passenger might be terrified during such an ascent, but this was all Menkar's doing. Waves of anger erupted from her body, causing the entire mechanism to shudder. It raced on. Floor 23, Floor 27, Floor 32. The lift came to a rattling halt. The doors opened to her residence. She let out a cry, and waves of frost and ice shot into the main room, splattering the ceiling and walls, forming icicles all about. She screamed into the room, "Markhab! You are such a fool!" The furnishings shook and jumped.

The largest wall of the room was all window, facing north to the low hill that separated the military sector from rest of the city. Menkar's residence did not look out over the tranquil black sea. Beyond the hill's dome glowed the lights of frigid Cronapolis. She raised her arms toward the window and let loose a shrieking scream. The entire view disappeared behind a sheet of ice.

Menkar closed her eyes. She took a deep breath. The tenseness in her body ebbed away, her shoulders relaxed and she exhaled. The angry lines of her face smoothed. She opened her eyes and smiled. Reaching up to the back of her head, she took out the pins holding up her black hair. She shook her head from side to side, shaking her long strands loose, giving back to them body and freedom.

She walked up to the ice window and jabbed the hairpins into its thickness. She had no illusions about privacy. She knew full well that Markhab had spying devices on that hill aimed at her apartment, among many others. She'd seen the surveillance images herself. And so she did not mind being seen as tempestuous and irrational. All the Commissioners were in these days of war. It seemed a good cover.

Menkar turned and crossed the room, entering her large bedroom. She peeled the military uniform from her body, her ghostly white flesh emerging naked as a new creature from an ugly chrysalis. She carefully set the uniform on a manikin bust in the corner of the room, taking care to hang it proper and cleanly. Then she strode across the room and sat at her vanity. She raised a finger and blew on it, then traced the perimeter of the mirror, giving it a frosty ice outline. Picking up a comb, she slowly pulled it through her hair, all the while humming a quiet lilting tune, staring into her own eyes, smiling.

She set down the comb. She opened a drawer and reached with a hand far into the back. Her finger found a tiny secret lever, and CLICK, a little panel opened next to the drawer. She brought out from the tiny compartment a small wooden box, light brown, hand carved. She set it before her beside the comb, still humming her lilting tune. She opened the box and drew out of it a sunburst shaped amulet wrought of white gemstone on a silver chain. It was one of the few rare Precession Star amulets made so very long ago. All disappeared when the military banned the religion of Precession several generations before. Menkar placed the necklace over her head, bringing it to rest around her neck, with the amulet resting just above and between her breasts. She loosened her hair from the chain, then she traced with a finger the delicate gem work radiating from its center.

Menkar got up and moved to the center of the room. She retrieved a wide circular pillow from the bed and placed it on the floor. She sat upon it cross-legged and began to meditate.

This would be an exciting night. Thanks to her subterfuge, Markhab's satellites would broadcast the Precession Festival from the polar Canine cities of Canoon straight into the homes and offices of Cronapolis. That would cause quite a stir. And there was very interesting news from Markhab himself. The missing Scorpion battleship from Wror finally showed up, battered and barely functioning, definitely not combat ready. Apparently Felines had attacked and swarmed across Wror. Markhab sent General Taurus up to the ship to take it to the shipyards of Keldo. That was one old man out of the way. It was even alleged he'd taken his whole family with him. And Markhab himself was leaving the city this very night, taking most of the other Commissioners with him to Lupus Minor. The attack on Canoon would not be long now.

"As Security Commissioner," Markhab had said to her, "You will stay here. Keep your heel on the city."

Menkar smiled in meditation, remembering those words. She had protested vociferously. It had been a good show. And that demon Corvus was still out of the way. She did not know where he had gone, but not here was where she most wanted him.

She took a deep breath and opened her eyes. She stood up, tossed the pillow back on the bed and returned to her vanity. She resumed humming her lilting tune. With her comb she separated her hair down the middle, then she proceeded to braid each side in tight ponytails, stiff and poking out backwards. She got up and went to her closet where, in the far back, she selected a wrinkled pale blue dress. She put it on. It hung loosely on her. She chose some flat plain black shoes and put them on. She selected a scarf and placed it over her head. Finally she drew out a long and tattered black coat. Her ensemble was almost complete. In the back of the closet on a shelf she pulled out a pair of gloves, one blue and one green. She walked back to her vanity to admire her transformation. She said to her reflection, "Hello Moona." Now she was ready, for Moona Menkar had a date. She turned and left the bedroom.

The ice on the large window in the main room was melting. The hairpins were dangling. One dropped. She gave another blast of frost, then walked calmly to a bureau against another wall. Heaving it aside revealed a tiny door. She drew out her amulet and set it in a groove inlaid in the door. There was a CLICK and the door opened inward. She crawled inside, turned and grabbed hold of one of the bureau's legs, pulled it back against the wall, then closed the little door.

Inside the little space in the wall were five things, a dim light, a helmet, a toboggan on a track, and Moona. She climbed into the toboggan, put on the helmet, strapped herself in, and pulled a lever.

The toboggan with Moona in it careened down a secret passage. The track wound its way noiselessly around and around and down between the walls and floors of the military residence building, picking up tremendous speed. Faster and faster, round and round, down and down she sped. The entire way was a pitch-black plummet. By the time she reached ground level she was traveling more than two hundred kilometers an hour. The track then straightened out into a gentle downward incline. On she raced at great speed. The track curved up to the right and up to the left at intervals to maintain momentum. Her teeth chattered from the motion on the tracks. On and on she went for several kilometers and many bone jarring minutes. The track in its narrow tube passage passed under the hill and beneath the streets of Cronapolis.

At length the track inclined upwards and her velocity slowed. Finally she coasted to a gentle halt. The tunnel in this place was tall enough for her to stand. Moona climbed out of the toboggan wobbly and unnerved. She giggled. She took off her helmet and dropped it onto the toboggan. Beside her was a metal door cast in a concrete wall. She drew out her amulet and pressed it to a dimple in the door. A latch clicked open and she pushed her way through.

She was in the storeroom of some business. Bags of flour were piled high all about. Moona gently pushed against the door and it locked closed. On this side, it melded in with the rest of the wall and was virtually unseen. She walked across the small room to a curtained door and moved the drape just a little with her finger to peer out. The street outside was dark and empty. She unlatched the door and stepped outside. The door swung closed and latched itself behind her.

The night was frigid and full of frost. Moona hurried down the street and turned onto a seemingly deserted alley. She walked cautiously, looking left and right. Someone was standing in the shadows on one side. She noted him shift his weight from one foot to the other. She knew who it was immediately, but gave no indication that she was aware of him.

Up ahead on the right was the side entryway to a large warehouse, lit by an overhead light. Moona walked determinedly up to the door and knocked. She spoke a password and the door opened. She slipped in quickly and the door was sealed closed behind her.

Three very tall and hunky men stood before Moona, hunky in the sense that they were massively bound in muscle, not defined, just composed of a couple hundred kilos each of thick meat. None were very pleasing to look at, frightfully intimidating if nothing else. *I could use men like this*, thought Moona. *Where do they hide?* One manned the door demanding passwords. One each stood before two long corridors.

"A hundred credits," said the man in the forward corridor.

"A hundred?" said Moona with surprise. "What if I don't have it?"

"Then you go with the pretty fellow over there, and no one ever sees you again." He nodded his head in the direction of his counterpart standing in the corridor to the right. Both smiled, but not in any friendly way.

"Fine," said Moona, letting her distaste be apparent in the word. She pulled a hundred credit vouchers from a pocket in her coat and handed it to the man in front of her.

He took the credit and gave Moona a wide grin. Despite his almost hideous appearance, as Moona increasingly thought of him, his teeth were white and perfectly straight. "Have an enjoyable evening, Miss." He stepped aside to let her pass.

"One minute," said Moona. She turned to face the behemoth manning the door. "What if I hadn't said the right password?"

The hulk stared at her in silence for a moment, then said, "See that button?" pointing to a black knobbed protrusion in the wall. "Wrong password, or no password, and I push the button. Trap door opens, and you fall into a pit. A friend waits down there for such 'guests.' No one ever sees you again."

"Thank you," said Moona. She turned and walked passed the hulk in the forward corridor. *No wonder this place was not on my radar,* she thought. She felt uneasy at the realization. *What else have I been missing?*

The corridors had brown walls with paint peeling. More areas were missing paint than were painted. Bare light bulbs hung from the ceiling. The floors were dirty with scraps of paper and debris. The further down the corridor she walked, the more she noticed a THUMP-THUMP-THUMP-THUMP beat reverberating through the floor and walls. At the end of twenty-five meters were double doors on the right. She pushed these open and found another corridor, fifty meters long ending in another set of double doors. The THUMP-THUMP beat was even louder here, and Moona could hear some form of screeching music emanating from the end of the corridor. She was intrigued. How many places such as this existed in the city? Her date, Craven, certainly knew things she didn't. She headed down the corridor.

At the end she heard a rattling sound mixed in with the music. The doors were vibrating, as seemed the floor and walls. Moona pushed open the doors with both hands and walked through.

The hall was enormous, bathed in red light with pulsing white strobe lights quite effective at disorienting her. The sound was deafening. It was called music, but it differed little from the portable leaf blowers used in the streets. There were hundreds of people here, possibly more. How did this number of people travel to one destination without being noticed? Moona saw quite clearly that the Commissioner for Internal Security was not doing her job properly. That was a concern. What other forces heaved in the underbelly of her own city?

The space was mainly a huge open pit with five levels, two above her and two below. Each level's floor was a five-meter wide perimeter around the huge rectilinear building. All about people were dancing, schmoozing, watching. Some darker corners had chairs, tables and couches where there were conversations, flirting, romances and sexual trysts. What an amazing place.

On the wall to her left hung a huge four story screen on which was projected images of the dancers gyrating on the ground floor amidst box dancers wearing little other than glitter. Through the sound system she heard a female voice bellow "Es musica des nudas."

To Moona's right was a coat check. She traded her scarf, jacket and gloves for a token, then proceeded down a staircase to the level below. Just as she stepped onto the floor a costumed effete sprayed her with a perfumed mist and said, "It's a party darling. Have some fun," and laughed.

Moona blinked her eyes and coughed, waving her hands in front of her face. "Why did you..." she began to say, but the effete had moved on, and Moona's perception became distorted. *A drug,* she thought.

She stepped to the rail and looked over the edge. Everything seemed bigger and the people more numerous. There weren't hundreds of people here. There must be thousands of people. And the space went on forever. The dance floor was filled with animals grunting and screaming in cries of sexual release. The music, previously just noise, now sounded complex and brilliantly composed. Moona could hear every note. She was sure she could actually see the music all around her.

The whole experienced calmed down after a few minutes. Moona rubbed her temples and turned. She needed something to drink. Standing right in front of her was Craven, holding two glasses.

"You made it," he said, beaming his awkward grin at her. He bent over and kissed her on the cheek. "Here, drink this." He offered her a glass.

"What is it?"

"Water. You look like you've been tripping."

"I got sprayed with something." She drank the glass dry.

Craven laughed. "Looks like your first time. Come on, let's sit down." He led her around to another wall where they found a sofa.

"This place is amazing, Craven. I can't believe I didn't know about it."

"That's not surprising. Yesterday it was a shipping and warehouse facility for potatoes and grains. Tomorrow the floor will be covered in flour."

Moona took Craven's glass and took a gulp. "Agh! That's not water."

Craven laughed. "No. I'm having vodka."

Moona handed the glass back to him. "I'd like some more water."

"Be right back." He got up and headed to a bar on their left. While the drink was being ordered, he snuck a glance at his watch.

Moona stood up and went to the rail, looking down at the dancers. *All these people are having fun, clandestine fun, even under the dark shadow of the Commissioners,* she thought.

Craven returned with her water. She took it, sipped at first, then gulped the whole thing down. She thrust the empty glass back into his hands, grabbed him by his shirtsleeves and said, "Let's dance."

They made their way down the last flight of stairs, like fish battling upstream amid the moving throng, to reach the seething critical mass of Humanity reveling in energies of their own creation.

Moona did not know the last time she had danced. Had she ever danced? It was freeing, exhilarating. Her eyes rolled to the back of her head and her arms reached into the air. Craven watched her, enraptured by her mysterious naïve wiles. Moona grabbed him and synchronized their movements in an unchoreographed repertoire.

Suddenly the music screeched, clicked and faded. The image on the huge screen distorted. Dancing and conversation stopped in bewilderment. Then the surprise happened.

A new music rose, a din of chords and harmonies, discords and disharmonies, unlike anything the people had heard before. The image on the screen came into sharp contrast. A satellite image appeared of the mountains of the north, the realm of the Polar Canines. The picture zoomed in, and crystal ice cities came into focus, beams of light shining in all directions, the light of the northern aurora shimmering above all. Then in even clearer focus, vast numbers of individuals gathered in hundreds of plazas, outdoor raves of light shows, fireworks and music. Such music.

Everyone in the great hall with Moona stood in raptured awe. None had ever imagined such a spectacle in their lives. Even Craven whispered, more to himself than to Moona, "Canines! I can't believe it. I've never seen one before."

The image on the screen focused on one individual, a huge Canine with a long snout of a face, tiny ears, and a thick white mane of fur around his neck. He wore a sparkling purple suit with a diamond crown on his head. He was the Emcee, the presiding figure over the seething throngs below him. Standing on a high dais working controls of music and light, he led the masses. He looked up into the sky, as if staring into the eyes of the satellites, seeing the Humans far on the other side of the world. He raised his voice to heaven and yelled, "Oi Ah, Raor Kai. Precession Haah!" The music blasted from the speakers, fires erupted behind him and the mobs roared.

In the hall where were Moona, Craven, and the underbelly of Cronapolis, the Humans raised their arms into the air, screaming back, "Precession Haah!" Tears ran down every face and the party went on.

Presently Craven slowed down and said to Moona, "Let's take a break." He led her by the hand up four flights of stairs to the highest level far above the dance floor. Up here the light beams arced and spun near the ceiling, but there were many dark and relatively quiet alcoves populated by small groups engaged in soft whispers with bowed heads.

Like a bunch of conspirators, thought Moona.

Craven found two comfortable chairs against the wall under a small light. He stepped away and quickly came back with two glasses. "Water," he said. "I'm parched."

"You're drenched."

"It's the dancing. I'm glad you came, Moona. I wasn't sure you would."

Moona sipped her water. She glanced passed Craven and watched a nearby couple. They were engaged in some ritual.

"You made such a deal over it. 'A New Year's party like you wouldn't believe,' you said."

"And?"

Moona smiled. "It's great."

"Someone's going to be in trouble over that transmission with the Canines," said Craven. "Someone high up."

"Mm," murmured Moona in mid-sip. "Most likely."

"Do you think Cornelius is going to show up?"

"Why? Did you invite him, too?"

"No. I'd just like to see him again. I've got a new knife move I'd like to show him."

"I haven't seen him for weeks," said Moona.

They kissed. Craven ran his hand along Moona's head and neck. Their tongues entwined.

She continued to watch the couple behind Craven. They had some bundle between them. She heard a high-pitched squeaking sound. The couple swooned. "That couple over there. What are they doing?"

Craven turned, craning his neck around to look. He turned back. "That's what I wanted to show you. The ultimate kiss."

Moona took another sip of her water. "Does it hurt?"

"Yeah, a little."

"Is it dangerous? I mean like an overdose?"

"Most things are dangerous in some way."

"Well that's the truth I suppose. What will happen?"

"It'll be like spending our whole lives together in one blissful moment."

"Is that as long as it lasts?"

"It seems longer. And there are some after effects that linger."

"How...."

Craven laughed. "My goodness you ask a lot of questions."

Moona observed him carefully. She took another sip of her water and said nothing more for a time.

Craven took her hand into his. They let the music flow over them, closing their eyes, nodding their heads. The Canine music was enchanting. At last Craven opened his eyes and stroked Moona's hand, coaxing her. She snuggled head to head against him despite being in separate chairs.

Moona smiled and opened her eyes. She drew in a deep breath and said, "OK. Let's do it, before I change my mind."

Craven sat straight up, a big grin on his face.

"How do we do this?" asked Moona. "Do we exchange credits with a shady character in an alley?"

Craven laughed. "Already did that. Stay here a sec." He got up and hurried around the corner to speak with someone in the shadows. Presently he returned carrying two bundles by top rings. They were draped with cloths so that whatever was inside remained unseen.

"What is this, exactly?"

"These are cute snuggly little creatures with furry faces. You take one and I take one. We let them, kiss us, then we exchange, and let the other, kiss us."

"So this amazing kiss is a vicarious experience for us. It sounds like they're doing all the fun stuff." Moona sounded skeptical on purpose. She had heard about this before during interrogations. She also knew that too much of one's mind can be shared. She was not about to blow her cover. She was equipped with a memory inhibitor pill. She needed to know more about this

Craven boy. She continued. "What exactly will I feel?"

"Well, besides a sting…."

"Sting? You said kiss."

"It's a tender love bite, actually."

"Oh-Kay."

"What happens is this. The bat's saliva mixes with our blood. It captures an impression of our thoughts, moods, emotions. Then we switch bats, and all that will transfer to the other host. Think loving thoughts of me, and I'll experience that in a rush."

"So we can control what we share? We can choose?"

"Pretty much," said Craven. "But there is a danger I need to warn you about."

"Here it comes."

"You might sense a dark place, agitated, even subtly appealing. Don't go there. Keep focused on me."

"Why? What's there?"

"Remember, there are four of us involved. Stay away from the bat mind. Once there, some people find it difficult to break away."

Moona became agitated herself. "This sounds a lot more dangerous than you let on. How many times have you done this yourself?"

Craven squirmed in his seat a bit. "A number of times. Really Moona, it's an awesome ride."

Moona gave Craven a thorough staring down. Was he actually as sane as he seemed? Moona had her, other vocation, to think of. She could not lose her edge to any debilitating drug. "What about diseases? Viruses?"

"Oh, these bats' saliva has a pathogen inhibitor. It's safe."

"Did they tell you that? The bats I mean?"

Craven smiled. "Of course you don't have to. I just thought it'd be fun to share something between us besides sex, and this party."

"Fine. Let's do it now before I consider changing my mind, again."

Craven beamed. He gently pulled off the fabric over the little cages. Inside each was a tiny child's hand size bundle of bat, wings folded and little hands clasping, big eyes looking out at Moona. They squealed and blinked.

Craven opened one of the cages and reached in gently to lift the little bat from its little perch. While he did this, Moona pulled a pill from a pocket in her dress and surreptitiously popped it into her mouth and took a drink of her water.

"Here," he said. "I'll hand him to you. Cup him in your hands. Be careful with his wings."

Moona took the little animal in her hands. "Oh, he's warm. And wiggly." She smiled.

"Now I'll get the other one." While turned away, Craven slipped his own inhibitor pill into his mouth and swallowed. With both animals out, he asked, "Ready?" Moona nodded. "OK. We'll both hold them to each other's neck. Now." Their hands extended, the bites were quick.

"Ouch," said Moona. Craven flinched at his bite. "I don't sense anything."

"Not yet. Now hold each to our own neck." The second bite was warm. "Quick, put them back into the cages." That was done. Just then the warmth spread to their heads. Moona and Craven both began to swoon.

The feeling was euphoric. The music faded into the background and their vision blurred. Moona saw three circles spinning in her mind. They merged into one vortex, blue in the middle, red near the outside, a black rim without. In the blue vortex images appeared, flashes that were memories, thoughts. She saw a young Craven swaddled in his mother's arms as a babe. Then he was a toddler, stacking lettered blocks on a wooden floor spelling out his name. *What a good boy*, said a female voice. The sound of that voice filled Moona with a trusting love. Focusing on the red vortex, Craven was riding a tricycle, peddling away down a sidewalk in the warm sun. Then he was crying, a feeling of loss and defenselessness as an uncle's voice told of the death of his parents. Next he was in school, head bowed while he worked diligently on math equations. Something hovered in Moona's mind, something she couldn't quite see. What was it? It was the black vortex, like facing a closed door. Moona concentrated. Something there. Something important. She sensed something beyond darkness. Something was holding her back, inhibiting her.

Behind her mind was a flurry of movement. Squeaking. Wings fluttering. She felt anxious, agitated. *Not that,* she thought. It was bat like. She drew away. She saw Craven building something, gadgets with wires. Then he was enjoying a meal, stew with chestnuts. It tasted so good. Moona licked her lips. And now Craven was kissing Moona. She felt his lips touch her own lips. Happiness. There was that darkness again. The inhibitor was hiding something. Moona tried to pierce the black with her mind. Then slowly she saw a tiny light, like looking through a keyhole. Yes, there it was, just there. Then she burst through the light.

She suddenly saw something she did not at first understand. It was familiar. It was a power station, the nuclear core. There were explosives! And Craven's voice saying, *Sine cosine, cosine sine.* Images of Craven at a meeting. Subversives. Someone saying, *If we succeed in blowing it up, it will mark the end of....*

Craven's mind slipped through Moona's memories. She was thirteen, and rows and rows of young men and women were in uniform. Next, she is singled out and chastised for carrying out a cruel prank. Then she was in her room before her mirror. She threw her brush at it, shattering the glass. But there was darkness next. He could not pierce it, yet he knew something was in the darkness. He pressed harder with his mind. Then he saw her, the real Her, in full uniform. She was....

Moona's eyes opened wide. She knew Craven for what he was, a saboteur! She bolted upright in her seat. The sounds of the rave and the Canine music rushed back in. She stared directly into Craven's eyes and yelled at him, "You!"

But he shocked her by exclaiming, "You! You're, Menkar!" He had seen through Moona's deceit just as she had seen through his. They both stood up, fear and cursing looks in each's eyes.

Moona lunged for his watch, flung open the dial and stared at the wiggling lights, now almost completely overlaying one another. She said, "Sine cosine, cosine sine. What have you done?"

Craven backed away. What a fool he'd been. This was the monster, the beast herself, the hated enemy.

Then all the music stopped. The images of Canoon cut away and the screen went white. The lights went out. Only candles offered illumination. People were yelling.

"It's happened, you fool!" shouted Moona.

Craven looked confused. He brought his watch up to his face. "No. It's not time yet. It's not the power plant."

Moona pushed him out of the way. She headed for the staircase amid the mob, barely finding a way through. She cursed and her eyes lit up. A deadening cold emanated from her, slowing everyone else as they shivered and rubbed their arms. She turned and yelled over the bewildering cries, "Craven, I will deal with you later. I know where you live."

Moona Menkar stormed out of the building and into the street, already crowded with people from all corners. She stopped short and looked up into the sky, her mouth agape with all the others. The frosty air had cleared. Streaming through the night sky was a veritable fireworks display. The satellites, Markhab's, and Menkar's, hold on the power of information, were burning up, careening across the breadth of Lupus, exploding. In the foreground to the south, Markhab's great transport ships were taking off, heading to the far northeast to Lupus Minor.

"What is happening?" wondered Menkar aloud. It was inconceivable that Markhab, or any of the Commissioners, was behind this act of sabotage, and it was beyond the ability of Craven. She knew that for certain. Was it something she had done? Impossible. It must be a Canine attack. Or Feline? It didn't matter at the moment. A nuclear facility was about to be destroyed. She had to deal with that, if there was time.

BOOM! The sky lit up like a sun. The sound of the blast knocked Menkar flat in the street onto her back. She jumped back up. With all her force she instinctively flung out her arms, her faced blazed with a terrible cold pale blue light. A freezing beam of energy burst out of her, aimed straight at the nuclear blast. A massive ice wall formed, containing the radiation blast on this side, diverting much of the destructive power away. But the outpouring of killing energy was persistent. The ice wall kept melting, and Menkar had to keep renewing her efforts to maintain the strength of the wall.

This was not all she had to contend with. The nuclear facility was situated above one of the spokes of the ancient spiral labyrinth where Craven hid out. The thought of it flashed through Menkar's mind. She had vaguely known of an ancient structure under the city, but it was not used by the military. Indeed, it was rumored to have been destroyed long ago. But from Craven's memories Menkar knew its shape and structure. This would be bad. The outcome was inevitable. The blast and the nuclear core's melt reached down to the level of the labyrinth. Menkar felt sick to her stomach. In seconds the nuclear force ripped through the bowels of the city, and like a choreographed pyrotechnic display, the other five nuclear power centers circling the city, all on the same spoked grid, lit up the sky all around. In the center of the city, the military edifice of the Forum exploded, its blast climbing high into the sky as a column of destruction.

Menkar spun in a circle, unleashing terrible waves of cold and ice. But she was one person, tiring. Radiation flooded the city. People were vaporizing, turning to ashen figures before her eyes, but she noticed something strange. Some people did not burn, a small few, and it occurred to her why this was so, for the same thing was happening to her.

Menkar stopped spinning. She held her ground, continuing to emanate powerful forces of cold and ice in all directions to keep the multiple blasts at bay. But she was changing. Her ears grew larger. Her fingernails grew long. Her face contorted. She felt her very DNA changing from the radiation. Her clothes had disintegrated. Thin flaps of skin grew and spread out from her fingertips, several of which extended into long boney rods. Fangs emerged from her mouth. It was the Kiss of the Bat, the animal's genome merging with hers.

Menkar's mind filled with thoughts and images wild and alien to her. She knew she had to get away from here. To her right she sensed a familiar smell. It was Craven. She turned, her piercing animal eyes staring, seeing the same piercing animal eyes staring back. He, and a handful of others, were fully transformed bat people, true vampires, like her. They all just stood staring at her, waiting for some command.

In a high-pitched shriek Menkar yelled out, "We must leave here. Fly east to the city of Dula, as fast as you can. Fly now!"

Giant bat wings took to the air. Menkar used her power to protect them from the fiery inferno engulfing the once timeless city of Cronapolis. Their cries pierced the night air for kilometers.

The city burned.

45 THE GATE

A Naemi gazed out the pilot's window at the evening's twilight. The sky was near indigo. The wispy clouds were fuchsia. Normally such a beautiful spectacle was fleeting, a rich ephemeral moment in the changing continuum of color coexistent with dusk. Naemi had been staring at the twilight and pink clouds for eight hours, lost in a rapture of seeming timelessness.

The invisible ship kept pace with the meridian of nightfall as it swept across the face of the Earth from east to west, starting in Egypt. Now they were above their intended destination, an ancient megalithic city on the high altiplano of South America's Andes. It was Tiwanaku, supposed City of the Gods from the very ancient days, before the time of the Annihilation of the Gods, and the exodus into space by their survivors. Tiwanaku. They were directly above it now. It was, according to Professor Altair, the place of the Gate, a machine of terrible power and source of the shimmering field. Professor Altair had convinced First Commissioner Markhab of that.

Naemi blinked her eyes and they flashed colors of blue and green, then blue and brown, then brown and grey. She only wanted a moment's peace, but that had been hard to come by with a younger Naemi beside her listening to radio news broadcasts and musical forms alien to her. And a much younger Naemi was in the main cabin with the others, Altair, Corvus and the security guard Blum. That conversation also echoed in Naemi's head, in all the Naemi's heads. Three Naemis with three Naemis' thoughts. No, there was no peace in older Naemi's mind. She blinked again, grey and green.

"This time we cannot draw so much attention to ourselves," said Altair. "I mean, we lost a man," casting a sideways glace at Blum, "And involved who knows what level of military attention."

Youngest Naemi stood apart from the others, leaning against the wall drinking from a glass of water. Altair stood beside the table, its surface cluttered with his notes, references and equipment. Corvus stood facing Altair, hands on hips, grinning with his usual mischievous smile. He had spoken little, listening to Altair go on and on. This Naemi was glad to be away from her other incarnations. They insisted on some autonomy. Naemi gave them nicknames. The sexy vixen she called Cheetah. The one with the funny eyes she called Blink. They found this amusing.

"We have to observe protocol," Altair said.

Naemi rolled her eyes. There was no protocol. This entire adventure followed a shoot from the hip strategy. They were making it up as they went along.

"My good Professor," said Corvus finally, his eyes shining strangely. "We will find what we're looking for. But do not lead us to cities and monuments for the express purpose of sightseeing architectural curiosities. This next city of yours had better provide more concrete results."

"We obtained vital clues in Egypt," replied an exasperated Altair.

Naemi interjected. "I have to agree with Corvus. This is not a scavenger hunt. It's possible we could have obtained your clues by more surveillance, without endangering our crew and mission."

"But this entire mission is an exploration. And whom do you think caused the scene along the frozen river?"

"Your Tiwanaku will be explored without interference by the Earth Humans," said Corvus.

"And how do you propose to do that?" asked Altair. "With more of your parlor tricks and magic? That will surely pique more inquiries into our presence."

"We are over the city now," said Naemi.

Corvus smiled. The light in his eyes twinkled, causing the hair on Naemi's neck to stand on end.

In the command cockpit, Cheetah tuned onto a news broadcast.

"…News from South America. This is Evening Report with Raul Castro. International tensions further escalated between Bolivia and its neighbors. The government has acknowledged that border checkpoints will close at nine tonight, local time. All tourists and day merchants must vacate the area around Lake Titicaca. No travel between the ruins of Tiwanaku and Puma Punko will be allowed after the borders close. The Bolivian military is coordinating the curfew.

"Now from Brazil. The last Palm Oil plantation in the Amazon Basin is set to cease operations this month. The wildly successful Amazon Restoration Project has worked over the past several decades to…."

Cheetah turned to Blink, who continued to stare out the window at her pink clouds. "Altair may get his wish. It sounds like civilians are being removed from the area below us."

Blink blinked her eyes brown. "Why don't you find something else to listen to? Provincial news is boring."

"Not if we're in the same provincial area. But ok." She found an alternative radio station.

An announcer spoke.

"…And from Current 93…."

Strange lyrics and music filled the cockpit. It went on for a short while.

"Lovely lyrics," said Blink. "How about something without words?"

Cheetah tried again. A male voice softly spoke.

"Serenade Number Thirteen for Strings in G Major, by Mozart. Eine Kleine Nachtmusik."

The cabin filled with an uplifting sound no Naemi had ever heard before. It was made up of beautifully orchestrated movements that at the same time were an entirely frivolous oeuvre. Blink gazed out the window and smiled.

Naemi in the main cabin smiled, too.

"What are you so smug about?" asked an annoyed Altair.

"I've been listening to the news, something you might have been trying. There is a developing political dispute between the government that administers Tiwanaku, and neighboring entities. Civilians are being removed from the area below us." She tapped her fingers against the wall to the strings and beats of A Little Night Music, though no one else in the cabin could hear it.

"Then the place is being evacuated," exclaimed Altair. "Excellent."

"Not exactly," said Naemi. "There's a political border just outside the city below. There will be military patrols."

"I can take care of that," said Corvus. "How long until we land?"

Naemi quizzically raised one eyebrow. "Whenever you wish. We are in place above the site, two kilometers. It is dusk."

"Then ready to land. I will ensure we are alone. I'll create a storm of cold and fog."

"How will we work?"

"Everyone must wear environmental suits. Do we have any?" He looked at Naemi.

She nodded. "There are four."

Corvus turned to the Professor. "And do you have any reservations?"

Altair stood up straight. "With the Earth Humans ethically removed, I assume I'll be able to take ALL the equipment I need?" He looked at Naemi.

She pressed her fingers to her temples. Music flooding her brain got louder. "Fine," she blurted out. "If you can carry it." She turned and hurriedly headed to the cockpit.

Altair said to Corvus after Naemi was gone, "Your abilities are amazing. Do you mind if I study you as you do whatever it is you're going to do?"

"Carefully," replied Corvus. "And Professor. Stand back."

Professor Altair went around to the backside of the table and sat down. He gathered some paper and a writing implement, and waited. Blum sat back on his bed cross-legged with his boots on, watching.

Corvus stood in the middle of the room facing the Professor. His feet were apart, arms out from his sides. His eyes focused on that middle distance used in meditation. His eyes were cold, bright and glowing. His very pale skin shined bright. The hair on his arms and head stood up. The temperature in the room plummeted. It hit Altair and Blum like a shock. The hair on their arms and heads rose, either from the cold, the electricity in the cabin, or both. It didn't matter.

Corvus raised his palms up. He grunted, "Yesss." The cold burst out of the cabin, out of the ship, as quickly as it had entered. Waves of energy pulsed out of Corvus' body. As the ship began circling down to the city of Tiwanaku, circular waves of frost descended with it, bringing a deadly winter.

Inside the cockpit, Blink was stretched forward, breathing against the window. The condensation fogged up a portion of its surface. Blink sat back and proceeded to use her finger to play a crosshatch game by drawing on the foggy surface. "I'm just saying," she went on, "that death is a transitory experience. I killed you. And then I died. But we both came back, and there's a third one of us to boot." She smiled, and her eyes flashed yellow and red, then red and yellow, then brown and brown.

Cheetah turned up the volume on the speakers. Night Music bounced off the walls. "But it only happened to us," she yelled over the horns and strings.

"How do you know what everyone else is doing, after they die?"

The door burst open and Naemi came running in, the fingers of both hands pressing against her temples. She shut the door quickly behind her. "Turn that music off!"

"I'll turn it down," said Cheetah. The Night Music faded into the background.

"Looks like it's back to work," said Blink. One eye flashed blue. She used the side of her palm to wipe away the rest of her game from the foggy window.

"You two have been out long enough," said Naemi. "Get back inside, both of you. We're going down to the city."

"The thrusters are already set," said Cheetah.

"Spiral course plotted," said Blink. Both her eyes flashed green.

Blink and Cheetah stepped forward into Naemi and all three merged. Naemi caught her breath a moment then sat down. She set the ship maneuvering into a spiral. Then the cold hit. It came through the door and the wall behind her, blasts of frigid energy. Naemi shuddered in her seat. She clasped her arms tightly around her chest. Breathing was labored. Then the cold ceased as suddenly as it began. *Evil genius*, thought Naemi. But then an unbidden thought from Blink proposed, *She doesn't really think he's evil.* Cheetah agreed.

Naemi regained her hold on the controls and the ship rapidly descended. It traced a circle spiraling ever tighter as the ship came down. Its contrails interacted with the waves of cold, and a twisting vortex was created. A plume of moist air traveling up and over the western slopes of the Andes merged with the vortex on the altiplano. A stationary hurricane, gorged with water in the form of ice and snow rapidly settled onto the plain. Lake Titicaca froze over. Any military units on the ground or in the air fled for cover. The invisible ship landed to the last horn and string of Night Music.

Blum led the way first out of the ship. He and the rest were outfitted in puffy white environmental suits complete with bubble helmets.

I feel ridiculous, thought Blink.

"Minus twenty-five centigrade," said Naemi. "Better keep the helmets on."

Even Corvus kept his suit on as waves of cold blue light pulsed through and out of him. Where stood Corvus, there lay the eye of the storm.

Within a half kilometer radius the air was nearly still. Any slight breath of air or footstep easily disturbed the ground fog. At the perimeter of the ancient city a column of wind churned. The plain down to the lake was a blizzard, and gale force winds battered the inland sea. To the north the ruins of ancient Puma Punku lay under snow.

"We'll need to use echo location if we're going to see anything in this fog," said Altair.

"Activate the blue button on your wrist," said Naemi. "The acoustics will transmit images from the helmet to your brain. We'll be able to see." Naemi turned her unit on. The walls and temples of the city appeared clearly in her mind. The images pulsed to the rhythm of the ultrasonic chirps.

"Spread out," said Corvus. "We're looking for the Precession Gate. We've all seen the pictures."

Cheetah and Blink separated from Naemi. "Hey," she said.

"What?" asked Corvus.

"Nothing," said Naemi. She felt foolish. "I'll go this way." She walked around the ship. Corvus and Blum headed in opposite directions, while Altair walked in a zigzag. He passed around a wall and stood face to face with a tall rectilinear statue.

"Now who are you?" he said aloud. He observed the statue's helmet, belt and artifacts in its hands. "These mean something, I'm sure."

Cheetah and Blink didn't need environmental suits. They headed to two entrances in a long wall that led to an amphitheater, a ball court. The wall they passed through was built of megalithic stone blocks, fitted perfectly together without mortar.

Through opposite gates they descended steps onto a platform overlooking the court. White blobs glowed in the walls. Blink stepped close to the wall and peered forward. "Oh!" she shrieked and jumped back.

"What are they?" asked Cheetah running up.

"Faces," said Blink. "Faces staring out of the wall."

Cheetah heard a murmuring of voices around her in the fog accompanied by a sound of wings fluttering. She quickly turned left, then right. No one was there.

"What is it?" asked Blink. She had heard it too, though from Cheetah's mind.

Cheetah turned slowly around in a circle. "This place is full of ghosts."

Naemi was on the far side of the ship relative to the others. There was little to see here visually, the fog was so opaque. Fuzzy echo images danced in the distance just out of the range of her device. One thing she did notice was everything getting brighter, much brighter. Naemi took a dozen steps forward. The shadowy dancers solidified into a massive monolith, a stone arch. A huge ball of light shone through it, visible because they were in the eye of Corvus' hurricane.

"The Gate! I've found it," she yelled. The others came running. "That light," she asked Corvus who quickly came up beside her. "What is it?"

"Some kind of surveillance device?" he wondered.

Professor Altair stepped up. "It IS the Gate," he said proudly, placing his hands on its carved surface.

"The light, Professor. Watch out," cautioned Naemi.

Altair laughed. "On this world, the unexpected should be expected. It is the moon, friends, and quite full. Now unless you want to marvel at any other celestial bodies, let's get to work on this thing."

Cheetah and Blink joined with Naemi. *The moon,* thought one sarcastically. The other giggled.

The Professor immediately had his tool bag open and began his preliminary investigation. He attached sensors to various locations on the structure to measure density, fault lines, internal crystalline formation and electrical resistance. A few taps from a hammer sent data flowing into the sensors. "Stand back now." He aimed a low yield gamma ray pulse gun at the Gate.

"Well?" asked Corvus after a moment. The Professor hunched over his instruments. "Is it a machine?"

"Oh yes," said Altair. "But it's not working right now."

"Why not?" asked Naemi.

"That crack is the most probable reason." Indeed, the others could now see that the Gate was actually split in two on a column.

"Then it's finished?" said Corvus.

"It's a circuit basically, made possible by seams of resonite in the structure, and beneath us. All we need to do is repair the circuit."

"Come on Blum," said Corvus. "Put your muscles to work up there."

"Not so fast," said Altair. "I have a more scientific means of repairing it. A reparative crystal matrix should do the trick." He pulled a spray can out of his bag. "Blum, do get up there. Spray this into the crack."

Blum jumped up onto the top of the Gate. The Professor tossed up the can. The solvent quickly filled the gaps of the crack with a material that crystallized on contact with the rock and air. Blum jumped down and waited with the others. Altair sent another pulse of gamma rays at the structure.

Mwummm. The Gate and its basal structure hummed. The interior of the Gate itself filled with a glowing mist. A portal opened inside. Shadowy shapes moved toward the entrance from deep within. Altair struck the Gate with his hammer. The monolith came alive with light.

Naemi suddenly got a headache. Cheetah and Blink separated, and moved away from the others.

"The carvings on the structure are glowing," said Naemi.

"Yes," said Altair. "You'll notice the rows of stylized Birds of Prey in seeming obeisance to the figure in the center."

"What does it mean?" asked Corvus.

"The proper question might be, what does it do?" said Altair. "The apertures on each side column are significant somehow. Blum, go reset the devices on the left. I'll do the same to those on the right. Now, strangely enough, if we only had some music."

"Music? Why?" asked Corvus.

"The Gate is a resonator. So it will resonate."

Corvus smiled. He stood before the Gate and began to sing. A deep operatic voice bellowed out of him. "Oh alteme, Tos attenes, Sons...."

The vortex in the Gate churned. Sparks crackled from the central figure and spread as lightning among the Bird of Prey images.

Corvus kept singing. The sound of claws scratching on stone clearly came from the Gate. The wind around them closed in and intensified. It sounded like a thousand flapping wings beating together. An orb of light formed in the center of the vortex. Suddenly it burst forth and struck Corvus square in the chest. He fell backwards several meters. He stopped pulsating. The wind stopped. The snow ceased. The temperature rose and the fog was gone. The stars shined down.

The Gate continued to resonate and glow. Naemi and Altair scrambled to Corvus. Naemi took off her helmet, then his. She held his head in her lap. Altair took his pulse. Corvus looked into Naemi's eyes and said, "The wind got knocked out me." She smiled and moved a lock of hair away from his forehead. He stared into the sky. "Look up at the stars," said Corvus attempting a smile. Then he frowned. "But they're so different here."

Naemi looked up. "We're far from home."

"He seems alright," said Altair.

"No more magic powers though." Corvus laughed then coughed.

"Pull him over here to the side," said Altair. Blum helped them.

"So Professor," said Corvus. "What is it? What does it do?"

Altair sat back on his haunches. "Very simple really. It's a frequency resonance enhancer. Input energy, regulate the frequency, and just about anything is possible."

"A power source? Why doesn't anyone else have something like this?" asked Naemi.

"We've tried," said Corvus. "Every installation exploded. How is it that this Gate didn't?"

"This whole city," said Altair. "Connected to the ground, the Earth, the whole planet is its reservoir."

"Do you hear it humming still?" asked Naemi. "It sounds like music."

The Professor got up and went to the entrance of the Gate, just pausing at the threshold. He turned back to the others and smiled. "It's Corvus' song. It's playing it back." He turned to the Gate and walked through.

"Wait!" yelled Naemi.

Altair was inside the shimmering field. The interior walls of the Gate dripped with glowing liquid metal. Along with the music, he heard murmurings and the flutter of wings. He was not alone. He felt the presence of a multitude. He waved his arms in front of him to try and dispel the vortex. He stepped out the other side.

"Well," he began. "That was...." Altair doubled over in pain. His body convulsed. He yelled, choked, growled, and changed.

Cheetah and Blink were back on the platform overlooking the ball court. They'd been drawn to the wall of faces as soon as the Gate had been activated.

"Corvus got zapped," said Cheetah.

"I know," said Blink.

"What are we looking for?"

"You should know that, sister of one mind."

Cheetah looked around. "The wind's died down and the stars have come out. See," she pointed up.

"Yes, strange stars. We're far from home. But here, the fog still persists though it's gone from everywhere else. Why, I wonder."

Mists twisted gently on the ball court. Then they rolled back and a scene unfolded. Ghostly spectators filled the stands, Humans on two sides, Birds of Prey on the other two. On a similar platform opposite Cheetah and Blink, Birds of Prey noblemen and judges stood. And on this side next to Cheetah and blink materialized Human noblemen and judges. They wore capes of feathers and loincloths of reptile skin. Their heads were strangely elongated. In their hands they carried boxy metal purses by metal rings.

"What is this?" asked Cheetah.

"History, I think," said Blink. Her eyes both flashed cold grey.

On the ball court itself stood four men, two Birds of Prey and two Human. They each wore heavy stone waistbands and leather loincloths. Their hands were tied behind their backs. Their feet were bare, bare claws on the Birds of Prey. The Birds with their majestic golden wings were tall, but the Humans were more muscular.

"It begins," cried a Human judge beside Cheetah.

Across the distance a Bird of Prey judge yelled back, "It begins." A rubber ball was thrown into the court and the game was on.

Using only their feet and bodies, the players dashed around the court knocking, kicking and deflecting the ball. The two pairs coordinated their moves. There was much thudding of bodies. A Bird of Prey knocked the ball into a small stone ring on the wall of the court, and cheers and riles erupted from the spectators. When a Bird of Prey pounced from the air onto a Human just taking aim with his hip, the crowd yelled, "Not fair!" The Human's neck snapped, crushed by the claw of his opponent. But the ball he'd just deflected hit the other Bird of Prey, putting out an eye and partially crushing the skull. He fell crumpled to the ground.

The remaining Human deflected the ball into the ring and scored another point. Tie. The remaining Bird of Prey leapt into the air to swivel his hip against the ball, but the Human hurled his body against the Birdman's chest with a thud. Recoiling, the Human spun around, kicked up the ball, and smacked it with his hips sending it flying squarely into the ring again. The crowd yelled and jeered.

The Bird of Prey launched his body into the air flapping his wings fiercely, but his stone waistband weighed him down. He plunged toward the Human's face, clawed feet extended. The Human fell and rolled underneath the Birdman. Back on his feet, he kicked up the ball and knocked it with his hip into the ring again. The Human spectators screamed.

The Bird of Prey now had the ball, was kicking it, giving it height. The Human came at him from behind jumping and slamming his body between the wings and shoulders of the Birdman, who screeched and fell forward. The ball knocked to the right. Both ran for it, but the Human got there first and sent the ball through the ring yet again. The Bird of Prey fell with all his might onto the Human, crushing his body to the ground. There was pandemonium in the stands.

The Human judge next to Blink stood and yelled across the court, "Four to One, Humans. Seize the survivor. He knows his fate. And seize all the Birds of Prey! For this was the wager." Spectators and guards streamed on the court and charged the Birds of Prey in the stands and far platform. Then the scene shimmered and faded, lost in the mist that returned.

Cheetah and Blink stood alone lost for words. Then Blink screamed. Something had grabbed her. Cheetah turned and also started. She pulled Blink's arm to drag her from the wall.

The ghostly stone faces murmured and moaned. They twisted their features and tried to speak. Then they rose, their opaque bodies stepping out from the wall. They turned en masse and marched up the steps and out of the ball court.

"They're headed to the Gate. We've got to get there first, sister."

"As fast as lightning." Cheetah and Blink ran wide and overtook the ghosts, then fled with all their speed back to join Naemi. The ghosts kept marching.

At the Gate, Naemi had run over to the stricken Professor. Corvus lay off to one side, propped up on an arm to watch. Blum stood beyond them watching intently, but not helping.

"What's happening?" Corvus cried out.

Naemi removed Altair's helmet. "It's his face, his skin, his body," she answered, shaking. "It's as if something is possessing him."

"Not possession," said Blum coming closer. "It's him. He's changing."

"What?" asked Naemi.

The Professor's body arched and his back split through the fabric of his suit. Bony scales and discs stuck out from his spine. His thighs swelled and the creature crawled away from the pile of shredded clothes. It looked up at her and snarled. His brow ridges stuck out over his eyes, which were wide open and red. His nostrils were huge. Foam and saliva bubbled and dribbled out of a mouth crowded with sharp incisors and huge blocky molars. A red narrow tongue flicked out and darted back in.

Naemi jumped back and screamed. "He's changed into some beast, some hideous, monstrous beast."

"Get away from it," yelled Blum. He stepped forward with his gun drawn on the transmogrified Professor.

The beast screamed.

Naemi yelled, "No!"

Blum fired five times. The creature hunched over, twitched, then lay still in rapidly spreading pools of blood. The stench of burning flesh filled the air.

"What's going on? Blum!" yelled Corvus. He struggled up and went to Naemi.

"He was in the shimmering field," said Blum coolly. "It changed his DNA.

He was reverting into a proto-Humanoid ape man."

"We could have tried to help him," said Naemi. She suddenly felt fearful of this overly large man with the gun who had just killed the Professor.

"No, we couldn't," said Blum.

"How do you know?" pleaded Naemi. "How possibly can you think you know?"

"I know," said Blum. "Now both of you, stay back."

Blum took off his helmet and climbed out of his uniform, aiming his gun at Naemi and Corvus. He was wearing a backpack of sorts. He undid his harness and it fell away, revealing a pair of huge golden wings unfolding. With a hand he pulled at his scalp and it came away along with his face. It was a mask. Beneath were downy tufts and the beak of a Bird of Prey. He stepped out of his boots revealing his clawed feet.

"You're changing too?" asked Naemi in panic.

"No," said Blum, and he laughed. "I AM a Bird of Prey. And I'm here to loose those of my kin imprisoned by this machine. I'm going to open the Gate."

Corvus and Naemi gasped.

"Stop!" yelled Corvus. "You take orders from me."

"These orders come from Gog. You will not stop me."

"Who is Gog?" demanded Corvus.

"Let me clarify. From Gog, by way of Markhab."

"What is he talking about?" asked Naemi.

"I hesitate to offer an explanation at this time," replied Corvus.

Blum flapped his wings and rose over the top of the Gate to land in front of it. "Ah, to spread my wings again," he spoke toward the Gate's entrance. "And you, my kin, soon you will feel the joy of air beneath your wings again."

Naemi and Corvus scurried off to one side. Blum stood with his hands on his hips facing the glowing Gate. He strode forward and with his fist punched the aperture on the left column. A horizontal shaft of light shone forth. Then he did the same to the aperture on the right column. Another shaft of light. The interior portal glowed and spun wildly, churning as a whirlpool. Shapes and forms jockeyed for position to step through the vortex. A jingling sound as of many bells rang out from the Gate. Cries of anticipation mixed with the flapping of wings also were heard. Then the shapes of great Birds of Prey stepped through.

"Return! Return!" yelled Blum in greeting. "Return to the realm of incarnation. Regain your forms. Come!"

A mighty Bird of Prey king, accompanied by his queen, led the host. Thousands lined up to follow them out.

"Hail Viracocha! Hail Mama Runu!" cried Blum.

"Breath! Blood! Life!" said Viracocha with great emotion, liberated from an eternity of banishment.

"Sight! Hearing! Smell and Taste, ah!" said Mama Runu, freed from her own banishment. They were oblivious of Blum and the Humans.

At that moment Cheetah and Blink returned and join with Naemi. She whispered to Corvus, "We've got to get away from here now. Something else is coming. It isn't safe."

The cries of exultation from the emerging Bird of Prey host were met by the otherworldly cries of the Human ghosts marching to the Gate. Naemi and Corvus gasped.

Viracocha took to the air and his queen followed. The host began rising in a roaring rush.

Blum turned and let out a cry. "No! This isn't possible!"

The ghost marchers quickly encircled the Gate and blocked the passage of any more Birds of Prey from coming through the vortex. They pressed forward with a ghastly moan, and the trapped Birds of Prey screamed and moaned. Blum was surrounded. He ferociously tried to fight the ghosts, but they hounded him and dug their ashen fingernails through his feathers into his skin. He howled. He tried to take flight. He was pushed screaming into the vortex. The ghosts climbed all over the Gate. The structure groaned. The electrical sparks radiating from the central figure sputtered. The Gate cracked in two, opposite the original repaired crack. The Gate ceased glowing. The circuit was broken. The machine stopped. The vortex disappeared.

The ghosts slowed and gathered before the Gate. One said in a chilling voice, "The wager. They who lost shall remain lost." Then they looked up into the starry sky at the Birds of Prey who'd made it out. They flocked back to the Gate in confusion. The ghosts vanished as a new danger manifested. A fluttering whirring sound quickly grew louder and came from the northwest. Searchlights beamed down from the black sky.

"More Birds of Prey?" said Corvus.

Naemi shook her head. "Human flying machines. We'll be caught if we don't get to the ship."

The frantic Birds of Prey scattered as the helicopters came down. Some flew right into the spinning blades, casting blood and feathers into the air. Most dove and darted and rose, and flew off to the mountain heights as quickly as they could.

"Maybe I can try to hold them off," said Corvus. He stood and tried to concentrate. His face glowed with a faint blue light, but he could affect no real effect. "I'm not strong enough yet." Suddenly search lights focused on their spot.

"Now you've alerted them to our exact presence," said Naemi with despair. "Run!" They raced to the spot where the invisible ship sat. Naemi pressed a facet on her ring and the door ramp opened. Up they darted.

Three helicopters were in the air above them wildly passing their searchlights across the ground. One landed, just missing hitting the ship. By the time the soldiers had disembarked, the ship was aloft streaming with all speed straight up into the sky through the atmosphere to the safety of space.

In the cockpit Naemi finally turned to Corvus and demanded answers.

"I can give you some guesses."

"All of them," said Naemi, "While we're on our way back to Lupus."

"No. Wror. First we must go to Wror."

"Then you'll tell me all you know before we get there."

46 IN THE BEGINNING

A tall Feline in a blue jumpsuit stood in a small green valley looking out a cracked transparent dome. He looked longingly upon a blue and green world far below him. "They say a beginning is a very delicate time. But where does one mark the beginning of a circle? It is arbitrary I suppose. But I have always considered the day I met a kindly Human female to be an auspicious day in my life. To me this is a tangible beginning, one to which I frequently revisit when melancholy takes me. It is generally how I remember it, yet I always see something new."

* * *

The cyclonic winds sweeping across the equatorial region of Wror whipped furiously against the Feline encampments on the caldera basin. It was not yet dawn. The dismantling crews were already at work taking apart the modular villages. Today was the day all would move into the completed ring cities of the island. Geothermal generators would turn on this day, powering the new Feline cities.

Galdinier turned in his sleep amid messed sheets, hanging onto a fragment of sleep while he could. But the banging of hammers and prying apart of metal walls drove away what sleep any still clung to. The wall behind Galdinier's head rattled, shook and clanged. In a tiny alcove above, a mechanical whip teetered, toppled and fell.

"Ow!" Galdinier woke with a start. The whip's canister handle struck his face, rolled off his chest. Galdinier tried to catch it but it tumbled, rolled and hit its trigger on the corner of the opening door. The whip's arm sprung out smashing a window, flailing into the wall, and dancing about in the middle of the room as if seeking a victim. Canopus entered the room, bent down to pick up the contraption and pushed the retracting button.

"Time to get up?" she asked.

Galdinier rubbed his head. "I'm naked."

"I see that."

I'm going to get a knot from this."

"One day you might wish you woke up on the other side of the bed," said Canopus.

"If that still hit me on the other side of the bed, I don't know how much it'd matter."

A gust from the windy vortex hit the encampment and the ceiling shook and rattled.

"Why are you here?"

"I'm not sticking around here today just to pack up juice boxes and tins of placalot meats."

"Hm. You've got to help out somehow. We're all supposed to be in the cities by the end of the day. Proper homes of stone, reliable energy. With all the resonite in the crust of this caldera, we'll have energy for a thousand years."

"And all evening unpacking boxes and tins? No thanks. Can I come with you?"

"I don't think that's a good idea. It's my alone time. And your mother will be wondering."

"I've already told my brothers." Canopus reached behind the door and lifted a daypack she'd laid there. Slinging it on her back and strapping it on, she stood hands on hips ready to start anything.

Today Galdinier was to head up into the encircling mountains to move the flocks of dorsein to fresher pastures. "I'll be hiking all day."

"We will."

"Hm."

"Give me a couple minutes to pee and get dressed. And I need a bowl of soup."

"I'm ready. You hurry up."

Galdinier pulled on some loose fitting knickers, shirt and shoes. Then he stepped out in the hall and disappeared for a moment. Canopus investigated the mechanical whip. He said he'd invented it himself and it had many uses, such as tapping the backs of dorsein to get them moving, snatching placalots from a distance, even plucking dust motes from a shaft of sunlight, though she had never seen him do any of those things with it. Canopus eyed a bolt sticking out of the wall. She touched the release lever, aimed and sent the whip's fingers speeding to the wall. With a gentle jerk and flip of her wrist, the whip delicately grasped the bolt, then rapidly spun until it was loosed from the wall. She retracted the whip and the bolt dropped neatly onto the palm of her hand, just as Galdinier returned. The wall detached from the ceiling and came crashing down upon the bed.

"Having fun breaking things?" he asked.

"This place isn't held together very well."

"The easier it'll be taking it all down then. Come on, let's go."

The narrow passageways of the portable warren resembled dark, dirty arteries guiding the movement of dozens of hurrying Felines. Rooms off to each side revealed the frantic activity this day before even the sun rose above the caldera rim, children packing and fighting and playing, parents packing and scolding. Galdinier and Canopus hurried toward an exit to the outside.

Gate 22-North was in a large room of several containers joined together with no inner walls. It was a bar, galley, meeting place, flop joint, warehouse, and exit. It was bustling when they entered.

"I have a locker over there with some extra jackets, if you want to borrow one," said Galdinier.

"Sure." Canopus trailed behind him, listening to conversations at tables and people passing."

"...Now you're being mad. No one is staying here after today. It's a filthy bog...."

"...Not good. There's too much resonite...."

Galdinier came up sipping soup from a bowl. "Still coming along? Canopus, are you still coming along?"

She startled. "What? Oh yes. Of course."

"Let's go."

Galdinier and Canopus donned warm parkas, slung provision bags over their shoulders and passed through the gate outside. The air was crisp with only a slight breeze now. As soon as their feet touched the muddy trampled grass, a hum and vibration from deep underground throbbed the surface. Flattened grass reached upwards, water droplets emerged from the mud and rose, hovering like dew centimeters above the ground. All about, the world seemed to exhale. Galdinier's spine tingled, his hair rose and his whiskers twitched. Canopus broke out in a giggle as if she'd been tickled. Then the sun rose above the rim mountains and warmed the caldera valley. Steam began to rise. Just then the humming and vibrations ceased, and a thunderclap sounded in the north.

"What was that?" exclaimed Canopus.

"It was a power-up test from the ring cities. They're going to be testing all day, phasing on the whole system till the ring is energized all way around. It's going to be an interesting day. The pedal pods are over there," said Galdinier pointing to the left. "Let's borrow a couple."

Canopus grinned. "I'll race you."

Galdinier shook his arms and shook his legs. "I'm stiff."

Canopus took off running. "And you're behind!"

"Ugh!" Galdinier grunted and sprang after her.

One hundred meters from the settlement was a metal platform a few centimeters raised above the grass. It was ten meters by five. On it was arrayed twenty egg-shaped pods, transparent, with three large paddle-like rotation wheels, two in front and one behind. Canopus arrived first and selected one for herself. She popped open the top and climbed in. Galdinier caught up, huffing a little.

"I thought you were in good shape," said Canopus.

"I am. You're better."

Canopus laughed. "Galdinier, the great dorsein herder, admits defeat."

He smiled. "A minor set back." He popped open the top of his pod and climbed in. The contraptions were pedal powered like recombinant bicycles. The pedals allowed for easy transport through the thick grasses of the valley. Galdinier closed his pod and backpedaled off the ramp onto the grass. Canopus followed. They positioned themselves facing northward and began pedaling. "I'll race you to the foothills."

"It's a deal," and she took off.

"Hey! No fair!" He sped after her.

The bright sun lit up the lush valley. Steam rose from the dewy grasses, moisture spraying all about as the pedals spun through them. They sped over puddles and plains. Above them motionless in the sky hung the shining armored asteroid like a sentinel. It had been several weeks since Galdinier's sister Eridani had died with so many others in the wave of epidemics that had greeted the Felines' arrival on Wror. It thinned the population by twenty percent, all because the medical container had not dropped from the asteroid. Was it still up there? Despite the tragedy, construction crews had finished building the ringed cities that would be their new permanent homes.

They pedaled for over an hour. The terrain got hillier as they climbed in elevation. By the time they reached the base of a hill marking the end of the plain, their pod shells were streaked with wet green from the grasses over which they'd ridden, and lots of bugs that had smacked into the pods, smearing the surface with yellow and green goo. Galdinier and Canopus rolled to a stop together. A tie. They climbed out of their pods and abandoned them. They started walking up the hill.

Halfway up they could see the sheer rise of City Block thirteen straddle the hilltop and the foothills for about half a kilometer in either direction left or right. There were windows and balconies, towers and turrets and parapets, the careful work of a modern civilization. All that was missing were the inhabitants. They would arrive this day with all the baggage and trappings of personal lives. Somewhere deep inside this city were the engineers fine-tuning the power generators. Another tremor in the ground, and the grasses trembled as another test pulse from the cities vibrated through the plains.

Galdinier and Canopus steadied themselves on the hill, still shaking. They were just below the city wall near an exterior stone staircase that led up in many switchbacks all the way to the top.

"Look at the ground," said Canopus. "Is that supposed to happen?"

Moisture from the ground and grass formed into drops like dew and hovered above the ground. Another pulse rolled out from deep beneath the city block. The floating dew vibrated and separated into smaller droplets. A breeze kicked up, dissipating the dew.

"Look at the grass," said Galdinier. About their feet and all over the hillside the grass went to seed. The new seeds fell, then sprouted, fell again and sprouted again. All the grasslands rippled in the rapid passing of generations.

Their feet tingled. The hair between their toes grew curly and wooly. Their calves stretched taut and their thighs bulged, not too perceptively, but they could feel it. Their arms were longer, stronger, shoulders thickening. They rubbed their muscles.

"Is this going to hurt us? What happens when all the generators are turned on together?" asked Canopus.

"Leave that to the engineers. We've got dorsein to find." They began climbing the switchback staircase.

Galdinier led the way, grunting and snorting. If the stairs were a direct diagonal this would have been easy. But every flight necessitated turning around and starting up again. Finally bounding up the last switchback, he emerged from the staircase opening onto the top of the wall. Canopus shortly emerged beside him. They sat on the wall for a time catching their breath, dangling their feet, surveying the animated scene of Felines streaming all across the caldera valley to the new cities. The verdant valley glistened.

All that moisture is pulsing to the surface, Galdinier thought. *It's going to turn the whole place into a bog. Liquefaction."* He looked up, blinking. He held up a hand to block the sun. There it was, the twinkling silent armored asteroid in its geosynchronous orbit above the island. *I must get there, somehow*, he thought. *Am I already up there, waiting to meet me?* Curious situation. While Galdinier mused, Canopus watched a slow coiling contrail spiral down through the sky. A breeze picked up. In a few minutes the contrail dissipated and was gone.

They both got to their feet as a new rumbling nearly knocked them back down, this time much further away. A different city in the ring was coming on line. Soon the generators would be pulsing all around the caldera rim until all were synchronized.

Galdinier turned suddenly toward the mountain ridge behind them. His ears perked and twisted. A bawl and a bay in the distance. "Dorsein. Time to move them to a higher pasture."

They scampered over the nearest of six overpass walkways, narrow catwalks that stretched between the plains-side and mountainside walls. Only two meters wide, they curved around in an organic lattice pattern far above the city. Below in the interior courtyard were trees, flowers, shrubs growing among homes, markets, media centers, public spaces, all designed with a Feline disposition, multi-levels, many balconies, lots of open arch doors and windows. Solar mirrors built into the walls directed as much sunlight as possible down into the expanse. The only thing missing was the population, but their approaching voices could be heard in the valley outside.

Galdinier crossed a hundred-meter expanse in a trot, Canopus right behind him. On the far side was another switchback staircase that led down to the mountain ridges and dells. Carefully they nonetheless hopped the way down, one leg then the other. One last hop and WHOOMP! A soft landing on a grassy rise.

A bawl, a bleat, a bay. The dorsein were beyond the ridge before them. Up a path Galdinier ran. It was beautiful, overhung by poplar-pines and pine-poplars, orange-red and yellow-orange blossoms, respectively. The breeze was cool.

The top of the ridge did not overlook the lowlands to the sea. Reaching its crest only revealed more grassy canyons and cool dells, and higher ridges. Galdinier and Canopus stood atop the ridge. No dorsein were in sight, though the sound of bays and baahs echoed up from some unseen canyon. Then a breeze picked up and carried a rich scent to the Felines' noses. They swooned. Grazimyth, growing among the sunny grasses, splotched white by their tiny flowers, filled the air with its intoxicating perfume. It drew them down. They ran down the ridge stumbling and rolling, laughing along the way. They fell over one another in a tumble of giggles.

Galdinier fell face down into a clump of white, the blossoms stuck up his nose. He inhaled deeply. Suddenly he flopped over, lips slightly swollen. He laughed hysterically. Canopus was kneeling in front of him, giggling and wiping laugh tears from her eyes. Galdinier jumped up and pushed her over into a thicker clump of grazimyth, but she grabbed his leg and brought him down, too. They fell silent in a happy heap, inhaling deeply, rolling over and staring up into the sky. They were caught up in an effluvial dream of colors and patterns. Slight but regular tremors swept through the ground beneath them. A three hundred and sixty degree rainbow arced across the sky along the planet's magnetic field lines. The generator pulses sped up into the air in circles like a hurricane of power with the caldera in its eye. The magnetic field lines bent, drifting away from the magnetic poles until their apex was the zenith above the Feline colony. Sparkling above the zenith point was the silent armored asteroid. It too pulsed in the beams from the resonite engines.

Long ghostly shadowy lines streamed through the skies from all four cardinal directions. They were invisible flying reptiles. They came down, circling around the pulse vortex of the island. Galdinier and Canopus could clearly see them now that their normal vision had blurred. They appeared as dragon beasts with emerald scales and cobalt blue plumage. They had long snouts with huge nostrils, rows of serrated teeth, waddles of bright red skin hanging from their throats. Red forked tongues hung from their teeth. Wide red eyes with cat-like pupils flashed bright. Bony cranium plates stuck out between backward arching spiral horns. The reptiles were up to twenty meters long from snout to tail club. Razor clawed talons from long arms and legs dangled down below their sleek bodies. Leathery wings spread out forty meters from tip to tip.

As the Felines watched, one broke from the vortex and flew in a direct line toward them. They remained frozen on the ground in clumps of grazimyth, barely breathing. Chirps and nasally cries erupted from the woods around. Suddenly there was the sound of cracking wood and brush as a dozen giant placalots stampeded up the grassy bank and just missed jumping upon the prostrate Felines. Some were red with brown stripes, others yellow with pink polka dots, others orange with green paisley patterns. They were huge, two meters tall and three long, fat and heavy. Their triple nostrils were enlarged, and their eyes wide with fright. The flying reptile swung low, arched its back and snatched a screaming red and brown placalot off the ground in its powerful talons. The dragon's neck stretched toward the sky, wings beating fiercely as it gained altitude. It flew off, the placalot screaming into the distance.

Galdinier stirred. He sat up. His eyes were glazed and his head was dazed. He turned. He could not believe what he saw, a vision of his sister beneath the trees. She took off in a run across the grassy dell and disappeared behind a shimmering mirage on a flat grassy shelf. He looked down at Canopus. Tendrils of rapidly growing grazimyth covered her. He shook her. Her eyes opened. He called her name. A tiny cry came from her face, and she too sat up.

"I'm hallucinating," said Galdinier.

"We both are," said Canopus. She rubbed her eyes.

"The dragons. Is that what you saw those weeks ago?"

"Yes, in the valley," said Canopus. "The day Eri...."

"Yes," said Galdinier. And he was quiet. He got up brushing and pulling the overgrown grazimyth from his arms and trousers. He extended his arm and pulled Canopus up beside him. "Did you see the giant placalots?"

"Yes. Scary."

"Not as scary as the dragons. There shouldn't be any dragons."

"I told you." Looking around Canopus suddenly exclaimed, "What's that?" She pointed to the flat grassy space. Something they had not seen before lay large on the grass. It shimmered slightly because it was otherwise invisible, but Galdinier and Canopus clearly saw it.

"A space ship!"

They dropped to the ground on bent knees. Caution. They sniffed the wind, which tossed around the dell in all directions carrying scents from the ship to them, and vice versa.

"I don't smell anything but grazimyth," whispered Galdinier. "And placalots."

"I smell other things," said Canopus. She crept forward cautiously, eyes stuck on the ship. But as they became more alert, their vision faded and the ship vanished. "It's still there," said Canopus. "We should be able to touch it.

"Careful," whispered Galdinier. But he crept forward right beside her.

They approached slowly but deliberately like a serpent aiming for a patch of sun. They reached the grassy flat. Canopus reached out an arm and – contact! She felt a landing leg. The tactile sensation was unnerving on an invisible object. Galdinier reached up and felt the hull. Canopus joined her hand to his. Together they moved their hands across the ship's surface. There were no seams, no rivets, no windows or doors. Then Canopus found a tiny spot that was warm. She pushed with a finger. There was the sound of motors and gears, and a hatch opened. A ramp descended. The ship materialized. The Felines jumped aside as the ramp touched the grass.

They gazed up into the interior of the vessel. Silence.

Canopus sniffed the air. "It's empty." She ran up the ramp and stood inside. Cautiously Galdinier followed.

They walked about the main cabin, taking note of the bunk beds, chairs, table. Galdinier laid his mechanical whip on the table and stepped up to the computer terminal in a wall panel. He began accessing files.

"Human, certainly," said Galdinier. "From Lupus. Look at all the entertainment content. But here, this is strange. Feline data files on Earth. But something is wrong. None of the protocol codes are familiar." He accessed the data tree configurations. He called up the core command galleries. "There it is. Incredible. This ship is Canine."

"Why does this ship have data from three different species?" asked Canopus.

"Maybe there is some alliance, or cooperation. But I don't smell Canines here."

"Neither do I. But I smell something else. Human, but familiar. Polaris."

"Interesting."

Loud sounds came from outside the ship, bleating and baying and baahing, growls and snorts.

"Something is wrong with the dorsein," said Galdinier. But the approaching sound of breaking twigs and footsteps on the ramp froze them in place. Canopus put a finger to her lips and whispered, "Shh. Someone's coming."

* * *

They hiked up through the grass and flowers, crunching twigs and leaves and stems on the way to the crest of the rise. As each footfall released its pressure from the ground, the grass and moss and soil sprung back higher than it was before. Naemi and Corvus climbed like shining giants, strong, erect and powerful. Their bodies grew stronger with each step. Limbs grew stronger, taller. Muscles bulged. Their clothes became unbearably tight and constricting. Finally Naemi had had enough.

She stopped. "I've got to get out of these clothes. I can barely move my legs and arms." She peeled herself out of them and stood triumphant, naked in the grass. Her hair danced in electric currents in the air. Her skin glowed. Her breasts were bulbous and blushed in the sun. She felt alive.

"I have to agree with you," said Corvus. Soon he too was naked. His muscles, strength and manhood were all enhanced. "This is liberating."

They crested the ridge and gazed down at the caldera valley, the ringed cities, the Felines streaming into those cities. And above all was a shimmering curtain of power fields forced up by the resonite generators. Corvus looked up following the light.

"Is it powering the great ship up there?" asked Corvus.

"Or is it the other way around?" Naemi contemplated the vessel she knew to be G's time ship. What was playing out here? He must be up there, watching me. Despite feeling such vigor just standing on this planet, breathing its pure air, basking in the lush magic of the place, Naemi felt uneasy under the certain eye of G. Was this somehow a test? Or was she even meant to be here? Were she and Corvus witness to something so sacrosanct that neither of them should be seeing it? Something more was here, she surely felt. Cheetah and Blink were also uneasy, but they said nothing.

"Those cities are advanced structures," said Corvus. "I don't know how they could have been built so quickly."

"Maybe they've been here for years. Maybe you just didn't have surveillance on them."

"Impossible. A Scorpion ship has been in orbit here for over a year. Nothing was seen." He looked up at the ominous shining asteroid. "Then the Drigan dorsein herders were delivered. Maybe there is a connection."

Naemi felt watched. "Perhaps it's time to go. We've seen what you came here to see. Let's get back to Lupus so you can make your report."

"Not so fast. I'm not done with my investigation yet." He stood tall and took a deep breath with his eyes closed. He slowly spread his arms out before him. Naemi watched him intently. The air about them crackled with electricity. Corvus' white skin radiated. When he opened his eyes they shown cold and bright like the brightest stars in the darkest night. He raised one outstretched hand in front of him, aimed it at the pulsing energy curtain surrounding the cities. A ball of bright light enveloped his hand and he let it loose. A ray of cold light shot forward. When it reached the pulse beams it passed through. At the point of contact, the curtain seemed to phase change and freeze. But cracks quickly spread in all directions like cracks in glass just before it shatters. It shattered. The pulse beams went on climbing into the sky. Corvus' beam drifted inside a ways, then dissipated into steam and just vanished. Corvus stood silent a moment, temporarily drained of strength. "Fascinating," was all he said.

"What are those energy beams?" asked Naemi.

"I don't know. But it's more than I can make an impact on."

Naemi bent down and picked up a branch. She threw it towards the valley. It soared over the top of the ringed city right through the beam. It continued a ways and dropped onto the distant ground. "At least we know normal things can pass through it."

Corvus nodded. "You have a good arm. Come on. I agree with you now. It's time to leave." He gave the asteroid ship one last furtive glance. Then he noticed the shadowy flying shapes move in and out of the curtain. *That's strange*, he thought.

"Are we going to visit the Humans in Bara-Band next?" asked Naemi.

Corvus shook his head. "No. I'm not here to catalogue their grievances or consult with them on anything. The Felines are here. Fact. Now the only thing is to report back to Command."

Naemi easily understood the rest. *Neither you nor the Human colonists can go up against so entrenched and defensible an adversary. Corvus might see himself as a hero, but never a martyr.* She moved in step behind him, following his path back down to the dell and grassy flat where hid their ship.

There was another thought that came to her, how strapping this young man looked, beaming in this new world, so tight and beautiful.

Not The Beast anymore? Interjected Blink.

And such a tight butt.

Cheetah responded, *Mm hmm.*

Is this the way? Naemi wondered. It was difficult to say they were even on a path. Out of each footfall the verdant verge bounced back and grew anew so that it was impossible to say Naemi and Corvus were retracing their steps.

"Are you sure this is the way to the ship?" she asked.

"Yes," said Corvus. "It should be. I think it is."

"Your confidence comforts me," said Naemi. Blink smirked and Cheetah giggled.

"The dell is right down here through the trees." He passed through dappled sunlight beneath the woods, then he stopped short. "A dell is here. But it's full of...."

"...Dorsein," said Naemi coming up beside him.

"These weren't here before."

"Because it's the wrong dell."

"We came down the wrong path."

"There wasn't a path," said Naemi.

"The ship must be that way," said Corvus pointing ahead and to the left beyond the dorsein. "It'll only take a minute. Come on." He stepped out from the shelter of the trees and walked right up to the herd, aiming to pass easily through.

Naemi watched him entranced. His white skin glowed in the sunlight. *He looks like a prophet going among his flock,* she thought.

A breeze passed through the trees carrying the scent of Humans among the herd. The mood of the docile dorsein changed. Naemi, Cheetah and Blink all felt a visceral change in the air. Cheetah noticed the cud chewing and snorting sounds of grazing were replaced by the huffs of tension and alarm. Blink saw a third of the herd turn to fully face them, necks craned, eyes wide and bloodshot, saliva dripping from bared teeth. Naemi watched Corvus wade right into their ranks.

"I think we should go around."

"Nonsense. They're docile as, dorsein," laughed Corvus.

The herd did not make much room for him. Corvus' laugh turned to impatience as he was forced to push his way through, protecting his manhood. A dorsein he pushed away with his hand shivered and growled. Growls went up among the herd. They pushed and jostled him, and despite his enlarged size, he was knocked down.

"Aaaaah! What the -?" Corvus yelled jumping up, holding a bloody hand, a finger bit off. "Naemi! Stay back. I'm hurt. This is very wrong." He turned back to try and push his way out. The herd closed in further. He tried to hold steady, but lost his purchase. He was kicked and brought down. He was bit in many places. "They're…Aaaaah!" His voice gurgled. Blood was in the air.

Naemi stood frozen for a fraction of a second. That was all it took to see curious dorsein rush up the slope towards her, gnashing and growling.

"Jump!" yelled Cheetah. Naemi sprung into the air, catapulting just meters over the heads of the herd. She had to be high enough. Their necks were so long. She soared over the herd right through the center of the dell. "Now separate!" Cheetah somersaulted to the left, Blink to the right, and Naemi straight away through. Cheetah hit the ground on the far slope hard, rolled back three times and came to rest against a tree. She shook her head and jumped up. Blink tumbled into a bush and came to rest on its far side. She jumped up. Naemi did a second somersault in the air and landed squarely on her feet facing the other direction. She spun around. All three looked out onto a macabre feeding frenzy.

The sound of the rampage was blood curdling. Growls and yells filled the dell. Human limbs were tossed in the air and fought over by the crazed dorsein. In the center of the herd they were pulling and ripping at the body.

Corvus' eyes were open, spilling a wild blue light in all directions, frosting the air as his head tousled on his exposed neck bone. All three Naemis could see into his rib cage. The blue lights went out. Some of the dorsein turned their attention to the women on the slope.

"We're out of here! Now! Follow me!" cried Cheetah.

All three took off running as fast as they could to the left toward the ship. Cheetah tore through the trees and undergrowth. She pushed branches out of her way and hopped over small obstacles of stone, grass and twig. Naemi was two steps behind keeping up pace, but was just behind enough to catch in her face the springing rebound of all the branches Cheetah knocked aside. Naemi cursed at each branch. Blink was three steps behind Naemi. Terrified at being mere jaw-snaps away from any dorsein giving chase, she violently snapped and broke every branch before her.

They ran along the ridgeline until finding the open dell where hid their ship, then raced down the steep slope, snapping and cracking the undergrowth with their bare feet. Shadows crisscrossed around them on the ground growing bigger and nearer. Blink looked up and scarcely had a moment to be afraid. A feathered dragon with great leathery wings ablaze in bright colors stretched out its talons just above her. "Drop! Now!"

Cheetah dropped immediately. The image was in her mind too. Naemi fell on top of her and they merged. Blink next. The beast screeched into the air and passed over them by centimeters, its wind rolling along Naemi's back.

She lay with her arms outstretched on the ground in front of her. On her right hand, her control ring to the ship vibrated and one of the gems glowed. "The ship is open. Someone's inside." Another flying beast took aim at her and soared down. Naemi rolled to the side leaving just grass for the talons to grab at. Blades of cut grass fell from its talons. Naemi got up and ran. She could see the ship and its ramp. She was almost there. A growing darkening shadow engulfed her and she leaped onto the base of the ramp. Feathers fell over her as the beast was forced higher else it hit the ship. Naemi crawled on her hands and knees to the ship's open door. She was inside.

The main cabin appeared empty of any intruder. Naemi looked around warily. She touched a gem on her ring and the ramp retracted, the hatch closed. Another touch and the ship was invisible again. She whispered to herself. *Cheetah, check the command center. And get us some clothes.* Cheetah emerged and headed to the forward cabin.

Blink too separated and approached the online access panel in the wall. "Someone has accessed the library files," she whispered. "Protocol base codes. Mission parameters. Flight plans."

"Sabotage?"

"Maybe."

Clothing materialized onto their bodies, latex bra and G-string with metal studs. Cheetah found clothes. Typical. Naemi glanced at the cabin table. Her breath stopped short. Lying on its surface was a mechanical whip, the same as the one G had given Cornelius. She picked it up. She heard a sound coming from the lavatory. In a quick movement she detached the whip and flung it at the door. Blink jumped aside. The mechanical pincers pierced the door and found its mark inside. A great wail sounded.

"Oww!"

Naemi pulled the whip back and the door came with it off its hinges. There cowered a Feline male clutching a bloody right ear where the whip had cut two deep notches. With terrible recognition Naemi and Blink cried in unison, "G!"

Just then Cheetah burst out of the command cabin dragging a young Feline girl with her. She stopped dead in her tracks. "G?"

"Let me go!" screamed Canopus wriggling out of Cheetah's grasp. She ran over to the ripped out lavatory door. "Galdinier, are you alright? You're bleeding." She turned to Naemi. "Help him!"

Naemi nodded at Blink, who retrieved a med kit and quickly began tending to the wounds. Naemi stood, hands on hips. "I'm sorry G. I didn't know you were here, obviously."

"I don't know who you are," said Galdinier, mewing and whimpering in his voice as Blink sterilized the wounds.

"I'm sorry we trespassed," said Canopus.

The pain subsiding, Galdinier asked, "What is a Human doing flying an invisible Canine ship with Feline command codes?"

"You can stop with the cover story, G. We won't muck up your plans. I know your time ship is up there. Are you surveying this illicit Feline colony?"

"Illicit?" scoffed Canopus. "We're the colonists."

Naemi was annoyed at the continued ruse.

Canopus sniffed at the Naemis. She looked with alarm upon Blink. "You're from Polaris. Are you three sisters? Or is this one your mother?"

Blink was immediately offended. She blinked her eyes at the Feline, green and blue, then grey and orange, then brown and brown. Canopus drew back.

"MOTHER? I am no one's mother! And we're not sisters," said Blink. "We are from Polaris. Don't worry. We are not from the Magistry."

"Enough of this game, G." said Naemi.

Blink finished dressing Galdinier's wound. "Naemi, come here." Blink pointed to Galdinier's ear. "You did this, just now. But there is no sign of his notches from before. Is it possible, this is how he got them?"

"Of course my ear wasn't cut before. What are you talking about?"

Naemi righted herself up straight, a concerned look on her face. "Join with me, girls." Cheetah and Blink walked right into Naemi and disappeared. Naemi shook her head. It still made her a little dizzy.

"What are you?" asked Canopus.

Naemi chose her words carefully. "My name is Naemi. I am on a secret mission for the Drigan government."

"But how can you do, what you just did?"

Naemi did not reply.

"Ok. Just let us go and you can continue your mission," said Galdinier.

Naemi opened her mouth to respond when suddenly the ship rocked to one side and everyone fell over. BOOM!

"What's that?" yelled Galdinier.

"The dragons," said Canopus.

Naemi jumped back up and ran to the command console in the front of the ship. She yelled, "Why are there dragons attacking my ship?" Then she turned to Canopus. "Why are there dragons on Wror at all?"

"They're flying reptiles," said Galdinier.

"Where did they come from?"

"We brought them," said Galdinier matter-of-factly.

"We have them on Polaris, too. You must remember," Canopus said to Naemi.

"They're not the same kind. They're supposed to be ephemeral, like ghosts."

"They're real here, some of them at least," said Canopus.

BOOM! The ship rocked again.

"I cannot fathom your logic," Naemi said to Galdinier. "But then I never could."

"What?"

BOOM! BOOM! Out the view ports, two dragons worked the front of the ship in an attempt to overturn it. Another was on the roof, striking the hull with its snout, ripping with its claws.

"We have to take off. There's nothing for it," yelled Naemi.

"Wait! You have to let us off this ship," cried Canopus.

Naemi turned to her and shouted, "No one is getting off of this ship." She powered up the engines. The ship shook in an attempted ascent, but the dragon on top was too much. Suddenly it began jumping into the air and landing hard on the hull. Again. Again and again.

BOOM! BOOM! BOOM! BOOM! BOOM!

"Do you have any weapons you can use against them?" asked Galdinier.

"No," said Naemi curtly. She pursed her lips tight in annoyance.

The ship began rocking back and forth again.

"I have an idea," said Canopus.

"Let's hear it, quick," said Naemi.

"The dragons are ancient Birds of Prey. They're brightly colored. They see colors."

"Your point?"

"You can make the ship visible. Can you change its color, too? Can you create patterns? Something to alarm them? Scare them?"

"That I can do. Yes." Naemi entered a series of commands onto her console.

Though they could not tell from inside the ship, from the outside the ship suddenly materialized in a blaze of pulsating red and black lights moving across the ship's surface. The dragons screeched and jumped back. The beast atop the ship leapt into the air and flew a distance away. Naemi throttled the engines on full and the ship careened up into the sky. The dragons took to the air to give pursuit.

The ship accelerated parallel to the energy curtain around the ring cities. High up, dragons flew in and out of the curtain, growing in girth, changing shape and color with each pass.

"Your energy beams are mutating them," said Naemi.

"I don't know how that's possible," said Galdinier.

"I've seen it before," said Naemi. "It's weaponized energy." Looking eye to eye with Galdinier, she added, "Whether you think so or not."

Up and up the ship soared, and the three dragons that had attacked them on the ground remained in pursuit. As the ship passed the area along the energy curtain where the majority of dragons flew in and out, they turned and joined the three in a climbing spiral. They approached the ship nearer and nearer until only the thinning atmosphere slowed them and they gasped for every breath. They fell back. Only one continued and raced ahead, the beast that had been atop the ship. Four kilometers above the ground it finally blacked out, went limp, and fell out of the sky.

"What now?" asked Galdinier. "Where do you intend to take us, if you won't return us to the planet?"

"I'll be returning to Lupus. Then later, if all goes well, back to Polaris." To Canopus she asked, "Would you like to return to Polaris? Don't worry, the Magistry will not be involved."

Canopus was surprised by the offer. The prospect excited her.

"You can't," protested Galdinier. Then he calmed down. "Take us to the armored asteroid. There is work I must do there. Drigans are allies of the Felines," he explained. "You must help us. I've been trying to find a way back to the asteroid. We arrived here with the Drigan colonists whom we dispatched far to the north. But our medical and communications containers did not drop with us. We have been unable to communicate with the captain. Not long after we arrived a terrible plague swept through the community. Tens of thousands died. My sister was one of them." He was emotional and his body held back tears. The whiskers of his face bent down and the tips of his ears bent forward.

He's telling the truth, thought Blink. *It's G's great grief.*

Naemi thought a moment, then agreed. "I can take you to the asteroid."

Canopus was quiet. She was weighing her own opportunities. "I will go with you, Naemi. Back to Polaris."

"We return to Lupus first."

Canopus nodded. "I understand."

"You'll give up your home, Canopus?" asked Galdinier. He was starting to feel this as a new loss.

Canopus explained. "I never wanted to be evacuated from Polaris, Galdinier. That was my home. Even though my family is below, I want to go back."

"Tell me about those dorsein," asked Naemi. She was now upset. "I did not come here alone. A companion of mine was savagely devoured by dorsein only minutes before I found you. It was an unprovoked, vicious attack. It goes against any knowledge or presumption of dorsein behavior. Just what are you Felines doing down there?"

Canopus looked quixotically at Galdinier. She was confused. "Dorsein ARE docile."

"They are," said Galdinier.

"They are NOT," said Naemi.

"Towards Felines. They were bred as defensive herds. They are loyal to Felines, but exhibit a degree of hostility towards other species."

"A degree of hostility," mocked Naemi. "Why?"

"There are Humans on Wror," said Galdinier matter-of-factly.

"Are you here to invade them?"

"Certainly not. "This is a shared world now."

"Hm. How much dialogue have you had with the Humans on your shared world?"

"None, I think. But I am not an official."

"No?" Naemi was unconvinced. "Are the Humans your enemies here?"

"No."

"Who bred the dorsein to be aggressive?"

"I did."

"Exactly." Naemi was upset. "But the Humans may rightly consider you a threat."

"I just need to get to the asteroid, to get those medical and communications containers down to the surface, to talk to the captain."

"I said I would take you," said Naemi. "But you have to learn to trust the Humans." That was all she said, and Galdinier said no more.

Above them growing bigger with each passing moment loomed the armored asteroid. Naemi knew this ship from a later time. It became a time ship, G's time ship. Was G up there now? Or was this really G standing just beside her? Time was a dimension that could be pulled and stretched, twisted back on itself in loops and knots. Whatever the distortion or direction, time was relative. Here, now, G was Galdinier, so it seemed. But was this Galdinier, G?

The asteroid appeared dramatically different from the one Naemi remembered. Canopus and Galdinier moaned at the sight of blackened armor seared from the attack by Markhab's Scorpion ship, though neither Canopus nor Galdinier nor Naemi knew anything about that. Of the five-domed environmental areas only one was intact. The others were cracked open or exploded. Anyone or anything once in them was now dispersed in space around Wror.

"How should we enter?" asked Naemi.

"With the right access commands, the armor plating should part creating a landing bay," said Galdinier.

"Do you know such commands?"

Galdinier said, "Yes."

"Then come over here and transmit them."

Galdinier nodded. He entered a series of command codes onto a COM screen, and Naemi pressed the transmit button. A single word displayed on the screen, the reply PROCEED.

One area of armor near the ship bulged outward. Naemi flew the ship through into a wide hangar bay. Small transport ships were docked about and two large containers sat in the middle of the hangar. And there were robots, everywhere robots, scurrying out of the way. Naemi landed beside the containers.

"Ok, we're here," she said. She powered down the ship. "Let's meet the greeting committee."

Galdinier, so eager, disembarked first running down the ramp. Canopus quickly followed. Galdinier was already engaged in conversation with a robot when Naemi stepped out onto the hangar floor.

"It is most pleasant to see you, Master Galdinier," said the robot.

"What happened here?"

"We were attacked by Humans just after you departed."

"Are these the medical and communications containers? Why did you not send them down?"

"We have been carrying out repairs since that day," replied the robot. "There was extensive damage."

"Yes. I saw. Where is the Captain?"

"We have not –." The robot paused when he saw Naemi.

"It's ok," said Galdinier. "She commands the transport that brought me."

"She is, Human, Master."

"Yes, but not with the ones who attacked. She fights them."

"And I will be departing soon," said Naemi, not actually trying to put the mecanique at ease.

"Continue," said Galdinier.

"We have not been able to contact the Captain all these months. He is locked in the command center and we cannot get in. I fear he may no longer be alive."

"Take me to him." Galdinier turned to Canopus. "Will you not stay with me?"

"I am sorry Galdinier. I wish to go with Naemi and return to Polaris."

"First Lupus, then Polaris," said Naemi.

Galdinier nodded. He could understand, after a fashion.

"Lupus, Master?" asked the robot.

"I will fill you in later."

"This is our exit then," said Naemi to Canopus.

The Felines embraced for such a period of time that Naemi grew uncomfortable.

"You will tell my mother and brothers, Galdinier? You will explain to them?"

"Yes, when I see them. And I will find you again one day."

"Ok," said Canopus finally to Naemi.

"I am in your debt, Naemi," said Galdinier. They shook hands. "If I can help you in the future, I will."

"Of that I have no doubt. Good luck here." She took Canopus by the hand and they returned to the ship.

Galdinier watched them depart. The armored asteroid closed. He had tears in his eyes. He turned to the robot and said, "Let's go see the captain."

* * *

Above them on a terrace where none could view him, an older and wiser

Feline stood watching. He was tall, wearing a blue overall jumpsuit. In his right ear were two old notches, battle scars he liked to think of them. He watched the Human ship depart, watched Galdinier and the robot leave the hangar bay. He nodded and smiled. "Thus it all begins again." Light swirled around him and for an instant the sound of breaking glass and grating metals erupted. Then all was empty and silent.

47 UNDER STARS FAR FROM HOME

Renender panted in anticipation. Yes, he panted. He stood in the Septum of Mine City. He was drenched in sweat. He felt hot and he had chills. But he was excited. Between the strange and beautiful, and strange and terrible, adventures behind him, and his past as a political mover and a business shaker, now stood a man in an enchanted suit. He considered himself a wholly new being, part Canine and part Human. His body was full of impulses strange to him, and in his mind he saw images entirely alien, Canine memories. The suit remembered.

The door was before him. What lay behind the green door? A city occupied and terrified. Beyond that, down the mountain in the horseshoe valley was more misery and usurped industries. Renender would save them all. He was the new hero, worthy of words and pictures in Uriel's book. He knew his responsibility and he was full of confidence, the hero of Lupus City.

The wild Canine presence within the suit ached to come forward. For a moment, Renender's head shook violently from side to side. In the blur, a snarling Canine face pushed through his Human skin to temporarily bare teeth and splatter saliva all about. But when the shaking ceased, Renender's Human visage returned. He wiped the spittle from his cheeks and chest.

He was tense. He squatted, his kneecaps snapping as he did so. He'd always had clicking, snapping knees. Some things didn't change. He felt faint for a second, but the time for action was now. He stood up, pushed against the green door, and went in.

The long hallway was pitch black, absolute darkness. Renender stood silently as the green door closed behind him with a deafening CLANG. He held his breath. Nothing. If he was going to proceed he needed light. His suit blazed forth in a kaleidoscope of colors, the light dazzling against the whitewashed hall. Dead light bulbs dangled from the ceiling. Security cameras were poised about the ceiling pointing down, threatening to reveal him, but they too were dead. No green lights, no red. Empty threats. Strange. Large numbers were painted in black on the floor beneath every lamp. Renender began his way down the hall.

Hundreds of meters ahead lay the sanctum of the Hypogeum. *My friends, prepare for your deliverance.* In that hallowed chamber he might find old Bordent, the Trickle Depth Miner. And if he could connect with Balthorelei, he could discover all that had transpired under the jackboots of Corvus and his fellow Commissioners. *Prepare to fall.* He marched down the hall.

Renender planned his triumphant return. He would need Jerembor's help. If he was still alive, together they could sort this thing out, evict the military. *This is going to be so easy,* Renender thought.

His mind drifted to his last night in Mine City. The woman Alice. No, that was not her real name, but it stuck. She was an ordinary woman who found herself in an unfortunate place at an outrageous moment in time. They became acquainted over a conversation about cave marmelots and star nosed moles.

He thought of the poor Escort named Jeaneau, so naïve, so delicious. He had a partner, Jeanette. Well, he hoped nothing nasty had happened to either of them.

And there was a particularly clever barista in the Hotel Empalasor. She could prove useful; though Renender imagined she'd just as readily go to the other side if it suited her. He could tell she was the type who grew up in Mine City and dreamed of getting away. Such a desire would play easily into the hands of the likes of Corvus.

The real prize of course would be Lupus City. Its onion domes, horseshoe valley and fleets of airships connecting the titanium mountain redoubt with the rest of the world. *Lupus City, and your beautiful balloons, I'm coming.*

Number 122 on the floor. Renender was half way there.

Renender's thoughts moved to earlier periods in his life from his recent experiences, his life in Lupus City. In his youth he had loved to race cars. Many an early morning Renender's father had collected him, again, from the Police Chief's precincts above the airship field. His parents weren't anything special as far as the rest of the community was concerned, a mere grocer and wife. Renender caused them many troubles when he would steal cars and ride them at top speed amid the airships. How many times had he sat waiting for his father to pick him up? A hundred? A hundred and fifty? If he hadn't been gay he might have spent many pleasant decades in some prison as a terminal troublemaker. But the Police Chief had a soft spot that often grew hard, for Renender. And so Renender had remained a bad boy ratcheting up the stakes, and the strikes, against him. But he was also very successful. Eventually Renender bought the police precinct the day after the old Chief retired. He turned it into his corporate headquarters. Renender Enterprises did very well. Business deals hitherto unheard of took shape in that building. Renender's businesses stretched as far as the great lakes, Big City, Shining City, Cronapolis, Dula, even further afield, and farther, but those were his secrets.

Number 91. Renender hurried down the corridor. His pendant danced. It struck his skin with its many points, each prick sending a warm wave of light through his suited body. Trot-trot and prick-prick.

He remembered his first day of Primary School. His mother had come into his room to see how was dressed. She looked him over, scrutinizing the suspender straps, the buttons on his vest, his shorts, stockinged legs and shiny black patent leather shoes. "Wear this," she said, handing him the pendant. "No one will cross a Pledge of the Precession Star." The first day of school was traditionally a costume party. The parents, administrators and public loved it. For the children, it set the pecking order for the rest of their school career.

Renender was very clever on that day. He'd overheard the school administrators discuss removing all the "adventurous" students to a special finishing school. Get them out of the way. Renender quickly organized a civic-wide movement championing "Reach out to the world." The student leaders quickly assumed policy-making authority in education. By the end of his primary school education, Renender had overseen the replacement of the Local Elective Authority with the twin Civic and Economic Councils. Crooked elective politics would no longer play a role in the development of Lupus City. Instead, enlightened leaders would set policy.

Number 10. There were only a few meters to go. Renender approached the cleft at the end of the corridor leading to the Hypogeum. Suddenly he grew dizzy and nauseous. A rumble moved through the mountain. He leaned against the wall to steady himself. The corridor seemed to move. The surface of the wall beneath his fingertips slipped and rippled. Then it was over. His stomach settled down and his head became clear. A quake? But it was over. Renender thought, *I'm coming back to my life. Where I've been is unreal. Bordent said such a journey could drive one mad. I'm not mad, am I? No. This suit is real. The Canine valley is real. No, I am not mad. But I will undo the deeds of those who are. I went away, not to run, but to gain aid. This suit, and I in it, are that aid. I'm back.* He shut off his light and stepped into the chamber.

The Hypogeum was dark, quiet and very dry. Renender raised a finger and it glowed. There was no one here. No smoke from incense or candles. Dust and ash lay on the floor. His footfalls stirred it up. There was smoke that had settled some time ago. Strange that this place might have been empty for a long time. It was almost never unoccupied. How long had he been gone? Surely only a few days. *Aren't there any miners at work? There should be votives for their safe return. Did no one light a candle or incense even for my return?* Renender spied a candle and half a stick of incense. These he lit. *For my own safe return.* He moved to the entrance.

Standing outside the red granite pilloried entrance was more evidence that things were off. Here too there was no light. Renender provided his own, again allowing his suit to pulse a kaleidoscope of colors with a rhythm that matched his own heartbeat. No guards. There was supposed to be at least one attendant at all times, each hour of each day of every year. But no one was here. On the desk was a timesheet on a clipboard. The last attendant signed out at 08:14:22, and nobody had signed in after. What time was it now? A clock on the wall said 08:15:00, and it kept showing that time. It was stopped. But what day? Had the clock stopped functioning? Or was time standing still?

Down the small corridor Renender passed out through a door and onto a small street. All was quiet, and other than Renender's own light refracting and reflecting off the titanium walls and glass windows, there was no other light.

Renender saw flowerpots beneath some of the windows, flowers all dried and dead, except for one planter with vibrant pink petunias. He walked up and touched a petal. Plastic.

A nagging strangeness that had tugged at Renender's mind finally found its cause. It wasn't all the missing people, or the lack of power. That was obvious. Rather it was a distortion of perception. The streets, the buildings, even some of the windows and doors, looked to be slightly pulled in one direction as if seen through a carnival mirror, or more succinctly, as if the city were made of taffy and it had been pulled in one direction. What was the explanation? The city was made entirely of titanium after all. Titanium was hard. Maybe it was a trick of his eyes, a product of the suit he was wearing.

A shiver ran up Renender's spine. His skin tingled. He felt dizzy and nauseous. Then he heard it, though its frequency was so low that he wasn't sure his sense of hearing was really involved in perceiving it. All around him the city stretched. Only a few millimeters, but it was everywhere, stretched in an upper left direction. Was it north or south, east or west? He didn't know. Presently the phenomenon ceased. Renender was perplexed. He decided to visit the city's security offices, and made haste to get there.

The offices of Mine City Security were easy enough to find. He'd been there many times, paying amicable visits to Jerembor the Sergeant, his friend. Like everywhere else, the place was pitch dark, silent, abandoned. Renender thought he might access some security logs, videos, anything that might give him a clue to what was going on, but all the equipment was dead. There was no power. The dusty surfaces reflected in Renender's pulsating light show. Counters and tables were bare of everyday artifacts. No pens, no pads, no coffee cups. Files were empty. Only dust. Whatever had happened, it was an organized departure. Then something caught Renender's eye. It stopped his pulse for a beat. Sitting neatly on the communications console was an envelope. Written in Jerembor's steady penmanship was a single word that kindled hope, RENENDER.

He tore open the envelope, anticipating answers to so many questions. But there was no note. What was there brought a smile to Renender's face nonetheless. It was the key card to his prized car, won in a card game from Jarbed. Perhaps everyone had left for Lupus City. That's where Renender would go. Home.

He was famished. Was any food to be found here? A sign on the door at the far end of the room read KITCHEN. Renender passed in and quickly rummaged through all the cupboards and storage lockers. All to be found were three sealed fiber bars and two liter-bottles of water. Renender ate all three bars and drank all the water. The bars were horribly dry, virtually tasteless. The water was flat, but at least it was something.

Key card in hand, Renender left the Security Offices and headed down the main street to the Plaza. The emptiness was depressing. The holographic projector was not functioning, so no serene lake lapped against the Promenade. The sign that read STAY AWAY FROM EDGE. NO BOTTOM still warned against the dangerous bottomless pit. Renender leaned over the edge and peered down into the abyss. Beams of bright light shot out from his eyes as he searched the depths. Nothing. Was it truly bottomless? Never mind such speculation. Across the titanium bridge, which was luckily extended, he could see into the arrival carport. There was a lone ground car, his ground car. Renender smiled. He sprinted across the bridge and stood a moment later beside his prize.

He inserted the card into its key slot, and nothing happened. "Hm." Renender was perplexed. A vehicle this state-of-the-art should not have a malfunction. Renender moved to the front. He bent down and felt under the chassis for the lever and popped the hood. Lifting it up, he set the guide bar. Some things were so classic that they never changed. He peered inside. None of the gauge lights worked. Strange. Everything seemed connected. The fuel cell was supposed to have a lifetime charge of, well, years. He snapped open the power compartment and drew out the fuel cell. Cold fusion was a basic concept. Inside the clear cylinder was supposed to be a palladium cathode in a deuterium bath. Yet the cell was dry. In place of the reactants was a jumbled crystalline structure that entirely filled the cylinder.

That shouldn't happen. The only explanation Renender could think of was the passage of time. Decades would have to pass for the crystals to form. Decades, or much longer.

The ground rumbled again and Renender felt dizzy and nauseous. Again, the strange stretching happened. Everywhere the mountain groaned. Then it passed. What was causing it?

He stood up straight, hands on his hips. He would not be riding back to Lupus City in this. He looked around. There in the corner of the cavern, sitting on its tracks was his salvation, a lone titanium transport cart, poised and ready to head down the mountain track. He would take it. Renender settled into the open bed, thankfully bereft of titanium ingots. He reached out and pulled the release brake lever. Gravity took over. He sped down the track into the tunnel on his way home.

The cart spun around the corkscrew tunnel and shot out the other side at breakneck speed. The track bypassed the seven gates of welcome to Mine City, skirting the flanks of the titanium mountain below the road. The distance to Lupus City was twenty-five kilometers, all downhill. There was gravel and sand on the track, but thankfully no rocks, boulders, or trees. Still, the journey was anything but pleasant. It was terrifying. Renender hung onto the sides of the cart with white knuckles.

He was still illuminated like a kaleidoscope. The sky was not quite dark, but twilight, whether it was dawn or dusk, Renender could not tell. He raced down the track like a mad speeding firefly. The flanks of the mountain passed in a roaring windy blur full of rattle, bump and screech. He bounced incessantly, nearly flying out of the cart many times. The kilometers sped by until the view opened up and the cart passed through the canyon lands and entered the horseshoe valley. Down, down until sudden darkness and a wrenching halt against rubber brakes stopped everything. Renender was in the smelting factory. All was silence.

Renender stood up on shaky legs. His nerves were shot. His heart raced. After a moment steadying himself he climbed out of the cart and looked about him at the factory. It was empty but for row upon row of empty carts. Dust and webs were everywhere. Windows were broken out and a weird purplish glow came in from the outside. Renender found an exit and left the building.

The purple glow was everywhere. It was the color of the sky. Twin purple suns hung low in the sky, dim and distant. A few stars shone through the weak light, strange stars set in constellations Renender had never seen before. Winged shapes flew high in the air, Birds of Prey. Above them a dark net crisscrossed the sky. It seemed to straddle the whole planet. The bands of the net were pinched in the east. Something, a massive ship, pulled the net. Below it all from where Renender stood stretched out the ruined remains of Lupus City, crumbling, quiet but for the wind, and empty.

Renender walked down the deserted streets surveying the decrepitude. Buildings were half collapsed. Onion domes that still perched on their towers were wind carved, their colors faded. The Civic and Economic Administration Building was cold and forlorn. Its doors hung open on broken hinges. The former greensward was a dry weedy field.

Down Renender went until he stood before own business headquarters on the edge of the valley field. A faded "R" was still discernible on the building, but the structure had collapsed. Renender felt pained. He would have liked to sit at a booth in his restaurant, exchanging jokes with Matta and enjoying her coffee. There would be no coffee today. The valley field itself, which had once berthed fleets of hundreds of airships, was pitted and overgrown with grass, brush and trees. The little stream running down the length of the field now cut a gorge near the far end, the valley's perimeter edge, and now a canyon. Waters gurgled there down the steep side of the mountain.

Renender felt dizzy and nauseous again. There came the low rumble, and the world stretched. When it stopped Renender shook his head to clear it. When he stopped, his eyes alighted on something in the field, an incredible relic. Renender ran out onto the field, hopping over holes, weaving around foliage. He stopped short. Lying on the ground was a square box gilded with gold and titanium inlay, and beside it was a long titanium trumpet. It was the box that the bandmaster would stand on, conducting his musicians and welcoming the return of the airship fleets arriving from the Lake Docks. But the band was gone, and so too presumably any airship.

Renender picked up the trumpet. It was a meter long and light weight. He stood up on the box and looked out over the field, the purple sky, the dim suns and stars, the net, and the sheer emptiness of the world. He looked up. Empty but for Birds of Prey high, high up. They paid no heed to the little light that was Renender far, far below. Still, he shut off his light lest he garner unwanted attention. He transformed. He was dressed in a fashionable tuxedo with tails. He wore a top hat. Hanging below his black bow tie was his amulet. A carnation was pinned to his lapel. Lifting the trumpet to his lips, he blew the welcoming sound from the greeting horn. Da da-da daaa. Da da-da daaa. Da da-da daaaaa. Its clear notes rang out across the forlorn valley, echoing back off the flanks of the mountains. The sound lingered, fell and finally died away. Silence returned.

Renender sighed. Then as he stepped down off the box a crash sounded, horrible crashing, like breaking glass and metal sheets scraping together. His amulet glowed. An arc of yellow light burst into being not three meters in front of him. Out of it stepped a figure. It was, "Naemi!" he exclaimed.

She stood tall in a red sequined dress. A star shaped amulet the same as Renender's hung from a silver chain around her neck, dangling just above her breasts. It too, glowed. "We've been searching a long time for you, Renender," she said.

"Wh...What has happened?" he asked.

"Specifically?" asked Naemi. She was calm, as if nothing was out of the ordinary.

"Everything!" he said exasperated. He spread his arms in wide arcs. "This!"

Naemi looked around at the field, at the city. She looked up into the sky, saying nothing.

"What is that, that thing up there?"

"That's the Kelden net," said Naemi matter-of-factly. Renender just stared at her. Finally she added, "It's moving the planet."

"Moving it to where?"

"Back, of course. It's being returned." Her eyes flashed green, then brown.

Alarmed, Renender took a step back. This was too crazy for him to process.

"I'm here to fetch you. Come with me."

"What? I don't know what's going on, but I'm not going with you."

"Oh for crying out loud," said Naemi. She withdrew a metallic cylinder concealed in her dress. She pushed a button and a long mechanical whip flew out. "I'm not putting up with this. You're coming with me." She drew her arm back, aimed and let it snap.

It flew at Renender, who had turned and broken into a run. The tip of the whip separated into three pincers. They snatched Renender right off the ground. He squirmed, he cried out. Naemi drew him back to her. She grabbed him, put her free arm around his waist and said, "Gotcha." They disappeared into the arc of light. The noisy din ceased and the light went out. Nothing but the breeze moved through the horseshoe valley beneath the purple sky.

48 THE SHIMMERING FIELD

The mountain vales of Lupus Minor were narrow and surrounded by sheer high craggy peaks. Scattered woods covered the lower vales while their upper stretches were boulder and gravel-strewn expanses cut by swift rivers and streams. These were the unforgiving locations of the titanium and uranium mines operated by the military. Forced labor was the occupation of the majority of residents in the gulag cities. Only Bafaria had a mixed economy allowing a semblance of normal urban life. Still, teams of workers streamed northward daily to join the ranks of gulag laborers in the mines and support industries.

From eyries high in the craggy peaks, Birds of Prey spied on the lines of Human workers marching up the rocky narrow valleys to their mines. With their keen eyes they could spot the frail, the weak, the old and young from the able-bodied. Just such a group of frail men were sighted in the valley now. From perches too far up to be seen by the Humans, Birds of Prey launched themselves from their ledges. They circled high above, adding more to their ranks with each loop. When two dozen were aloft, they descended.

Barandin was middle-aged, a longtime widower. His years in the mines had aged him into an old man. Yet four days a week he joined his line and made his way up to the titanium mines in the craggy mountains with little complaint. Despite being born to the gulag life, he was hardy and healthy. He trudged along the workers path with the care and sureness of any expert Sherpa. But today he was lost in the reminiscences of long ago days. He thought of a little boy he once knew who lived with his mother and sister across the hall of a tenement building. The boy was smart, friendly and helpful. He always ran around pretending to fight monsters. On occasion he would play chess with Barandin. Those were memorable days. Then tragedy befell the family and the boy went away. What was his name? Oh yes, Cornelius. As Barandin smiled at the memory, he twisted an ankle on a loose stone. He fell tumbling out of the line. Two of his mates helped him to his feet. He waved off offers to rest and continued the march, though as a straggler bringing up the rear.

Watching, and aware of everything, the Birds of Prey struck.

The Humans became aware of their danger only as fast moving and rapidly growing shadows raced across their line. They broke into a mad run, but the terrain was hazardous, and many tumbled. Black and Silver wings were upon them in seconds.

Barandin could not run. Instead he hopped. His balance was off and he zigzagged back and forth, left and right. His pained antics made him an unpredictable target until he careened off the path, arms and legs akimbo in what might have been a cartwheel but for the resulting broken limbs. Lying in the dust and rocks, he could only stare as the dark shape seized him in its talons and bore him aloft. Up, up he went, the sound of beating wings filling his ears along with the cries of his compatriots. The ground receded to a terrifying distance. The slate grey cliffs rushed by. Then with a thud he was dropped onto a narrow cleft of rock, his body broken, but his spirit still temporarily intact. His eyes stared at the sun until a monstrous shadow stepped before him. The cold black eyes of the huge Bird of Prey pierced his mind. Then the beast spread its wings. Streaks of silver in the feathers seemed to pulse. The Birdman shrieked a thunderous scream. Barandin was struck dumb. Only one thought still inhabited his mind, the last thought he'd enjoyed before the attack, the little neighbor boy who had wanted to grow up one day and fight monsters. A tiny smile cracked his lips and he mumbled the name, "Cornelius."

The great Bird of Prey stabbed him with its beak, tearing out his entrails in a sport of blood and gore. A fellow Birdwoman shrieked and fluttered and came to alight beside the corpse. She said nothing, but turned her head in jerking motions first in one direction and then another, her eyes pitch black and cunning. The killer ended his meal and stood up, shoulders back and chest out. His face and beak dripped red and blood ran down the feathers of his chest. He shook his head, splattering blood.

"Go ahead, finish it," he said to the new arrival, who promptly plunged her beak into the chest cavity of the Human.

"He said something before he died," said the first Birdman. "Someone's name. It was Cornelius."

The Birdwoman pulled and pulled and pulled until her head came out with a broken rib bone in her beak. She swallowed the bone and meat whole. She cocked her head up in the direction of the one who spoke. Her eyes only saw red, but not through the red of blood. She couldn't speak for the bone wasn't down all the way yet. All she could muster was a cluck. She leapt off the cliff just as a host of red-feathered Birdmen bore down upon the eyrie from above. The first Black and Silver Birdman only had time to turn around to see a golden spear launched from the hand of Casimir the Red Falcon find its mark straight through the heart in his chest.

Casimir, friend to men, and a hundred of his loyal Falcons fell upon the gluttonous Black and Silvers, routing their feast with golden spears and claws until none were left alive, none but the sole Birdwoman who soared down the airs above the river valley, still trying to swallow the old man's rib bone. The Falcon Cholima sent her spear at the fleeing Black and Silver. Both spear and Birdwoman soared out of sight.

Red wings filled the sky. They hunted each last Black and Silver until the mountain crags and gravel grounds were littered with wind blown feathers, only a portion of which were red. But no red Birdman was among the corpses that fell from the sky that morning. Casimir's host alighted on the ground to survey their work. Casimir directed the fallen Humans be buried under a rocky mound, while the Black and Silvers were heaped onto a pile and set ablaze. The Red Falcon host rose into the air as the foul stench of burning flesh filled the rocky valley. They set their eyes to the southern distance where lay the city of Bafaria and headed in that direction, each Birdman wielding a golden spear that twinkled in the sun.

The lone Black and Silver raced southward. She sought out any thermal she could find to maintain an average altitude and as much as possible not beat her wings. The Human rib bone was still lodged in her throat. She could barely breathe. The barren rocky canyons gave way to less warm grasslands. They followed the river's courses south to meander in the nitrogen bogs just north of Bafaria. There the air was heavy with moisture, mists hovered above the swamps, gently disturbed by the heavier moisture-ladened air moving up from the great expanse of the forests of Aran, and south of there from the sea.

There were no more thermals here to steal lift from. She gasped for air. She beat her wings, each flap an agony. She passed over the nitrogen processing facilities, huge round tanks set amid the swamps collecting the gas and processing it for industrial use powering the city of Bafaria. The city itself spread out beneath her now along the river near where it joined with the Great River of Lupus in the canyon-lands. She would not be able to make it that far, to deliver her message to Gog the Great. She soared between towers and residential blocks of the city. Here the wind churned between buildings and the air was hotter, dryer. She caught an updraft and rose as high as the tallest building. On its top the Birds of Prey had set up a sentry.

She arched her wings and pulled them forward. Her feet hit the surface and she tumbled, rolled, came to rest at the feet of the chief sentry, a mainly silver Bird of Prey. He jumped back, floating a moment in the air with his great outstretched wings.

"Eh. What? What news?"

She gasped for breath. Blood trickled from her mouth. One wing was broken.

"I am Giloth, from the sentries above the titanium mines in the mountains." Cough. More blood. "We were attacked. They are coming. Casimir and," cough, "and, Cornelius-lius."

Just then the swooshing sound of an object shooting through the air rushed at them. A golden spear struck through her chest and lodged itself in the building top.

The sentries leapt into the air. The chief cried out, "To the great river canyon. We must alert Gog." They raced south.

* * *

The First Commissioner's bullet train snaked through the river canyon lands from Bafaria south to the Forward Base. This stretch was carved into a groove of the cliff face itself two-thirds up from the healthy flow of the Great River's spring flood. The blue and black striped train was fifty meters long. It glistened when the canyon swung out to face the eastern sun. A road snaked along the opposite cliff top. Men and women trudged along the road singing half-hearted songs of the march, spurned on by armed captains along the way. The train and the marchers approached the same destination, the frontline where the assault on the north would commence. This was the day.

The narrowest part of the canyon was where the red cliffs were but half a kilometer apart. The high roiling spray of the tumult spotted the windows of the train. The tracks were wet and crowded with colonies of bromeliads, orchids and ferns. The train slowed around the green watery bend. The tint of the light of day dimmed as a curtain of shade swept up from the south covering the sky. As the train came out of the bend, rocks tumbled from above. It was a quake. Rubble cascaded down bouncing and loosing more cliff fragments. The open tunnel collapsed onto the train shattering windows and crushing the fuselage. The train did not move again.

The marchers on the opposite road stopped to stare in amazement. The captains were confused. They yelled and struggled to get the lines moving again.

Then suddenly the whole world seemed to CLICK and reverse frames as in a moving picture of unreality. The number of people on the road doubled. All were in military uniform. Flags waved in the breeze and they sung in loud voices patriotic songs of military might. Again the train approached the narrows, this time at a high speed and did not slow. The river was higher and the tracks exceedingly wet. The train entered the green turn but its centrifugal force was too much for such a wet track. The tint of the sky darkened. The cliffs shook and the First Commissioner's train jumped off the tracks. It turned on its side and plunged into the torrent followed by a sizeable portion of cliff.

Then CLICK, reverse frame. The whole scene changed again. Flying barges patrolled the river canyon hovering meters above the lowered water. It'd been a dry winter and spring in Lupus Minor. Armed snipers filled the decks of the barges aiming at the lorries creaking along the road laden with men and women, workers or prisoners, depending on one's definition. They poked fingers, hands and faces out of the titanium cages on the truck beds. The line of lorries trailed kilometers from the center of Bafaria to the Forward Base. On the other side of the canyon the train tube was completely enclosed in a titanium casing. Titanium awnings protected the tube from debris that might fall from above. Awnings below protected against moisture splashing up from the river. Only mosses and lichens grew on the rock face below the bottom awnings, nothing else.

The First Commissioner's train traveled along its course at a constant velocity. Its progress was only evident by the frost that spread along the tube's outer surface, rippling forward and condensing into a fog along it course. A sheet of darkly tinted sky swept across the horizon followed shortly thereafter by a rumble of ground and tumble of cliff. The train snaked by without impact. However, screams were raised on the other side as a lorry swerved and rolled on the shaking road. A piece of the cliff broke off taking part of the road with it. The lorry careened into the river and rocks far below. The flying barges did not attempt rescue. Instead, one hovered closer to the road. A voice bellowed through a loudspeaker, "Keep away from the cliff. Maintain your progress. Keep up. Keep up."

The frost from the train twisted in the winds blowing through the canyon, some swept up by the outflow jets of the flying barges. Any remaining wisps quickly evaporated in the warm sun of the day.

The train continued to weave its way through the canyon another five kilometers until the cliffs fell back revealing a colossal military base of domed buildings, rectangular platforms and crisscrossing connector ramps. All was made of reinforced titanium. No buildings had windows. Flying barges hovered everywhere. Some were landing on platforms, others lifting off. Two bridges connected the complex on either side of the river. On wide bays on both reaches of the water were large fenced-in camps where Humans were corralled. They represented the foot soldiers at the ready to march north across the high plains to Canoon. For now however, they were just prisoners collected from all parts of Lupus Minor.

The train slowed and pulled into the forward station below the largest domed building. It stopped. Doors slid open on only one car. A cold blast of air erupted from the opening and one man stepped out. Frost filled the air. Ice covered the ground. The Human, tall, strong and forbidding in black leather, sported a wide black beard and puffed on a cigar. He stood still. Markhab looked up. Black and Silver Birds of Prey flew overhead. Others perched on the rims of the dome buildings.

Where is Corvus? he thought to himself. His eyes glowed and an ice roof stretched from the top of the train to a roof of an enclosed walkway. Markhab hated the ever-present Birds of Prey forever spying on him. There were too many. He intended to maintain the Human advantage in the coming battle.

Below Markhab in the caged pens, the men and women of Lupus Minor saw him. Cries of hate and anger rose up to meet his ears. Fists were raised at him. Guards along the outside perimeter of the cages stuck electrified prods through the fences antagonizing the prisoners. Other guards crowded the prisoners even closer together to allow room for more and more prisoners arriving in the lorries. "Schnell! Schnell!" the guards shouted. It was a dirty ugly thing. Markhab walked the length of the metal platform above them watching, puffing on his cigar, nearing the staircase that led up to the large domed building.

Markhab stoically regarded the pitiful aggregation of Humanity below him. He stared with sharp eyes that passed through the wretchedness, seeing only materiel for his war plans. Chattel. He kept puffing on his cigar, which helped mask the vile scent of so many unclean. He chewed on the end of the cigar, puffed a huge cloud around his head, and sent it drifting downwards into the pens. The prisoners choked and coughed. Markhab grinned, puffed again, and resumed his walk along the metal corridor.

A wide support beam momentarily blocked his view of the prisoners below. Suddenly a bright light enveloped him. The sound of breaking glass and metals rubbing against each other filled his ears. He vanished.

A moment went by when nothing happened. Then the sound and light show erupted in the same spot Markhab had stood. He stepped out, a smirk on his face. He vanished again in the same manner. Again he appeared, puffing on his cigar and glaring down at the prisoners in disgust. He turned and started down the metal corridor again. He jammed the end of his cigar into the palm of his hand, biting his lower lip to not flinch from the pain, but his face contorted in a grimace. But then the light and sound came back and Markhab was gone again.

Time ticked by. The prisoners groaned below. Flying barges traversed the canyon above the water. Black and Silver Birds of Prey circled high overhead. In a tremendous flash of light and deafening sound of glass breaking, metals scraping together, audible only to the rabble below, Markhab again stepped out of the ring of light. The brilliant cacophony ceased. Markhab sucked and puffed on his cigar, taking absolute pleasure from it. He turned and walked the rest of the length of the metal walkway with surety of purpose, never once looking down at the prisoners. At the end of the platform he climbed a metal staircase up the cliff face. Up he went one hundred and ninety-two steps, each one a clang of his boots against the steps. At the top, a gravel path led directly to the largest domed building. It was the Headquarters of the Military Commission. He entered, never pausing or looking around.

The antechamber was huge, thirteen stories tall and fifty meters square. Twenty-four guards stood in two rows four meters apart lining a blue and black checkered marble floor leading from the external entrance through which Markhab had just crossed to an inner double door, the full thirteen stories tall, that led into the main chamber. The blue and black standards of the military draped from the walls, ceiling to two-thirds of the way down to the floor. Markhab pressed ahead. The entire cordon of guards saluted as Markhab passed them and he saluted back, though glancing neither left nor right. The hall was chilled. Each footfall echoed. Markhab reached the inner doors. He entered his security ID code into the locking panel. The mighty doors swung open. An icy frost escaped. Markhab marched through the heavy doors, which silently shut and sealed behind him.

The interior chamber was the single largest enclosed structure still standing on Lupus. It was one hundred and fifty meters tall inside, straight up to the concave dome, which soared to an additional twenty meters at its apex. The diameter of the chamber was one hundred and twenty-five meters across. And inside it was cold. Ice crystals covered the walls, growing outward like gypsum flowers. But the circulating air smoothed the sharp edges and created swirls and ribbons streaking up to the heights. Carbon dioxide condensed too and dripped out of the air. Stalactites cast long spindly fingers down from the domed gloom. They dripped liquid CO2, which pooled and ran in rivulets grooved in the floor. In the coldest recesses, even liquid nitrogen formed.

Faint bluish light seeming distant slowly pulsed through the ice crystal walls. The constant slow motion growth and movement of the crystals caused shadows to creep through the space. Five figures stood on five stations near the center of the floor facing one another around a slowly rotating semi-sphere globe of Lupus, itself five meters in diameter. The figures turned to look at Markhab. Markhab walked the long distance across the floor's radius to stand at one of the open stations beside the others, his boots crunching the ice. These were the surviving Commissioners of the Human military government. Markhab puffed on his cigar. The smoke he exhaled fell as hail onto the floor.

"Corvus, is delayed," Markhab said, his voice a cold murmur. The other Commissioners nodded their understanding. "What is our status?"

At his queue their eyes burst forth in cruel light and their faces shined. Then each, Markhab included, grew to enormous height seventy meters tall. The globe rose up on a pedestal revealing the entire sphere of the planet. Up it rose fifty meters. One of the Commissioners, a woman with red hair, pointed to two locations above the globe. A holographic projection of two tiny silver-shaped spheres moved over its surface.

"We have two surviving satellites," she said. One drew an arc across the planet above the locations of Star City, Cronapolis, Dula and Aran City. The other drew an arc across the Canius Mountains from Lupus City, the Great Lakes, Big City, the Cantons, and the Great River. The chamber's walls projected images from the satellites.

Another Commissioner spoke. "Aran City is burning. Floating mines cast into the sea at Star City and transported by ocean currents led them into the Bay of Aran. The monsoons pushed them all the way up to the city where they detonated." Images of the conflagration filled the chamber with red and orange light.

A third Commissioner spoke. "The Canines and Humans are amassed on either side of the Great River north and west of our position fifty kilometers passed the river gorge." A scene of encampments appeared on the wall.

Markhab spoke. "The Human cities can be rebuilt. Everything is in place now for our sweep north in a wave of victory to annihilate the Polar Cities of Canoon. The encampments along the river will be routed like flotsam, to finally float downriver as thousands of corpses. But we must be vigilant against the Birds of Prey. We use them as a means to an end, but they are full of treachery. They seek to turn our victory into their own ascendency. We will deprive them of that. Now listen carefully. This is what we are going to do."

* * *

Outside the domed building, more and more Birds of Prey collected around the dome top, perching on the rim looking outward. A tinted curtain of light swept across the sky, followed by a rumbling along the cliffs. The bedrock beneath the domed building shifted. The structure creaked and groaned. Dozens of Birds of Prey lifted into the sky. Below them, the great doors of the building opened up. Huge swaths of frost and dry ice cascaded out, flowing from their density down the sides of the cliffs. Great fogs spread out across the river's surface and rose into the air, concealing all from the startled Birds of Prey. It continued to spread until it eventually thinned in the heat of the sun.

Markhab and his five Commissioners emerged from the structure silent and purposeful, back in their normal sizes. They sparkled and glittered like ice diamonds. The swirling fog mists twisted away from their forms as the air popped and crackled with electrical discharge. They marched in single file along the cliff top path leading away from the complex toward a command observation platform overlooking the river.

Flying barges crowded and hung together over the cages holding Markhab's prisoners. Birds of Prey circled over and around the observation platform. Standing on the platform was the largest and mightiest of the Birdmen. It was Gog, resplendent and terrible. He was three and a half meters tall. His eyes were pitch black as were his feathers. Shimmering silver patterns pulsated through his feathers in iridescence. He towered over a silver Birdman who had just touched down beside him. Gog spread his glorious wings stretching six meters tip to tip. The light of the sun dimmed around him. He bent his head to listen to the messenger.

Markhab approached the platform while the other Commissioners held back. Gog nodded at whatever the smaller Birdman was saying. As Markhab stepped up beside Gog, the messenger spread his wings and flew off. Gog folded his wings and turned to Markhab. The Bird of Prey's unblinking eyes sough to pierce Markhab's mind, to no effect.

"Welcome, First Commissioner." His voice boomed. "We are ready."

Markhab's face glowed blue white and his eyes shown bright as the sun. He grew in stature and rose to the height of Gog as electricity crackled in the air, popped and shimmered. "Begin this, such that we may rid Lupus of its Canine yoke."

Gog smiled. Visions of rivers flowing with blood filled his mind. He held before Markhab a device, simple in its design with two buttons over one. "This controls the Shimmering Field generator. Based on the designs you provided from your fellow Commissioner Corvus, the exo-scaffolding built into the canyon walls will affect the transformation of your army into its full and terrible purpose. But first, I will demonstrate another aspect of this Shimmering Field."

Gog pressed one of the top buttons with the talon of one of his fingers. A creaking rumble sounded from the cliff faces as the exo-scaffolding contracted. He pressed the bottom button. The canyon hummed a deep sound. A vortex of light appeared above the river, its center a deep blue. A wind blew through the canyon carrying the rustling sound of flapping wings. Ghostly shapes took form. The flying reptiles long adrift in Lupus' skies descended from their airy haunts and flew through the vortex. Suddenly a rush of Black and Silver Birds of Prey emerged one after another until a stream of hundreds materialized. Markhab registered no surprise on his face, though deep within his calculating mind he realized the treacherous intent of Gog's plan. Black feathers and silver feathers swept passed Markhab. After materializing, the army of Birdmen rose high in the air circling over the military complex, blackening the sky.

Gog laughed. "Now for you." He pressed the other top button on his device. The exo-scaffolding contracted further, changing the humming frequency. Then he pressed the bottom button again. The vortex elongated and changed to a pink shimmering hue that flooded over the river and its banks. The light swept through the prisoner's holding pens. The men and women cried out. They screamed. The metamorphosis took hold and soon an army of fanged beast men, snarling through teeth dripping with rabid saliva, hungered for blood. Their agitation rattled the cages and the fence groaned. The guards retreated back to a safe distance. The beast men began fighting one another. More cries went up as first blood was spilt.

"The Armies of Armageddon," yelled Gog. He shrieked and his cry split the sky. Thunder shook the world.

"Open the gates," yelled Markhab to his Commissioners below. They relayed the order to the Captains in the flying barges. The mad beasts rushed the open gates. Markhab's voice boomed. "North! Leave none alive!" Along the riverbanks rushed the army, with Birds of Prey above.

Gog tipped his head to Markhab. "A question for you, First Commissioner. Do you know of a man named Cornelius?"

Markhab considered the question. "Cornelius? Cornelius. Commissioner Menkar had an informant named Cornelius, a door-to-door purveyor of knives. A minor contact. A man of no consequence. Why do you ask?"

"His name has come to my attention," replied Gog.

"He would have died in the conflagration of Cronapolis along with Menkar."

"We will see," said Gog.

49 RAPTURE

Cornelius dreamed. He was running. He ran across plains so vast that it was days before anything changed. Tall grasses, little rivers and rolling hills were his world. The sun made its journey across the sky many times while he ran. The stars turned in their courses for many nights and still he ran. He never tired. He did not sleep. Running was his existence, his being. What thoughts he had that might have spawned in his mind, never encountered his consciousness.

Finally one day as he ran the terrain changed. He entered foothills and rocky ground, but his feet never stumbled. Stones rolled away before his footfalls and tipped back into their eternal resting places after he passed. By nightfall he was bounding through wooded mountains. He found paths and crevices that only dorsein should know, but he knew them too. Up mountains he ran passed swift rivers full of torrents and white water. He ran higher and higher until the very ground beneath his feet was no longer ground, but vast slow moving columns of ice so high and so thick that only the cold wind was his companion.

Then he ran under great arches of ice and streets of frost through cities of towering spires. No inhabitants dwelt more in these ghostly realms. His passing was marked only by lonely winds and he was a sprite, once there and suddenly gone.

The cities of ice behind him now, Cornelius scaled glaciers and ran even higher. Finally one midnight he stopped on the top of the world, the universe of stars over his head. Colors burst and danced in the dark, boreal auroras far above, so far that their cries and screams could not be heard. Grey white fields of ice spread in all directions around him. He knew that from here, every direction was south. Nowhere was anyplace that could be said to be north. He was north and nothing else.

In the ice fields of this place he found round crystal domes spread all about, each reflecting the auroral light, and radiating an inner light of their own. He bent down kneeling in the ice and snow leaning on the domes with his hands. Into the deep crystal spheres he looked and was amazed at the magic within them. Never in his life could he have guessed at this place, nor imagined what he saw. They were mirages, miracles kept safe by time, secrets hidden away from the world.

Finally, finally he grew tired, his body remembering its long flight, this journey to the top of the world. He lay down and the veil of sleep took over. He was at rest at last.

* * *

Naemi's invisible ship streamed through the quark soup, riding the proper eddies and avoiding the wrong whirlpools. The distance to return to Lupus was vast. The journey through the quark soup would only take minutes. Within those precious minutes Naemi sought to find her mental balance, keep Cheetah and Blink tamed, and keep an eye on her new charge, Canopus. The young Feline was full of questions, about Lupus, about Polaris, about Naemi herself. Correction, about Naemi her-selves. All were good questions, and Canopus should be equipped with all the answers. But Naemi simply didn't have the time.

She sat at the command console, eyes closed, with the bright pink of the quark soup outside illuminating her face. She inhaled deep breaths, held them, and slowly exhaled. Again. Her thoughts found that deep calm when all time slowed to near nothingness. Her body lightly shuddered as tension fell away. The creases of her mouth bent upward into a contented smile. This was the perfect moment. Then....

"What are we going to find on Lupus? Is there danger? Are we picking up more friends to take back to Polaris?"

Naemi's smile straightened to a frown and her eyes burst open, flickering in colors of red and green, accentuated by the glow of the soup. She took one more deep breath and kept her lips sealed tight. One more exhalation and her eyes softened. Finally she spoke.

"I asked for a moment of peace and quiet." *And I suppose I got that,* she thought to herself. "You must be prepared. There will likely be danger and violence, even death. At the least there will be intrigue."

"Are you a spy? Or maybe an assassin? A princess fighting an evil villain?"

Naemi nearly choked as laughter tumbled from her mouth. "All at once, I suppose. I am who I need to be at any given moment. At this moment, I am apparently your informant. Very well. We return to Lupus to aid my friend Cornelius fight an evil dictator's regime with the help of the Canine Alpha."

"What is a Canine Alpha?"

"Someone, if in whose presence you find yourself, you will not ask that question. He is the leader of the Canines on Lupus."

"Like a chief councilman? Or a king?"

"Well, not ex…sure. You can think of him like that. But I must help Cornelius."

"Is he Human? Or Canine?"

"Cornelius? Human. Of course, Human."

Is he your mate?"

"My WHAT? Ha! He wishes."

A buzzer sounded and lights on the console flashed.

"You can make your mind up about that soon enough. We're coming up on Lupus. Now sit down."

Naemi took command of the ship's controls. Canopus watched intently. The pink glow of the quark soup grew brighter and still brighter, then it vanished. Naemi and Canopus blinked their eyes from the sudden change.

After their pupils found their proper dilation, a blue planet floating among a sea of stars lay before them. The globe was fully illuminated by the light of a nearby sun. The planet's face was of a round blue sea surrounded by a continental rim.

"It's beautiful. Look at all the water. Is it an ocean world?"

Naemi smiled. "Quite the opposite actually. There is a southern ocean and a few lakes. But mainly land, just land, mountains, rivers, deserts, plains. We're over the southern pole. Let me position us above the equator."

The ship changed position and the planet moved. Half the sea slipped below the southern horizon. River deltas licked the extremities of the vast single continent at its edge with the sea. The mountains of Canius soared into view and as the planet turned, the great forest of Aran spread green below them.

"It looks so exciting, so perfect," exclaimed Canopus.

"Everything looks perfect from such great heights," said Naemi. "Down below it'll be a different matter." She touched the gem on her sunburst pendant hanging around her neck. "Where are you in this big world, Cornelius?" she mumbled aloud. As if in answer to her question, her gem glowed warm. Naemi searched the globe for a like-glow.

"Can you find him?" asked Canopus.

"Mm." Naemi closed her eyes. In her mind she saw a river, a canyon, far below northern mountains. She opened her eyes. The ship was directly above the great river of Lupus that flowed from the polar mountains of Canoon all the way south to the Sea of Aran. Naemi's eyes traversed the course of the river. At a particular place her gem warmed more. It grew hot, and she knew. "Got him." She turned to look at Canopus. "Yes. We're going down."

"What can I do?"

"Stay put, that's what, for now. Blink, I need you to keep an eye on her." And Blink emerged from Naemi, blinked twice blue and blue, and smiled at the young girl.

"Come with me," she said, extending her hand to Canopus. "Let's give Naemi a little space." They moved to the back of the ship.

"Now to avoid Markhab's satellites," Naemi said. "We may have only one shot at this." The ship spiraled downward.

* * *

The blue-grey cloak of pre-dawn chased away the stars revealing furtive movement along the banks of the Great River. Dark shapes of great structures on the water began to take discernible form as the world lightened and mists curled and rose. Humans and Canines hurried to and fro the riverbanks from a gravel beachhead where thousands of motorcycles were parked. Like industrious ants, they removed the odd bits and parts they had transported from the Roadhouse near Big City and carried the wares to the river. With haste and purpose they were constructing ships. Skeletal ribs and frames went up first, then were filled in by the building of ramparts, decks and fittings. From shoreline reeds, women collected flashing and flickering slugs into woven baskets. These were passed from hand to hand in lines straight to the ships where the baskets were emptied into holds and the slugs joined and spread out to work their magic. Gurkbuzzel, and the ships became whole. From another direction, desert Stilt Walkers converged on the scene, each tall walker beneath an umbrella hat transported backpacks of metal canisters with a large red "R" on each, titanium gas from Renender Enterprises, and they were loaded into huge gun blasts on the decks of the ships. Finally ready, Canines and Humans ascended rope ladders and climbed aboard.

Then suddenly the sun burst from its gates below the eastern horizon. Its first rays struck the eyelids of a sleeping figure in the grass on a hillside above the gravel beach. Cornelius awoke instantly. He stirred, stood and stretched. He blinked and rubbed his eyes. He wore only a loincloth, and his skin was dark, almost black from his time under the sun. His chest was hairy; his body lean with muscles taut from use. On his head grew long and matted dred locks that fell to his shoulders. His beard was full and black and curly. Cornelius yawned, taking in a huge breath that pulled the world's airs to him. His breath was so deep that the winds of the warm moist sea thousands of kilometers to the southeast were drawn to him, drawing with it waters and kelps and any floating thing to the shores of Aran. The winds swept over the great forests, up the river and through canyons to form clouds above the river plain. Cornelius breathed several more times, then let his attention focus on the activity below him.

Construction of the great floating fortresses was nearly complete, and Cornelius chuckled to himself at the brilliance of the concept. It had not occurred to him that all the misshapen parts and pieces carried by the motorcycles across the plains would be fit together as river boats. Ingenious. There were seventeen ships in all. They shimmered in psychedelic color displays that played on the lightening waters of the river.

Alpha Trifid came up beside him. The Canine's eyes were alert, expectant and bright. His ears turned in several directions as he became aware of all sounds in the world. "You are finally awake, Corneze."

Cornelius smiled a bright wide smile with teeth white as alabaster. "I always enjoy a good night's sleep."

"Especially if it lasts through to mid morning."

"Only till the dawn this time."

Trifid reached into a tiny bag about his waist affixed to his loincloth. He removed two small yellow seeds. He offered one to Cornelius.

Cornelius shook his head. "These little blossoms work better for me." He bent and plucked some tiny white flowers that grew in bunches all about the land. He brought them to his nose and crushed them between his fingers and inhaled deeply. His eyes dilated and he swooned for a moment, as did Trifid, who bit and swallowed his seeds.

The world suddenly grew brighter and revealed many of its hidden secrets to their sight. Away to the north, invisible Canine ships soared into the sky up to orbit and beyond.

"The last ships are leaving for Puppis," said Trifid. "The Polar Cities are empty."

Cornelius nodded. Above the river and streaming toward the canyon lands, they watched the invisible flying reptiles gather. "More Birds of Prey are finding a way out of their ghostly existence and into this plane."

"Adding to the gathering storm," said Trifid.

A whooshing sound emanated from the sky above them. An invisible ship spiraled down, leaving a circular contrail in its wake. The sound of the ship aimed straight for them. In a flurry of wind and dust, it came to rest beside them.

The ship remained invisible. The hatch extended and out stepped one long awaited.

"Naemi!" cried Cornelius. He ran to her. They embraced and he took her up in his arms and lifted her off the ramp. He jumped and spun in the air in a circle. They landed feet on the ground among white flowers. Then they pushed one another away to gaze in wonder at the changes in both of them.

"You've had some adventures I'll wager," said Cornelius. He could not stop beaming his smile at her.

"And you Cornelius," said Naemi. She touched his broad tight hairy chest, then felt the great mats of dred lock hair crowning his head. "You are changed."

"For the better I hope. I want you to meet someone. The great Alpha!" But Alpha Trifid was gone. Out in the river Cornelius saw him swimming to one of the large ships. "Well, later then."

"Markhab's forces are amassed through the canyon lands," said Naemi. "This looks like it's going to be a battle of annihilation." She gave Cornelius a wily smile. "There'll be plenty of sport for both of us."

"It's not what you think," said Cornelius. "It's marvelous. It's actually a RE...." But he stopped short his revelation. The air hummed and the ground vibrated.

"Look at the water," said Naemi, pointing. Out from the canyon entrance a pink light spread across the river's surface. The light danced and sparkled on the waves just as Alpha Trifid finished climbing up onto a ship's deck.

"I've seen this before, twice," said Naemi. "What follows is not good.

Canopus might be able to help us."

"Who?"

"A Feline I picked up on Wror."

Just then a shriek split the sky. It was everywhere at once. It pierced the flesh and mind of everyone on Lupus. Naemi clutched at her ears and fell to her knees. Cornelius pulled at her shoulders to bring her back to her feet. Then a thunderous roar filled the air. Floating barges emerged from the canyons. They were manned by snipers. They launched several shots among the running and scurrying Humans and Canines along the shore, but most barges raced upriver. The Polar Cities were their destination.

Then the sky grew dark. The wings of thousands of Birds of Prey blotted out the sun. They rose from hidden perches in the canyons and swarmed the lands about the river. Everything was covered in shadow. Cornelius' blood boiled in rage. The toes of his feet curled and his heels sunk into the ground.

"We can use my ship against them," said Naemi. But the ship was gone. A rush of sound and flurry of wind was all that marked its retreat. Naemi pressed the gems on her ring repeatedly. She thrust her hand into the air at the sound of the ship as if to launch a magic beam at it, but nothing happened.

"You brought a Feline to Lupus? Don't you know what that means?" said Cornelius.

"Obviously I don't," said Naemi.

Cornelius turned to his forces along the river. "Defenders of Lupus! Spears!" His command bellowed across the riverbanks. Beside each man and woman a mighty spear rose out of the dirt and rock as if thrust up by Titan warriors from the underworld. Each defender took up his weapon just as the sky closed in with Black and Silver feathers.

"I've got to get to Alpha," yelled Cornelius. Her started for the water.

"No!" shouted Naemi. "You must not go into the water." She tried to bar his way but he was not to be deterred.

"Move aside," barked Cornelius.

"No! You do not understand."

Cornelius tried to shove her away but she stood firm. Then she seemed to vibrate and pulse for an instant. Suddenly there were three Naemis. Cornelius stopped short, eyes wide in wonderment and confusion.

"You must not go into the water," said Cheetah.

"It would be your undoing," said Blink, and her eyes flashed from orange to red to yellow.

"Listen to us, Cornelius."

Then ten thousand beasts roared and stampeded out of the canyons.

"What witchery is this?" yelled Cornelius.

"It's not witchery, but it is evil," said Naemi.

"Look at the boats!" said Cheetah, pointing.

Men and women in the water flailed and screamed as they metamorphosed into devolved beasts. Cries rose from the Humans and Canines on the ships. Even from where Cornelius and the Naemis stood, they could espy figures falling to their knees, writhing in pain and pulling at their hair. Then the ships themselves changed. They listed, drifted, then seemed to ripple. Spotted and striped patterns raced across their surfaces, and from each ship a dozen tentacle arms erupted outward. They flailed in the air just as the Birds of Prey descended into their midst. The arms swatted and plucked Birdmen out of the air as if they were catching flies.

"Gurkbuzzel!" yelled Naemi in delight.

Then CLICK! Everything changed, moved backwards in time and vanished.

Cornelius awoke with a start. The bright first rays of dawn struck his eyelids and warmed his irises. He opened his eyes. It was only then that his ears registered the bass roll of the flowing river, its splashes along the banks, and the shouts of men and women, Canines and Humans, working along the shore. His nose encountered a welcomed smell of hot soup simmering over a fire down by the water's edge. Cornelius got up onto his feet and stretched. He inhaled a deep breath and drew half the airs of the world toward him. He lowered his arms to his side.

Where was Alpha Trifid? Cornelius spied a group of people that had gathered around a steaming outdoor kitchen where the soup was being served. Trifid was there. He accepted a bowl from a Canine woman and, turning toward Cornelius up on the sandy bank a hundred meters away, smiled and waved and called out. Trifid broke from the group and strode to Cornelius, careful not to spill the soup from its bowl.

A curtain of shade swept across the sky. An instant later, the river heaved from its banks. The dune on which Cornelius stood gave way, sending him cascading down the avalanche of sand while still upright. He stopped right in front of Trifid, the sand just covering the Alpha's furry toes. Beyond them, the river spilled its banks, creating a slurry of quicksand. The ground continued to shake. Then, CLICK! The world whooshed, spun, blurred

The sound of the river filled Cornelius' ears. The water's wide course was pinched as it entered the canyon lands, resulting in a roaring rush. Cornelius opened his eyes and sat up. It was cold.

"Good morning, my friend," said a placid voice beside him. "For once you are up before the sun."

Cornelius turned and smiled at Alpha Trifid. "There is a first for everything."

Alpha nodded. "Today is a good day for firsts."

"In my dreams I have seen amazing things. I'm not sure what is real."

"Everything you saw in your mind is real. I have no doubt of it."

"What I have seen then changes what we are fighting for."

"The danger we face is no less reduced because of your dreams. Danger races toward us."

"I would like some soup," said Cornelius.

Alpha laughed. "I've had it waiting for you this whole time. It might even still be warm." He lifted a gourd bowl of steaming broth and handed it to Cornelius.

He took the bowl from Alpha with both hands. He breathed in the warm aroma, took a sip, and let out a contented sigh. Then he swallowed the rest in three quick gulps.

"Easy there," said Alpha. "Is there a rush?"

Cornelius set down the empty cup, licking his lips. "The ground will move. I didn't want to spill."

"Now are you ready for what comes next?"

"Yes," said Cornelius. "I know exactly what to do." He stood up and repeated to himself, *I know exactly what to do.*

As Cornelius stood, the sun's first rays shot through a gap in the eastern hills and illuminated his face. His skin soaked up the power of the sun, turning a deep bronze. Cornelius inhaled deeply and drew all the airs of the world to him. His whole body was gold. His muscles shimmered in hues of onyx and cinnabar. He exhaled and the winds of the world swirled around him in a vortex of racing mirages. His hair danced like crackling flames. His heaps of dred locks rose and waved in the wind. His stature grew as the sun darkened from the gathering clouds. Cold, dry air from the north mixed with warm, moist air from the south. Thunderheads formed and lighting flicked over the river. Thunder rocketed across the land. Cornelius' eyes glowed gold and shown out across the expanse, lighting all. He looked down at the river's near shore and saw the construction of the gurkbuzzel ships just being completed. Then the sky tinted as a swift moving curtain of shade raced across the sky.

"Get ready to slide, Alpha! The bank will collapse. Ride it down. Stay on top!"

"Now you're a fortune teller?"

The ground lurched forward and the high riverbank burst in a cascade of sand. Cornelius and Alpha surfed it down to the shore. The river jostled and tipped as the land shook. The gurkbuzzel ships were drawn into the main current. Few men were aboard. Most were suddenly stranded on the exposed mud flats.

"Get away from the shore! Quick now!" Cornelius yelled at the men. They tried, but were scarcely able to make any progress before the wall of water rushed back at them. Cornelius and Alpha leaped into the air and landed on a bedrock outcropping. The others disappeared beneath the surging water.

The Canine ships bowed and reeled. They surged toward the center of the river. The turbulent waters sloshed against the cliff gates full of white foam, loosening boulder and gravel into the rush.

"Corneze, gather the Fifty Guard," yelled Alpha Trifid. "The thunder is coming and we must meet it."

"To Alpha!" cried Cornelius, and they came. From all directions, the elite commandos hastened to their leader at the speed of sound. Two, eight, twenty-four, thirty-five, forty-nine. With Cornelius, all were present. Just then another tint of shade crossed the sky. The bedrock rumbled. Part of the canyon cliffs on their side of the river collapsed, leaving a road-like ledge parallel to its length. The cliffs vibrated again. Now a pink light shot out from deep within the canyons, a shimmering horizontal beacon tickling the surface of the flood and illuminating the ships entering the gates.

A blood-curdling cry ripped through the air splitting the sky. Its percussion force blasted through the atmosphere and circled Lupus three times, echoing and finally dying down, but not before it was replaced by a yelling roar from thousands of tortured lungs. The mad host approached on the new road.

"This is it!" barked Alpha. "It's up to us to take them out. Form a mighty anvil to shatter the hammer blow. Corneze!"

Cornelius shouted his orders. "The biggest brutes in front around Alpha. Ten wide with the rest backed up behind. Crouch!" Each locked their heads and arms to their comrade's before and beside. Cornelius was cheek to cheek with a growling tensing mass of torsos, butts and thighs. Canine fur was in his mouth, and musk filled his nose. "Bind!" Fist and fingers clutched skin and muscle.

"Wait for it! Wait for it!" yelled Alpha.

The horde of wide red-eyed, fanged and clawed post-Humans rushed the Canine anvil. Twenty meters, ten meters, two meters.

The pink light shown over the Fifty Guard. Cornelius was at the Eight position in back. His head and eyes facing down, he noticed a light glowing bright, and brighter. It was his precession star amulet. At the same time, the feet, calves and thighs nuzzled around him morphed. Nails grew long into talons. Limbs thickened. Growls turned to agonizing grunts. What was happening?

"Set!" Cornelius yelled, and the hammer struck.

The frenzied metamorphs crashed into the Canine anvil. BOOM! Dozens of the mad post-Humans in the initial impact were bounced into the air. More beasts piled into the fray, crushing the beasts before them. And now a new force met them. Markhab's floating barges streamed out of the canyon gates. The beasts flung toward the river smacked against the oncoming barges, and into the water. The Fifty Guard maintained their scrum pack against the onslaught. The Canines advanced.

From his position in back Cornelius heaved and strained to maintain the push forward. His face was buried in the muscle of the Canines. His head was down and he could barely see through his squinting, stinging eyes. He was drenched in sweat. The frictional heat from all the bodies sent wafts of steam billowing around him. The Guard was changed. They were now a mad snarling mass of werewolves, but they shielded Cornelius from the pink light. What was going on? There was no time to think on that.

Now more trouble as a thunder rippled across the ground and the sound of crashing metals and breaking glass erupted all around.

"Aahh! You're kidding me," groaned Cornelius under his harried breath. He heard the sound of blasters and explosions, but he did not lessen his thrust. Even so, the hammer force of the beasts actually lessened, dropped off and vanished. The Fifty Guard shot forward in a heap, tumbling and rolling along the road over the crushed bodies of beasts. Any remaining alive were fleeing for their lives. Cornelius looked up to see why.

The gurkbuzzel river ships glowing in the pink light had morphed into floating tentacled fortresses. Huge arms with toothed suctions flayed back and forth in the air. With deliberate action they snatched the mutated beasts off the road and threw them into the river or smashed them against the cliffs. By twos and threes and dozens, the creatures were swept off the road. Cornelius and the werewolf Alpha and Guard rolled out of the way of the tentacles, crawled, scooted and ran. The ships passed through the canyon gates, raking away all the beasts as the ships moved downriver.

Cornelius looked upriver. Hundreds of pairs of Nut-Nuts were materializing all along the shore. They were out-fitted with shoulder-to-air launchers, and were blasting up at the floating barges.

* * *

Naemi struggled to control the ship's descent. A moment before, the ship had been gently circling down through the planet's atmosphere. Then the shockwave had hit, a wrenching cry that split the sky sending a powerful blast buffeting against the ship's fuselage. They spun in mid-air, somersaults and cartwheels in the sky. They careened down through gathering storm clouds toward the river valley. Onboard there was mayhem.

Naemi was thrown out of her pilot's chair and smashed against the door. It slid open. Blink separated, tumbled on through, knocking into Canopus who was kneeling, screaming. As the ship spun wing over wing, Cheetah separated and fell hard against the ceiling. Using the ship's motion of centrifugal force, Naemi clawed her way back to the pilot's chair, fortunately fixed to the floor. In one huge heave, she pulled herself onto the chair and activated the safety force belt. Secured, she brought the ship under control. It rocked. It sheered. It slowed. The landing struts extended. In half a second the ship struck the ground and shuddered and was still.

Naemi caught her breath. She released herself from the safety force belt and stood up, wobbly. Cheetah and Blink picked themselves up from where they'd slammed into the floor upon landing. All were bruised. They stood together in the cockpit. Three mechanical whips rolled to her feet.

"Three?" asked Cheetah.

"The others appeared when that shriek split the sky," said Blink. They each picked up a whip. Only then did they notice the cacophonous mayhem outside the viewports. Flying barges soared through the air, trading fire with Nut-Nuts on the ground. Amazing!

"Let's get out there," said Naemi. "Keep Canopus inside."

Canopus was crouched beneath the table in the main bay, luckily bolted to the floor. She lay prostrate, whimpering. The others filed out.

The ship was still invisible on the rocky ground above the road ledge. The ramp came down and three Naemis marched out, Naemi in front, Cheetah and Blink behind on either side. Their hair blew behind them in the chilly air. Goose bumps broke out across their bare skin, barely covered by their latex lingerie. They stood still amidst the maelstrom.

Flying barges streamed out of the river canyon heading north. Each supported a complement of half a dozen rifle-toting marines. All along the riverbank and in the water itself were flailing, struggling Humans and Canines dragging themselves to shore. Some watery upheaval had overwhelmed them. Passing just now into the canyon channel were huge Canine gurkbuzzel ships, grotesquely morphed into floating squid-like leviathans, their arms raking the air to pull down the floating barges, smashing them against the cliffs. Others swept up hideous marauding creatures that may have once been Human that were pouring out of the canyon on the road just below Naemi's ship. There, a group of Canines fought against the horde, but as they fought, they screamed and crumbled on the ground, caught in a pink preternatural light that emanated from deep within the canyons. Then out of their ranks a figure shot upwards into the sky, circling slowing a thousand meters above the battles. It was Cornelius, and he spread his arms, gathering storm clouds around him.

Flashes and crashes erupted all around Naemi, Cheetah and Blink. Dozens, hundreds of pairs of Nut-Nuts appeared all along both banks of the river. Some pulled people out of the water, but most took up offensive positions beneath the floating barges. The Nut-Nuts quickly set up mobile gun launchers on round-geared rotors that made the whole contraptions look like canons. They shot into the air at the barges rings that looked like spiral soap bubbles. Upon contact, the barges began to melt, some quantum burning taking place. The barges dissolved beneath the feet of Markhab's marine gunmen.

The winds over the battles whipped faster and faster round as Cornelius drew more of the airs of Lupus toward him.

Naemi released her mechanical whip and flung it up to crack in the air. Naemi turned to her companions and yelled a battle cry. "Come on, ladies. Let's smash some shit!" They yelled in unison and cracked their whips in unison. Naemi and Cheetah made contact with two barges and jumped, reeling themselves to their targets. They landed steadfast on the rushing barges knives unsheathed and commenced hand-to-hand combat.

Blink was still on the ground. Just then a rush of wind around her marked the invisible ship on take off. From atop a barge Naemi yelled, "Blink! Get that Feline!"

Blink rushed back up the invisible ramp, disappearing into the craft as it retracted. The ship whirred away.

Naemi and Cheetah continued snapping necks, severing limbs, raining blood out of the sky. It was then that she saw the next oncoming threat. The sky became black from the dark wings of Birds of Prey. Gog's minions were upon them.

* * *

The pressure in Canopus' head was terrible. She felt like her brain was trying to expand, but was instead being crushed by her own skull. It was the same feeling she had when the dragon screeched and flew at her on Wror. Her forehead throbbed, her third eye pineal gland trying to open, ever since that world piercing shriek split the sky and this ship smacked right into it full force. Canopus had tumbled between ceiling and floor, wall and wall, door, desk and window in the near free fall to the planet's surface. She cowered, whimpering and mewing beneath the fixed table in the main bay of the ship, while Naemi and her strange doppelgangers prepared to leave.

Canopus' neck craned forward, low on the ground. Her eyes were wide.

They darted back and forth, up and around, seeking something. They rolled up so far her pupils nearly disappeared into her head, leaving just opaque hazel orbs. She started making a grumbling sound that was almost a purr, until it finally came out as a chirp. "Chirp-chirp. Chirp-chirp", aimed at some distant point nowhere above her.

She heard the outer ramp descending, the door opening, the others leaving, the sound of Naemi shouting back, "Keep Canopus inside!" The door closing.

They were gone. Canopus got out from under the table, stood up and composed herself. She looked about. She calmly walked to the control room, entered and sat down in the piloting chair, closed the door and locked it.

Outside the window viewports, storm clouds swirled. Flying barges full of armed men streamed by. The ground shook in myriad explosions. Canopus looked down at the console and ran her fingers over the many controls, caressing them. She had paid special attention to the pattern of buttons Naemi had pressed, executing various commands. Canopus knew how to operate this ship. She retracted the ramp and maneuvered a controlled ascent, turned, and aimed the ship through the gates of the canyon lands following the course of the river. Before her were bizarre tentacled things that might be boats if they didn't have arms, or they might be polyped mollusks if they hadn't had ship hulls for bodies. She maintained her distance from the flailing arms.

The cliffs meandered in broad swipes first to the left and then to the right, back and forth again. The ship dipped left, dipped right, keeping pace. Canopus executed perfect control over the craft. The tentacled river ships swept the banks of the river clear of mad beasts, a vermin horde. The last of the flying barges passed overhead.

There was a commotion behind the cockpit door. Someone was in the main cabin. There was yelling and banging on the door. Canopus glanced quickly behind her for reassurance that the door was still undamaged. Then BOOM. RIP. BOOM, CRASH. RIP. Blink was prying the door out of its frame. Canopus rocked the ship left and right to unbalance her. Cursing came through the door, then a thud.

Canopus allowed a tight smile to briefly cross her face. Her destination was just up ahead. Then CRASH! The door was gone. Blink stood there, red faced and furious, her whip retracting as it let go the door. And her eyes, her eyes! How they blinked at Canopus.

"You mustn't interfere," said Canopus. "Just stay back there."

"You ungrateful bitch!" yelled Blink. "Get out of the way so I can turn this ship around."

"It isn't turning around."

"You are."

Then the sky went dark. Black wings over silver wings over black stretched across the sky. They blotted out the shafts of sunlight breaking through the churning clouds. They blotted out those clouds. They flew above the level where the barges had flown, out of the reach of the tentacled ships.

"Birds of Prey," Blink uttered. "Where did they come from? Definitely there were no Birds of Prey the last time I was on Lupus."

Canopus' eyes were wide and unblinking. Her mouth opened a crack in wonder.

"Girl, look at me," said Blink.

Canopus refocused her attention on flying. She did not turn around. "Stay away from me." She prepared the ship for landing.

Blink didn't want to endanger the ship, or her life. She patiently waited for the landing maneuver to complete.

The ship settled on a cliff ledge far above the river. The ledge was crossed by a gravel path leading up from a complex of domed buildings to an eerie lookout with a commanding view of river canyon in both directions. Atop the eerie lorded a huge Black and Silver Bird of Prey. He gazed north, overseeing the winged host as they swept over the canyons. The great Birdman became agitated, sensing something nearby that he could not see, could not pinpoint. He let out a shriek, but nothing about him he could see caused his distress.

In the ship, Canopus too became agitated. She fell to the floor behind the piloting chair, prostrate with her neck extended out. Her eyes rolled to the back of her head. She opened her mouth and chirped, and chirped.

Blink was fascinated by the behavior, but became alarmed when it looked like Gog might discover their presence. He appeared to react to the Feline's chirping. Out the window Blink could see the Birdman's black eyes searching here and there.

From her vantage point it looked to Blink that Gog stared right at them, piercing through the invisibility of the ship. Then Gog straightened his back, unfurled his wings and fluttered them, the glint of silver shimmering all around. The glint sparkled off the controls in the ship's cabin. This shouldn't be possible, thought Blink. Somehow the silver light was penetrating the invisible shield. Canopus continued to chirp.

Blink lowered herself to the floor opposite Canopus. She had to stop this attention the Feline was apparently drawing. Blink began to hum, low and slow at first, then rhythmically faster and louder. Canopus tensed at the sound. She stopped her chirping. Canopus looked at Blink, whose eyes were flickering through a barrage of different colors. The patterns complemented the humming. Canopus' eyes dilated. Her head began bobbing up and down. Then her eyes glazed over and her whole body slumped. She was out.

Blink stopped blinking but continued to hum. She got up slowly and returned to the cockpit where she sat down at the controls. She strained her neck to look out the window at the Bird of Prey outside. Gog was no longer looking at, or looking for, the ship. Something had drawn away his attention. That is when the cliff collapsed beneath the ship. Gog took to the air, narrowly evading the collapse.

Blink was thrown out of the cockpit and through the air. She landed against the outer door, snapping her wrist. By a twist of ill fate, her ring activated the door. Blink fell screaming out of the ship, falling with it. She crashed onto a gurkbuzzel boat, and the invisible ship fell onto her. The boat exploded and changed into a swirling mass of slugs that sank into the river, then emerged, wriggling for shore.

The other gurkbuzzel ships then used their tentacles to reach deep into their holds and come out flailing with canisters of titanium gas. They flung them far over the canyons, directed toward the city of Bafaria and its nitrogen swamps. The chemical reactions of titanium and nitrogen created a nuclear like flash that consumed the gulag city in flames. The blasts followed pipelines of nitrogen that subsequently engulfed the satellite gulag cities.

The explosions teamed up with another quake, and the scaffolding of the cliffs' shimmering field generators cracked. Ribbons of pink energy erupted in all directions.

In the river, the invisible ship materialized, rose to the surface, and floated for a time, just long enough for a shocked wide eyed Feline to crawl from the open compartment door, slide into the waters and swim to shore. She pulled herself up onto a road beside the waterline just as a shimmering ribbon of pink light enveloped her body.

* * *

Naemi and Cheetah danced in a whir of motion on the bank of the river, far enough upstream and away from the melee of monsters. The grotesque transformation of Humans and Canines was a daytime nightmare of shrieks, cries, growls and howls between fanged apes and werewolves. Let them wipe themselves out. Naemi and Cheetah flung their mechanical whips in the air at the floating barges. Cheetah's latched onto a steersman and yanked him out of the ship. Naemi's locked onto a rail. She catapulted up and landed on her feet atop the barge. She tipped backwards and with a kick, dispatched a sniper, who fell back knocking over another. Naemi steered the barge onto its side sending two others overboard. Then she turned the barge around and drove it straight into the path of an oncoming barge. She leaped out just as the two collided that ripped both vessels to pieces. Naemi landed on her feet right where she'd been standing before beside Cheetah. Then they did the same to two more barges, and two more after.

All around the Nut-Nuts were busy taking down more barges. The air was full of fire and explosions and black clouds of smoke and falling debris. Then a darkness closed, but it was not from the circling clouds. A thousand

Black and Silver Birds of Prey dove out of the sky. They swooped down and snatched startled Nut-Nuts from their defenses, carried up, and dropped them to their deaths.

Naemi and Cheetah attacked the Birdmen with their whips. Feathers and blood rained down everywhere. Then one Bird of Prey seized hold of Naemi's whip and yanked her up into the sky. She retracted whip and soared up to meet the Black and Silver. But his outstretched talons grabbed onto her first. She swung by her feet. Then he dropped her. She fell, and blood splattered across her face. Turning upward to see the cause, the Bird of Prey tumbled passed her, a golden spear lodged in its breast. Naemi saw red everywhere. Hundreds of Red Falcons streamed out of the sky sending golden spears through the ranks of Black and Silvers. Spears were quickly retrieved from dive-bombing Falcons, and up they soared again to wreck more death.

Naemi tumbled. The ground rushed up. Centimeters above the river's surface she was snatched back into the air. A Red Falcon carried her to the river's edge and released her safely. It was Casimir. He landed beside Naemi, who lay dazed on the ground. A short distance away, a falling barge crashed and exploded, taking Cheetah with it in the inferno. Naemi could only watch with glazed eyes. Casimir was aloft again. A blinding explosion erupted far down river. The flash obliterated Bafaria.

The ground trembled and rumbled and yawned. The course of the river spread open in a great crack, a seam that unzipped from south to north. The waters fell into the depths and steam billowed up amid flames and molten sparks. The river was on fire.

* * *

Far above, Cornelius saw everything. The gathered airs of North and South swirled around him. Tall cumulus clouds rose up from the convergence, topping off with flattened anvil tops. The churning airs buoyed Cornelius. He hung in space as if standing on firm ground. Lightning arced around him, reflecting in his eyes. Thunder clapped abound him. All the hair on Cornelius' body stood on end. His skin twitched and tingled. He watched the events below play out.

Alpha Trifid and his Guard were busy dispatching Markhab's horde. Two Naemis and myriad Nut-Nuts battled the floating barges. Casimir and his Red Falcons were subduing Gog's Black and Silvers. Blood rained from the sky. Blood seeped across the land. The river ran with blood. And a lone Feline survived disaster and escaped from Gog. Bafaria ceased to be, in a flash of destruction. The river burned. Cornelius waited for the sign. Then he saw it. Three aged Canines maneuvered on the ground in an abandoned, ruined section of the battlefield. Three kites with reflective mirrors flashed in the sky trained by three ugly women, now beautiful Canine girls.

Gog, aloft, also saw the shining sky markers and flew toward them. But from the collapsing cliffs behind him, shimmering ribbons of light rippled across the sky. Gog flew directly into one large beam. He contorted in mid air. His size enlarged by three times. His feathers turned to scales. His wings became leathery. Arms became clawed forelimbs. A pointed tail emerged from his lower spine. His neck elongated. His snout protracted. His Black and Silver coloring faded. He was left a ghastly bone white dragon. He screeched, beat his wings and rose higher in the air.

Cornelius dropped out of the sky. He aimed toward Gog, and he was not alone. From the cliff road, a lone figure leapt, a great sabre cat beast rising into the sky to meet the dragon. The sabre cat made its mark, sinking her teeth into one of Gog's hindquarters. The dragon screeched. And he continued to fly.

From the river's cliff gates, another figure left ground and ascended in a great leap. A werewolf with long snarling snout filled with rows of razor teeth and fangs. It caught the dragon's other hind limb. And yet he flew on.

From one side, another figure fell onto the dragon. It was Casimir. He landed on Gog's lower back. The beast screeched again and writhed in the air. Then came Cornelius barreling out of the sky to arrive on Gog's neck. He held on. They all held on.

"Now, dear dragon," said Cornelius in the beast's ear. "All moments are now. This was your goal all along. We will help you. But every goodly deed requires its sacrifice. You are ours." He stroked the dragon's neck, and north they flew.

665

They followed the burning river through the Canoon flat lands, then foothills. Up ahead, cliffs of rock and ice faced off against the river of fire, an ice wall keeping the Polar Cities frozen. But it was no ordinary glacier field. Six great figures in the forms of giant Commissioners pulsated about the field, blue light connecting each, perpetuating the cold against the river of fire. On one, a brighter light shone, an amulet blazed, a Precession Star. Cornelius' amulet also burned bright.

"Now my dear dragon, our mark is set," whispered Cornelius in the beast's ear. He glanced back. Canopus, Alpha Trifid and Casimir held on. "Now Gog. You must take out that one. Breathe fire. Do it Gog. Do it now!"

The dragon inhaled, and his internal furnaces ignited. His stomach burned. The flames shot forth and smothered the figure with the bright light. The reaction was instantaneous. The cold blue light connecting the Commissioners broke its connections. An explosion equal to that which destroyed Bafaria consumed the ice field. The superheated flash instantly melted all the ice of the polar mountains into a cauldron of searing steam. The Polar Cities disappeared. The shock wave expanded and slammed into Gog. The dragon and his companions were struck and knocked out of the sky.

At the top of the world, the northern most plateau steamed, and a most amazing thing happened. The iridescent orbs on the north pole cracked open. Streaming out of them into the sky were Birds of Prey of every ilk, Golden Eagles, Falcons, Hawks, Owls, Kestrels, Herons and others. The skies of Lupus filled with the beating of new wings, newborn, yet fully formed. They rode the airs to all parts across the globe.

But the dragon Gog and his companions could not see the vision of rebirth. Gog struck the land, BOOM! his fall leaving a chasm half a kilometer across. Around him positioned at the four cardinal directions of the world, fell Cornelius, Alpha Trifid, Canopus and Casimir. BOOM! BOOM! BOOM! BOOM! into four new craters. The force of their four impacts rebounded in the bedrock. Rising out of the devastation were four small hills of slag. On each of their summits was a rocky statue in the rough guise of its entombed, a Human, Canine, Feline and Bird of Prey.

The skies above echoed in choruses of new song, while below lay a world mostly quiet. It began to rain.

50 THE WRITTEN AND ILLUSTRATED HISTORY

A quiet wind stirred up dust and ash, mixing it with the steam and smoke rising from the chasm in the ground. Every now and again there was a hissing sound as rivulets of water snaking down from the warmed and snow-free mountains found their way through cracks to the superheated rocks below the riverbed. In time, the rocks would cool and the river would return, when snows fells again on the Polar Mountains.

Naemi sat with her back against the crude statue of Cornelius projecting out of the ground beside the chasm. Three other crude representations stood nearby, those of the Feline Canopus, the Canine Alpha Trifid, and the Bird of Prey Casimir. Stony, eyeless visages gaped down at the chasm's depths, keeping silent watch over the remains of Gog.

Not too far to the north near a rubble heap Naemi heard music. It was slow and somber. Naemi stood up and looked in the direction of the music. She shaded her eyes as she scanned for the source of the sound. Approaching the pile of rubble was a strange contingent. Walking in single file, a line of Canines navigated the ruined terrain on tall stilts and wearing umbrella hats. Behind them were a half-dozen Canine children. They wore robes with red ribbons that fluttered in the air. They played flutes.

Naemi stood quietly and watched the bizarre procession. When they reached the top of the rubble heap, the children began overturning stones searching for something. Before long, their search was over. At this distance it was difficult for Naemi to see exactly what drew their interest. It looked like a body was being excavated and lifted off the ground, but by the way in which the form stretched and draped, Naemi concluded it was only an article of clothing, some body suit. Naemi wondered who had worn it, and why it was significant.

The Stilt Walkers turned around and lead the troupe of children back across the wilderness away south and westward, carrying the suit solemnly with them. Before long they vanished in the hazy distance. Once again, only the wind and hissing steam spoke in the world.

* * *

The sun shined low in the sky in the Canius Mountains. Shadows stretched long in the valley. Flame maples still bloomed, overarching the little stream. On its far bank stood the Great House. As the shadows deepened at the end of the day, lights came on, torches and the great fireplace dancing in reds and oranges from the windows.

Before the fireplace, the Canine children were gathered together after their communal meal for story time. Uriel held up a big old picture book and was relating a new story, a new chapter.

"New Birds of Prey were born into the world, while the evil Gog met his end by the efforts of all four species. It was a new age, a new age of wonder and flight and discovery for Lupus."

The children clapped as Uriel finished her story. She put the big old book down on the long table and started arranging cushions and blankets for the night's slumber. Aleph drew closer to her and looked at the illustration on the book's open page.

"That was quite a story, Uriel. I'm confused about something in this picture, however."

"What is that?"

"In this picture, the ancient eggs hatch and the world fills up with newborn Birds of Prey. Gog tumbles out of the air. But above all of this is some object high in the sky. What is it?"

Uriel looked over Aleph's shoulder at the picture in the book. "Oh, that's the sky ship. Didn't you see it? It was so big and bright."

"It looks like there are people in it."

"Yes! See here on the lower level? There is a Feline surrounded by robots. They are peering down watching everything play out below."

"And what is above?"

"On an upper level is a great Bird of Prey. He is peering down watching everything play out below. See how his wings flutter?"

"And above him?"

Uriel looked closely. "It looks like another Feline."

Below the Great House, in a basement lit by torches, was a large dais. On it propped on a stand, a suit lay extended, kimono fashion. The suit reflected a thousand different colors on the walls from the torchlight. An amulet hung from the suit's neck. It glowed a bright blue. Suddenly, the suit blazed in a kaleidoscope of color, patterns rippling along its surface. The suit was alive, ever waiting.

* * *

Naemi dozed against the rocky facsimile of Cornelius. The sun had set. Cold stars shined overhead. There was nothing to be heard but the wind. Even the hissing steam had died down. Suddenly there was a huge din, like the sounds of breaking glass and scraping metals. Naemi awoke with a start, leapt up and jumped back. All four statues shook and trembled and collapsed in four bright circles of light.

The End

ABOUT THE AUTHOR

B. Michael Hill was born and raised in rural California. He has a degree in Political Science. His career has included working for a major metropolitan newspaper, and more than two decades at a leading financial services firm. His interests include hiking, gardening, cooking and learning about ancient mysteries. He is married and lives in Alameda, California. Precession: Age of Descent is his first novel.

MAP OF THE PLANET LUPUS

Thank you, dear Reader

Thank you for purchasing *Precession: Age Of Descent*. If you enjoyed this book, please consider writing a brief review for the online bookseller of your choice. Your positive review encourages others to read *Precession: Age Of Descent*, and is extremely helpful in getting it out to as many people as possible. Thank you!